An Immaculate Illusion

To

Gwen

All Best wishes

for.

D-A. Panon

An Immaculate Illusion

D. A. Panama

Troubador Publishing Ltd
Unit E2 Airfield Business Park,
Harrison Road, Market Harborough,
Leicestershire. LE16 7UL
Tel: 0116 2792299
Email: books@troubador.co.uk
Web: www.troubador.co.uk

ISBN 978 1805142 010

British Library Cataloguing in Publication Data.
A catalogue record for this book is available from the British Library.

Printed and bound by CPI Group (UK) Ltd, Croydon, CR0 4YY
Typeset in 12.5pt Adobe Jenson Pro by Troubador Publishing Ltd, Leicester, UK

I would like to thank Catherine who patiently read the early drafts and gave me inspiration for the cover.

Prologue

Springtime in Berlin 1945

The government section of the shattered city is a mere ghost of what it once was.

There in the shadows can be seen what remains of the once magnificent New Reich Chancellery. If observed from the Wilhelm Strasse side of this still imposing but now partially destroyed building, slightly to the right one can see what appears to be a garden hut. It is in fact a concrete entrance. It has a door and beside it stands a large, battered concrete air vent. Beyond that door is a set of steep stairs leading to a massive warren of rooms and tunnels. It is a bunker. Two bunkers, in fact: Upper (Vorbunker) and lower (Fuhrerbunker). And down there murder and suicide are being mooted as the only available options. But options for whom – and are the proponents of such measures truly in earnest? Conspiracies which have been promulgated for years are still running their murderous course and will travel on far beyond the conclusion of this massive conflict.

That aside, one salient and emotive fact felt by those entombed within and without the bunker, is that no matter who lives and who dies, the myth of the Third Reich must continue for eternity. After all, nobody wants to die as a fool.

April 20 1945

The stench was now pretty well unbearable to anyone that had not been incarcerated almost seventy feet beneath the surface and forced to breathe in recycled and barely filtrated air for weeks without end. This is the Upper Bunker and it adjoins the New Reich Chancellery. The reek of unwashed bodies, fear induced sweat together with only occasionally functioning plumbing is made all the ghastlier because there is no escape from the offending odours. Here and there laughter can be heard. Admittedly it is laughter bordering upon the hysterical but at least it is better than listening to the shrieks of the wounded. Those poor souls are left lying where they have been dumped at the foot of the initial flight of stairs of the Upper Bunker entrance. A medic might get to them at some stage but probably not. Sympathy, empathy and respect for the nation's wounded soldiery has long since evaporated. Now, they are largely ignored unless one of them begins to scream too loudly, in which case he receives a resounding kick from one of the SS guards. Even at this late and decidedly terminal stage of the war various notaries seek an audience with the Führer and must be shielded from such obvious signs of defeat. The whole situation is depressing enough as it is.

Deep in the bowels of the complex the conference room is shoulder to wall packed with army and Reich leaders.

Condensation runs in little rivers down the cracked plaster walls. The currump of exploding shells landing directly overhead makes even the reinforced concrete ceiling shake like sails before the wind. Flakes of whitewashed plaster drift lazily downward where they spread themselves almost uniformly over the officials in the room.

"I will die here," bellowed Hitler. "Here in Berlin, I shall end my life, if necessary by my own hand."

Oh, please do it soon, was the thought echoing in the heads of those present.

"I fought through the first war. I have no fear of death. Indeed, it will be a blessed release from all the dreadful problems that beset me."

Fought – him? From what those gathered in the conference room had heard, Hitler had never been more than anything but a safety seeking postman.

"Treachery. Let down by those that I trusted." The Führer's voice rose higher. It wouldn't be long before the shrieking started. "My orders disobeyed and the daily instances of betrayal. Death will be welcome. Make no mistake, I shall go gladly!"

CHAPTER 1

Earth erupted all around him and utter terror, fear of an impending and hideously violent death coupled with the agony of mutilation reduced the Private soldier to a whimpering wreck. The blasts of exploding shells and the whistle of countless hundreds of discharged bullets from British small arms had him jerking and writhing uncontrollably in a pointless effort to evade that which could not possibly be seen nor avoided. It would simply arrive when it was ready and remove him, together with his various constituent parts, from this life on earth: this wretched hell on earth!

He had volunteered so readily and with such happy excitement. He and the rest all singing merrily as they marched off to war. Off to fight for the Kaiser and the fatherland. Oh, such joy they had experienced. To be real soldiers: real men!

"I want to go home." He shrieked as bullets thudded dully into the earth around him spitting up clouds of dust into his wide terrified eyes. "Please! Please help me. I don't want this anymore!" Tears and snot ran down his youthful features. And then he heard it. A shriek even louder than his own. Pure, unadulterated mortal terror from a soul in torment. Even Dante could not have conjured up a more hellish scenario than that of Ypres in October of 1914.

Away, the young soldier had to get away. He crawled across the now barren and blasted landscape blindly, without even the vaguest idea of direction.

Earlier that morning they had climbed, as a disciplined infantry unit, out of their trenches and advanced readily, with brave determination, toward the enemy lines. That advance had remained a disciplined line for less than two minutes before it dissolved into a mob of panic-stricken young boys running willy-nilly in each and every direction. Officers and NCOs fell first and then total panic ensued. The green young clerks and shoe salesmen from Bavaria found that their first introduction to mortal combat was, for many of them, their last.

As he crawled, desperately hoping that a sniper wouldn't see him, the soldier attempted to stay as buried from sight as was possible, whilst at the same time keeping up a forward momentum. It was so painfully slow. Agonizingly, his fingers gouged into the tough, dry earth as he dragged himself onward. He shrieked as two fingernails on his left hand were torn away under the pressure of his own weight and desperation, but terror gave him strength and fortitude far beyond his normal means. Sharp-edged stones ripped at his cheeks and his blood was flowing freely from superficial wounds and scratches.

He was dimly aware that his rifle was gone and, ludicrously, the thought entered his head, he would be punished for such gross carelessness if his superiors found out. As if it mattered now.

Spatter-spatter-spatter-spatter! A neat line of small calibre bullets ran across his field of vision a mere six inches away. His bladder gave up completely and his bowels threatened to follow suit at any moment.

"Oh, dear God what am I doing here?" He sobbed. He wanted his mother. The woman that had cuddled and cradled him for so many years before her painful death from cancer. She who had nurtured and given him everything; never saying no to whatever her pouting, demanding charge demanded. Now she was gone and could protect him no more.

"Oh bugger-bugger-bugger!" Sobbing, he crawled on. Direction no longer mattered. He just hoped that it was away from the enemy. A corpse blocked his way and he fearfully peered over and around it. He almost died from shock as the 'corpse' reached out a hand to him.

"Help me! Please help me!" The voice was high pitched, almost squeaking. "Water, please. Water." The wounded man's searching hand found the young soldier's tunic lapel and began tugging frantically. "Oh God…. please help me!" He was blind. His helmet and the entire right side of his scalp were gone. One eye hung horribly down and rolled forlornly around his cheek; the other had been obliterated along with his scalp.

"Get the hell off of me!" The young soldier hissed. Once again verging close to panic. "Son of a bitch. Let go!" He twisted and turned the offending wrist but still that hand clung on. "Why don't you just die!" Bullets began to thud around them and what he had thought to be a corpse now truly became one. Trying hard to control his breathing he backed away and then around his dead comrade in arms.

The shelling, whilst still hammering the life out of the once verdant earth, was moving further northward and the small arms fire a little further south if his ears were to be believed. That meant only one thing.

"Oh, to hell with the Kaiser," he moaned. A counter attack!

His crawling increased in speed. With the slight return of his equilibrium, he now had a rough idea of where he was. Or at least, which was north, south, east and west. He didn't dare yet crouch or in any way present a larger target. The artillery barrage might have moved on but the machine gun and rifle fire were still very much in evidence. It looked as though the German offensive, in this area at least, had not gone to plan. How many of them had gone down in that first three to four minutes – thousands?

Bavarian Infantry Regiment 16. Where the hell were they? They must have advanced deep into the enemy front. His own unit of the 1st Company List had not advanced very far before being slaughtered like sheep and for the most part, haring around in total panic.

He cried out as he tumbled into a large and deep shell hole. There were bodies lying in puddles of water and he rolled down and over two of them before sliding to a stop at the feet and ankles of a curled and trembling form of another utterly terrified and broken soul.

Huge deep-set blue eyes stared into fear widened light blue ones as recognition sparked in one set of orbs.

Lieutenant Karl Lieberman, officer commanding 1st Company List had disgraced himself utterly. The moment they had come under enemy fire he had lost it completely. Out in front, some fifty metres from his start line and bravely waving his pistol and shouting at his men to advance bravely and do Germany proud, he had vomited with disbelief as his command quite simply ceased to exist. Machine guns and rifles had opened from a line of enemy that he hadn't even known was there. What kind of military intelligence was that? The enemy had been sitting less than two hundred metres away and they had walked right into them. All his training, breeding and determination to serve his Kaiser, had deserted him at that horrific moment.

What now – what to do? Lieberman had no idea. He raised a trembling hand toward his fellow soldier in mute greeting. Tears that recently had been trickling down his begrimed youthful cheeks were hastily wiped away. He, Lieberman, needed to buck-up.

The young soldier stared right back at him. Not in a deliberately disrespectful way but in shock at seeing his commanding officer, the God of Gods, he who must be obeyed and all that, in the same trembling state that he was himself. The man was terrified. Even more so than he, if that were possible.

"Lieutenant Lieberman sir." A longish pause as Lieberman stared, and then nodded slowly as though acknowledging a previously doubtful fact. He didn't recognize the soldier in front of him but the man was from his, Lieberman's, own unit. Somewhere in the back of his strangled mental state a warning sounded. This was not how the fatherland envisaged its glorious leaders. Little men in a blue funk and

4

mocked by those in whom they were supposed to instil respect, fear and adoration.

"A bad state of things, I fear." He tried to sound manly and confident but was acutely aware that his voice was trembling like butterfly wings in a strong breeze.

"What's that sir?"

"I'm all cripped up, private. That's all." The lieutenant clumsily pointed to his ankle. "Took one hell of a tumble whilst under fire, you know. Can't stand on the wretched thing. Damn nuisance!"

They both flinched as a briefly sustained burst of gunfire whistled over their heads.

"Well, sir." The private glanced nervously about and then looked up at the sky. What to do? If the enemy advanced in a counter attack, they would be found and taken prisoner. If, however, their own troops caught them up in a retreat, what in God's name could they say? Other than the *stated* ankle sprain, the lieutenant did not appear to be wounded. Neither of them seemed to have been damaged in any way other than the private's quite severe scratches due to his speedily enforced movement away from combat. His various little cuts were bleeding quite freely, giving him the superficial appearance at least of a wounded fighting man.

In spite of their hazardous situation the private was beginning to feel better. He had found somebody even more contemptible than himself.

"Sir." The soldier reached out a tentative hand and gently, almost caressingly shook his lieutenant's foot.

"What? What did you say?" Lieberman tried to clear the frantic, jumbled thoughts from his head. Who the devil was this scruffy apparition from hell? Ah, yes. One of his own men. Oh GOD! Bile rose up in his throat as he remembered, as everything came crashing back into his unwilling consciousness. He was a coward. A snivelling, weeping coward and now it would be known by all. He sobbed as his knees jerked spasmodically up to his chest.

"Not my fault," he muttered brokenly. "Not my damn fault."

"Of course not, sir." The private spoke soothingly. "Look sir. I know how it is."

"You do?" Fear tinged with relief, then a mask of total fear. "You.... you do."

The private reached across and drew the rifle of one of their dead comrades toward him. Loaded but not fired. Pathetic! Already, within the confines and comparative safety of the shell hole he was becoming belligerently judgmental, ignoring completely the fact that he had no knowledge of the whereabouts of his own rifle due to an identical finger paralyzing panic. He shoved the rifle into the lieutenant's limp unwilling hands. An idea was forming in his formerly disordered but now rapidly calming mind. The young soldier was possessed of a survival instinct second to none. He was, as yet, unaware of its true propensity but it would prove to be a powerful tool in the future.

Noise from the south. Was that men yelling? If so...in which language?

"Now, sir." The private fastened his lieutenant's hands more firmly around the rifle. "Listen to me."

"Mind your tone!" For an instant Lieberman's natural feelings of superiority over anything even remotely sounding working class, asserted itself.

"Will you just listen!"! The soldier hissed. No time for the niceties. Things were happening out there and he – they, needed a story. If he couldn't come up with something soon, the lieutenant would be disgraced and he, the non-ranking piece of cannon fodder, would most likely be shot. That of course, was if it was their own troops coming toward them. But if they were British: what then?

"Do you speak any English, sir?"

Lieberman nodded. "Yes, a little."

"Good. If Tommies appear in front of us, throw up your hands and tell them that we surrender." Lieberman nodded his understanding, really not caring too much about anything other than survival.

The private cocked an ear to one side and then scrambled to the edge of the shell hole. Peering over he gazed intently outward. The firing was no longer coming in their direction. It appeared to be moving further to the right. All so uncertain. He threw himself back beside Lieberman.

"They're ours and they're running. Running this way. Back to us. Now here's what we do."

T he soldier's little plan worked perfectly. He and Lieutenant Lieberman were swept up in the general retreat and very few questions were asked. The first battle of Ypres, 'Slaughter of the Innocents,' as it later became known, was not something that the German high command, lower command nor even those in the corporals' mess, wanted to remember, let alone discuss in detail.

September 15: 1915

K arl Lieberman fingered the nice, shiny Iron Cross 2nd class that lay on his makeshift HQ desk. Awarded to him for valour at the battle of Ypres 1914. He, or rather, his low-ranking saviour, had bluffed their way to safety and awards. After all, who would ever dream that an officer, a German officer, would lie? Especially when a private soldier had so earnestly regaled their debriefers of his commander's incredible courage under fire. All histrionic gobbledygook but their listeners, whether they believed any of it or not, took it all at face value. Germany needed heroes and reports of heroic deeds.

Lieutenant Colonel Phillippe Engelhardt had authorised the forwarding of the recommended decoration, and Captain Karl Mayr had done so with raised eyebrow. Lieberman was a Jew, and unless Mayr was mistaken, a homosexual, to boot. All of which the blonde, very Aryan Mayr found distasteful. The fact that the Jewish homosexual in question also had blonde hair and very blue eyes and looked more Aryan than the average German could ever hope to look, made not an iota of difference to his feelings about that officer. The man was a fraud. Mayr could smell it. But with all that was going on and going wrong, best left for the moment. The army didn't need scandal or defeatism. It needed heroes; even pretend heroes were better than none.

L ieberman placed his decoration back in its little box and then into a desk drawer. He rarely wore it, knowing as he did that he quite simply did not deserve it. It was a lie. That lie, though, had saved him. Saved him and his clever friend both from an awful and highly publicised fate.

He shivered as the soldier in question moved closer, and laid a handwritten message before him. The former private, now lance corporal's hand, lightly and oh so briefly, brushed the side of his exposed neck. The lieutenant almost bent his head toward that hand, desperate to feel its touch on his face, his skin, anywhere and everywhere. He breathed in deeply.

The lance corporal smiled at his commanding officer. He wore the Iron Cross 3rd class and was Lieutenant Lieberman's top messenger at regimental HQ. A nice cushy job well behind the actual battle lines. The occasional round or random shell might pop in now and then but that was infinitely preferable to squatting in a flooded front line trench day in and day out. The HQ trench was clean and spacious; barely a trench at all, really. Inhabited by the company commander, a rarely seen sergeant major, a sergeant and seven company runners, life was as good as it could possibly be under the circumstances and each one of them knew it.

Alsace was quiet at the moment. Tranquil even. As he stared out over the parapet of the tidy HQ trench, memories of the horror of Ypres came flooding back. The lieutenant, the fear, the affair. They had kissed in secret and fondled with dramatic intensity. Even with his sweet friend, August Kubizek in Linz, it had never been like this. He frowned. It was dangerous territory but his relationship with the lieutenant protected him from combat, from death!

Of one thing he was certain. There would never be another Ypres, not for him. He, Adolf Hitler, had no intention of dying in a pile of mud. His new job was about as cushy as it was possible to get in this massive killing war. Regimental runner meant being miles behind the front line and occasionally sauntering from one rear area to another delivering more or less important messages between more or less important officers. His closeness to Lieberman had got him this job and he wanted above all to keep it. He had a little bit of rank now, just enough, and a little extra in his pay packet. He was a corporal. Adolf smiled thinly. Who in Braunau am Inn would have thought it? He, Adolf Hitler, an army corporal. A man with responsibilities.

CHAPTER 2

April 22 1945: Berlin, The Bunker

"Where is Steiner – WHERE IS STEINER!" Spittle flicked from mauve coloured lips. Adolf Hitler's eyes rolled in a frenzy of ungovernable rage. His feeble fists clenched and unclenched as they waved in pathetic unison above and around his head.

"Why has Steiner not attacked…. why?"

All eyes in the conference room turned to General Alfred Jodl, who in turn looked to General Hans Krebs. Pale, straight backed, handsome but stern faced, he seemed the very epitome of the upright and invincible German warrior. His job it was to coordinate the joint attacks from army detachment, Steiner attacking from south to northeast, and General Busse of the 9th army, attacking from south centre to the north in order to join forces with Steiner.

Hitler had been confident that this joint offensive, born from his own monochrome imagination, would be hugely successful for the German army. The reality, of course, was vastly different. There had not been and would never be any offensive. Busse was barely clinging on and had long since given up any hope of relieving Berlin. 9th Army was now fighting for its own survival and working its way west, away from the Soviet armies bent on its destruction.

Steiner's Battle Group? Krebs almost choked at the appellation

'Battle Group!' Little boys, old men, some sailors and a handful of ancient, broken-down French tanks were all that made up Battle Group Steiner. Confidently promised reinforcements and ammunition had not materialized. There had been no attack, not even the pretence of one. When pressured by Field Marshall Keitel and General Jodl to get a move on, Steiner had less than politely told them to fuck off! He had since disappeared with a handful of his men, gone west somewhere.

Keitel looked hard at Krebs as if expecting some kind of sensible reply to the Führer's impossible question.

Sweat ran in small rivers down the stressed general's neck, seeping uncomfortably on down and deep inside the high collar of his restricting service jacket. It was stifling in the conference room and he could barely breathe. The air conditioning had stopped working yet again, and all that was being circulated was the foul air inflicted by constant and uncontrolled human flatulence.

Krebs suddenly felt an almost overbearing urge to burst into tears. God dammit! His lower lip was trembling like a fleshy worm on an oven ring and there was nothing he could do to stop it. It was all so wrong, so stupid. None of this made sense anymore. He had once adored National Socialism and its harsh intolerant methods. It got things done. He had even at one time believed in the Führer. Now though, he saw it for what it was. All horribly mindless and chance grasping. No great political cause or theory, and certainly no guiding genius at the helm. But here he was; stuck in this blood soaked and criminal rut with no way out. It *had* to end. It must!

Gathering himself he stammered, "There has been, there…. there was no offensive my Führer. According to latest reports, General Steiner was unable to penetrate……."

A howl of anguish tore through the conference room. "Betrayed…. Betrayed! You vile, hopeless army bastards have betrayed me. Spineless scum the lot of you. I want you dead. D'you hear me – DEAD!" Retching sounds came from the Führer's throat.

Krebs's mouth hung open. The smelly picture of insanity before him was truly terrifying. This was the supreme leader of the Third Reich in all his wretched reality! With one word, or a thousand, this ranting wreck could condemn them all to death. Death in a variety of unpleasant ways. Even his close colleague and Hitler favourite, General Burgdorf was trembling.

Keitel, forgetting his high rank and the need to keep up appearances, was chewing nervously on his fingernails and not caring one bit what he looked like. The Führer had gone off on one before, but never like this!

"The war is lost! Thanks to you, you scheming, cowardly sons of bitches, the war is utterly lost. After all my efforts, my sacrifices… This is how you repay me. With cowardice and treason. Bastards – all of you! It's done. Over! You hear me? I give up. My orders disobeyed even by the SS. I shall die by my own hand and what a relief that shall be. Now get out you gutless sacks of dung…. Get Out! It's over!"

H e sank back, as his Generals and staff left his presence, filing slowly and nervously out of the conference room.

Shocked, stunned and bewildered. Did he mean it – over? With soldiers still dying in their thousands as they desperately tried to defend him, was the Führer now simply going to give up and quit like an irritated waiter?

Martin Borman, the party secretary and Hitler's most indispensable minion, frowned angrily. Damn! The Führer's death would not suit him at all…. not yet, anyway. He, Borman, ran this dungeon madhouse with an iron fist and he, Borman, decided who did what and went where and who saw the Führer, and he, Martin Borman, would decide if and when the dribbling, half blind, pain riddled Führer might die, and if necessary, how!

Fixing a beatific expression over his round, rather brutal face, Borman turned back to his Führer.

"Perhaps I should fetch Doctor Morell," he softly suggested. His expression ludicrously ingratiating.

"Yes," the Führer hissed his reply. "Have him come to my quarters as soon as possible. Now, get out." As Borman moved obediently to the door he was pulled up short by his master's next utterance.

"Keitel, Jodl, you stay. The rest, out!" He suddenly seemed quite calm; or at least calmer. As the two officers eased their way back into the room, Borman coughed like a waiting receptionist. The thought of being left out of anything appertaining to the Führer was anathema to him. "Should I stay as well, my Führer?" Vocal tone and facial expression were both unctuous in the extreme.

"Borman, just go will you! Get Morell and then get on with doing what you normally do." Face set into an ugly mask of compliance, Borman did as he was bid.

"My Führer," Field Marshall Keitel came swiftly to Hitler's side as he staggered slightly. "Should I call Linge, as well?"

"Yes," Hitler nodded. "I need to rest and take tea. Lots of tea. And then, then I shall plan my end."

"No my Führer, no!" Keitel gasped and fretted. "Do not say such things, What shall be done without you, my Führer? You are our lives, our inspiration."

"Do you intend to make peace, my Führer?" asked Jodl, very nervously. There was no telling whether or not his demented chief might change his mind.

"ME?" Hitler scoffed, and for a moment Keitel and Krebs feared that he might lapse into shrieking mode once again. But he merely slumped back into the high-legged wooden chair and swept his right hand across the map table, spilling the flags and symbols of unit designations willy-nilly, as though they no longer mattered. "No. If it's peace you're all so set on, Goering can manage that far better than I.

"Now, listen. I want squads sent out to apprehend Steiner and his traitorous little gang. When found, hang them from the first lamp post their captors can find. See to it Keitel." Keitel nodded. How he was supposed to find, let alone apprehend, Felix Steiner and his fellow gun toting hell-hole escapees amongst all the existing chaos in and around

Berlin, he didn't know. He did know, though, that now was not the time to argue with the Führer.

"And you, Jodl. Take over the running of what's left of the defence. As of now. I don't want to be bothered with minutiae any longer. Can't be doing with it." General Jodl somehow swallowed the bellow of outrage that almost flew from his throat. Minutiae? The destruction of the Reich's first city and the slaughter of its people, minutiae? Krebs felt his heart constrict savagely, as his outrage threatened to overwhelm his better sense. Only with the greatest difficulty was he holding himself back from physically confronting his Führer.

Hitler sighed heavily and fought against giving way to his chronic meteorism. Tension played havoc with what remained of his digestive system after years of lettuce leaves, cream cakes and arsenic based medication.

"Linge!" Keitel's self-important bellow echoed from the walls.

"Herr Field Marshal." Came the reply from out in the corridor now used as an anteroom.

"Help the Führer to his rooms."

"Of course." Obersturmbannführer Heinz Linge stepped smartly, almost delicately into the room and went straight to his Führer. He looked as always, neat and tidy with not a hair, a lace or button out of place. His cologne made a decent combat against the variety of odours which clung everywhere and never seemed to lessen. His glance flicked for the briefest of moments over the scattered symbols on the map table, and then, all business, fastened on the Führer. With familiarity gained through long years of close contact and confidentiality, Linge gently grasped Hitler by his forearm and armpit. Known for his unquestioning loyalty and obedience to his Führer, Linge's rank was out of all proportion to the position that he held. His SS rank of Obersturmbannführer was the equivalent to that of an army lieutenant colonel. His job, as Hitler's personal valet, servant and general factotum made him something of a nattily uniformed butler. A butler with SS rank and status, though.

Heinz Linge was in close proximity daily to Hitler, and in his professional capacity as trusted and devoted servant had almost unchallenged access and intimate knowledge of all that went on in his Führer's small and now pretty well non-existent private and professional life. A life that had once been so sensationally exciting and all encompassing, was now reduced to fear and inactivity in a few underground rooms. Rats in a trap. Linge kept his own counsel but he was no fool. He knew well enough what was coming. Nevertheless, he made no requests for favouritism and his emotions seemed to be completely in sync with those of his leader; as such he remained much valued and trusted by the eternally suspicious Führer.

The faithful Linge was privy to all that went on around the Führer and his inner circle and had been a shrewd witness and observer for many years. Even Martin Borman could not budge the SS uniformed valet from the Führer's side, and heaven knows he had tried often enough with veiled hints of bad behaviour, alcoholism together with doubtful loyalty. All to no avail. Hitler trusted his sweet-faced, always compliant servant and so promoted and protected him.

Leaning heavily upon his valet, Hitler shuffled from the conference room. Running waist high throughout the length of the lower bunker complex was a wooden safety rail. This had been installed in order to assist the failing Führer's weakening legs, unpredictable equilibrium and worsening sight. Eyes weakened by doses of strychnine swallowed for years as a tonic to combat listlessness, along with arsenic-based capsules taken for intestinal problems. These remedies, amongst others, were heartily endorsed and lovingly prepared by his personal and very controversial physician, Dr Theodore Morell. Morell's care and creative use of powerful and dangerous chemical and plant extracts had taken their inevitable toll on his health. What had once helped, superficially at least, was now killing him. Ageing him way beyond his fifty-five years. He looked like a terminally ill geriatric on his very last legs. But his system refused to give up.

The Führer's weight was bearing down heavily on the slimly built Linge. Hitler was muttering to himself as they moved slowly towards the Führer apartment. Linge nodded and smiled his usual agreeable smile whilst wondering how much longer any of this could continue.

Rochus Misch, the bunker switchboard operator with the rank of SS Scharführer, lurched out of his cubby hole. Nothing came over the airways or landlines without Misch's knowledge. His state-of-the-art Siemens switchboard was so advanced that only he knew how to competently work it. It shone with the sometimes static and at other times brightly flickering, attention demanding lights of five designative colours and kept him busy, informed and shut off from the never-ending bustle of the outer rooms and corridors of the Führerbunker.

A tall, well-built man, Misch was the genie who understood the mass of leads, wires and plugs that made up the bunker's communication system. He was their window to an ever decreasing outside world.

"Misch."

The Scharführer glanced over and smiled. Only a few days ago he would have clicked his heels together and saluted like a well-oiled but noisy machine. He was a handsome man, and even down here, with all its peeling plaster, dripping leaks and claustrophobic nooks and crannies, he looked ready for a parade. No regulation salute, however, was forthcoming. Linge could raise hell and insist upon it, of course. But that would simply mean embarrassment all round. The food stains, the dribbling and the shaking limbs, commanded precious little in the way of love and respect for the ailing and now sad excuse for a leader. No more God-like status. Just a sick, demented and very sad old man trying to stay alive just a little while longer. There was still the unquestioning obedience, though. Amazing, that…. how they all, himself included, continued to obey. Once, before the joyous advent of National Socialism, he had been a lowly bricklayer but always with an eye open for the main chance. The Nazi Party and the SS had been his main chance and he had seized it eagerly. Linge had hopped on board the SS train of advancement and good things and followed Hitler, obeying him at every turn. When the time came, on that fateful day in 1933 to swear allegiance, he had happily sworn the SS blood oath to willingly lay down his life for the Führer at the drop of a hat: as if! Of course, at the time he hadn't envisaged that such a thing might actually come to pass. Now, though, it seemed that just about everybody in Germany was dying for the man, whether they wanted to or not. It was absurd!

"Over here, Misch. A little help if you please."

The large, always friendly seeming Scharführer Rochus Misch ambled over and obligingly took Hitler's weight on his powerful left arm. Being so much taller than Hitler, his six-foot one-inch frame towering over the Führer's stooping five foot seven inches, he had to bend considerably in order to lend support and take the ailing Führer's weight. With a barely concealed sigh of relief, Linge moved away and led them forward toward Hitler's apartments. Odd thing about Misch, he thought. A man never to rock the boat. He would fit in wherever he was placed. He had been chosen as one of the lesser members of the Führer's entourage years ago simply because he was big, bright, deferential and obedient. No trouble at all. Linge, however, had taken the trouble to go over his record, very carefully. Misch, amazingly for a young man in such a position, close to the Führer and the heart of the Reich's decision makers, displayed no inclination whatsoever to further his career. Scharführer Rochus Misch, it seemed, was a man with no ambition; none at all. He merely wanted to survive in the easiest, cushiest way possible and went out of his way not to draw attention to himself. He was very intelligent and would have done well at any middle ranking university, had he ever attended. Indeed, his teachers had pleaded with his grandfather to allow young Rochus to go on to university in order to progress further with his education and fulfil his obvious promise. His academic form at school had been excellent and he was also a fine sportsman, excelling at football and boxing. But grandpa Misch, Rochus's guardian since the death of his parents a few years previously, was adamant. His grandson must learn a trade and bring in some money. And so young Rochus travelled the route of apprentice, with some day release technical college visits thrown in. Not that he objected to the route chosen for him. Rochus went along with it all, comfortably travelling on the wind. Nevertheless, everything he did, all his technical college results and such, displayed a superior intelligence to the norm in his subject grouping.

All that and no ambition? What an amazing rarity of a man. One thing, however, that Linge had picked up on. Misch was uncomfortably close to the very scary SS Gruppenführer Johann Rattenhuber, Hitler's uncompromising personal security chief and therefore a man to be wary of regardless of his lowly rank. Clearly someone that enjoyed anonymity and calm, Misch gave the impression that he intended to see out the war as comfortably and as safely as was possible. If that meant kissing the Führer's rear end with a smile, or, equally obligingly, and in his polite and unfailingly charming manner, putting a bullet in the great one's brain, then, he would comfortably execute whichever one ensured the path of least resistance. That, Heinz Linge felt for certain, constituted the essence of SS Scharführer Rochus Misch.

The thick, blast-proof steel door to the Führer's apartment squealed angrily as Misch heaved it open and ushered the Führer into his tiny suite of rooms. Entering the study and stopping just in front of the bedroom door, Hitler tapped him gently on the arm and nodded his thanks. Misch, wincing slightly as his back clicked from the enforced bending, clicked his heels smartly in acknowledgement.

Linge gave a slight wave of his hand as he dismissed Misch and motioned him to leave the blast and gas sealed door ajar. As Misch returned to his switchboard duties, Linge made a show of dusting the single telephone and straightening it.

"Doctor Morell has been sent for, my Führer. He should be here presently. Shall I fetch tea, sir?"

"Yes, Linge. Camomile tea will do. And some cake, Linge, some cake."

"Of course, my Führer. At once."

Hitler eased himself into the sofa and allowed his head to drop back. He winced at the steel door's metallic grunt as Linge drew it closed.

Morell would doubtless have something that would make him feel better, for a while. But what was the point now? It was all truly coming to an end. This thing, this lengthy *Gotterdammerung*, which even in a total lunatic's version of reality should never have come to anything at all, was drawing to its ruinous conclusion. Who would have guessed, eh? He, Lance Corporal Hitler, was der Führer. He, the former corporal, had become the feared and hated destroyer of the world, the eradicator of mankind! Cleanser, more like. Pah! Even Wagner couldn't have thought up this flame-lashed finale. As for his beloved Germany? Beloved? How could he possibly love this train wreck of a nation? He shook his head. He had little idea of what it was really like out there, where all hell now reigned supreme, or so he had been told by various visitors. He hadn't been outside for what seemed like an age. The stairs were a problem now, of course. And then there was, well, who the hell needed to see first-hand the bomb blasted ruins of their own massive failure? No! Not his failure; theirs. Those incompetents that had promised to obey him and who, instead, had disobeyed, criticised and wrecked his great plans. The military, the Gauleiters, even his own inner circle. Cowardice and betrayal by all of them. As for that fat oaf Goering: was there a greater fool anywhere on the planet? Unless it was von Ribbentrop, of course. Monumentally vain and stupid. Thing was, they had all been chosen by himself for precisely those mundane and less than admirable qualities that were so useful to a leader: ambitious but basically stupid bullies, unable to mount a challenge to their lord and master, nor able to function fully without him. He scratched lazily at an itch that was persistently nagging his inner thigh and puffed out his sagging cheeks with the temporary relief that his scratching brought. Well….you get what you pay for. No doubt about that!

The Führerprinzip. It had worked well enough, although it made for a lonely existence with him, the Führer, the bestower of all wealth, influence and title. It had once hugely amused him to observe how small men with tiny minds loved such big titles and fancy uniforms. Not much left to bestow now, though.

The trembling of his arms and left leg was worse today, and his eyes hurt dreadfully. Was he talking to himself? Need to watch that, he mused. Can't have people thinking that I'm losing my mind. Where was Morell? More importantly, where was his tea? He sat alone, his head nodding oddly out of time with the trembling of his limbs. Was it really all over? Well, yes, of course it was and had been for some time! Only his persona, his psyche, had kept people believing in an impossible victory, as he self-destructively steered this onrushing Armageddon thundering to its inevitable conclusion. From 1942 onwards, as news of successive disasters and retreats battered down the walls of his confidence, he had, like a spoilt and spiteful child smashing his favourite toys because the giver had done something to upset him, thrown away one army after another, one elite division followed another into torment and oblivion as he, the Führer, eased his fury by smashing his human and mechanical toys against the rocks of his enemy's hatred.

He had learnt a good lesson from that Bavarian company sergeant major in 1915. One of those hard-as-nails, touchy-feely types that abounded wherever a lot of young men were closeted together.

"It's all an act," he'd said. "Every damn thing for higher-ups is an act. When you're in charge, sonny, no matter who you are, you can't come out of that act, see? Not ever – not even for a second. 'Cos if you do, then those around you will realize that you're no different from them. Just a thieving, rutting lump of meat waiting to die, afraid to die. Scared to death of it all. And 'cos humans is fickle bastards, through n' through, they'll turn on you. Got it, Junge? Now. Squeeze 'arder. Guter Junge"

The Junge had indeed got it. He had obeyed that wise dictum as though it had been sent by God himself, and, as tempered by a master, it had worked astoundingly well!

All gone now, though. Well, nearly all gone. There was nothing left to do but die. Oh, hell and damnation – to die – an end to everything? He simply could not imagine it. How does one imagine death, he mused? His unpredictable stomach clenched and rumbled unpleasantly as a wave of nausea inducing fear ran through his being; his body and brain immediately and strongly rejected all thought of deliberate death…. of any kind of death. There must be a way, something left to try. What about Field Marshall Ferdinand Schörner? His army group was still intact in Hungary. Perhaps an attack toward Berlin could be launched from there. No – not enough time. He sighed. It was all so unfair. All his work, his dreams, not to mention his genius, gone to waste. Let down by them all. All those that simply could not understand his, his what? A limp hand waved at the air. Why did he forget things so quickly these days? His memory had once been his greatest tool. Always ready with facts and figures that he had recently read; not understood, but certainly read.

Amazing, how it had all happened. Yes it was. A few moments from the past drifted before his tired eyes. What a bunch of morons. He coughed and noisily swallowed a large, slimy gristle of phlegm. For the life of him he could not bring to mind his political ideas and foundation. It had all just seemed to snowball out of nothing. The war? Ah yes, this bloody war. Doomed. All that came into his fevered mind now were varied strains of a mixture of Wagnerian symphonies accompanying a manic Siegfried waving a shiny sword.

He had said repeatedly that death would be a blessing for him. A release from all his trials and woes. He would take his own life, he had told them, more than once. Now, that time was fast approaching.

"Die?" he whispered. "No, I don't want it to end. It can't. It just can't. I won't let it." At the back of his mind, though, the truth nagged at him. Yes, you must die, and soon. Do it soon.

Adolf Hitler's final battle was about to begin. As he, the man responsible for snuffing out the lives of millions, sought desperately for a way of prolonging his own. The irony, of course, was completely lost on him.

Theodor Morell carelessly threw several vials of anti-gas capsules, heart pills and stimulants into his cracked and worn medical bag. These were followed by a fistful of powerful opiate concoctions prepared by himself, all of which Hitler voraciously consumed each and every day. The bottles of capsules packed and rattling like chipped castanets, were followed by syringes, needles and iodine. The veins themselves were receding, shrinking as plaque took over and the heart showed signs of giving up the unequal struggle. Powerful eye drops made up this cornucopia of drugs and medicines. Morell popped a 'mother's little helper,' Pervitin, into his mouth. Enjoying the quick rush it gave him he took hold of his bag. Time to treat his drug addicted Führer, hopefully for the last time. There was surely no point in his remaining in this concrete coffin. He intended to beg Hitler for command of the German Red Cross. That title should see him safe after the war when the inevitable war crime arrests began. And surely, surely the Führer would agree that he, Morell, deserved the reward.

Short, revoltingly overweight and with the personal habits of a warthog, doctor Morell was disliked by pretty well everybody in the upper and lower bunker. That had never bothered him. His rise, his fame, the plethora of splendidly disgusting, slutty women now available to him, made the dislike of his peers and fellows totally irrelevant. Now, though, he was sweating. He knew what his system of medical practice had done to the Führer, and so did Stumfegger, the SS surgeon now living in the bunker, and Dr Werner Haase, the new stand-in for emergencies. And that valet, Linge, liked to observe a tad too closely for his liking.

The word 'quack' was being ever more frequently bandied about, and Morell had the distinct feeling that Hitler was, at last, listening to the warnings. His fleshy, ugly lips twisted with anxiety. It wasn't his fault that the Führer had unremitting intestinal problems, foul breath, bad sight and trembling limbs. He'd had some of those things, and worse, when Morell had first been recommended by Hitler's splendidly alcoholic photographer, Heinrich Hoffman.

Morell had prescribed, Hitler had ingested and the initial results had been joyously effective. The problem was, the wretched man insisted upon taking more and more of Morell's prescriptions and in ever stronger doses. How many times did he have to explain to Hitler and the rest, that belladonna was a poison; be careful with it? But the wretched man had no willpower. He'd get an ache, a spasm or a cough and off he would run to the medicine bottle. And if that didn't work *immediately*, then he would go into a hissy fit and demand something that did.

Nevertheless, because of his association with the Führer, Theodore Morell's meds were widely sought after and many folk swore by his treatment and methods. Many others, however, did not. Was it his, Morell's, fault if people were so stupid as to ignore his warnings as to overdosing with strong medicines, and go stuffing themselves to oblivion with his remedies?

Anyway, it was time for him to get out of this underground madhouse. Desperate to leave, he had tentatively broached the subject with Joseph Goebbels. The propaganda minister was the only true and loyal friend remaining to Hitler. The problem was that Hitler didn't much like him. Seemed to think a lot of his wife, Magda, though. Goebbels advised against a direct approach, however, as the Führer was by now heartily sick of people using all manner of excuses to abandon him. As like as not he would fly into a rage and order his arrest, even his execution. But Morell didn't dare leave it any longer. It was becoming almost impossible to venture more than a few hundred metres from the Chancellery. If he didn't get out now, the chances were that he never would. Perspiring heavily with fear, the good doctor girded his mental loins and prepared for his meeting with the Führer.

There was tea and cake but only one cup and no second plate. The Führer looked like death on an off day. The quivering was now quite severe and his breathing ragged. His eyes, however, though yellow-tinted and heavily bloodshot, were focused and quite calm. Alone together in his tiny, cell-like bedroom, any physical secrets were out of the question. Hitler hated to strip in front of others. Most thought that it was because of his scrawny physique and a wish to keep the Führer aura intact. There was, however, as Morell well knew, an entirely different reason for Hitler's modesty. Many years ago, shortly before the first world war, Adolf Hitler had been examined by an Austrian army medical board and had been rejected as being unfit for military service. With a rare concern for thoroughness, the Austrian military doctor concerned had picked up on something that most army medical boards worldwide would have missed, or even ignored. It wasn't his physical weakness that had barred Adolf from Austrian military acceptance, although he certainly was undernourished and somewhat feeble. It was his severe, although operable, Hypospadias which made even the most straightforward of male bodily functions an absolute nightmare. That together with a testicle that had stubbornly refused to drop, made young Adolf Hitler undesirable for the Austrian army.

The German army though, had no such qualms. They never even noticed.

Rochus Misch was fielding one call after another when Morell came bundling by. The good doctor was happy and in a hurry. The Führer had refused point blank his request to be given overall responsibility for the German Red Cross. He had, though, sacked the portly quack and, making sure that he left his bag of medicines behind, sent him from his presence. Werner Haase would take over for whatever time was left.

Morell was delighted. Up and away! Moving rapidly for such an obese individual, he barely waved goodbye to anyone. He'd left most of his gear in his room, which, apparently, Joseph Goebbels would now be taking over. He was more than welcome.

Morrel headed for the stairs and the relative freedom of the bomb hell that was Berlin.

It was time to put all this behind him and begin afresh. He doubted very much that a reference from his former employer, Adolf Hitler, would be of any future use.

Scharführer Misch was in a quandary. His state-of-the-art switchboard was nearing a catastrophic breakdown. Overheating barely described it. Since the recent refusal of the Führer to have anything more to do with command decisions, no orders, commands or requests had gone out. Nor had the Führer, or anyone else, responded to the desperate pleas for orders and information pouring in from the various, abandoned commanders in the field.

Misch's opinion of the high command was diminishing rapidly. How could they simply let men die like this?

"Outflanked and no ammunition. Send ammunition and reinforcements…please respond!" This from a frantic major, commanding what remained of the 7th Volkssturm Grenadiers.

Misch stared forlornly at his switchboard. There was nothing he could do except sit there whilst this tragedy unfolded.

"Is there anybody there? Answer me you sons of bitches. What am I supposed to do?"

"The best you can. What else?" Whispered Misch, as he leaned forward and withdrew the copper-coated diode from the board in front of him. There would soon be nothing from the switchboard. Constant shelling, bombing and small arms fire were making repairs to the frequently broken lines of communication almost impossible.

Misch sat back and observed Linge walking toward him accompanied by the bunker's resident snob, Major Freytag von Loringhoven. They both wore a conspiratorial look as they glanced at him. Misch ignored them. Such furtive looks were common these days. He stiffened in his seat when a heavy hand from behind slapped him on the shoulder. Misch turned to see who it was.

"Misch, my good fellow." Martin Borman gave him a smile that was about as genuine as a black-market Rolex. "I want this message sent immediately." Misch's eyes widened as he noted the addressee, but he nodded acceptance. "Yes, Herr Reichsleiter. At once."

"And no blabbing. Got it?" Borman's sausage like fingers lightly twisted Misch's ear. In another place that would have been a colossal mistake.

"Of course not, Herr Reichsleiter. Have I ever?" The tone was bland, inoffensive. Nevertheless, Misch's irritation at having his ear tweaked and his professionalism questioned penetrated even Martin Borman's thick skull. He slapped the Scharführer's shoulder again with an overload of false bonhomie as he walked away. "Good man, Misch. Good man."

"Isn't there any way that you can stop her, dear?" Magda Goebbels crossed one elegant ankle in front of the other. "After all, you still have considerable influence and she is such an attention seeking pain."

Joseph Goebbels looked over at his wife; his long-suffering wife. The wife that he didn't much care for anymore. Never really had, in all truth. It was the Führer who insisted that he marry, and Magda had been available. Richly available, as it turned out. It had been at a time when the Führer was striving for respectability, and trying desperately to move away from the horde of psychopaths and sexual deviants that had for so long made up his coterie.

Magda came from a well-to-do family. Nice properties, nice manners and lots of money. True, her stepfather was a Jew but they had muddled their way through that small misfortune. Unlike the dark eyes, black hair and almost Semitic look of her husband, Magda was true Nordic. All wavy platinum blonde hair and widely spaced blue eyes. And for some reason she, and many others, found the Führer, Adolf Hitler, sexually attractive. A real turn-on, in fact. Power did things to women, Joseph knew. He need only look at himself. Five feet four inches tall, buck-toothed and with a club foot. Yet he had only to click his fingers and the most glamorous females in the Reich would come running. Well – they would have, at one time. The ladies might not find the prospect of an evening with Joe Goebbels too enticing these days. He smiled; he'd seen the day, though.

"She insists, my dove," he replied. "Says she wants to share everything with the Führer, and all that kind of stuff."

"Histrionic clap-trap," snapped Magda. "She's an airheaded ninny. What on earth can our glorious Führer see in such a creature?"

What both Goebbels and the Führer had seen in Eva Braun was normality. A not stupid but not terribly bright, compliant attention seeker. Eva was perfect for the *supposed* sexual needs, as the average German saw it, of the Führer, Adolf Hitler. Marriage was out of the question. The people, though, must be led to think that Hitler's appetites and needs were normal and above reproach. He could remain single but it was necessary that he have a woman in tow. And so began a deliberate and ongoing charade. The fantasy of an illicit, *almost* hidden love affair between the dedicated leader of his people and his loyal, devoted, but rarely seen, woman. Just the one woman, mind. The people must see that their Führer was steadfast and no philanderer. Goebbels had judged it all to perfection and it suited the fantasy loving Eva perfectly.

The knowing nods, winks and elbow nudging from the populace at large were signals of his success in this endeavour. Joseph had frequently congratulated himself on his own genius. Eva might not be the brightest soul but she did, with surprising insight, fully understand the role that she had so happily accepted. In it, she had surpassed even Goebbels's expectations with her ability to continue in the part so expertly. The out-of-a-bottle-blonde had turned out remarkably well. There was no talk behind closed curtains about the Führer needing a woman: he had one.

Lately, though, she had begun fantasizing and truly believing that she was the first lady of the Reich. Airs and graces that she had never displayed whilst Germany was storming to success on all fronts, had come very much to the fore in the wake of German defeats and disasters. She was becoming an absolute pain!

Joseph knew how much Eva liked to show off. Even an audience of one was enough to provoke and satisfy her exhibitionist tendencies. In the seclusion of the lake area at Hansbach, where she cavorted almost naked and enjoyed swinging from the branches of trees whilst a trusted somebody filmed, photographed and applauded her antics, no real problem. Discreetly placed and hidden guards ensured total privacy.

Likewise at Berchtesgaden it had not been so bad, as she made no effort, then, to assume feigned sophistication. There she had been wheeled out and displayed to all and sundry and allowed to waffle and cavort away to her heart's content. An indulgent Führer would smile and nod as his *secret* paramour flirted, pouted and conversed in her frivolous way with the high and mighty of the Third Reich. They, the insignia laden and oft heavily uniformed big-wigs of the new Germany, easily tolerated Eva's fatuous chatter and easy manner. Many of them were on a similar intellectual level and so conversational embarrassment was rarely a problem. Many of the men liked her. The women and wives of the inner circle, however, did not, and refused to take her seriously.

Not ugly but certainly no beauty, without hairdo and make-up Eva was really quite plain, almost homely. A strong athletic figure topped off with something of a large, pudding face. Not completely unattractive; merely somewhat typical and ordinary, which of course, was precisely the idea. Time and experience, though, had changed Eva somewhat. Now skilled dress sense and expert use of cosmetics could have the dowdy Eva Braun looking, from a distance, almost as good as Hedy Lamarr.

The bold attentions of one or two of her SS escort, big blonde, beautiful types, were received and reciprocated energetically by Eva. Always with the utmost discretion and secrecy. And always initiated by herself. Had to be that way, as no SS guard would dare step toward her uninvited, so to speak. Provided the boat wasn't rocked, Adolf let things ride.

Eva had gotten above herself once or twice, but bringing her sharply back to earth was never a problem. A couple of highly dramatic but decidedly non-lethal suicide attempts had gained the Führer's attention and irritation. But nevertheless, he had increased her circle of freedom and became more attentive.

"Keep her away from firearms and barbiturates," were his somewhat hypocritical commands.

Eva knew only too well upon which side her bread was buttered. She had trained herself, learnt from her mistakes and everything had worked superbly. But now, things were getting rocky and Eva's version of reality, like Adolf's, was veering somewhat off-centre.

Great heaven! Magda leant forward to remonstrate with her husband. "She's not pregnant, is she? Dear God in heaven what could be worse?"

"How could I possibly know?" Goebbels sniggered. Pregnant? What a riot that would be! As if the Führer would, or could, ever father a child.

Magda, for whatever reason, failed to see that the Führer's sexual leanings, such as they were, went in a totally different direction to that which she imagined: and she no doubt imagined herself to be somewhere close to the centre of those leanings.

"Then why is she becoming more and more loud and foolish? The Führer won't put up with it for much longer, Joseph. Something should be done. Have a word with her and put her right." She was still leaning forward as she spoke and her heavy breasts swung slightly beneath the expensive silk of her full shouldered dress. The slow unintended movement reminded Joseph of all those admiring women that once lined the streets of Berlin as Adolf passed by in one of his motorized cavalcades. Wide-eyed, heaving breasts, up-down Nazi salutes and hysterical adulation. It had been an amazing, and really rather erotic phenomenon. It was the Reich's women that had finally propelled Adolf Hitler into the Chancellery. Too many men had been suspicious and afraid of the unsophisticated corporal, or just downright jealous of the big-mouthed Austrian lording it over his German betters. Well, Girl Power had won the day and Adolf Hitler made it to the top.

Goebbels shook his head slightly. Why did he bother with these foolish thoughts? All was tragedy and hell. Ye Gods! His brain sought to lock onto the frightfulness of his, and Germany's situation; the destruction, death. The entire bloody world was being disembowelled!!

"Don't shake your head at me like that, Joseph." Magda, not realizing where her husband's train of thought had drifted, assumed that his head shaking was directed at her. "This is important. Morale is going to the dogs. She bosses the SS men around as if they were her servants. It won't do Joseph – it simply won't do."

"Magda," Goebbels thrust out his hands, palms up. "Please, my dear. We have so much to think on. To sort out."

"No, Joseph. Now you for once will listen to me. I mean, really, Joseph. You are the minister of Propaganda."

"And Enlightenment, my dear. Let's not forget. Propaganda *and* Enlightenment."

"Can't you at least try to not look so depressed all the time?"

"Difficult. You see, Schatzi, it is a surfeit of the aforementioned enlightenment that promotes my depression." He intertwined his fingers, making a little house beneath his nose. Was it even marginally important now what Eva Braun, or anyone else for that matter, might say, or do? No, not at all. Magda, though, needed to pretend that things still mattered. That proper form should be observed, regardless. Oh well, then. Let it be so.

"Honestly, Joseph." Magda waved an exasperated hand at him. "You of all people, should be setting an example of confidence and faith in final victory. Things will shortly turn for the better and the situation will be resolved. This I know to be true." Magda smiled, smugly, her left eyebrow raised in an irritatingly know-it-all fashion.

"You know – how?" Goebbels flipped both hands toward his wife. "Exactly how do you know this truth? A little bird, perhaps?"

"I know, Joseph, because," she nodded as though speaking to a slightly backward child. "Yesterday, I spoke with the Führer and he assured me that all would soon change for the better. He will be using a secret weapon, Joseph." A look of supreme confidence and smug superiority sat on her handsome face. "We shall all be saved by his genius."

Goebbels felt a nit-picking despair arise from the lower region of his stomach. This woman that he had married. Always so superior. With her breeding, family connections and money. At times like these he found her impossible to tolerate.

"A secret weapon," he muttered. Now completely beyond the sarcasm for which he was noted. "A secret weapon, you say?"

Magda nodded enthusiastically. "Yes. He has one in mind. He said so. He has one in mind."

"Really? Has one in mind? Then one wonders why, just a short while ago he raved and screamed that the war is lost and is now contemplating suicide. He has abrogated all responsibility for the war, for us, for Germany. So, where is this secret bloody weapon you naïve old gas-bag?"

CHAPTER 3

May 1919: Augsburg, Bavaria

Army barracks are rarely places of tranquil beauty, and in the pouring rain on May 17 1919, Lechfeld barracks near Augsburg in Bavaria was anything but a thing of beauty. Gone were the pristine pathways and freshly painted barrack walls. Soldiers still lived there. Or, rather, soldiers of a sort. The catastrophic defeat in 1918 had changed things beyond all recognition. The once immaculate army barracks at Lechfeld was now grubby and paint flaked. Soldierly cleanliness was a thing of the past. The rows of barrack rooms, line upon line of them, resembled more a camp for the homeless.

Adolf gazed around less than affectionately. It was home. His home and he felt grateful to have it. But what a state to let things get into. Lucky to be here, though. He knew that well enough.

Upon his return to Bavaria, Adolf had talked himself into being elected to the soldier's council. As a representative of that body he had done quite well, respectfully putting the returning soldiers' requests before the civilian authorities, displaying a degree of eloquence that none of his colleagues could match. He had also shouted down mercilessly any gainsayers on his own soldier's council. Adolf had gained a small reputation and he liked it. Then that fool

Eisner, the Bavarian government leader, had gone and got himself assassinated. All change! Soldiers' councils were already a thing of the past. Mutant Socialism was rearing its ugly head and Adolf wanted no part of anything even hinting at communism, which was unfortunate because the Bavarian Socialist Council fairly reeked of it. There would be more changes, violent changes, and very soon. Had the world ever been so topsy-turvy unpredictable?

Always a hater of the commonplace or predictable, Adolf shuddered with anticipation. He could almost feel the winds of change whistling in his ear.

The slouching lance corporal scuffed at a lone cigarette end that clung determinedly to the toecap of his right boot. His lip curled. Filthy habit and too many took advantage of it, in his opinion. The campgrounds were littered with dog-ends and assorted rubbish.

The war was done and he had survived. Survived without having to actually fight in a single battle. True, he had been in attendance at some of the biggest blood baths that the world had ever seen. But, with the exception of Ypres in 1914, it was as a rear-echelon runner and well away from the hell of the front line. Not bad going, keeping himself in one piece after four long years of relentless killing.

His relationship with Lieutenant Lieberman ended when that officer had been removed forcibly from this earth by a random shell, which had unkindly blown him to the four corners whilst he was walking to the latrine. With that unfortunate event it looked as though his protection might have gone. However, Lieutenant Lieberman being a Jew had helped enormously. Adolf's next commanding officer, Lieutenant Hugo Gutman, was also a Jew and he read Lieutenant Lieberman's reports very thoroughly. Lance Corporal Hitler, was, it would seem, an absolute gem of a man and a loyal and conscientious soldier. A glowing reference from one Jew to another was worth more than a Mason's handshake. He had remained out of harm's way until, as rotten luck would have it, a random shell sought him out in 1918.

He was wounded, mildly compared to many, and the projectile with its accompanying mustard gas had done him a huge favour.

The barrage containing the offending HQ shattering shell had been part of a massive opening salvo directed at the front lines some four miles away. Adolf and two others had survived. Stretchered away and hospitalized at Pasewalk in Pomerania, far away from the horrors of war.

When he regained consciousness, Adolf found that he was unable to see, or speak. The gas had blinded him and done something awful to his throat and lungs. The doctors told him that he would be fine, but he didn't feel fine. His eyes hurt terribly, all the time. When he tried to speak it felt as though a sharpened garlic grater was being pulled over his vocal cords. In November the eye bandages were gently removed and the doctor pronounced that all was well. But Adolf resolutely refused to see. The battlefront beckoned with its death dripping finger and he wanted no part of that hell. Here at Pasewalk he was, and here he intended to remain for as long as he could. Arm dramatically thrown across his now unbandaged eyes, Adolf moaned loudly about his need to return to his duty at the front. To serve the fatherland with his comrades in arms. He must regain his sight.... he must!

As lance corporal Hitler was a holder of the Iron Cross 1st class, the attending physician hesitated to take him to task over what was, to say the least, an outrageous piece of play-acting. The moaning corporal's eyes were fine and his throat and lungs were almost completely healed.

Adolf was more grateful than ever for that Iron Cross. No one would doubt him, not overtly anyway. Lieutenant Gutman had put him forward for the award after enduring an awful lot of wheedling and ear-bending from his lance corporal. He never boasted about his prized decoration. To do so would have meant making up a story about how he had won it, and that was something best not gone into in any depth.

The doctor, frowning as he stared down at his charge, began writing on his clipboard. He would call in the hospital psychiatrist to study this possibly malingering individual. Forster could sort it all out. He, Brandt, had other work that needed doing. In the meantime, he wrote at the bottom of his notes: 'Undergoing further treatment.'

One day later, when news of Germany's defeat filtered through, the psychiatrist, Doctor Forster, found his skills very much needed throughout the hospital wards. Not least was his attention directed to Lance Corporal Adolf Hitler who, upon learning of Germany's shameful capitulation, fell into a shrieking, demented nervous breakdown. Lance Corporal Hitler had not taken a single life for the fatherland during the course of four years of bloody warfare. Not once had his hands closed around an enemy's throat, nor had he felt an enemy's bayonet press against his flesh. And yet, the thought of defeat drove him to the brink of madness.

"Oi, Hitler. Get yer arse over here." Sergeant Franz Hepper bellowed at the lounging junior NCO. Adolf glanced up, his pale blue eyes fastening upon the beckoning finger of his immediate superior. He hissed through his walrus-type moustache. What now? The days of his grovelling before meaty mouthed sergeants were gone but, nevertheless, respect for the rank must be shown if he wanted to keep and perhaps even progress in his new job with the Information Office of the Military Administration. He desperately wanted to undergo the next political education course being held in unit 17 of the barracks. He would be good at it, he knew. If he could get himself on to that cadre he would be trained on how best to put forward the Bavarian government's ideas on political correctness and all things Bavarian. To watch out for and report any subversive elements that he might see or suspect to be at work around him. Yes, of course he could do that. Delivering a lengthy harangue to a captive audience of obedient private soldiers would not pose a problem for him. His voice, since the gassing of last year, had undergone a very definite change. With normal tone and inflection, his vocal levels were now more nasal with a strange resonance, like a voice speaking in an empty room. But it was when he increased the pitch and volume, putting pressure on his vocal cords, that the change was truly astonishing. People sat back, grown men became wide-eyed and people listened in a way that they never had before. As yet it was a rough tool and one of which he was becoming daily more aware. His voice had become, courtesy of the contents of that gas-filled British shell, forceful and attention gaining. This new job, if he got it, would enable him to hone his new talent. Ideas were beginning to form in young Adolf's mind. He was canny enough, though, to realise that he needed experience. Captive audiences would be a good start. No heckling. Just obedient listeners eager to please.

"Yes, sergeant," he puffed, trotting over to where Hepper stood waiting. Adolf's 5 foot seven and a bit inches of height towered above the sergeant's five foot five. Hepper, though, had wide shoulders and a barrel chest, whereas Adolf's shoulders more resembled an old, sagging coat hanger, and he possessed nothing in the way of a chest that was worth mentioning.

"Get yourself over to Captain Mayr's office. Double time now. Chop-chop!"

"What's it about, sarge?" Even as he asked, Adolf knew the futility of such a question and the response that it would provoke. Inwardly he cursed his stupidity at giving the abrasive Sergeant Hepper an excuse to bully and shout. Hepper loved to exercise his sergeant's voice. The Kaiser and his Junkers might be gone, but he, Sergeant Franz Hepper, was most certainly still here.

"Well, here's the strange thing, laddie. Our beloved leader fails to see the importance of allowing me, his most humble sergeant, any kind of insight into his all-knowing bloody mind. So, in short – I don't soddin' well know. Alright with you, corporal?"

Adolf smartly brought his heels together.

"Yes, sergeant." He mumbled.

"What's that, corporal? I can't hear you."

"I said – YES, SERGEANT. I UNDERSTAND!"

Hepper blanched and stepped back. His face registered momentary shock at the powerful vocal blast to which he had just been subjected. Where the hell had that come from? Quickly pulling himself together he waved his swagger stick toward Mayr's office. "Right! On yer way, then, Hitler. Be smart about it now."

Adolf right turned and slammed his foot hard into the ground. "Yes, sergeant."

Hepper watched the tall, skinny lance corporal as he double timed away. A strange bird that one and Hepper had loathed him at first sight.

He went rigid as something stiff poked powerfully into his back, just above his lumbar region. Spinning rapidly around Hepper found himself confronted by Sergeant Max Amman.' "Who d'you think you're pokin' Max, eh?"

"I'd watch it if I were you, Hepper." Amman's harsh features were set like a meat-hungry rottweiler. "You don't want to keep pushing him like that."

"Says who?" Hepper sneered but there was a slight catch in his voice. Amann was a hard case and mixed with other hard cases.

"Says me," Amann replied. "That soldier, Corporal Hitler, as is, has some nifty mates, let me tell you. And they won't appreciate you doing your pre-war song and dance routine at his expense, Got me?"

"Now look Max," Hepper began to bluster.

"Don't now look Max, me. Last time, unless you want a nocturnal visit; do we understand each other? Lay off Hitler!"

"Alright – alright." Hepper raised a placating hand. No harm meant, Max."

"Right, then." And with that Sergeant Amann strode off.

"You think this Hitler can cut it?" Captain Karl Mayr looked without enthusiasm at the report before him and then at his junior, Lieutenant Ludwig Stiller. Mayr tapped the report. "I'm aware of this fellow, you know, Stiller. Saw the colonel's report on Gutman's recommendation for the Iron Cross. I forwarded it myself. *Had* to forward it myself. Questioned it but was told in no uncertain terms to mind my own, etc."

"Happened a lot," Stiller commiserated. "What could you do – what could anybody do?"

"Good men, deserving men going unrecognized, Stiller. Whilst tripehounds like this…this corporal Hitler skulked at the rear picking up medals and citations. A bloody disgrace!" Mayr's face was reddening under the stress of his growing anger.

"I know, I know." Stiller shrugged. Sod it! He would have done the same given half a chance. So would a lot of other men. The fact that lance corporal Hitler wanted to survive, had survived, did not, in Lieutenant Stiller's view, make him a bad man. "A nasty wound he picked up, though. Gassed, wasn't he? Pretty awful, that must have been."

"Whilst bravely charging the enemy?" Mayr sneered. "Not likely."

"Well, sir, when you consider what we have to work with, Hitler's a bit of a find, really."

"You say so? Well, the truth of that will out at some stage. We'll see – we'll see." Mayr's eyes flicked across the bottom of the page he was reading and an expression of disbelief crossed his handsome, fierce-eyed features.

"What's this about him having his own room, eh? Outrageous! Even the sergeants have to double up these days, Stiller." Mayr bent his head once again to the report in front of him. "Transfer from the room, eviction more like, was requested by his fellow roommates? Nine men wanted him moved -why? I've never heard of such a thing."

"It's, er, it would seem that the other men object to his personal habits, sir."

"Personal habits? I don't understand. These are nine hairy-arsed veterans we're talking about. How bad can Hitler's personal habits be? Oh, hells teeth. He didn't come on to them, did he? Need to be seen to if he did, you know."

"No sir. It's nothing like that. From what I can gather it's his, how to put it, lack of intestinal restraint and the mess that he leaves the lavatory in, at times."

"That's no damn excuse to give a man a private room. How bad can it be, for God's sake?"

"Apparently, sir, it goes beyond being merely, bad."

Mayr sat disbelieving and shaking his head.

"And sir," Stiller made a shape with his hands. "Hitler's room is in reality a broom cupboard. Not enough room to swing a rat's tail. The sergeant just shoved a bed in and voila! Job done. Lance Corporal Hitler seems quite happy to be in there and it keeps the others quiet."

"And he's good, you say?"

"Best of the bunch, by a long chalk, sir. Mostly what we have here are old sweats that are barely able to utter one word without following it through with an expletive or a dirty joke. Hitler is different. He speaks well, sir. Not high German, of course, and he does have that rough Austrian accent, but truly, for a man of such limited education and intellect, he really knows how to put a point across. Honestly, sir, there aren't too many like him."

Mayr looked hard at the lieutenant. "Are you by any chance, Jewish, Stiller?"

"No sir. Why do you ask?"

"It's just that this fellow, Hitler, seems to get on very well with Jews. Is he a Jew, d'you know?"

"No idea, captain." Stiller wasn't too sure that he liked where this conversation might be leading. Jews had been getting something of a bad press of late. Heaven knows why. Many of the Jewish faith had served with distinction during the war. People just needed someone to pick on, he supposed.

"Says here," murmured Mayr, that he's Catholic. Ever see him go to church?"

"Hah!" Stiller's loud outburst had Mayr widening his eyes.

"What was that?"

"I beg your pardon, sir. But church going believers after four years of the hell they've all been through? I doubt very much that Jesus plays much of a role in Hitler's life, or the rest of them, come to that."

June 1919. Augsburg.

An apprehensive Adolf Hitler stood at rigid attention before his commanding officer. He had been granted placement on the political course held at Unit 17 and, once recovered from his initial shyness, had impressed the instructors with his verve and fire. His written work was woeful and full of grammatical errors but nobody cared much about that. Once that yap was open and in full flow, he was one hell of an orator. Bordering on persuasive demagoguery they, his instructors, had said. But with all that, a natural speaker with a dramatic style which seemed to please all. Lance Corporal Hitler was given a pass mark with recommendation that he begin giving indoctrination courses immediately.

Captain Mayr would never like him, but even he had to admit that Lance Corporal Hitler was a first-rate motivator with the lower orders. On Lieutenant Stiller's recommendation, Captain Mayr had sat in on one of Hitler's sessions with young recruits. Adolf now ran a five-day indoctrination course which extolled the virtues of the Bavarian government and all who served it. He was, Mayr realised, almost brilliant. Mayr himself had come away from one of Corporal Hitler's afternoon sessions with his head swimming. The wretched man had almost convinced him, *him*, for God's sake, that Bavaria was run by saints and philanthropists. Incredible! Karl Mayr knew very well that Bavaria was run by crooks and self-seekers. But to hear Hitler tell it, the place was a paradise of cherub cheeked fairness and an enemy of corruption.

Another officer had dropped by and lingered. Clearly captivated, enthralled almost, judging from the expression on his scarred and somewhat ugly face. He had gazed at Corporal Hitler with rapt attention. Rather too rapt, in Mayr's opinion.

Captain Ernst Rohm was certainly enthralled by young Corporal Hitler's eloquence and delivery. He was attracted in another way, as well. Mayr knew of the rumours concerning Captain Rohm's barely concealed sexual preferences. It was said that he had fucked his way through every frontline trench from Verdun to the Somme. Nobody had done anything because Rohm was such a terrifying man and was easily capable of scaring the wits out of other terrifying men. He was also someone that collected the secrets of others. Dark and in some cases life and reputation destroying secrets that were kept within a grey cache deep within the confines of Ernst Rohm's unpleasant mind. The savagely gouged duelling scar embedded in his left cheek, just below dark expressionless eyes, spoke of a man never to be messed with. His round close-cropped head sat atop a smallish, chubby little body which totally belied the fact that the squat captain Rohm could, in an instant, transform his seemingly harmless body into a mass of destructive fury. The man was a killer of the old school. Ernst Rohm killed because he liked to inflict harm. He found it a great joy to remove everything that a man, or a woman for that matter, could be or ever had been. A real bastard, in fact. And now, as Karl Mayr could so clearly see, the bastard had his eyes set on young Adolf Hitler.

"Now, Corporal Hitler. You've done very well with your assignment thus far. However," Mayr paused, clearing his throat for effect. Adolf felt his pulse rate quicken alarmingly. Was he being sacked – given the boot? He had worked his backside off. What in heaven's name might have gone wrong? Too much shouting – arm waving? Surely not. Nobody had said anything or passed on a warning. His naturally hysterical inclination was threatening to overcome him. He could certainly feel and almost see his heart pumping away beneath the sweat inducing woollen service jacket. He liked his job; needed it. What on earth would he do if Mayr kicked him out? His eyes were bulging and breathing was becoming more and more difficult. Rising panic had him close to gasping for air. Was he having a heart attack? His chest hurt. Luckily, his thick moustache prevented Mayr from seeing the way his teeth were grinding into his upper lip.

Mayr looked up at the now uncertain, and to say the least, strange expression on Hitler's face. Good, he thought. Wouldn't do any harm to bring him down a peg or two. Hitler had done nothing wrong. Quite the reverse, in fact. He was *too* good. Over the past few days, the lance corporal had taken to strutting around like he owned the place. Doe-eyed adulation from some of the younger members of his course was part of the reason for his sudden conceit and self-confidence. Also, the attention of Captain Rohm seemed to have bolstered his opinion of himself no-end. Lance Corporal Adolf Hitler now reckoned himself to be someone of importance. The men on his five-day courses hung onto his every word and treated him like some kind of ancient Norse sage. And God alone knew what he and that Captain Rohm saw in each other. To which end Captain Mayr had decided it was time that this rising star, as he saw himself, was moved along to other duties. Not sacked, though. Oh no. That would be foolish. Mayr needed worthwhile and useful subordinates and Hitler might prove to be extremely useful in the future.

"**A** new and somewhat different assignment for you, Hitler. One which, I am sure, will suit your abilities admirably."

"I wish only to serve, sir," whined Adolf almost weeping with relief. He wasn't to be sacked. His small rounded shoulders trembled perceptibly and rounded even further inwards. It was his moustache, though, that Mayr was staring at.

"That'll have to go, corporal." He turned to Lieutenant Stiller. What d'you think, lieutenant?" Stiller, gazing at the almost hand-wringing Corporal Hitler, looked blankly back at his commanding officer.

"Sir?" He didn't have the faintest idea what Mayr wanted to see gone. The corporal's chameleon like change from classroom firebrand to the whinging ninny standing obediently before them had come as something of a surprise. Not least because of the ease and speed with which it had been accomplished. An empty vessel, then? Clearly! Stiller gave a tut of disappointment. He had been certain that there was more than self-serving interest to the man. Oh well!

Captain Mayr glared at him impatiently and then flicked his gaze in the direction of Hitler's jowl-tautened face.

"That!" Mayr inclined his head sharply toward the distinctly uncomfortable NCO.

"The bloody moustache, man. Look at it."

"Ah – yes. Bit on the bushy side, I'd say."

"Damn thing's massive," growled Mayr. "Looks as though it's alive. Get rid of it Corporal Hitler. Today. Clear?"

Adolf gulped and nodded. "Yes sir. Today sir."

"A moment, sir. If you please." Stiller walked the four paces to where Adolf stood and then stared hard at his face. After a few seconds, he stepped back and nodded as if endowed with a sudden great wisdom.

"Well?" Mayr spread his hands questioningly. Stiller approached and bent to his left ear.

"Might be a good idea to let him keep it; or something, at least," murmured Stiller, keeping his voice low.

Mayr glared at the lance corporal and then turned back to the whisker close face of his adjutant. "Why? What on earth are you talking about?"

"Nasty little mouth," hissed Stiller.

"What?"

"He's got a nasty little mouth," Stiller's voice rose dramatically as he straightened up. "Weak, oh, I don't know. Hard to define, really, but it looks a lot better with something covering it."

Mayr rose from behind his desk and strode over to Hitler. Neck craning forward he gazed hard at the offending moustache, and then reached out and tugged it up. Adolf squeaked in surprise and alarm.

"Quite right, Stiller. Quite right." He smiled and patted Adolf's cheek in a paternal manner. "Well, corporal. None of us is perfect, eh?" He returned to his desk and seated himself. "I have the answer." Two pairs of eyes were glued to him. "When you leave here, corporal, and before you set off on your new assignment, you'll visit the barber and have that lip-devouring monstrosity clipped down to a toothbrush cut. Heard of it? 'Course you have. Kaiser had one and looked bloody good with it. Clear?"

Needlessly, Adolf slammed his booted right foot into the office floor. "Yes captain, sir, Got it, sir. I shall arrange to have a toothbrush style moustache, sir."

"Speaking of toothbrushes, Corporal Hitler. Whilst you're at it, you might see fit to use a toothbrush more frequently; unsparingly, to be precise. Your breath…." he waved his hands disdainfully. "You take my meaning, young man?"

Adolf was crimson with embarrassment. His moustache, his mouth, his breath. What else did this son of a bitch want to complain about? He felt resentment bordering upon hatred rising up from within. Fear, hate, disgust at himself; it was all bubbling up to a nervous and ungovernable rage. Careful now. He must be wary lest he do or say something which might so easily be regretted later. He who pays the piper, etc.

"Yes sir. Begging your honour's pardon. I have been remiss. It won't happen again, sir."

"Good. Now", Mayr leaned back into his deeply curved chair and waved a sheet of paper in front of the discomfited lance corporal.

"See this?"

Adolf's brain worked like a steel trap to close off the prompt response that rose immediately and insubordinately to his tongue. A rapid fire, 'Of course I can see it, you brain dead idiot!' made it no further than his quivering epiglottis. Instead, "Yes Herr Hauptman. I see it."

"It is a list," Mayr shook the A4 sized paper noisily. Adolf assumed that some kind of response might be required, so he nodded his head vigorously!

"A list, sir," Adolf repeated obligingly.

" And it contains," Mayr continued, "five names of new and burgeoning political parties which must be investigated thoroughly. And I mean *thoroughly*, corporal Hitler. Understand?"

"I do sir," Adolf stopped himself from nodding again.

"You, corporal, shall attend these meetings and report back to me with your findings. I want the names and occupations of all those who are, or purport to be, in charge; running things, and so on. You will make a written report upon which I shall decide if further action is required. Do you understand, corporal?"

"Yes sir. All very clear." Excitement tingled his veins. A spy. Great heavens! Life was becoming more worthwhile than he had ever imagined it could be.

"One last thing, corporal."

"Sir?"

"Jews. Do you get on with them – or have a problem with them – anything we should know?"

Shit! Where the hell was this going? It was so difficult to know where some people's mindset was with regard to Jews Some were for, some violently against and always, either way, it was virulent.

He didn't reckon either Mayr or Stiller to be Jewish, but he couldn't be completely sure. Gutman had been a Jew and he looked more Nordic than a Wagnerian Siegfried. So too had Lieberman, come to that. In fact, he had always got on well with Jews. Nothing against them one way or another. Just people scrubbing along. Although, as he thought on it, they did seem to scrub along better than most. Cleverer, he supposed. As he thought back, he remembered his mother's doctor had been a Jew. She had died of cancer and, out of sympathy for the bereaved young man, the doctor had never remitted his bill. A thoroughly decent type, that one. Then, there was that awful night in 1913 under a bridge in Vienna. Freezing and alone, flat broke and close to suicide, he had been approached by an elderly man who had shared his meagre ration of food with him and then made a present of his overcoat. That big woollen coat had saved his life. No! The old Jew had saved his life and he had done it out of common decency and regard for another human being. Good people!

"I've nothing against them, sir."

"Good. Keep an open mind, corporal, at all times and no false accusations. I won't stand for it. Understood?"

"Yes, sir." Adolf agreed. "Fair play to all. I get it sir."

"But not at the expense of our own, mind you. Remember that all true Germans have had a terrible time of late, corporal. We must see to our own first. Right?"

A slight confusion entered Adolf's brain. What was this commissioned oaf hinting at? He grasped the bull by the horns.

"Meaning, sir, that Jews aren't our own?"

"Of course they bloody well are man; after a fashion, anyway. Just not quite as much, that's all," Mayr's voice rose. "Now do you take my meaning?"

"I do sir." How could he not understand such contemptible logic?

A slight but noticeable change had come over the previously timid seeming corporal. Stiller looked closely. Was that a smile tugging at the NCO's lips?

"Off you go then, Hitler. Do a good job and it could be the making of you."

Adolf saluted, then accomplished what was, for him at least, a smart about turn and marched off to his new life.

CHAPTER 4

April 23 1945: Berlin, The Bunker.

Genius. Pure genius. He shot up from his fabric covered easy chair with remarkable speed and agility for a man in such physically enfeebled condition. "This is why I was always destined to lead Germany to her destiny. It is why the people are so right to put their trust in me, in my abilities and intuition. Only I could come up with such a plan to save the Reich. Do you hear me, Eva? Only I!"

The two of them were sitting in Hitler's tiny drawing room, whilst above them countless Soviet shells continued with their now largely ignored but nevertheless still intrusive hammering.

Eva sat with legs curled under her on the sofa, idly touching more gloss to her fingernails. Her mind, though, was very much elsewhere. She looked over at him. What in God's name was he going to do now? None of this was how she had envisioned things would be. Like so many others, she had hitched her frock to this strange man's coat tails and then just let the good times roll. And oh, how they had rolled.

Eva knew what people thought of her. Not too bright, a gold digger, a clothes horse not fit to be the Führer's woman; officially or otherwise. How wrong they were. In 1929 she had been a mere chit of a girl. Seventeen years of age and all ambition but no talent. Her employer, Heinrich Hoffmann, often used to mention Adi when they worked together in his little studio in Munich. Adolf had been sort of notorious in his fame, and Eva had reckoned that Herr Hoffmann was spinning a yarn. She knew that Herr Hoffmann had taken some official photos of the man who liked to be called, der Führer, but had no idea that they were in any way close. Her surprise when Adolf Hitler, the well-known and much talked about politician, turned up at Hoffman's photographic shop and addressed her employer by his first name before turning his attention to her, had left Eva all of a tremble.

Such a famous man and he was talking to *her*. Asking how she was and what sort of things she enjoyed doing. There was he, all of forty years of age, and she a mere chubby cheeked seventeen. Eva had been flattered in the extreme. She could never truthfully say that she found Adolf physically attractive or a turn-on in any way, at all. But he certainly had something. The something in question was most likely the lure of danger, excitement and uncertainty. All covered, though, by a blanket of safety and strength. Big cars carrying big strong men with guns and overflowing with confidence. And all of them obedient to the strange man who seemed to find her attractive and even, yes, interesting!

Sex never came into it. From the very beginning Adolf treated her like an expensive and delicate pet. Pampered, cossetted and tolerated. She would have the grand life, was the given promise, live in luxury and within reason be obeyed by those immediately around her. True enough, Eva thought as she stared at her Führer awaiting his next great revelation. She'd had it all.

Eva had entered a world of make believe. It was all such fun! The attention, the secrecy and so many important people, plus the feeling of being hugely important one's self, of being at the centre of it all. It was totally irresistible and she had treated it as a sort of game for grown-ups. It was Adolf's game, of course, and whilst he controlled it nothing could ever go wrong. That had been her firm belief. Until now! It was clear that all the fun and games could, and indeed were, coming to an end. A violent and filthy end. Getting into Berlin from Bavaria had been a nightmare of reality. The city and its people were being systematically butchered from ground and air. She had never dreamed that it could be this bad. Her initial hand waving insistence that she should join her man in his hour of need had been for display only. No way was there any real intention of remaining in the hell-hole that was now Berlin. Playing the tearful, handwringing paramour refusing to be separated from her lover had been a convincing performance. She had really enjoyed acting out her lovely little drama before all, secure in the knowledge that Adolf would never let her go through with it. But he had: the selfish old git!

Well, I got that well and truly wrong, she mused.

"The world knows that you will never give up, Liebling. And neither shall your loyal followers." She smiled at him expectantly. She almost always smiled at him expectantly. It's what he liked but, oh hail Mary, she was getting so utterly sick of it! More than fifteen years of gormless grinning and warbling inane platitudes. It used to be so very her, but now she could barely be bothered with any of it. Survival was the thing uppermost on her mind and she didn't much appreciate the way Adi, der Führer, persistently waffled on about suicide. Perish *that* thought!

Adolf looked down at her and waved a finger. He didn't notice, or simply ignored, the slightly glassy stare in Eva's eyes and the tautness of her features that spoke of a woman driven to distraction by the combined elements of fear, boredom, disgust and despair, all wrapped up inside one ghastly mental cul de sac. She was trying to keep up appearances, but living down here in this foul maze of rooms and cubby-holes, in this filthy grave, was too much to take.

"I was wrong, Eva," he wheezed. "The war is far from lost. I shall crush and destroy my enemies. And then, then, I shall hang those traitors from meat hooks. I've done it before. Oh yes! Mark my words. I've done it before." He nodded, and a ridiculous jack-the-lad expression crossed his ravaged features. Full of opiates, digestive aids and heart medication, Adolf, her Adolf, seemed more like a washed-up music hall comedian than Führer of the Third Reich. Jesus, she almost sobbed out loud. What was happening?

Nail fluid was starting to seep over Eva's fingers and skirt as she squeezed the small container savagely in her hand and tilted it all unknowingly into her lap. The strong smell of chemicals quickly began filling the small drawing room but Eva hardly noticed.

Meat hooks? What was he talking about? She had heard something about the trials after the July 20th assassination plot. But surely not. He wouldn't, couldn't have *really* hung the perpetrators from meat hooks.... could he? Oh, what did it matter, anyway? She had herself to worry about in the here and now.

He was tugging open the big blast-proof door. "Get this damn door open." Eva ignored him. If he wanted the door opened he could tug on the wretched thing himself, or use the bunker's interconnecting phone to call for immediate attention, as was usual.

With a loud, high-pitched squeak, the door inched ajar and he thrust a shoulder into the gap that appeared and heaved with all that remained of his strength to open it further. "Keitel, Where is Keitel?" he yelled out into the corridor. "Fetch me Keitel, now!"

If Wilhelm Keitel had one supreme talent, it was to appear, as if by magic, at the merest mention of his name when uttered by Hitler.

Whenever his much loved and adored Führer needed him, Wilhelm was always there to obey unconditionally his master's commands. Even Linge couldn't match his unswerving devotion.

Tall, high stomached and with a permanently pompous expression etched across his stern, moustachioed face, the field marshal stood before his shambling Führer.

"Yes, my Führer." Keitel didn't allow surprise to show on his features. A tiny twitch of concern was sufficient. He knew very well that the Führer unfailingly noticed such things, and he, Keitel, had long since mastered the art of extreme unctuousness.

"The conference room, Keitel."

"Yes, my Führer?"

"Get them all in there. Mohnke, Weidling, Jodl, all of them, Keitel. Now…don't waste time!"

Keitel's jaw dropped fractionally. "But, but you said…"

"I said that I want the commanders and communications chiefs, local and frontline here now. At once, Keitel."

The field marshal's head rolled from side to side with discomfort. He was not a particularly good general, nor was he an outstandingly bad one. And he certainly was not in any way an idiot. He was, though, totally under his Führer's spell. Wilhelm could in no way stand up to Adolf Hitler, not even in his present feeble condition. The Führer, in Keitel's opinion, was a genius and must be obeyed. Genius or not; the oath he had taken, which they had all taken, bound him totally. He could no more forswear that oath of obedience than he could gouge out his own eyes. Could not, and would not. Not ever!

Hitler's demands now, however, pulled him up short. Weidling was somewhere north and up to his neck in Russians and shells. He had been out of radio communication for the last three hours. He might be dead for all anyone knew. Last reports stated that he had been attempting to shore up Brigadeführer Krukenberg's crumbling defence line on the north side of the Tetlow canal.

A detachment of French volunteers had just recently arrived in Berlin and was being rapidly thrown into the battle.

"Yes, my Führer. At once." Turning on his heel the field marshal stalked off.

Alfred Jodl patted his colleague firmly on the shoulder. "Calm down, Keitel, there's a good chap. No sense in losing it now."

"How on earth can I get hold of Weidling?" Keitel's voice was naturally of a harsh timbre. Now, though, it was more of a harsh whine. "Where in God's name is he?"

"All you can do is keep the switchboard at it and send out messengers."

"What's the damn point, Jodl? The switchboard either can't get through, or it's jammed with nonsensical bleating from hysterical civilians complaining about the Russians. I send messengers and they don't come back. Killed or done a runner. No difference either way. What a bloody shambles!"

"Pull yourself together, field marshal!" Jodl became stern. He and Keitel knew one another very well.

"**H**err General." A large figure filled the doorway of the small room that two senior officers shared for their work duties.

Both men turned hopefully toward the SS Scharführer in charge of the communications switchboard.

"Yes, Misch — what is it?" Keitel waved an impatient hand.

"General Weidling has been located, sir. I relayed your orders as instructed."

"And….and.?" Keitel was almost beside himself. Jodl frowned at the field marshal's lack of deportment before a lower rank. He really should get a grip. This would not do!

Rochus Misch had his almost permanently engraved half smile fully in place.

"General Weidling states that he will be here within the hour, sir. That's if, well…."

"If what, man? Come on. Spit it out."

"That's if he's not blown up, shot or captured. He hopes that the trip will be worthwhile, sir. Those were his, the general's, own words. Said I was to relay them to you verbatim sir."

Oh, did he now," muttered Jodl.

"He did, sir. In precisely those words."

"Yes, yes, alright, Misch. Off you go back to your switchboard. Keep up the good work." Jodl gave him a tight smile.

Misch clicked his heels, nodded politely at the two general officers then took his leave.

"Damn cheek," hissed Keitel. "I've a mind to discipline that young man. SS or no SS."

"Leave it Willy. We need him. He's good at what he does and he's still here to do it. Think on that, eh?"

Once again, like the cast of an awful and unending movie, the same characters gathered within the cramped confines of the conference room.

Weidling turned up as promised. His uniform was covered with dust and various particles of detritus that were best not too closely examined. He looked unutterably weary. Brigadeführer Mohnke, too, appeared pretty well close to exhaustion. Both of them had been dragged away from the full-on violence of battle and neither of them appreciated the dream-like air of lunacy pervading the entire bunker complex.

There was the usual jostling for space within the close confines of the small conference room. Most of those present were bewildered and depressed. What was he up to, the Führer? Only a few hours ago he had given up and gone off in a monumental sulk. Now here he was shambling around bright-eyed and speaking of ultimate victory.... again!

Twelfth Army. Wenck's army. That is the key, gentlemen. I shall turn Wenck away from the Elbe. He must gather all his available forces and smash the Russians here." Hitler's finger stabbed at a mark on the huge table map of Berlin's northern sector. "He will attack from the south, take Treuenbrietzen and then link up with Busse's 9th army. Holste's XLI Panzer corps will coordinate with a devastating attack on Konev's front here," his trembling hand waved vaguely over the proposed offensive area, a gesture which in reality, encompassed some seventy miles from left to right.

"Such an attack gentlemen, so unexpected at this stage, will shatter the exhausted Russians. They will collapse and turn tail. Victory shall be ours. Here in Berlin we will shatter the Slavic hordes." His wrinkled, liver spotted hands pounded into his chest, and his eyes shone with a brilliant, unnatural glow. "They will drown in their own blood," he shrieked. "They will howl for mercy and there shall be none! You hear me, gentlemen? NONE!"

"Oh, my Führer," Bormann enthused. "Such genius – such perfection." He turned his large, ugly, grin-plastered face to the others. "God has blessed us with the divine intuition of our beloved Führer. All hail to the Führer!"

The packed room did not exactly reverberate to the somewhat less than enthusiastic, in fact almost groaningly resentful chorus of Heil Hitler that followed Bormann's brief paean. The Reichsleiter glared with barely concealed fury at the assembled worthies.

Goebbels chimed in with a supporting, "Long life to our beloved Führer. Success is assured and under his leadership we shall overcome and advance to glorious victory."

A brief silence followed. The only sounds being the shuffling of nervous feet.

"Precisely." Hitler's eyes flicked over them. He knew it was all guff and flannel but it kept them in line. That old sergeant major's dictum of so long ago still held and, if anything, must be held to more strongly than ever before. Mustn't let these bastards into his mind. Keep them obedient. He wasn't one of them. He was different, apart, and he must stay as such. And stay alive. Remain living and alert until fate, destiny, something, forced the worm to turn just once more. He had been lucky in the past, so why not again? He was a survivor. All that was necessary to carry on was to keep these defeatist whiners in line.

"Keitel."

"Yes, my Führer."

"You will travel to Twelfth Army headquarters and inform General Wenck of my decision. His offensive must begin within the next few hours. It is vital that he link up with Busse before Konev's next assault on our lines. Clear?"

"Yes, my Führer. I shall leave at once."

Hitler nodded and waved a peremptory hand. Keitel, after a long look at Jodl, departed on his mission. It was Jodl who, just a few hours ago, as Hitler went into a nervous collapse after the Steiner debacle, had suggested this outrageous and clearly hopeless military manoeuvre as a sop to calm Hitler down before he ordered the slaughter of all his remaining generals. It had never been meant to be taken seriously. But now Hitler was claiming the idea as his own streak of undeniable genius. On paper, of course, it was possible. And that's all any of it was, paper. But he, Keitel would order the accomplished Walter Wenck to relieve Berlin and thus complete his duty to his Führer.

Generals Krebs and Burgdorf threw back a large glass of neat schnapps apiece. Burgdorf had always been one of the Führer's staunchest supporters. An utterly loyal soldier who would be true to his oath – to the death.

"What did you make of all that, Hans?" General Burgdorf poured them both another large measure of schnapps

"I'm just wondering," Krebs threw back his drink in one gigantic swallow. "How much longer we must continue taking that man seriously."

"Hush!" Burgdorf hissed warningly.

Krebs poured yet another overly generous amount of the clear corn schnapps into his glass. "Hush – why?" Krebs waved his glass around. "Afraid we might be overheard?" The general grinned at his colleague. "And who's going to do what, Wilhelm? Does anybody really care anymore, eh?"

Both of them jerked back with shock as the large, lantern-jawed face of Otto Gunsche, SS Sturmbannführer and Hitler's personal adjutant peered around the door of their bunker office.

"Might I have a word, gentlemen, seeing as how you are both taking a little personal time?" The smile was wolfish. Gunsche towered over the pair of them and not for the first time, Krebs wondered at Albert Speer's supposed architectural talent. The Führer's so-called genius architect had constructed a multi-roomed warren for dwarfs when many of the supposed dwarfs were well over six feet tall. What a nonsense!

"Of course, Gunsche. Come in. Drink?" He proffered the bottle to Gunsche, who accepted with a nod.

"Business for the Führer?" Burgdorf asked, nervously.

"Oh yes. Always." That wretched wolf's smile was still there and it was annoying the hell out of Jodl. What came next, though, pulled him up very short indeed. He had indeed been in touch with Goering in a reply to the Reich Marshal's enquiry as to the state of things in Berlin. And now.....?

"Oh, that fat fool," muttered Jodl.

"Isn't he, though?" Gunsche's grin merely served to enhance his ugliness.

Jodl turned and explained to Krebs. That man nodded. "Well, he's got it coming with all said and done."

"True enough," answered the always phlegmatic Jodl rising from the table. "I'd better have a quick word with Bormann."

"Yes," Gunsche smirked. "I reckon you better had."

CHAPTER 5

September 1919: Munich, Hotel Furstenfelder Hof

A dolf sat, barely listening as the man, Drexler, droned on and interminably on. Outlining for the umpteenth time his party's plans for a better Germany. Not bothering to suppress a yawn, Adolf glanced down at his notes. Nothing here of interest at all. This was his second visit to the DAP, The German Workers Party. Working now as what the Army called an Intelligence Agent, in reality, a lowly paid eavesdropper, Adolf was thorough and painstaking. He wanted to keep this job. It paid him a minimal wage, clothed and fed him. Being without educational qualifications of any kind, work outside the army was impossible for him to find. And things were getting worse. Mayr had told him to double check on this German Workers Party before he moved on to his next assignment. He knew that he must keep his reports flowing, accurate and interesting. Trouble was, his grammar was bad, his spelling appalling and his prose woeful. Mayr now regarded him as a glib chancer but nothing much else. He would speak to his lowly lance corporal as though addressing a mental hunchback. Adolf hated the man but really needed this job.

He folded his little notepad and placed it carefully inside his jacket pocket. There was nothing more for him to do here. There was, however, something, or rather, someone, he wanted to look at more closely.

There were some fourteen men sitting in various places around the rented hotel room. He had garnered the names of the three leaders of this rather sad little excuse for a political party and had carefully written down their stated political aims.

Anton Drexler, the individual speaking, and badly, at the moment, was the nominal leader. He was backed by the supposed intelligentsia of the group, a poet of sorts, named Dietrich Eckart. Gottfried Feder a self-taught economist, made up this trio, and of the three he alone had any ideas worth mentioning.

Adolf had difficulty in referring to this group as a political party even within the privacy of his own mind. The one thing that they all possessed in common, though, was an intense dislike of Jews. Adolf noticed, as they waffled on, how the backsides of those attending would twitch and slide noisily around the leather covered chairs and benches, as if in sympathy with the speaker's tones and nuances. It occurred to him that these crass amateurs were missing an opportunity here to whip-up emotions. Groups of political answer-seekers like these were invariably just begging for a cause to follow. For someone to fill their eager minds with unified reason to hate. The more loudly and more vehemently, the better. Hate was, in Adolf's opinion, the one certain common denominator guaranteed to bind people together. The only thing needed was a focus point. It struck him that Drexler might have hit upon something with his racist views of the Jews. Interesting, but not enough to warrant further attention.

What had gained his attention, though, was the decidedly handsome young man sitting just a few feet away and opposite. Slim, dark good looks and delicate hands. Those hands were, at that moment, idly caressing a tall glass of chilled Weissbier. Adolf watched as a slim index finger traced a wavy line in the condensation which was covering the high, cool glass. The finger stopped, and then dipped neatly into the frothy head atop the beer. Adolf almost gasped out loud as the finger transferred itself to its owner's mouth. So casually erotic! It was electric. He tried to look away, but after a life of ugliness and deprivation, Adolf was now confronted with the most beautiful thing he had ever seen.

The young man looked up and met Adolf's gaze. He smiled gently and Adolf felt the blood rushing to his face. He couldn't look away and felt himself just sinking into those dark inviting eyes. For all his former, fully clothed and clumsy assignations with two others, Adolf was a novice when it came to flirtation and physical expressions of interest in another.

His minor genital deformity made physical contact difficult and meant that he would never willingly allow anyone to see him unclothed. He would not stand to be mocked – ever! But this smiling young man before him. Oh dear! Adolf had known only minor stirrings of lust before this moment. He had once thought that he yearned for affection but then realized that he simply needed people to do what he wanted. He wasn't at all sure what he wanted this handsome young man to do for him, only that he wished to know him, to be with him.

Pulse racing and all at sea, Adolf sat trying desperately to think of something to do or say that would interest the object of his interest.

"And we shall push for Bavaria's separation from the rest of Germany, with all the strength at our disposal," Drexler waved a triumphant arm. "Bavarian independence can, and shall be accomplished within our lifetime." Drexler had raised his voice with this latest pronouncement. Bearing in mind that such a statement was definitely illegal, and uttering such could carry a prison sentence, it was pretty daring. Unfortunately, delivered as it was in Anton Drexler's dreary monotone, it fell rather flat.

Not to Adolf, though. Drexler had hit a nerve. Bavaria to pull away from the greater Reich? Germany to be split and turned into independent states – again? Back to the dark ages? Not if he, Adolf Hitler had anything to do with it. The war had crushed Germany and left her weak. Those bastards, the French and the British had rammed the Versailles Treaty down Germany's gagging throat, humiliated her and then repeatedly raped the corpse of German nationhood. And that rape, by those misbegotten French hounds occupying the Ruhr, continued month after month. To hear some fool prate on about willingly splitting Germany even further asunder was not to be borne.

The handsome young man had stopped caressing his glass and was staring at Adolf with even greater interest. He rolled his eyes, clearly in full agreement with Adolf's assessment of Drexler's last statement. Without realizing it, Adolf had risen from his chair with set jaw and wide staring eyes.

"WRONG!" Head back and index finger of his left hand pointing accusingly at Drexler, Adolf glared about him. "The man is wrong!" All heads turned to look at the newcomer. A few recognised him from a meeting the previous week, but none knew him. Adolf hesitated, now aware that he was the centre of attention and he had nothing prepared.

"Really?" Drexler smiled down at him condescendingly. "Have you listened to everything that I have said, young man? Do you understand fully what it is that……"

"Do *you* fully understand the meaning of what you have just said?" Adolf didn't precisely snarl the question, but the tone of contempt was palpable. He nodded at the three men on the dais and marched determinedly toward them. Drexler, uncertain what to do, looked at the other two for assistance. Eckart merely shrugged and looked the other way. The advancing figure with the manic gaze didn't seem one to pose any kind of physical threat. Feder stared with interest. God alone knew that this little group needed livening up. A total of fifteen members on the books and no sign of more wanting to join. Perhaps this scruffy oik might spark the proceedings up a little. What harm could he do? Ill dressed, as were so many these days, no threatening flesh on his bones, he looked as though a strong puff of wind could knock him over. He glanced at Drexler, nodded and smiled.

Drexler took the hint and waved an encouraging hand at Adolf as he approached. Adolf clambered onto the dais and stood before Anton Drexler and the others. His height surprised them. From a distance he had seemed decidedly puny, and generally speaking he was, but he was taller than he appeared and there was something about him that Drexler found horribly unsettling; or was it exciting?

Stepping back, Drexler turned to the sparse audience. "Gentlemen. Tonight, it appears, that we have a guest speaker.

"Allow me to introduce…." He turned to Adolf expectantly.

"Hitler." Adolf turned to face the now more interested audience. "Adolf Hitler."

It was a minor triumph. Totally ad-libbing from the start, Adolf began his unrehearsed speech in a moderate tone. He explained the foolishness of separation from the greater Reich, not in a learned way, as if from books and university study, but in his own way. In short, he made it up as he went along and they loved it.

As though standing outside himself, Adolf observed the movements and reactions to his statements, and his mind recorded every single nuance and flinch. Gently he broached the subject of Jews, and, with a slight raising of his voice, condemned them as usurers. Whether or not they were, was beside the point. He must test the waters of local feeling. Then, with a raised fist, he called them 'parasites' that should be removed from German society. This truly got them. The small group was rapt with attention. Feder and Eckart both nodding enthusiastically. Adolf mentally marked down the number one hate on the list: Jews! They hated them beyond reason. Well, that was what defeat and humiliation did to folk. Someone had to be blamed. He personally blamed the command structure for insisting that the armistice be signed. Politicians had in the end, gone along with the signing of the Versailles treaty so, they too were culpable. Were there any Jews in the government at Weimar? He wasn't sure. It didn't matter, really. As long as Germans themselves weren't blamed. Very well, then. Jews it would be. And so, never expecting to return to this room, he played and toyed with his audience and when he had finished they cheered him to the rafters. Glancing at his wristwatch he was astonished to see that he had been speaking for almost one hour, and yet here they all still sat, their ears ringing with every improvised and made-up statement that he had uttered. Not an iota of factual worth in any of it. Yet look at them, cheering and clapping as though he were some kind of Messiah. Unbelievable! Well, the fun time was over and he needed to be going.

Perspiring slightly, Adolf nodded his acknowledgement to them all and made to leave. The object of his earlier attention was smiling and applauding wildly and he wanted to speak to him. But what to say – what to say? As it turned out, he didn't have to open the conversation with him before departing. His life was about to change on that night in pretty well every conceivable way.

Climbing down from the dais, he was moving toward the lower end of the room when a light touch on his arm made him turn enquiringly. It was Drexler, all smiles and almost fawning.

"Wonderful speech, Herr Hitler. I had no idea that you were so knowledgeable." The locksmith, for that was his trade, thrust out his hand. "A true pleasure to meet you. Here," with his free hand he withdrew a business card from his inner pocket. "Please take this and do please join us. We very much need chaps of your quality and capabilities. You have such style, Herr Hitler. Real style!"

"Style? Me?" Adolf smiled and returned the pressure on hand heartily pumping his. "One does one's best, Herr Drexler. We all must work for a better, stronger Germany."

"Oh, indeed, indeed. And please call me Anton." Drexler smiled even more broadly as he waited for Adolf to respond in a similar fashion. Precious little chance, thought Adolf.

"Then, Anton, it shall be." He released the locksmith's hand, bowed slightly, then turned abruptly on his heel and left the bemused Drexler staring after him.

"Number's on the card," called out Drexler. "Same time next week?"

Adolf waved a non-committal hand. He had a lot to think about. Speaking, as he just had, had been an incredible experience. These men weren't a captive audience of unwilling soldiers. They sat and listened and applauded because they wanted to; they wanted to listen to *him*.

His eyes flicked around the lower end of the room. The beautiful young man was gone. Oh, well. He shrugged inwardly. You can't have it all. What he did have, though, was plenty of food for thought. Might there be a future in politics? He had thought often about it. He had the talent, of that much he was sure. But ideas? He would need people with ideas. Just basic simplicity. Nothing fancy. Don't confuse folk with paradigms they could not possibly understand. Most of the speakers that he had listened to and observed over the past few weeks swamped their meaning with high sounding, and to the common man, totally incomprehensible claptrap. They thought that it made them sound clever, educated and more knowledgeable. No! Not to Adolf's mind. The average man, and woman, must be able to clearly understand the message. That was a problem, though. What message? Needed some thought, that one.

Bread, a roof, sufficient heating in freezing winters; that sort of thing. Give people security and they would die for you.

The door swung shut behind him as he stepped out into the street. There had been a great deal of back-slapping from smiling well-wishers as he departed, so the tentative touch on his wrist did not alarm him as he took the final step onto the pavement.

Taking a half step forward, he turned and found himself gazing into the deep brown eyes of the young man from the hotel.

"That was magnificent. Hope you don't mind me saying."

The smile was captivating. Adolf automatically stuck out his hand and found it immediately taken. He then did something that he couldn't remember ever doing before. He introduced himself using his first name. "My name is Adolf," he said, still gently shaking his new acquaintance's hand.

"I know. I heard. I'm Emil. Emil Maurice."

A friendship was born in that moment. A friendship that would last throughout their individual eternities right up until their final tragedy.

CHAPTER 6

April 24 1945: Berlin, The Bunker

The atmosphere in the bunker had changed. It still wreaked of body odour and fear, but now something else had crept in. Almost tangible, but not quite. Little groups gathering out of nowhere, and then, as abruptly, splitting apart. Privates and majors, corporals and generals; briefly huddled together and seemingly gossiping like old friends. Something was up. Conspiracy, perhaps? Or could it be just men coming together and sharing mutual terror and despair? That this final charade had lasted so long was beyond belief. The neatly uniformed military aide sniffed. If only Hitler would have the decency to die. Perhaps, mused the young officer, the Führer might be given a helping hand into the next world. It certainly wasn't before time!

Major Freytag von Loringhoven wrinkled his splendidly bred and aquiline nose in unconscious distaste. Filthy place. Cleaners came only occasionally when, and if, they could get through the bombing and shelling. The entire complex was served by only one resident cleaner. A slim, thirty to forty-something Portuguese woman. How the devil she had found her way to bomb shattered Berlin was anybody's guess. Loringhoven sniffed disdainfully. She would be unlikely to get out. As would any of them. The young major's thoughts were constantly on ways of escaping this madman's labyrinth. He was every inch an aristocrat and looked it. Tall, handsome, a graceful mover even through the narrow rooms and corridors of the claustrophobic bunker. Hitler seemed to quite like him, which was something of an achievement, bearing in mind that some years previously good old Uncle Wolf had deliberately slaughtered or imprisoned thousands simply because they *were* aristocrats.

Freytag von Loringhoven was an old school blue-blood and a complete snob. He had first met the Führer in 1944, so he was quite the new boy compared with some of the time servers in Hitler's extended military family. He'd never seen the Hitler of the early days of Nazism, only the new model Führer with attendant bad smells, shrieking fits and, in Freytag's mind, hopeless mental incompetence.

Somewhere in the bunker, someone was smoking. A pastime so absolutely taboo to Hitler that Loringhoven felt a shudder of apprehension run through him. Even though he had only been with the Führer's entourage for little more than one year, his entire system was now geared for survival against the manic savagery of his leader and the constant plots of the inner circle one against the other and, for that matter, any underling that might have crossed them.

The tobacco smell was drifting down from the upper level of the bunker and it was quite faint. Not faint enough, though. The whiff of burning tobacco stirred Loringhoven's own craving for nicotine. Surely, the Führer would, at any moment, demand that the perpetrator be dragged out and shot; at the very least thrown into a camp somewhere. Ah, but of course not. Not whilst the drug demented fool lay recumbent in his quarters behind that heavy blast and gas-proof door. He would remain oblivious to anything going on within the rest of his subterranean hovel until such time as that hinge-squeaking gate of his was opened.

Sleep, even drug assisted, came with ever increasing difficulty. And awaking from it had become something which he dreaded.

His every return to full consciousness after slumber was pure horror.

It had been so ever since Stalingrad. That dreadful feeling one had of, *it was all so real*, upon awaking from a bad dream, or a nightmare, followed by the overwhelming sense of relief that came with the realisation that it had all been nothing more than a bad dream and that everything was well with the world. But then, with full consciousness returning came the train crash of despair, as one realised that it hadn't been a dream, that the ghastly cries of shrieking accusation, of failure and the death of millions, was all grim reality which must be faced by the monster responsible – by him! Awful – unbearable! And it was never ending.

He rolled onto his back, gazing up at the ceiling. His eyes hurt. Great heavens, everything hurt. Even lying here on his steel framed bed his limbs trembled uncontrollably. He bit hard on his lower lip. Another day to face. Another day of unremitting hell and pretence. He rubbed both hands over his face and then forced himself into a sitting position. His ability to push reality to the back of his mind was impressive, even to himself. But Adolf knew the truth well enough. He had known that the war was lost, or rather, could not be won, after the halt before Moscow in 1941. And he had worked on the premise that, by seemingly believing in ultimate victory, he could induce others to believe it as well. And it had worked splendidly. Not any more, though. It was pretty much all over.

Should he call Linge for help with his shaving and dressing? He had tumbled to the floor a couple of times in recent days as he attempted to thrust his feet into his trousers. As for shaving? Very risky. It didn't do to have the staff see those blood seeping little nicks and scratches on his face after shaving. He would get Linge to do it. Ah, yes, but of course. He gave himself a sharp slap on the cheek. He was becoming badly forgetful. As previously arranged, Linge would be banging on the door if the Führer didn't appear before a specified time. Any minute now.

Wenck. How was he doing? Had Twelfth Army's offensive gained any ground, and if so, where? He fought down the familiar fluttering of arrhythmia inducing apprehension as it ripped through his trembling system and made his heart bounce erratically against his ribs like a mishit tennis ball.

How much more? God's rotting teeth, how much more? Did the people, his people, and his soldiers.... did they, any of them, realise the hell that he endured on a daily basis? Did they realise the sacrifices that he had made for Germany?

"I have given my life for Germany," his guttural yell was all unheard behind the stout metal door. "My very life!" A tear of self-pity rolled down a yellow tinged cheek. "It's all ending," he whispered, his hands balling into tight knitted fists of hopelessness. "And I can't stand it!"

He thought longingly of more carefree days, when he and Emil had planned the future of Germany together. So many wonderful ideas. Ideas that had come to fruition beyond their wildest dreams. Ideas that had become material facts, but now lay as rubble and dust beneath the feet of their destroyers: the Slavs and, yes, damn them all to hell the Jews! He paused, mentally as well as physically. Staring at his nightmare haggard reflection in the small table mirror; for the life of him he could not remember when it was that his hatred of the Jews had burst forth. Now, think, Adolf, think! The Slavs. They had to go because they were in the way and he, or rather Germany, needed their space. Simple. It had gone horribly wrong thanks to his useless generals; nevertheless, the premise spoke for itself. But the Jews? It was all becoming so vague. A sudden dizziness threatened to overwhelm his already unsteady balance; these damnable opiates were destroying his brain, throwing his cognitive functions completely askew, but his reliance upon them was total.

"I know I hate them, and I have come so close to eliminating international Jewry. So close! But for the life of me," he stared at his reflection and then looked hopelessly around his sparsely furnished bedroom, "I can feel a natural hatred for that Semitic scum. I want every last one of them dead, but can't remember why!"

About time, Loringhoven reckoned, to chance oblivion and go outside for a cigarette. Also, to discover, if possible, who it was that dared smoke anywhere in the bunker. He gave a brief thought to the habit that so many of them had. Nicotine addiction was the very devil of a thing. The smokers residing in the bunker, and there were many, would sooner go outside and risk bomb, shell and bullet, rather than deprive themselves of their nicotine fix. The evil of smoking was something the Führer was always droning on about. One way or another, smoking will kill you, he never tired of saying. Loringhoven clicked his front teeth in annoyance. Bloody hypocrite! The wretched man dosed himself daily on an assortment of powerful drugs and yet had the nerve to criticise others for their habits. What a complete nonsense.

He glanced down at his watch. The next briefing was scheduled for 11:00hrs but would, as usual, be more likely to be held when the Führer decided ad hoc what was going to be done. Plenty of time for a few hard drags on one of his cheap and nasty, but still obtainable, Ekstein's.

Turning into the bunker's narrow lower corridor, he almost bumped into a worried looking Field Marshal Keitel. Only recently returned from his highly risky fifty kilometres jaunt to Twelfth Army's HQ on the Elbe. Keitel waved his marshal's baton at Loringhoven as the younger man moved aside for him.

"All well, sir?" he asked, smiling politely.

Keitel paused, opened his mouth to speak, and then, clearly deciding that the young major didn't carry sufficient weight or gravitas for his pronouncement, shut it again and moved on. Loringhoven made to continue upside when he was pulled up by a curt demand from the field marshal.

"Führer up yet?"

It was 09:30hrs and here, at the heart of the greatest disaster known to mankind, was one of its chief flag bearers asking if the final arbiter of the entire seething mess had deigned to get out of bed.

"I wouldn't know, sir. Probably not." A smart clicking of the heels and the major moved quickly away before he said something that might cause him trouble. The field marshal loved his Führer and would not tolerate any real or imagined insolence.

Easing his way through the overcrowded upper corridors, Loringhoven was astonished to see the writhing, twisted bodies of wounded soldiers littered pretty well everywhere. Yesterday there had been but a dozen or so, but now the place resembled the overflow of a badly run hospital. Moans, groans, the occasional scream of unbearable pain, all mixing in with the clack of typewriters being hammered by overworked, grey uniformed young men, furiously typing out incomprehensible orders to unit commanders who, in all likelihood, were dead before the last sentence was completed. And there, puffing away as if nothing mattered, like a man waiting for a nightclub introduction, was Fegelein. SS Gruppenführer Hermann Fegelein. Loringhoven's lip curled with distaste. Charlatan! That smooth face, handsome if one liked the gigolo look, was completely unlined. Whatever worries Fegelein might have, they in no way showed on his creamy white features, nor in his smug, self-satisfied expression. To look upon Gruppenführer Fegelein was to look upon a man at ease with the world; well, his world anyway. Loringhoven hated him. Indeed, he despised all those jumped up ex-waiters, bricklayers and such like, that lorded it as they strutted around in their snazzy Hugo Boss styled uniforms. As far as the aristocratic Major Freytag von Loringhoven was concerned, they were ill-bred scum.

Sadists, perverts and conscienceless deviants; like their bloody leader. But Fegelein's SS rank was equivalent to that of a Wehrmacht general, and thus vastly outranking a mere major.

Loringhoven forced a smile of greeting onto his face but refrained from saluting.

The lightly built former stable boy come jockey, so very popular with the ladies down in the bunker, returned Loringhoven's insincere smile with a much-practised movie-star style lopsided grin. Married to Eva Braun's sister, Gretl, Fegelein considered himself to be a thing of glory; smart, quick-witted and popular was how Fegelein saw himself. In fact, though highly regarded by women, most male colleagues held him to be a thief and a cheat. Below average height, he was handsome enough, and he certainly had a way with the ladies. He only had to waft by the secretarial pool to send them all of a quiver with anticipation and fluttering hands. And more than one of them had fallen willing prey to Hermann Fegelein's own searchingly fluttering hands. Gretl Braun had fallen for him at first sight, and Eva herself was even more susceptible to his oily but persuasive charms. Hermann, however, could never remain faithful to any one woman, not even when married to Adolf Hitler's sister-in-law. He led the poor girl a merry dance with his shallow ego and meaningless promises. She still adored him, though, and tolerated his deficiencies and misdeeds with Wagnerian fortitude. It wasn't only women, however, that fell for the Fegelein personality trap. Himmler, the feared Reichsführer SS, had liked and promoted the glib Hermann Fegelein so that he now occupied his present position as SS liaison officer representing the Reichsführer directly to the Führer himself. At one time, that would have been the golden job. Things now, however, were changing rapidly.

"**G**ood morning, Major." The movie star smile that rolled across his cheeks like melted butter, had Loringhoven longing to slap the smarmy little SS man's face with a pistol butt.

"Come." Fegelein waved a beckoning hand inviting Loringhoven to follow him to the bunker exit just a little way above them.

Easing past two surprisingly immaculate but not terribly attentive SS guards, Fegelein stepped into the chancellery garden where he turned and waited; the smooth smile now replaced by an amused smirk.

With his first step outside the bunker Loringhoven lurched heavily to one side. He felt as if his feet had been planted upon some fairground dare-devil ride. The impact from countless high explosive shells detonating uncomfortably close by made the ground heave and buck beneath him. Shrapnel whistled all around, unseen and deadly as its tempered steel horror searched out soft yielding flesh in which to bury itself. Its impact as it gouged its way into concrete and wood could clearly be heard. As could the occasional but infinitely more alarming *ping* of a smaller piece of glowing hot metal ricocheting from a nearby wall or metal frame.

These bombardments, heralding the closing ring of vengeful Soviet forces, had been nerve twistingly close for days. But this! It was as though they were lobbing shells from the next street. Terrifying!

"Great heaven!" He looked over at the smirking Fegelein.

The Gruppenführer, remaining theatrically calm, inclined his head briefly to indicate direction. "They've moved up heavy artillery less than eight hundred metres away. Been banging away since early this morning. We might launch a counter attack later, but I wouldn't put money on it." He waved his cigarette like a party sparkler. "Just over there; north of Beckman's Fine Arts." He giggled like a small boy telling a dirty joke. "Precious little fine about it now, eh?"

"So close?" muttered Loringhoven. He moved forward a dozen or so paces past Fegelein looking anxiously to left and right. Fegelein roared with laughter as he watched him.

"What the hell is so amusing?" Concerned and annoyed, Loringhoven glared at the laughing Gruppenführer.

"For heaven's sake man," the chortling SS leader croaked just as a fresh salvo thundered all too close by, nearly knocking them both off their feet. "The way you're looking up and down the street. You look as though you're waiting for a bus!"

Loringhoven, seeing the point and feeling foolish, placed his hands on his hips. To be spoken to in such a manner, by a man like this, was almost beyond bearing.

"Come on, major." Fegelein moved back to the relative shelter of the concrete doorway. "Have your cigarette before you're blown to pieces."

Loringhoven lit up as he joined the suddenly pensive Gruppenführer. Moving back past the guards and further into the upper bunker confines, he inhaled deeply. If Fegelein could light up here, then by God, so could he. It was becoming clear, and more so by the hour, that the old taboos were being cast aside, ignored. Discipline was slipping. It was all starting to seep away. The Führer's commands, whilst still sending countless obedient soldiers to their deaths, in Berlin and elsewhere, now carried less and less weight down here.

Oh, they still clung on, many of them, to some kind of shared fantasy that it would all be alright and that something would turn up and make everything better again. It was a fantasy which remained because they communally wished it to become reality. For so long had Hitler been 'the magic man' it was simply impossible for them to think otherwise. Others, though, were well aware of the truth. He could not save them, himself, nor even one tuft of German grass.

Loringhoven dragged deeply again on his cigarette. The awfulness of defeat. The certain knowledge of an impending catastrophe that was going to be hideously destructive to their way of life and everything that they knew made his knees weaken. For many days now it had simmered cloyingly beneath his skin, this feeling of utter helplessness, along with mind-numbing apprehension of what the future might hold.

"I wonder if my apartment still stands," muttered Fegelein.

"Your apartment?" Loringhoven stared at the Gruppenführer questioningly.

"Yes. I keep a place in Bleibtreustrasse. You should pop in sometime," he added jokingly.

"But my dear Gruppenführer," Loringhoven was stiffly polite, but intrigued by the fact that high life loving Hermann Fegelein kept an apartment in Berlin. "Bleibtreustrasse is how far from here?"

"No more than four kilometres, and before you ask there are still four roads open in that direction."

"Dangerous though," stated Loringhoven.

"And this isn't?" Scoffed Fegelein, gesturing about him.

"I was more thinking of the patrols; our patrols. If what I hear is anywhere near the truth, they like nothing more than stringing people up for any crime that those military chain-dogs can think up."

"Oh, I know," Fegelein nodded carelessly. "I saw them hang a ten-year-old girl and her parents from the same lamppost. That would be," pursing his lips he looked hard at Loringhoven, "three days ago."

"Why?" Loringhoven made little effort to hide his disgust.

"Because," Fegelein gave his annoying little smirk, "all the other lampposts were similarly occupied."

Loringhoven ground out his cigarette butt in annoyance. "No, I meant...."

"I know what you meant, major. And the answer is I don't have one sodding idea. They do it because they can; that's all there is to that. As for me? I am a decorated Gruppenführer, a Waffen SS General and a confidant of the Führer. To stop me or even attempt to do so would mean that *they* would find themselves hanging from a lamppost – by their balls, mate!"

"You didn't think to intervene, I take it?"

"None of my business." Fegelein's facial expression was utterly dismissive of any such thought. Then, cynically, "The law must take its course, major. Wouldn't you agree?"

"Yes, quite so," Loringhoven sniffed. What a vulgar little man this SS oik was. Awful!

Their attention was taken by a minor disturbance further down in the bunker, on the lower level. Raised voices and rushing bodies.

"Best check on that little kerfuffle." Fegelein nodded towards the concrete steps. "Another disaster to tempt our jaded palates, eh?"

"More than likely," Loringhoven followed him down the stairs. Could it be any worse? Had Wenck's offensive been wiped out so soon?

At the bottom of the stairs the anteroom, really nothing more than a large corridor which led off to all the other lower bunker rooms, buzzed with uniformed men, gesticulating and twittering like disturbed magpies. Goebbels was nodding disdainfully at an enraged looking Martin Bormann. Krebs was listening with dismay to a loudly expostulating Keitel. Loringhoven moved toward his chief, intending to discover what lay behind this latest episode of bubbling hysteria.

"Gruppenführer Fegelein. Over here if you please." Bormann crooked an impatient finger at the SS officer. Goebbels also added his own totally irrelevant hand fluttering at the smilingly compliant Fegelein.

Damn! Whatever it was that had happened was a bloody nuisance. Hermann Fegelein had his own plans to be getting on with, and wasting time with these ninnies was not likely to prove helpful in bringing them to fruition. He needed to get to the switchboard and, more importantly, get to his apartment before the routes were completely blocked off by the Russians.

"Herr Reichsleiter," Fegelein's smile might have charmed the skin off an unripe banana, but it could in no way charm a man who didn't even know the meaning of the word. "Something?" Hands clasped behind his back he bounced up and down on his toes hoping to give the impression of out and out readiness and efficiency.

Bormann, party secretary and probably the most powerful man in the Reich after Hitler, and quite possibly before that man, handed a red typed message to the Gruppenführer.

"Read that. Just read that. Of all the opportunistic, treacherous pieces of garbage ever issued from that fat oaf, this takes the cake."

"Does seem a tad pushy," muttered Goebbels, pursing his lips. "The Führer is livid; quite out of his skin with rage."

Tell me something new, thought Fegelein as he read through the offending missive. Officially worded, and quite diplomatically, too, in his opinion, the message simply stated that the sender, Chief of the Air Force, Hermann Goering, required clarification regarding the situation in Berlin, as it would appear that the city would soon be completely encircled and the Führer with it. Goering, as Reichsmarshal and Hitler's designated deputy, wanted to know if all was well and if not, should he take over the duties of Führer as stated in the Führer decree of 1938? The offending sentence read, "If I do not hear from you by 18:00hrs I shall assume that your freedom of action is restricted and so assume that, most regretfully, I must take over the duties as leader." This was followed by protestations of goodwill and loyalty. Even this late in the day, the pernicious and vindictive Martin Bormann saw clearly how he could bring down his old rival. By the time he had finished denouncing the fat leader of the now almost defunct German air force and reiterating his many failures, Hitler was close to death with rage.

"He's attempting a coup," snarled Bormann. "The Führer agrees."

Load of bloody nonsense, thought Fegelein. None of his business, though. He just wanted to get on with things that concerned him personally. All this internecine backstabbing was so utterly moronic. Did they not realise that there was nothing to stab for anymore? Pratts!

"Disgraceful," agreed the Gruppenführer. "Thoroughly reprehensible." He handed the message back and smiled inwardly. He loved using big words. Being a general had done him the world of good. He could now bandy long words with the best of them – so he thought, anyway.

"Fegelein," Goebbels moved to stand slightly in front of Bormann.

"Wait," Bormann thrust himself forcefully back in front of the diminutive propaganda minister. "I'll handle this."

Goebbels frowned with annoyance. True, he reckoned Goering to be nothing more than an overweight, contemptible hedonist; but Bormann was something entirely different. A loathsome creep of a man. Totally untrustworthy. Hitler swore by him, though. Nothing could be done and no one could be seen by the Führer without the shadowy Bormann's permission. Vile, secretive and now, almost all-powerful. The party secretary had worked behind the scenes for years to get into this position; whining, wheedling, destroying, and now he held sway. Pah! Goebbels shrugged. Much good may it do him, the invidious pig.

Bormann wrapped a paternal arm around Fegelein's shoulders.

"You are the SS liaison officer. So now I want you to liaise. I have sent a message to the Reichsführer SS and you must back up that message by stating in the clearest terms to your boss, the truth of this matter. You will inform Reichsführer Himmler of Goering's treachery and state that, as per the Führer's directive, signed by him and on its way to the Reichsführer as we speak, he, Himmler, is to arrest Goering at once. Whatever it takes, the man must be apprehended and locked up until the Führer decides upon the death penalty or not. Understand?"

"Arrest Goering?" For once the normally glib and adroit Fegelein was speechless. The air force chief kept an entire division of Luftwaffe infantry on hand as a personal and very powerful guard. Reichsführer Himmler also kept a personal guard consisting of a division of SS troops, complete with tanks. That these two powerful and mobile private armies might be better utilized at the front seemed neither here nor there. Goering had fervently promised the Führer Luftwaffe troops for the Berlin front on the occasion of his birthday a few days previously. None, however, had materialised. Would Goering submit to arrest?

"At once, if you please, Fegelein." Bormann's thick, ugly head was thrust forward pugnaciously, and his expressionless eyes bored into the Gruppenführer's searching for any contradiction to his demands. Fegelein had always managed to conceal his covert desire to inflict pain and violence upon others. Not for nothing had he been placed in command of the Death's Head SS cavalry brigade in Poland in the war's early stages. He had killed many men, women and children with his own hands. It was an urge that he kept covered with an oily smile. Now, though, the urge was on him again. It came as a powerful physical desire to clamp his teeth over Bormann's bulbous, pockmarked nose and chew until the blood flowed. It was most definitely sexual. Killing and maiming had always been deeply gratifying for him. The sheer pleasure of slaughter quite simply could not be equalled by anything else. And he was, he knew, just one of many. The Führer of the Third

Reich allowed, covertly promoted even, rule by absolute deviance. Thus keeping himself free from the morays and social strictures of those closest around him. Not one of them could criticize his behaviour and not one of them did.

The Gruppenführer's smooth, round face betrayed just the slightest tick, as he took one step back. "Of course, Herr Reichsleiter. At once." Turning on his heel, he stalked off to the communications room. Much as he loathed Martin Bormann, and much as he baulked inwardly at any delay in what he needed to do, this little scenario, so pathetic in its amateur drama group production values, might fall in nicely with his purpose. As he thought on it he smiled. Yes indeed. This could all work out very well.

"I'll have him shot. No, hung. I'll hang the traitorous oaf and display his fat corpse as a warning to others. Yes, that's what I'll do. Betrayed, why am I so betrayed by all and sundry.... why?"

He had stripped the Reichsmarshal of all his offices and degraded his name and rank, but still Adolf hesitated to give the final order for his execution. Goering, he who had once been so loyal now revealed in all his treason. It was treason, wasn't it? Oh, yes. Beyond doubt. Fat Hermann was making a final bid for power. No chance of that, my friend, thought Adolf, none at all. But still....to kill his old colleague and disciple? Maybe-maybe. He would have to think on it.

The Führer had dismissed everyone from his presence whilst he attempted to recover from the numbing shock of treason by his former Luftwaffe chief. He felt his mind beginning to wander again. Where was Wenck? The offensive should be well underway by now. That Russian flank was just begging to be broken into and smashed. And the other commander, the one entrusted with the armoured thrust: who was it now? Damn – it was gone, opiate transported to some hidden recess within his fading memory.

As visions of generals, battles and failures drifted away from his conscious mind, so thoughts of Munich all those years ago, those optimistically carefree years, came flowing into his tortured and dying brain.

CHAPTER 7

May 23 1928: Munich, Thierschstrasse 41

There is always something so enjoyably comforting and comfortable about listening to a howling wind and pane-slapping rain whilst within the warm, cosy confines of a well-furnished room in front of a crackling fire. That's what Emil thought anyway, as he lay with his dearest friend in front of a blazing fire soaking up the warmth from the flames and basking in the affection emanating from his bright-eyed, chatty lover.

They had been the closest of friends for, well, it seemed like forever now, and they cherished each and every nuance of one another. That night when he and Adolf had first met, he had known that great things lay ahead of them. They had taken over Drexler's little DAP and turned it into something quite different. No real programme to speak of, just the usual politicking and waffle, with vague and empty promises. Neither of them had known or had any real idea of what they were doing or what to expect. It had all seemed not much more than a semi-serious game done in the hope that eventually someone might take them seriously. And incredibly, quite a few had. Somehow it had grown out of all proportion to their expectations. Confused at first, they had grabbed onto the reins of their flyaway dream with eager and determined hands.

Adolf had moved quickly and carefully and under his leadership the NAZI party had flourished. He had, for a while, been circumspect in his dealings with folk, always cleverly seeking out their weaknesses and using them against real and potential opponents. And speak? God how he could speak. He practised constantly, gestures, facial expressions but, above all, that incredible voice. Just thinking about Adolf in full flow had Emil all of a quiver.

Things now, though, were changing. Emil was very much aware of what had at first been a barely perceptible change in his friend, into what was now a full-blown metamorphosis. Together they had mounted the Bier Hall Putsch and together they had endured, although *endure* wasn't perhaps quite the right word, imprisonment in Landsberg. Whilst confined at Landsberg he, Emil, had taken his friend's dictation and written in his own hand Adolf's great opus, Mein Kampf. And it was he, Emil, who had discussed well into so many nights, the various methods of getting people to follow them without question. The *them*, however, had very soon become *him*; Adolf Hitler.

And Emil's greatest contribution? Nothing less than the idea for a totally new style of bodyguard. As they had chatted away some three years ago, exploring all sorts of airy-fairy ideas, Emil deftly captured Adolf's turgid imagination by describing a fearsome group of black clad warriors, tall, broad-shouldered and devoted to a leader for whom they would joyously give their lives. All waffle, of course, nobody ever gave their life joyously. In his mind, Emil had modelled this breathtakingly over-the-top group of goose-stepping protectors on the ancient Band of Thebes, a dedicated band of homosexual warriors in fourth-century BCE Greece. It was they who, for the first time in ancient memory, had achieved the unthinkable and given the macho, but every bit as gay, Spartans a good thrashing at Leuctra in 371 BCE. Adolf immediately squashed the idea of actively promoting military homosexuality. It wouldn't suit his *real man* image, as portrayed to the working class. And image was everything. Adolf had enough trouble keeping the rampantly homosexual Rohm and his Brownshirts under control without taking on and being responsible for another group of sexually overactive and pathologically violent dim-wits.

As long as the new paramilitary force *appeared* to be devoted to the rule of law and decency and all things truly German, then the charade might well be a glowing success. Sleight of hand – that was the thing. Emil remembered how he had pondered for days over an effective name for his new creation until finally coming up with something worthy: Shutzstaffel. SS for short. Excellent! He had even designed some cute little metal insignias. The lightning flashes for the SS uniform lapels had been a masterpiece, Adolf had said so. And the silver piping around collar and rank badges added a very definite snazz to the carefully tailored uniforms. There would be nothing ordinary about the SS uniform, nor about the SS themselves, for that matter. Emil had engaged the services of a clever and willing designer, who, due to the current recession, had precious little in the way of work and was only too happy to turn his considerable talents to military design. He had brilliantly realised Emil's ideas, delighting both Adolf and Emil with his flair and aptitude. Hugo Boss would be a valuable addition to the party, when, and if, he decided to join. With the economy in its current state, fashion designers were living a hand-to-mouth existence and many of their studios had closed down. Hugo kept going only because he and Emil got on so well and because of the work that Emil at times managed to put his way. The new uniforms, though, really were a winner and who could tell how many of them Hugo might have to knock up?

Emil's idea had come to brilliant fruition, and his little group of rather cutely muscled guards had grown in numbers. And they were certainly needed. Ernst Rohm, the tough, formerly indispensable commander of the Party's para-military wing of some ten thousand brown shirted ruffians, was growing too powerful for his own good; certainly too powerful for Adolf's peace of mind. Rohm had been gently warned, no point in antagonizing him, but he seemed unable to resist the call of power through violence.

The new guard formed a totally independent protective circle of elite warriors around Adolf, much to the annoyance and bewilderment of Rohm and his brownshirts who considered that Adolf Hitler's protection was their job and theirs alone.

Emil, certain that he and no other would be the overall commander of the newly birthed SS received a firm and hurtful slap-down from his beloved friend. The job went to Schreck. Something of a Hitler look-a-like, almost his double truth be told, Julius Schreck became the Shutzstaffel's first Reichsführer. Emil had to be content with the honour of being the second man on the SS membership list behind Adolf. Adolf was the number one and Emil number two, with the highfalutin title of Oberführer. It hadn't seemed like much at the time, but one day soon, because of that all-important #2 on the SS honours roster, everybody would know that Oberführer Emil Maurice was the de facto creator of the SS and as such, he would be greatly admired, respected and in some quarters regarded as a demi-God. The only fly in that particular jar of ointment thought Emil, 'Is That I'm a Jew!'

There had been times, many months earlier, when he would curl up with laughter as he thought about how they had created it all. The applicants must be tall and blue-eyed, Adolf only half-jokingly insisted. True Aryans, that's what we need. Truth was, of course, none of Adolf's closest associates was either tall, blue-eyed or in any way handsome or indeed seemed very Aryan at all.

Racial purity was the main thing, spouted Adolf. None of these eastern looking types, no Muslims. Africans and certainly no Jews.

"You know how people hate Jews," Adolf had intoned. "And we must encourage that hatred."

"Yes, but to what extent?" Emil had enquired with a certain amount of trepidation. He was well aware of the necessity for a communal and largely superficial hatred to permeate and thus bind the membership together in a tightly disciplined arrow of nonsensical bigotry. It was a proven and effective political tactic.

"What have they done to us, really?" He looked his friend straight in the eye with the question.

"Nothing, of course. Not that I'm aware of, anyway. But that's neither here nor there, Emil. It's a group large enough, rich enough and most importantly, ethnically unsound enough, to warrant hatred and persecution. We need a target to aim at, Emil and the Jews are going to be that target. We shall insist upon getting rid of the evil, economy staining Jews from our wonderful nation. The sanctity of the German bloodline: blah-blah-blah. Mindless, esoteric guff, true. But damned effective, eh?" Adolf waved his hands contemptuously. He would target pregnant women and the elderly if it suited him. "We must get the volk behind us and drive this message home, daily, hourly, every goddamned second of our existence!"

Emil would never forget how he had shuddered at the change that came so swiftly over his friend. Was that hatred real or just another splendid act?

"You seem, pensive, Emil." Adolf laid a soft hand upon Emil's shoulder.

"My Jewish blood. It's going to hold me back. I know it!" He spoke with a small catch of despair. His shoulders slumped as he shook his head in a slow negative fashion. True enough he was only part Jewish. That, however, was going to be quite irrelevant if the rules that he himself had drawn up were to be in any way literally construed. Jews were to have no rights. Jews were to be expelled from all reputable institutions. Jews were to go – clear out, or else! Oh hell! What a bind. It had started out as a bit of a laugh, written with many accompanying sips from the schnapps bottle and loud, frequently vocal applause from Adolf. Now, though, it threatened to engulf him with its bigotry and awfulness. What was it the English poet, Shakespeare, had written, 'hoisted by his own petard?' Well, that's me alright, he thought, well and truly hoisted. He bit hard on his bottom lip, wishing now that he had thought out this SS business more deeply and a great deal more sensibly. From a purely personal point of view, he was worried sick about how all this was going to turn out now that the party was gaining so much momentum. They were growing in power and influence. The Nazi party now had some real clout in the Reichstag and on the streets. Just as important, they had the backing of some big businessmen with more, hopefully, ready to jump on the bandwagon. People were listening and falling in with the Party line. It wasn't just the Jews that Adolf condemned in his outrageous but immensely popular speeches. Homosexuals also came savagely into his firing line. Hell's bells, did he fear nothing? Certainly not the truth. Straight 'A' for hypocrisy, my dear friend, he thought. Let's just hope that we're never found out. Emil was suddenly feeling horribly uncertain and sorry for himself.

"D'you know, Adi, I feel like some reincarnated Judas. Honestly, I do!"

"Don't worry about it," comforted Adolf. "No one will ever know, and if they do I'll sort it. You, my dear Emil, need never worry about anything."

Emil leaned forward and clasped his friend's hand in gratitude.

"Now," Adolf smiled. "Just one little thing."

"Oh yes," Emil smiled back in anticipation and began unbuttoning his shirt. The thought of what was to come made him feel decidedly better. Pepped up, almost.

"No. Not yet." Adolf gently pulled Emil's hand away from his shirt buttons. Later. Just a little later."

"OK," Emil nodded acceptingly. "What then?"

"You must be aware, Emil, that things are changing, taking shape so to speak."

"Uh-huh."

"I've realised that I must take control of everything…and I *mean* everything concerning the Party and its leadership."

"Of course, Adi. I completely understand."

"No. I don't think that you do. None of you do." Adolf rose from the floor and stood purposefully with legs apart before the fire.

"To continue to advance, to succeed, this casual first name basis which other parties insist upon using, must stop. It is so stupid," he threw his head back as he searched for the right word, carelessly hand flicking his hair back from his eyes in a decidedly feminine gesture. "American! Yes, it is ridiculously American and lacking in respect. As of now, all that is going to change."

Emil swallowed dry spit. What the hell had Adolf thought up now? Didn't they have enough crack-pot ideas bubbling insanely on a dozen different rings?

"In future, I shall be addressed as Führer. By you and everyone in the party. No exceptions."

For a while it looked as though he might burst into one of his endless monologues, but he contented himself with standing legs apart, hands on hips, chest thrust determinedly out and his coat-hanger shoulders stretched back as far as they could go. Eyes shining with self-worth and affection, Adolf now only needed a photographer. Unfortunately, none such was available, so he contented himself with some manly nodding, a trick he had learnt from the Italian dictator, Mussolini whom he much admired.

Oh dear God, call me Mayer, thought Emil as he stared up at his wide eyed, overdramatically glaring friend, Führer, lover, whatever. This sounded very much like friendship, common decency even, being thrown into the waste bin of ego. He had seen it coming, and now here it was. A man insisting upon being called the Führer by everybody around him, even those closest, was on a short and unhealthy trip to total isolation.

"You, Emil, dear friend as you may be, shall from this day onward address me as Führer. Clear?"

Emil nodded, not at all sure how to respond to yet another skin-shredding metamorphosis by his friend.

"And now," Adolf glanced back at the crackling fire and then suggestively at Emil. "Come here."

Despite his trepidation, Emil could barely wait. Nevertheless, a degree of caution made him incline his head toward an adjoining door at the far end of the sitting room. "Shouldn't we….?"

Adolf smiled his recently developed and rather smug Führer smile. "Not a problem. They're all out until gone 16:00hrs, at the earliest. An hour should more than suffice, wouldn't you say? In fact, by the look of you my sweet friend," he winked knowingly, "just a few minutes might do!" He gave an uncharacteristic half giggle and Emil found it somewhat off-putting as he realised Adolf's mirth was directed toward his rapidly rising tumescence.

"But if it makes you feel better," Adolf sidled to the door adjoining his private study. "Shall we?"

Geli sauntered into the pantry of the big apartment. Her cutely styled but now soaking wet beret hung dripping alongside her coat in the hallway, and her shoes sat surrounded by a pool of gently leaking water beneath them. Her wool stockinged feet left damp imprints as she moved across the tiled floor. Outside, the rain still fell but more lightly than earlier in the day. Her eyes flew over the crumb covered worktop and followed their trail to a lower cupboard which she gleefully opened. Goodie! Mummy had done a little baking before departing for the shops. She would doubtless have coffee with her friend Elise whilst out and spend time chatting about recipes and such like.

Geli attended the Dekner pre-university school for young women on a daily basis where she was busy cramming for her entrance exam to the Ludwig Maximilian University. Medicine was the subject and a medical degree would be the happy pinnacle of respectability for the Raubals, to the doting mother, at least. Geli was a bright, lively girl and no one anticipated any problems with her enrolment at the prestigious Ludwig Maximilian. Her exam cramming, however, was half-hearted. She had no real interest in medicine or healing people. At nineteen she should have been, according to her elders, maturing into a forward-thinking young woman determined upon advancement and a career.

The truth was, though, that Geli simply wanted to have some fun and excitement out of life. The university and medicine thing had merely been to keep her mother and uncle Adi happy. She had passed her early exams with ease and learning wasn't the problem; boredom was! Bright and clever as she was, Geli now realised that she was not cut out for the life of a doctor, medical researcher or anything at all along those lines. It was all so boring. Sooner or later she would have to tell her mother and then, perhaps, her mother could tell uncle Adi. Yes, that would be best.

School had finished early today because the Dean's assistant had suffered a massive and rather public stroke, so the head of faculty had sent all the girls home, as they, the poor things, were bound to be suffering emotional trauma from such a shock.

Geli smiled. It was good to get away from that musty old place a couple of hours early. If the faculty wanted to think that she, or any other of the teenaged girls at the Dekner, cared one way or another about the salty and constantly grumpy old assistant Dean, Fraulein Fisch, let them. She giggled loudly. Perhaps a whole bundle of them could die and thus give the girls a few weeks off from their interminably boring academic chatter.

She wondered idly what her mother would be bringing back from the shops. Food played a big part in Geli's life. She loved nice tasting things whether sweet or savoury. And mumsy always ladled out generous helpings. Recently, uncle Adolf had taken to noshing vegetables and cakes in preference to meat. Turning vegetarian, it seemed. Silly, thought Geli. At least he didn't insist that his household follow his example with this new fad. And good old uncle Adi still adored his liver dumplings and the occasional slice of well-cured ham. Not yet completely vegetarian. Perhaps time would wean him away from this curious obsession with vegetables. Geli could easily understand the love of cakes, cream, jam and stuff. She had the self-same weakness for those naughty bites. And these days, thanks to the rise in their standard of living, she was able to eat as many of them as she chose. Wonderful – but she knew that she must watch her waistline carefully, or it would all catch up with her at some stage in the future. She looked down at her wrists. They were naturally thick and her medical studies had shown her that she was of a body type that easily, all too easily, gained unwanted pounds. Watch one's weight! Easy enough to say, but life was so good now, and where others struggled to make ends meet with all the ups and downs of an uncertain economy, the Hitler political circus and extended family were doing OK, thank you very much.

Things had looked up ever since uncle Adolf had asked mummy to take on the duties of live-in housekeeper and occasional cook. Angela was uncle Wolf's elder half-sister, and although she quite strongly disagreed with some of uncle's ideas and methods, she was nevertheless extremely grateful for the leg-up he had afforded them. Uncle paid mummy well and bed and board were provided free. "As it should be," her mother opined. "We're family, after all."

There they were. Sitting enticingly on a cloth covered metal tray; small, perfectly rounded cinnamon cakes with sweet apple centres. Gorgeous. Just too much! Geli carefully lifted one of the soft cakes from the tray and took a sniff.

"Oh, sod it," she whispered conspiratorially to herself and took another. Mummy made such wonderful cakes. Her staple cooking wasn't so good, but her cakes and buns were superb.

One cake down and one still to go, Geli made her way to the pantry exit. At the ancient wooden, metal framed door she stopped. Should she get a plate before journeying out into the hallway? Her mother would moan like a Valkyrie with toothache if she found cake crumbs on any of the apartment floors. With the unerring balance of youth she spun around, snatched a plate from the shoulder high shelf and munched contentedly away at her tasty little prize.

Geli Raubal had all the joyous flush of youth shining from her unlined skin. Although a little on the heavy side, she was nevertheless attractive in a fresh open-faced way.

Geli liked, enjoyed even, being Adolf Hitler's niece. Uncle Adi wasn't just famous hereabouts, he was downright notorious. There was an incredible thrill in being associated with him. The other girls were constantly asking questions about his habits; what was he like – what foods did he eat and……did she fancy him?

As to the latter; no she certainly did not fancy him but she did find him fascinating and yes, very overbearing. He seemed to think that he owned everything around him, especially people. Yes, that was it. Uncle Adi liked to collect people and get them to do what he wanted. Geli was young but certainly no fool. He was interesting, yes, but her doting old uncle liked to surround himself with deferential types – deferential to him, that is. His associates were invariably either ugly, flat-nosed creatures with a penchant for violence but little in the way of brain power, or they were educated types, well-spoken but with no volition of their own; simply limp wristed marionettes waiting for their strings to be pulled. A bit like actors. They all had one thing in common, though. They looked to the great intellect, uncle Adolf, for leadership and knowledge of what must be done. Geli wasn't at all sure as to the extent of uncle Adi's intellectual prowess; she had heard him speak to his colleagues and such, and he sounded more hectoring than intellectual to her mind. But what did she know, or care for that matter? Uncle Adi seemed able to get what he wanted, when he wanted it. He was certainly an amazing man, her uncle, and she loved basking in the aura of such brightly reflected glory.

More to the point; she placed the last of the delicious cinnamon cake into her eager mouth, was that gorgeous driver of his, Emil. She lay the shiny clay plate carelessly on top of the rectangular occasional table in the centre of the hallway. Would he be home or had uncle Adi sent him out on some errand? She had spoken with Emil on quite a few occasions. He was bright and funny, and that smile! She felt her heart begin to thump harder against her chest. She had messed around as most girls do when they pass puberty. But there had never been anything serious. Nothing to make her flip her lid, so to speak. Then, that primitive emotion love, or lust or whatever they liked to call it, had rocked up and twisted her heart in one huge, terrifyingly delicious squeeze. That first time she had set eyes upon Emil Maurice. Oh Wow! She shivered even now as she thought of him. Yes, he was only a driver but he was high-up in uncle Adi's party. They went almost everywhere together.

Almost two years of unrequited love. Emil had personality and wit. He treated her with charm and respect, and on the rare occasion when their bare flesh, a hand or an arm, touched, electricity had flowed through her entire body so violently that it felt like a seizure.

But *was* her affection unrequited? The way he looked at her, at times. The smiles, the expression in those gloriously deep, dark eyes; he fancied her, really. She was sure. Well, she was going to take the lead and do something about the turmoil within her. She was nineteen now, and not some silly child. When she looked at Emil she found herself imagining things and situations, with him that she would never have believed she was capable of. She didn't just want him to do things to her: she wanted to do things to him. Yes – it was all so disgusting. It promised to be so disgusting that she could barely wait!

A quick glance out of the west facing side window into the courtyard showed that the car was parked on site. Emil was home, but where might uncle Adi be? In his study, probably, working on yet another speech. The longish and surprisingly wide corridor led to four bedrooms, two of which lay beyond a small ornately curved archway above the deeply recessed living room door. At the far end of the hallway lay a small, spiral stone stairway which led down, rather too steeply, to a large tunnel shaped double cellar. That place, as Geli knew, was full of Nazi impedimenta; flags, banners and such-like. It was also where Emil slept and passed his quiet time, whenever he had any, that is. Down in his cellar he would often ponder on new designs for his party ideas, a deft new way of slanting a cap, perhaps, or a new touch to an already existing badge, and so on.

Geli placed her ear against the wall and listened. Nothing. So she moved quietly down the hallway until she was standing right outside uncle Adi's bedroom door. Ear to the door but again nothing.

Now it was time to test her youthful courage, take her burgeoning lust by the scruff of the neck and do this thing!

Gently she tip-toed down the cellar stairs until she reached the thick oak entrance door. She tapped nervously but there was no response. Tapping became a firm knock followed by a sharply hissed, "Emil. Emil. Are you there?" No sound, no answer. Tentatively she tried the door handle. It came as no surprise to discover that it wasn't locked. The only door in the apartment that uncle Adi ever allowed to be locked, was his own. She glanced about her as she moved amongst Emil's belongings and the SS paraphernalia that lay in neat piles all about the place. So neat and tidy. There was the pleasant smell of an expensive after-shave. His clothes were hung in neat and pristine order. Her Emil; her glorious shining Emil.

Well, she turned round and about. If he wasn't here, where on earth was he? The garage, perhaps. If the car wasn't going to be used today then at some stage Emil would park it in the wood and brick garage come workshop. He would probably give it a good clean whilst he was at it. Emil had been known to tinker a little beneath the bonnet of the supercharged Mercedes, but that wasn't really his thing. They had Julius for that. Emil disliked getting grubby, and God forfend that he get so much a smidgen of oil or dirt on his clothes. Emil's slightly over-the-top desire to be always nothing less than at his pristine best was something of a puzzle to her, bearing in mind that not so very long ago he had been quite happy to batter the living daylights out of anyone who dared confront his boss in a disrespectful, or God help them, physical manner. Emil was a toughie, alright. She hugged herself with secret pleasure. So good looking and cute and neat, and he was a real hard case. Like a movie star; all good looks and invincible. So adorable!

Running her hand over his rail hung clothes she moved back to the door. Feeling a little disappointed she made her way back up the stairs.

She supposed, as he wasn't in the kitchen, pantry, garage or his own quarters, that he must be in the living room and probably with uncle Adi. There was the small drawing room of course, but nobody ever went in there. It was just too pokey and dull.

Back up in the hallway she moved toward the living room. Two small carpeted stairs took her down to the recessed mahogany door. It was heavy but thanks to regular oiling and dusting the hinges didn't creak at all. The brass door knob, though, rattled ever so slightly as she eased open the door and popped her head around, displaying a gay smile as she did so. Uncle Adi liked to see his niece smile; lit up the room, he said.

Nobody here, she mused, Now that *was* odd. She knew someone was in the apartment, they had to be 'cos coats, hats, car and so on, were all where they should be. These days, whenever Emil went out with her uncle, day or night, he wore his SS uniform. He wasn't merely uncle Adi's best friend; he was his driver and bodyguard all rolled into one. Emil only wore civilian dress when he went out privately or on days at home.

The living room was large. Even so, uncle Adi was looking for somewhere bigger. Heavens, thought Geli, we'll be living in a palace next.

A rectangular table sat off centre of the room and around it were eight carver style chairs. Its original use had been as a dining table, but now it was used to host meetings with uncle Adi's NSDAP friends and associates. Again off centre was a sumptuously upholstered sofa facing three wide armed leather chairs, all surrounding an ornate Chinese coffee table. This little lot sat on a wide and well-worn imitation Persian carpet, which had badly curling edges. The furniture arrangement was quite deliberate. It gave carefully planned space for uncle Adolf to march up and down and swing his arms as he regaled his guests with his plans and ideas. Once seated, it would be impossible not to see, or hear, uncle Adi in full flow. Her uncle simply could not abide being ignored, and in this room there was precious little likelihood of that happening.

An overly long cabinet with garish, bronze door handles was the only other large item of furniture. It was old-fashioned and heavy; like everything else in the room. To Geli's young eyes it was aesthetically all at sea; very masculine and dry. No bright colours or happy pictures. Just dull honeysuckle paint and oversized chairs. Awful!

There was one bright point, though. Sitting almost sedately atop a small occasional table beneath one of the two wide bay windows, was a much-prized Nauen radio. Its tone was amazing and Geli loved to listen to modern music on the rare occasions when uncle Adi allowed her. That such technology existed, that music being played hundreds of miles away could be brought in an instant to her ears through this little plastic box was truly amazing!

She stood staring down at the modern technological marvel and was sorely tempted to switch it on. It wasn't just music that could be relayed through its magical little speaker. Drama, poetry readings and current news also came tumbling out upon demand.

What was that? A moan? And there it was again. What the devil? She craned her neck searching for the origin of that strange sound. Across the room, the door to uncle Adi's study was closed. Probably locked. Uncle Adi never allowed anyone into his inner sanctum unaccompanied. But that moan had come from within his private study, of that she was sure. What if he were ill? He rarely drank and never smoked, but he did keep insane hours. Geli's medical studies had shown her that people could become ill, even drop dead for no apparent reason, within a second of appearing normal. With a slightly nervous giggle, she moved over to the study door. The thick American style carpeting muffled any sound that she might have made.

She felt suddenly and inexplicably nervous. The sound of heavy movement came from behind the thick study walls and there was that awful moan again. More like a groan this time. Nothing for it; forbidden or not she had to open that door. Someone was clearly in distress. Uncle Adi could be ill in there, or even Emil. They might need her help and, such as it was, her medical expertise.

"Harder, Emil, much harder!"

"Yes Adi.... I mean my Führer." Emil stamped his shoed foot hard down onto Adolf's flaccid and heaving belly. As he stood over his writhing, ecstasy filled friend he stamped and ground the sole of his shoe into the soft pink flesh, and then aimed a kick at the wobbling little jelly rolls of fat around Adolf's midriff. At the same time he began pleasuring himself as he stood dominantly astride his recumbent Führer. "For you my Führer – for you!"

Like two frenziedly braying donkeys both men released the sounds of their orgiastic pleasure at precisely the same time.

Geli's head jerked back. Those dreadful cries. Surely howls of unbearable pain. She didn't stop to think that there had been two almost harmonizing bellows of what must surely be someone in agony.

"I'm here, I'm here," she called bravely and threw open the door, prepared to offer whatever assistance might be required. One step into the study, slowly followed by just one more.

"Oh my God!" Tears sprang to her eyes and both hands flew to her mouth. She might have experienced many reactions, and indeed she did. They flew through and across her psyche in an instant. Horror, disgust, disbelief and the shock of betrayal. Betrayal most of all. Her uncle, the great man, the would-be ruler of the world lay there, naked. He half turned as he gazed up at her in shocked disbelief. The bastard!

And Emil, her lovely Emil. Well, he looked rather less than lovely now, his trousers and pants thrown carelessly aside and his shirt tails sticking to his sweaty back-side and his leather shoed foot firmly between uncle Adi's pasty little legs. Yuk! .... oh, hell's bells, this was just too much!

She stared at Emil and then back down at her uncle. Silence now reigned as the three of them just stared at each other. Geli wanted to leave, to run, but for whatever reason her feet seemed glued to the floor. Her face was contorted with horror, shock and fear. Adolf's face was an absolute picture of blood engorged rage and terror. Emil's expression was one of drooping despair.

Geli managed a step back when Adolf snarled from the floor; "Get out!" Spell broken she needed no further urging. Clumsily she fled that scene of male abandonment and made for her room. She wanted out of this carnal hellhole. The horror of what she had just seen was seeping more and more deeply into her consciousness with each passing second.

Throwing open the door of her bedroom she ran in and threw herself on the bed before rolling swiftly off it and remembering to slam the door shut. There was a lock but no key. Uncle Adi held all those secreted away somewhere in his study. Was he going to come and barge in on her, and go on one of his self-righteous monologues? Make excuses? What? Someone had to say something, sometime. How on earth could she look him in the eye ever again? What he had been doing with Emil was against the law, wasn't it? She wasn't one hundred per cent sure, but it was certainly frowned upon. Even uncle Adi frowned on it, or so he had said. Germany needs proper men; he'd repeatedly stated to all and sundry. No room for shirt-lifters in Hitler's manly Germany. What a bloody hypocrite. Geli's slim fingers curled around the top cover of her single bed. But he would, she knew, hate her and rage at her because of what she had witnessed, and seen his absolute and rather untruthful self. Yes, uncle Adi was a liar; an out and out liar.

And Emil. Her shoulders trembled with hurt. Such an utter letdown. She knew that he liked women, but clearly he liked men as well. Was that possible? And yet she was still interested in him. There had been nothing objectionable in the ruggedly sturdy body that Emil had been displaying. The shock of the knowledge that, if anything, right at that moment she wanted him more than ever before almost had her running for the bathroom. How the hell could she still be attracted to such a man? Was she, too, a pervert?

At least two minutes passed before Adolf managed any semblance of pulling himself together. The secret was out. How the devil could he have been so stupid, so blindingly idiotic? To risk everything for a tacky sexual urge. He cursed himself for a weak fool. Never – but never again! Viciously wiping himself clean he snarled into the air, "I'll be finished if this gets out. D'you hear me, Emil? God damned finished."

Emil had managed to dress remarkably quickly. Far more quickly than his stunned leader, anyway.

"Not to worry, Ad…" this was bloody ridiculous, "my Führer. It's just one of life's little accidents."

Hitler glared at him. "Accidents like that are wreck and ruin. Are you truly so dense that you can't see it?"

Emil felt anger rising and had to hold hard onto his own frazzled emotions. Was it his fault that his over-eager Führer had wanted sexual release so badly that he couldn't wait? Always someone else's bloody fault. Typical!

"Please…. please don't get upset." Emil crooned. "I'll sort it. I'll go and have a word with her. Convince her to stay quiet. She'll listen to sense. I know she will. Your niece is a very sensible girl, you know."

Now almost completely dressed with just a little tidying left to do, Hitler froze. Emil found himself staring at a rigid finger pointing at him like a pistol barrel.

"Take that tone with me ever again, Emil Maurice, and I'll have your head clubbed to a pulp and sent on to your damned mother. D'YOU HEAR ME?"

From rising anger to a state of almost abject terror, Emil nodded.

It was no threat. Adolf Hitler had merely foretold the immediate future should he be crossed. Emil knew his friend, or rather, perhaps, erstwhile friend. If he put a foot wrong now there was no telling what his lover might do; certainly, though, it would not be pleasant.

Now at last moderately presentable and calming more with each passing minute, Hitler turned thoughtfully away. This needed careful handling. Little Geli, and mouthy Emil. He needed their silence. Emil wasn't a problem. He had as much to lose as himself. But Geli, his niece. What to do about her? How on earth could even he, force closed the mouth of a lively, feisty and wilful nineteen-year-old who was so full of herself? Pursing his lips, he knew what he must do. He would do it because he had no idea of any other solution and because it always worked so well. Geli would be quiet and acquiescent under the threat of terrible retribution. The fates of Geli and her mother, their joint futures, were in his hands. Defiance would see the full horror of uncle Adi's vengeful fury unleashed. Yes, that was it. Nevertheless, a bad feeling, a feeling of unease lingered in his belly and simply would not go away.

"You Emil, will do and say nothing. I'll get around to you later."

"Around to me....?" Emil's jaw went slack. "My – my Führer. What do you mean – around to me?"

Hitler half smiled at this very abrupt, drastic even, change in their relationship. "Exactly what I say, Herr Oberführer Maurice. Remain here until I am ready for you." With that he swung away and left the study and a very uncertain Emil Maurice stewing on the recent events. Emil leaned back on the thick legged desk. His mind was racing: Oberführer – was that a promotion?

"Now, child." Hitler sat on the edge of Geli's bed and spoke more as a father than her uncle; her debauched, depraved and dishonest uncle. She had once thought that he was quite a man. A pompous but dynamic force of light and truth. Not anymore. She knew now what he truly was; a liar and a hypocrite. It was all so confusing. But why did she care so much? It wasn't as though it was any of her business. Because she had seen it, that was why. Witnessed what they had been up to. Probably what they had secretly been doing for many years. It was just so ugly and Geli didn't like ugliness in any form. Emil hadn't been ugly, though. But he had looked silly, which was just as bad, really, in Geli's estimation. Where was he, anyway, and what the hell was going to happen now?

As if picking up on her train of thought Hitler rose from the bed and stood over her. Geli stared up wide-eyed. She was normally of a brave, forward disposition unwilling to take lip or insult from anyone.

But now, for the first time in her carefree life, she felt afraid of another human being. Geli had thought that when her uncle appeared with his explanations as to what she had witnessed, she would feel contempt and loathing and that she would display her contempt in no uncertain manner. Well, she certainly felt the loathing but dared not display even a smidgen of contempt. This was a different uncle Adi. He was just too damn scary to mess with; not like uncle Adi at all. But of course, as she knew deep within her, this is what he had always been,

"You understand, child, that you must obey my diktats at all times, and without question. You are never to leave this apartment unchaperoned...."

"But uncle Adi, please.......

"NEVER! Do you understand, girl – Never?"

"Yes, sir," she whispered, almost humbly.

"D'you think that I don't know how you feel about Emil?" His voice rose, harsh and accusing. "You disgusting little harlot.... WHORE!" Transferring his own guilt and fear made him feel immediately better. It was her fault. Yes, far better that it was all her fault. He had already convinced himself where the blame lay. Truth became just another of those little annoyances that were best ignored when inconvenient.

"I've seen the way you look at him, enticing him and leading him on. You won't, you can't have him, my girl. Understand? He-is-not-for-you, you brazen hussy."

Geli trembled with shock and disbelief. Who in heaven's name was this man? Mad! He's bloody mad, she thought, as even greater fear enveloped her. His eyes were manic and his voice, well, it was theriomorphic, terrifying!

"Please, uncle Adi, please. I didn't do any......"

"Silence!" He bent forward, his face thrusting at hers almost touching. His hand moved as though to grab hold of her hair but then dropped away. They were nose to nose. Geli shrank back: God, his breath was vile. She shuddered and rolled her young head from side to side, desperate to get away from this awful, vile man.

"You may speak," he hissed "when spoken to and not before. Clear?"

She nodded, shamefacedly. Why couldn't she stand up to him, the raging bully?

"ANSWER ME." He roared. Geli started at the power of that command.

"Yes, uncle."

"Good." Suddenly he was calmness personified. "There's a good girl. All's well that ends well, eh?"

"Yes uncle," Geli nodded frantically, tears running down her fear frozen features.

And then he was gone. Just like that. Bastard, she thought but without any real anger or resentment. All she felt was shame at being handled in such a manner. She felt – pathetic!

So this was how it must be. Sacked, thrown out, discarded; as good as anyway. The Führer, that two-faced son-of-a-bitch whom he'd worshipped and obeyed for all these years, had abruptly terminated his employment.

"It's for the best, Emil," Hitler had cooed. "A good long rest and then we'll think again. But right now, Emil, what we've had, well, it has to end. The risk." He fluttered his hands in one of the absurdly feminine gestures that he allowed himself when alone with Emil. "It is far too dangerous for something that is, relatively speaking, so unimportant."

Unimportant? "Jesus H Christ!" Emil's curse was loud enough to attract the attention of the four other occupants of the bus, all four of whom turned and frowned at him. Three men, one woman, all elderly and bossy looking, as only cantankerous old folks at odds with their fading and unloving world can look. To hell with them, the wrinkled old bastards. He rammed the rim of his hat hard down over his eyes as his mind raged at the unfairness of his former employer.

Wasn't unimportant when that pathetic little gnome of a penis raised its dirty little head, was it Adolf, you ungrateful whore. No more Mercedes for me thought Emil. The bus from now on, eh? His attention wandered to Geli. Poor kid. She had done nothing, and yet Adolf's full and hateful fury had descended upon her, and to a lesser extent, her mother, his half-sister.

Oh well. Emil was a survivor and survive he would. His belongings packed into a small suitcase with a promise from Hitler that anything else would be sent on to his forwarding address. Back to watch repairing, then, thought Emil. The small rental lock-up property on the corner of Engle Strasse was his for the asking. Hitler hadn't fired him from the SA or the SS. Well, try it, thought Emil. I invented that crazy idea in the first place. His name, Oberführer Emil Maurice sat atop the honours list of the SS directly beneath Hitler's. It might not mean very much right now, but that honours list could well become a thing of high regard, one day. Oberführer, me, he thought. Ought to be bloody Reichsführer in all truth. Well, not to worry. It was Oberführer of sweet bugger all really. But there was no telling what the future might hold. Sighing he sat further back into the worn and rock-solid bus seat. He withdrew from inside his overcoat pocket first his SA membership, and then the much more carefully cherished SS card with photo and rank. He felt almost paternal toward his creation. Pretty boys in pretty uniforms might not count for a lot right now but who could tell what the future might hold? He smiled fatalistically. One day, perhaps.

Nine days had gone by since Emil's departure and Hitler had to admit he missed his long-serving chauffeur/bodyguard/lover. Emil it was who had written down in long-hand those copious early notes for Mein Kampf. His own writing was pretty poor, something which he had never truly mastered. Grammar, writing, spelling and punctuation were all still pretty much a mystery to him. He simply didn't have the patience to tackle lengthy tasks. No problem, though, when there were others to carry out those mundane necessities.

He might allow Emil back into the mainstream, one day. Not into the immediate circle, mind, but some sort of reward for his past services. At the moment it was too dangerous. The slightest whiff of opprobrium now would mean ruin. He, Adolf Hitler, would never engage in sex acts again. In future, humanity, even useful humanity, would be kept at a firm emotional and physical distance. No more mess and no more whining lover's demands. That was the end of it! Without even being aware of it, his cognitive and emotional empathy had become nothing more than a self-reflection.

He determined that even casual familiarity must be a thing of the past. He was the Führer and the familiar address of Du when he was being addressed by others would no longer be tolerated. In future it would be the formal and far more respectful, Sie. No more errors, no more pandering to base appetites such as sex, alcohol or tobacco.

As far as the Party was concerned, things were going well and with any luck the economy would plummet again within the next few days. Inflation promised to rocket, along with the price of staples. Which meant, happily, that the less fortunate working and non-working classes would become even more restless than usual. Party membership was reasonably steady but he needed an increase in dues paying members. The new apartment on Prinzregentenplatz was ready to move into. It was palatial and far grander than he needed but he wanted to be seen to be on the rise. Party funds would be paying for some new furniture and, of course, the lease.

He whistled tunelessly as Angela, his sister, placed another slice of apple pie and cream in front of him. She was hugely puzzled by the abrupt change in the relationship between her brother and Geli. Geli rarely spoke first to her uncle and the former warmth that had existed between the two of them was gone. Geli at times looked downright fearful and her brother's expression whenever she caught him looking at her seemed so guarded, unreadable, but certainly not affectionate. What on earth had gone wrong? Angela had probed and questioned her daughter but to no avail. And her brother's response to anything outside what he wanted to talk about at any given time did not encourage the asking of personal questions. These days he seemed to discourage general conversation of any kind. Whatever the problem might be, Adolf had even less intention of confiding in her than had Geli. No matter. Sooner or later, one way or another she would drag the truth out of her daughter. Then they would see.

"Is it sweet enough for you," she asked with a smile, knowing full well that Adolf could never scoff down enough sugar.

He nodded slowly, helping himself to more cream. "It is a work of culinary genius, Angela, as are all your pastries." It was true enough. Angela's pastries were extraordinarily good. Happy with the compliment she moved silently around the pantry and then to the kitchen to complete her daily chores. She was making a vegetable lasagne for dinner tonight and unlike her pastries, her main dish cooking was never quite as good or as certain, no matter how hard she tried.

Hitler shoved the empty plate contentedly away from him. Excellent! Nine days on from that unfortunate escapade and all seemed well. His dependent female relatives would do as they were told. Angela, his loving sister would continue to keep house and ensure that everything ran well. As for Geli? Now he frowned. He could feel that old sense of unease returning, and to this day he had never once been proved wrong when acting upon it. Difficult. This was so very difficult. As long as she obeyed his strictures all would be well. But would she – and for how long? He began clicking his fingernails-click-click. His niece was young, and he had many things that necessitated his being away from Munich for days, weeks even at a time. He simply couldn't be here on tap. If she were *too* closely guarded then she might blurt out the truth to her chaperone, whoever that might be. Young females had a bad habit of opening up their hearts to sympathetic listeners. There was no telling what she might come out with. She had seen too much. Seen him as he had never wanted to be seen; just another hopelessly sex obsessed male. More to the point, she had seen his penile misfortune. Whereas he had once had affection for his niece, he could now barely look at her without feeling contempt and loathing for himself – and her. Damn her to hell for being such a nosey bitch!

Geli was already displaying signs of depression and unrest. Her attendance at the pre-university college had been terminated and the little work remaining for her entrance exam to the university would be accomplished from home. But she was showing no interest in further study. She had even indicated that she had no intention of attending any university, that she was done with studying. There was no telling what might be going on in that young mind. He needed to keep a wary eye on her. She must not be allowed to hinder his march toward political success, in any way whatsoever.

He wanted to be gentle with her, to be kind, he really did. If she behaved – *if* she did, then all would be well. And if she didn't? Another few seconds of finger clicking. He would sort that out if and when it came to it.

CHAPTER 8

September 17 1931: Munich, Hotel Krone

A dolf had just finished one of the most important political pitches of his life. The Party was flying high to the extent that important politicians now travelled to see him along with industrialists, big business types and press barons. The tattered economy and factionist in-fighting amongst the many political parties in the Reichstag meant that no clear course could be navigated. Any good idea or halfway sensible plan for the future would be immediately shouted down and crushed by energetic filibustering from self-seeking opposition groups. The streets were places of pure terror as violent gangs roamed the thoroughfares and dark alleys of all the major towns and cities. Death and injury had become commonplace. The police were powerless to prevent the now highly organized para-military gangs that roamed the streets from inflicting violence upon whomsoever they chose. Sometimes the less than partisan police forces of various towns joined in the mayhem with baton swinging joy. Berlin was the crux. The capital was a hell-hole of discord and misery that made Dante's Inferno look like happy families playing softball on a Cannes beach. Only one Party and one man now stood out. The Nazi Party was a disciplined force. It was run, controlled completely, by one man. It could unleash ten thousand, uniformed and directed, heavy fisted yobs on the streets of Berlin alone. And the man commanding that army of thuggery, and ruling it with an iron hand, was Adolf Hitler.

Adolf Hitler, leader of the now very powerful Nazi party that had more than one hundred deputies in the Reichstag. With yet another new election in the offing and with the Nazis looking good to gain substantially more Reichstag seats, many industrial and political fence sitters were looking to the Nazi party as the unlikely guardians of future German prosperity. Strength was what was needed; not mollycoddling democracy. Hitler's speeches were dynamite. The masses were swinging behind him in droves. His enemies waited for him to overreach himself but Adolf was boxing clever. His aim was the very top, and any lie, subterfuge or act, no matter how vile, would do just so long as it served his purpose.

Joy-Joy-joy! He smiled broadly and whacked his trenchcoated thigh with the now ever-present riding crop. It gave off a most satisfying crack. Good for the tough guy image, he had decided a little over one year ago. He liked to whack a table or chair back now and again just for effect. It looked and sounded authoritarian. It said clearly; don't mess with me! Over the past months he had practised his vocal delivery, his body movements, his every gesture daily. He had taken as his role models some American actors. A certain George Raft was Adolf's favourite. The man was small but moved in front of the cinema camera with an aura of undeniable menace. Edward G Robinson was another. Both men frequently portrayed tough, no-nonsense sorts of men with a penchant for killing. Adolf admired Al Capone. Now there was a man who knew how to get what he wanted and took it; a man who made others tremble. That was the way to be in this modern day and age.

The humble and frequently mocked beginnings of the early DAP were long behind. Spurned, insulted and attacked in turn, he had survived. How? He couldn't really say. He knew that he had an odd knack of making folk believe in him. Women, for all their famed intuition, seemed to take in every last bit of blaggarding that he chose to throw at them. It meant, of course, that he always had protective cannon fodder around him. Escape was easy if necessary.

Those with money and influence had avoided him at first. Now, though, a good few wanted him and more were showing open interest. He was being courted by truly powerful men, but he knew that one wrong move would be his undoing. He had come this far by using a lot of bluff and, as the Americans liked to say – Bullshit. He had built a house of cards and glued it together with human weakness, gullibility and perversion. Useful tools but, like a diseased mucous membrane, only loosely binding. All of them were weak and eager to follow but he had to have a more concrete base than the violent and often deviant men he had chosen to be around him. Yes, he could count on their loyalty but to what extent? As long as he kept feeding them the crumbs of success they would follow him. But he needed more, and for that he must dig strength and courage from out of the working class. His new SS appointee showed great promise: Heinrich Himmler, an odd, chinless man, but an amazingly effective administrator and utterly subservient to his Führer, Adolf Hitler. A talented bully born to grovel and obey; precisely what Adolf needed and as many more as he could entice to his banner.

He turned briefly to glance back at the hotel foyer. Kretschmer, owner of several iron foundries throughout Bavaria, waved a smiling farewell.

Rich as Croesus, that man, and he had seemed almost deferential. Yes – a good meeting. Adolf was fairly sure that he had impressed them all with his abundant perspicacity.

He threw himself into the back of the huge supercharged Mercedes and firmly tapped his driver on the shoulder with his crop. "Prinzregentenplatz, Schreck. Nice and easy, if you don't mind."

His driver, Julius Schreck nodded compliance. "As you say, my Führer. Nice and easy." He had known Adolf Hitler for years. He even looked a little like him, truth be told. There had been a time when it had been Julius and Adolf. All first names and great buddies. But those days were gone and Julius was fine with it. He had always known that Hitler was an oddball – an excessively oddball. So being on more formal terms suited him very well. The pay was good, he had respect and a good life. What more could a man ask?

Hitler had just that moment departed and white jacketed waiters were clearing the dining table as the group of men and one woman drifted to the adjoining private room for coffee and cigars. Business had called him and anyway, he knew well enough that they would want to discuss him out of earshot.

The lone female, Frau Gertrude Huber, owner of a very large international publishing house and four national magazines snapped her fingers at a tray-burdened waiter as she placed between her over large lips, a gold, jewel encrusted cigarette holder with an oval shaped Turkish blend poking out from the business end, and waited impatiently for a light. Ostentatious barely described the item, but then it did little enough as an adjective to describe Gertrude Huber. She was short, massively plump and possessed a chin shaped like an Arab's scimitar. The waiter, quickly giving up the vain attempt to light her cigarette whilst retaining control of his tray, dumped the tray onto the cushioned seat of a nearby chair and then lit Frau Huber's cigarette.

Without even a nod of thanks, she inhaled deeply and far more noisily than was necessary before releasing a powerfully projected stream of tan coloured smoke into the room.

"For God's sake, someone open a damn window. It stinks in here. That wretch farted on the way out."

Otto Krause, now ensconced in a thickly upholstered leather chair grinned up at her. "Are you sure that it was him?" He grinned his charmingly boyish (so he believed) schoolboy grin. He didn't like Gertrude Huber, nobody did. But she was wretchedly powerful in the publishing world and quite disgustingly talented at getting what she wanted. She was dangerous to those who crossed her due to her propensity to call in favours from powerful acquaintances in high places.

Otto was on the wrong side of fifty and tried oh-so-hard to look younger, but the encroaching dewlap and receding hairline gave the game away. His vast wealth came from mining iron ore and mineral deposits in Czechoslovakia and Belorussia, where his ruthless disregard for workers' rights won him few working-class friends but drastically increased his profits. So, as far as Otto Huber was concerned, stuff the workers! Charming, urbane and once handsome, before gross over-indulgence of alcohol, sex in all its forms and his gastronomic weakness for gargantuan quantities of pate de foie gras and schweinshaxe, took their inevitable toll on his arteries and complexion. His body was pudding soft but had quite remarkably not yet run to massive layers of fat. If he had any degree of solid muscle about him, though, it was impossible to see as Otto Huber disliked all forms of physical exercise unless directed toward carnal effort. He did, however, maintain a savagely funny wit and a droll outlook on life. A life which he knew would in all likelihood leave him before very much longer. But what the hell? As far as Otto was concerned, life was for living and enjoyment; not sitting around aimlessly and waiting for it to end.

"Well, then. What do we all make of our, what should we call him – Führer, was it? What a nonsense!" Hans Becker, shipping magnate and enthusiastic owner of the Asus race track in Berlin, simply let himself drop into a chair and stuck his legs out in front of him. Drawing greedily on a cigar that was only slightly less formidably thick than his index finger he made to speak again but another voice piped up before he could continue.

Max Richter, already seated, smoking and sipping upon a heavily flared glass rather rudely filled to the brim with brandy, stabbed an equally massive finger at Becker. His cigar smoke mingled with Becker's and already the darkly furnished and draped room was becoming a carcinogenic nightmare. "That's what his minions call him. Or so he says, anyway."

"Really? And they go along with that, do they, those brainless morons?" Becker looked doubtful.

"I can assure you that they do." Friedrik Lehman, the most thoughtful looking of the small group of super-rich individuals in the room, spoke softly but clearly. "Brainless – moronic – downright vile? Yes, all that and more. But they obey that man, Hitler, to the last letter of whatever command he chooses to give."

"And how would you know all this?" Richter enquired.

"Because he has someone on the inside. Don't you my love." Gertrude Huber waved her cigarette holder in a dramatic circle, creating a pretty loom of yellow smoke. "Right up the mouthy Austrian's rear-end, I shouldn't be surprised." She laughed throatily at her own rough humour, choking a little as she disturbed a small mass of cigarette induced phlegm.

Lehman's left eyebrow raised fractionally in distaste. What a loathsome woman. But he turned toward her with a full-lipped smile. "Clever, as always, Gertrude." The smile dropped abruptly and it was as though it had never been there. "Don't underestimate that man." Lehman was serious, they could all see that. But none of them apart from Lehman seemed overly impressed with the would-be Chancellor of the German Reich.

Krause eased one leg over the other as he made himself more comfortable. He too had found the man, Hitler, to be a bit of a nonsense, but nevertheless malleable and eager to please. Part bellicose sergeant major and part whinging serf, Hitler came across to him as a man capable of combining, or discarding, as many characteristics as he needed to at any given time: an actor, of sorts. The perfect politician thought Krause. With just one glaring exception. "He doesn't have any kind of worthwhile platform." He sniffed, then sipped at his fresh brandy before going on. "Other than an obvious penchant for achieving his ends by means of violence, what does he offer us – bearing in mind the millions that he's begging us to contribute?"

"Well, let's see," Becker chimed in. "His main points seem to be Jew-baiting and destruction......"

"He never said destruction," pointed out Richter. "Merely suggesting their permanent removal to other climes."

"Or else," laughed Huber. "Just watch that space my friends."

Horst Weber, armaments manufacturer and the only other member of the group bestirred himself. "And what about all that guff concerning living space in the east? What does he think – that the Poles and Russians will just let us march in and steal their land?" Secretly Weber would love such a scenario. War, perhaps just a small one, would mean huge orders and profits for his business.

"When did he mention all that?" Questioned Becker. "I never heard him say any such thing." He looked around at the others and was greeted by shaking heads. Hitler had not mentioned living space in Poland, Russia or anywhere else for that matter, during the course of their lunch meeting.

"Have none of you ever attended his meetings?" Demanded Huber, glaring around. "Or read his political agenda?"

"Agenda?" Richter almost roared the word. "Rip up Versailles, take back the Rhineland, stop paying reparations and eliminate the communists, and of course, knock the Jews about. You call that an agenda? The man is an empty-headed chancer without an ounce of originality in his head. Violence is all he knows. Not that I give a shit if it works, but that fool is asking for our support and our money. He is nothing more than a yappy twat!"

"A yappy twat with an army of obedient thugs," pointed out Lehman quietly.

"Oh, for goodness sake!" Gertrude Huber squeaked exasperatedly. "Like we need an honest politician; as if we could find one. This man, Adolf Hitler, is precisely what we *do* need. Mindless and bordering on moronic, yes! Ruthless and self-serving, yes! Greedy, grasping and with no conscience whatsoever, certainly!" She threw her arms toward the ceiling in a dramatic gesture; "Malleable and ready to grovel on demand – YES!" Gertrude Huber's eyes glittered with an Amazonian triumph. "What, I ask you gentlemen, could be better? The man is perfect. He will obey us, be ruled by us in all that is important and," she smiled joyfully at them all, "we shall ride him like a horse."

Her rhetoric had stirred the others. Becker leaned forward and said, "By harnessing him we harness the power on the street and control the only weapon capable of stopping those damned communists. And might I remind all here that there are more than thirty political Parties to choose from in that wretched kindergarten of a Reichstag? It's a bloody joke. All of it, nothing more than a bad joke!"

It wasn't a joke, of course, and not one of them regarded the increasingly deteriorating situation as such. Regardless of whatever else they might think, or whether they liked or disliked each other, the one thing that they all agreed upon without reservation was, the communists and their allies must at all costs be stopped. The plethora of smaller Parties could easily be crushed or absorbed, but the far left posed a more serious threat. The economy was rocky, the communist run unions were way too powerful, all the time forcing employers such as themselves to pay out more and more in wages and health benefits. It had to stop. And if the raucous lout commanding those uniformed thugs on the street could do that, then he would have their unlimited backing and blessing.

"The fact is," said Krause, "I can't find it in myself to trust the man. There's something very," he paused for a second as he searched for the right word, "*off* about him. I can't put my finger on it, but I find him sort of, well, unhealthy is how I would put it."

"Unhealthy?" Laughed Richter. "Now that is rich, coming from you, Otto. Since when did we put health before wealth, hmm?"

"You know what I mean," Otto waved an admonishing finger but in a friendly fashion and they all smiled.

"Course I do, dear boy. Just tweaking that golden chain of yours. But here's the thing, the way I see it. Herr Hitler is not top drawer," that remark was greeted with choked laughter and agreement. "He's a joke as a politician and yet he has gathered around him the most powerful army of thugs seen since the early days of the Weimar and the Frei Corps. Whatever else he might be, our tame cretin is bloody dangerous. Now.... isn't that precisely, as Gertrude says, just what we need? Our very own tame and compliant saw-dust arena scrapper? Control him and we control not just the streets and those communist wretches but, once we get him into power, we control legislation. Think of it, my friends. We can legislate, through Herr Hitler and his minions, tax exemptions, duty exemptions and...and," he paused, raising a waving hand at his eager listeners, "wait for it – business sanctions against those that don't toe the line, our line, that is. All that for a few million Marks."

"Billion," cut in Becker. "More like a billion."

"But think what we can get out of all this." Richter was now deadly serious. "We may never have such an opportunity again. Like it or not, this man Hitler wields awesome power out there and he has asked for our help. He can't do without it, *but*, he might, he just might be able to find backing elsewhere. Those are my thoughts on the matter, anyway." With nothing more to say, Richter leaned back silently in his chair.

They all gazed at one another in turn.

"That is a point well taken," said Gertrude Huber.

Like a boxer trying to liven himself up, Becker slapped his heavy jowls. "Right. We take him on, back him and put him where he wants to be and he makes us the czars of business and industry and we make our own rules as to how German business is conducted. I've got that right, I think. Yes. I'm all for it. Use the little git and then toss him aside when we're done."

Lehman smiled his little ghost smile at them all. "A government run by business can only be for the betterment of all," he softly said. "We shall all benefit and through us so shall the nation benefit."

"How saintly you are, Friedrik," scoffed Gertrude Huber.

Lehman momentarily widened his smile. All of them filthy rich and powerful but not one of them half as clever as they thought. He had seen more than two years ago the way things were moving and had moved to cover all foreseeable eventualities. He was a hugely successful entrepreneur with a variety of business interests dotted across the country; more to the point he held a vast store of readily available cash ready to force entry into any worthwhile and immediate business opportunity. Friedrik Lehman had a finger in many pies, and one of those fingers was lodged deep within the activities of the Nazi party. Not merely that, thanks to the offices of a good friend, he was now a high-ranking member of the SS. These were the coming men; he had sensed that from the start. Tunnel visioned, one track minds. Perfect fodder when controlled by a first-class brain. He didn't know Hitler personally, indeed until today he had never met him. But Friedrik was very well acquainted with the head of his particular department within the Party: Reichsführer Heinrich Himmler. His report to the Reichsführer would make interesting reading to both Himmler and at a later date, his boss, Hitler.

The conversation continued for another hour before the meeting broke up. All those attending were in agreement. A massive fortune in Reichsmarks, plus a substantial reserve, would be made available to Herr Hitler and his Nazi party. Horst Weber had been the only possible dissenter, but once he discovered, courtesy of Lehman, that Paul Krupp of Krupp Industries was already on-board he quickly went along with the general consensus.

Krupp was the ultimate industrial power in Germany. If Krupp and his board reckoned that the strange Austrian with the odd voice and mannerisms was a man to back, then, as an arms and fuel systems manufacturer, that was good enough for Weber. And in all honesty, anything that could crush those bastard profit destroying communists would be a blessing for Germany in the long run.

CHAPTER 9

September 1931: Munich, Prinzregentenplatz 16

He loved his big, black supercharged Mercedes. Travelling along the wider main roads outside town gave him a sense of real freedom. It was a little large, he supposed for the smaller streets of central Munich but it sure as hell got him noticed and that was the general idea. He didn't drive himself, always had trouble with the gear stick, but Julius Schreck did the job very well and was threatening enough to scare off all but the most determined admirer or attention seeker.

Cruising at an amiable twenty kilometres per hour the black Mercedes crept through the upmarket Bogenhausen area of Munich and into Prinzregentenplatz and Hitler's large and luxurious apartment. The meeting had gone well and Adolf was feeling quite upbeat. He would, he was certain, get an aircraft out of all this. He needed one desperately if he were to get around Germany and canvass effectively. He mulled over the various topics and comments from the rich and influential group that he had just met. He also mulled over their various personalities. Vile scum, the whole damn bunch of them. Greedy, self-seeking and utterly obnoxious in every way that mattered. With the exception of Lehman. There was an interesting man. He knew of him, of course, already a valued backer of the Party, but this was the first time that he had seen the rich Berliner who liked to gamble vast fortunes at sometimes long odds. That one, Adolf thought, might well have more uses than just supplying money. As for the rest? Pah! Hateful but necessary. He would give them what they wanted for only as long as it suited. He had made some outrageous promises to them and he marvelled at their combined stupidity. Did they truly believe that he would surrender one iota of power to a bunch of money-grubbing merchants, scribes and tool-makers? Imbeciles! However, it was by no means certain that he could accomplish the final uphill stretch of his journey. A giant leap of faith and boundless confidence would be needed if he were to realize his dream of becoming Chancellor. Not merely a party leader but Reich's Chancellor, second only to that inbred Prussian egotist Field Marshal von Hindenburg, the incumbent Reich President. Sooner or later he and that stiff-necked Junker were going to cross swords. Apparently, according to various reports, Hindenburg considered Adolf Hitler and his men to be nothing more than noisy, quarrelsome louts. The old field marshal had often been quoted as saying that Hitler and his Nazis should be stamped out; that they were trouble-making thugs and a danger to Germany's burgeoning democracy. Paul von Hindenburg loathed Hitler and his Nazi Party with a vengeance. Adolf sniggered slightly. The old fool was right, of course. Democracy was the first thing that he, Adolf Hitler, intended to eradicate. It was a cancer that should be cut out, and then the flesh of the German people harshly cauterized, in order to cleanse it of the filth of Jewish mantra! Jews had nothing to do with democracy in Germany, of course he knew that. But it was good to have a muscular yet naïve target to thrash and cripple. The Jews were serving that purpose very nicely. His downtrodden Herrenvolk, after years of being bullied and humiliated by the seedy French, cowardly Italians and overbearing British, needed a scapegoat. A *thing* large enough and easily identifiable as the villains of the piece. Something for them to blame and attack. And under his virulent leadership, that is what they were doing with ever increasing ferocity. So much so that the hatred that he and his slogan spouting cohorts had managed to engender in his followers surprised, nay, astonished even him. Might need to get a grip on it at some stage, but not just yet. They might not be aware of it, but the Jews were, at the moment, serving a valuable cause: his cause.

He allowed his head to loll back slightly. He could still barely believe what he had accomplished. There was no doubt about it, due to luck, providence, call it what you will he had been far more successful than he dared hope. He had chosen his closest supporters well, though. It was they who suffered and toiled and believed in his genius, or at least pretended to. Who the hell knew what really went on in the minds of weak but ambitious men when they were on the make – as they all were, himself included? And so from one step to the next, they had lurched and now here they were. Knocking on fortunes door. It was all so frighteningly surreal.

His home,16 Prinzregentenplatz loomed up before them. This address was a huge step up from the others. Berchtesgaden was nice but not nearly as plush as this place, although they were working on that building to add more space. Lovely view, though, no doubt about that.

His mind went to his niece, Geli. What to do with that foolish, wilful girl? It never seemed to lodge firmly enough in his mind that Geli was now twenty-three years of age and sick to death of being closeted by her paranoid uncle. In the years since she had witnessed his *secret* he had barely left her side. Either he or someone else, a bodyguard or pretend friend, was always around.

He slapped the top of his leather documents case. Look at what she wanted now. To be a singer! Was she off her silly head? His niece, Geli Raubal, had the singing voice of a lark – a lark that was having its throat slowly and painfully stretched by two pairs of badly serrated pliers. Awful! He knew that she needed male company and he had tolerated the occasional, very occasional boyfriend. Geli, to put it mildly, was very much into sex. Nothing much wrong with that. She was after all a normal, healthy young woman. Well, he sighed, possibly not completely normal. Her hysterical outbursts were becoming more and more difficult to contain. She had quit her medical studies and taken up music, with her own voice as her chosen instrument. A disaster which she failed to realise. Poor Geli had no talent at all but Adolf paid for various teachers to run her through her studies and practice. But now, her latest demand? She insisted, pleaded violently, that she be allowed to go to Vienna and there study under a dynamic whizz-kid of the voice, Helmut Strang. No way! Adolf didn't have the time to go to Vienna just now when all his energies must be devoted to electioneering and canvassing. The wretched girl was demanding more and more of his valuable time and patience, the latter of which was fast running out. Clearly histrionics ran in this family. His own were timed and directed; was it the same with his niece – did she really think that she could indefinitely mess him around like this? Little minx! No, there would be no living in Vienna with some music teacher for Geli; she would do as she was damn well told or he would know the reason why.

"Shall I put the car away, my Führer?" Queried Schreck.

"No." Hitler came out of a reverie in which things had been taking a far more satisfactory turn as he envisioned himself administering a sound thrashing to Geli's bare back-side "Park up outside the apartment. I shall be leaving for a meeting soon and I don't intend to be late." Bruno Gesche, his ultra-tough bodyguard leapt out of the back of the Mercedes and opened the front passenger door for his Führer. "Should I accompany you to the apartment, Führer?"

Hitler shook his head in a negative. "Just wait in the foyer until I come down. I must shower and change then we'll be away." He gave Gesche a tight-lipped, eye-to-eye smile. His fondness for the powerfully built, and hugely intimidating bodyguard was ill-concealed. Above average height, horse-faced, physically very powerful and utterly devoted, Bruno Gesche was a truly frightening creature. Adolf knew that he could rely upon his SS Untersturmführer absolutely. People were in general automatically afraid of Gesche without him having to do a damn thing. Slightly crossed eyes stared out coldly from a heavy head with a long jutting jaw. Gesche was a ruthless and utterly without mercy brawler. Men very much larger than he, had crumbled broken and whimpering beneath the ferocity of a brutal Gesche attack. He loved to stamp on heads until he heard them crack and he could see the brains bubbling through shattered cranial bone. Fingers, knees, eyes and genitals, all these were things that Bruno Gesche enjoyed destroying, slowly if possible, but in the end, any way would do. He had been with Adolf since the school in the barracks back in the early twenties. He had latched onto the Austrian for no reason other than he had become bewitched by his voice and fire-like gaze. Charisma had taken over Bruno Gesche and he would be forever loyal to his friend and employer. Like a faithful hound he obeyed his master implicitly and would savagely bite off any hand that was raised against he who fed him.

The heavy wooden door swung open and Gesche stood to one side as he allowed Hitler to stride past him. A secondary inner door, upper half glass panelled, Hitler thrust open himself.

This apartment block boasted a resident porter who, when free of various odd jobs, could be found, as now, seated behind a small, highly polished table complete with telephone and register book in which were recorded residents' calls to the porter and the comings and goings of all those whom the porter noticed entering and leaving the building. Both the neatly dressed porter and his wife came with the building. What did not come with the building, though, was the heavy set, grey jowled man wearing an all-brown SA rigout complete with a highly polished Sam Browne belt and a swastika buckle. High bellied and with all the appearance of a man who would die rather than ascend a flight of stairs, the SA warrior abruptly jerked up from his casual stance leaning against the hallway wall and threw out his right arm.

"Heil, my Führer." Werner Kempka, another of Hitler's double-necked bodyguards saluted his boss who threw a half-hearted and rather limp wristed salute back in return.

Richard Fleiss, the porter looked on all this with a carefully concealed attitude of utter contempt. Who the hell did this man, Hitler, think he was? He trolled around Munich, adoringly trailed by folk who treated him like he was the second coming! 'All together and sieg heil Jesus, is it?' he thought. Fleiss was in his early sixties and had never in all his years of service as a porter witnessed such patently obvious used car salesman's guff. As for the majority of the weirdos that came through the apartment building doors on business for this self-proclaimed Führer, well, he'd sooner keep as great a distance between them and himself as was possible.

It wasn't that Herr Hitler and his associates were noisy or disturbed the other residents in any way. It was just, well, that they were uniformly awful! Fleiss and his quiet, doe-eyed wife were used to gentlemen coming and going with, on occasion, a smart well-dressed lady of breeding in attendance. There was nothing gentlemanly about Herr Hitler nor the oafs that surrounded him. And that young woman, his niece, was hardly ladylike. More of a party girl, that one. Loathsome. All of them.

"Good afternoon, Herr Hitler," Fleiss simpered. "Are we well today, sir?" He stood but refrained from the ridiculous salute that Kempka had thrown out. He allowed Kempka to stay on duty in the foyer because Herr Hitler insisted upon it: for security reasons. Really! These wretched people. Bodyguards stamping around everywhere like there was a war on or something. Did this Hitler fellow honestly believe that his life was in danger? Stuff and nonsense as far as Fleiss was concerned. It was all for show: smoke and mirrors with precious little in the way of substance.

The metal heel taps of Hitler's bespoke shoes clicked noisily against the foyer's stone mosaic floor. God! Thought Fleiss, why must he enter the place sounding like a bloody flamenco dancer?

"Any calls?" The question was voiced abruptly.

That voice; – horrible! Fleiss felt himself shrinking, shrivelling even, and almost took a step back as Hitler came close and stared him in the eye and Fleiss looked away unable to meet that gaze. He couldn't understand his complete fear of the man. There was no reason. Yes, he was a thug and he employed thugs to do his bidding; just like in those American gangster movies. But here, in these nice very upper middle-class surroundings even this type steered clear of outward displays of aggression. And Herr Hitler had no reason whatsoever to bring harm of any kind to the friendly live-in porter. But then, as Fleiss was well aware through life's experience, men like Adolf Hitler rarely needed a *reason* to bring pain and harm to anyone. They just did, that was all there was to it.

"Herr Strasser called, sir. Said he had tried your private line but there was no response. He asked when you might return, sir."

"And you said?"

Fleiss felt the onset of bodily trembling; small beads of perspiration began to show on his temples. He knew from what he had overheard that Herr Hitler and Herr Strasse did not get on, see eye to eye, so to speak. There had been a disagreement of some sort but beyond that, Fleiss knew nothing.

"I informed the gentleman that I was not at liberty to disclose the comings and goings of the residents, sir. I told him so quite firmly, if I may say."

"Please see that you continue to do so." Fleiss shuddered as Hitler gave him a friendly tap on the shoulder. "Good man, Herr Fleiss. Keep it up."

"Of course, sir." The porter breathed in deeply with relief as Hitler gave the SA man a questioning look.

"Still upstairs, my Führer. Said she didn't want to go walking today."

Not surprised, thought Fleiss, with a monster like you in tow. Poor kid. Common as muck and openly flirty but he felt sorry for young Geli Raubal. Why Herr Hitler kept her closeted up all the time was anybody's guess, but it wasn't right; not in his opinion. Not that he had any intention of voicing an opinion around or about Herr Hitler.

"Good. Wait here. I shall be down within the hour. I want you to remain on duty until I return from my evening meeting. Clear?"

"Clear, my Führer."

A brisk high-kneed trot up the few stairs leading to the second-floor landing saw Adolf outside his own apartment's front door.

It was some two years since he had purchased the place, or rather, the Party had purchased it for him. The family that had owned the basement property had long since moved out leaving only the Steiners on the top floor, who for some reason were never seen. Adolf had instructed the Party office to put in an offer to purchase the entire property. He liked it here; suitably middle-class with precious little in the way of ostentatiousness. No one would ever be able to accuse him of living like a degenerate Byzantine emperor. The eight rooms, two bathrooms and two kitchens were more than adequate for his needs. He had the entire second floor, which was capacious by any standards, so space and privacy were not a concern. There was ample room for all his needs.

Geli was sitting by the desk in her room when she heard Uncle Adolf enter the apartment. With tightening lips she geared herself up to face her formidable uncle in his own lair and, if at all possible, beard the patronizing pig. She had had more than sufficient of being treated like some sort of cherished but rather cheap bazaar trinket. Enough! She was going to Vienna whether Uncle Adolf gave permission or not. Twenty-three for God's sake and yet still he treated her like an untrustworthy and impetuous child. This was 1931, not some plague riddled year in the sixteenth century. Women had rights these days. True, she held his secret. But surely he must realise, if she had ever intended to disclose it to anyone she would have done so by now. A cowardly, paranoid ninny, that's what he was. Well, now she was going to stand up to him. He didn't scare her and she wasn't one of his trembling, black uniformed pretty boys. She was Geli Raubal and Geli Raubal had had enough of blustering, patronising males in razor-creased uniforms to last a lifetime. To hell with them and him. There were some nice men out there, not all Nazi types or gorillas waiting for lunch. Gentle, thoughtful and imaginative men who could make her laugh and feel alive.

Cocking her head to one side she was sure that she could hear him pottering about doing something or other in the hallway. Head back, shoulders squared she marched to her bedroom door. And that was another thing, there was no lock on her door. Who did he think he was, forbidding locks on any door but his own? Crazy! Time to sort a few things out with uncle Adolf.

He was standing over the bureau which stood half way down the hall and just a few feet from her room. He half turned as he heard her door open and from the corner of his eye he observed her as she came full shouldered out of her room. Something about her posture alerted his self-preservation instincts. Adolf didn't like sudden posture changes in the people around him. It was unnerving and never did bode well. Geli normally crept around him, edging side-on through doorways, seemingly always trying not to be noticed. Today, though, something was different. Was that a flash of defiance in her eyes? Geli was a well set up girl. Nothing delicate about her bone structure or musculature at all. Heavy-set and probably quite powerful with wide shoulders and a thickish neck. She came towards him with a definite air of determination. Damn! Of course. This silly business of going to Vienna and canoodling with some Austrian baritone. His mind had been on personal security as he entered the apartment, which was why he had gone to the bureau to check on his Walther automatic. It normally lay behind the locked bureau, the hinged flap of which now lay open revealing various compartments all containing little secrets of some description. The armed and cocked pistol was now in Adolf's left hand as he turned face on to his niece. Her eyes fell upon the weapon instantly and he casually placed it back onto the bureau flap.

"Well then, Geli," he smiled in an avuncular fashion. "And how has your day been?"

"I need to talk with you, Uncle," Geli's voice was raised to an unnatural pitch and volume due to the nervous tension that now ran through her system making her appear more threatening than she felt or intended to be.

"Do you now!" He was not at all accustomed to his niece speaking to him in such a peremptory fashion. "Then be quick. I have a meeting to attend shortly."

There was no point in faffing around with uncle Adolf so Geli just grabbed the bull by the horns. "I *am* going to Vienna to study and you don't have the right to stop me."

"Oh, but I most certainly do, young lady. This is my roof and the food that you eat is paid for by me, not to mention the clothes that you stand up in. I feed and house both you and your mother and don't you forget it – EVER!" His sister, Geli's mother, was still employed by him but was these days used to care for the house in Berchtesgaden. The threat was implicit and, he knew, cowardly. In these uncertain economic times housekeepers were ten-penny and easy to find. But he would not tolerate underlings, family or not, falling out of line. Obedience was everything!

He could feel the anger rising within him as it always did whenever anybody had the temerity to disagree with him. How many times had they gone over this self-same scenario? Too damn many! This ungrateful, pampered minx dared to thwart him after all he had done for her and her mother. Family or not he was of a mind to throw her physically from the apartment. Let her roam the streets and see how independent she felt then. No. Of course he couldn't do that. She would trundle off to Vienna the very second he evicted her. Did she have money? She must have. The vindictiveness of his run of thought became abruptly more pensive and questioning. Where and how the devil had she managed to garner it? Suddenly it all began to sink in. He had been bamboozled by his niece. Not once had she mentioned money and clearly did not expect him to pay for her journey to Vienna nor for her lodgings whilst she was there and nor, it would seem, for her *supposed* tuition.

Realisation dawned on him. First shock, then a small tremor of surprise and bewilderment, and then, yet again, anger. "You ungrateful little slut!" He hissed like a suddenly trod upon serpent. "You've arranged it all behind my back. You have been with him, haven't you? God's rotting teeth you....you. You've been with him *here*! In my home? Answer me or I swear to heaven I'll cut out your black little heart!" His right hand flapped against his thigh in a frenzy of exasperation. No acting now, Adolf was downright furious. Of course; it came to him in a flash of revelation. That's why Geli was so confidently determined. She was already having an affair with this Austrian music teacher-cum-singer. How the bloody hell had she managed to carry on romantic trysts without his knowledge? Bodyguards, informants, surely someone must have noticed something.

Geli stared at the spit-speckled face of her outraged uncle with loathing. To think that she had once adored this dreadful man.

She hadn't been anywhere near Vienna and apart from some delightfully realistic fantasies, which she had so naughtily and delightfully shared with her unmet and distant beau in Vienna, she had done nothing untoward. They had not met, she and Helmut Strang had merely spoken once on the phone and communicated, hesitantly at first and then gradually more robustly, by letter. It was thus far all fantasy between two lonely people. The sexual undertones of their correspondence, though, had gradually become more and more graphic until now, each ached desperately for the other. And where was the harm, they asked? He was twenty-nine years of age and she twenty-three. Adults and ready for commitment and adventure as they chose. It should be their business and nobody else's. But then, not everybody had Adolf Hitler for an uncle. And Adolf, as Geli knew, regarded anyone within his sphere as his personal property to be disposed of at his pleasure.

As her uncle took another step toward her, Geli did not flinch or step back. Her determined jaw thrust out as she leaned forward. Caution flew to the winds. It was all too much, this constant shrieking, carping and foot stomping. Her own rage flooded her being, reddening her face and restricting the muscles of her throat, turning her voice into an ugly crow-like blare.

"You vile old man. Vile-vile-vile! Damn you and everything about you. I HATE YOU!"

Adolf froze. He had never heard his niece use foul language before. Nor had he seen her look anything other than demure and self-effacing. He was unprepared for the virago that now stood threateningly before him.

"Go on big uncle Adi. Hit me! Why don't you? You know you want to you lame old git!" In her fury she did something that she had been wanting to do for ages. She stamped on his foot, hard! The hoped-for shriek of anger and protest, however, was not forthcoming and Geli realised that she had made a dreadful mistake. His features froze into a mask of something that she could not recognise and his eyes. Oh, dear God those eyes. Her anger fled as quickly as it had arrived as she remembered what her uncle was capable of, of what she had heard about him over the years.

Like a hedgehog caught in a car's headlights, she watched as his upper lip slowly began to curl over his teeth. The blow, when it came, was almost an anti-climax. Shock rather than pain stiffened her body, as she staggered back and fell. The taste of blood filled her mouth and a dislodged tooth slid lazily over her swelling lips. Geli saw his foot the second before the heel made contact with the bridge of her nose and she shrieked as the steel-capped heel was twisted savagely into her flesh, turning her nose into a gory mess of ripped cartilage. Something inside her cracked and broke, as that same foot began a ferocious kicking and stamping spree all over her lower body. Geli's mouth opened in pathetic efforts to scream again but her own blood choked her. Incoherently she begged him to stop but he, her uncle, her protector, was too far gone. He stamped and kicked, his eyes shining with the unnatural delight of an in flagrante sadist.

Suddenly he stopped and just stood for a moment staring down at her. Geli knew that she was quite badly injured. Hopefully not fatally, but certainly painfully. He turned away from her and briefly disappeared from view. Then, abruptly, horribly, he was kneeling across her and lowering himself onto her chest. His rank breath swamping her badly broken nose with its ghastly exhalations.

"Now what do I do with you, Geli, eh? Silly girl!" The pistol was in his hand and he stuck the barrel into her soft, yielding throat. "Poor little Geli," he whispered. His face contorted with a pervert's delight. "Geli must be punished for being bad, mustn't she!"

Her eyes widened in absolute terror as his finger tightened around the trigger. His weight on her chest was suffocating as he ground himself harshly against her. She tried to raise a pleading hand. The gun barrel thrusting against her throat, combined with the flowing blood from her badly broken noise, was making it impossible for her to breathe.

"Please," she managed to gasp, "please stop. Uncle Adi," it was a blood-splattering sob, "please don't hurt me anymore. I'll be good. I promise."

"Yes-yes!" He was making guttural, unintelligible noises. Barely human, he seemed more like a thoughtless, brainless thing.

Desperate now she managed to grab his wrist and, astonishingly, slowly began forcing the gun away from her throat. His pleasure suddenly curtailed, Hitler stared nonplussed at his moving arm as though it weren't part of him.

"Stop that, you stroppy bitch. Stop it now or I'll kill you." His teeth gritted as he exerted all his strength. There was no getting away from it. His niece was remarkably strong. Damn her to hell! He jerked and pulled but still Geli held on and in this trial of strength, she was slowly getting the upper hand. Youth and pure terror lent her the strength that she never would have believed that she possessed. She jerked beneath him, throwing her hips up and then to the side, taking him completely by surprise. As he lost balance and rolled from her, his finger inadvertently squeezed the trigger tight. The retort from the gunshot was muffled by the close proximity of two adult bodies but nevertheless, a gunshot it unmistakably was.

Adolf sat staring at her in disbelief. Slowly, like an uncomprehending child, she turned her head toward him and he froze in shock as he watched the life flee from her eyes. She said nothing, but the last expression that her young face ever revealed was one of terror as death made its premature claim on her young life. A small fountain of blood bubbled up from the wound directly in front of her heart, and then it stopped. Geli Raubal was dead.

Slowly, Adolf rose and looked all around him. The stupid girl, what a damn silly child she was – had been! Provoking him like that. It was all her fault of course, but now it was time to sort things. His niece was dead and he had killed her. The fall-out from this would be highly damaging to his electoral chances, to say the least. A murder charge – even manslaughter? Out of the question. What to do? Oh...hell and damnation – what to do! Had the shot been heard and if so by whom? He needed to get this thinking straight but it just wasn't possible. He was in one hell of a damned mess, no mistake! Why wouldn't his mind work? He needed a plan. That, of course, was the immediate problem; or one of them, anyway. He rarely planned; it wasn't in his nature. He simply went ahead and hoped for the best, using the tried and tested methods of violence, bribery and threats; any planning was generally done by others more suited for that kind of thing. That was it. He needed one of his henchmen. But who! There was no one to hand. He was pleased to notice that his hands weren't shaking, although his right foot hurt like the very devil from where that appalling strumpet had stamped on him. Oh.... now there was a point. Angela, Geli's mother was going to be, to say the very least, upset and demanding of an explanation. She would have to be sorted, hopefully without too much obvious pressure.

The small automatic was still his hand and he thrust it into his trouser pocket until he could decide what to do with it.

An idea drifted into his action shocked brain. Suicide. How could he arrange all this to look self-inflicted? He stood, thinking, or trying to, of a way out of his predicament. A tap came at the door and he almost fainted with fright. His body frozen rigid, his eyes turned like painted golf balls toward the front door of his apartment.

Outside the apartment Bruno Gesche tapped again, more firmly this time. A sound had indeed been heard but no one was too sure what it might have been. To those in the foyer, it had sounded like a distant car misfiring; but from where Gesche had been waiting, outside by the big Mercedes, it had sounded rather like it *might* have been a gunshot. Surely not, of course. Not from inside Hitler's apartment, of all places. But one could never be too sure and caution was a good habit to have. Better safe than sorry.

"Is everything well, my Führer."

Hitler almost collapsed with relief. "Are you alone, Gesche?"

"Yes sir. Should I call the others?"

"NO!" Hitler almost shrieked. He went to the door and opened it ajar, peering fearfully out. His audible sigh of relief as his eyes fell upon the ever-loyal Gesche had even that man's nose wrinkling beneath the onslaught of his Führer's breath.

"Get in here," snapped Hitler.

Gesche stared down at the now death befouled Geli Raubal. He turned to his leader questioningly.

"An accident, Gesche. We were conducting small arms practice and the damn thing went off."

Went off – just like that? Giving her a broken nose along with a bullet straight through the heart? Not a likely scenario. Bruno Gesche, however, was not a man to ask questions of his leader. He traded in loyalty, his loyalty, and loyal he would forever remain.

"What went off, sir?" he enquired pointedly.

"Oh, yes. This bloody thing!" He dragged the small Walther from his pocket and displayed it on his palm. Gesche looked from the gun, to the body on the floor and back again, all the while avoiding eye contact with Hitler.

"It won't wash sir."

Hitler knew very well what he meant. Loaded firearm practice in an apartment hallway followed by a fatal accident looked like rampant stupidity; the bloodied and broken nose along with the detached tooth made it look even worse. He raised a 'what-then' hand and let it fall limply by his side. Like it or not, he was in Gesche's hands.

"You have to get to your meeting, sir." Gesche meaningfully tapped his watch. A gift from the Führer for his thirtieth birthday. He walked slowly a few feet along the hallway and pointed to a half open door. "Might that be the young lady's room, sir?" Hitler nodded, waiting for what might come next. If anyone could sort this out, at least in the short term, it would be Gesche. His bodyguard held out his right hand. "If you please, my Führer. The gun."

Wordlessly Hitler handed over his pistol. Pocketing the weapon, Gesche bent and lifted Geli Raubal's corpse from the floor as though it weighed less than a packet of biscuits. With his burden firmly held he went to what had been Geli's room and toed the door further open. He disappeared from Hitler's view for a moment as he lay Geli's dead body on the floor of her bedroom and then, after first giving the pistol a good rubbing with his kerchief before wrapping her hands around it, placed the pistol on the couch to the left of her bed.

Exiting Geli's room and still not meeting his leader's eye, Gesche said, "I urgently suggest that you go to your meeting immediately, my Führer. Without me, I'm afraid as I have things here which need my attention; if you know what I mean." Now he raised his eyes and met Hitler's full on. "You may expect, my Führer, to hear some very bad news later in the evening concerning the unfortunate demise of someone close."

Hitler stared at his bodyguard for a moment, then without a word strode to his study where he picked up some papers. He had understood Gesche's meaning completely. Time to go. He must get on with his day and put all this behind him. Once out of the study he quickly washed his hands and sloshed his face clean. No time for a shower, he needed to get out of here. There was blood on his jacket and shirt so he rapidly threw them off, trousers as well, and put on his party jacket and black trousers. A quick tidy-up to look as normal as possible and he was done.

Leaving the apartment he saw that Gesche was no longer in the hallway. He could hear the man doing something or other in Geli's room. He poked his head into the room.

"My clothes, Gesche," he dropped the shirt, jacket and trousers on the floor. "They seem to have become rather...."

"As good as done, my Führer. I'll have replacements ready by the time you return."

With that final item sorted Adolf exited the apartment. Thank fortune for good staff. Gesche had saved the day. The main thing was for him, Adolf Hitler, to get out of the apartment post-haste and give his bodyguard time to work whatever magic he had concocted. Gesche would in all probability call in the services of the new security chief, Heinrich Himmler. There would be publicity and it would need careful handling and manipulation.

"Tegernsee," he instructed Schreck. "Take your time, we're in no rush."

Julius Schreck obeyed and made no comment on the strange fact that his leader was sporting a rather large scratch mark beneath his left eye. And was that bruising on his right hand? Looked pretty severe. What had his Führer been up to? Schreck allowed the tiniest of smirks to move his thin lips. None of his damn business, right? Right then!

"As you say, my Führer. Nice and easy does it." The Mercedes slid majestically away from the curb and on out of Munich.

CHAPTER 10

April 25 1945: Berlin, The Bunker.

Hitler lurched through the Bunker, feeling his way carefully through this, the last of his kingdoms. The generator had broken down again, meaning that the toilets had stopped flushing and every area stank to high heaven. Spreading puddles of water had formed on the concrete bunker floor, and atop one of them circled a tobacco shredding dog-end. Although some of the more robust souls maintained a fatalistic attitude, the general ambience was one of blunt despair as the inevitable rushed toward them all. It seemed to many that only yesterday they had been partying and celebrating beneath crystal chandeliers and toasting the praises of the Führer and the invincible Third Reich. Now here they were awaiting the unthinkable; death, torment, rape and hell itself.

Hands fluttering before him gave Hitler the appearance of a zombie seeking to grasp and consume the closest human being to him when in fact, as his sight was now so negligible, he was shooing them out of his way. The shambling, leg-dragging gait, which had him drifting uncertainly from side to side, threatened to send him head-first into a wall.

He had exited his quarters all unexpected, and without the faithful Linge his progress was erratic, to say the least. Orderlies and clerks, secretaries and military officers, made way for the shambling wreck of a man with the wide staring eyes. But not even one of them looked at him with the respect of just a few weeks previously. Pity and compassion sat on the faces of some, whilst loathing and contempt lay barely concealed on the faces of others. A cigarette was stamped out further down the corridor, but not in any particular haste. Sacrilege!

"All will be well," the flaccid cheeked Führer of the Third Reich managed the semblance of a smile. He attempted a wave with his lesser trembling hand but the effort sent him lurching all unbalanced into the condensation-soaked lower bunker wall. A dozen or more pairs of eyes stared at him as he groped for the support rail. Mouth wide open and gasping for breath he struggled to regain his equilibrium. A tiny sob sounded from somewhere, and ahead of him came a giggle of amusement.

Suddenly a thick-set figure dressed in a brown party uniform appeared at his side.

"My Führer. What are you doing unattended? Linge!" Bormann shouted loudly enough to wake the dead. "Where is Obersturmbannführer Linge?" Those who had previously been watching the inept display of mobility by their ramshackle leader now found urgent tasks that needed their immediate attention.

Neat, precise little steps sounded as Heinz Linge rushed to his Führer's side.

"I thought that you were still sleeping, my Führer, he almost stammered. Heinz Linge did not ruffle easily but he took his responsibilities very seriously indeed.

"Any news – what news is there?" Hitler's plea for information left both Bormann and Linge baffled for a moment. Linge looked pleadingly to Bormann for help.

"Shall we just get you back to your quarters until the morning briefing, my Führer?" said Bormann in the unctuous manner he always used when addressing his commander-in-chief.

"Linge. Here!" Bormann gestured to the high-ranking valet and they both placed a protective arm around Hitler's shoulders.

"Take your Goddamned hands off of me," shrieked Hitler. Eyes wild with sudden fury. "I demand to know – what news is there?"

The tall figure of Rochus Misch poked his head out from the telephone switchboard room.

"Ah! Misch, Misch. What news man – where is Wenck?" He turned to all those in his immediate vicinity. "Twelfth Army will soon turn this tide. Mark my words. All will be well. Oh yes! Have no doubt. Have faith all of you and you shall soon see what comes to pass. Victory! I have seen it. Oh, such victory shall be ours. Here in Berlin we shall deliver to the Russian beast a defeat such as no army has ever before suffered. You'll see. Very soon now. You will all see."

"My Führer," Linge again attempted to steer Hitler away from the switchboard room and the man in charge of that area, Scharführer Misch.

With surprising strength for a man so enfeebled by opiates and ill health, Hitler roughly pushed past his valet and shambled up to the Scharführer and repeated his question.

"There has been nothing since the report of General Wenck's advance on Halbe and Ninth army's attack around the Spree forest, my Führer."

"Ah-ha! They advance. You see? *They* obey my orders. Not like those traitorous buffoons who think they know better than their Führer, eh? You see, gentlemen, what happens when my orders are obeyed? Things immediately become more concise due to my unobscured objectivity; My genius will not be denied. It can be neither thwarted nor denied. All one needs is faith. FAITH!" He looked gloatingly around. "I was right all along, you see?" He turned and tapped Bormann's chest and then shambled back the way he had come waving his good arm at the busy clerks and aids. "I told you all that everything would work out in the end. Yes I did. And is it not so, eh? Tell me, is it not so?" Turning back again he lurched past the now somewhat confused Linge and lunged toward the switchboard room. "Have faith," he spluttered, as he gazed at the man in charge of the now pretty well defunct state-of-the-art switchboard. "Victory is assured; have no doubt! No doubt!"

Misch stood aside so that Hitler might pass if he so wanted. He did and shuffled untidily past the towering SS man and on into Misch's lair which was simply an enclosed space partitioned off from Martin Bormann's office. So typical of Bormann to ensconce himself directly beside what had once been the constantly buzzing hub of information. Misch was the only man fully conversant with the bunker switchboard and he assiduously took care to remain so. However, its use now as an instant information relay and receiver was problematic, as most of the outside terminals and command centres no longer existed. The line to Weidling's HQ was, more or less, operating and the inner lines of General Mohnke's HQ still functioned, just. Both these lines needed constant repair due to heavy shelling, therefore information was sporadic. General Wenck's command post and HQ, however, were completely off the air. It had been a while since their last communication so, as far as the bunker's main occupant was concerned, the climatic offensive launched by Wenck's twelfth and Busse's ninth armies was still underway and going to plan. It had not occurred to Hitler, yet, that neither of the battered and ill-used armies concerned, had any particular interest in rescuing him and his cronies. They were in fact, and all unbeknownst to him, fighting like blood-crazed maniacs to batter their way out and get as far away from Berlin and the Russians as possible. General Busse's attack toward Wenck's Twelfth Army was a last desperate effort to save what remained of his encircled army, not an effort to unite and attack yet again against impossible numbers in order to save Adolf Hitler. Hitler wanted to live and he saw it as his soldiers' duty to ensure his continuing existence by rescuing him no matter the cost. But as far as generals Wenck and Busse were concerned, Adolf Hitler no longer had any relevance in the scheme of things. For them, and the majority of their command, the Führer of the Third Reich had gone destructively beyond his sell-by date.

Rochus Misch had long since guessed what was going on at Halbe. He also knew who was doing what to whom down here in this death hole. Holding true to his SS oath was all very well whilst it suited him, but now he was uncertain what to do for the best. Most assuredly someone *had* to do something and soon.

Hitler sat heavily on the one decent chair in Bormann's office.

"We should be hearing good news anytime now," he intoned. "Any time at all. We need patience, Bormann. We should not be too hasty when things are going so well, eh?" A pathetic attempt at a smile to which Martin Bormann immediately responded in his toad-like way.

"Of course, my Führer. Not long now. Your judgement is, may I say, my Führer, faultless as ever. Providence guides you and protects us all." Goebbels, with his totally unnatural ability to sense whenever Bormann had the Führer alone, eased into the cluttered little room that was the Reichsleiter's office.

"Bormann is correct, my Führer. Future generations will laud your abilities and the sacrifices that you have made for our German Reich."

"Oh, indeed. Indeed!" Bormann agreed, smiling like a man with a grin sliced on by a machete. He loathed the little Propaganda Minister and he hated being addressed simply as 'Bormann' by anyone other than Hitler. Who did this conceited little jackass think he was? Just look at him with that Jew's face, club foot and bony, ridiculous body. Bormann looked away lest his hatred of the diminutive Joseph Goebbels begin to show. He would have him, one of these days. He would do for the little bastard, make no mistake, he promised himself.

"The Reich's Propaganda Minister is so right, my Führer." Bormann was almost simpering and Goebbels could barely suppress a grin of satisfaction. He reciprocated the Reichsleiter's hatred fully and then some. Brutal, cruel and more utterly self-serving than Hitler and his entire circle combined, he was now probably the most powerful man in the German Reich. Much good may it do him, gloated Goebbels, bearing in mind that there was precious little Reich left to lord it over.

Out in the corridor typists clacked away at their machines as corporals and the like bustled around self-importantly carrying sheaves of now largely irrelevant documents typed with orders, demands and commands from one desk or room to another. Anything to look busy and avoid being sent outside.

Winnie Stenz looked over at her colleague, Gertie Mueller. "Wasn't he going to kill himself, or something?" she hissed.

Gertie glanced left to right. "That's what he said. So I was told, anyway."

A teenage gefreiter with one arm and only half a face dropped some eagle emblemed documents onto her desk. "He changed his mind. Reckons we got a chance of winning after all. Choice, eh?"

"Changed his mind….again?" Winnie threw up her hands. "Well, I never did. One minute it's all over and then the next it's stick with me everybody It'll be alright. Lot of old crap if you ask me!"

"Why can't he just die?" moaned Gertie. "Then we could all just go home and forget about it. OH – Sorry, I didn't mean…." She lurched back in her chair and gazed about her in a minor panic. She looked pleadingly at the teenage wreck standing before her. "I'm so sorry. I didn't mean to sound de, defea….oh dear!! Tears filled her eyes as she realised that she could at any moment be denounced dragged outside and shot. The young gefreiter had only to utter one condemnatory word and she was doomed.

"Don't worry." The soldier placed a calming hand, his only hand, on her trembling shoulder. "But honestly," he leaned forward and whispered in her ear. "If you've still got a home you should go there and not come out again 'cos the Russians will be banging through this front door anytime now, a few hours maybe, and they don't treat girls nice. They really don't. I've seen what they do, miss. Get out while you still can. As for him?" The young private nodded in the direction in which Hitler had disappeared. "He won't kill himself. Pratts like that never do." One year of hell on the frontline had given the young man a lifetime's experience in human behaviour. "He'll always find an excuse.

Mark my words." A Scharführer appeared and beckoned the soldier. "Gotta go. Take care." His smile was a horror but Gertie felt a rush of affection for the young man. Affection and pity. What hope for youngsters like him? None!

25 April: Halbe near the Spree Forest. 17:44hrs.

Pristine they had been. Shiny, proud, fear-inspiring and hugely impressive to the eye. Not anymore! The once mighty, huge cannoned Tiger Tanks, twelve of them all brand spanking new and shipped to the 21st Panzer division only days ago, lay as unevenly spaced, smouldering piles of metal junk. They shared their death space with a variety of half tracked vehicles and countless bits of bodies that were once attached to firm jawed young soldiers of the Third Reich.

The ground still shuddered beneath the constant barrage of heavy guns from the Soviets and their German adversaries. Von Gluck it was that had been given the unenviable and pathetically ill-advised task of opening a corridor through to central Berlin so that civilians might escape that roaring inferno. The Soviets had quickly seen through the hastily thrown together effort. Even with the redoubtable Tiger Tanks, such a breakthrough was hopeless to contemplate. The sheer numbers of Russian men, tanks and guns that fell upon all sides of von Gluck's understrength offensive overwhelmed them within one blood-soaked, horrific hour.

A sop to the Wehrmacht High Command's demand that their glorious Führer be rescued by the latest saviour to arrive on the scene of national destruction, the blond, very blue-eyed and by now thoroughly pissed off, General Walther Wenck, had destroyed the most effective part of his exhausted army.

Lying trapped beneath the violently detached armoured turret of the lead Tank, writhed Leutnant Horst Manstein. The joy of his mother and pride of his father for all his twenty years, the handsome blonde head of the young officer rolled erratically from side to side.

He was only just regaining consciousness after being blown from his tank following a hit from a Soviet 100mm M1944 anti-tank gun, and the real and absolute horror of what had just happened to him was about to sink in. The M1944 was one of the few mobile field weapons that could cope with the might of a Tiger's armour plate. Its projectile had ripped through Leutnant Manstein's vehicle, delivered from an expertly sighted gun crew more than a kilometre away. Manstein and his attack group had run into an unending barrage of armour piercing ordnance from fifteen of the simultaneously firing and very mobile M1944s and had lost eight of their twelve tanks before their infantry could get to grips with them. And when their infantry had finally come face to face with the guns and their crews, they were swamped within twenty minutes by an entire Guards division backed up by some fifty T34s. Soviet superiority in all aspects of ordnance was now so vast as to be beyond worthwhile challenge. The Soviets were superior in everything bar raw courage, and courage was never going to be enough.

Blue eyes began to widen as the pain became gradually more and more evident, more real. Trying to reach a sitting position using his elbows he attempted to heave himself away from the ugly bulk of the formerly protective turret. The huge black swastika so lovingly painted on by his constantly joking driver, Obergefreiter Karl Lankse, was now red and plastered with what appeared to be flesh. Was that someone's leg splattered over the upper crook of the swastika emblem? A sudden stab of agonizing pain ripped through his lower belly forcing him to stare down and notice for the first time the utter ruin of the bottom half of his body. A soft cry, followed by a bewildered sob, then a shriek of pain. His attempt to heave himself away from the Tank had in effect separated his upper thighs from his legs. Tendrils of his once firm ligaments and flesh now lay slapped in messy disarray either side of him. The massive turret sat there, no longer a protecting friend but a monster of agony inducing cold steel" Oh dear God – Oh dear God in heaven. Help me. Please," he sobbed loudly knowing full well that soon the pain would become something which would be utterly unbearable but which, until merciful death claimed him, must be born; he might last like this for ages. Just a few minutes would be a few minutes too many.

When moments later, as a wave of pain came like a tsunami from hell, and his body protested about the manner of its vile destruction, he found it was every bit as bad as he had feared it would be. His shrieks, when the full agony set about him, rang through the forest and surrounding dirt roads. He was a Manstein. Scion of an aristocratic Prussian family, respected warriors from centuries past. His uncle was the greatest living general, none other than Field Marshal Erich von Manstein. A roaring blaze of agony wreaked through the sad remains of the once handsome young officer. As he screamed, he writhed and twisted, rolling two to three feet away from where his legs lay crushed to a pulp beneath the turret of his burning Tank.

"I don't want to die," he wept. "Not like this. Oh…sweet bloody Jesus help me!" For one brief comforting moment he thought he felt his father cradling his head in his arms and whispering soft, encouraging words to him. But it wasn't his father; the uniform was very different indeed.

Something sharp was prodding his gaping wounds. Mouth open and head rolling he stared up. Russian brown and on the business end of a long bayonet attached to a worn and filthy rifle. Prod, prod, stab! The Soviet private soldier stalked slowly around the dying, pitifully whimpering German officer. He teased and taunted the poor youngster with the sharp point of his prodding bayonet. The Soviet had a round, smooth featured face which might under normal circumstances have been deemed of friendly and obliging countenance. Not now, though. He was speaking in his Slavic tongue, his words beyond Manstein's comprehension. Other than two much repeated words: "Nazi Scum – Nazi Scum!" The point of the bayonet slit the German's eyelid before the Soviet continued to gleefully stab at his enemy's writhing half-body. He giggled loudly as Manstein attempted to roll onto his stomach and heave himself away from his smooth faced tormentor, leaving a trail of blood and bits as he grovelled slowly in an elbow propelled and erratic half-circle at the feet of his gloating Soviet tormentor. A vision of his mother came before his tear-streaked face and he held out a desperately seeking hand toward that vision of comfort and love. The bayonet sliced clean through back-to-front of his hand, nailing him in position. A boot was ground harshly into the back of the neck, forcing his horrified face deeper and deeper into the battle-churned earth.

"I don't want to be here," he whimpered, just as his neck broke. "I don't want to be here anymore." Thankfully, life then departed the last uniformed Manstein under the age of fifty-five.

25 April. Spree Forest south-east of Berlin. 18.30hrs. General Walther Wenck's HQ

Wilhelm Keitel slapped his Field Marshal's baton across his leather gloved hands in a noisily melodramatic manner. Like a proselytizing fundamentalist in uniform, he strode up and down the dusty excuse for a road that ran alongside General Wenck's ramshackle, wooden hut HQ.

"This will not do, General Wenck. D'you hear me? It just will not do. Where is your armoured spearhead? Where is your attack, man?"

"Attack?" Wenck looked at the baton waving Keitel and made a superhuman effort to remain calm. Beside him the commanding general of the Ninth Army, a thickly bespeckled Theodor Busse, wiped a splodge of grime from his exhausted looking face.

General Wenck tried hard not to frown as he answered his superior. "Attack with what, if I might ask, Field Marshal? There is precious little left with which to mount an attack."

"But you've just linked up with Busse here," Keitel favoured the haggard Ninth Army commander with a nod, "and the entire Ninth Army. Surely now you can thrust with your combined forces into the Russian flank and relieve Berlin. Surely you can do that now, Eh? Yes – of course you can." He nodded and raised a small cloud of dust as he stamped twice with a highly polished booted foot as if to validate his point. "It can be done, Wenck, my dear man, it can, and you shall do it. Clear?"

"Might I point out to the Field Marshal," Busse interjected, "That Ninth Army now has less than thirty thousand men, no tanks and no artillery? Ninth Army is in no state to launch any kind of offensive anywhere at all. Not at this time, and frankly Herr Field Marshal, not at any time in the foreseeable future."

Keitel pouted with annoyance. "Are you telling me that you've managed to lose eighty thousand men and eight hundred tanks in less than one week? Dear God in his heaven man, what the damn hell have you been doing?" Keitel was known to dislike the use of coarse language, but the revelation that the Red Army could now thunder through the twenty-mile gap left by the disintegrating Ninth Army came as an almighty great shock. Only supply problems could now slow down the Soviet advance.

"What was *I* doing?" Busse's eyes became flint behind his well-worn and smudged spectacles. "Well, Herr Field Marshal, *I* was fighting the goddamned Russians who came at us with more than one million.... yes, sir, over one million men and who knows how many tanks; two, three thousand? Don't even mention their wretched artillery; constant rolling barrages over a narrow front from at least twenty thousand large calibre guns whilst we, obeying the Führer's orders, just sat there and soaked it all up. Every-Goddamned-Bit-Of-It!" The Ninth Army commander's hands were clenching and unclenching with alarming rapidity. He was quite clearly a man close to the end of his tether. "And so, with regards to gathering sufficient men for your next great offensive. Well," trembling now with rage and exhaustion, Busse pointed to a small convoy of open-backed trucks packed full with wounded and broken men as it drove slowly past them. Vacant stares, open and festering wounds, they rolled and jerked in time with rough and agonizing synchronicity to their vehicle's harsh, unyielding contact with the deeply rutted road. Behind them came long lines of marching infantry. Shuffling infantry might be a better word. Many of them were walking wounded and all of them wore the same blank expression. To a man they shuffled along with round, drooping shoulders and faces made ugly by exhaustion and despair.

"There are the men that must fight in your next great battle, so why don't you ask them how they feel about it, sir? Better still, how about giving them a good old national socialist pep talk? Bound to do the world of good."

Wenck laid a friendly but restraining hand on his colleague's shoulder. They both looked at Keitel, waiting for the inevitable outburst. But none came. He looked from them to the battered hopeless soldiers filing past him. His voice softened and the bombast fled. "You can at least try." he appealed. "One last effort, eh?" No response came from either general and Keitel turned to look again at the troops slouching past him. He might be Hitler's office boy, as his detractors liked to say; he might be obedient to the point of servitude to his Führer. Nevertheless, he was still a soldier and even he could see that it was hopeless. These men were done. They had had enough and could do no more. He looked helplessly around him for a moment, then, "Do the best you can, gentlemen. That is all that I ask."

Wenck and Busse nodded silently and saluted as the Field Marshal climbed back into the dust begrimed staff car. He paused for a moment. Stupid! A staff car with fluttering OKW pennants in the middle of a war zone. He should have used a Kubelwagen. Nondescript, safe, but not good for an already shrunken ego. Ah well. Returning the salute through the open rear window he sat back and closed his eyes. It was all over. Done. But what in God's name was he going to say to the Führer? The end was imminent. Was it a good idea to return to the Bunker? No – probably not. He would drive to Furstenberg and try to get through to the Bunker from there. That was about it. He tapped his driver lightly on the shoulder with his marshal's baton.

"Furstenberg, Hartmann. As quick as you can."

CHAPTER 11

May 1932: Berchtesgaden, Obersalzberg

Adolf sipped delicately at his green mint tea, savouring the fresh, natural flavours and loving the smell that arose from his bone china tea cup. This was the life. High altitude fresh air, obligingly respectful company and excellent food prepared by his cook, Margarete Roloefs. Cakes lay on large three-tiered stands in a neat line all down the length of the thick legged oaken dining table. Closest to him lay the stand containing his favourite apple cake with nuts and raisins. Already three of those delicious cakes had disappeared down the Führer's eager gullet. Nobody said anything, or even looked, as he wolfed them down. It was his *thing*. It did not seem to matter who might be at the table, anywhere or anytime, when it came to apple cake, cream cake, or perhaps.... apple *and* cream cake, Adolf went into scoff mode. He couldn't resist them. His special cook, Frau Roloefs was a true mistress of her art and the Führer wouldn't part with her for all the art works in the Vatican.

A light breeze drifted across the assembled company causing the bushes and small trees surrounding the garden to rustle and sway in pleasing harmony. There was plenty of coffee for his guests and a variety of cakes and sweetmeats. Enough to tickle the palate of even the sweetest tooth. The coffee was from South America and large pewter pots of the stuff were being rapidly emptied and refilled by white jacketed flunkies as the guests chatted and laughed together.

Adolf smiled and nodded as he looked around, crumbs snickering down the front of his grey tie and on to his neatly ironed white shirt. His casual, charcoal coloured jacket lay open, thus avoiding the small avalanche of crumbs and he smiled lightly as he brushed away the offending confection. An open jacket front was the only concession Adolf made these days to informality. He encouraged neatness and uniformity in others and constantly practised the same himself.

A small female hand reached across and with easy familiarity brushed away the remaining crumbs from his shirt. He frowned at first and seemed about to push the overly familiar hand away, but then thought better of it and instead offered a winning smile.

"Thank you, Eva, my dear." Adolf patted her hand in a paternal fashion and she responded with a girlish twist of the shoulders, a full lipped pout with tilted head and a cheeky gleam in her eye. The pout became a full faced Eva Braun smile as she leaned back in her chair. "There," she simpered. "All better." Her eyes flicked quickly and expertly to all sides to gauge the reaction of those present. She was laying her claim and she wanted all to know it. *She* had a place here and it was at the *top* of the table!

Most here didn't like her, she knew that well enough. They considered her to be a lightweight gold digger and attention seeker. They did not understand what the Führer could see in someone like her. Not much in the way of intellect, education or charisma. To most she was rather dull. Well, she treated the table to one of her slightly vapid smiles, let them think whatever they like. The Führer, Adolf Hitler, *her* Adolf Hitler, was on his way to the very top and for his own very good reasons, and hers, he insisted that she accompany him on the journey. She knew why. The appearance of normality was important and she helped make Adolf look normal to the outer world. It was no love match, although she occasionally simpered winningly when they were being observed by those of any importance. In the early weeks, she had been excited by his charisma, his power and the way he so easily got what he wanted. She had met generals, politicians, high-flying businessmen – all sorts. She had met people, ex-royalty even, seen and done things she could never have imagined in her former life; the life before Adolf, or LBA as she liked to call it privately. All this whilst being his supposedly *secret* amour. Thankfully, he was not interested in a physical relationship; not with her, anyway. It had puzzled her at first, his lack of interest in her sexual charms. She was after all considered by most to be, if not an outstanding beauty, at least an attractive young Fraulein with her bits in all the right places. But he had made it clear that he was not interested in any way in her *bits*, nor anyone else's for that matter. An odd character, her Adolf. She regarded him as her Adolf because he was determined to possess her in every platonic way imaginable, to own and control her and if possible manipulate her very thoughts. Well, two could play that game. He was her ticket to grandeur and riches; a life of effortless comfort and respect. Far better than some schoolgirl romance followed by a cute little house and a brood of snotty, shrieking children. This was the life – her life, and she intended that nothing interfere with it nor Adolf's progress up any ladder that he chose to climb. She did at times feel quite strong sexual urges which would tempt her to glance at one, or even two of those gorgeously wide-shouldered and snaked-hipped SS types with ill-concealed longing. Adolf had noticed, alright, but seemed inclined to ignore it. He might possessively dominate her will, mind and life, but was uninterested in her body. Odd, she curled a whisp of her attractively long light brown hair around her middle finger. He possessed her pretty well completely but displayed no willingness to own or discover the sexual side of her nature, nor indeed to insist that she refrain from any activities in that area. What was it that the strange little Propaganda man, Joseph Goebbels had said? 'Be discreet my dear and all will be well. Be discreet but never silly, hmm?' Yes, that's what he had said. Odd little man: well, they were all odd, this lot. Alright, then, she would be discreet. But there was no way that she intended to deny herself life's natural pleasures, especially with him being away most of the time.

She threw Adolf a smile and shared the same with the very interesting looking Albert Speer. Now there was a wonderfully handsome younger man. Might have to be careful with that one. She smiled inwardly. She found her supposed beau, Adolf, to be physically repugnant. There was no way in anybody's world that she could physically desire a man like him. Apart from being so physically unattractive up close, he was a non-stop windbag. On and on and on, he could go, and did go, all too often! Repeating himself over and over again. Yuk! Thanks be to God, that as far as Adolf Hitler was concerned, she, Eva Braun, was nothing more than a necessary ornament. To put it bluntly, (it wasn't as though he didn't know) he was her uber-powerful meal ticket and protector. All she had to do was play her undemanding part with grace and gratitude and everything would be permanently and gloriously fulfilling. Let's face it, she thought, as she reached across and daintily picked up a small chocolate cake, it wasn't as if she was ever going to have feminine opposition. Sexual female wiles were never going to work on Adolf, that was for sure. However, she glanced almost furtively at young Albert Speer; she wasn't quite so sure about the other side.

A dolf also glanced more than once at the debonair young architect. They had met last year at one of his more successful rallies and had happily clicked on some strangely esoteric level. A bond had been forged almost immediately and for the life of him, Adolf could not understand why.

Reaching for yet another cake he hesitated as Speer looked toward him. That strangely cold but undeniably attractive face was so compelling. Was he as haughty as he appeared, this Albert Speer? Certainly, when he was with Adolf Hitler, he gave little sign of such weakness. But Adolf was pretty sure that he could spot the signs of overweening self-love in young Herr Speer. Nothing wrong with that. It was a weakness that might be exploited at some stage. Self-love meant the desire for advancement. Ambition! Oh yes indeed. Adolf could always use men with high ambition for they were the most malleable and obedient of all.

He nodded to the hovering waiter who then refilled his cup with the light green liquid that was his mint tea. It didn't require stirring but nevertheless, Adolf lifted the silver tea spoon and lightly dabbed it into his tea. He played thus for a few seconds as he returned Albert's gaze. The younger man smiled and for one awful, no, for one delightful moment, Adolf felt as though he were dropping into paradise. He sometimes missed Emil Maurice and had at one time held great affection for that ever-loyal man. But it had been nothing like this. This overwhelming feeling of…what? He could not put a word to it. His eyes bored into the smiling architect who abruptly, and sensibly looked away. Adolf's face was set like granite. He had no idea, of course, of the scary visage that he now projected. This was the face of the covetous Hitler; the man who would not be denied. The moment was brief and Adolf smiled as he powerfully slapped his mental equilibrium back into place. Such things as he had momentarily envisaged could not ever be; not any longer. Nevertheless, though, what a wonderfully fascinating creature young Speer was, to be sure.

He glanced around the table. Hess sat with his wife as they both chatted animatedly with the Ribbentrops. Now, there was a man who thought that he was God's gift to humanity. Joachim von Ribbentrop. Conceited but clever, thought Adolf. Useful in quite a few ways but needed keeping on a tight leash. Seated at the far end of the table with his odd, outrageously ugly little Frau sat Himmler. He and his wife sat quietly gazing around at their surroundings. Physically quite feeble, probably one of the few men that Joseph Goebbels might beat in a fist fight, Heinrich Himmler was devoted to his Führer in every way. He was also utterly terrified of him. A word from Adolf would immediately galvanise the po-faced SS Reichsführer into frantic and obedient action regardless of what that action might be. Adolf could barely tolerate the man and hated even being in the same room with him, but he was so very useful and the perfect head of security. Cold, fearful of his master, obedient and utterly without any true feelings of humanity. Excellent! Himmler it was who had so expertly handled that embarrassment over the sad and sudden death by suicide of his niece. He had handled the story, the publicity and the dampening down of any pertinent or difficult questions for his Führer. Luckily he had been in his Munich office at the time, so the quick-thinking bodyguard, Bruno Gesche, experienced little trouble in contacting the bespectacled SS chief, who these days favoured sinister looking silver rimmed pince-nez spectacles. His arrival on the scene, along with Hermann Goering, who just so happened to be in Bavaria at the time, ensured that as little odium as was possible clung to the Nazi party leader. A job well done by his SS chief.

Someone else's eyes were boring into him, he could feel it. Rohm. Ernst Rohm, the SA chief sat there with a sardonic smile on his face as if knowing precisely the thoughts that were travelling through Adolf's head; which he probably did. He could smell Adolf out in just about anything.

My dear friend Ernst, thought Adolf. The one man he allowed to address him with any semblance of the old and comfortable familiarity. Tough, lippy, brave and puffed-up little Ernst Rohm. He's done so much for me, Adolf mused. But now he was becoming one hell of a pain in the rear-end. Sometime soon, he knew, there would have to be a reckoning with his ambitious and so *dear* friend Ernst.

Adolf realised that he was still idly stirring his tea and committing the social sin of seemingly ignoring his guests. He hadn't, of course, ignored any one of them, not really. Even though he had been staring with his intense gaze into the distance he was sizing them all up. Now that things were changing and the Party growing daily more influential and important, how would these individuals handle true power and responsibility? Nobody had said anything to him or attempted to gain his attention during the course of his prolonged silence, most of them assuming that he, their genius leader, was contemplating some great stroke of political wizardry. It was certainly time that he spoke to them all as one. The next massive election loomed and his efforts now must of necessity be fully devoted to the campaign trail and travelling all over the Reich in his nice shiny Junkers 52. It was time to heave that old fossil, Hindenburg, out of the President's office and into retirement.

Goering's loud, hooting laughter drew his notice and he grimaced slightly as he observed his deputy's wobbling chins and neck. He was about to tap the side of his cup to gain attention when Friedrik Lehman came and stood respectfully at his side.

"Might I have a word, my Führer?" Such a respectful tone from such a well-bred and hugely rich man was always music to Adolf's well-tuned ears. It was to Lehman's house that Adolf and his guards had fled on the evening of Geli's death. The fine holiday home at Tegernsee, one of several owned by the urbane and almost unknowable Lehman, had proven to be a fine sanctuary with its delightful surroundings, fresh mountain air and respectful, even worshipful staff and neighbours. A place where, the moment he was informed of his niece's sudden and violent death, he had immediately engaged himself in a bout of grief-inspired histrionics, the shrieking amateurishness of which had rendered even the normally unflappable Hermann Lehman utterly speechless. The many sympathetic well-wishers, ghouls and nosey-parkers that had turned up to offer their condolences had been treated, one and all, to a performance of such staggeringly tearful mediocrity, that not one of them came away convinced of anything else other than that, in all likelihood, there was a lot more to the story than the wishy-washy press releases that the Party were handing out: 'Poor sweet girl, troubled by exam failures and accidentally ended it all – so very tragic!' etc, etc. Hitler's performances of avuncular anguish fooled nobody. Murder was the word on the tip of many tongues. On the tip, but never beyond it. If the Führer was slaughtering his family what business was it of theirs? They had their own lives and families to consider.

"Yes, Lehman – what is it?"

Lehman gestured with a slight nod that it might be better to move away from the table but with a peremptory gesture Adolf waved him closer. Lehman now held the rank of Gruppenführer in the SS, a reward from Himmler for his aid throughout the Geli Raubal crisis. A nice high rank and ensconced deep within the coming power in the land suited him very well; the uniform, however, did not. To Gruppenführer Friedrik Lehman, the flamboyantly tailored Hugo Boss designed uniform was just too pretentious; mere fancy-dress frippery, even if he did look rather good in it. Never display what you truly are, was his motto and SS uniforms displayed only too obviously what the wearers were. Nevertheless, he bowed to necessity and wore the wretched thing whenever he deemed it suitable or advantageous. He had to admit that, as a statement, the black uniform had enabled him to get his way on more than one occasion. People were afraid of it, or rather the man who wore it.

Eva looked on, her round face wearing a smug expression. She would be able to overhear every word.

With a small sigh Lehman leaned into Hitler's ear and whispered something. All Eva was able to catch were the words. "Von Papen," before Hitler shot up out of his chair, his face a mask of fury and hatred. Lehman was not merely very rich, his contacts were of the highest quality and he moved easily between the rough and ready world of National Socialism and the rarefied atmosphere of the high and mighty Junkers, aristocrats and upper middle-class with their sweetly observed good manners.

Albert Speer was craning his neck in an effort to gauge what might be going on.

"He said that – about me?" Hitler almost shoved Lehman out of his way as he strode out from his place at the table.

Total silence now reigned at the formerly bee-hive noisy table as all eyes became glued to the very irate Führer. He moved, stiff legged in his anger to the ornate balustrade and slammed both palms flat on the carved stone ledge. Leaning over it he kicked at the flared baluster knocking a piece of stone down into the garden below. With no warning, he turned and let his blazing gaze fall upon each and every one of his guests. Then, arms crossed and with the same stiff legged gait, he returned to his place at the table.

"We are going to knock this decrepit old fool, von Hindenburg, from his ivory perch and then consign that imitation of a man, von Papen, to the bin of forgetfulness. Unless......." He paused allowing his features to recompose and his tone to become less violent, "I decide upon something different for the oaf; as and when I may!"

The threat was not lost and all those present, including the wives, nodded in agreement even though not one of them, with the exception of Lehman, had the vaguest notion of what Hitler was going on about nor what might have angered him to such a moustache chewing degree.

Lehman smiled inwardly. The Führer had gathered around him what could only be described as the most mentally bereft bunch of obediently violent half-wits and sycophants as could sensibly be gathered in one place. Speer was certainly no half-wit, though. And to anyone with eyes to see, he was rather more than a self-seeking sycophant. A dangerous man for all his suave manners and dimpled smiles. Curt, abrasive even, to underlings; charming and subservient to those that outranked him. Very much a player.

Much like myself, thought Lehman.

He had just relayed, as ordered by Hitler, the exact details of a meeting between the current Reich Chancellor and the Reich President. The precise wording came from Otto Stenner, personal secretary to von Papen and unbeknownst to the President, Reich Chancellor or Adolf Hitler, a very well-paid associate and informant of Friedrik Lehman. It was the very preciseness of the wording which Hitler had insisted upon, that made this message delivery so enjoyable. Those two worthies, Hindenburg and von Papen, had been discussing a projected meeting with the Nazi Party leader, Herr Hitler. The *Herr Hitler* designation was as far as their verbal courtesy extended. Hindenburg had referred to Adolf as a rabid animal, the Austrian corporal and a thick-headed swine not fit for government.

Von Papen had stated that the man Hitler was nothing more than a dog but that he could be domesticated and made obedient. He, von Papen, would undertake the said domestication and see that the feral beast, Hitler, would be made suitable and malleable enough for them all to get by and keep Hitler's block of National Socialist deputies in line. He could be easily controlled, promised von Papen, with the offer of a meaningless ministry and, perhaps, something for one of his barely literate underlings. Just enough to keep his working-class little ego polished. With that mundane task accomplished, they, the Chancellor and the President, could then get on with running the country. Hitler, they had decided, would be given the Post Office, Agriculture, or some such. Oh, how they had laughed.

And oh indeed how Gruppenführer Friedrik Lehman did so enjoy tarting up that message, just a little, before delivering it in his calm, urbane manner to the blustering hysteric who would be king. It wouldn't be presidents, their chancellors or hapless Reichstag deputies that would be running the country once Herr Hitler was successfully ensconced in office. Not a chance! A select group of ultra-powerful tycoons was standing by, ready with their clout and billions to run the country as it deserved to be run. A proper management team with not one fuzzy-headed idealist amongst them. The world's first corporatocracy would soon come into being with every chance that the Nazi Führer, Adolf Hitler, would never so much as have an inkling of it. Friedrik Lehman and his associates knew very well what the rest of Germany had yet to realise; Adolf Hitler didn't have a single worthwhile political idea in his violent fantasy riddled head. Lehman knew all too well that once seated on the throne of power, be it the presidency or the chancellorship, Herr Hitler would, once the euphoria of gaining power had worn off, be completely lost. Surrounding oneself with ninnies, drug addicts and alcoholic no-hopers was one way of ensuring that no real challenges would be made against his leadership; it was also a certain way to turn even the most prosperous of nations into economic trainwrecks. What this potential government by deviants and perverts would need would be toys aplenty, and a few *supposed* economic miracles to keep them quiet and malleable whilst the real rulers of the Reich got on with their work of making Germany the mightiest industrial power in the world. Hitler and his gang would be dumped when they had served their purpose. The industrial magnates, backed by the Junkers and the army, would see to it that power was removed from the mental vacuum of Nazism. Even so, as he observed the strange mannered and gravel voiced man before him, Lehman mused on the near future. Best be always on guard and don't take anything for granted. These people were hallmarked nut cases and he would need to be ever vigilant. It never occurred to the brilliant Lehman, nor his clever colleagues, that they might have already severely underestimated the common little Austrian corporal.

Magda Goebbels looked sweetly over at Eva and smiled. God, how she loathed that upstart little slut. That she, a working class, conceited hussy should sit so close to the Führer was almost beyond bearing. She knew only too well that vivacious, glowing skinned Eva Braun was nothing more than a favour selling gold-digger. A randy slut, to boot.

'I have only to catch you out just the once my girl,' mused Magda, 'and then, my dear, see what the wolf does to you.' She almost threw her head back with the pleasure of that thought.

Eva smiled down the table at her. Did she know – could she sense Magda's hatred and resentment? The beguiling innocence of her return smile seemed to say no; but the small though determined thrust of breasts which were larger, firmer and a good few years younger than Magda's own quite generous appendages, lent lie to that premise. The entire movement, so small as to be noticed only by the seething Magda Goebbels, said, see them and weep, dearie! Magda didn't weep. But she most certainly ground her teeth and would have spat if she could.

Most of the round, staring eyes now glued to the arms akimbo, almost messianic figure standing before them were full of awe and abject devotion. Craned necks and eager postures awaiting the prophetic words from their infallible saviour, their reason for being, their Führer. Magda Goebbels, even with her husband Joseph sitting eagerly beside her, could barely stop her chest from a crazily voluptuous heaving. When Adolf Hitler went off on one he was absolute dynamite!

Not all eyes present stared with such complete devotion, though: not quite.

His arms began to rise slowly out from his sides, palms upward and blue eyes curving dramatically toward the heavens as he spoke. He spoke loudly and many of the guests' fingers gripped the table edge with painful pressure as that strangely magnetic voice washed over them, drenching them all in their Führer's needs and desires, and commands!

"It falls to me to rescue Germany. Providence has decreed that my genius and mine alone can save The Fatherland from the vileness of the Jews, Masons and perverts that permeate every corner of our great nation. EVERY CORNER!"

Rudolf Hess leapt to his feet. "Thank God for the Führer. We are with you my Führer. Sieg Heil."

Himmler was only marginally behind Hess in the jumping out of the chair stakes and, with eyes glowing fanatically from behind his rather ludicrous light reflecting pince-nez spectacles, threw out his right arm in a bone-rigid Nazi salute and shrieked, "Heil Hitler!" To which the entire assembly rose and shrieked the same thing with outflung arms and various degrees of vying enthusiasm.

Goebbels' Heil Hitler roar turned to a shriek of pain as Göring's much larger hand collided with his halfway during their joint upward trajectory.

Briefly gripping his small and abused hand, and then bravely releasing it, he used his entire stock of pain resistance in an attempt to ignore a broken finger which throbbed hurtfully and completed his salute to the Führer micro-seconds after the last hand had gone down.

The grin on Hermann Göring's face was smugness exemplified as he mouthed, "So sorry, dear fellow."

Adolf had noticed the small interchange between his two stalwart lieutenants and chose to ignore it. Such things pleased him. Keep the staff at each other's throats and thus keep them, all of them, off balance with only himself, their rightful Führer, able to provide any kind of balance. It worked perfectly.

Palms downward he gestured for them all to sit. Beckoning to the two hovering waiters he pointed meaningfully at the few still unopened bottles of wine and then proposed a toast. He would not partake of neat alcohol himself but did on occasion have a glass of white wine. Now was such an occasion.

When all was done and everyone present had a full glass before them, he raised his glass and made a sweeping motion that encompassed them all and, in fact, the entire area.

"Victory – success – and full reward for faith and hard work! These things I solemnly promise to all of you, my friends. We cannot be defeated nor discouraged. We shall prevail in all our aims. Yes – success shall be ours!"

Table thumping, foot stamping and heaven only might count how many choruses of Heil Hitler rang out. But they were all deliriously happy, because success, one way or another, was assured.

CHAPTER 12

April 27 1945: Berlin, The Bunker 13:00 hrs.

The urgent tapping on his shoulder had Rochus Misch turning and frowning deeply with irritation. He was attempting to glean any information that he could from the static-filled transmissions that flew across his switchboard and then vanished with infuriating swiftness. He was sick to death of majors, colonels and even generals constantly barging into his little electronic cubbyhole and interfering with his increasingly difficult job. They demanded news of the outside world and some even had the temerity to demand phone access to their wretched families – as if!

"Is there any news? The Twelfth Army. Is there any news? They should break through anytime now. What news is there, hmm?"

The frown slackened immediately. Misch would recognize that voice anywhere. The Führer, shuffled up and down the inner bunker corridor, incessantly asking the same damned question over and over again. 'Is there any news?' NO, Misch wanted to scream out. 'And if there ever is, you can bet your sagging arse that it'll all be bad!' But, of course, Scharführer Rochus Misch said no such thing. His habitual and generally endearing smile seemed glued today quite harshly to his face, as he replied, "I'm afraid not, my Führer. So much static and many trying to use the same line,"

"Same line?" Hitler appeared confused. "But Wenck's HQ has a direct signal capability to this transmitter, receiver, whatever. By my authority he has a direct line. I ordered it, Scharführer. So why isn't it working – WHY?" At that moment Bormann appeared.

"My Führer," he spoke as though he hadn't seen Hitler for a month of Sundays.

Misch hung his head. Dear God in heaven! Now he had two of them to twitter away aimlessly about future victories and the glories of The Fatherland. Beans-on-broomstick would this lunacy never end?

"I need news Bormann, news from the front."

"Why is there no news, Scharführer," Bormann demanded in his always annoying and peremptory tone. "You know very well that the Führer needs to be kept up to date. Constantly up to date with all the latest information."

"Indeed sir, I do but…."

"Then why are you not doing your job, Misch? Must I replace you?"

"Tut-tut, Bormann. No need for that. The Scharführer is doing his very best, I'm sure."

Odd thing about the ailing, pretty well brain-dead boss, thought Misch. He invariably stood up for his lower grade workers. A strange man. No doubt about that.

"Always, my Führer. I have given and still give of my very best." He made as though to stand but Hitler's trembling hand briefly caressed his shoulder as he rose, indicating that he remain seated.

"I know, I know." He turned and shuffled out, turning once more just before he left.

"Let me know. The second it comes in, give me all and any news. Understood?"

"Of course, my Führer. The very instant."

"Good man." With that, he was gone followed by the rotund Bormann whose belly rudely shoved against the put-upon Misch as he passed.

"Keep your eyes and ears glued, Scharführer. At all times."

Misch now beyond politeness, and caring less with each passing second about military protocol, didn't bother to answer. He simply adjusted his headset and waited.

He didn't have to wait long. His switchboard went blank for a few seconds before flickering back into working mode. His headset hissed and buzzed as he strained to make out the staccato delivery from somewhere way above and beyond.

"I can't make that out. Speak up, speak more slowly." Misch was almost pleading with the operator on the other end of the line. It was a message right enough, but from where and from whom? A brief silence followed by a harsh, still intermittent but now more recognisable voice. Misch's fingers closed around the pencil by his wrist. It was Keitel. None other than, at last, the somewhat tardy Field Marshal. The Scharführer began scribbling frantically, desperate to get the garbled facts down before the line was lost again.

"I see, sir. Yes Herr Field Marshal, I got all that." Misch's face had paled a little as he digested the message fully. He alone had the responsibility of giving this news directly to the Führer. Just damn well great! God alone knew to what new heights of blood curdling hysteria the Führer might yet reach when he received this latest piece of front-line disaster. It would undoubtedly send him soaring over the edge – again! Perhaps he should just hand the message to Bormann and let him carry this latest blow? No point. The Reichsleiter would simply hand it straight back to him with a lecture on how the Führer would so much prefer to hear all and any news straight from the horse's mouth, or as close as he could get to it. A hiss of clarity came over the beleaguered communications line and Misch was able to ask the pertinent question; where was the Field Marshal and when might the Führer expect his return?

"Furstenberg, sir? And….no way through…. Russians blocking and encirclement complete. Yes sir, got it. Of course, Herr Field Marshal. I shall inform the Führer of your undying loyalty and devotion to the end. Yes, sir, you may of course rely upon me to relay the message in its entirety." He yanked out the headset and mouthpiece assembly with a savage pull.

"Everything okay Misch?" The tall dark figure of Brigadeführer Wilhelm Mohnke loomed over Misch's left shoulder. "You're looking slightly miffed." The slim, rather cruel features of the SS officer's face twisted into a friendly smile. They had known one another for a long time. From similar working-class backgrounds, they had even faced each other on opposite sides playing football for their respective villages. A game at which both excelled. That, however, had been back in the twenties. They met up again after both men had, for very different reasons, joined the SS. The career driven Mohnke had risen quickly to the rank of Hauptsturmführer and was for a while Misch's commanding officer. Misch, never a man to court fame or promotion, had seemed content, insistent in fact, upon remaining a mere SS Oberschutze. Rochus Misch was a man who kept his light hidden firmly under a bushel. He was possessed of many talents and Mohnke had used some of those talents to further his own and certain other rather secretive activities of the SS and Misch could be relied upon never to mention them.

Wilhelm Mohnke had a soft spot for Rochus Misch. Admiring his unflappable coolness under fire and the way that he always seemed to get a job done with so little fuss. After providing sterling service to his employers at home and abroad, and receiving a severe wound, Mohnke had had no hesitation at all in recommending him for a newly vacant post on the Führer's personal staff. From there Rochus Misch had progressed to trusted courier and switchboard operator. Not just any courier or switchboard operator. In his time Rochus had carried messages and carried out furtively arranged assignments from the Führer's head of security, Johann Rattenhuber. Assignments, some whispered, that had decidedly nefarious connotations. When Rochus travelled, he had travelled first class and with the wonder key of a Führer 'Assist this man in all his endeavours' order in his pocket. The state-of-the-art Siemens switchboard that he now worked was a thing of wonder and confusion to all except Misch. And he had craftily listened in to and cleverly decoded many verbally coded conversations that would have dropped the jaws even of Bormann and Goebbels et al. Typical of him, whilst recovering from his wound, he had applied for and taken every single course appertaining to signals, codes and telephony.

Mohnke and Rattenhuber were good friends and both knew that despite his always charmingly deferential demeanour, Scharführer Rochus Misch was the most intelligent man in the Bunker; he was also, in all likelihood, the most dangerous. Mohnke, Rattenhuber and the rest all thought that they could gauge a man but good old Rochus was a conundrum. No one really knew him or what he believed in nor even what he wanted, other than a ticket out of this place, the Bunker.

"Oh, good morning, sir!" Misch turned in his seat and directed a respectful nod to his superior officer.

"Morning, Misch. Someone get your goat?" He nodded toward the glowing switchboard. "Another excuse maker wanting to bail out?"

"That and a bit more, sir." It was against protocol but Misch handed the high-ranking SS officer his hastily written notes with a nodded invitation to read.

Frowning deeply, the SS General read Misch's always neat and legible handwriting.

"Ah-ha!" He breathed in deeply for a count of two and then exhaled through pursed lips. A sure sign that he was more than a little perturbed. "That, Scharführer Misch, my old comrade in arms, would appear to be just about it. Although," his slightly buck teeth appeared as he attempted a worldly smile, "it's been about *it* for some time now. Wouldn't you say?"

"More than my life's worth, Herr Brigadeführer." Misch allowed a knowing smile to cross his handsome features.

"Which, my friend, isn't much in today's coin," Mohnke responded with exaggerated dolefulness. "I have to report to the Führer so you might as well deliver your bad news alongside mine, eh?"

Hitler sat calmly staring at Misch and then down at the notes that Misch had only moments ago brought to him.

"All of them – retreating?" He whispered. His eyes were dull and he made no attempt to hide or control the shaking of his arm or leg. He just sat, glancing from the notes to Misch and back again.

"According to the Field Marshal, yes My Führer. The drive toward Berlin has been, erm…. discontinued due to overwhelming enemy forces crushing both flanks. The Field Marshal said that……"

"It no longer matters what Keitel said or did or did not do. It's over." He raised a trembling hand. "Get back to your switchboard. Go…. go!"

With a muttered "Yes, my Führer," Misch turned and left the Führer's presence. Mohnke gave him a raised eyebrow and a slight nod as he left, which clearly said, "We'll speak later."

"They're running, Mohnke. Running like scared children. Betraying me. Those loathsome swine. Just like all the rest. Those spineless bastards."

Mohnke kept his face neutral and said nothing. Just a few hours ago Walther Wenck had been Adolf Hitler's beloved blue-eyed boy. His wonderous saviour, along with the rapidly retreating Twelfth Army. Now, because he had had the temerity to call off an insanely futile suicide mission that would have meant the horrible deaths of thousands of already wounded German soldiers, he was a swine, a dog and a lump of loathsome filth. General Wenck had clearly decided that Adolf Hitler was not worth any further sacrifice and that, in Adolf Hitler's eyes, was an unforgivable sin.

"I'll have him shot, of course." Hitler's eyes showed some of the old animation. "Or perhaps hung by wire on a meat hook like those other fools that thought they could disobey me. Disobey me? ME! The Führer! I'll show them, Mohnke. I'll show them. Send men and arrest that traitorous wretch and his entire HQ and that gutless dog Busse, as well. You hear me? Arrest them at once!"

"Of course, my Führer." Just where the alternate eye-rolling to tear-shedding Führer thought that he might find men to send out into the hell-hole that was now Berlin was a mystery. But a fairly typical mystery when one considered the atmosphere that reigned in the Bunker and had pervaded all of Hitler's dwellings, temporary or permanent, since he, Wilhelm Mohnke, could remember. A dreamland, once so believable but now clearly nothing more than an increasingly bad nightmare. Nevertheless, thought Mohnke, we must salvage something from this hideous mess. Not Hitler, for sure. But something, at least. Otherwise, they would all, every one of them, go down in history as brain dead lunatics and *that* quite simply must not be allowed to happen – not in any way whatsoever!

Warrior heroes: misled, but patriotic and brave. Yes, that was the way it must be.

His own news for the Führer; that they had two days at the very most before the Russians gobbled up the tiny perimeter that Mohnke and his last few remaining SS Leibstandarte, some forty old men past sixty-five and thirty-seven twelve-to-thirteen-year Hitler Youth boys were tenaciously holding, had been received with barely a flicker of interest. General Weidling's forces were now scattered throughout the ruins of Berlin. Still fighting in quite large but in the face of the massive forces arrayed against them, inconsequential groups of resistance. It was now purely death for no reason.

"My watch doesn't work, Rochus. Look." She handed him the offending timepiece as if expecting that by the merest wave of his hand he could make it function immediately.

Misch took the watch, white gold and very expensive, a gift from the Führer, no doubt. "I'll see to it, Fraulein." He gave Eva Braun his lopsided devil-may-care smile and she moved instinctively closer. "You are the nicest person down here, Rochus," she smiled back at him and her hand lightly fluttered against his. Rochus Misch was one of the few of Hitler's working circle that had any time for Eva. He, in fact, quite liked her, even though she was an incorrigible and rather dangerous little flirt.

"We must help each other whenever we can, Fraulein Braun."

"When d'you suppose it might be ready?"

The bunker was not likely to boast an array of skilled watch technicians, although, one could never tell.

"Just as soon as I possibly can, Fraulein. I promise."

April 27: The Bunker, Berlin 17:00 hrs.

They had ensured that the coast was reasonably clear here in the pantry of the Vorbunker. No inner lock on the door of course but they hadn't intended to go this far with their death risking dalliance. An important and very quick chat, he had said and she had agreed.

She stared at him in disbelief. "Leave the bunker, with you – now?"

He nodded. "Yes, my sweet. I have everything that you might need all stored away in my apartment in Bleibtreustrasse. Perfumes, only the best for my girl, and some lovely clothes that you'll adore." He didn't mention that the store of laid-in clothes and perfumes along with various other items of ladies' personal grooming had been gathered over time, left by visiting females from many different parts of the Third Reich. "You must leave with me now, and I mean right now! Those Asiatic scum are here, not at the gates but right here at the front door. I have a Kubelwagen and there is still an opening to the southeast but it won't stay that way for much longer. If you stay here you die or are captured. D'you want that – do you?"

"I can't, Hermann." Eva was breathing heavily as fear began coursing through her veins like a slow moving and sluggishly claiming cancer. He was right. She knew that. But surely, a little longer and she would receive what she came for; her due! And there were bound to be escape plans. No one but a lunatic would willingly come down here to die. Well, nobody but *him* anyway. The soldiers would know what to do and Joseph Goebbels would most certainly have thought of a clever plan. Why else would he have brought his lovely but noisy children down here if not to ensure their future safety? No, she would not go with Hermann. It was far too dangerous. Love, infatuation, call it what you will, did, after all, have certain sensible limits.

The Kubelwagen bumped its way crazily over huge potholes, the smartly uniformed SS general leaning expertly from left to right as he steered around great, gaping craters in the road. The once glorious Wilhelmstrasse had certainly seen better days, and unless the driver of the small, battered military vehicle was wrong, the machine gun fire that he could hear was less than two hundred metres distant. Far too close for comfort!

Fegelein had suborned the battered old Kubelwagen from the motor pool under the very eyes of Hitler's personal driver and motor pool commander, Sturmbannführer Kempka himself. It wasn't so much the car that Kempka had objected to letting go, God knew there were enough of them lying around in the underground Reich Chancellery car park, it was the fuel necessary to make it run. All fuel, whether petrol, diesel or even ersatz was now horribly scarce and Kempka's orders were to husband every single drop of it. Fegelein, however, was as always over-the-top persuasive. Kempka knew that the smooth-talking and showy SS officer had an apartment in town and that he came and went pretty well as he pleased. He was Gretl Braun's husband, an intimate of Hitler himself and a trusted functionary of Reichsführer Himmler. As if that were not enough, he was a decorated Waffen-SS General and an active SS-Gruppenführer to boot. All of which made him a difficult and dangerous man to cross, even for a Hitler favourite like Erich Kempka. In the light of which he had allowed one ten-litre can of fuel for Fegelein and elicited a promise that the Kubelwagen, *with* some petrol remaining, be returned by muster the next morning. Not a hope! Hermann Fegelein had no intention of returning. He was done with the war, with Hitler, Himmler and the whole lot of them. It looked as though he was also done with Eva Braun, which was a shame because he liked her quite a lot. Certainly a lot more than her sister, to whom he was married and who was heavily pregnant with their first child.

Well, that was just too bad. They would have to fend for themselves; every man for himself, and all that. He'd only married the adoring Gretl to get closer to Hitler's inner circle; a career move that he now deeply regretted and was trying desperately to cover up. He would get home, dump this wretched uniform and all the decorations along with anything else connecting him to the Nazis and Hitler's old gang. It must be done before the Russians kicked down the door. But carefully, despite the need for haste. What was the saying? Do in haste – repent at leisure? Unlike many of his Nazi colleagues, or accomplices as von Loringhoven liked to term them, Hermann Fegelein was sensibly aware of the type of retribution they might all expect. He had allowed his darker side full rein in 1939 when, as a young Hauptsturmführer in Poland, he had happily engaged in all manner of murderous activities to gain the approval of his superiors. He had certainly gained respect for his kill quota which, in numbers and enthusiasm, had been surpassed by very few. The young Hermann Fegelein's devotion to duty had been held up as a fine and noteworthy exemplar to the then newly formed Einsatzgruppe. Thirty or forty men, women and children forced to their trembling knees and shot in the back of the head? Such actions did not present a problem for the superbly enthusiastic young SS officer, Hermann Fegelein. Sometimes, if the mood took him, he would smash their brains out with a short, infantry soldier's trenching tool. Messy – but impressive to see; or so he thought, anyway. The proof was in the pudding, as they say. He spat powerfully out of the rackety Kubelwagen. Oh, yes indeed. His supposed ice-hearted cruelty had won him contacts and promotion and here he was, a top Nazi general, pretty well at the pinnacle of where he had aimed. Often photographed chin-wagging with the high and mighty, he was easily recognisable to anyone looking in his direction.

"Just typical of my sodding luck," he cursed loudly and spat again.

"That shit-for-brains twat had to go and lose us the bloody war! What a bloody mess. Moron!"

He slapped a hand angrily against the thin metal of the Kubelwagen door and cursed again as the flimsy over-worn latch gave way and the door swung open. Hastily reaching out he grabbed the flapping door and heaved it shut. He needed to be more careful. Stay calm and avoid drawing attention, at all costs. Capture by the Soviets for any SS or Party members would, in all likelihood, mean a fate worse than death. Excuses through ignorance, feigned or otherwise, were not going to work. The bill for all their self-indulgent fun, games and State encouraged sadism was about to be presented, and smooth Hermann had no intention of being around to pay for his share of it. At his apartment he had money, gold coins, papers and travel documents ready for his next move. He also had top secret documents appertaining to his immediate boss, Heinrich Himmler. "Ho!" He laughed out loud. "If Adolf and the boys could see that little lot." He shook his head as he drove. He would destroy the incriminating documents later. First, he must change out of the fancy SS get-up and into more appropriate civilian clothes. As Eva had declined his well-meant offer of escape, silly cow, then, he would grab a hold of Erika Lanz; a nice piece of slightly more downmarket totty living close by. A couple would in all likelihood have a significantly greater chance of escaping notice than a lone male or a nubile young female on her own.

He drove on gradually getting closer to his once very upmarket address in Bleibtreustrasse and totally ignoring the hanging bodies that had been strung up at every available lamp-post. Death squads, commanded by bloodthirsty junior officers and NCOs from the quite recently formed Order Police, scoured the ripped and torn streets of the capital in search of victims. Anyone caught doing anything at all that might be regarded as a misdemeanour, no matter how trivial, was summarily shot and stacked up against any available wall. Being hung from a lamp-post was now becoming something of a rarity, as pretty well all Berlin's lamp-posts were either flattened or already occupied with grotesquely dangling showpiece corpses.

Hermann congratulated himself on being able to get away from that underground madhouse. He had money, papers and a route out of Berlin. What poor Hermann Fegelein did not know was that he was clean out of time. Even as he drew up outside his apartment with its boarded windows, fate conspired against him.

For days now he had loitered around the upper regions of the bunker with nothing to do. As Himmler's liaison office to the Führer, his position had become more or less irrelevant as the Reichsführer fell out of favour and was seen and heard from less and less. Fegelein, though still present, became largely forgotten and ignored. He had nothing to do. That state of affairs, however, was about to change. Reports were at that very moment reaching eager ears in the bunker of Reichsführer Heinrich Himmler's treachery. He had been discovered negotiating with the allies, or trying to. He had put out peace feelers and the BBC had mentioned his activities over their foreign news service.

As he trotted up the war-scarred steps to his front door there was emitted from the bowels of the Führer bunker just a few kilometres away a feral howl: "Where is Fegelein? Fetch me Fegelein!" Poor Hermann had no idea of the storm that was about to be unleashed upon his unwary head.

Eva moved disconsolately down to the lower bunker, the Führer bunker; the holy of holies, the inner sanctum, the foul-smelling hell-hole where they were cooped up like unwashed peasants and mine workers. Awful! Had she been right in refusing Hermann's offer of escape? She was now doubting her wisdom in ever coming down here. It had seemed like such a good idea at the time. Join Adolf, her Führer, her master, in his hour of need. Do all the ever-so-loyal cooing that he liked so much and state loudly that she was here to share *all* the current trials and tribulations with her adored Führer, the greatest man ever to lead the German Reich. Stress, of course, should have been placed upon the word, 'current'. It had never occurred to her that this might be a permanent state of affairs; the end. It could not possibly be so. She knew that things were bad, of course she did. She had come from relatively untouched Berchtesgaden to the pure unadulterated horror of what was left of Berlin. There had been no rationing or shortages of any description at Berchtesgaden, Adolf had seen to that. Sometimes she would sit out on the terrace and gaze up at lots and lots of aircraft, American probably, as they flew on their lazy, quite prettily contrailed way toward various siren wailing targets.

So unfair of them, she had reflected, as the aircraft passed many thousands of feet overhead, to drop bombs on innocent and defenceless people. Where was the justice in that? As for Berlin; beyond belief! How could all this have happened? Of course, she wasn't silly. She knew that things could go a little wrong, not quite to plan and such-like, in a war as big as this one. But Adolf had always been so reassuring with her, with all of them. 'Don't worry. All will be well,' and so on. And despite the grim looks on faces around her as time wore on, she chose always to believe him. It was so much easier that way. After all, as she would tell the staff and anyone else who might listen, *He* was the Führer and *He* knew best. Of course he did. All those cowardly sillies and their moans full of whining self-pity. She had given a good scolding to more than one over the past few months. But now? Well! She hadn't thought for one minute that they would remain down here in this underground hovel for any great length of time; a temporary expedient, a stop-gap, until one of Adolf's massive counter blows or new secret weapons struck terror and defeat into the enemy. Somehow her mind had created a gigantic movie set within her egocentric imagination and had cast her as the glowing, ever courageous heroine.

"Oh, God!" Her hand flew, knuckles first, to her mouth as a huge bomb, shell or something highly explosive shook the thick vorbunker ceiling; it was quickly followed by another and then another. In swift succession a whole series of the terrifying things crashed into the ground directly overhead, loosening plaster and masonry and bringing down a cloud of lung-choking dust and dirt.

Eva reeled back against the bunker wall. She wasn't made for this. This was not a movie. It was terrifying and horrible and she was not too sure how much longer she could keep up the pretence of being the loving and loyal little woman to that sad old man downstairs in his Führer quarters. It had never been any kind of love match but Eva just so adored being a potentate's favoured woman. But even she, with all her talent for self-delusion, now had to face the fact that her Führer, Adolf Hitler, the king of kings, as once was, so to speak, was a down and out loser – big time! Men! Damn the conceited, lying fools all to hell. Why couldn't she have found one with a nice job and lots of money? That's all she had ever wanted, she thought tearfully. To be looked after and cared for. "It's not bloody fair," she whimpered as tears began coursing down her still quite plump cheeks. She made a half-hearted attempt to wipe tears and dust away from her face. "I won't stay down here," she hissed almost to herself. "I damn well won't."

"Fraulein Braun. Are you alright? Have you been hurt?"

Von Loringhoven reached out a helpful hand which Eva was sorely tempted to swipe away. Snobbish, landed gentry git. She knew that Major von Loringhoven did not think too highly of her, and she fully reciprocated that feeling.

"Thank you, major. So kind." Oh Hell! Eva felt depression seeping into her brain. Here we go with the pretence….again!

"The Führer wants to see you, Fraulein. At once, if you don't mind."

As if it ever mattered what I minded, she thought. But smiled through the caking dust as she accepted his helping hand down the remaining steps to the Führer bunker.

"How could I possibly mind, major? But I really should tidy myself up a little after my recent dust bath, don't you think." She attempted a gay, full lipped and shiny toothed smile which didn't fool von Loringhoven for a moment. But at this stage of affairs, Freitag von Loringhoven didn't much care about anything; certainly not Eva Braun, anyway.

"As you say, Fraulein." He returned her smile with an equal lack of warmth. "Unfortunately the generator has ceased to function, again. There is still some clean water in the Anteroom latrine. I shall have some brought to your quarters."

"So very kind," Eva simpered as she moved to pass by him.

Von Loringhoven gave a tiny bow from the waist. Her feeble effort to mask her working-class Bavarian accent had always rankled. Ghastly! She might just as well have said, "Ta ever-so."

Eva made her way toward her quarters at the deep far end of the bunker.

"Oh. By the way, Fraulein Braun," von Loringhoven called after her. "You wouldn't happen to know the whereabouts of General Fegelein, would you."

Eva gulped hard and turned briefly. "Good heavens, no, major." She waved a now somewhat grimy hand. "Officers come and go all the time. I barely notice anyone anymore." Had Adolf noted Hermann's absence already? That spelt trouble for the bolt-hole seeking Hermann and Eva wanted none of it. She did wonder though, how far he might get.

"Any particular reason?" The moment that the question was out of her mouth she knew that she shouldn't have asked. Why should she, Eva Braun, care where her brother-in-law may or may not be?

Von Loringhoven stared at her for a few seconds with his wide, innocent seeming baby blue eyes. "Something about the Reichsführer, Fraulein. That's all I know. The boss is mightily upset, though." With that he left her and continued his search.

I need someone, thought Eva. I can't do this alone but I need someone to help me. She bit hard on her lower lip as she forced herself to move deeper into the dank half-lit recesses of the bunker. She wasn't at all sure how much longer she could go on with this charade before cracking up completely.

CHAPTER 13

August 13 1932: Berlin, Presidential Palace.

Rohm, former army captain and Brown Shirt bully boy, stood with clenched fists, his duel scarred face a frozen mask of concealed hatred. Beside him stood his friend, the man to whom he had pledged himself, his ability, his loyalty and his undying friendship. That man, to whom he had entrusted his fate, looked about ready to grovel before the seated, giant figure of the six-feet-five-inch president of the shambolic Weimar Republic. Paul von Hindenburg sat behind a massive oaken desk and in front of that desk, also seated and facing them lounged the insufferable Reich Chancellor, Franz von Papen. All these snobbish and unbearably supercilious 'Vons' had Ernst Rohm ready to spit. At least he and Adolf shared a similar lower middle-class background. Hitler's father had been a minor customs official and Rohm's a railway ticket inspector. Both had been stern, uniformed men used to being obeyed.

Paul von Hindenburg, the president, and his chancellor, Franz von Papen, were both of the landed gentry Junker class. Born to rule, entitled to riches and comfort. They oozed culture, charm and refinement. Their very aura of superiority and breeding had men like Rohm and Hitler almost trembling in awe. Centuries of subservience had instilled an almost pathological hatred of such proud and mightily lineaged men. Hitler kept his eyes downcast, as was appropriate for a man of his class when confronted by such august greatness as that which now sat solidly before him. Rohm, however, had had more than enough of these entitled boobies and their airs and graces. To hell with them!

"As I am sure Herr Hitler understands," von Papen droned mellifluously, "all and any agreements reached here in this office are dependent upon Herr Hitler imposing stricter," he paused here and glanced at the hulking figure of Hindenburg, "might I say *far* stricter controls and limitations over the actions of his, that is, his Party's supporters,"

President Hindenburg nodded heavily in agreement. "Must exert greater control, Herr Hitler. All this street violence. Won't do you know; just won't do. Get a grip on it man." The hugely heavy jowls of the eighty-four-year-old president of the Weimar Republic shook alarmingly. The old man was ill, overweight and sick to death of running a country that was voluntarily rushing to hell in a burning handcart. Vicious, animalistic brutes seemed to be springing constantly from the far right and the far left of the political spectrum, all eager to devour anyone standing in the middle. The old and ailing president truly cared for his people but could feel only despair as he watched them being exploited by malignant forces too clever and too strong for them to resist. What in heaven's name had happened to his once staid and law-abiding countrymen? Driven to rampant hatred by the stupid unfairness of the Versailles treaty? Yes, that was part of it. But the pogrom of orchestrated violence in which so many took delight, baffled his senses and left him feeling deeply dispirited. Only the ghastly little man standing so respectfully in front of him seemed able to exert any kind of control over the savage and unending spiral of street violence that pervaded the streets of every German town and city. It had to stop! He gazed hard at the Nazi Party leader. The fellow didn't have a seat in the Reichstag himself, yet he led the powerfully supported Nazi Party and its Reichstag deputies with absolute and single-minded authority.

That in itself, that kind of unyielding discipline was frightening for it meant that it was all, every thought and action, under a single and utterly dominant entity.

Herr Hitler worked under the guise of democracy and care for the people but as far as Hindenburg could see, there wasn't a caring bone in the Austrian's body. However, that ruthlessness, control and single mindedness were precisely what were needed just now. Order had to be restored and the nation set on an even keel. Enough of this constant stream of elections and street brutality by both left and right. Hitler was demanding the chancellorship for his support; not a hope in hell! Not whilst there was breath in the well-bred bodies of the upper class, and certainly not whilst Paul von Hindenburg was alive. Something, though; he had to offer the man something.

Hindenburg's massive body moved uncomfortably within the confines of his high-sided chair and his mind wandered slightly to other things; he knew that he really should think about losing some weight. Chairs, uniforms, walking, all of it was becoming more and more difficult these days. He laid a bear like hand on top of his desk. He mustn't antagonize this Hitler fellow too much. Dislike him as he may, look down on him as he most certainly did, and not only by virtue of his great height, he now had to face the reality that Herr Hitler controlled more than two hundred Reichstag deputies and many thousands of uniformed SA men who roamed the streets of every town and village in Germany. This man, this former corporal, now led the largest single Party in the Reichstag and although not able to gain an outright majority, they could block completely any and all government legislation if they chose; and that is precisely what Herr Hitler was threatening to do. He could, if he so wished, bring government to a halt.

Von Hindenburg felt his normally quite feeble pulse quicken and flutter alarmingly. He liked to be thought of as a good man, a caring leader devoted to his people, but having to tolerate being faced down politically by a man of Hitler's background was really, just too much.

The fellow was, with all said and done, little more than an ill-educated peasant; and an Austrian to boot! Here, in this very office, he behaved in a manner out of all proportion to his natural status and ability. Ability? He sighed so loudly that even von Papen's eyebrows raised questioningly.

Hindenburg shook his huge head. What ability did this Hitler fellow have? Precious little as far as the president could see. He had read and re-read the many lengthy reports on Adolf Hitler, his huge outdoor rallies and so on. And at not one meeting, rally or interview had he espoused so much as a single civilised or original political thought. Bread, pensions and social security for the workers? Yes – fine. But it was a heartless con. Nothing more than a pro tem piece of verbal chicanery spouted out to gull the masses. And who would have to pay for it all? Why – the masses themselves of course and right through their collective nose. Then there was the Nazi leader's favourite topic; Lebensraum – take more living space by moving east. The German people needed and deserved more living space, he said, and the Nazi Party, would ensure that they got it: fine. Was his assumption then, that the inhabitants of those coveted regions might simply just up and leave, happily wandering off into the sunset, and by so doing obligingly make way for the space-seeking Germans? An unlikely scenario even for a fantasist such as Hitler and his geopolitical expert Karl Haushofer. And in any case who in God's name was going to fight and die, not to mention pay and supply the necessary weaponry, for such a lunatic venture? The Nazis conveniently omitted to mention that millions of people lived in the areas earmarked for the supposedly 'eager to move' Germans. Paul von Hindenburg knew his people better than Herr Hitler, it would seem. There was no way that they would willingly move to the arid plains of the Ukraine or the disease riddled, weed clogged lakes of the Pripet.

And, of course, there was the constant Nazi refrain, the galvanizer, the vote winner: destroy Jewry and the Jews before *they* destroy Germany. What total codswallop! The man was a dangerous bohemian chancer who had a knack of telling people what they wanted to hear, what *he* wanted them to hear and making them believe it. Nevertheless, a common-as-muck chancer he may very well be, but circumstance dictated that he be dealt with in as cordial a fashion as was possible.

One of Hindenburg's problems right now, apart from his always painfully nagging gout, searing dyspepsia and chronic constipation, was his Chancellor, von Papen. Whereas Hindenburg nurtured a deep-seated albeit patronizing affection for the peasantry and working classes of Germany, von Papen nurtured only contempt mingled with ill-concealed disgust whenever close to them. Seen and never heard, was his motto. They should be grateful if they had a roof over their heads and a doctor to look after their many ills and scabrous, overbred families. They were there to serve their betters, nothing more! All this trades union nonsense needed to be nipped in the bud and cut clean away from the body politic. Workers with a say over their own lives was not something that Franz von Papen countenanced. And that, of course, as far as von Papen was concerned, was where the fiery, violence loving Austrian came in. Herr Hitler had already, in private, promised to eliminate the Unions; not something that the working classes were in any way aware of, at the moment. What a hoot it would be, the chancellor thought, when they found out! Oh, what a day that would be. In the meantime, though, he and the president must somehow get this loud-mouthed lout on board and obedient to their will.

Eyes deliberately downcast and hands wringing like a broken suppliant, Hitler cast a surreptitious glance at his companion. He could sense his SA commander's anger and hostility toward their surroundings. Ernst was too volatile for this situation but the president himself had expressed a desire to have the ferocious little former army captain present. Adolf realised that Hindenburg was well aware of who led the men on the streets and wanted him here so that he could listen to and take in the president's warnings about the continuing street violence. 'Stop! Or the army would intervene.'

Adolf smiled in his most convincingly servile manner as he nodded agreement with the elder statesman. Army brought in? He might say so, the old president, but it would not be so. Adolf had already ensured that enough of the army top brass were sitting comfortably in his pocket. Indeed, a few of its leading officers had voiced open approval of Adolf and his Party's aims. As usual, though, threats and blackmail along with sincerely delivered promises for the future expansion of the Wehrmacht had brought forth many more of the required promises of loyalty and support. As long as they had lots of tanks and guns to look forward to playing with the army and its leaders would be easily led. The military mind, as far as Adolf was concerned, was simplistic and basically very childish. Feed them, clothe them, tell them where to go and presto, they were happy. Keep them in bratwurst, bullets and promises and that should be quite sufficient. Not forgetting, of course, to occasionally stroke their military ego with batons and high-sounding titles. All so easily done – if one had the vested power.

The time for his next great move was almost upon him. He rolled slightly on the balls of his feet, rather like a stationary policeman.

Adolf could barely believe what had happened nor quite understand his remarkable good luck. How had all this come about? What had once been nothing much more than a violent, almost thoughtless way of covering his own academic and emotional deficiencies, had become his passport to notoriety and election success. The crippling insecurities and rages which he had feared would hold him back, had in fact propelled him forward into the limelight and his bid for power. He could now control his rages and his vindictiveness and used them to enhance his acting performances on the speaker's rostrum at his many indoor and outdoor rallies. Those rallies attracted thousands of hysterically adoring supporters. His political statements, and here he almost laughed out loud because his political statements, invariably plagiarized, were acclaimed by many as the thoughts of a genius. Just how stupid could people be? In a collective mass, very, as it turned out.

His thoughts, pronouncements more like, were invariably Wagnerian dream-world foolishness! Lots of shouting and yelling and verbal provocation, over all of which, he had come to realize, he was a natural master.

Chaos reigned across Germany's entire political spectrum, and chaos was the creator of opportunity. Chaos was to be encouraged, not denied, for within its cold heart lay the seeds of random good fortune. Men such as he could never prosper and thrive in a calm, peaceful society. Chaos and mayhem needed to be denied to the exclusive well-bred circles of society and instead be distributed unevenly amongst the poor, the miserable and the dispossessed. Thus might a man like he, Adolf Hitler, gather the reins of all those singular rivalries and turn them into one, single destructive force. That is what he had done and he was pleased with the results thus far. Turning the unacceptable, or rather making it *appear* that he had turned the unacceptable, into a fundamentally decent and proper way of behaving because it was for the good of the state.

Adolf knew very well what they truly thought of him, these high and mighty types. The group of business folk and industrialists who thought that they would control and dominate him when he came to power: Really? And these mental hunchbacks who called themselves politicians. Did they truly believe that he hadn't seen right through their clumsy little schemes? Morons! Nobody and no system was ever going to control him. Ever!

Chaos was reigning again but this time it had a firm-handed conductor giving it direction. So, of course, it wasn't chaos at all. It was merely Adolf Hitler having his way.

Rohm's breathing was harsh and obvious to all present. Once again Adolf mused upon just how much longer he might feel inclined to tolerate his erstwhile friend and collaborator. The friendship, at least for Adolf, had ended months ago. Ernst saw things differently and remained loyal but far too outspoken for Adolf's liking. His collaboration, though, was still necessary. More than ten thousand SA men were a potent force and Adolf needed to tread carefully to avoid antagonizing them. Their time would come – but not quite yet.

"The position, Herr Hitler, as I am sure you will agree, is one commensurate with your," Von Papen waved a condescending hand, his smirk of superiority clear even beneath the covering of his huge moustache, "shall we say, lack of experience in other fields."

Hindenburg frowned deeply. Did his chancellor have no common sense at all? He was deliberately antagonising a man who took precious little to antagonise at the best of times, and this was damn well NOT the best of times. Wretched fool! Von Papen had insisted that they offer Herr Hitler the post of Minister without Portfolio; essentially a non-position where he could do little harm. If he refused, then, they might go a little higher and throw him transport; but no more than that. Von Papen relied heavily upon overawing the peasant-like Hitler and assumed that the oaf would be over-the-moon with the offer of any ministry at all. After all, men of his type couldn't realistically expect to reach the highest office. That would be just too silly. The trouble was, though, that Franz von Papen seemed hell-bent on insulting the handwringing Adolf Hitler at every possible turn.

"Well, then." Von Papen smiled sardonically at the Nazi party leader. God, how he loathed this creature. Foul smelling, working class and with eyes like a caged badger with myosis. "What do you say, eh? Not a bad offer, bearing in mind that your citizenship is Austrian." He waved a beautifully manicured hand as if revealing some unpalatable news and glanced smugly back at the president. He pointed a long finger at Hitler. "Austrian," he repeated with a snigger.

Von Hindenburg sat expressionless, trying to quell the rising anger within him at his chancellor's gross incompetence.

Hitler's hands untwined and his servile demeanour vanished quicker than thought. Ignoring von Papen as though he were less than a speck of dust, he stared Hindenburg straight in the eye.

"As you must surely know, excellency, and as *you* surely should," he threw a witheringly contemptuous glance at von Papen. "I fought against Germany's enemies, for four long years. I was wounded twice whilst carrying out my duties for the fatherland. Also, just so that you know, Herr Chancellor," Adolf's tone could have cut through a dozen slabs of frozen meat, "I have been a citizen of the Reich since before last February. More than thirteen million people voted for me and my Party." His gaze was full on Hindenburg, those eyes so abalze that the even the all-powerful Reich President found it hard not to swallow. "Therefore, your excellency, I refuse your," he paused so that both Hindenburg and von Papen might clearly note his contempt, "so *generous* offer. I demand the position of chancellor. The trust and faith of the voters deserve no less. Make me chancellor and I shall see that government works properly, as it should do. Refuse it and, well...." He left the rest, the threat, unsaid but it hung in the air like an anvil waiting to drop on their toes.

"Hauptman Rohm." Adolf gestured to his colleague as, without waiting for formal dismissal, he turned his back on the president and chancellor. "We are leaving." Ernst Rohm grinned like a toothy hyena. This was the Adolf that he knew and adored. He'd just stuffed it right to them!

"But Herr Hitler, please." The now panicking von Papen called after them. "Let's negotiate. Surely we can come to some arrangement, an agreement acceptable to all?"

Just as he reached the door Adolf swung back to face the president again and, still ignoring the flustered chancellor, he said loudly, "You know my terms. Chancellor or nothing. Non-agreement will mean every political road blocked. I promise you, your excellency, all government activities will grind to a halt. Give me what I ask," he was careful not say demand, although demand it most certainly was, "and I shall not let you down. I would die first." With that, he directed a short bow from the waist to the president and departed the Palace.

Gesche threw out his right arm in a smart Nazi salute and then pulled open the door of Hitler's huge Mercedes. Both men, Rohm first, climbed into the back and sank heavily into the thick leather upholstery. The indispensable Bruno Gesche gave a slight click of his heels and looked the question at his poker-faced boss. Adolf nodded. "All went well, Gesche. Better than expected." He gestured briefly with a light wrist flick, "Frau Benner's, I think. Time for a little relaxation before we pay Goebbels a visit." Gesche nodded and eased in behind the wheel. Several passers-by on the Wilhelm Strasse bent over to peer inside as Gesche started up the powerful motor and engaged the gears. The general public in this area was well used to seeing important political figures on a daily basis. This was after all the government quarter. But Adolf Hitler was already more than just any boring, staid old politician. He was young, dynamic. Adolf Hitler was a star! His picture was everywhere, and unlike the president and other big-wigs, Herr Hitler could be seen in movie theatres and giving speeches in theatre halls and such like. Oh yes, Adolf was one hell of a character.

"Führer, Führer, Führer," came the cry from outside the car as it pulled away. Adolf waved and smiled. "We should have had the hood down," he murmured as he smiled at a pert young woman who wanted nothing more than to climb into the car and be with her hero.

"Too much more of your cake eating, Adolf," Rohm playfully tickled Adolf's burgeoning little paunch, "and those pretty young things won't be looking at you in the same way." Rohm laughed raucously. "Dear me no, my old friend. Not in the same way at all."

Adolf stopped the deep frown from occurring in the nick of time. Ernst was looking at him all friendship and bonhomie and pretending to be completely unaware of the offence he had just caused. He was just Ernst being Ernst, and that meant being a domineering Alfa male son-of-a-bitch and refusing to toe any kind of line. Personnel movements and staff replacement rattled briefly through Adolf's brain.

"Ernst," Adolf spoke firmly but politely. "Once again I must ask you to refrain from addressing me in the familiar. It is Führer, Ernst. At all times!"

"Of course it is," Rohm patted Adolf's thigh in a proprietary fashion. "Of course it is."

Adolf, aware of Bruno Gesche's tight-lipped grimace of disapproval from the driver's seat, curtly swung his head away from his SA leader. He had more important things to mull over at the moment. That drooling young woman had brought home to him that he must concentrate more heavily on the female vote. In the end, it would all depend upon them. They had dragged up pretty well the very last of the male votes. There might be some dregs but the women were the important target now. Without them, Adolf knew, he and the Nazi Party would fail at the polls. He had little doubt that Hindenburg would ditch von Papen and agree to his, Hitler's, demands. If he didn't? Well, they would simply bring all government business to a standstill. He had the majority of deputies in the Reichstag and therefore he could veto any damn thing that he pleased...and he would!

Chocolate cake, topped with cream, a lot of cream, sat invitingly on a beautifully inlaid Bareuther tea plate. Adolf slowly pushed the multi-trayed cake tower away, just a little, and observed Rohm as he clumsily slapped an apricot and apple pastry and a mouth-watering slice of Posen gateaux drenched in cherry cream and melted caramel, each pressing into the other on his rapidly overfilling plate. Rohm was, in fact, on his best behaviour bearing in mind the company and the venue. A lot of movie and theatre folk popped into Benner's exclusive patisserie to sample the delicacies. There was the usual neck craning as the effusive little Hungarian waiter had shown them to the corner table where they could view, if they wished, the comings and goings of Frau Benner's.

"You think that the old man will give in?" Rohm asked, still deliberately refraining from using the term Führer.

"Over this chancellor business? Of course. He might try and throw Kurt Schleicher a bone as a delaying measure, though."

"Schleicher? He might be dangerous. Nobody's fool, that one."

"Schleicher's problem is the same problem that they all have," was Adolf's rejoinder.

"Which is?" Rohm sat back, cake crumbs tumbling in splendid disarray down over his shirt and jacket front. He didn't give a damn. His chubby, unpleasant face bore an arched expression as he gazed at his companion.

"Me, Ernst. They underestimate and misjudge me. Just as," he glanced at Rohm and returned his arched expression, "so many others blindly insist upon doing."

Rohm nodded and fiddled with his cakes, somehow conjoining the lot and making an inordinately ghastly mess on his small, ornately inlaid tea plate. He knew that these days he trod a very fine line with his friend, Adolf Hitler. But he could not for the life of him cast himself in the role of the grovelling inferior to this man. Their shared history forbade that. It was his pride, his ego, he knew, that might eventually bring him down. He must, if he were to survive, not just politically but *survive* in any way at all, be prepared to subordinate himself to this man beside him. Body and soul. No half measures with Herr Hitler; Herr bloody Führer? Damn cheek!

"Do you think, that," Rohm spoke softly, trying to sound deferential "we might be pushing the populace too hard with all these elections? They are sick of it."

"I know." Adolf smiled. "And therein lies the secret, Ernst."

"How so?" Rohm allowed himself to look slightly bewildered; although, in fact, he was precisely that.

"Once I have taken the chancellorship I shall, by virtue of, shall we say, governmental unrest, challenge for the presidency and force a national presidential election."

"You can't be serious!" Rohm's arms flew up over his bullet-shaped head. "You are already challenging for the presidency and, might I say with respect, losing right royally. The people love old Hindenburg so president he will stay."

"For now, yes." Adolf smiled.

Rohm shook his head. Adolf was not a patient man. When he said for now, he meant literally, right now – immediately!

"You are quite right. The public is sick to death of all these elections and there is no way that I, or anybody else can topple that old bonehead from the presidency. So," he raised a restraining hand as Rohm made to interrupt, "Once this election is over and, let's say, we have surreptitiously encouraged civil unrest to reach a new peak of awfulness, along with the appropriate amount of public despair, we call another. The people will see only too clearly that the NSDAP alone can bring a return of peace and prosperity. Mark my words, they will vote for me in droves….or rue the day!" His meaning was clear enough. Adolf wanted to do things legally but his patience was limited.

Rohm scratched at his fleshy thigh. "The polls again – after all the nation has been through?" He looked doubtful. Referring to Hindenburg, he said, "You know, the old boy is sick and frail. Even the thought of another presidential campaign will probably bring on a stroke. His constitution is shot all to hell. No pun intended." Rohm roared with laughter at his own witticism. "Anyway, it was only under the severest pressure from that imbecile Bruning that he's running at all. The aristocrats are scared witless 'cos there's no one else who can stand against you and hope to win."

"Precisely," Adolf had a wolfish grin. "His heart is erratic and barely beating and his arteries are so severely clogged that he survives on mush mixed with boiled water. He is nothing more than a corpse looking for its coffin. Every time he awakes from a nap is a surprise for that old man."

Rohm almost slammed his hand on the table as full comprehension of Adolf's plan dawned.

"So, Hindenburg presumably turns up those gnarled old toes, which…?

"Which leaves me as chancellor and the man in charge of everything."

"And then?"

"Then, my dear Ernst, I shall take what I want and abolish the office of the president...."

"You'll what?" Rohm almost choked.

"Abolish that office for good."

"And replace it with what for crying out loud – with what?"

"A new office and a new concept. I, Ernst, I shall be Chancellor *and* Führer. Don't waste your time with doubt, my friend." Adolf threw Rohm a condescending smile. "Such a thing may well be impossible for others to even envisage, let alone accomplish. But I shall *make* it possible. The Führerprinzip is the only way to save the Reich. Once that is accomplished we can throw out all the current democratic garbage – for good!"

Ernst Rohm found himself sweating. Excitement – fear? It was hard to say. "But look here," he expostulated rather more loudly than intended. "You're talking a coup de main and if I remember correctly, the last time you tried that things didn't exactly work out! Seriously, Adolf," he pulled himself up short as he noticed the expression of anger and exasperation cross Adolf's face.

Adolf's right hand raised just a little above the tablecloth as he leaned ever so slightly forward, toward Rohm.

"Keep your voice down, Hauptman Rohm and you will use the term Führer when addressing me. Clear? Got it? For the last time Ernst. Say it, say it now and damn well mean it!" The tone was low, almost a hiss but Rohm felt as though his eardrums had been assaulted by an orchestra's percussion section.

Sweat flowed freely now. He was twice the man that this so-called friend of his thought himself to be, yet it was this friend that held every card and every option. How the hell had it happened? The reversal of their fortunes was complete. Fearless Ernst Rohm, the man who feared nothing and nobody, was trapped and had no choice but to give in, toe the line, obey. Bastard! No choice, though. None at all with this manic dreamer sitting in front of him. Manic, but going places, that was for sure. He breathed in deeply and could feel the well of Hitler's patience finally reaching its shallow end. Placing both hands on his thighs, he leaned back into the comfortably upholstered seat, puffed out his substantial chest and said, in a calm and almost matter-of-fact manner, "Yes my Führer. It shall be as you say." He gave a respectful half nod which made his double chin wobble slightly and at the same time threw in a seated half bow, "My Führer!" He immodestly finished these gestures of obedience and respect with a loud belch. "So sorry, Führer. All this rich food, you know. A bit too much, perhaps." It wasn't a victory, nor even close to one, but it was, at least, something.

Adolf smiled. It mattered not a jot that Ernst didn't mean a word of what he had just said. The SA leader had said it, 'Führer', and that was all that was important. Not long now and the mighty Ernst Rohm would be begging for scraps.... or dead!

Adolf looked contentedly around the patisserie. It was done.

"Time to go, Ernst." There was no bill to pay. The Benner family were staunch National Socialists and were only too pleased to entertain Herr Hitler whenever he wished. The little Hungarian waiter did a roaring trade in souvenirs; a napkin that Hitler had used; a spoon, a fork, etc. He made sure that the Nazi leader knew nothing of his little side-line, though. Doubtless Herr Hitler would be monumentally enraged should he discover that his name, indeed the very items that he had touched, were being taken in vain and sold on to the hoy-polloi. Best keep it to himself. Poor fool. As if such a thing could be kept secret for long, let alone indefinitely. Two weeks later the transplanted Hungarian was jobless and on his way back to Budapest.

Easing back into his seat, Rohm, trying very hard not to show how rattled he was by his leader's plans, asked the question.

"How, precisely, do you intend to provoke a situation that can ensure that you become president *and* chancellor at one and the same time?"

"With your help, Ernst, of course. You, my friend, will order the SA out onto the streets for one last, almighty heave."

"Of violence?"

Adolf waved an airy hand that could have signified anything and any meaning. He knew well enough which way Ernst Rohm would take it.

"Nothing in writing, of course," Ernst smirked.

"Don't be so obtuse, Ernst, not even jokingly. Clear?"

Rohm pursed his lips. They had come a long way since 1920. Adolf was barely the same man; or rather, he was the same man but wearing a much more expensive coat. Not quite bulletproof yet, my little colleague, mused Rohm. Not by a long shot. He still needed Ernst Rohm and his SA protection.

"So, then?" Rohm's look was questioning and he clearly needed an answer.

"Think about it, Ernst. Riots on the streets, violence on every corner and the police not able to cope," he gave Rohm a knowing nod, "You can picture all that, Ernst, I'm quite sure. Not only picture it but, shall we say for the sake of argument, that you might enjoy painting on that particular canvas."

Rohm grinned hugely. He was getting the bigger picture and it was quite brilliant. "And you, our Führer, will of course see to it that the Reichstag is hamstrung and, like a constipated hog, passes nothing but wind; thus ensuring that, to all intents and purposes, Germany is rushing to her doom and can be saved only by …."

"Precisely, Ernst. Me!"

"But the enactment of laws and so on. How on earth do you intend to…"

"Think, Ernst – Think!"

For a moment Rohm was stumped. What kind of government machinery could enable Adolf to take complete control of everything whilst still keeping up the outward appearance of legality? The answer was there and it came like an epiphany.

"An enabling act? Surely not even you would dare?"

"And who do you suppose will stop me, eh – or even attempt to do so? With the Reichstag full of spineless, weak-kneed cretins begging for guidance, the nation demanding the restoration of law and order; who will they turn to? Yes, my friend, the short answer is *me*, along with an Enabling Act which will allow me free rein to do as I deem fit and necessary." His face was flushed with triumph at his own brilliance. "Well," he added. "And the party, too. Of course, the Party before all, eh Ernst?" Rohm sat upright "Oh yes, Germany and the Party before all; always and forever."

Adolf nodded in agreement but Rohm could sense insincerity. Not for the first time he felt a nagging doubt about Adolf's motives and true aims. People were afraid of Ernst Rohm and few men in high places trusted him. He did, however, have one redeeming grace, and that was his utter loyalty to any cause he embraced as long as that cause put Germany and the Nation's rise and well-being before anything else – even family. Ernst Rohm was loyal to Germany, to the death. He was not so sure about his Austrian friend. Adolf had always been a strange one. A firebrand of a speaker that could rouse people to staggering heights of nationalistic fervour; he could whip even normally staid and sensible men into a murderous frenzy with that voice of his. In the early days, when the young Hitler had been grateful for any kind of job, he had been easy to control, malleable and eager to please. Ernst and his cronies, like so many others, had figured that he was little more than an easily controllable puppet. That misconception had been kicked into the stratosphere quite a while ago. Rohm hadn't worried too much. He liked Adolf and found that their ideas were similar. Now, though, he realised that it was he who had been used, not the other way around. How and when it had happened, when the roles had been reversed, he couldn't say. But there it was. Problem being, he no longer had any idea of what Adolf Hitler was about; what he believed in and what he intended. Had the man truly fooled everybody? Did he have any idea himself what the bloody hell he was going to do once he attained the total domination that he sought?

Rohm cast a quick look at the man he wanted still to regard as his friend. Could this *Führer* of his do anything, get anywhere without him, without Ernst Rohm? Damn right he couldn't and pretty soon now Ernst was going to put him straight on a few things. But not yet. 'I'll keep an eye on him,' mused the SA leader. But right now the future was looking full of possibilities and Ernst Rohm was not going to go rocking this particular boat. Later, perhaps, if the need arose.

CHAPTER 14

April 28 1945: Berlin, The Bunker

Down in the depths of military hell a dictators shriek of anguish yet again rent the stale, odour filled air. Tears flowed down drawn and withered cheeks as dirty fingernails tore at unkempt hair. Out and into the crowded corridors of the Führer Bunker roamed the demented, foot-dragging leader of the Third Reich as he, and not for the first time, howled about his misfortune, the treachery and ingratitude of others.

Major von Loringhoven, trying desperately to remain calm and continue with his façade of perpetual sangfroid, took the forty steps that were necessary for his longish legs to reach Goebbels office with the speed and grace of an Adlon sommelier. He struck the closed door just once, and heavily, with the central knuckle of his right hand and immediately cursed as pain shot from hand to wrist. All these lower Bunker doors were heavily made and the Propaganda Minister's was iron covered.

"Come in." The voice that called to Loringhoven sounded tired and uninterested. Not at all like the always optimistic Joseph Goebbels. Von Loringhoven eased the door open and slid inside the small office.

"What is it major." Von Loringhoven couldn't help but be struck by Goebbels's wan and utterly 'pissed off with it all' countenance. His mood seemed to have sunk even further since the arrival of his wife and children. All six children, five girls and one boy spent much of their time playing in the upper Bunker and being spoiled by the secretaries and uniformed clerks. Their happy shrieks as they played could even be heard down here in the depths. Loringhoven was puzzled as to why the Goebbels' would want their kids to be in such a place at such a time but it wasn't his business to question the wishes of his superiors. Magda Goebbels was, if anything, even more devoted to the Führer than her husband. Von Loringhoven could not see the attraction but, for whatever reason, Frau Goebbels revered her Führer. Doubtless they had made plans to get the kids out but they sure as hell were leaving it late. A difficult situation for them, as Joseph Goebbels couldn't leave whilst Hitler was still alive – none of them could!

"It's the Führer, Minister. He's badly upset." The sounds of Hitler's raving came clearly through the still slightly open office door. "He's calling for you, sir."

"Yes," Goebbels tapped the folder on the desk where he sat. "But why – by that I mean, what is wrong? What all-consuming disaster must we face now, eh?" Goebbels threw his arms out wide in a splendidly dramatic manner, "What the hell else is left to go wrong?" He stamped his clubbed foot hard on the concrete floor. "Germany is in ruins, our armies destroyed, we endure the odium and await the revenge of the entire world; we are, to all intents and purposes right royally stuffed, major. Wouldn't you agree? Utterly and irrevocably wrecked, disgraced, defeated. So, major, do please tell me," He favoured the shaken von Loringhoven with a ghastly doom-laden smile, "Just what is it that ails the Führer at this precise time? A splitting headache, cream gone off, another army disappeared from his little war board?"

Von Loringhoven's mouth hung open just fractionally and only for the briefest instant. Never, but never had he heard Goebbels, or any other member of the leadership, speak in such a way.

"Ah," he said, almost conspiratorially and giving an ever so slight rein to his sense of humour, "but minister. Surely we must never forget the genius of the Führer nor the wonderful weapons that he intends to launch at *any* given moment."

"Oh, for God's sake shut up! Seriously, major, you believe all that guff?"

Von Loringhoven gave an elegant shrug and decided to be all seriousness. "Now that you mention it, sir, does seem a tad far-fetched."

"Just a tad?" Goebbels almost choked on a running saliva bubble of high-pitched laughter. "Well," Goebbels manfully forced himself into serious mode, "perhaps you're right, major. But you know, my young friend......." he was almost whispering

"Yes sir," Loringhoven was all ears.

"You might want to stop trying to sound like those SS clowns." Once again that odd giggle threatened to take over the diminutive Propaganda minister. "Not likely," he waved a warning finger, "to be in vogue for very much longer. Already wearing more than a little thin, I'd say."

Von Loringhoven decided not to join Goebbels in his slightly hysterical jocularity. Danger lurked in those dark corners. One never knew when these formerly fanatical types might revert to the all-grovelling sycophants of a few weeks, days in some cases, earlier.

"Speaking of the SS, minister. That is why the Führer is calling for you."

The door suddenly flew open, hurling von Loringhoven into Goebbels's desk where he clutched frantically at falling files, folders and various state papers, as Goebbels leaned back as far as he could go, which wasn't very far, to avoid contact.

"Have you heard the latest?" It was Bormann and he was clearly ready to go on a rant.

"My dear Reichsleiter," intoned the somewhat put-out Propaganda minister. "How nice of you to drop in. Seriously, always a pleasure."

Bormann hesitated for a moment as his gaze took in the absurdly ill-balanced young major who now resembled a terrified ostrich with bad knees and an arthritic neck.

"What are you doing here, Loringhoven? Be about your business."

"The Führer sent him, Herr Bormann, so a little patience if you don't mind. This is *my* office with all said and done. Hmm?" Glibly said but there was no hiding the dislike beneath Goebbels's tone. Neither man could abide the other but that was Hitler's way of ruling. Keep them all at each other's throats with him as the final and absolute arbiter.

There was no way that von Loringhoven could leave the cramped office without severely disturbing the thick-set Martin Bormann from his position at the door. The damned man blocked it.

"You were saying, major?" Goebbels smiled beatifically at the harassed aid.

"The...."

"*I* was saying," snarled Borman in his guttural and always unpleasant way."

"Fegelein! Where is that treacherous swine, Fegelein!" Hitler's voice cracked with emotion as it howled all along the lower Bunker corridor.

"Damn! Later." Bormann flicked a peremptory hand and went to wait upon his Führer.

"Honestly, sir." von Loringhoven managed to straighten up at last, his lips curling with distaste and irritation. "The Reichsleiter's manners are intolerable."

"Calm down, major," Goebbels spoke reassuringly. "We tolerate him because we must, for now. So, chin up. I know the pressure that you're under but we can't afford to get all histrionic." He nodded deliberately at Von Loringhoven. "We get enough of that from certain other quarters, wouldn't you say?"

The young major took a deep breath and signalled his agreement, as Goebbels continued. "Now, what's this about the SS and why was Hit....I mean the Führer yelling for Fegelein? What's that piece of dirt been up to? Nothing good I'll bet."

Von Loringhoven, relieved that Bormann was out of the way, at least for the time being, related his shattering news. Taking another deep breath, he began, "It's the Reichsführer SS, sir, Reichsführer Himmler,"

"Yes, yes, major I do know who the Reichsführer SS is. Come on man! Out with it."

Years of very upper-crust breeding began to split at the seams of Major Freytag von Loringhoven's rapidly disintegrating sang-froid. As the Bunker's resident snob, he had felt it his duty to maintain an icy but aristocratic calm before the frightfully vile and ill-mannered elite of the Nazi party; their drug-addled eccentricity of a leader included. But to be constantly spoken to and denigrated by these thugs in such a manner was now more than he could stomach. It had all gone on for far too long. He was a Baltic nobleman who, before the Nazis came to power, had commanded and received respect by virtue of his birth and centuries old family history. His male ancestors had been masters of the order of Teutonic knights: true German nobility. He had survived Stalingrad, Normandy and countless battles. He was a holder of the German Cross in gold, a much-respected honour. Yet here he was stuck in this hovel beneath the ground being patronized and treated like a lackey by people far beneath him in breeding, education and indeed, every damn thing that mattered. Were these tears springing to his baltic blue eyes? Yes, they were. Von Loringhoven was hovering on the brink of a nervous breakdown. Here in front of him half sitting half standing like some mischief bent Satyr, was one of those sublimely perverse mental hunchbacks who earnestly believed that their brand of ghastliness should enshroud the entire world. This creep, Joseph Goebbels, had at least some small modicum of education. Laughable, really. They strutted around, or they once did, loudly proclaiming the glorious superiority of the German race, the almighty Aryan. Invincible and magnificent in its blue-eyed blondness. The wondrous Aryans who most certainly should rule the entire world and dominate the Untermensch that inhabited so many parts of it. Yet one of the staunchest propounders of that fair and flowing ideal was nothing like that in any sense at all. He most certainly wasn't blond and blue eyed.

Reich Propaganda minister Joseph Goebbels looked more Semitic than a rabbinate Jew; club-footed as well. How had such a man climbed so high? God in heaven: how had any of them?

In the meantime, Goebbels required an answer to his question.

"It would seem, Herr Reichsminister, that the Reichsführer has been attempting to negotiate with the allies. He has, it is alleged, offered peace terms."

Goebbels rose slowly to his full five feet and five inches. "He's done what?" For once even Goebbels was lost for words. "How do we know this."

"It came over the BBC earlier today, sir. The Führer has a transcript. There's no doubting it, I'm afraid."

"The 'true oh so ever true' Heinrich has gone and betrayed the Führer, all of us, to those Russian scum. Is that what you're saying?"

"No sir. From what we can gather of his negotiations, I should say attempted negotiations because the allies apparently turned him down flat, they were directed solely at the British and Americans."

From outside, not far from the office door, Hitler's voice reached a piercing squeal. "I don't care, Bormann. Get me Fegelein and arrest that son-of-a-bitch Himmler. And, come to think of it, arrest Fegelein, too, when you find him. Arrest all of those SS bastards. D'you hear me, Bormann, all of them!"

"Come, sir, my Führer," Bormann risked placing a heavy protective arm around Hitler as he attempted to shuffle him away and back to his apartment. Anywhere out of earshot of the many SS men loitering around the upper Bunker and down here in the lower area.

"It's all over," howled the Führer. "The treason of all those around me is unbearable. I shall take my own life; end it all. Death is nothing. It will come as a glorious release. I welcome it."

"Of course, you will my Führer," whispered Bormann. He had no intention of allowing his meal ticket to slip from his meaty grasp just yet. Although, he suppressed a sigh, it looked as though he might have hung on for too long. His many and varied attempts to convince, cajole and wheedle Hitler into leaving Berlin whilst it was still possible had failed miserably. Without his mighty Führer, Reichsleiter Martin Bormann was nothing much more than a cipher. If he were to survive with any of his current power at all intact, then he must soon make a move and distance himself from the others down here. But not yet, not yet.

"My Führer, my Führer." Goebbels rushed up to them, his face a mask of almost filial concern, his club foot hammering noisily down against the Bunker's concrete floor as his right leg attempted to keep up with his left. Goebbels at speed somewhat resembled a marionette being controlled by a drunk on a speeding Ferris wheel. Every jointed part of his body travelled in a different direction. The visual result was the kind of physical comedy that people would happily pay good money to see, which was why Joseph Goebbels normally moved very slowly and with well-intentioned grace. Suppressed giggles came from all around. Never before had anyone dared so much as smile when the great ones passed by. The giggles were at least covered by a hand or breathily gulped back; for now, anyway.

From further down the corridor, possibly the routing clerk's little alcove, there came a long sinuous tendril of cigarette smoke followed by the smell of burning tobacco, and someone, somewhere dropped or threw a glass at the wall. It was beginning to look as though the inmates might soon be taking over this oxygen deprived asylum. One of the female clerks shrieked with stress induced hysterical mirth as the thick, mightily reinforced concrete ceiling shook horribly beneath yet another massive dropping of bombs and, or, artillery; who in God's name could tell the difference anymore? Caked in chalky white dust she stood up from behind her shared desk and waving her hands with palms out she gazed down, still giggling hysterically, at the white dust spread over her previously unblemished sky-blue skirt.

Wide and glassy-eyed she gazed around at the still ranting Führer, down at her chalk covered clothes, and then, as if seeking some kind of explanation, down at her pretty and overworked hands. "That's me, I'm afraid." She spoke quite calmly, and then, like a dazed drunk and using walls and desks to maintain her balance she staggered away, along down the corridor toward the steps leading to the upper bunker and from there nobody would ever know.

Hitler hadn't so much as noticed. He also bore the dusty white detritus shaken down from above, but he was far too engrossed in his own drama to bother with such things. Rochus Misch, leaning out from his switchboard sanctuary quickly ducked back again. The scene that he observed before him looked like something out of an absurd American comedy. He shook his head and sat attentively gazing at his switchboard and hoping that no one would call him to aid the Führer. A call came through. Misch straightened up as he recognized the voice. It was Fegelein.

"Look at this, Goebbels. Look at this!" Hitler waved the offending scrap of paper around as though everyone in the Bunker could and should see it. "Betrayal, Herr Goebbels. Filthy, vile betrayal." Tears began flooding from the trembling Führer's eyes. He turned his painfully protesting body around, hands outstretched like a supplicant in a badly written Greek tragedy and jowls wobbling like a Turkey's finger-slapped dewlap.

"What have I done to merit such treatment? I ask you – WHAT?"

A young, face-damaged gefreiter, Hans Jung, sat at his desk some ten feet from the current drama being enacted by his enraged Führer. He slowly turned his ruin of a face to the pretty young secretary standing beside him and mouthed. "*Seriously?*"

It was too much. Getta, for that was her name, clutched at her stomach and let out a howl of mirth so loud that even Hitler and his group were pulled up short and started with surprise.

"Ooh-Ooh!" Bent double with mirth she waved a conciliatory hand at her Führer who simply stared back uncomprehendingly.

"Sorry," she gasped.

"Have you seen this, my girl?" Hitler waggled his condemnatory piece of paper high above his trembling head. "Look – look! You see? You see what I must contend with? This, this treachery is now a common bond between such scum. Scum! All of them."

Getta had stopped laughing in the face of a shower of spittle from Hitler as he closed with her. "I told you. Didn't I tell you all that we could lose only through treachery – didn't I? And here it is," he turned so that all could see. Well, they could see the paper at least but not what was written on it. "The proof. The out and out proof that I am betrayed. That is why I must end it all. It is over.... done.... finished!"

Goebbels raised his eyes and Loringhoven felt his hands itching to close around the Führer's sagging throat. Bormann, however, renewed his attempts at placating and moving Hitler to his apartment.

Hitler suddenly became calmer and almost listless.

He pointed a finger at von Loringhoven. "See to it that Fegelein is apprehended and questioned." To Bormann, he said, "Have Himmler arrested, stripped of his titles and rank. He is to speak to no one. Clear?" To poor young Getta he simply said, "Go and rest child. It has been a long and trying day." With that, calling for his valet, Linge, he turned and shuffled back toward his rooms.

N ow settled in his small armchair Hitler sat back, sipped his tea, took a large bite of his cream-filled sponge cake and glanced at the projector sitting on the table beside him.

"The same movie, my Führer?" Linge hovered respectfully, the metal canister containing the anticipated film held across his left arm as he displayed it like a fine wine.

"Yes, Linge. And more cake when you have the thing running.

"Of course, my Führer." Linge began threading the film through onto the sprockets. His master never tired of this particular movie. There had been a time, years ago now, when the Führer had enjoyed watching westerns and historical epics. He would sit for hours with those of the invited inner circle and watch, spellbound, the antics of various actors and actresses. Now, though, there was just the one movie and he always watched it alone. Linge sighed inwardly. His master had much to put up with and much to suffer. Perhaps this odd little vice wasn't so bad. He wished though, that the Führer would find some other more wholesome entertainment than tonight's offering. It consisted, this one-hour long movie, of a series of naked men being hung on meat hooks using piano wire. The Field Marshalls and Generals involved in the July 24th plot to kill him had all been dispatched in this manner. They had been executed in such a way on the Führer's express order and each separate execution lovingly filmed in every ghastly detail. The condemned men's final agonies and humiliation as they writhed and jerked out their last moments, covered in their own filth, were now artistically framed in celluloid, there to remain permanently for the Führer's delectation whenever he wished to view that horror, which he did quite frequently.

"Perhaps," muttered Hitler, "I shall add Himmler to this little list. Yes, I think that I shall."

"A splendid idea, my Führer," agreed Linge. The feared and detested Reichsführer SS hung naked on a meat hook would bring a smile to many a face, German and non-German.

CHAPTER 15

August 8 1935: SS HQ, Berlin, No:8 Prinz-Albrecht-Strasse,

Reinhard Heydrich was not known for his sense of humour but he most certainly had one. As he strode toward his boss's office, number 8 Prinz- Albrecht-Strasse, he could easily conjure up in his mind's eye the frozen-eyed stare of the feared head of the SS, his direct superior, Heinrich Himmler. Himmler had risen, by virtue of crafty manipulation, back-stabbing and an amazing ability to grovel and fawn at the right time. Up from a scrawny little non-achiever to be head of a three hundred strong Führer security group back in 1929. It had been the time when Adolf Hitler had decided that he needed protection from his own SA as much as from the armed and deadly communist opposition. From that modest beginning, and using those same talents, now fiendishly well honed, he had expanded the SS to fifty-five thousand men: virtually his private army. Very clever, very crafty and very worthy of respect. He might be a physical weakling but the man was one hell of a ruthless bastard! Reinhard Heydrich, however, knew his man, and he had, so to speak, his number. As far as Heydrich was concerned, possibly rather too smugly, he had the number of every one of them. Unbeknownst to Himmler and the rest of the Nazi big-wigs, he had a file on everyone who was anyone in Hitler's Third Reich. He had continued with his file gathering and in-house spying ever since an accusation against him stating that he, Heydrich, had Jewish heritage; a charge of which he cleared himself only with some difficulty. He had managed to destroy the incriminating evidence lodged in the small records section of the parish hall of Rieda in central Germany. That record had pointed to a Jewish great grandmother from Silesia, a pretty girl by all accounts, who had been a servant in the Heydrich household. The revealing document no longer existed and the registry page was now conveniently altered and all traces of Jewish forebears eliminated, along with the poor fool who had first mentioned such a vile calumny. There was, however, nothing he could do about his great beak of a nose. At school they had mocked him, calling him Moses Heydrich; let them dare now! Anyway, apart from his curse of a nose, he looked suitably Aryan and as far as he was concerned, he was. He had once said to Albert Speer, Hitler's arty building friend, that it would be virtually impossible to find a German man or woman, or anybody else in Europe for that matter, that was free of Jewish blood. Those folk had traversed the four corners of the world for hundreds of years and whatever arts, acts or fashions they practised; celibacy was not amongst them. Speer had nodded in that non-committal but always agreeable way of his. They were like minds, he and Speer. Neither of them gave a damn about Jews, racial purity or anything else appertaining to that pie-in-the-sky nonsense. It was all just a means to an end. Speer got to play with brick buildings and he, Heydrich, got to wear fancy uniforms, have lots of beautiful women and in general, indulge his every taste and whim whilst at the same time treading down inferiors and destroying utterly those that he didn't like. Sadism? Yes, he supposed that it was, he knew it and didn't give a damn. A gentleman should always be a sadist; it gave him an aura of mystique that women found irresistible and men found terrifying. He loved it, and being in such total control only increased his appetite for more. And there was more, so much more, to be had.

Reichsführer SS, Heinrich Himmler was devoted to Adolf Hitler. Devoted, terrified and in awe of the great man. Great? Heydrich clicked his tongue against the roof of his mouth. To some fools, perhaps. But Reinhard Heydrich saw through the showman's façade of the Nazi leader. Clever and cunning certainly. Self-serving and devious? Without a doubt. But great? Hardly! Well, a half-smile twitched at the thin lips of SS Gruppenführer Reinhard Heydrich. Credit where credit's due and all that; the Austrian former corporal's acting was quite superb and that voice was to die for. Reinhard's voice was out of all and any proportion to his six feet in height and his cold, menacing, blue-eyed stare. It was, to say the least, squeaky and totally at odds with his admittedly handsome, but rather pointed and grim visaged features. Oh, yes. He envied Adolf Hitler his voice. But things were, all in all, going Reinhard's way. From a formerly disgraced junior naval officer in the old navy to the equivalent rank of a major general under the current rather more tolerant gang of social misfits, wasn't bad going. He was no more impressed by his boss, Himmler, than he was by any other within the Nazi hierarchy. A good administrator but a mouse. Loyal to the Führer, Adolf Hitler, to the very end of days; or so he constantly repeated to anyone who would listen. Putting it bluntly, the greatly feared Reichsführer was scared to death of the Führer; he was about as violent and scary as an irritated gerbil. Himmler might look ice-cold and intimidating but the man was riddled with deficiencies and self-doubt. He could sign away a man's life but in no way could he ever personally commit murder, slice innocent and defenceless flesh, or even personally light the faggots beneath a curse shrieking witch. Reinhard Heydrich could do all those things whilst eating a good meal or sipping on an expensive cognac. Pain, terror and threat were the stuff of life, of success and requited ambition.

His highly polished boots, of the very finest quality, clipped neatly on marble cased stairs as he made his way up to Himmler's office. The Reichsführer kept his lair at the very top of the massive building and anybody wanting to beard him, so to speak, had to enter after a quite lengthy, public and twisting climb of the wide circular staircase.

At the top of his climb, Heydrich paused for a moment to adjust a slight crease that had formed on the red general's stripe of his trousers just above his right boot. The black helmeted SS Guard standing outside the entry door to the Reichsführer's office slammed a highly polished booted foot into the marble flooring and threw up his right arm like an Olympic athlete throwing a javelin.

"Heil Hitler."

Heydrich's response was decidedly more casual. His arm simply flipped back as if swatting away an annoying insect.

The guard turned to open the door and as he did so an SS officer exited a side door from further down the ornately ornamented landing.

"Herr Gruppenführer," with small finicky steps, the rotund figure approached and puffed himself to a halt in front of Heydrich. The pathetic Heil Hitler salute that flopped up from the smaller man to his superior elicited an amused sneer but absolutely nothing else.

"Can you spare a minute?"

"As long as it is a minute, Boss. What is it?"

Oberführer Hugo Boss's, round oily face creased into a smile of gratitude and supplication. He was afraid of Reinhard Heydrich, as indeed were most people. The Gruppenführer was a man who could do favours or cause pain and ruin with just a glint of those ice-cold, Teutonic blue eyes. It was never possible to tell which way the redoubtable Heydrich might turn. Sensible men remained always on their guard when Heydrich was around, or, more sensible still, took themselves completely out of his way.

"Well, sir, the latest order for my uniforms – the one's with the death's head design on the lapels."

"What of them?" Heydrich liked Boss's SS uniforms very much indeed. He was wearing a Boss designed, or rather a Boss tailored item, himself. Boss made the things, neatly tailored and beautifully cut, but it was Oberführer Karl Diebitsch who came up with the ideas and designs. In truth, Boss was merely the factory man. It was Diebitsch who was the shining light of creation in Boss's little outfit. A light that would remain hidden, sadly for Diebitsch, as Hugo Boss, rotund and harmless as he might look, would kill before he gave away what he considered to be his personal set of Nazi laurels. Himmler had agreed that both men, Boss and Diebitsch should have honorary SS rank. It tied them, and others like them, to the SS and its Reichsführer, Heinrich Himmler and, indirectly of course, to Reinhard Heydrich. Diebitsch was an airy-fairy artistic type, easily cowed, whereas Boss was a natural born bully, an imitation alpha male. So, it was Hugo Boss who ruled and not his designer. It was the Führerprinzip in miniature being worked by (so he thought) Heinrich Himmler. In reality, it was Heydrich who suggested and arranged most such honours. They weren't real SS men of course but both were active members and supporters of the Nazi Party happily going along with whatever line the Party demanded of its members. In return Boss would occasionally ask a favour and clearly, this was what he now had in mind. Heydrich quite enjoyed occasionally dispensing largesse to eagerly panting underlings; it made him feel powerful and let them, the underlings, know from whence that power came.

"Well, Herr Gruppenführer," Boss hesitated slightly, possibly in the hope that Heydrich might give him permission to drop the formality and use a given name – not a hope! He breathed in deeply through small even teeth. "We are having some little trouble with output."

"So?"

"The Reichsführer stated quite specifically that three thousand of the new uniforms be ready, must be ready by the end of next week."

"And so?" Heydrich shifted the folder he was holding with a degree of impatience.

Bull by the horns, thought Boss. "Can't be done, Herr Gruppenführer. I don't have the staff…I mean, enough men in the cutting room."

Heydrich looked into his subordinate's shifty little eyes. The concentration camp construction programme had been accelerated sharply and now there were more than fifty such completed camps all requiring uniformed guards and staff. The Death's Head brigade, as they would become known, were specially chosen individuals with particular skill sets. Himmler wanted them neatly uniformed and he was a complete fusspot when it came to things like outward appearance for his growing gang of concentration camp controllers. Commandants, their deputies, even the attendant doctors and surgeons were required to wear the snazzy new Boss tailored uniforms. All the way down to the bog-standard lowest rank SS Schutze (private). The way things were going, the guards of the ever-increasing number of concentration camps were going to be better dressed than royalty, and certainly better turned out than anyone else in the Third Reich. There was even talk of a fighting arm of the SS to be created along Wehrmacht lines, the Waffen SS, and that would mean many thousands more, if not quite so snazzy, SS uniforms for Hugo Boss and his designer colleague, Diebitsch, to churn out.

"How many," drawled Heydrich, knowing full well what Boss was after. A rapidly growing pool of available labour resided in those concentration camps. Some of it was skilled but most just provided brute force labour and little else. That would, of course, change as time went by, as the camps gained access to more skilled individuals. As it was, at the moment there was labour aplenty and it was free to whomever controlled it. The camp commandants controlled that labour, but Theodor Eicke and Reinhard Heydrich controlled the commandants. Favours were doled out and promises exchanged. It had already become extremely profitable to the growing number of officers involved.

Boss gave a mini shrug and limply waved both hands a couple of inches from side to side. "Quite a few, Herr Gruppenführer, bearing in mind the Reichsführer's diktat." Boss turned his shiny, some would say greasy face upward toward Heydrich. "Time is of the essence, and that sort of…"

Heydrich cut him short with a peremptory flick of his right index finger. The wretched man was not only sweating quite revoltingly, he was also simpering like an importuning catamite.

"Three hundred do you – four, five? Jews, I imagine? You'd prefer Jews? I hear they make good tailors. Trainable and such like, hmm?"

"Five… five hundred? Oh yes, yes sir, that would do ever so nicely. I don't know what to say. A life saver Herr Gruppenführer. I can't tell you how grateful I am. Truly, sir!" He was, too. Over the moon style grateful. The most he had hoped for was a hundred or so social deadbeats. To have real live Jews, natural born tailors in his opinion, was an absolute God-send. Result!

Heydrich nodded his dismissal and Boss trotted off a happy man. The Gruppenführer was such a fine fellow to deal with.

Heydrich turned his thoughts and his person back to the course at hand. This next should be highly amusing. It was the kind of situation that made his life so very much worthwhile, worth living for the sheer hellishly insane fun of it. Childish he knew, but then wasn't that childlike charm during a confrontation every psychopath's one redeeming feature? If it weren't then it damn well should be.

He eased his way into the plush, and absurdly ornate office of his chief, Heinrich Himmler. As an office it was too large, a typical national socialist failing, in Heydrich's opinion. Everything designed to be big, to awe and overpower the senses. It didn't work in his view. Neither did the imitation art works dotted around the walls and tables. The Rembrandt was real enough, though, but who the hell wanted a Rembrandt anyway? Oversized, over-painted and in this case hung over the wrong wall.

Pushing the door closed behind him, Heydrich smiled at the Reichsführer. Here, before his feared and revered chief, his persona was subtly different. Exuding his usual cold menace, yes, but cleverly mixed with a barely detectable deference to his direct superior. He strode toward the desk behind which the incredibly neatly uniformed Heinrich Himmler sat all unmoving.

Himmler looked up and observed his advancing subordinate. A

dangerous man, this deputy of his. He had personally seen to his early promotion and then, equally as personally, sought to bring it to a halt. Reinhard Heydrich was, as far as the Reichsführer was concerned, his most dangerous threat and rival. Yes, rival! Himmler hated that word but Heydrich had outmanoeuvred him and become so utterly indispensable that further promotion could not be denied him. Hitler himself had been so impressed with the ice-eyed blond that he had insisted upon his further advancement. Hitler had, of course, as was his way, spotted a future rival for his tame SS puppet to deal with. It certainly kept him in a constant state of musicless en-pointe. One might not hear but could certainly sense the feral hissing from a resentfully self-protective Reichsführer.

Himmler liked to sit so that the sun, when not clouded over, reflected from his pince-nez spectacles. He needed glasses sure enough but the steel rimmed pince-nez were pure affectation. He thought that they made him look sinister and he was right, they did. His slightly mongoloid features and high cheekbones gave him the appearance of an inscrutable Chinese mandarin bent upon some diabolical mischief. He looked about as Aryan as Genghis Khan swinging a scimitar.

Himmler didn't return his subordinate's smile but spoke in a surprisingly guttural tone. Heydrich wasn't sure whether the glottal throttling rasp was an effort to imitate Hitler or something that came naturally. He had never heard Himmler shout, nor even so much as raise his voice. Reichsführer Himmler firmly believed that self-control made the man and that all men, particularly those with authority over others, should at all times maintain iron composure.

Such self-control showed clearly that a man was worthy of high office and trust; Heinrich Himmler was a man who loved his homilies and mantras and would, with great seriousness, expound at least one of each every day as though he were the originator of an original thought. Original thought from that quarter was an unlikely prospect as far as Reinhard Heydrich was concerned.

Both men locked eyes as Heydrich came to a halt before the Reichsführer's desk, halted and threw out a faultless salute and a high-pitched bark of "Heil Hitler." Apart from the oddly soft and squeaky voice, it was beautifully done: the sharp clicking of the heels, the crisp snap of the knife-edged creased uniform sleeve at the apogee of the spear-like salute, even the slightly jaunty angle of his superbly tailored SS cap looked good. Himmler felt his dislike and envy for this man rise like uncorked bilge. Nevertheless, he managed a smile, of sorts, and greeted his subordinate with a nod and a growled, "Hrmmph! Yes, Heil Hitler, Gruppenführer Heydrich." Himmler rarely used his subordinates' names without their titles. He disliked what he considered to be overfamiliarity. Such things bred contempt, he believed.

"What do we see today, then, Herr Gruppenführer?"

Ignoring the strange phraseology, Heydrich half turned toward the heavy oak chair placed a little to his left. Heavy oak it certainly was but it was tiny in comparison to the Reichsführer's massively carved mahogany throne chair with its high back and twin eagles perched menacingly on each beautifully polished wooden shoulder.

Himmler nodded his permission to sit and glanced at the green file in Heydrich's left hand. A green file meant SS history on someone or other. Interesting. Himmler enjoyed gossip as much as the next man; surreptitiously, of course.

"Something for me?"

Oh, for God's sake, thought Heydrich. Why does this man insist on speaking the obvious? Covering his contempt with natural aplomb, he nodded. "As a matter of fact, yes, Herr Reichsführer. A matter of some considerable urgency, I should say."

Himmler nodded in a self-important, avuncular way. "Continue, please."

Heydrich crossed his legs and felt the sudden urge for a cigarette. The Reichsführer, however, like his master, Adolf Hitler, frowned on that unhealthy and foul-smelling practice. There were no ashtrays anywhere near where the revered Reichsführer might be likely to tread. Heydrich raised the file slightly. "It concerns, Herr Reichsführer, a certain individual's request to marry. As you know, all SS members must seek your approval and permission before they can marry."

"Just so," responded Himmler. "In order that I," now he smiled, slightly, "or rather we," he waved an encompassing hand the sweep of which took in the icy figure of the Gruppenführer, "can ascertain that his bloodline and that of his intended spouse are of pure Aryan stock. We can tolerate no mixed blood, Herr Gruppenführer. Applicants must be pure blood Aryan: no exceptions." Himmler waited for Heydrich's nod of agreement before continuing. "The idea being, as you know, to maintain the purity of the SS and the Aryan race in general and, I believe, that I personally have succeeded in keeping much of the Jewish menace at bay."

"Yes, Herr Reichsführer, I heartily agree."

"Of course, you do," Himmler decided that he could risk being condescending, even a little patronizing. "Now then, I trust that all this means that we shall have no such racial problems with our latest applicant for knot-tying, eh?" He nodded smugly at his flippant turn of phrase. "That, presumably, is his application?"

"It is indeed, sir." Heydrich felt a burst of heart constricting joy rise within his chest as he leaned forward and handed Himmler the file containing the request. What stood out at once was the bulk of the thing. It seemed fairly obvious that it contained something more than just a request with an accompanying personnel report and recommendations. These were normally only three to four pages in length. What Heydrich was handing over bore more resemblance in size to a PhD student's dissertation.

"So, who do we have here?" Himmler took the file with a small, well-manicured hand. A hand that had never in all its forty-plus years done so much as one second of manual labour. Heydrich had on one occasion been obliged to shake that floppy paw. Weak, damp and sponge-like, was how he had found it. Not a man's handshake at all.

"The request, Herr Reichsführer, comes from Oberführer, Emil Maurice." Heydrich sat back and awaited Himmler's response.

"Maurice – Emil Maurice? The Fuhrer's former confidant? The progenitor of the SS! Our founder?" Himmler was fast resembling a beached guppy, with his mouth opening and closing. He had never met the man upon whose ideas, dreams and fanaticism about racial purity, the entire ethos of the modern SS was based. Emil Maurice was a God to all SS members. He was openly acknowledged as the creator of the organization and idolised accordingly.

Heydrich nodded happily.

Himmler eased himself deeper into the wide shouldered back of his chair.

"Oberführer Emil Maurice," Himmler was smiling with happiness. "The creator of the SS. The man whose ideas made us what we are.

"The very same, Herr Reichsführer." Heydrich smiled back. His smile was almost genuine for he too was happy.

Oberführer Maurice was a man respected by Reichsführer Heinrich Himmler to such an extent that he had only recently commissioned a life-sized bust of the progenitor of the SS to be placed in the SS headquarters entrance foyer. For some unknown reason Emil Maurice had withdrawn from the limelight of his creation, content to retain a purely ceremonial role and limited powers within the organization. A great man, indeed. Job done, he had, to all intents and purposes, nobly stepped aside to make way for younger men.

"Well, my dear Heydrich," Himmler was now all smiles and bonhomie. He often used such as a tactic to keep subordinates off balance, although it wasn't likely to work with Heydrich. "Hardly necessary for the good Oberführer to seek permission from us, eh? Of course, he can marry. No need to go any further with all this checking and authentication on the man who is, with all said and done, our very creator," he looked down at the file in front of him, then frowning slightly, he glanced up at Heydrich. "Checking, which I see, you appear to have already carried out."

"I follow, as always, Herr Reichsführer your very own example in thoroughness, which, if I may say, sets a fine example to us all."

"Yes, yes, very good." If he saw or even sensed the sarcasm behind the Gruppenführer's toadying remark he had decided, wisely, to ignore it.

The file lay before the Reichsführer still unopened and it seemed that he was content to leave it that way. But tempted though he was to push the A4 laden file back to his subordinate, Heydrich's calm immobility stayed his hand. A slight angled movement of his neck from the blond officer seemed to indicate the file. Like two cobras gifted with identically bobbling Adams apples the icy-eyed SS chiefs stared each other down. Almost without realising it Himmler's hand gently caressed the front cover of the file. It wasn't that he was losing face or nerve before Heydrich; rather, it was now clear that Heydrich knew something that he, Himmler, didn't. Damn the wretched man!

Heydrich smiled as his chief looked down, opened the file and began to study its contents. He waited. Himmler read slowly, turning the pages with exaggerated care. His professionally detached manner gave away no sign of anything untoward. He sat reading, face like a champion card player; no expression at all.... until – Heydrich's head stretched forward just a little. The Reichsführer's hand trembled, and to Heydrich, it seemed as if his neat pince-nez spectacles had widened to accommodate his suddenly bulging eyes. Yes, that normally cold Himmler gaze now held an expression of insupportable horror. The hard lump of laryngeal gristle that formed the Reichsführer's Adam's apple bounced around in his gullet like a ricocheting table tennis ball as he gulped for air. His soft, inoffensive little hand closed into a less than impressive fist, gathering the pages beneath it into a creased bundle.

There, there it was: Oh Joy! Heydrich almost shrieked with pleasure. The Reichsführer Heinrich Himmler sat there with bared teeth, and expressions of rage, disbelief and horror, all rolled into one. Like a big round rubber mask, Himmler's face contorted in extreme rigor and then grimaced horribly. His clenched hand, the one grasping the file, he raised and pointed at Heydrich. Loose sheets of printed A4 scattered over the floor as Himmler stood and hurled the offending file and documents from him. He panted, gasped and lurched slightly before regaining his balance by holding on to the front of his desk.

His eyes travelled from side to side, upward and then from side to side again. It was as if Heydrich weren't in the room.

"Are you quite well, Herr Reichsführer?" Heydrich asked solicitously, now all kindness and concern. He stood so that his six feet three inches could tower mightily over the more diminutive five feet seven and a bit of his anguish riddled chief. "Can I do anything?"

Himmler's eyes fell upon him and shone with hatred.

"The man is a Jew!" The noun was spat out as though his tongue were covered in acid. If a whisper might ever be referred to as a shout, then that was the sound that the Reichsführer SS managed to emit. Even Heydrich was taken aback by the intensity of the hatred, the force of loathing behind his superior's utterance and demeanour. Here was a Heinrich Himmler that neither he nor anyone else had ever seen. The true beast inside an outwardly always calm, inoffensive little man who revered and obeyed his Führer.

"How has this happened?" Himmler was deathly pale but gradually recovering his composure. He hadn't got where he was by being an over impassioned fanatic with no control over his emotions.

"Tell me, Gruppenführer Heydrich. How long have you known?"

"I brought it to your attention the moment the file came into my possession, Herr Reichsführer," Heydrich evaded. "I am, of course, every bit as shocked by this appalling revelation as you, sir. A dreadful thing, indeed." Actually, Heydrich thought the whole thing a terrific hoot and he had known for quite some time about Oberführer Maurice, his religious ethnicity and his various doings here there and elsewhere. Little of importance escaped Reinhard Heydrich within the Third Reich. And now, he knew precisely the right switch to flick with regard to his pasty-faced boss, Heinrich Himmler.

"Well, we need to get ourselves out of this damn mess. It could ruin us all, Herr Gruppenführer."

"Just so," Heydrich nodded sagely.

"The man who created the SS, wrote down its code of behaviour, laid out our governing rules with regards to recognizing the inferiority of other races, the Jews in particular; devoted his life and career, not to mention seven whole pages of instructions covering the devilment of the Jewish race and the need to remove them from our living space, is in fact, himself a Jew! We can never, Herr Gruppenführer, allow such a revelation to become public knowledge. Clear? Now, how the devil did it come about in the first place? Was this the man's idea of a sick joke? Damn it all to hell, man – It's lunacy, Heydrich. Pure lunacy."

"Yes, indeed. I take your point, Herr Reichsführer. I shall, of course, implement whatever course of action you order with the greatest alacrity. I can assure you, whatever you decide, it shall be acted upon swiftly and with the utmost thoroughness."

Of course you will, you snake, thought Himmler. He had calmed and was almost back to his normal icy self. There was no way that even Heydrich could have arranged such a scenario as this. But by the same token, he was enjoying his immediate superior's travail. Not for nothing was Reinhard Heydrich now known as 'Beast Heydrich.' The son-of-a-bitch would have happily circumcised Emil Maurice himself if it meant getting one-up on his boss, or anyone else for that matter. Heydrich needed to be watched these days, twenty-four-seven with no let up. The man was more ruthless than that murderous ancient Roman psychopath, Caesar. Himmler needed to be rid of his rival but he must take his time and take Heydrich all unawares. As yet, no such opportunity had shown itself but sooner or later, one way or another, Reichsführer Himmler fully intended to move Reinhard Heydrich on; away to pastures new. A nice promotion, perhaps, but somewhere as far distant from the hub of power as possible. He was too dangerous and becoming far too influential for Himmler's liking. He would wait, he had to. He had nurtured this incredibly dangerous and clever viper to his bosom and now he must somehow detach the limpet-like influence that Heydrich was slowly wrapping around parts of his SS.

In the meantime, the wretched Jew, Oberführer Emil Maurice.

"I shall inform the Fuhrer of this travesty," murmured Himmler, not looking at Heydrich as he worked out a solution to his problem. Heydrich remained silent, watchful.

"Did he know, d'you suppose, the Führer – about Maurice."

"Oh, surely not," Heydrich feigned shoulder squeezing outrage.

"I'll have the wretch thrown into a concentration camp," Himmler continued, "and then quietly done away with. That should solve the problem."

Heydrich gave no warning of what he had gleaned during his lengthy and thorough investigation into Oberführer Emil Maurice. Nor did he mention the fact that this was a problem best ignored, glossed over, and forgotten because it was a no-win scenario. Lock Maurice up in a camp and sooner or later the truth would out. Maurice himself, in all likelihood, would bellow the truth behind his incarceration to all and sundry. Hitler had once been close to this man, and still regarded him as a friend; not that Heydrich had any intention of letting Himmler in on that little snippet. Let him discover it himself, quite possibly to his cost and Heydrich's advantage. Either way, nothing lost in keeping certain things to himself. The best way out of this was, of course, to end the offending Jewish Oberführer's existence as soon as possible. Himmler, though, would not countenance that, as Heydrich very well knew. Himmler was his master's obedient dog, and such permission as he thought might be needed could come only from the Führer himself. Rule breaking went against the grain for Heinrich Himmler, and murdering an SS Oberführer, Jewish or not, who just so happened to be personally acquainted with the Führer and who also happened to be the creator of the SS, was to the Reichsführer's pedantic mind, breaking a rule too far. No! He would go and see Hitler and demand that Maurice be stripped of all his rank and titles and thrown without further ado into one of the new concentration camps. There was a state-of-the-art centre being developed at Sachsenhausen that would do nicely.

Without saying anything to Heydrich the Reichsführer picked up the phone and tapped for a line. He would demand to see the Führer at once.

A muffled voice answered at the other end of the line and Himmler spoke with surprising courtesy. "Henke? You will call Hess at the Chancellery right away. I need to see the Führer on a matter of the utmost urgency and importance. It is a matter of national security. No, Henke, you will tell them that I am coming straight over. Vitally important. Got it?" He replaced the receiver and shot Heydrich a quick glance. "I must be away Herr Gruppenführer, so let's gather up these papers before some nosey little clerk comes in and sees what they should never see." He smiled coldly. "It would cost them their life were they to do so."

I t was only a five-minute walk to the Reich Chancellery but nevertheless, Himmler took the smaller of his open-top Mercedes. He liked to be seen but not brushed against, as so often happened when ordinary people accidentally-on-purpose got themselves too close to those above their talents and their station. He could have gathered a small army of stunningly uniformed SS men but that would have taken too much time. His normal driver would be quite sufficient for his purposes today. The offending file lay safely within the confines of his heavy briefcase which he held tightly to his side. Nobody, other than the Führer, not even God himself, must see what that file contained.

The air was good, as this part of the city remained relatively free from the belching pollution of diesel driven buses and heavy trucks. Himmler loathed exhaust fumes of any description. Frightful, unhealthy and in his opinion, deadly. But needs must, as he well knew. Things had to be shifted from one place to another, so, petrol, diesel, even synthetic fuels were necessary for the ever-increasing volume of transport. Offensive fumes, though, played havoc with his rather delicate system. He hated coughing and choking in front of others so he practised regular breathing exercises which enabled him to hold his breath for longer than he might otherwise have been able. He had learnt the technique from a book by some long dead Chinese yoga master, and that in turn had led him to investigate various other remedies concerning several different ailments and infirmities. All very interesting. So much so, that he had set up an SS-funded institute devoted solely to the exploration of the copious amount of guaranteed longevity and healing techniques that permeated writings from the East. He was quite convinced that many of them, with the correct application, would work.

The Mercedes pulled up outside the Reichstag entrance with barely a sound from its expertly applied brakes. The driver leapt out and opened the door for Himmler to alight from the shining vehicle.

"You will remain here," Himmler brusquely ordered his driver.

"Yes, sir." The man threw up a neat Hitler salute, then deftly closed the car door as Himmler climbed out and marched with purpose and solemnity up the wide stone steps leading to the main chancellery doors, outside of which stood two marble-like and gigantic SS guards. No one would be likely to make any attempt to have the Mercedes moved from its present position. The Reichsführer's SS pennant fluttered threateningly from the bonnet and was more than sufficient to deter any traffic-cop busybodies.

The towering 1.95m plus guards with their polished silver helmets stood frozen, like recently scrubbed and dressed statues. They observed wide-eyed as the Reichsführer, head of the SS, their direct lord and master, mister scary himself, advanced toward them. A slight puffing of his rather loose little cheeks did nothing to spoil the effect that Himmler was having upon his huge, devoted and scared witless underlings. Their wide, knuckle scarred hands slapped with a loud unison crash against the wooden barrel shrouds of their rifles as they saluted the Reichsführer. He in turn favoured them with an icy, pince-nez magnified glance and nodded. The massive wooden double doors of the chancellery swung open beneath the effortless and uniform pushing from the guards and the Reichsführer SS marched manfully through and on to the great one's lair.

The high ceilinged, massive windowed and partially mosaiced

hallway echoed to the sound of Himmler's steel-tipped heels as he strode toward the Führer's office. The few individuals that he came across either froze into Heil Hitlering immobility, or scuttled away like mice hoping that they hadn't been seen. Himmler loved it. What bothered him, however, was the outrageous lack of any worthwhile security within these mighty and splendidly adorned walls. He made a mental note to review and immediately rearrange the Führer's security protocols. As he marched regally, or so he thought, down the full length of the absurdly long hall he could just see, if he squinted hard enough, another tall, just the one, SS guard standing outside the door to Hitler's office. The Führer was a difficult man to protect because he hated, truly hated, being surrounded by big beefy men who were more immediately intimidating than himself. One bodyguard he could tolerate but he loathed to be shepherded by them. Himmler had left that task to Otto Meisner and the man had failed miserably. His head would, metaphorically, soon roll courtesy of the Reichsführer's sharp blade.

Hitler sat at his overlarge desk fiddling with some papers which he was supposed to look at and probably sign, he wasn't too sure. They seemed full of details about exchange rates, GPD, balances of various payments, and so on. With a loud grunt he slapped a hand over those papers and, yawning massively, stood, stretched, and then strode to the eight-foot-high window and gazed longingly at the outside world. Boring! He was bored out of his skull. A couple of years had passed since he had brilliantly seized power; seized yes, but all done legally and with care. He was now Reich Chancellor and Führer all rolled into one and all completely legal. The office of the presidency was abolished and he, Adolf Hitler, was the supreme head of state. It was a year since the armed forces had sworn a personal oath of obedience to him, Adolf Hitler, as their supreme head, their glorious leader. An individual oath from each man. Never before had such a thing been done; at least, not since the days of Arminius. The army generals were cock-a-hoop and thumping each other's backs with masculine joy at the prospect of seeing their responsibilities and the size of the army more than quadruple.

They weren't expecting a war, of course, they simply enjoyed having more toys to play with and more shiny medals to stitch onto their uniforms. Adolf knew well enough that most of them thought of him as nothing more than a jumped-up corporal. Just a cheap relic left over from the last war. They reckoned that they would be able to control the former NCO and boss him about; blind him with military science and such-like. Fools! Others had tried that approach and every one of them, individual or group, had failed. Adolf now truly believed himself to be superior to others. How else could he have so easily and so frequently blind-sided and fooled them? Destiny was his friend and guide. Much of the time he felt invincible! And he would be, once he managed to bring all three military arms up to scratch.

Right now, though, he was restless. He hated getting up early and steadfastly refused to do so. Ruling the nation was not the exciting journey he had thought that it would be. People had such mundane methods and expectations. The actual nitty-gritty of everyday governing, planning and economic recovery groups was of no interest to him at all. The price of bread, vegetables and coal didn't interest him in the slightest. His finance wizard, Helmut Schact, had been warning him of late over his military spending and the amount of public spending he was so determinedly and quixotically authorizing. The man was clever but he was also a pain. Adolf needed a big army, navy and air force to accomplish his many future aims; and public spending, big buildings, massive new roads and town improvements, were precisely what people noticed and admired about his leadership.

He loved the parades, making speeches and massive displays of government power; creating huge awe-inspiring buildings, great parks and delivering on seemingly impossible promises concerning welfare and pensions. Anything that could be conjured up quickly. Speed above all was essential lest his adoring public became disenchanted with the new order. That was his style of politicking, not all that 'should we increase the price of bread' verbiage.

Ministerial and vested interest group meetings smacked of democracy and Adolf Hitler was having none of that in his government. It was government by the Führer and of the Führer. Nothing else. He handed out responsibility and then dealt with problems on a one-to-one basis. If something looked like becoming an overwhelming nuisance then he quite simply ordered the man he had placed in charge to create a committee to oversee and clear the problem. Other than that, Adolf did not like to be involved with problems. He had, after all, so many things to do. Schact had pointed out that this policy of ruling had already created an entire army of under ministers, clerks-in-charge, huge numbers of secretaries which all, in turn, meant new offices which in turn created yet more committees needed to solve the problems created by the previous committee or committees. The result was utter confusion, which suited the Führer very well for in such a miasma of political ineptness only he, the Führer, could give any kind of truly effective ruling. Confused people rarely posed any kind of threat or challenge. So Adolf Hitler firmly believed.

The tap on the door of his office was light. Adolf turned toward the door and then sat down behind his big, ugly desk. The room was big, far too big for him to enjoy working in. His bohemian mind preferred more cosy confines. Warm fires, thickly upholstered living room chairs, chintz and lace, these were Adolf's preferred domestic surroundings. The great hallway leading to his office could easily contain, lengthwise, a couple of football pitches and this office of his wasn't much smaller than a tennis court. He felt lost in it and so, as a result, spent as little time here as possible. The day was fast approaching when he would cease to use it at all. He had given his splendid young architect, Albert Speer, the go-ahead for a new Reich Chancellery and the way that young fellow worked, and was so in tune with his own ideas, it shouldn't be too long before the building was completed. It would be even bigger, more glorious and more grandiose than anything in the government quarter built before it. But he, Adolf Hitler, would use it purely for ceremonial purposes; to meet, greet and overawe foreign dignitaries as they ventured into his lair.

In the meantime, what did his finicky SS leader want? According to Hess the Reichsführer had stated that it was a matter of national importance. Adolf didn't much like Himmler. The man was pedantic and, in many ways, rather stupid. But he was an able administrator, an excellent clerk and obedient to a fault. Like a dog, Heinrich Himmler basked and glowed whenever praised by his Führer. Adolf rarely, if ever, looked for excellence in his associates and underlings; merely a moderate amount of ability and total obedience. The last thing he needed was to be surrounded by men of ability and individual opinion. Perish that thought! Morons might be impossible to like but they were far easier to control.

"Come!" He used his deep, guttural command style voice. Best keep his trembling little Schutzstaffel boss on his toes.

It was almost comic. Himmler popped his head around the side of the wide office door like a character out of a badly drawn cartoon. The terror of the German Reich knew very well who his master was.

Adolf did the Reichsführer the courtesy of rising from behind his desk. "Himmler, my dear fellow. What brings you here in such a rush, eh?"

Himmler came into the room marched up to the desk and saluted his Führer. He became flustered when Hitler offered his hand, as his own was only half way down from his perfect Nazi salute. A confusingly quick up-down-up-down by the hands of both men resulted in Hitler withdrawing his hand and leaving the Reichsführer with his own hand outstretched, ignored and looking for all the world like a blind man groping for a support.

"Ah-hem," Himmler began. "Yes, my Führer. There is something of great import, which is truly most shocking, and which I believe necessitates your immediate attention, my Führer." He coughed politely behind a flattened palm. "At your convenience, of course, sir."

"I see," Hitler sat, leaned back and glanced up at the ceiling, whilst at the same time gesturing his permission for Himmler to sit. Despite his prim and proper exterior, the outwardly dull and boring SS chief had a penchant for occasionally veering toward outrageously wild courses of esoteric investigation. Some of Himmler's underlings were quite firmly convinced that he intended to seek out and introduce himself to God; others believed in him to such an extent that they were equally firmly convinced that, once he had discovered the correct formulae of potions and spells, he would do precisely that. The astral plane world of the Reichsführer SS was a strange place and he had no trouble in populating it with like-minds.

Adolf had learnt of late that his near-sighted Reichsführer had recently initiated research into the occult, black magic, satanic rites and all manner of religious faiths and ideals at his SS leadership school at Wewelsburg Castle in the picturesque Alme Valley. Under the Reichsführer's orders, and with the SS footing the bill, the ancient castle had been refurbished and transformed into something quite different. Gone was the SS leadership school. The entire edifice was a now feared and avoided SS Occult research centre. Like the castle from Bram Stoker's novel, Dracula, Wewelsburg castle, or castle Wolfenstein as it had become known by the locals, loomed threateningly over the picturesque little village of Alme. Although there were no fearfully related stories of an evil, blood hungry count issuing forth from Wewelsburg at night seeking victims, the locals swore to anyone who would listen, that the sounds emanating from that menacing castle when darkness fell were all too often inhuman and terrifying.

All complete rubbish, of course. Himmler loved playing mister scary and using his black-clad SS to frighten common people. All to the good. It kept them in their place and saved him, Adolf, from having to look like the ogre of the piece.

"Explain." He looked sharply at Himmler and then at the file he was withdrawing from his briefcase. The Reichsführer hesitated, remembering all too clearly his initial reaction to the file when he had first read it. The last thing he wanted was to stand, sit or be anywhere near Hitler if he flew into one of his violent rages. They were terrifying and so nervously debilitating for the sensitive Reichsführer. When confronted by such, Heinrich was inclined to feel incapacitated for days afterwards. He quite simply could not mentally withstand such monumental assaults upon his psyche as those which his Führer was capable of unleashing upon him, and others, too, come to that. Adolf had the knack of being able to shriek, at will, like a demented Titan.

"Well, my Führer," the tone was, he hoped, suitably obsequious. "It concerns a high-ranking member of the SS."

Adolf sighed and with avuncular reassurance said, "You cannot be held responsible for the failings of all those under your command, Himmler. You take too much upon yourself. Bad for the humours, you know; and you can take that from someone with an exhaustive knowledge of such things. Oh yes. So, then, out with it." He gave the SS chief a friendly nod.

"It concerns a certain Oberführer," Himmler threw his gaze off centre hoping like crazy that Hitler would pre-empt him. The Führer, however, just sat waiting impassively, although a slight tapping of his right foot from beneath the desk displayed a stealthily emerging impatience.

"This Oberführer," continued the Reichsführer, "is well known to the Führer. Very well known. He is, my Führer, non-other than your old comrade in arms, Oberführer Emil Maurice." Himmler sat back and awaited Hitler's response.

A few seconds of complete silence passed as Hitler gazed deep into his underling's eyes; a gaze that Himmler tried but failed to hold. He looked down instead at his folded hands.

"Oberführer Maurice?" Hitler's tone was soft, inviting and pleasant to the ear. Trouble! That tone spelt trouble. "Ah, yes. I remember him very well. I personally, personally, found him a position in Becker's ministry for trade. A quiet post for a quiet man. What can he possibly have done to so upset you, Himmler?" Adolf waited for an answer. Truth was, of course, his old friend Emil Maurice was anything but the quiet sort. He stayed silent because he knew what was good for him. There was always the chance, though, that he might burst out of his silence. If that were the case......well it would have to be sorted!

"Sir. My Führer." The Reichsführer rose and stood rigidly to attention. "I regret, that I must inform the Führer, that it has come to my attention that Oberführer Emil Maurice is a.... well sir, the Oberführer is a Jew." There it was. He'd got it out and now all he could do was await the inevitable explosion of rage from his leader as he digested this unpalatable fact.

A brief silence, no outburst, no shriek of rage. Not even a change in facial expression. Himmler stood, waiting and puzzled, as the Führer leafed idly through the file before him barely pausing as he turned the pages.

"Ah!" The Führer's left index finger tapped hard against the last page in the file. "So that's how all this has come about. He seeks permission to get married."

"Yes, my Führer. That's quite right, sir. We have not yet run a complete check upon his illegally desired paramour but thus far it would seem that she is of good Aryan stock. A credit to our race. Such being the case, my Führer, as it would seem to be, then I shall, of course, initiate criminal proceedings against this fellow, Maurice at once."

Hitler looked up at him questioningly.

"The despoiling of German womanhood, my Führer. The mixing of Jewish with Aryan blood. It is now a capital offence under the Nuremburg Laws."

"Laws which are not yet fully promulgated."

"A matter of days only, my Führer. We shall merely be a little in advance of the final ruling."

"Ah." Hitler puffed out his cheeks a little and looked to one side. He almost felt a slight degree of jealousy that his old friend Emil had found solace in the arms of a woman. But then, that was Emil, any old port in a storm and Emil Maurice was not a man to deny himself his creature comforts for too long. It was this 'permission to marry' clap-trap that was causing all the kerfuffle. Without that, the likelihood of anyone ever discovering Emil's Jewish ancestry would have been hugely remote. Silly, silly man. These checks had been Emil's very own idea all those years ago when he had first dreamt up the SS. Talk about chickens coming home to roost. Oh, Emil. What a damn comedy.

"I must, of course, immediately strip Herr Maurice of his rank and titles within the SS and I am toying with the idea of sending him to one of our new camps and letting him rot there. It is horribly awkward my Führer, to order the execution of the creator of the SS even though that is what he so richly deserves. Unless, sir, you wish me to adopt another course of action. I brought this to your attention, my Führer, because as the supreme head of the Reich it is only fitting that you, yourself, should judge this perfidious individual and pass what is, in your view, my Führer, an appropriate sentence; or should I say punishment?"

Adolf closed the file with care and said, "You shall do nothing. Understand, Himmler – nothing?"

The Reichsführer stood aghast and disbelieving. Had he heard right? "Nothing, my Führer? Did you say do nothing?"

"I did, Himmler. I did say that. Oberführer Emil Maurice is to be regarded as an Honorary Aryan from henceforth. Clear?"

"A WHAT?" Himmler almost shrieked the word. It was the first time in his life that he had raised his voice to the Führer. But this madness; an Honorary Aryan? What sort of hollow blaggarding was that? A man was either an Aryan or he wasn't. And Emil Maurice wasn't!

"I don't understand, my Führer." Himmler's sudden borderline apoplexy was bubbling dangerously close to the surface and threatening to undermine his normal Führer induced servility. "You have so often stated that we must, even if it cost us our lives, our nation, our very souls, we must defend, purify and keep pure our Germanic bloodline."

"True." Hitler puffed himself up in fluffing pigeon style. "Are you questioning my edicts? You choose to query my genius?"

"God in heaven no, my Führer, never! I merely seek to...."

"Do not seek anything other than to obey me, my commands and my will. I have made you what you are, Herr Reichsführer Himmler. And I can make you even more. By that very same token," his voice rose to a terrifying pitch, his face contorted into a mask of demonic (and thoroughly staged) evil, "I can transform your puny existence into one of absolute and unremitting hell."

"I.... I," Himmler trembled and began to feel very afraid and tearful. "My Führer, I sought only to......"

"I don't care what you sought. I seek only your unquestioning obedience. Mark that word, Himmler. Unquestioning! That means my perspiring Reichsführer, I command, you obey. Clear?"

"Yes, my Führer. I obey. My loyalty is my bond, my Führer."

"Good," Hitler waved an airy hand. "I shall decide who shall and who shall not be an Honorary Aryan. Such folk might be of future use to the Reich and the decision shall be mine alone."

"I understand, my Führer. I shall quash all mention of Oberführer Maurice's religious ethnicity."

"Do so at once."

"Yes, my Fuhrer."

"That is not to say, Herr Reichsführer, that we will go soft on the Jews. Continue with your otherwise excellent work with your customary flair, yes?"

Recognizing his dismissal Himmler saluted. "I understand fully, my Führer. You may rely totally upon me and the SS."

"Good. Now, remember that next year we are hosting the Olympics, so you may increase your standard arrest and imprisonment efforts for the time being but be prepared to scale them back as we close in on 1936. We must attempt to promote an atmosphere of brotherly goodwill to all men; that kind of thing. Alright, old fellow?"

"Yes, my Führer. I shall see to it all." Himmler favoured his leader with a fearful sick smile and left.

Now he had to face the long walk back along the imposing Reichstag hallway. When he had arrived some thirty minutes previously the place had echoed emptily, like a rarely visited mausoleum. Now, though, it teemed with streams of people, military officers, politicians, clerks and all sorts, cluttering up the wide expanse of marble floor and gathering around the impressively framed high windows. A mere thirty minutes ago, upon his arrival through the massive doors of the Reich Chancellery, he had stridden the length of the ornate hallway like Achilles himself; mighty in his SS regalia but, unfortunately, with no one around to admire his uniformed magnificence other than a single and far more impressively built and turned-out SS guard. With all thoughts of personal splendour departed, he now found himself crawling back like a maggot through molasses. Every step he took was a struggle for his ego whipped equilibrium. He was certain that all those around were craning their necks for a glimpse of the humbled and chastised Reichsführer. Sons-of-bitches! Had they heard the Führer chewing him out? No – impossible. The rooms were very effectively soundproofed. Himmler squared his scrawny shoulders and threw back his becapped head in a neck-curving arch. Führer or no Führer they would all, one way or another, learn to fear Heinrich Himmler. He just needed to be careful not to tread on his beloved leader's toes.

The short journey back to his HQ was swiftly accomplished and Himmler lost no time in getting straight down to the task in hand. "Get me Gruppenführer Heydrich," He barked at his aid, Wolfgang Henke. "At once Herr Reichsführer." Hanke snapped out the affirmative response together with a very smart click of his booted heels. The boss was clearly in a vile mood.

The Reichsführer didn't have to wait very long for his chief subordinate to appear. Heydrich was desperate to know what had transpired between two of the most powerful men in Germany. One look at his chief told him that possibly things had not gone too well. Himmler rarely displayed anger, or anything much in the way of emotion unless he felt that he had been vilified in some way. And then? Well at such times, he could become quite astoundingly egocentric, blathering on interminably about unfairness and the harshness of his life, etc. The Reichsführer, Heydrich decided, was no iron man. That blancmange spine of his would bend double under the first sign of real pressure.

"Sit," Himmler commanded in a brisk but not too unfriendly tone.

Heydrich eased his six-foot-plus frame into the leather covered English Chesterfield that sat just off right to the Reichsführer's desk. Himmler eyed him over his gleaming pince-nez. He had meant for Heydrich to sit in the oak chair in front of him, close to his big carefully arranged desk. Heydrich sitting himself at the somewhat greater distance left the Reichsführer feeling not quite so much in control as he would have liked. It also meant having to raise his voice slightly. It would, of course, seem petty to order his subordinate to move to the less comfortable solidity of the oak chair; might make him look small minded. Or would it? He rolled his lower lip as he pondered yet another of the day's problems. Pah! Too late. The moment had passed and he needed to get on. He would think of a suitable Heydrich put-down later in the day. Something really mean and trivial that would get right up his subordinate's nose. His dangerous subordinate, though. He mustn't forget that, not for an instant. He evinced an emotionless smile at Heydrich who, quite reasonably confident in his own burgeoning power, ignored what he took to be his chief's odd little grimace. He did not doubt that Himmler had managed to work out that he, Reinhard Heydrich, had known full well that Hitler and Maurice had once been close friends and that the Führer had every intention of protecting his friend of yesteryear. Himmler was doubtless fuming over the fact that he had marched himself before the Führer without the requisite information, thus making himself look a complete fool before his feared and revered lord and master. He would be looking for someone to blame. That someone had to be Gruppenführer Heydrich. Why had his deputy not warned him, informed him, of the full facts of the matter? Reinhard crossed his legs elegantly and made a point of studying his well-manicured fingernails. He would simply protest ignorance of the Führer's former liaison with Maurice. After all, they really should consider it a feat of brilliance on his part that he had unearthed this snippet of information in the first place. He had done his job and would strenuously deny any knowledge of the friendship that existed between Hitler and his Jewish buddy. It was hardly his fault if the Reichsführer hadn't done his homework. He should have made it his business to know. The fact that his reputation and ego might have been somewhat put-out by his failure and dressing down by the Fuhrer (oh yes, Reinhard knew, alright) was certainly not the fault of the hard-working, hugely talented, if rather determinedly ambitious, Gruppenführer Heydrich. Complete hogwash, of course, because it most certainly was all his fault; every last deliberately aimed shit-stirring drop of it. Heydrich blew contentedly across his fingertips. He was satisfied. As far as protestations of innocence went, his should sound more than adequate if it became necessary to trot them out.

Himmler felt his pulse rate increase very slightly as he observed the always immaculately turned-out Heydrich blow over those slim, elegant, musician's fingers. Himmler did not possess slim and elegant fingers. He did not, in fact, possess a single physical trait that might be described as even remotely in keeping with any common notion pertaining to male attractiveness.

What did give him immense satisfaction, though, was the inescapable fact that, despite his sporting prowess, fencing, swimming and shooting, the Gruppenführer was possessed of what might best be termed as, childbearing hips. They were too wide for his otherwise well-toned torso and legs. Not that anyone ever, ever, dared mention this strange physical characteristic of the Gruppenführer to his face nor anywhere near him. He was a fearsome and lethal opponent who went for the jugular every time he engaged in any kind of combat. Fear inspiring and terrifying, were precisely the correct words to use when describing Gruppenführer Reinhard Heydrich. Had they really mocked this man at school? It seemed barely believable but the reports stated that it was so. Oh well. Himmler hoped profoundly that Heydrich's torment had been severe and nightmare forming.

"I have just returned from a meeting with the Führer." Himmler spoke calmly but the tiniest tick flickering at the bottom right corner of his lip betrayed the still festering resentment bubbling close beneath the urbane surface of the SS commander-in-chief.

There was a brief, unexpected silence and then, like a fair-ground-pop-up, the Reichsführer shot rocket-like out of his chair and stood rigid.

Even a man as powerful and confident as Reinhard Heydrich wouldn't dare sit whilst his ranking chief stood, so he rose and waited for the thunderclap, which he knew was coming, to break out over their heads. Inwardly, he knew that he had pushed Himmler to something. The man's face had all of a sudden become quasi messianic. A ghastly smile crossed his pale, mongoloid features.

"There is something I want you to do, my dear Gruppenführer.

Heydrich drew himself up to his full height. Shoulders back, belly in. Every inch the splendid Teutonic knight; apart from those slightly over-round hips, of course.

In his own superlatively urbane manner Heydrich responded.

"The Reichsführer has merely to command." A slight bow and deft incline of the handsome blond head, and Heydrich returned to the erect at attention position. His deferential sentence had been nothing more than a sarcasm laden trickle of drool but Himmler missed that completely, as Heydrich had known he would.

Himmler raised his right hand with index finger extended. The movement and the following pose were a direct copy from the Führer repertoire of fancy poses and arm waving. Might look good enough on the Austrian oik, thought Reinhardt, but on Himmler, no; not at all impressive. Nevertheless, he waited and Himmler continued.

"The Führer," Himmler mouthed the words as though he were invoking a vision of God. A wide sweep of his right arm followed by an upward and all-encompassing thrust from his left, palm up and fingers curled. "The Führer," he intoned for a second time. Heydrich watched with barely concealed amusement. The Reichsführer looked for all the world like a man conducting an imaginary orchestra. Himmler's right index finger pointed suddenly at Heydrich.

"The Führer sends his compliments, Heydrich, for the diligent work that you have carried out on his behalf. To serve the Führer is to water the greatness of the Third Reich."

"A greatness before which we all make obeisance and vow everlasting fealty, Herr Reichsführer." How he got that out without laughing like a donkey on nitrous oxide, Heydrich would never know. It was all too silly but the Reichsführer loved, absolutely adored, the high blown over-stressed phraseology which was rapidly becoming identified with SS terminology. Fine, if that's what it took to keep the fool calm, then so be it. No wonder, he mused, that Hitler himself thought the SS to be boneheaded morons good only for one thing; doing as they were told. But what the devil was it that Himmler was going to ask, to demand of him?

"Now," Himmler became smooth, almost smarmy as he carefully folded his arms and leaned back slightly on his raised SS booted heels. "As you know, next year will see us here in Berlin hosting the Olympic Games. The XI Olympiad, in fact," he added self-importantly. "I believe that you are yourself hoping to gain a place on the German fencing team, Herr Gruppenführer."

"If my duties permit, Herr Reichsführer it would be an honour to represent the Fatherland."

"Of course, of course. It will be such a pleasure to observe one of our own in action." Himmler smiled a shade too smugly. He would make it his business to ensure that the fearsome Gruppenführer would be positively buried beneath a mountain of duties. Far too many to allow any of that leaping about with floppy swords rubbish. Something to look forward to thought Himmler. It should be well worth the wait to see his subordinate's woe-hung face when he realised that the only Olympic action he was going to be involved with was going be the arranging and supervision of the Führer's security detail and that of every single foreign dignitary that chose to attend the games. Enough work there to keep him more than just a little busy.

"However," continued the Reichsführer, "with a view to the coming Olympiad: the Führer has stated that your activities with regard to the Jewish question, in effect the Jews themselves, you see, might need to be, in fact must be scaled back before the inevitable rush of foreigners crosses our borders and witness things that might cause them to arrive at a complete misconception of what we are trying to do here in Germany. They are…."

"Not likely to understand that we want the Jews gone, or dead?"

"Just so," Himmler's face was now completely expressionless. The actions with which we are cleansing our house, along with," he glared pointedly at Heydrich, "such language as you have just used, must be put aside until all this running and jumping nonsense is done with. Clear?"

"Absolutely, Herr Reichsführer."

"Now to the point, my dear Heydrich. The Führer requires that for the next two months, we increase drastically the level of severity concerning our actions against the Jewish population nationwide, but not so much so in Berlin. You, Gruppenführer Heydrich, shall oversee, in the wider sense, all activities and monitor such. You will report directly to me. You need not take account of the Gauleiters' demands and wishes. Some of them are wishy-washy and prone to sentiment; ideologically soft. You know the type. They can be weeded out later. You answer only to me and, of course, the Führer should he wish to become directly involved. You see and understand the scope of all this,

I take it?"

Heydrich nodded, calmly awaiting the final thrust of his boss's statement. Hitler most certainly would not want to become directly involved with anything that required hard work, odium or blame. Of that he was sure.

"Finally." Himmler's chinless little head arched back slightly as he prepared to deliver his carefully primed bombshell.

"The Führer requires that you, Herr Gruppenführer Heydrich, and let us be perfectly clear, you personally, undertake a task of the utmost importance. It would not be an overstatement to say, of national importance. As such the implementation of this vital task falls to you, Herr Gruppenführer, a tried and tested warrior to the cause of National Socialism. Heil Hitler!"

What on earth was the man blathering on about? "Oh, yes. Heil Hitler." Even rolling headfirst out of a bunk-bed Heydrich would have accomplished the dramatic Nazi salute with infinitely more grace and form than his pigeon-chested boss.

Himmler lowered his arm and stood, staring triumphantly at his subordinate.

For heaven's sake, thought Heydrich. If the fool's not going to tell me, then I'd better ask.

"And the great task with which I am to be entrusted Herr Reichsführer. What, precisely, might that be?"

Himmler smiled with, what was for him, something approaching genuine warmth. "The Führer requests, that you, Gruppenführer Heydrich, take upon those broad shoulders of yours the responsibility of designing, creating, and eventually putting into action a final solution to our mutual problem." The lie fell easily from those well-practised lips. The idea was his and his alone but once under way the Führer would never in a hundred years veto or countermand it. Not even the glorious Führer could stop what was going to happen. Not that he would want to; but if he did, he wouldn't be able to, so that was that, almost.

"And what, sir, do please pardon my obtuseness, is our mutual problem?"

"The very one that you, Heydrich, are going to sort out. You can set up a new department because it will doubtless become highly detailed and very," he nodded conspiratorially, "very hush-hush. You understand me?"

Reinhard knew that he was being goaded. Himmler was teasing and deliberately trying to provoke him to anger. It wasn't working. The fact that he would dearly love to take his scrawny little leader's neck in his hands and wring it was simply par for the course. He felt that urge every day. The mere thought of forcing those puffy little eyes to burst bloodily from their mongoloid sockets gave him a thrill of sexual pleasure. Even the idea of viciously slapping that insipid, idiotic face of his and witnessing the terrified surprise that would cross those soft little features, brought on an erotic tingle. But, that was as far as it would ever go. Reinhard Heydrich, despite his faults and foibles, was nothing if not well-bred; a gentleman. His father had created the famous Halle orchestra and he would die before he lost self-control before this overpaid clerk. So, he said nothing and allowed his ice-cold and highly menacing stare to do his talking.

Himmler cleared his throat. "What you are going to do Herr Gruppenführer is create a solution, a way, method, design, call it what you will, of ridding us of the pestilence that pervades Germany. Rid us of it PERMANENTLY! Is that clear enough Herr Gruppenführer?"

"The Jews?"

"Of course the bloody Jews. Who else, man?"

There it was again. That total, unreasoning hatred. Heydrich didn't mind at all getting rid of all the Jews with whatever method suggested itself; but by the same token he would be happy enough to carry out the same procedure on old women, Catholics, children and pretty well anything else that popped up. He realised, though, that the Reichsführer was deadly serious and was demanding a long-term and permanent solution. Such a thing would take time, possibly years and would in all likelihood become its own steamroller. Heydrich didn't know that Himmler was lying about the order coming down from the Führer but that didn't matter. Nothing of this description was ever likely to be put down in black and white, anyway. As if hearing his thoughts, the Reichsführer said, "Needless to say, Heydrich, there will never be anything in writing that directly corresponds to whatever action you take.

" Understood, Herr Reichsführer." Heydrich's rather high-pitched voice was silky smooth with menace. Truth be told, he was feeling quite flattered and pretty good about things. This most recent commission suited his talents and temperament admirably. There were more than five hundred thousand Jews still in Germany and they were soon all to be his; to flay, torture and kill as he saw fit. Joy!

"It shall be done, Herr Reichsführer. Heil Hitler!"

Himmler nodded, returned the salute and breathed heavily with satisfaction as Heydrich left the room and returned to his lair to already begin the planning of human destruction.

Himmler sat and spread his hands out over the desk. His mind went over the many conversations that he had entered into with Hitler concerning the Jews. Hitler it was who constantly screamed about the perfidy of the Hebrew race. Now, though, it was on/off, hot/cold. NO! That was not the way. To hell with the Olympiad. Well, alright, if it had to be, he could wait until late next year but then – then? Himmler's face became a revolting mask of a weak man's hatred and bile. The Führer had belittled him; behind his back Heydrich mocked him. "I will give you something to chew on," he said out loud. "Mock me, will you – laugh at me, will you?" His voice rose and perspiration ran freely down his face as he waved sweat dampened hands. "I shall fill your gullets with the corpses of dead Jews. Their Rabbis, their women, their children, their stinking old men: I shall fill Germany to overflowing with dead Hebrews, Gypsies and other riff-raff. See if you laugh, then. The future will hail me as one of the greatest Germans of all time. And as for you, Oberführer Emil Maurice," his face twisted with all the ugliness that only complete, unreasoning hatred can produce. His next words came out in a serpent's hiss of pure venom. "Think I can't get to you, do you? Well, we shall see. The Führer sees fit to protect your vile Jewish being. So, for the time being, you still walk this earth but I can get to you Emil Maurice in so many different ways, as you shall see!"

CHAPTER 16

September 9 1935: Augsburg, Bavaria

SS Obersturmführer Franz Maurice trod his deliberate way toward his office on Kleber Strasse in the municipal centre of ancient and lovely Augsburg. No need for a car on a warm and cloudless day like today. He lived just a ten-minute walk away from his place of work, the central office of the SS-Verfügungstruppe in Bavaria. Despite a recent scare, he had good reason to be content and at peace with the world. Brother Emil had done well enough for all the family. From a humble watch repair man to the dizzy heights of SS Oberführer stationed in Berlin was one hell of an achievement. And now Emil had married a girl from an upper middle-class background, thus elevating the working-class Maurice family to a social position far above anything they might have realistically envisaged before their rise to prominence as loyal enforcers of the Nazi regime. Franz allowed himself a sly grin. The social elevation was nice and made him feel good. And their luck was holding. Franz sometimes worried whether even his brother's relationship with Hitler would be enough to hold back the slavering hounds of antisemitism should the world at large discover the truth about the Maurice family. Being highly respected pillars of National Socialism and all its ideals would not likely count for much. Such beer hall respect would evaporate into the ether if their secret become generally known. Franz, although not wanting such thoughts to spoil what promised to be a beautifully sunny morning, simply could not keep a nagging apprehension at bay. In his opinion, Emil had made a huge mistake in filling out that SS-Permission to Marry application. He must surely have known that they would check, and check thoroughly, too. The trouble was Emil's insatiable ego. He'd clearly reckoned that his position as the creator of the SS would protect him. Wrong! Himmler was now the number one in the SS and wielded enormous power. The organization was nothing like the entity that Emil had dreamed up all those years ago. The damn thing was massive, unwieldy and had taken on a multifaceted life of its own. Emil had underestimated Himmler, overestimated himself and was lucky in his relationship with Hitler. That luck, however, would only go so far in this surreal world of odd-sods and barrow boys. The main complication had arisen solely because of Emil's total infatuation with his new wife, Hedwig, and an overwhelming desire to impress her. She was a lovely girl in all respects and the daughter of a serving Wehrmacht colonel. Nothing could ever be too much trouble for his wonderful bride, the love of his life. Fair enough, the girl seemed to love him right back, doted on him. She truly believed that her SS beau, now husband, was every bit as important as he loudly proclaimed himself to be. Emil, regarding himself as untouchable, and besotted with his beautiful Hedwig, had blundered on regardless and walked blithely into a storm of trouble. Thankfully, his long-standing relationship with the Führer had seen him through the crisis of Himmler's hatred. For some reason *other* than Emil's Jewishness, the SS Reichsführer had taken a massive dislike to him and desired his end by whatever means possible. The Führer obviously had a high personal regard for the recently married Oberführer Maurice and the Reichsführer would have been blind not to notice it. But the truth behind his hatred for Oberführer Maurice remained a mystery.

Himmler knew of Maurice's deep involvement with Hitler on the Night of the Long Knives, where Maurice, supporting his Führer against supposed enemies in the riotous and no longer reliable SA, had ruthlessly gunned down the homosexual Edmund Heines and his boyfriend in cold blood and in flagrante delicto. It was also rumoured that he had aimed a kick and spat messily at the SA's former leader, Ernst Rohm, as he was led away in disgrace to his ultimate execution a few days later. None of that cut any ice with the vindictive Reichsführer. Once he developed a hate, or even a minor dislike for someone, they were permanently in his sights, on his 'to-do list', so to speak. Even Himmler, though, could not gainsay the Führer of the Third Reich. So, Emil, Franz and the family Maurice survived Himmler's wrath and did all they could to stay well out of his way.

Franz was enjoying his walk to the office and the automatic respect that his natty insignia laden SS uniform drew from passing strangers. Tall, powerful men docilely moved aside to allow him ease of passage; women lowered their heads and directed coy smiles toward him. Franz was on the short side and in no way a fighting man. That sort of thing he left to his older brother Emil. Emil was tough as old bricks; just rather too lippy with it was the only drawback. Nevertheless, he thoroughly enjoyed playing the 'tough SS man'. It felt good to know that big strong men who really were tough guys were afraid of him. Yup, they were afraid of little old, scared stiff Franz Maurice; a man who would run a hundred miles to avoid any kind of physical confrontation that might involve bodily harm, pain or injury – to himself, that is. In high good humour he crossed the road just a few yards from the main entrance to his office.

The car that hit him was travelling at more than fifty miles per hour, or so witnesses later testified. No registration number was forthcoming and there was nothing much by way of an investigation, despite the rank and occupation of the deceased. Poor Obersturmführer Franz Maurice died instantly and never knew what killed him.

Ten kilometres away in Dierdorf a tall young man in a plain grey woollen suit climbed out of the newish but now slightly dented DKW F5. Young he certainly was, twenty-two, or so, if even that. Well set up, he moved gracefully around to the front of the car. A couple of dents but nothing in the way of blood and gore. The impact had been precise and luck had been on his side. At a shade above forty-five miles per hour the wide-fronted DKW with its inverted bull bar chrome bumper, had lifted the small SS man clean into the air and forward from the murderous machine and driver bent upon his destruction. Just as he hit the ground, stunned and unable to realise what was happening to him, his head was cracked open by the jutting kerbstone which he unhappily struck with great downward force. Within a split second the car struck him again, crushing his already shattered head and grinding his ribs deep into his lungs. He was dead before the rear wheels rolled over his shattered body.

It had all gone very smoothly, as far as the young man was concerned. Surprisingly so, as this was his first assignment. There was no way at all that his uniformed victim could have survived. The sound of Franz Maurice's head hitting the concrete road almost immediately after impact told its own story. The explosive skull cracking pop had resounded like a bottle of champagne being uncorked.

He turned and walked briskly to the front door of the wide fronted, three storied house in Rosenweg, a wide cul-de-sac in the village of Dierdorf where even the meanest properties were expensive. Pretty well this entire area was owned by Friedrik Lehmann, the owner of the house that the young driver was about to enter. The man who greeted him at the open door, though, bore no resemblance to the suave and urbane Lehmann. Sturmbannführer Johann Rattenhuber was built along the lines of something wide, thick and decidedly unpleasant. His chiselled features looked to have been cast by a sculptor enduring a grey day in hell. To say he was ugly would be a ludicrous understatement. But in a world where physical ugliness and psychological deviance were prized attributes, he was bound to do well. So well in fact, that he had succeeded the ever loyal and now promoted Bruno Gesche. But whereas Gesche had been merely scary; Rattenhuber was a howling horror! Standing at five feet and eight inches in height he was a good deal shorter than the young, athletic man approaching him. Very broad across shoulders and back, with thick arms which bulged uncompromisingly through tunic sleeves that would have comfortably encased the thighs of most men, he exuded raw physical power. His gaze, like a temporarily satiated raptor surveying its next prey, was one long, cold, dead-eyed stare, which would stay dead until something or someone rekindled his appetite. Then one might notice life, of a sort, fill those dark eyes. He had once been a career police officer but police work in civilian life gave nothing approaching the personal fulfilment and overall satisfaction that he imbibed on an almost daily basis working as the Chief of the Führer's security detail. He had the power to make generals grovel; he loved that power and he used it, constantly.

Just being within a few feet of Johann Rattenhuber was enough to raise trembling goosebumps in his subordinates and the hackles of his equals. But not those of the young fellow walking easily toward him, though. This man didn't give a monkey's toss about hard cases, flattened noses and evil reputations. He was a man, young, it was true, who made those noses flat and delighted in destroying inflated tough guy egos. He greeted Rattenhuber with a brilliantly winning smile that crossed genuinely over his handsome face. He saluted briefly and Rattenhuber responded politely enough with a quick right cross of a salute. His eyes were asking the question, although a call had come through within minutes of the event in Augsburg.

"No problems, sir. A complete success and no pursuit. All satisfactorily completed, Herr Sturmbannführer." A smart click of his civilian heeled shoes was accompanied by another winning smile.

Rattenhuber shook his head in amusement. This lad was something else, he really was. He had just killed one of the highest-ranking SS men in Augsburg and here he was talking about it as though he had just been chosen to play a minor league game for the Hitler Youth. The grim-faced Sturmbannführer couldn't help himself and cast a friendly grimace at his protégé.

"Inside, laddie. There's someone due to arrive shortly and they'll want to meet you before we send you on your way."

The young man obeyed at once and strode into the house, noticing as he did so an open door behind which a large group of people were chatting and filling the place with cigar and cigarette smoke. They looked to be important folk, top drawer. The smell of expensive cologne and perfume mixed with tobacco smoke wafted out; all rather sensual.

Rattenhuber gestured to a smaller door by the wide staircase and the young man entered and waited. Then he crooked a finger at a shirt-sleeved individual standing idly by one of the flowerbeds. The man became at once a ball of energy and rushed to stand before him. Rattenhuber gestured to the front of the car and said, "Sort it and clean her up."

"Yes sir. At once."

The DKW was driven to the four-car garage at the far side of the house, and within a few short minutes had a brand-new set of number plates; less than fifteen minutes after that the dents were straightened and the car as clean as a whistle. All done and very neatly, too.

CHAPTER 17

September 9 1935: Dierdorf, 10:30hrs

Friedrik Lehmann was going to be both pleased and relieved when his associates departed. However, as most of them had only recently arrived he would have quite a long wait. And the guest of honour, Heinrich Himmler, had yet to put in an appearance. Their formerly quite small circle of wealthy industrialists, businessmen and newspaper owners had grown considerably since they had ploughed in the necessary money and influence to ensure that their occasionally charismatic puppet, Adolf Hitler, became duly elected by all legal means. Together they had succeeded beyond their wildest dreams. But it was Hitler who had accomplished the seemingly impossible by overturning heavy percentage odds and brilliantly taking advantage of his opponents' weaknesses and mistakes. However, none of them, not even Friedrik Lehmann, had foreseen the incredibly audacious move by Hitler of seizing the Presidency, and then dragging out and enforcing an all-encompassing Enabling Act, with the effect of making him dictator by consent of the Reichstag and therefore, the people. He then boldly announced that he, *he*, had decided to abolish the office of the Presidency and that henceforth he would rule alone, as supreme commander and Führer of the Third Reich. Even his closest associates had been stunned by the speed and nerve of his actions. Hitler had not, Lehmann now realised, deeply planned any of those moves. There had been little or no deliberation whatsoever. The wretched man had quite simply chanced his arm: all or nothing and if nothing, why then, what the hell!

Incredible! The Party, Gauleiters, SS-Leaders and such, were still cock-a-hoop and so were a majority of the electorate. As to the group attending here today, though? Well, there was some deep-seated doubt being voiced. Softly and with great caution, it was true, but voiced nevertheless. His associates, mused Lehmann, were not sieg-heiling morons to be gulled by the aimless waffle of a street corner bookie. Nevertheless, gulled or not, every man and woman here was profiting right royally from their generous fiscal association with mister wonderful himself, Adolf Hitler and his idiosyncratic party. Their closest association, though, was with Heinrich Himmler. The number one SS man, a fellow with infinite human resources at his disposal and with yet more to come – or so he had promised. He was a man whose still growing influence seemed to permeate the very air breathed throughout Germany. A word from him to any dignitary involved and a contract was as good as awarded, regardless of the frequently outrageous claims of the submitted tender. Excellent.

Now, they even had their very own little club. Strictly members only, of course. 'Friends of the Reichsführer' had been the circle's early designation. For it had, after all, been through the influence and foresight of Reichsführer Himmler that the many lucrative contracts and favours which the circle now enjoyed had been provided. It was all very symbiotic. Under his auspices the members of the circle thrived, and under their generous patronage the Nazi Party had grown, become rich and now ruled through new and impressively constructed buildings, some of which were so spacious that they resembled the glittering palaces of old. All that was down to Hitler's latest favourite-in-chief, Albert Speer. Speer was clever and in Lehmann's opinion might well outlast many of the Führer's current mish-mash of inner circle acolytes. At present, however, he was too much a small fish to be considered a serious threat. Other more important concerns required immediate attention. Hence today's ad hoc meeting.

Cracks were beginning to appear in the united front normally presented by the circle. The natives, it might be suggested, were becoming restless. True, every member of the circle was making obscene amounts of money. Weapons, tanks, aircraft and ships, bullets and bayonets the manufacture of which had made Friedrik Lehmann even more obscenely rich than he already was. And it was true enough to say that, idiosyncratic and revoltingly deviant lunatics though they may well be, the Nazis knew how to create previously unthought of ways of making money whilst at the same time preventing any bureaucratic interference from slowing down the immensely profitable gravy train that they were all so comfortably riding. As long as everybody toed the same line, all would be well. That, however, was one of the problems; small at the moment but it might grow. Some toes were shifting away from that line.

The Keppler Circle, for as such they were now known, was a gathering of filthy rich and massive egos. No one in the group could tolerate being bossed about. They had, all of them, fondly imagined that it would be they who did the bossing over these moronic louts masquerading as politicians and soldiers. It was now becoming ever clearer that they had badly underestimated Herr Hitler and his cronies. None of them, not even Lehmann, had been given any say at all in government policy or actions. They had anticipated being listened to, of giving firm and obediently followed directions to the ship of state. Such had not happened. Their advice was neither asked nor sought. The Nazi ship was sailing right enough but the direction was, to say the least, erratic.

True, the wonderfully profitable contracts continued to roll in but it was *their* obedience that was demanded, expected and insisted upon. Pay your dues, and that meant millions, and manufacture what we say. Those were unalterable commands from the Nazi hierarchy. Some members were even beginning to feel that they might be in danger if they displayed hesitation or unwillingness. It was Lehmann's job to keep this particular vehicle on the straight and narrow, massage their egos and persuade them that all was well and that it was a wonderful thing to have such a strong government protecting at all times the interests of the filthy rich, of which they were such shining and exemplary lights. He hoped they would listen, because even shining and exemplary lights were not above having their toenails removed, tongues torn out or family members abruptly disappear.

But it wasn't simply unrest within a small part of the Keppler Circle that was concerning Friedrik Lehmann. He had an eye to the future and it bothered him that the Nazi's method of governing, and that meant Adolf Hitler's method of governing, was not in the real sense any kind of governing at all. The French had a phrase for it; laissez-faire. There was far too much of 'let them just get on with it, it'll all work out in the end'.

Lehmann shrugged. It was the Nazi way. Divide and rule. It had to be altered, though, at least a little, else the entire edifice would come crashing down around them. Only the week before he had found it necessary to become directly involved with sheet metal production at his new factory in Dusseldorf. An order placed by the Army requested two thousand tons of 4mm plated and worked steel for delivery before April 1936. Wonderful! A first-class money-spinning order to fill for the Army. Couldn't go wrong. A growing and insatiable, metal devouring monster whose demands were only ever likely to increase. Lehmann had been in high good humour. Production had commenced almost immediately and then the waters broke, so to speak. The civilian branch of the Wehrmacht procurement office located within the Ministry of Defence in the Wilhelmstrasse, Berlin, had written stating that the previously ordered 4mm plate must in fact be 3.8 because of the pre-planned rivet sizing. The Wehrmacht procurement office, based in the same building but two floors down, was enraged, and at once countermanded the order from the Ministry of Defence office. Lehmann, always hating to become personally involved on this level, sent his high-flying personal representative, Karl Döhring, to sort matters out. Matters were not sorted out. Döhring was confronted with obstinacy and obtuseness and an introduction to the overall big cheese of armament production, who headed yet another department in the same building. He was an ancient relic named Field Marshal Walter Bacher. Bacher had smiled, then looked stern and then said that he would rule on the matter later, after he had interviewed the heads of the departments concerned.

Which of course, he never did. He merely forwarded the complaint and correspondence dealing with it to the Ministry of Economics who sent it back to the Wehrmacht Procurement Office for their opinion. Ludicrous! Matters were made worse when yet another missive landed on Lehmann's desk. This one stating that until further notice, all, and that meant every cubic centimetre of available plate steel, including all calibres, measures and weights, worked or unworked, must henceforth and until further notice by the issuing authority, be reserved solely for the newly formed Luftwaffe. Germany's splendid new air force must now take priority for *all* available steel; plate or otherwise. The order was signed by none other than Hermann Göring, President of the Reichstag, Prime Minister of Prussia and absolute commander of the Luftwaffe. A man who was greedily grabbing as many reins of economic power as he could.

All pretty hopeless, thought Lehmann. Too many of the current crop of quasi leaders within Germany's myriad, and often pointless, offices and organisations, seemed to think that they merely had to snap their fingers to make a thing happen. Click, and hey-presto! One hundred cubic tons of steel at the door. Why did they refuse to realize that things had to be paid for, planned, husbanded and spread out, conserved, protected and all the other nasty things that the Nazis could neither understand nor abide? They had no patience: everything had to be *now*. Himmler would be here soon and Lehmann, along with the rest, intended to place firmly before the Reichsführer the stark facts of the matter. There was no order, no method or uniformity within the national industrial or political framework. Without change, Germany was on the fast track to becoming an economic train wreck.

At the back of his mind, Friedrik Lehmann, influential and massively rich, owning high rank within the feared SS, began gradually to form an exit strategy. A wise man kept more than one chicken to lay eggs.

Rattenhuber ignored the reception room with its bigwigs and their interminable conceit. He knew Friedrik Lehmann only superficially and didn't trust him. He was too smooth by half. Talk of Midas. The man seemed only to have to think of money to make yet another million. Himmler had bestowed the rank of Gruppenführer upon the suave, well-spoken and always immaculate Friedrik Lehmann, which put that man out of Rattenhuber's reach. But only for the time being, matey, mused the rock-hard Sturmbannführer. I know your type.

His thoughts were pulled up short as he heard a car approaching. This must surely be the Reichsführer. Rattenhuber would have preferred that his chief not meet the young fellow waiting in the ante-room. But Himmler had, this time, insisted upon looking upon the features of Rattenhuber's latest killing acquisition. After all, this last effort had been more than just a little personal.

Himmler eased himself from the rear seat of his supercharged Mercedes 770 and stood for a while by the open door being held obediently by the towering figure of his SS bodyguard. From around the other side of the Mercedes came his aide, Hauptsturmführer Conrad Eicke. Unlike the splendidly wide shouldered and glowing blondness of Himmler's bodyguard, Eicke was of middle height, brown-haired, grey-eyed and with soft-cheeked features supporting a slightly turned-up nose. He was yet another SS officer who gave lie to the Nordic ideal of muscular Nazism allied to superior intellect. Rattenhuber, watching from the front door, reckoned that only the miserable, downtrodden working class possessed the Nordic attributes to which the Nazi ideology was so devoted and enamoured.

He could barely stop the ugly grin from crossing his features. The Aryan Superman, then, was a brain-dead, muscle-bound lump of grimy-fingered neurosis. Mind you, though, a thought brought the encroaching grin smack down off his face; there was always Reinhard Heydrich and his ilk. Even Rattenhuber was ever wary of the SS Gruppenführer.

Himmler waited while Eicke approached with a polished attaché case and shiny silver baton. The baton he handed to the Reichsführer with a respectful bow whilst tucking the attaché firmly under the crook of his elbow. Taking the baton without a word, Himmler strode purposefully toward the waiting Rattenhuber. He modelled, or at least attempted to imitate, his gait and mannerisms upon those of a famous actor, Hans Albers. All the rage was Albers. A man that could move with God-like grace and speak in tones that were able to sway movie and theatre audiences all over Germany and Austria. Albers had the natty trick of wearing his overcoat draped over his shoulders. The effect was one of devastating physical charisma. Women drooled over and men envied the handsome actor. Himmler had attempted the same method with his impressively styled ankle length leather coat but with rather less than the desired effect. On each attempt to casually wear his coat in the cavalier Albers fashion, the wretched thing immediately fell from his too scrawny shoulders into an untidy heap around his ankles. He had given up and relied instead upon his Hugo Boss tailored, cut, re-tailored and re-cut until perfect, uniform. His cap had a raised front and a slightly slashed peak giving him a rakish, bit-of-a-devil look which he liked immensely.

"Heil Hitler!" Rattenhuber's arm shot out in the regulation Nazi salute.

"Heil Hitler," Himmler responded with a theatrical flourish of his shiny silver baton, as Rattenhuber showed him into the large open hallway.

"Herr Reichsführer. Such a pleasure to welcome you to my home." Lehmann appeared with the ease of a butler in a B movie and saluted with the grace of a ballerina accepting a bouquet.

"Which home, Friedrik, you have so many?" Himmler laughed at his own humour and the other two men chortled dutifully.

"Everything ready?" Himmler enquired.

"Oh yes, indeed Herr Reichsführer. We are all gathered and eager to hear your word. As always." The unctuous manner washed over Himmler like an acceptable melody. The Reichsführer clearly relished Lehmann's version of charm and good fellowship. Jesus wept, thought Rattenhuber. Doesn't this wheedling ponce have any shame? The answer to that, he already knew. No!

"Good," Himmler glanced at Rattenhuber. "And the other matter?"

"Ready and awaiting your attention, Herr Reichsführer." The Sturmbannführer didn't bother to smile. He knew that it only made him look even more threatening. He gestured to his left. "In the anti-room, sir."

"Very well. I'll see to this little matter first, if you don't mind, Lehmann."

"But of course not, Herr Reichsführer. Everything shall be as you wish. We are, all of us, at your complete disposal."

"Excellent. "You are acquainted with my aide, Hauptsturmführer Eicke, I believe."

"Yes, we have indeed met." Lehmann smiled at Eicke who returned the gesture with a slight downturn of his lower lip, a click of the heels and a strictly formal, Prussian-style bow. Himmler smiled broadly. He loved the correctness of military and Prussian manners and morals. All so stiff, formal and easy to control.

"Show me," he snapped to Rattenhuber. All business now. It was time to get on.

The Sturmbannführer thrust out a guiding arm and led Himmler to the anti-room where the object of their interest awaited. Himmler was pleased with the way things had gone. If what he had been told was true, the youngster had acted in the manner of a well-seasoned assassin. He'd shown no sign of nervousness before or after, had followed instructions to the letter and to top it all, had accomplished his task and withdrawal from the scene with the minimum of fuss. Hardly the actions of a callow youth. Such men were rare and Himmler secretly envied their cold ability to physically, at first hand, snuff out human life with such nerveless precision. They weren't mere killers, not the best of them. It was an art form. Practised 'til became beautiful. He too, Heinrich Himmler, snuffed out lives, that was true enough. But with him it was more cerebral; all done with the stroke of a pen. And the pen, of course, must always remain mightier than the sword.

He found himself looking up at the young man. The fellow smiled down at him as he threw up his arm in an almost casual salute that from anyone else might have been construed as insulting. But the young man quite simply oozed charm – buckets of it. At around 1.85 metres and a splendidly proportioned ninety kilos of solid muscle, he was certainly impressive enough. It was his manner, though, which so rapidly captivated the Reichsführer. Likeable – was that the word? How could a man with his talents, and obvious lack of scruples, be so intensely likeable at first glance to a total stranger? The smile was genuine and the blue eyes twinkled attractively. The broad shoulders and obvious physical power of the man did not appear to be in any way threatening; at least, not at first glance.

Himmler sucked in his breath. This man was a jewel. He could be sent anywhere and pass any muster asked of him. He didn't have even so much as an iota of the assassin or hard man about him. Yet he was both those things and more. They'd found him, or rather Mohnke had, at a fairground shooting range where the young shooter smilingly beat all challenges. It turned out that they were already acquainted through small-time amateur football tournaments a few years previously, the pair of them being talented sportsmen. They also shared a similar background in carpentry and suchlike.

Friendly persuasion by the naturally convincing Mohnke had steered the younger man in the right direction and a modicum of training had shown him to be a natural. Well-spoken for a lower-class individual he was also surprisingly well-read. Further background checks revealed excellent school grades and glowing reports from impressed teachers. He learnt quickly and soaked up like a sponge the surroundings of wherever he was. He wanted one thing out of life. His own survival and comfort. He was theirs!

Himmler smiled and stuck out his hand. "You have done well. I congratulate you on your success. The SS greatly appreciates your loyalty and diligence."

The young man smiled that winning smile. "My duty only, Herr Reichsführer."

Himmler's forefinger began tapping the young man's lapel and his features creased as if a thought had suddenly occurred to him.

"You know what?" he turned to the ever-grim Rattenhuber. "I have definite plans for this young fellow. Loyalty and talent should be rewarded in equal measure. Don't you think?"

Rattenhuber nodded agreeably. He had no idea what the Reichsführer was droning on about but it was always best just to agree.

"You will return to Berlin where you will report to Hauptsturmführer Mohnke. Once there, take your orders from him and him alone until I instruct you otherwise. Clear?"

The young man nodded without showing the slightest degree of curiosity. Himmler gazed up at him quizzically. What, he wondered, went on in this young fellow's mind? He seemed to take all and everything in his stride. No tick of apprehension or jerky hand movements betraying nervousness. He seemed totally at ease, unflappable. The Reichsführer realised now precisely where he wanted his young apprentice to be. Outwardly he would become a member of the recently formed Waffen SS unit, the Leibstandarte Adolf Hitler. His real work, though, would come through the offices of the SS-Sonderkommando Berlin, where he would be at all times available for whatever duties his master, the Reichsführer-SS, Heinrich Himmler, considered suitable for his talents.

On a sudden impulse he asked, "Have you read any Goethe?"

"Just a little, Herr Reichsführer. We were made to recite some of his work at school."

"Ah!" The Reichsführer nodded sympathetically. "And?"

"Sir?"

"Your opinion, man. What do you think of the great one's works?"

"In so far as I can accurately gauge any such work, Herr Reichsführer, I found that his warnings about the evils of romantic love and, indeed, marriage, worthwhile and succinct."

"Really?" Himmler glanced over at Rattenhuber with an expression of mock surprise.

"No sir. Not really."

Himmler turned back to the completely straight-faced younger man and tapped him firmly on that broad chest with his baton.

"What then, eh?"

"To be perfectly honest, sir. I found it not worth the cost of the paper it was printed on."

"So that's your expert opinion of our greatest poet, is it?" Rattenhuber leant back slightly on his heels. Had the young fool gone too far? Himmler was constantly harping on about honesty from his subordinates but if that honesty didn't coincide with the Reichsführer's own opinion, then, things could get nasty.

"Of all of them, sir."

"Go on."

"Poets and their drivel, sir. I have no time for any of it. Hopelessly self-obsessed fools, sir, and writing for the same."

Himmler's mouth dropped slightly. Not because of the strength of the opinion but from its source. How utterly excellent. The man had spoken words that were music to his ears. Urbane, charming and super likeable he may be, but the fellow didn't have a single romantic bone or thought anywhere about his person. Perfect!

Himmler stepped back. Turning once more to Rattenhuber, he

said, "Does he have everything he needs?"

Rattenhuber looked at the calmly waiting young man, who nodded respectfully.

"He does, sir."

"Then," Himmler tapped his shoulder in a friendly, avuncular fashion. "Off you go. Listen carefully to Hauptsturmführer Mohnke. He can teach you a great deal about the comings and goings in Berlin. You understand?"

"Yes sir."

"Good. We shall meet again in a few days. I shall expect to hear of further good reports."

Himmler watched as Rattenhuber saw his subordinate to the door and then beckoned him over. "Things are moving quickly, Sturmbannführer. I may shortly have to move Mohnke on and up, so to speak." He looked from side to side as if fearing eavesdroppers and then gave Rattenhuber a knowing look. "The Leibstandarte is going to need top men. Loyal men than I can trust. Mohnke is first rate."

"Indeed, sir," Rattenhuber nodded his agreement.

"Think you can handle the Sonderkommando? It will mean a lot on your plate and a total disregard of any previous mores and opinions that you might have held or still hold."

Johann Rattenhuber couldn't suppress the flash of pure satisfaction that crossed his features at that moment. Promotion to the big-time.

"You may always count on me as your most loyal servant, Herr Reichsführer."

Himmler nodded and gave the Sturmbannführer an icy smile. "I am quite sure that I can. Be in Berlin before Thursday next. And keep a close eye on our young friend. I have certain plans for that one." Waving Rattenhuber away Himmler turned and entered the room where Lehmann and his guests were waiting with ever lessening patience.

Outside, the object of Himmler's interest entered the passenger seat of an Opal and lit a cigarette. Born in Oppeln, Silesia on the Polish border, life in his shambling out-of-the-way village had been tough. Both parents dead at an early age, brought up by a strict grandfather and never experiencing anything that might be considered as comfortable let alone luxurious, Rochus Misch was more than happy with the way things were going. He was on the up and up, with a standard of living already beyond anything he had previously hoped for. He had subsidised travel to all sorts of wonderful places and all he had to do was be obedient and not rock anybody's boat. Easy enough. OK, he had been a little puzzled about the killing aspect of it at the beginning, but it had been carefully explained to him that such actions were necessary for the well-being of the people and the state. There were some very bad people out there and they, like a vicious cancer, needed to be removed with all possible dispatch. Rochus hadn't believed a word of it. What he had wholeheartedly believed was that if he didn't comply, then things could go badly for him and the chances of the good life would be swept away. And anyway, he didn't really care too much. If eliminating the nation's enemies meant a comfortable and secure life for him, then so be it. After all, he reasoned, it wasn't as though he was being ordered to kill children or anything like that. No. Life was good. Rochus smiled happily and wondered who might be next.

CHAPTER 18

April 28 1945: Berlin, The Bunker, 18:00hrs

Rochus Misch blinked back a painful tear caused by dry eyes due to the inefficient half-light of the Bunker with its dank, airless rooms and passages. He adjusted his belt. It was noticeable now that his waistline, never thick or flabby, was considerably less than it had been a year or so ago. His mind went back briefly to those halcyon days of Berchtesgaden, Augsburg and other lovely places. When it was all free travel and youthful curiosity about the future. Well, he couldn't help the rueful smile that crossed his still handsome features, the future was not looking so bright now. Himmler gone. Done in and finished, bar a miracle. Heydrich, long dead. There was, though, still the rock-steady Mohnke. A general now and commander of the inner ring of Berlin's defences. He had risen high, had Mohnke. Rochus, however, had not risen high in rank and position, and that had been his only demand for such skilled devoted service. High rank meant being noticed; noticed by pretty well everybody who counted and many more who didn't. Being at the forefront of Joseph Goebbels's all-encompassing state publicity machine, and being lauded (loudly) as a hero of the Reich, would inevitably have led to an agonizing death somewhere during the course of yet another of Hitler's regularly occurring military catastrophes. In truth, Germans preferred their heroes to be well and truly, albeit heroically, dead. With all said and done, dead heroes were easier to tolerate than the all too frequently crippled and disfigured survivors. With the living, the fuss just ran on for too long.

Rochus had brilliantly avoided coming to the full notice of the great and the powerful, with, of course, the exception of Reichsführer Himmler. He had obviously met Hitler; he had met them all but to them all he was a mere cipher. A cipher they trusted because he always seemed to be around. There had been a close and uncomfortable moment when he had crossed Reinhard Heydrich's path. Heydrich by that time had risen to the rank of Obergruppenführer and was actively seeking first-rate men and commanders for his brand-new brainchild, the Einsatzgruppen. Rochus had done well to avoid any kind of relationship with that particular gang of cutthroats and their dreadful commander. Reinhard Heydrich had given chase, determined to ensnare Himmler's favourite assassin, for such he had become. Heydrich didn't know it for fact, but he guessed, could smell, the abilities that Himmler so prized in his handsome subordinate and he, Heydrich, was keen to utilise those abilities for his own ends. Rochus had then called on the favour of the almighty Reichsführer-SS. He had, he politely pointed out, performed his duties with exceptional diligence and loyalty. He demanded nothing from his superiors in the way of huge amounts of money, vast leaps in rank nor large and overbearing houses with maids and flunkies. To be left alone to do his job was all that he requested. Other than for the basic necessities, money had precious little appeal for Rochus. He travelled first class and was shown deference by those he came into contact with. He wasn't required to go and throw his life away senselessly at the battlefront. He was well clothed, well fed and well looked after. What else could a man possibly want? Sometimes he had, of necessity, to take a life. At other times in order to gain information, it had been sadly necessary to inflict great pain upon his victim. On occasion he had had to kill women, and although he found that particular act to be mildly distasteful, it was his job and doing it well meant that he lived well – very bloody well. Until now!

The 8mm projector's constant whirring sounded like an army of cocaine fuelled cockroaches scampering over old newspapers. The Führer of the Third Reich, however, barely noticed the noise. His ghastly, yellow filmed eyes widened yet again as the flickering 8x4 home-movie screen displayed the naked figure of sixty-four-year-old Field Marshal Ernest von Witzleben writhing and jerking in his death agony, as he hung from the piano wire that entwined his slowly stretching neck.

Hitler had personally instructed the executioner to hang the perpetrators of the July 24th plot like carcasses of meat, and the man had obeyed his instructions to the letter. Cameras were carefully placed at several different angles, all with powerful zoom optics fitted so that the Führer's delectation not be impeded in any way. The close-ups of the broken and dying men hanging from meat hooks and wriggling grotesquely in their final obscene agony, were works of art that, as far as Hitler was concerned, easily equalled those trashy Jew-inspired efforts turned out by Hollywood.

The executioner, briefly turned movie producer, Fritz Grosch, enjoyed his work immensely and he had worn a leer of joyous satisfaction throughout the entire day's work. Witzleben was the last of the eight condemned men to suffer this ordeal. Stripped, humiliated, and now hanging in agony from the thin wire cord around his neck, he had not made a single sound. No pleas for mercy, no shrieks of terror or pleas to the almighty. Bit of a let-down but never mind, thought Grosch, just so long as the Führer got his jollies; that was all that counted. He turned to the camera, widening his leer as he lashed a small metal studded leather strap across the dying Field Marshal's shrunken genitals.

Hitler jerked in time to the dying Witzleben's camera lingering heave of agony. A moan of pleasure escaped the Nazi Führer's lips and his hand closed around the almost-but-not-quite rising of his nether regions. He didn't care about mess: this was his pleasure. He had had the entire series of executions filmed in this way and he watched them regularly. Even now, ill and facing ruin, he found pleasure and release from watching those ingrates, those traitorous bastards suffer. Yes! And the suffering was far from over for all the vile scum who had betrayed and deserted him. For all he cared, it could all fall in ruin and the nation of whining failures with it. Let them all die in agony; screaming and grovelling as their children burned and were crushed by bombs and broken buildings. "Yes-yes-yes!"

He called for Linge to come and clean him up and remove the projector and screen. If only he could get his hands on Himmler. That back-stabbing lying piece of fantasy devoted bilge would suffer a fate more awful than anything even his most imaginative concentration camp deviants could think up.

The movie projector and screen were all packed away. The round occasional table was littered with crumbs and small globules of jam, butter and God alone knew what else. As was the front of the recumbent figure slouched in the worn armchair. Linge had long since given up any attempt to keep his Führer neat and tidy. Small jam and butter stains surrounded greasy shirt buttons and his trousers were a disgusting mess.

Heinz Linge looked with some pity at his once all-powerful employer, the mighty Adolf Hitler.

He's gone completely, mused Linge. Hitler's grasp on reality had grown less with each passing day. His once awe-inspiring perseverance and refusal to countenance defeat despite appalling losses of men and material was revealed as a charade. It hadn't been, as they all so fondly imagined, the iron-willed display of a courageous leader determined to ensure his nation's survival. No, just the opposite. Linge, and others, now realised it had been nothing more than a staggering degree of insouciance. The man didn't care about the people, about anything other than himself. He was a creature devoted to hate and his need to feed that hate. But hating what? Heinz Linge sucked in air; for him, that was possibly the most awful thing about the entire last twelve years. This man, his Führer Adolf Hitler, Führer of the now doomed Third Reich, didn't *know* why he hated, only that he needed to give physical expression to that pulse tripping emotion. And then, to become completely fulfilled, the surge to have others join him in a mutual hatred of something, any shared villainy would do. From there he could work upon that emotion, feed on it and replenish his strength, as others fed from him in order to supplement their diet of belief – in him!

It had led, in the end, to precisely what the Führer had always wanted. He had brilliantly surpassed the efforts of all preceding slayers and destroyers – easily! In comparison, as Linge saw it, Atilla, Napoleon and Genghis Khan now came across as nothing more frightening than peevish babies screaming for their rattles. Destruction on a huge scale. A world in flames spinning to the tune of countless millions of screams. And he, Heinz Linge, had witnessed every energy pulsating moment of it. They all had, and many of them had enjoyed every awful moment of it. Their rollercoaster ride of ultimate self-indulgence was about to come hurtling off its single track, but what an amazing ride it had been.

Unbeknownst to most Germans, however, in Hitler they had a warlord who suffered constantly from the disturbed child's abnormality of spitefully breaking his own toys; and his very last toy was Berlin.

Linge gazed down at the instigator of their mutual destruction, the sleeping Führer. He observed as the fleshy nostrils of his leaders somewhat bulbous nose flittered in and out under his laboured breathing. A shame he thought, such a dreadful shame. In 1939 it had all looked so good, so promising. The Führer had duped them all; himself as well in all probability. Oh, yes. Heinz Linge was no fool. He'd been captivated for a while, yes, but he was not stupid and had come to know extremely well the man that he had served so intimately for the past ten years. There had been warning signs in the early days, of course there had. But they all, ambitious users and devoted disciples alike, ignored them. Hitler had given them – hope! His bewildering ability to convince others that it was in their interests to turn *his* dreams into solid reality, was by far Hitler's greatest talent. And, in truth, they had all willingly gone along with him. By his will alone Hitler had created Armageddon! Linge sighed heavily. The man that he had served and once honestly admired for becoming something out of nothing, was in reality, nothing more than an ephemeral opiate with which a gullible people had sniffed at once too often.

The sounds of exploding shells directly overhead made him look up at the immensely thick ceiling. Even down here, so many feet beneath the ground, the sounds of battle permeated the Bunker with unregulated frequency. A familiar gut-twisting sadness hardened Linge's normally smooth features. He had overheard Hitler's instructions to Albert Speer and knew of his wildly insane plan and desire to see Berlin destroyed. His final breakable toy.

"No, my Führer." Linge bent and did something that no other person in the Reich had ever dared do, not even Eva Braun; he lightly kissed the creased and dream twitching forehead of the man he had once admired.

"Not Berlin. That must not be."

Bormann watched as Linge made his way out of the Führer's quarters. A hiss of annoyance escaped the Reichsleiter's lips as he saw Rochus Misch, that wretched underling, just waltz into Hitler's private apartment as if he owned the damned thing. Like too many others these days, the man was just so damned full of himself. Was this what it had all come to? Only a few days ago he, Martin Bormann, had been the only way anyone at all, regardless of whom they were, could get to see the Führer. He, Bormann, had guarded the entrance to the Nazi oracle for the past four years and had come to view the Führer as his personal property. Like ancient Cerberus, he guarded the gates to hell and arbitrarily slathered his venom upon any unwelcome approach to his master's realm. For years they had feared him because of his massive influence over their supreme leader. It was he, and he alone, that relayed orders or loaded suggestions to Hitler's countless minions at home and abroad daily. He had done so for so long that he had forgotten what it was like to be just plain old Martin Bormann. He was Reichsleiter Bormann, head of the Party Chancellery, and as such he controlled all Party promotions and appointments and even drew up Hitler's daily schedule and appointments calendar. Not that there was much of any kind of schedule to draw up these days. Bormann, though, was still the shadowy figure behind the Führer; the grand inquisitor, as he liked to hear himself referred to. The trouble was, even a die-hard like Bormann had been forced to acknowledge the unpalatable truth. The war was lost and it must soon be every man for himself. Problem: 'Every man for himself' did not include Adolf Hitler. It had become very clear to Bormann that his erstwhile leader and protector could not now protect, lead or administer anything at all. The man was done. Lip service was still paid, but just barely. The various unit commanders still attended the ever more useless military conferences and briefings. Such meetings were now completely pointless but the colonels and generals still obeyed because they knew no other way. Without a chain of command those military die-hards were lost. So he, Bormann, or Krebs, now that Keitel had done a disappearing act, simply took what information they had to offer and told them to hold at all costs. Now, however, there was precious little remaining to hold. The Soviets were almost at the Bunker door and they would not be knocking politely for entrance when they finally arrived. Hitler had been droning on incessantly about killing himself but clearly didn't have the stomach for self-removal from this earth. Until he was gone there was Damn all that any of them could do.

Bormann frowned, whistled and then hawked. He had to get out. Hitler or no Hitler. If he were to salvage anything from the wreckage he must get to Plön, where Admiral Dönitz and the rest of what remained of the *supposed* Nazi government were awaiting events. He needed to safeguard his position in government. Without the Führer's backing, though, he might have trouble maintaining his eminent status within the Reich; or whatever remained of it. Hitler had refused from the outset to leave Berlin, a cast iron decision which had left Bormann flummoxed. He had been convinced that he could persuade his Führer, a man who trusted him implicitly, to leave Berlin and go to the south where they could continue resistance indefinitely. Hitler, however, had refused. He was determined, he had said, to die in Berlin. All well and good if the son-of-bitch had stuck to his word and had the bloody decency to die. But no…he lingered on, and on, moaning, and crying and well….just constantly bellyaching about everything. To get on with what Bormann had in mind, they needed Hitler dead. There were official forms and dockets and most important of all, official seals at hand. All of which only he, Reichsleiter Martin Bormann had access to and they were stashed neatly in his own personal cubby-hole. He had long ago mastered the art of forging Hitler's signature; something any halfway competent secretary could do.

True, Goebbels and Walter Hewel, a loyal and busy foreign office aide, had official stamps appertaining to their offices, but only Bormann had the wherewithal to write and stamp something which stated the Führer's personal command. Or, at least, appeared to do so. Incredibly, even now, throughout the Reich, many millions of folk still regarded a Führer order as tantamount to a command from God. That situation, however, was likely to alter very soon.

He must act quickly. Bormann was thinking hard, giving his devious mind full rein as it explored the murky corridors of trust and survival. Who to trust? He had a plan forming and it just might work. It should suit the more hidebound die-hards that might have to be involved and equally appeal to those who, like himself, were determined to survive at any cost.

Upstairs, in what had once been the rooms allocated to the Führer's physician, Doctor Morell, Joseph Goebbels harangued his wife, Magda, and she verbally slapped him right back. What had begun as a calmly enunciated discussion concerning what, if anything, might remain of their current options, had sunk swiftly to an unpleasantly low level of mutual denigration and loathing.

"Why didn't you follow Speer's advice and leave? He could have got you to a place of safety. Relatively, anyway. Anywhere but here."

Magda glared at her complaining and routinely unfaithful husband. Less of the unfaithful these days, of course. Bunker existence didn't much lend itself to the seeking out of affairs of the heart; the ambience now geared itself more to the immediate and hygienically undemanding type of sexual encounter that required no thought or feeling other than that of release. Some of the impromptu parties that seemed to spontaneously roar themselves into being in the Vorbunker were precious little more than drunken orgies. Any excuse, any bottle, anything that moved. There was enough alcohol, morphine and a host of other mind-numbing substances to make life, for a short while at least, appear to be a real joy. Odd. Neat spirits of all kinds flowed like water, yet not enough petrol could be found to run a small car for more than twenty or thirty miles. Lunacy!

She had always been wary of Albert Speer, once a very close friend of the Führer. That man had fallen somewhat due to his insatiable ambition and his obvious contempt for those around the Führer, including her husband, Joseph. That, after such short acquaintance, the Führer had developed a large degree of trust and affection for Speer and, on a personal level, clearly much preferred him to her ever-loyal husband, caused Joseph great chagrin. Hard to take, for a prideful man like Joseph, whose entire life revolved around the Führer, as indeed, did hers. As for Speer? Nothing, not Führer, state or family came even close to rivalling Albert Speer's love and promotion of self. Hitler, unfortunately, had not initially seen it, not that is, until much later when Speer's cold and naked ambition had revealed its gnashing teeth. Nevertheless, at times even long-standing enemies came together before a mutual threat. Speer might well have been able to get the Goebbels family north to Dönitz and the awaiting provisional government. Magda assumed that that was where Speer himself had headed off to.

"You spent months trying to bring that man down," she hissed. "I saw you work with Himmler to destroy him. You tried to assassinate him, with Himmler's help. Yes, you did!" She raised an imperious hand. "Don't bother to even think about denying it. When the man lay helpless in hospital you got Himmler to send in his SS doctor to finish the job. But Speer outwitted you and got away."

"Utter rubbish," protested Goebbels but his demeanour inferred that his wife was telling the truth. What did it matter now, anyway? The truth was that, with no exceptions, the entire inner circle, all of Hitler's closest associates had, at one time or another, plotted the downfall of one or all the others. Sometimes working alone, but more often than not working in alliance with another member, against whom they would turn at a later date and for more or less the same reason, to gain more power and influence. Göring, Himmler, Ribbentrop, Speer, all of them, right down to the lowest little clerk in the Wilhelmstrasse. Thus, as a governing group, a hierarchy, they ruled their departments with the kind of selfish inefficiency which Hitler had come to expect, and appreciate. His worms remained tame lest they be trodden upon, and that was good. It was quite simply the way that the Führerprinzip functioned.

"I don't judge your political or personal misapprehensions, Joseph, I never have. It was not my place to interfere but you might have done better to make an ally of Herr Speer rather than align yourself against him. The Führer has always loved that man."

"It's done!" Goebbels almost shrieked at her. "There is no further point in speaking like this. I merely said that you were unwise not to accept Speer's offer of help. Now I must think of another way of getting the children to safety. What in God's name possessed you, Magda? What the bloody hell were you thinking of to bring them here?"

Magda, in a fit of overwhelming loyalty to the man she adored and who, it seemed, was now being deserted by all, had not merely brought herself down into the Bunker. She brought her six children as well. Five girls and one boy. Their happy shrieks of joy as they played throughout the many rooms and cubby-holes of the stairwell and lower Bunker brought smiles to the faces of some, grimaces of irritation to others, and to some few others, glances of affectionate bewilderment. Had nobody thought that this was the very, but truly, very last place for a small group of beautiful and happy children to be brought? It was said that there were more than one million vengeful, murderous Russians just yards away. What had Magda Goebbels been thinking of?

"Where else could I take them, Joseph? Tell me. Where?" She ran a well-manicured hand over her beautiful blond hair and stared him down.

Joseph hated these face-to-face family disagreements. His ministerial rank meant nothing and he was well aware, because Magda ceaselessly reminded him, that it had been Magda's wealth via her Jewish stepfather, that had enabled them to keep up such a high standard of living before the war. Magda was a force of nature, no doubt about that. The Führer thought highly of her, and she in turn adored her Führer; worshipped the ground he walked on, even now. Joseph, though, had long since ceased worshipping anybody's damned ground be it Hitler's, the Pope's or Jesus of Nazareth. The time for dreams and cartoon characters was gone. It was fair to say, that he was even sick to death of the Führer. Nasty old realism was the picture now and that meant, well, it meant death. He sighed and lightly kicked his polished toe-cap at the frayed carpet edge. It was rug more than carpet but it ran almost wall to wall. "Well, Magda," he spoke softly. "What do you suggest that I do with them now, hmm? Vanish them into thin air – magic them to the safety of Bavaria with a click of my fingers?"

"I don't suggest that *you* do anything, Joseph. I am their mother and I have decided what must be done."

"Oh have you now," he snapped back. His voice was laden with sarcasm. "And what, if I dare ask, might that be."

"You will know in good time." Magda's tone was contemptuous. "When I see fit to tell you."

He took an unsteady clubfooted step toward her. "When you what?" he growled. "Let me tell you madam that you will......"

"Tell you in due course." Magda raised her hand in an almost

Hitlerite gesture of command. "Now, I have things to do." With that, she turned on her heel and left the tiny apartment.

Joseph was stunned into silence. A rarity for him, to have no rejoinder. He tried to fight down the anger, the fury that rose within him. "You damn well come back here this instant," he yelled. To no avail. Wherever Magda had gone, and it couldn't be far, he would find her soon enough and then give her a good dressing down in front of the children. Yes, he'd let her, and the children know who's boss in the Goebbels household. He rammed a small fist into the side of his head, rubbing his temple almost savagely. Silly – childish! He was being just too bloody silly! It was all pretty well over and here he was worrying about his authority being supplanted by a wife who, in all honesty, had always ruled the domestic roost anyway. He turned back into his room and did something that he would regret for all that remained of his life.

He decided to let it go.

Albert Speer drew heavily upon his half-smoked cigarette. He was exhausted but there was still much to think on. Although he had precious little to do in the way of his professional duties, he still had a good deal to accomplish when it came to covering his well-trodden tracks. The trip from shattered Berlin to his present location in Hamburg had been one of unremitting hell. A few days ago he had visited the Bunker, ostensibly to say an emotional, tearful even, goodbye to his beloved, besieged and beleaguered friend and Führer, Adolf Hitler. The meeting had not gone well. The journey had been fraught with danger and personal risk to himself.

The government quarter, where Hitler had entombed himself beneath countless tons of protective steel and concrete, was under constant shelling and aerial bombardment. Not to mention those revoltingly murderous little SS wannabees running around and shooting anyone they thought might be a deserter, a thief or a skiving defeatist. They would shoot at anybody, it would seem, rather than the advancing Russians.

Speer's visit, on the surface a purely altruistic demonstration of loyalty and support for his ailing and defeated Führer, was nothing of the kind. True enough they had once been enamoured of one another. Speer because Hitler exuded the beauty of raw power and offered an open door to riches and influence, all of which Albert had enjoyed; Hitler because Albert Speer was artistic, irresistibly enigmatic and when it came right down to it, just so incredibly handsome. It became a love affair of the mind, for nothing physical ever passed between them other than the occasional and ever-so-slight loving touch, as they passed one another at a desk, table or narrow doorway. But their minds, in those heady early days of the Third Reich, had been as one. A shared dream of art and the creation of great buildings that would last for centuries as monuments to their towering artistic genius, and thus elevate them far beyond the dreary realm of mere mortals. All so wonderful!

That was when clever Albert had played his little game. He knew damn well that he was no genius, but if the charismatic and emotionally myopic leader of the Reich chose to see him that way, well then, he had no intention of disabusing him of that pleasing notion. Let the truth take care of its sanctimonious self.

Back then, in the early thirties, catching Hitler's eye was somewhat akin to catching a golden goose by its long neck. Albert caught it alright, and kept a strangler's grip around its sinewy throat, until much later in their relationship, when he felt it being dragged forcibly from his weakening grasp by increasingly powerful enemies and then, by his once beloved Führer himself.

For years, when at the height of their friendship, they had chatted endlessly about art, discussed building projects when he, Hitler, should have been concerning himself with the approaching economic disaster. It required total attention and hard work if they were to avoid what was coming. He had been warned, several times, that a 1920s doom scenario was just around the corner if he failed to act or to appoint someone who could act independently. Back in 1936,

Schacht the finance minister had bluntly informed the Führer, not in so many words but his meaning had been clear enough, that it was time to put away childish toys and get down to work. But Adolf would have none of that. The Führer had his own plans. He loved to talk, and dream, and then talk some more.... a lot more, about his pet subjects, in particular architecture and, of course, himself.

Adolf and Albert adored one another's company and, using a variety of multi-coloured Lego bricks, built one pretend city after another. Germania was their favourite, with super wide boulevards, avenues and ludicrously tall, thick-walled buildings running along each street. They were both so pleased with the wonderfully realistic dimensions that they discarded the Lego and had the thing rebuilt using balsa wood and Paper Mache. The model was huge, a work of art in itself and it was changed in size and design regularly. Like little boys with a table-top train set, Adolf and Albert would chop and change the cutely made buildings and lovingly move around the little plastic cars that added, for them, so much realism. The only thing missing from this and, in fact, all of the make-believe cities they built, was any sense of proportion. Adolf had no sense of scale at all and Albert, who did, was too sensible to advise him about his woeful lack of it. Castles in a Baron Munchausen sky, as Ribbentrop once mockingly observed to his aide, Walter Hewel.

And so, on the 22nd April 1945, Albert had trotted down into Hitler's subterranean hidey-hole and laid out, ever so carefully and with great respect, why he thought that the mighty Führer should stay in Berlin and why he should take his own life; preferably by using a pistol. The German people, he explained, those that came after them, must have something to look up to, of which they could, as a nation, be proud. The Führer of the great German Reich must go down in a blaze of glory, fighting to the very last for his volk and his Reich. In no way, and here Albert had allowed tears of anguish to roll down his cheeks, in absolutely no way must they allow the Soviets to capture their beloved Führer alive. He must never fall into their evil hands. The disgrace would destroy what was left of the nation's pride.

Hitler had remained silent throughout Speer's elaborately convincing pitch. Thus encouraged, Albert continued. "So much I have learnt from you, my Führer, so very much. And the people know of our close association, sir. They will accept me as your most natural and faithful successor." He smiled sadly and nodded sympathetically to the shrunken man standing before him. Still there was silence. Albert shuffled his feet. It occurred to him that the Führer could easily have him shot on the spot. Had he put his pitch too strongly? Surely Hitler didn't think that he could survive this all-encompassing calamity. Could he really be *that* delusional? But then, he had, after all, just suggested to a sick, totally paranoid old man that he blow his brains out. Had *that* been the wise thing to do? God damn him, thought Speer. It was Hitler himself that constantly carped on about ending it all. Droning on interminably about how rough and tough and awful his life was. He'd been mentioning suicide since, well, way back, since 1942, after Stalingrad.

Albert realised that he had been meeting Hitler's eye. In the old days not something he would have dared to do. Had he really found this man attractive? That nose was horribly bulbous. It seemed to be spreading over the Führer's face with a life all of its own. He took a deep breath. The bad air, stale and recycled, had made him feel nauseated and light headed. He had said the wrong thing. Well, not the wrong thing, perhaps, but said in the wrong way. Damn! Now he had to figure a way out of it. He spread out his hands, palms up in a conciliatory gesture. It came across to Hitler as a patronizing affront.

"You stuffed up, ungrateful piece of dung." It wasn't a shout, nor delivered like invective. Hitler's tone was almost conversational with a hint of regret.

"You, of all people. You want me dead!"

"Ah, no, my Führer, I merely.......!"

"You merely what, Herr Speer?"

"My concern is the future of the Reich, my Führer. And for your name, your legacy. Your all-important legacy." Yes, Spear's mind raced, that was it. Puff up the old man's ego with a lot of guff about how the nation would always remember him; that he would never be forgotten, and such like. Hitler liked praise, and over-the-top flattery had always stimulated a good mood in him.

"Your dream, my Führer, must and shall live on through your unquenchable will." Not bad, thought Albert, bearing in mind the situation.

"Oh, do shut up Speer. I see right through you. I don't blame you for being what you are. I am too old, too tired and no longer care about you, Germany, the people or sod all else. It's done. Now. For old times' sake, do yourself a favour and go." He was almost whispering now. "Just go, Albert. I have nothing more for you."

For the first time in his selfish life Albert Speer felt true sadness and sympathy for another human being other than himself. He suddenly realised how much he meant what he had just said. With outstretched hands he appealed to his Führer one last time.

"Adolf, please. End it. Don't let this go on. Look at you. How you are suffering! This has to end, please."

Hitler raised a trembling arm and pointed to the blast proof door. "Go." With that, he turned his back on his erstwhile friend and said no more. Speer stood for a few seconds and then, head low, he departed Hitler's presence for the final time.

Was he dead yet? Speer wondered as he lit yet another cigarette. Hitler had looked as close to death as any man could be and yet still be alive. Fifty-six years of age and he had looked well past eighty; and a very sick eighty, at that. His mind ran back to 1938 and the last of his personally designed Cathedral of Light rallies at Nuremburg. What splendid wonders they had been, and all his creation. The very first time that he had used them, Hitler and his entourage had gone into thigh slapping paroxysms of ecstasy. The way the gigantic Nazi flags were caught in shadowy and all enfolding masculine detail, had been masterful. His greatest, triumph, though, had been his ability to badger Goering into loaning him more than one hundred and fifty anti-aircraft searchlights, enormously powerful things they were, too. It had been the lights, each one of them carefully placed in the exactly correct position by himself, that had given the display the surreal, primaeval and, yes, barbaric but still so frighteningly well-disciplined aura of German invincibility. Those powerful lights had criss-crossed and arched like massive interlocking gables of luminescence, garishly highlighting the giant Swastika flags which hung from the grand, crescent shaped Tribune of Honour Auditorium and the Luitpold Hall. Speer had not designed the buildings, not even the smaller ones that dotted the perimeter of the Luitpold arena. But the decoration, the tarting-up, so to speak, was all Albert Speer. And it had been awe-inspiring. Magnificent! Never to be forgotten. That first rally, in 1934, when the searchlights first flashed into life in one extraordinary blaze of light, would live in the hearts and minds of all those who attended for ever more.

And that was the problem. He drew hard on his cigarette. Being famous had now lost every last iota of its former attraction.

For weeks now, Albert had been frantically covering his tracks. Hitler's final great command, the Nero order, which stated rather cruelly, that all German means of aiding their existence must be obliterated, as they had proven themselves unworthy of his sacrifice and genius. Bridges, water mains, food depots, factories, all and everything were to be destroyed and thus denied to the enemy. The German people would just have to die, and that was that. They should have fought harder. It had been said with a careless wave of the hand by a man who didn't give a damn about anything other than his everlasting love of destruction and his determination to annihilate, even now, at every opportunity no matter how small. It was the one thing that had remained solid and utterly predictable about the Führer; it could always be relied upon.

Since the Führer's issuing of the lunatic Nero Decree in mid-March, Albert had made a big thing of visiting commanders in the field, and various gauleiters, ostensibly to plead with them to ignore the dreadful and transparently spiteful Nero order. The fact was, of course, that every single one of them had ignored the wretched thing anyway. Not one of them intended to destroy his people, their families or themselves, let alone deprive the entire nation of its means of subsistence. Most had remained obedient to the will of their Führer until that point, but that last insane command was too much. They disobeyed, and thereafter, Hitler's will, along with his charisma, lay like a writhing, loathsome slug seeking an escape from an unexpectedly encountered repellent.

But, Albert reasoned, by assuming the mantle of a brave, concerned citizen who, with no thought for himself and at great personal risk, went rushing about the danger zones in total disobedience to the will of an enraged and demented leader, must assuredly go down well later, when, as was certain to happen, they were all caught and thrust into prison cells like the condemned men they would undoubtedly become; already were.

Some of his colleagues were astoundingly stupid. Himmler, for one, truly believed that the Allies would welcome his policing expertise and would be eager to employ his various talents to control the defeated but possibly still volatile population. Jodl, Keitel and many others thought that the excuse of merely doing one's duty would be more than sufficient to ensure their survival. They were, after all, merely obeying orders. Fools! Albert had more than enough savvy to know damn well that the allies, the Soviets in particular, would demand revenge on every single one of them. Many millions had died, directly or indirectly at their hands. Albert knew better than most that there were no innocents in the Nazi hierarchy, not even at mid-level. A government of sexual deviants and murderous psychopaths had been allowed to run amok and enjoy a five-year killing spree; an orgy of death and sadism on a never before envisaged scale. Hitler, his Nazis, and that, mused Albert Speer, includes me, had shown the world what humanity was capable of, of what it truly was. Out loud he said, "We merely held up a mirror. They will not forgive us for that."

In the meantime there were still papers, documents and the like to be destroyed. He had been clever, had Albert. His only direct link to anything truly bad was Himmler. That was Albert's weak link and he hoped fervently that the Reichsführer might soon meet his end. He had been sensible enough to channel his orders through his deputy, Franz Dorsch, and only occasionally directly through conference with Heinrich Himmler. But had he put his signature to anything meaningfully bad? He was pretty sure not but one never really knew. He had tried his utmost to be like his Führer in not appearing to be directly responsible for anything connected with the as yet little-known Final Solution. However, any thorough investigation would reveal that *Europe's economic dictator*, as Dönitz had liked to call him, controlled all movements of stock, munitions and labour. That was a fact. He had been number one and responsible. In the short term, it depended upon whether or not the Allies dug deep enough to find anything incriminating. Hopefully, with all that would be going on, they wouldn't be too much bothered. Then, after all that, he would have to rely upon time itself to erase any memories of that bad past.

In the smaller scheme of things, he was confident that he might be at least halfway believed if he said that he had been tricked, hoodwinked by mightier powers than he; insisting that he was a mere technocrat with no real idea of what was going on within, and without the Third Reich. He might just get away with it. It wouldn't be easy and he would have to lie and be more sincere in his very professional insincerity than he had ever before been. He had spent his life at it, waffling and being charming, now his life would depend upon it. The fly in the ointment? The wretched Himmler. That man could provide information proving beyond any shadow of doubt his, Speer's, involvement with the death camps and their methods through his transport system for shifting workers, slaves and Jews from one place to another. Might prove awkward.

Well, almost time for his appointment with Dönitz. There was little point in worrying about it now. All he could do was take each day as it came and be ready at all times to think on his feet. 'And remember Albert,' he spoke smoothly to his reflection in the full-length mirror as he adjusted his hat. 'Rub some warmth into your cold old heart and be charming and deferential to all.' He smiled and went off to see the man who was to be the next and final Führer of the rapidly shrinking Third Reich; Admiral Karl Dönitz.

CHAPTER 19

March 1939: Tegernsee. Bavaria

Friedrik Lehmann smiled at his guests and waited for the muted chatter to die down. They had been joined today by the president of the Reichsbank and former minister of finance, Hjalmar Schacht and a debonair American by the name of Thomas McKittrick.

Horst Weber sat with Ernst Krupp and Germany's most powerful banker, head of the Deutsche Bank, Karl Kimmitch. They were chatting amiably with much nodding and smiling. Hans Becker, though, was not smiling. His ear was being bent by the always voluble Gertrude Huber and she was making a great deal of sense with what she was saying to the shipbuilder and owner of Germany's largest cruise fleet.

"Boats sink, Hans, yours just like any others. If it comes to war, what price, then, for your pretty boats?"

"Ships, Gertrude. They are called ships. Boats are little wooden toys that children play with."

"Pah," Gertrude Huber waved a fleshy green-nailed hand. "They float, Hans, so they are boats, yes? Just so. Don't be so pedantic. Boats float: ships sink." She chuckled throatily at her little play on words. Becker looked thoughtfully at her for a moment. Green painted fingernails didn't suit the stocky and redoubtably grim-visaged Gertie Huber. But then, no kind of feminine adornment was ever likely to soften her rather forceful appearance. Nevertheless, her dailies and various glossy magazines had done the Party proud. The glowing articles and endorsements churned out relentlessly by her publications had massively boosted their popular vote, and her tame editorial economists obligingly played with statistics thus drastically improving the picture of the economy which, sadly, was sinking into a parlous state – again! She had even managed to bolster up the Nazi Party's falling popularity when things had been looking desperately uncertain back in thirty-two and thirty-three. Not even the State's very own rag, the appallingly slap-dash Volkischer Beobachter, had done better when it came to glorifying Hitler and the Nazi regime. Gertrude Huber had a rare knack for sniffing out first-rate and totally unscrupulous writing talent.

Becker favoured his rotund colleague with a smile. The necessity of maintaining good publicity for his expensive cruise line meant that it was always a good idea to avoid ruffling the feathers of this particular press baron. Besides which, those investigative reporters of hers were all too good at digging up the varied and numerous peccadillos of high-ranking Party members. Chances were that her well-hidden files on the indiscreet were more damning even than those that Heinrich Himmler possessed. Becker trod a careful and respectful line with Gertrude Huber. He liked her more than most and enjoyed her sometimes outrageous teasing. Today, though, he wanted some questions answered by the government finance boys in the room. So, dispensing with levity he turned away from Huber and glanced across the room at the always suave and urbane Friedrik Lehmann. Gruppenführer, now for God's sake. Did the man's penchant for intrigue have no bounds? Clearly not.

"Well, Lehmann," Becker's harsh Berlin accent rasped loud and guttural. "What will it be? Where are we all headed, eh? You and Herr Schacht seem closest to the Führer. Who, by the way," he stood and gazed around at the others, "these days can't be bothered to return my calls. Not even from one of his blasted henchmen. Can you credit that? A couple of years ago he couldn't stop himself from sniffing around like an eager puppy, fawning and whining for the smallest scrap of attention. Now – the wretched......."

"HANS!" Gertrude laid a rough hand on Becker's arm. As he swung toward her, she glanced meaningfully at Lehmann who was standing quietly and observing the irate Hans Becker with feigned avuncularity. Becker glared briefly at the debonaire Lehmann before looking away. They had all worked and plotted together for years to get that loud-mouthed little Austrian hysteric into power and none of them much enjoyed being side-lined and ignored. Not when it was their millions that had put Mister Hitler where he was. Becker could remember when the man who now revelled in the title, 'Führer' had been nothing more than just another whinging, cash shy politician on the sweaty handed make.

How different it was now, though. His all-powerful mightiness, the Führer, had not spoken to the group as a whole, nor any of them personally, with the exception of Schacht and possibly, Lehmann, since 1937. Becker, and Huber, both seethed with resentment but now knew where the absolute power lay. They had been hoodwinked, betrayed and treated like spoilt rich children. Presumably as a sop to their combined egos Himmler had approached them, arranged an occasional meeting and spoken about the future. In general though, he delegated the smoothing of ruffled feathers to his able deputy, Friedrik Lehmann. The Reichsführer SS was rather busy these days with his castle Wewelsburg and the formulation of many new plans for the future. Lehmann, however, was by now quite certain that his boss lived on another plane to the rest of humanity. He trod, like a giant jack-booted rabbit, the astral plane of Rosicrucianism, alchemy and various other mystical codes, creeds and nonsense. It made him malleable, but it also made him unpredictable, so Lehmann moved with great caution at all times. Now, he prepared himself with a gentle squaring of his shoulders, it was time to spout some reassuring Party blurb to quieten the natives.

"First, let me assure you all that I have the Führer's solemn word that there will be no war." Lehmann smiled at them all. "He truly does know what he is doing and we are blessed to have such a genius to guide and lead us in these troublesome times."

"Well, I say," muttered portly Horst Weber. "Who'd have thought that we would ever see genius IQ in single figures?" Those around him chortled. Most were under no illusions about their Nazi Führer/Benefactor. Reports of his meetings, his aims and his acts all pointed to the same thing. The man, Hitler, didn't have the remotest idea about how to run a country, order the economy or effectively delegate. Which would not have mattered had he, the Führer, simply done as he was told and obeyed the instructions relayed to him from his betters. That had been the initial agreement. But, as one or two of the more cynical amongst them had always suspected that he would, harum-scarum Adolf Hitler had gone right off their neatly planned rails and not only defied them, he had threatened three of them with concentration camp internment. They were stuck with it and with him. True, they did indeed have the power to break free if they so desired, but what then of their massive investment? Did they really want to see all those millions go to waste for the sake of a little ego bruising and bad housekeeping? They had mutely decided to leave it and continued to throw their money, influence and resources toward the smiling and outwardly grateful Hitler and his cronies. They had been rewarded with fat contracts and high ranks within the SS. There wasn't a man or woman in attendance at Lehmann's house that held an SS rank lower than Sturmbannführer. Plus, they had those gorgeous uniforms to wear whenever they pleased. Small in-jokes were frequent and tolerated. But no doubt Horst Weber's comment referring to the Führer's lack of intelligence would filter its way to the Führer's ear. That was a man who demanded that he be regarded as super-intelligent; beyond the norm: a miracle of modern humanity! He wasn't, they all knew that. Chances were that Horst's amusing but unwise remark would, sooner or later, come right back and bite him savagely in his rather plump rear-end.

"No war, then?" Otto Krause sounded relieved but wasn't one

hundred per cent sure that he believed Lehmann.

"Certainly not one that will be started by us." Lehmann nodded firmly. "The Führer is ever cognizant of his promises to his friends. Profits we have all made," he glanced around and theatrically raised his hands, "in abundance, I should say. Or do I hear complaints?"

The assembled worthies laughed dutifully. Lehmann, though, could see that they were far from convinced. Walther Funk, the current Minister for Economics had made his profuse apologies to Lehmann and declined to attend. He was, he tactfully pointed out a truthful man and didn't want to risk the Führer's wrath. Particularly now, when, with all said and done, he, Funk, was pretty well at his wit's end. He was a loyal Party man and a staunch Hitler follower, but the Führer simply would not listen to sensible advice. There was trouble brewing and there seemed little hope of avoiding it, so it was probably best that he stayed away. Least said, soonest mended, and all that sort of thing.

After some suitably calming rhetoric, Lehmann formally introduced their American guest. If any man in that room could possibly match Friedrik Lehmann in suaveness and urbanity, even surpass him, it was the immaculately dressed and beautifully poised Thomas McKittrick. He charmed them all with his well-chosen words and sensational revelations as to US fiscal policy with regard to Germany.

"There will never be another recession such as the one which the entire civilized and industrial world suffered a few years ago," said McKittrick. His German was flawless, as one might expect from such a well-educated man. The American smiled winningly and pointed to Karl Kimmitch. "Today, gentlemen, and lady," he bowed slightly from the waist to include the only woman amongst the group, Gertrude Huber, "Herr Kimmitch and I concluded our business negotiations and put our seals, so to speak, to a joint venture that can only be of immense benefit to both our great nations."

N
ow here was a thing! Heads turned; eyes widened. No one present, apart from McKittrick and Kimmitch, had known a damn thing about business negotiations between the two men. Whatever it was, it was bound to be big. The head of the Nazi party's friendly Bank did not waste time with minnows, and the American's reputation preceded him.

All heads, some beautifully coiffured, some bald, or, as in Huber's case, rinsed with some dye of indeterminate colour, were turned toward the speaker. Kimmitch was smiling broadly. Quite a coup they had pulled off, he and the American. The Führer would be delighted, or at least, should be.

"BIS," McKittrick said, proudly. "An answer to all our fiscal prayers."

"BIS," Kimmitch rose and looked round the room, enjoying his moment. "Yes indeed. I hear you all ask, what is BIS?"

"Were you thinking of telling us any time soon?" growled Max Richter. "Or must we get drunk on the suspense?"

The explanation came fast and precise.

Every person in the room leaned forward as the formation of McKittrick's and Kimmitch's brainchild was laid out verbally before their eager ears. The Bank for International Settlement or BIS, as it would be known. Excluding inflation, McKittrick first made clear with a gracefully wagging finger, the BIS set-up would guarantee Germany's finances, regardless of whatever state the nation finds itself in with regard to other, even non-friendly nations. What this meant, the American glibly explained, was that he and Kimmitch had together devised a method for international monetary and financial cooperation that went far beyond anything yet attempted. To the representatives of Krupp, I.G Farben, Max Richter and others, the implications were crystal clear. Should war come, and most felt sure that it would, sooner or later, then money between nations, even throat slicing belligerents', would continue to flow. Business, their business, that is, would continue as before. The plan was excellent. A work of genius.

"When you say international," piped Gertrude Huber, "just how international do you mean? It all sounds good, but perhaps too good to be true."

A general nodding of agreement and some coughing. McKittrick still had his audience but Huber had made a valid point. She continued, "For a venture such as the one you propose to stand any chance of success, it will first be necessary to gain the cooperation of all the major private banks of the world; or at least most of them. Then obtain, at least tacitly, the agreement of the National banks. They will have to agree unanimously to work from then on in complete accord, despite whatever else may or may not be going on in the world. Not an easy scenario to envisage, Herr McKittrick." Huber looked around her and saw agreement. She had thrust her point home well.

Like well-rehearsed vaudeville players Kimmitch and McKittrick both smiled together.

"I did not come here to waste your valuable time," said McKittrick. A beautifully executed spread of his beautifully manicured hands said it all. More than thirty heads leaned forward in anticipation. Could this golden egg laying American have pulled off the impossible, and all in secret from the world at large?

"We have the signed agreement of all the major banking houses worldwide. Italy, Japan, France, the USA and," he beamed around at his audience, "Great Britain. That's just to mention a few. In total, ninety-seven countries, my friends. Rest assured that government involvement will be minimal and in most cases, non-existent."

"A pity the same can't be said about your US trade policy," said Richter. Although he was pleased enough with what he had just heard. McKittrick shook his head sadly. "Precious little to be done about the vagaries or simplistic posturings of elected nincompoops no matter from which nation they hail." He turned to Schacht with a winning smile. "Any present company excepted, of course."

"I can assure you, Herr McKittrick," Schacht smiled back albeit rather coldly, "there is not a man in this room that has been elected."

"Your government's policy," Horst Weber said, "is certainly not friendly to Germany. Their trade agreements with the British and the French are hugely disadvantageous to us."

"Ah," McKittrick raised a hand. "Gentlemen and lady. I must point out that, although we will control much of the world's finances, we will not control, not completely anyway, government policy. However, I can assure you all that the USA has only the kindest and best of intentions toward Germany and her Führer. America, shall always be the truest friend of Germany and the German people. Believe me when I say, and this is from the very top at home in the USA, none of you has anything to fear from America, now or in the future. Business rules the world and will always make the wisest choices. We Americans are born to business and we will, with all due diligence and good faith, nurture and increase our business with your great Third Reich."

If a man like McKittrick, a personal friend of prominent Republican and presidential advisor, John Foster Dulles, could make such promises and declare categorically that Germany had a free hand, then, surely, all was well. Any war would be local and winnable without involving powers that Germany could not possibly defeat with her limited resources.

A feeling of goodwill permeated the room, and earlier mistrust had been whittled down to watchful caution. The rich folk were feeling very much better.

Weber in particular, along with his I.G Farben associates, felt particularly fine. Gustav Krupp was almost ecstatic. Small wars were wonderful things. He leant across and slapped Weber's podgy left knee. "Not such a bad day after all, eh?" Pleased as punch he rose to leave. Building tanks and big guns were all very well, but so much better when they had to be constantly replaced due to battle losses. Yes! Today was a good day for Germany and Krupp Steel.

Chapter 20

March 1939: Wewelsburg Castle

Almost three hundred miles away in the tiny and picturesque village of Wewelsburg, evening had fallen. The valley nestling a little group of houses, all placed prettily but haphazardly around the village's single tavern, were quiet; drawn curtains and closed shutters, not even dogs barked. High up above them, atop the grim lined rock-face, Wewelsburg Castle was seemingly in motion. Lights flickered and giant shadows fell hither and thither. The people of Wewelsburg knew well enough that tonight things were going on in the castle. The Castle of Doom as it was known. A towering monstrosity of satanic evil and a place to stay well away from was how the trembling villagers furtively described it to anyone from the outside who took the time to listen. The rooms within the castle, so it was said, were all themed after various historical and mythical figures from the distant past. Within those frightening walls and towers the SS acted out their demonic rites and experiments. They dressed in strange devil worshipping robes and, so it was rumoured, performed blood sacrifice on the very young, or the very old – or indeed, anyone at all. So it was said, anyway.

Cars had been arriving throughout the early part of the evening. Long-bodied, armour-plated Mercedes saloon cars with their fluttering

SS pennants and black uniformed occupants sitting menacingly grim faced within their leather upholstered confines.

Sometimes, so the village folk said, you could hear hideous screams, shrieks of unbearable human agony issuing forth from the frightening hilltop castle. It might simply, of course, have been the wind howling around the craggy rock face and crenellated walls with their high and sinister turrets. The huge red and black Nazi flags and emblems lifted and waved threateningly even in the mildest breeze.

The tavern was empty of customers on this night. When SS groups came from a great distance on a castle visit they sometimes dropped into Gunther Hertz's quaint little Gaststätte for schnapps and fried chicken. Their drivers, all hard, unpleasant looking men, would wait outside smoking and just looking downright mean. The SS officers didn't always visit the charming Gaststätte; it would depend upon their schedules. But when those cars thundered up and parked, the locals stayed away just in case they did. The men that occasionally visited Castle Wewelsburg were not the kind of people that any normal being would want to associate with. They were very different in a distinctly odd and unsettling way.

The great fire in the castle's King Arthur room crackled and spat dark charred slivers of bright burning wood out onto the white marble floor of the realistically designed medieval Arthurian throne room. Realistic, that is, if this were a film set. Twelve stone pillars stood thick based from floor to the several stone arches beneath a high vaulted ceiling. At each pillar stood what was referred to as a sacred fire. The twelve pillars represented the twelve knights of the fabled King Arthur.

Standartenführer Mikel Olandorf adjusted his long, irritatingly flowing medieval robe. His chain-mail corslet hung heavy around his shoulders and the ridiculous bloody lump of tin adorning his sweat dripping head was a ludicrous monstrosity. His hand closed angrily around the ornate hilt of the sword which hung clumsily from his hip. The blade was the real thing, so he had been solemnly informed by the gefreiter in charge of the vintage weapons store. It certainly felt like it but Olandorf knew that, like everything else in this fair-ground horror show maze of caverns, it was a fake. It was sharp, heavy and made his back ache like crazy. The imitation rubies and diamante crap adorning said hilt were doing sweet sod all for his ego, mood or feeling of contempt for his surroundings. But – needs must, and all that. If one wanted to get on in this world then one had to comply with the various idiosyncrasies of one's superiors, no matter how insanely idiotic they may be. So here he was, an SS officer on the rise, on the make, and hopefully on the right track. Today he had been designated as Sir Belvedere; whoever the hell that was or might have been. Standing across from him, rigidly staring straight ahead was SS General Theodore Eicke. A mightily feared SS commander of the highest order and hugely respected throughout the SS. Olandorf felt privileged to be in the same company as such a man as Eicke. The stockily built and plump featured General Eicke exuded none of the bonhomie that his features might suggest. He was the Inspector General of Concentration Camps and had less congeniality than a burning snake; and like the snake, he hissed a lot. He was a friend of Himmler and an enemy of Heydrich. Heydrich had stolen one of Eicke's favourite toys from him, Dachau Concentration Camp, and Theodore Eicke was not a forgiving man. He was probably the only man in the Third Reich that did not fear the ice-cold Reinhard Heydrich. Which, of course, meant that Himmler made sure to constantly play one off against the other just as he had learnt to do from his adored master, Adolf Hitler.

Others were standing less than majestically before the great stone pillars. Each attempting to look engaged and thoroughly au fait with the proceedings and each, to a greater or lesser degree, failing hopelessly. They resembled beer hall boozers awaiting the start of a fancy-dress ball. Chief amongst them was Obergruppenführer Sepp Dietrich. Once one of Hitler's bodyguards he had, like many of the Führer's minions from the early days, risen to high office. Few though, had risen as high as the tough, redoubtable and perennially thick-headed Sepp Dietrich. He was loyal, one paced and tunnel visioned. It was his complete and unwavering loyalty that had ensured his success; that, and an infallible ability to eliminate the Führer's enemies en masse. He was the kind of man that Hitler prized above others who possessed so much more talent. As with all, when it came to trust and promotion, the Führer valued loyalty ranked alongside stupidity as the most bankable of commodities. Sepp Dietrich was adored by the men under his command. His bluff exterior, genial grin and firm handshake neatly concealed the well sewn cloak of professional mediocrity that was more a part of him than his own skin.

Dietrich was having trouble concealing his boredom. Now there, thought Olandorf, is a man just itching to take his ungentlemanly boot to a few puffed-up British backsides. Obergruppenführer Sepp Dietrich still smarted over the outcome of the first world war and longed to exact an entrail tearing revenge over those, as he referred to them, chinless and snotty nosed islanders. Olandorf rocked back on his heels slightly as he felt the swelling of his ankles and feet press hard against the ungiving and unforgiving metal of his wide-toed sabatons. No doubt at all that Dietrich and his Leibstandarte would put the fear of God into anyone.

Making sure not to move his head, Olandorf cast his eyes over the assembled 'round table' company. Why, he wondered, would the Reichsführer choose an ancient and probably mythical British king for tonight's little get-together when he could have chosen Charlemagne, or one of the German Henrys or Frederiks? The castle had many such rooms with gloriously Teutonic names inscribed across their arched lintels. An odd choice, in his opinion. But, then, with all said and done, Heinrich Himmler was an altogether odd individual. He allowed his gaze to rest momentarily upon the Reichsführer. The supreme head of the SS was resplendent in full plate armour over which lay a pure silk surcoat emblazoned with a dragon rampant. Olandorf was pretty certain that the race obsessed Reichsführer had not the slightest idea that the full plate armour in which they were all so uncomfortably and ridiculously encased, was unheard of until the mid-fourteenth century. Such glorious raiment would have been totally beyond the imagination of the fabled Arthur from the seventh, eighth or ninth century, whichever one he was supposed to have lived in.

"Herein we pledge our allegiance," intoned the Reichsführer, "to the might, glory and steadfastness that is the true Germany."

'Oh, lord," thought Olandorf, as they all dutifully recited word for word the Reichsführer's droning incantation. "Why does the wretched man insist on making a sodding church service out of it every time.' Like a priest with a thick tongue and severe laryngitis Himmler continued. Withdrawing the specially made sword from its long gold inlaid scabbard, he held it dramatically aloft. The sword had been crafted especially for the Reichsführer because of his sad lack of physical strength and his total inability to raise the real thing any further than knee height, and even that had proved to be problematic.

"The glory that is Germany shall be burnished by we, her servants. For all eternity we shall serve without question whatever orders and commands delivered to us from beyond. Valhalla is our home and the blood of Odin flows through our veins. Our earthly Führer, Adolf Hitler, may the sons of Odin cherish his name, brings the word and oversees our obedience. Through him, we beseech the great ones to accept our obedience for all time. THIS WE SWEAR BY ALL THE GODS IMMORTAL!"

Olandorf and Eicke roared with the rest of them as the pagan ritual continued and became ever louder and more blood curdling as each man sought to outdo the others in shrieks and displays of metal encased foot stamping loyalty.

Swords held high and pointing aggressively upward, somewhere toward wherever they all, by mutual consent, supposed Valhalla might be, they roared in unison; "Germany and her life forever: always victorious! No compromise and no mercy for the enemies of Germany. Germany above all – always! Sieg Heil!" With Himmler adopting what he fondly believed to be a heroic Arthurian pose, the sieg-heiling continued for, perhaps, just a little too long before he brought it to an end with an imperious wave of his now ungauntleted hand. With swords calmly replaced within the safer confines of their scabbards, Himmler stood, legs apart and arms akimbo as he prepared to address the assembled worthies in more moderate tones and on more mundane issues. His armour shone and the white silken surcoat with its emblazoned dragon rampant was, even on him, quite impressive. Atop his head sat a silver bascinet and on top of that lay a solid gold circlet denoting his kingship. He, at this moment, was King Arthur. The effect, however, was somewhat spoiled by the glinting pince-nez spectacles and his unfortunately rather mongoloid appearance. He resembled more an overlooked and weedy addition to the family of the long dead Genghis Khan. He was certainly no Siegfried. What the hell, thought Olandorf. Did the Führer, really go along with all this clap-trap? It certainly looked like it. According to Himmler, the possibilities were endless. He had even mentioned controlling the weather. Amazing! Hitler therefore allowed him to continue with his investigations into all manner of strange things and asked few questions of his SS leader.

A shriek rent the air making all heads, bar one, look up in alarm. It came from somewhere behind or below but because of the castle's odd acoustics, its exact location was a mystery. It came again, this time louder, making the sound easier to pinpoint.

"Ignore that gentlemen, if you please. Just some minor unpleasantness." Himmler half turned toward the sound which had emanated from behind and to his right. "That door Ober Scharführer, as soon as you can." The massively proportioned senior NCO standing guard some fifty feet away from the high-ranking group of SS luminaries, lumbered to obey. His attire, as far as Olandorf could ascertain, was, more or less, that of a sixteenth-century Spanish Conquistador. At more than two metres in height and weighing at least one hundred and twenty kilos without the armour, the Oberscharführer was not going to get anywhere very quickly. The shriek, for whatever reason, rang out again.

"Quickly, you oaf,"

A confused expression, doubtless often used, crossed the Oberscharführer's grizzled features.

"Which door might that be, Herr Reichsführer, sir?" He asked attempting to keep his naturally rasping voice as low keyed as possible.

Himmler was now looking somewhat disgruntled. His performance had been interrupted and he didn't appreciate it one bit.

He spread his hands and spoke as though to a complete moron.

"I don't know, man. Just find the thing and CLOSE IT!"

The Oberscharführer clumped off loudly. His metal shod feet giving off a resounding and echoing clang with each weighty step that he took. Certainly the sound emanated from the area around a flight of circular stone steps. Only one door at the top of the stairwell could be seen from where Himmler and his group stood, and over its lintel was inscribed Orthodontic Inquisitions.

The Oberscharführer lumbered back, his halberd tapping the marble floor like a third foot.

"With respect Herr Reichsführer, sir, the door is closed. All the doors up there are closed sir."

Himmler stamped his size seven foot in a petulant manner and immediately threw his head back and glared at everyone as he realised that he had made himself appear less than kingly. The shriek, now turning to a howl of unbearable agony beat against everybody's ears.

"What the hell......." Dietrich pursed his lips as he cut off the remainder of the sentence. Swearing before the Reichsführer was not the done thing. Especially here in this holy of holies. But some poor sod was being given more than just a once-over. It sounded like the application of hot irons or electric cables being placed unkindly over sensitive parts.

Himmler's normally weak and watery grey eyes were now alight behind his rimmed pince-nez spectacles. "Gentlemen, I must apologise for the unseemly noise. I shall have the culprit apprehended and punished."

"Sounds as though the poor sod's been punished enough if you ask me."

"What's that, Herr Obergruppenführer?" Himmler's tone was acid. He didn't much take to the former butcher/bodyguard come top SS General; Hitler, though, set great store by him, so he tolerated him but just barely.

"Nothing at all Herr Reichsführer. Please forgive the interruption." The stocky Dietrich covered his hard face with a cold smile which didn't reach his eyes but did manage to slightly reveal his teeth. He gave a small bow in Himmler's direction and then stared pointedly ahead.

"We shall adjourn immediately to the Wessel room, gentlemen. I wish to speak to you on an important matter. So, I think perhaps that the less informal surroundings of that room might lend themselves better to our needs."

"With or without armour," Eicke asked in all seriousness.

"Oh, without, I think." Answered Himmler in all equal seriousness. "These things do," he squirmed a little. "restrict one in a most alarming way. However did those heroes manage to fight all day in these things, eh? Real men, my friends. Yes, indeed and real heroes too. We must all, we German men, aspire to the glorious ideals of manhood that were held by our forefathers."

"Rape and pillage," muttered Dietrich. "Just the thing!"

Unarmoured but unfortunately still sweating, the group of men sat waiting and attentive in the Wessel room. Their leader and speaker stood before them now clad as they were more used to seeing him. In sharp contrast to the oddly faux aspect of the majority of rooms in the castle, the Wessel room had a decidedly more modern look to it. No burning log fire spluttered and spat here, and there was no sign of antique bronze and iron fire surrounds. Instead, four big, wide rimmed and round bodied central heating radiators pumped out constant heat. Heinrich suffered from the cold and was inclined to be a martyr to a wide variety of different ailments, all quite debilitating, should he not take proper care of himself or, as he much preferred, to be taken care of.

Eicke lit up a cigarette and Himmler glared at him. The concentration camp inspector immediately ground it out on the shining wooden floor using the sole of his even shinier shiny leather SS boot. Strands of crushed tobacco spread out at his feet along with a small patch of black ash which Eicke idly shoved away with the raised side of his knee-high boot.

Sepp Dietrich, however, did not put out his cigarette. To hell with Heinrich bloody Himmler and his foibles. Sepp needed a gasper and Sepp was going to have one.

"Obergruppenführer," Himmler spoke kindly and smiled benignly, masking his intense irritation. He gestured to Dietrich's smoke swirling cigarette. "If you wouldn't mind."

Dietrich took a long hard drag of his long-awaited and desperately needed cancer stick and then rose slowly. Taking another lungful he strode toward a window. The vile stench of his Russian blend Cebeb cigarette filled the room within seconds. Himmler waved an offended hand in front of his nose as, upon reaching the window, Dietrich took another huge lungful of the vile Russian concoction and then let the smoke stream out through his nostrils. Even hardened smokers like Eicke and the also attending Lothar Heimbach were feeling somewhat nauseated by Dietrich's imported Russian horror.

Angrily now, Himmler spat out, "Herr Obergruppenführer!"

Pulling open the window, Dietrich turned back toward the Reichsführer, took another deep drag, waved the cigarette pointedly in the air before throwing it out into the night.

"There, now," this time his smile was real. "All done." He returned to his seat where he waited as though nothing had happened. Himmler composed himself and prepared to continue. The window remained open.

After some ten minutes of general expostulation against those foreign nations that seemed determined to oppose the Third Reich and its rightful place in the world, Himmler came to the point.

"What is said here within the sacred confines of these walls must never be repeated. I want that to be clearly understood, gentlemen."

Murmurs of acquiescence drifted up from the expectant company seated before him. Himmler's high cheekbones glistened and the pupils of his slightly slanty little eyes dilated from behind his pince-nez. These men and their subordinates would be his tools for the realization of his dream: the total obliteration of Jewry. Annihilation by any and all means.

"We come to the Jewish problem. Let us not beat about the bush, gentlemen. We want them gone and they shall be gone! Gone from this great nation of ours, and gone from Europe, gone from the East – for good!" He looked around as though he had just imparted some great, previously unheard piece of wisdom or knowledge. Which, indeed, he just had.

"Europe!" Questioned Olandorf. "How, if I might ask, Herr Reichsführer, do we manage that?"

"The East, you say, Herr Reichsführer!" That was Eicke. "It sounds splendid, sir. But how – when?"

Sepp Dietrich sat studiously examining his fingernails. Himmler had gone too far. Dietrich knew well enough what was being planned in the Fuhrer's mind. Himmler, though, had only an inkling. The Reichsführer knew, or thought he knew, what Hitler wanted but in reality, knowing what Hitler would like to do and knowing exactly what it was that he was going to do were two very different things. Men like Himmler did things because they thought that was what Hitler wanted them to do, not because he had implicitly instructed them to do any such thing. Himmler believed that his leader Adolf Hitler wanted every Jew on the planet dead, ergo, he, Himmler must strain every nerve and muscle to obtain a favourable result for his master.

Sepp knew what his boss, Adolf, really wanted. The man wanted an easy life and would happily destroy the world to get it: simple!

"Then, if you'll forgive me Herr Reichsführer," said Heimbach, "You mean war. We are going to war."

"Oh, not so fast, young man," Himmler gave his famed icy smile as he wagged an admonishing finger at the youngest officer present.

It was clear, though, that the SS leader was speaking of a major and massive conflict, else why mention that he intended to dispose of millions of Jews within the territories that he had just mentioned? Heimbach, young and idealistic, gave little or no thought as to what such a war might mean. But the others knew well enough. There was some nail clicking and tongues pensively running along the insides of clenched teeth as the implication of Himmler's seemingly indiscreet remark sank in. Or had it been indiscreet? The stone-cold SS leader was not prone to making verbal errors. Clanger dropping was not a Reichsführer weakness; the very reverse, in fact. Had he just ever so slightly set ajar the window of the big secret? Food for thought indeed and muttered questions began drifting back and forth in something of a verbal jumble. Must it be war, then? Did they have enough tanks, ships and aircraft? No one thought to ask about the availability of the sinews of war, the real necessities such as manganese, iron, nickel and chrome and a host of other things desperately needed to prosecute a war. Not one of them thought to ask such questions. After all, that was the Führer's job and he would surely provide. If the Reichsführer SS and their great leader Adolf Hitler were confident of military success then Germany must assuredly be well prepared for such a venture. Excitement filled the room. All bar Dietrich, who knew better, had suddenly taken on the glowing complexions of great excitement and joy. Himmler quickly shushed them down and returned to the major theme: disposal of the Jews within German borders first, and then without.

The meeting droned on with suggestions as to how best eliminate as many Jews as quickly and efficiently as possible.

"The numbers might run into many thousands," suggested Heimbach to an indulgently beaming Reichsführer.

"Hundreds of thousands," Olandorf corrected.

"No," Eicke stared around the room at his death discussing companions. "Millions, I tell you. They are everywhere."

The conversation soon took in Gypsies, homosexuals and the mentally retarded. Any large and non-Aryan group could be fair game in the coming racial clean-up.

"As for the Retards," said Himmler. "Well, who or what could be less Aryan than those brain befuddled monstrosities, eh?"

Only Sepp Dietrich looked doubtful and that was purely because of all those present, he seemed the only one able to envision the colossal manpower that such an operation would entail: manpower that might well, at some later stage, be greatly needed elsewhere.

"I suggest," said Himmler. "That you all study the methods used by the USA during their extermination of the Native American Indian. They turned genocide into an art form and are to be commended for showing us and the rest of the world the way to eradicate unworthy races."

"I thought the British led the way in that sort of thing," said Olandorf.

"Oh dear me, no," the Reichsführer chortled self-importantly. "True, they gave us the fine idea and method of the Concentration camp from a system they devised in South Africa. But really, all they managed to eliminate were fairly useless and innocuous women and children. The deaths of those women and children were quite simply allowed to compel the Boars to surrender; which of course they eventually did. Frankly, I believe that the real reason why so many thousands of those women and children died was down to pure accident; accident mixed with carelessness. The British, from what I can gather, did feed them, not much I grant you but they didn't starve the wretches. No, the reason those women and children died was because the British, quite typically, forgot to allow them any kind of medical facility. Not so very different from the way that they have always treated their lower orders. No medicines, no unguents and a quite appalling lack of hygiene. All very messy, very public and not at all what we want."

"Then what do we want, Herr Reichsführer," questioned Dietrich, whose own family had lived in a filthy slum, mired in squalor made bearable only by his, Sepp Dietrich's determination to improve their lot. And improve it he had. From slum dweller, to butcher, to Nazi thug and then to SS general. Not too bad at all.

"Privacy, Herr Obergruppenführer," came Himmler's icy reply. "We do not want to attract, under any circumstances, the attention of the outside world. We have much to accomplish and there are sure to be those who will refuse to understand our holy mission."

"Yes," mused Olandorf. "There are sure to be our detractors but more to the point, Herr Reichsführer," he paused as Himmler gestured for him to continue. "How, sir, do we accomplish a thing like this on the scale which you, and of course, the Führer, wish to see accomplished?"

"As I said previously," reiterated Himmler. "Study closely the American methods of genocide. Also their method for keeping undesirables down and under control. The American negro is kept in a permanent state of fear and dependency and their relative freedom is completely at the will of their white superiors. Many of the aforementioned methods of elimination and control, gentlemen, were and still are effective and first-rate, in my opinion. Their greatest industrialist, Henry Ford, lauds most loudly any method used to keep down or eliminate those unworthy types that infest all areas of our globe."

The Reichsführer leaned forward, both hands waving ever so slightly at the wrist, drawing in his audience. "Now, see here," he continued, warming to his pet subject and briefly fixing his beady eyes on each man present before going on. "To expand their empire and ensure success for their imperialistic aims, they needed to eradicate the Native Americans. This was in part accomplished by the white colonists, basically still Englishman but with muscles, poisoning the very earth in which the natives sowed their crops. What could have been simpler, my friends? Just poison the earth and then just watch and wait for the natives to die. They also injected them with smallpox and engaged in very basic elimination techniques such as wholesale slaughter. I am given to understand they had some excellent and effective commanders in the field of violent death. Although to be honest, gentlemen, unlike those old American exterminators, I consider bludgeoning and hands-on slaughter to be both time consuming and lacking in finesse. Nevertheless, even using those somewhat dull and unimaginative methods, I believe that the Native American population declined from some eleven million in the eighteenth century to less than three hundred thousand by the end of the nineteenth. So you see, gentlemen, it can be done and it shall be done."

"And you mean to use the camps for this purpose, Herr Reichsführer?"

"Just so, Eicke. And, unlike our American friends, we shall introduce methods of extermination that will scrape the filth of Jewry from Germany and as many other places as our will to succeed can reach. Sieg Heil!"

Here we go again, thought Dietrich as he rose, threw out his right arm and sieg-heiled manfully with the rest.

Chapter 21

itler's office within the new Chancellery was huge. He hated working here, or anywhere else for that matter, but this marble-walled echo chamber he loathed most of all. True enough, when Speer had shown him the designs and layout of everything it had all seemed so wonderful. A building fit for the Gods, with an office befitting the mighty Führer of the Third Reich. A room in which he could overawe supplicants and opponents alike. The trouble was it also overawed him. The sky seeking ceilings with chandelier lighting that needed an army of cleaners and electricians to keep it all functioning. The massive, recessed marble walls with their door sized windows dwarfed him, his ideas and his sense of himself as the mighty one. He felt like an immature midget in this place and now hated all of its four hundred square metres with a vengeance. His voice echoed whenever he spoke in this room, as did the voices of any others that might be invited to speak. The more he frequented the New Reich Chancellery the less inclined he became to do any work in it. There was no doubt about it, the damned place stifled his creativity.

The desk behind which he stood was every bit as ostentatious as the room which it was supposed to compliment. Gold inlaid top, solid gold ink pots with platinum pens laying gracefully unused beside them. White calacatta marble busts of himself and Frederik the Great were placed on either end of the great desk. There was an ornately upholstered chair with wide armrests placed some ten feet in front of the desk. It was from here that a visitor, foreign dignitary or some such, would be expected to request, demand, beg for, whatever it was that he or she wanted. It would also mean raising one's voice in order to be heard satisfactorily each by the other. Hopeless! Hitler had felt, for the first time, a small niggling doubt about his favourite architect, Albert Speer. The man had messed up big time with this monstrosity of a government building. The Führer, though, had to continue pretending to adore the wretched place for fear of making himself look foolish and indecisive, and that would never do. Also, Albert was the sort likely to go off in an enormous huff if his architectural designs were criticised.

Adolf strode to one of the huge windows and peered out. He gestured to his companion, Walther Funk, Reichsminister for the Economy, to sit at one of the smaller chairs ringing the wall.

"I am confident of your ability to get on top of things, Herr Funk. The ebbs and flows of national economy, dousing incipient inflation and suchlike; those are things that chaps like you are so good at sorting out. Whereas, they quite simply mystify other mere mortals." He favoured the harassed looking Reich Economy chief with a winning smile.

Walther Funk was certainly harassed, stressed and at his wit's end. He was experiencing what Finance Minister Schacht had been forced to endure just two days previously, and that was the Führer's absolute refusal to listen to financial or logistical reason. He would not, or could not comprehend that just because he had gained supreme power within the Reich, he could not change the stark reality of the world's international or domestic financial system simply because it suited him. International bankers didn't deal in abstracts or political huffle-puffle. For them, money was a stark reality.

Funk was a loyal party man but had by now realised that the Führer thought in purely bourgeoise, almost peasant terms. Germany was rushing headlong into a deep recession that would be fuelled by overwhelming inflation unless the Führer took his head out of the sand and wised up to the reality of political and financial life.

"We have already taken desperate economic measures, my Führer." Without asking, Funk rose from his seat and faced Hitler directly. "Sir, you must, must cut back on government spending."

Small lights appeared to dance dangerously behind Hitler's eyes as he stared down at his even shorter Economics minister.

"Must? Did you say MUST? Careful Herr Minister. Do not presume to lecture or command me, your Führer."

Funk trembled but held his ground. The future of the Reich could well depend upon what was said or decided, here today.

"Forgive me, my Führer. But you have been spending vast amounts on armaments; importing ores and items that Germany does not possess. Nickel, manganese, iron, chrome – even food."

"I have given the people work," Hitler waved an impatient hand in front of Funk. "When I came to power there were six million unemployed. How many now Herr Funk, eh – how many?"

"I believe some three hundred thousand, sir."

"Hah! Just so," the Führer spun triumphantly on his booted heels. "And yet, and yet Herr Funk, you see fit to criticise me."

Funk sighed deeply and hoped that the Führer would not see the exasperation and despair in his eyes. The man had completely ignored the central problem and had just gone on about how clever he was.

"I would not dream of criticising your genius my Führer," said Funk placatingly. "But, sir, all those people that you have put into work have been promised pensions, medical care, cheap cars and holidays. True sir, you have built great roads, the autobahns are a miracle of design but sir, we do not have the money to pay for all that. We do not export anything like enough to cover even a fraction of what we have been importing. My Führer, to put it bluntly, we are billions in debt and I see no way out."

Hitler placed his hand on his hips and glared at his Economics minister. True enough he had promised pensions, paid holidays along with all sorts of other tempting inducements and he had produced those things for a grateful people. They loved him. He'd done it all because he knew that the only way a man like him could stay in power was to ensure that the populace remained docile and obedient. And the best way to do that in the short term was to give them what they wanted. Later, things could be done differently. Unfortunately, later seemed to be arriving somewhat earlier than he had anticipated.

"Sir," Funk continued. "Our international borrowing is now more than sixty per cent of our GDP."

"I annexed Austria and the Sudetenland," snapped the Führer. "Are you saying that those two valuable acquisitions aren't enough to ease our balance problems?"

"Nowhere near it, sir," responded Funk heavily. "Our spending," he diplomatically refrained from saying your spending, "on the armed forces has been and still is astronomical. The goods purchased from the east alone for the military is almost ten per cent more than our GDP."

These damned politicians mused Hitler. They seemed always to want to put a damper on things. From his perspective, things were going very well indeed. He was respected, and a little feared, by the outside world. When he threatened, the leaders of other nations, great nations, trembled. And yet here was this mealy minded little politico rambling about misfortune to the man who was nothing less than the saviour of Germany.

"And the advice, then, which you are itching to propound, is what, eh? Start a war and steal what I need?" The Führer's stare became piercing and his pupils dilated at his own mention of war.

Funk shuddered. War was becoming an ever more likely option, as his master's lack of forward planning and reliance upon fate and uniformed lackeys to see him through began to bear unpleasantly tainted fruit. Germany was years away from being ready to engage in a major war. Because of the enormous sums spent on the fighting arms of the military, the supply system had been neglected and was

hopelessly antiquated. It had not the remotest hope of keeping up
with mechanized infantry and armour whilst still using horse and cart
and there simply was not enough money remaining in the allocated
budget to even partially assist in modernisation. Hopeless! Funk knew
only too well that sooner or later Hitler would have his war. The man
dreamed of glory and conquest and he was itching to get on with it.
But it must not be yet. Somehow he, and a few others with more than
half a brain, must keep the Führer reined in. "I can see only one course
open to you my Führer."

"Which is?" enquired the Führer, clearly not expecting much.

"Seek an alliance, sir, with an economically stable state and arrange
favourable trade rates in exchange for German military expertise. You
do have sir, after all, a large and potent army, navy and air force. It
might be a good idea, now that you have personally destroyed the evil
that was the Versailles treaty, to use those assets. In a relatively peaceful
manner, of course."

Damn this annoying man. Hitler slapped his thigh quite savagely,
never a good sign for those in his company. He might have a point,
though, this finickity economics chief. He had received complaints
from all arms of the forces demanding more cash for their individual
expansion; industry moaned that it was groaning beneath the weight
of the increased wages authorised by the State, meaning the Führer,
and all his financial advisors were warning him to tighten his belt,
pull in his horns and just about every other cliché known to man in
their rapidly combining efforts to hold back the two programmes
which interested him the most: the armaments industry and the
grandiose architectural plans that he had allowed Speer to talk him
into. Massive new buildings, streets and avenues in Berlin and other
cities in the Reich were already under construction. A new capital,
Germania was envisaged and already on the drawing board. Great
and wonderful projects and a powerful enough army to allow the
Third Reich to thumb its nose at even the most powerful of nations.
What was it that Funk had said? Was it millions or billions that they

owed? Surely it couldn't be billions. Nobody on earth could owe that much money.

Funk reaffirmed his statement. Billions! Dammit! Hitler bade good day to his Economics Minister and chewed at the tip of his moustache. He had to find a solution, and fast!

After dismissing Walther Funk from his presence, Hitler called his ubiquitous personal aide and Party secretary, Martin Bormann, and instructed him to inform Foreign Minister Joachim von Ribbentrop, that his presence was required at the Chancellery immediately. Unfortunately that rather snooty worthy had the cheek to inform Bormann, whom he loathed with a vengeance, that he was rather busy at that moment. He would, he said, try to get there within a couple of hours. It was a four-minute walk or a one-minute drive and Hitler flew into a monumental rage at the Foreign Minister's flippant rejection of his Führer's demand for immediacy.

Bormann, always on the lookout for ways to drop others of the inner circle into the mire of Hitler's wrath, had not relayed in any way the urgency of the Führer's demand for his Foreign Minister's attendance. He had put it across as more of a polite request, speaking softly and obsequiously about how nice it would be to see him, and how much the Führer looked forward to hearing all his latest foreign news, and so on. The Reichsleiter was an absolute master of verbal chicanery. He smiled as his boss demanded the phone and almost grinned widely as Hitler shrieked at Ribbentrop to get his sorry backside over to the chancellery right away or there just might be a new foreign minister by this time tomorrow.

Ribbentrop and his aide were standing red-faced and puffing before their Führer in six minutes flat.

Hitler acted as if nothing untoward had happened. He left Ribbentrop standing in the centre of his huge office whilst he walked around in staggered circles like a peripatetic teacher making a point to a dense student. With his arms jerkily waving about as he made some point or other, he repeatedly turned to Ribbentrop and waited impatiently for agreement to whatever it was that he had just said.

Joachim von Ribbentrop's greatest misfortune, apart from his innate stupidity, was that he had been born with a rigidly pronounced po-face which made his natural facial expression appear to be one of supercilious boredom. Worse still, he constantly held that po-face in a nose tilted up position, thus making it seem that he considered himself to be vastly superior in every way to the rest of humanity. Ribbentrop, was in fact, one of those people who looked to be exactly what he was; a pompous fool. He had replaced the former Foreign minister, von Neurath because Hitler, for some inexplicable reason, considered him to be a brilliant man of international affairs. Which, as far as the former Foreign Minister and his peremptorily sacked colleagues were concerned, didn't say an awful lot for Herr Hitler. The Führer, in his insightful wisdom, reckoned that the former wine salesman and now newly minted Foreign Minister would be a first-rate choice for the important post of overseeing foreign affairs because he was so well travelled. He could not have been more wrong! Well-travelled Ribbentrop certainly was: Canada, the USA, Turkey and quite a few other places to boot. Yes, he was travelled, but his personality was a mockery inducing disaster. Steadfastly devoted to the Führer he might be, but squint-eyed Joachim was really something of a bad-tempered joke within the close Führer circle. Although he could function well enough on a lower level, if ever placed under pressure of any kind he was unable to respond actively to stimuli or emergency surroundings. Unforeseen, unexpected events were total anathema to dozy Joachim. He became tongue-tied, foolish seeming, and found it impossible to react as was needed. He was loyal, though, and Adolf Hitler was the only man alive of whom Joachim von Ribbentrop was afraid. And, as yet, Hitler still had faith in the man's abilities.

"Do you take my meaning Ribbentrop?" growled Hitler, voice dropping to a normal level as he suddenly felt very tired. He had been up since ten-thirty am, rather too early for him, and it was now close to 13:00 hours. He had not taken tea or cream cake and was feeling utterly exhausted with the morning's work. It was now afternoon and he needed to rest. This feeling of being overworked always left him feeling somewhat martyred; almost saintly. People must realise that their Führer was not an infinite resource; he needed rest and sustenance. Yes, indeed he did.

Ribbentrop nodded like a wooden dummy with hooded eyes. He always nodded when his Führer spoke. He found it best in the long run.

"I understand perfectly, my Führer," Ribbentrop felt that terrifyingly familiar lump of sludge entering his mind.

"And?" Hitler stood with legs apart with his arms beckoning expectantly. Ribbentrop took half a step forward as if expecting the Führer to demand a hug. He pulled himself up just before completing that ill-advised step.

"And, er, what, my Führer?"

"What are you going to do?"

"Erm," Ribbentrop looked helplessly toward his aide who, though more than willing to help his boss in any way that he could, found that attempted communication through rapid eye-blinking semaphore and contrived facial expressions was no substitute for imparting information in the good old verbal fashion.

Bormann wondered if he might not be experiencing his first heart attack as he fought down the howls of laughter that threatened to explode from his person at any moment.

"Well?" Demanded Hitler, now becoming thoroughly irritated.

"Do about what, precisely, my Führer?" The aide turned away in despair mixed with terror and behind Hitler, Bormann bent double with barely concealed mirth.

Hitler's teeth were beginning to appear from behind his thin snarl forming lips. The aide, realising that their careers, both Ribbentrop's and his own, were on the line with very likely worse in store unless rescue of some kind were to be effected, raced the six paces to his floundering boss and whispered urgently into his ear.

Poor old Ribbentrop turned back toward his Führer; still the same immobile facial expression, as though nothing at all was wrong. Only the stream of perspiration running freely down his forehead and face betrayed his acute anxiety. Sweat lay and then became absorbed by his formerly immaculately arranged shirt collar and tie. He was aware of it well enough and the effort he was making to look as though nothing was amiss, that he was in complete control, was comical in the extreme. It was pure Ribbentrop.

"I have just such a plan my Führer." He coughed and a rather sick looking smile spread over his perspiration glowing face. Bormann was loving every single moment of this show.

Ribbentrop raised himself up on his toes and then rocked back again. He raised a hand in an airy gesture and gave a solemn and wise man style nod. Bormann sniffed loudly and the Foreign minister's eyes flicked briefly toward his hated enemy.

"And, Herr Ribbentrop; what might that plan be?" Hitler turned his back on Ribbentrop, tapping his right foot and waiting for the great revelation.

"I have, my Führer, er, ahem, for some time now been acutely aware of our sundried international problems."

"A most remarkable admission for a Foreign Minister," smirked Bormann.

Engulfed by rage fuelled terror at being made to look a fool before his Führer, Ribbentrop almost broke. "You son of a...."

Hitler turned with raised hand. "Your plan, Herr Foreign Minister. If you don't mind, I should very much like to hear it."

Ribbentrop's breath came in short, close to panic gasps. He pointed to Reichsleiter Bormann. "It is most secret, my Führer. He, sir, should leave. We can't have just anybody knowing about the high level of diplomacy which we are proposing to undertake."

That wiped the smirk and all semblance of amusement from Bormann's face.

"Just anybody? I am not just anybody you jumped up booze peddler!"

Ribbentrop's fists closed and he took three rapid steps toward the stocky and eagerly awaiting Reichsleiter.

"ENOUGH!" The Hitler roar stopped Ribbentrop dead in his tracks and had Bormann looking steadily at the floor beneath his highly polished brown demi-boots.

Hitler glared theatrically at the pair of them in turn. In truth, though, this kind of thing bothered him not one jot. It enforced and reinforced his command system. Keep the snapping position seekers at each other's throats and well away from his own; that was his system and his motto.

"The Reichsleiter," said the Führer, almost kindly, "remains here. He is privy to all things State. Relax now, Ribbentrop, my dear fellow. We are all friends here. Our mutual trust is our unbreakable bond. True?" He looked at them and smiled that special Führer smile.

"Oh, so very true my Führer," said Bormann with seemingly great feeling and genuine emotion. "As the SS like to say, Loyalty binds us. The perfect motto, if I may say so." Bormann was almost simpering.

"Actually," chimed in Ribbentrop, "it's, My Honour is Called Loyalty."

"Oh is it really?" Bormann almost snarled and it was Ribbentrop's turn to feel smug. "Yes, Herr Reichsleiter, it really is." Ribbentrop's po-face was looking ever more supercilious as his nose turned up a ratchet or two. Bormann could swear that the wretched man almost smiled.

"The aide can get out," snarled the Reichsleiter. He turned toward Hitler with an ingratiating smile. "With the Führer's permission, of course."

The aide couldn't wait to get leave. The idea that he had just so briefly passed on to the Foreign Minister was one that, in all likelihood, would send the Führer into a shrieking, froth spitting hissy-fit. There simply hadn't been time for him to dream up anything else. He had mentioned his lunatic little scheme to his boss a few days ago and Ribbentrop had stared at him as though he were completely mad. "An insane idea," he'd scoffed. "Save it for the fairies."

Actually, thought the aide, as he bowed and took a step backwards, it wasn't such a bad idea at all. A little time, a little polish and he might have come up with something very presentable. Well, that was all that they had so it was now up to the Minister to convince the Führer that he had indeed been working hard on some kind of dynamic mould busting deal that would aid the Third Reich in its hour of need. The Foreign Minister, like his Führer, loved the use of grandiose phrases and now was the time to think up a few new ones.

Ribbentrop gave his aide a despairing look as he departed. Poor Joachim was almost in tears when Hitler came unexpectedly to his rescue.

"Let the young man stay," he commanded. "It's good that younger members of our elite gain first-hand experience within the true corridors of power, eh young man?" He smiled condescendingly at the dapper young aide. "Stay with your boss. I may even have some questions for you later." Not daring to speak, the aide dropped his eyes and nodded coyly. A handsome young fellow in the physical mould of the Führer favourite, Albert Speer. He stood closer to the much taller Ribbentrop and waited for his master to begin, all the time feeling like the straight man in a badly under rehearsed variety hall double act.

"Right, then, Herr Foreign Minister. Let's hear it."

"My Führer," Ribbentrop moved closer to Hitler and the aide moved in time and step with him. It was beginning to look more like a comedy double act with each passing moment. Hitler barely noticed the slightly comic aspect of his underlings as Ribbentrop made to speak more loudly. He was used to men, and women, making themselves look foolish when in his presence: much as he himself had done when he first met Mussolini in Rome. They'd said that he looked like Charlie Chaplin. Bastards! Well, he'd paid them back for that one, alright. Oh yes indeed! The Press wrote admiring prose, glorified the Party line or were left with nothing more than nail extracted stumps to scribble with.

A few minutes passed before Ribbentrop managed to get into any kind of flow but he was finding his feet and a strange sort of rhythm as he went on. Much of what his aide's initial premise had propounded remained in his mind; it was just his inability to find the right words. Three words, though, brought instant response.

"The Soviet Union – Did you say, the Soviet Union?"

Hitler stood with legs wide apart, his fists clenched and his expression a mixture of shock and disbelief.

The aide leaned into his boss's ear and gabbled something. Soft little hands waving and flapping as he spoke. Ribbentrop, leaning to the left in order to hear what he was saying suddenly pulled away, withdrew a kerchief from his trouser pocket and disgustedly wiped away the glistening deposits of bubbling spittle from his ear. With a less than gentle shove he thrust his well-meaning aide away from him.

"Yes, my Führer. Purely temporary, you see. We make agreements, like the Americans did with their natives, and then we just ignore them. No one expects civilized people to take inferior scum like Slavs or American Indians seriously. The usual rules quite simply do not apply."

"Nincompoop!" This was Bormann, now quite beside himself with rage and, yes, joy. Ribbentrop had sunk himself now. Trade, or any kind of deal with communists would be a like inflicting a cancer on the Reich. Was the man completely mad? He had to be and things were all the better for it. At last he could see the end of the pompous bird brain and his entire useless team. The Führer would surely now crush him like the bug that he was.

Ribbentrop, surprisingly, ignored the insult.

"Ores, nickel, chrome, petroleum, wheat and many, so many other essential items my Führer." He tried desperately to recall the myriad other things that his aide had imparted to him but nothing came. As it was, though, he had already caught Hitler's attention with the words, nickel, chrome and petroleum. He turned and with an "If I may, my Führer," he beckoned his aide to complete the list.

Hitler listened and Bormann, thinking he saw his chance to make the final lethal stab at the Foreign Minister butted in.

"How dare you even mention, let alone suggest that the Führer even so much as consider for one minute any kind of relationship with those Slavic dogs, the anathema of everything decent and German. Communists! Our most hated and despised enemy and here you are pleading their case, their cause and God alone knows what else. You go too far, Herr Foreign Minister. I say you...."

"Be quiet, Bormann. I need to think."

"But my Führer," Bormann gasped theatrically. "See what this man espouses. An insult to...."

"Shut up, Bormann or get the hell out! I said, I need to think."

True enough, Hitler mused, as he paced rapidly up and down, the Soviets and their vile communist doctrine were the Reich's most deadly enemy. Nevertheless, needs must when the devil drives and the devil was certainly driving now. Stalin, however, as the Führer knew, was having his own problems. Hitler rather admired the man, in truth. He knew how to get things done. Rumour had it that the Russian dictator had totally purged his officer corps. Innocent of sedition or not, Stalin simply got rid of them. A damn good idea. Those military types with their airs and graces all so full of minion bolstered superiority, were an absolute pain. They needed taking down a peg or two, although Stalin had, perhaps, gone a little too far. The Soviet military leadership, never of the most impressive quality, was now emasculated and relatively useless; for the time being, at least. And Ribbentrop was correct. Russia had all those lovely assets just waiting to be traded with Germany if an arrangement could be made. OK, it meant going back on all that he'd previously said about the evil Russian empire but he could manage that. Goebbels and his propaganda machine would sort out the relevant hogwash, and he, the Führer would nod and smile sagely in a wait-and-see kind of manner; and they, the people, millions of obedient lambs and tail-wagging dogs, would be firmly convinced that their genius of a leader was planning something very special and all for the good of the Reich. If the Reich flourished and survived then so would he, Adolf Hitler, flourish and survive. It was all one and the same, and so yes, he would be working, very hard, for the future of the Reich. It would all require very careful handling, though. Was the battering ram that was Joachim von Ribbentrop the right man for the job? Yes! The Russians needed to be under no illusions about what was required, and there was nothing illusory about Ribbentrop at all. He needn't be told the Führer's innermost thoughts, just enough to keep him going with the coming charade. Time was of the essence. The Soviet high command wouldn't remain moribund forever. And just look, thought Hitler as he mused on affairs, of what Napoleon accomplished with a bunch of over promoted corporals and sergeants. Time to move things along at a pace.

He threw back his shoulders. Germany desperately needed a massive share of that Soviet wealth. He realised, as he pondered and his minions waited expectantly, that he would prostitute every tenet that he had previously espoused if he could get some kind of deal going with Joseph Stalin. Hell – he would even prostitute himself!

He spun around, paused, and then marched like a man on a mission straight up to the somewhat taller Ribbentrop. That man flinched slightly and barely managed to stop himself from taking a step backward.

"See to it, Ribbentrop. It's an excellent idea. Get it done – get it all and offer anything that we have…within reason, of course. Get to Moscow and do what you have to do. Promise those bastards anything that pleases them. I must have," he spluttered slightly as he waved his hands beneath the Foreign Minister's face, "Damn it, man, you know what we need! See Funk, get a list and go make a deal. Understand? Greatness calls you my friend. So go, be great for Germany!"

Caught up in his Führer's enthusiasm Ribbentrop fairly glowed. "It shall be done, my Führer. Sieg Heil!" His arm swept up in the familiarly over dramatic Nazi salute.

After a few more words, Ribbentrop and his aide departed. Ribbentrop's face was full of eager anticipation and joy at his Führer's faith in him to accomplish this vital task. The aide, though, was positively beset with angst. How on earth were they to arrange a meeting with such an inveterate enemy, whose loathing of them at the very least equalled theirs of him? The aide's mind dwelt upon what their leader would do to them in the event of failure.

Bormann stood with hands behind his back. Calmly surveying his powerful master. "Are we sure that this can work, my Führer? It is a big ask."

"When the time comes, Bormann," answered Hitler. "I shall take what I want from those Soviet horrors, as and when I please. But right now," he sighed and glared at the Party Secretary. "I need time. We are not ready for war, not yet. And honestly, Bormann, we probably won't be for another three to four years."

"With Russia, you mean?"

"Yes, of course I mean Russia. Who else? The Poles, though, now that's a different matter."

"They are certainly running scared," noted Bormann.

"And so they should be. Danzig is ours by right and by God, Bormann I'll see it returned to the Reich very, very soon. What's more important though, is all those rich minerals that the Poles are sitting on. Copper, Zinc, Lead, Sulphur and so on. If we can get our hands on that little lot, then we'll have enough in reserve to take on anybody, in the short term, that is."

"But we need Russian cooperation to accomplish it?"

"Yes Bormann, we do. So, backup Ribbentrop in this and see that he has all the support and material that he needs. Stomp on anybody that so much as even looks as if they disagree. Clear?"

"Absolutely, my Führer."

"Now. Send in those damned generals."

CHAPTER 22

August 23 1939: Rue Saint-Rustique. Paris

Montmartre was an interesting slice of Parisian antiquity for any visitor who enjoyed the surroundings of old but modernised buildings, quaintly cobbled streets, French cafes, bistros and a kind of old-fashioned way of life which the spreading of the great city of Paris had not yet quite extinguished. Somehow this suburb, although now completely engulfed by the vastness of the ever-spreading city, had retained its old-world charm. It fought daily a valiant but losing struggle against the ever-increasing number of street widening city planners with their nagging insistence upon change and total modernisation.

The quite steep hill upon which Montmartre was situated provided something of a breath stealing challenge for some, but not for the fit, broad shouldered young man striding along the rue Saint-Rustique. He was happy and bore the look of a man content with the world and his lot in general. Though the weather was rather warm for the smartly tailored but unseasonable blue serge suit that the young fellow was wearing, he exhibited no sign of discomfort whatsoever. He had taken time to visit the Basilica of the Sacre Coeur and adored the lines and wonderful antique feel of the ancient church. It was cool and restful in there and it had once, so it was said, been a place of pagan worship. He had found that snippet of information to be intensely interesting, but did not have enough time to investigate further. Indeed, he should not have taken even such a small detour but he felt that he deserved it. Now, though, as he walked along the rue Saint-Rustique, he admired the ivy and other creepers that grew, lovingly tended and cut back, on each of the narrow fronted, terraced houses. Three stories high, some of the lovely little houses had creepers surrounding each window of their frontage.

The entire place, thought the young man, was a joy. He had indeed fallen in love with Paris. Well, as the saying went, didn't everybody? He smiled as he arrived at his destination; 17 rue Saint-Rustique. From the outside, his destination was every bit as neat and tidy as the rest. Continuing upward some twenty more metres, he turned left into a tiny alleyway leading to another wider alley at the back which allowed access to the rear of the houses on rue Saint-Rustique. Strolling slowly downhill, and happily taking in his surroundings from all around, the young man came to a halt outside the rear entrance of number 17. Casually he glanced around as he lifted the latch on the wooden gate and let himself in. It was just as he'd half expected, a lovely little garden with a small pond and a water-spouting Eros. Lovely. What a fine place to be!

Otto Wels sat back in a corner of his living room. He was happy enough today. The sun was shining, he had money in the bank, he lived well considering the circumstances, and this nice little house gave him the anonymity that he craved. The house, furniture, everything was rented. Otto didn't own so much as a stick of it. The furniture was a little sparse but certainly comfortable. Otto preferred leather upholstery and panelled walls beneath oaken beams but beggars could not be choosers. He certainly was no beggar but times and things in general had most decidedly once been a whole lot better. Nevertheless, he leaned back and lit a cigarette, after all that had happened he really shouldn't complain; at least he was safe and that counted for a lot. In fact, it counted for everything and he thanked

God for good friends. Cloth upholstery and flowery wallpaper were small prices to pay for one's freedom and safety. Compact though the charming little house might be, it was more than large enough for a single occupant. It boasted three bedrooms and two WCs both separate from the modern bathroom. An adequate kitchen, scullery and basement for storage; a dining room off the kitchen, a nice drawing room and the sitting room in which he now relaxed and spent most of his time. All this and a couple of small box rooms. More than enough room for one.

Heaving his spare frame out of the high-backed easy chair, the sixty-six-year-old Wels crossed to the bay window beneath which was a circular table. In the modern style, it was a dropleaf; a useful adaptation but not one which Otto much appreciated. He preferred the old fashions and styles in clothes as well as furniture and décor. Only one hard-backed chair sat at the table and that was set before a splendid old Mercedes Superba typewriter.

"Sod it!" He cursed a little as he realised that he'd left a trail of cigarette ash on the cashmere rug covered floor. Never mind. Hilda Kemp, his twice weekly cleaner come laundry lady was here today and with some stern reproachful glancing she would clear it all up for him. Hilda had come with the house. They rarely spoke. She would simply turn up and begin working.

He sat before his typewriter and loaded it up with a sheet of A4 paper. There were some sixty sheets of the cheaper type of A4 neatly stacked to the right of his machine.

Otto glanced out of the window. Bright sunshine glowed over a street which was at the moment devoid of pedestrians and traffic. It was generally fairly quiet here, although it could get noisy at times when the more boisterous holidaymaker decided to come out to play. Luckily, after visiting the holy Basilica most trippers preferred the far livelier night-time entertainment of the always lively city centre.

What a lovely city Paris had turned out to be, Otto decided. A lively if not always welcoming people inhabited the French capital. Voluble, always opinionated but never boring or intrusive, that's how he saw them. He had been uncertain when he first began his exile; or rather, when that son-of-a-bitch had taken away his citizenship and *forced* him out of his homeland. What a cowardly swine. Otto remembered that fateful day when he had confronted Hitler in the Reichstag, waved a finger in the then would be Führer's face and told him bluntly, on the 23rd of March, 1933, the day that German democracy ended, "You can take our lives and our freedom, but you can *never* take our honour." In private some hours later, with Hitler attempting desperately to reach an accommodation with the upright leader of the SDP, he had told Hitler to his face, "You, Herr Hitler, are a monstrous liar and a thief!" Those were the last words that he had spoken to the German leader, but not his last words of defiance. He had fled Germany and the Nazi dictator's vengeance, and with the steadfast help from friends at home and abroad, had finally found a safe haven here in Paris.

He was still determined as ever to strike out at Hitler and his gang in any way that he could. And that way was the ego ripping stab of the truthfully written word, hence his typewriter at the ready. Otto still had plenty to write about, and these days he was not as reticent as he had once been about exaggerating the woes and horrors of the German Third Reich. Adolf Hitler, that brainless, perverted irritation on the anus of humanity, must be stopped, got rid of in any way possible.

Otto's finger, he was a two-finger typist, hovered above the shiny keys of his beloved machine. The intended digit was just about to make its first impression of the day on one of the keys when he felt the barest whisper of a draught on the right side of his neck. The very last thing that he ever felt was the hand that gently, almost caressingly cupped his jaw. There was the smell of cedar wood, not unpleasant, was Hilda wearing perfume? How unlike her. Then – nothing! The irresistible forward pressure of the left hand on the back of his neck, combined with the awesomely powerful pull of the chin holding right hand, brought death instantly and without pain to the broken necked Otto Wels. He would no longer be a propaganda problem for the

Third Reich or anyone else.

The young man looked with satisfaction upon the successful completion of his day's work. The woman, probably a maid, was unfortunate but unavoidable collateral damage. Wrong place at the wrong time for poor Hilda Kemp.

The young man gently, so as not to disturb anything on the table, eased Otto's lifeless body out of the straight-backed chair and placed him carefully in the empty armchair. There, he moved the lifeless head a little to the left. Poor Otto looked quite restful. Now, the woman. He didn't like mess or scruffy work, this young assassin. He had eased Hilda Kemp from this world as she turned all surprised at his soft entrance through the back door and into the scullery where she had been scrubbing down the large brownstone sink. The sharply delivered left hook to her flabby little jaw had rendered her immediately unconscious and the large but well-manicured hand that caught her by the throat as she fell, maintained pressure on her carotid artery until she ceased breathing permanently. All done without noise or fuss.

He liked to be neat and he also had something of a sense of the theatre. The ever-present demi smile suggested the presence of impishness within the handsome young killer. Not so; not even nearly. It was quite simply the way that his features arranged themselves when in repose. Which indeed said a lot about the young man, bearing in mind that his features were in repose in his current situation. Such was the handsome openness of his expression, that no one could possibly conceive that this nice-looking young man was about to rip the life from them.

He had not received any orders to search or go through the dead man's belongings, so pandering to his ever-present sense of neatness and order he quickly went back to the scullery and placed Helga's body in a neat cross ankle position on the floor with her dead hands clasped over her chest. The place was beginning to whiff quite badly now as both bodies were emitting their final fluids pretty well simultaneously. Time to go.

Cotre Leval was waiting in a blue Citroen some three hundred metres away at the rue Damremont. Leval was a sergeant in the local police force and was thoroughly sympathetic to the aims and ideas of the Third Reich. He also enjoyed the generous stipend paid to him monthly by the German SS which had allowed the easy purchase of a handsome little riverside cottage outside Paris.

Leval would drive him from Paris to a private airfield in Crail where a Fieseler Storch waited to transport him back to the fatherland. Once there he would report mission accomplished and await events.

Rochus Misch left the smart little house in Montmartre and made his way to the waiting Citroen.

September 3rd: 1939

In late August all hell had broken loose in the political corridors of Berlin, Moscow, London, Paris and just about everywhere else in Europe. Excitement, bewilderment, joy, the entire gamut of human emotion swept through the German people as the unbelievable news of the Führer's latest display of his unerring genius hit the streets. Radio broadcasts and high pitched almost hysterical updates from loudspeakers placed on what seemed to be pretty well every street corner in every town screamed out the news. A trade deal and a non-aggression pact with the awful, evil and downright scary Soviet Union had been agreed, signed, sealed and delivered. Some few were furious and condemning of the treaty; the majority, however, were delighted that the menace of Russian expansionism was, for the time being at least, manacled to a signed peace document. And a trade deal, to boot. Excellent! Unemployment, lower than it had been at any previous time in Germany's history, had been showing unsettling signs of increasing, along with small but significant price rises of staples and much larger hikes in luxury goods.

In the eyes of the majority of the adoring populace, The Führer was a true genius. His greatness would shield them all from harm and want.

All that joy and euphoria had been less than one week ago. Now, however, a palpable shudder of apprehension ran through the Reich at the unexpectedly huge volume of military traffic that came roaring through the streets of German cities and towns on its tarmac ripping way to the Polish border. Apprehension became dread as the familiar sound of Jackboots, thousands of them, heralded the approach of marching columns of combat ready men; all heading in the same direction: East!

Hitler was furious. Why weren't the people out cheering their brave soldiers? Could they not see and hear the mighty men and machines of war that he had created and now paraded like Mars himself before them?

Goebbels clucked and reminded the Führer that the German people had not been aware that he planned to annex, or rather, defend Germany against Polish aggression and their evil anti-Aryan ways. He would have it all out in the Press tomorrow. By the evening, he promised Hitler, the entire population would be shrieking Heil Hitler. They probably wouldn't, of course. The people didn't want another war. The horror of the previous conflict was still well within living memory of most Germans. They had accepted the takeover of Austria and the Sudetenland because those places were German by right. But surely, as the Führer had promised, that was all done now, wasn't it? Hadn't the Führer himself agreed; no more territorial gains were being sought by the Third Reich?

Goebbels smirked. Not much hope of that. Not with Germany being so needy, and not with Hitler being determined to regain the old city of Danzig from those thieving Poles. He wanted his little war but only if he could be absolutely sure of winning it. Goebbels knew his Führer probably better than anyone. Uncle Wolf, as the Goebbels children liked to call him, was wound up like a taut spring and needed to unwind with some ego satisfying violence. The destruction of a few Polish cities should do nicely, along with a suitably massive body count of slaughtered Polish soldiers.

As hostilities had loomed ever nearer Goering began evincing symptoms of a panic attack. He was certain that his splendid Air

Force was up to the job, but then, as niggling little doubts crept in, the heavily jowled Luftwaffe chief's smile faded; were there any certainties in war – or in life, for that matter? Oh dear! It took all his willpower to prevent himself from rocking back and forth and rubbing his hands like a worried old woman. It was his Luftwaffe that was leading the attack. What if it all went wrong? He pursed his plump lips. Too late to worry about possibilities now.

Ribbentrop on the other hand was prancing around like some sort of third-class demi-God. His meeting with Molotov and the ensuing pact with the Soviets had sent Hitler into an almost orgiastic frenzy of fist pumping delight. From being the satirized dummy of the inner circle, Ribbentrop had gone to being lauded as greater than Bismarck, more far sighted than Goethe in all of his imaginative scribblings. His selection as Foreign Minister was surely just another sign of the Führer's unwavering genius.

Himmler, away in his office and closeted with his closest aides was rubbing his soft little hands at the merest thought of all those tens of thousands of Jews waiting to be annihilated by the cleansing necessity of the Nazi extermination machine. A machine which, though not perfect, was improving all the time and was always open to inventive personnel and new ideas.

Less than a week after the signing of the pact, the Führer had shown clearly to the world what his heartfelt promises of peace had meant; German forces hurtled across the Polish border and began an orgy of killing and destruction that left Poland's erstwhile allies helplessly wailing and flapping their hands. He had stuck it to the British and the French and left them feeling emasculated and helpless; which they now were. The British wouldn't fight, promised Ribbentrop. He knew them all too well, he said. They were trembling ninnies afraid of another war with the resurgent and powerful Germany. The French had missed the boat and proven their lack of will. They might make threatening noises from behind their big defensive wall, the Maginot Line, but that was all those spineless cowards would do. Poland was there, ripe for the Third

Reich's taking and breaking! Thus spake Joachim von Ribbentrop, Foreign Minister and Germany's new man of the hour.

"So be it!" Had roared Hitler, and the order was given to some surprisingly unenthusiastic Generals who suddenly seemed none too confident of the outcome and espoused downright horror at the thought of war with France and England should they come, as promised, to Poland's aid. But after some less than gentle urging from their Führer, they went ahead anyway. Sixty divisions, more than one million five hundred thousand men, two thousand tanks and more than one thousand aircraft thundered like an apocalypse across the Polish border in the name of the Führer and the glories of all conquering Nazism. Hitler now felt that he was truly a God. He had unleashed never before seen power against the over confident and militarily naïve Poles. The world watched as Hitler and his friends capered and sang as they stripped away the ages old layers of humanity and replaced them with the puss seeping skin of all embracing vileness. It had taken time, but Adolf Hitler had at last achieved his subconscious aim in life; he had opened the gates of hell and invited all who revered that which was loathsome and disgusting to join him on his crusade for the rights of criminals and deviants like himself to torture and destroy all who were in his eyes, inferior, or even, simply disagreeable. The queue to join was depressingly long.

Sunday: September 3rd 1939. Hitler's office in the New Reich Chancellery.

Now was the time for strong nerves, and the Führer was displaying nerves of steel even if inside he was a quivering jelly.

He stared around at his colleagues all of whom were exhibiting signs of extreme nervousness. All bar Ribbentrop, that is, who stood with hands behind back, nose in its usual upward pointing direction. The tiniest smile played at the corners of the Foreign Minister's lips. Everything was going splendidly. He had been right about everything up to this very point. Yes, of course the British and their French allies had threatened war if Germany continued with her Polish invasion. They had even sent an ultimatum which was due to expire in a few more minutes. It was all bluster, of course. What else could the British government have done after being so stupid as to openly guarantee military assistance to a country more than one thousand miles distant and in an area where they had no military personnel or equipment whatsoever? What on earth had they been thinking of? Did they honestly think that the German Wehrmacht was made up of the usual type of British opponent, spear waving tribesmen wearing grass skirts? Clearly that fat little chatterbox, Churchill, had not the faintest idea of the true power of the Reich. Bellicose and bullish, as far as Ribbentrop could see, begging for war. All wobbling chins, bouncing jowls and hot air. He reminded the Foreign Minister of their very own Hermann Goering. Well, to hell with Churchill and his warmongering cabal. If they did attempt anything foolish they would receive a bloody and abject lesson in humility. The stupidity of the French and British merely served to make him, Joachim von Ribbentrop, look supremely brilliant. And, he breathed in deeply, so deeply that he felt a moment of dizziness, surely a worthy successor to the Führer should he become incapacitated or, heaven forefend, die prematurely. He enjoyed seeing the nervousness of Goering and the others. They knew nothing of diplomacy, foreign policy or the devious tricks of international politicians. He, Ribbentrop, knew them all and had triumphed over them all. The greatest glory of that triumph would come when the British, as they most assuredly must, backed down from their ultimatum and gave an abject apology to the Third Reich for daring to even *consider* interference of any sort, and agreeing that Germany had acted completely within her rights of self-defence and self-determination. Yes, when that happened, then he would have truly scaled the greatest height of all.

I t was just after 11 am when the marble encased telephone began to ring. No one said anything, not a word, as it rang merrily away, waiting for someone to pick up the receiver and answer. Hitler turned and stood staring at his Foreign Minister. Goering began to sweat even more heavily than before and Goebbels rocked back and forth on his club foot trying to appear unflappably calm. Hess looked worried and uncertain, his slightly forward protruding teeth biting constantly on his lower lip. Ribbentrop, calm and controlled, gestured to his aide, Wosner, to answer the phone. The aide did so and spoke softly and rapidly into the mouthpiece. A tense and oppressive silence followed as Wosner listened with rapt attention to whatever was being said to him from the other end of the line. He then turned towards Ribbentrop and said, "It's for you, Herr Foreign Minister." The aide stood with hand outstretched as he offered the phone to his boss.

"Oh, for fucks sake!" Goering exploded. "Answer that bloody phone, Ribbentrop, will you?"

"Quiet, Goering." Hitler's voice was soft as he gestured Ribbentrop to take the offered telephone receiver.

Ribbentrop strode over to Wosner and snatched the proffered device from the hand of his trembling aide. Placing it to his ear he made a great show of calm complacency which stood out in stark contrast to the unseemly display of temerity from the rest of the inner circle as they awaited the fateful news. Ribbentrop displayed no such uncertainties and fervently hoped that Hitler was taking on board the steadfastly confident demeanour of his Foreign Minister whilst others were wilting under pressure. He, Ribbentrop, dealt in cold hard certainties and facts; there was no room for doubts and misgivings. Without so much as a facial tick to convey his feelings the Foreign Minister listened intently to what was being said at the other end. He nodded, muttered, "I see," and then replaced the receiver as though it were loaded with dynamite. He stood with his back to them for a few moments and it was Goebbels who noticed a thin stream of sweat trickling down over the Foreign Minister's right ear lobe. Could that be a good sign? Not likely, he thought, as a tightness began winding its way around his gut.

Hitler waited stern-faced for his Minister to break the news. The tension became unbearable as the unusually reticent Foreign Minister stood silent, searching for words and then blanching visibly as the silence was shattered by Goering as he rose in all his obese majesty and roared, "WELL?"

Ribbentrop turned to them and spread his hands.

"Oh shit!" That was Hess. "I guessed this would happen."

"Ribbentrop," hissed Hitler. "Would you like to share your news?"

"Yes," the Foreign Minister nodded, "of course, my Führer". The confident, bombastic Joachim von Ribbentrop had disappeared and left in his place a craven, almost tearful sniveller.

"They have declared war."

"The British?" Goebbels queried.

"Bah!" Hess growled with exasperation. "Who the hell else – a troop of fat Latvian midgets?"

"Yes," Ribbentrop sighed heavily, "the British. Prime Minister Chamberlain spoke at just after 11 am. It would seem that Great Britain and its Empire have declared war on Germany. The French are expected to follow suit within the hour."

"My God, Ribbentrop." Hess rose and pointed a finger at the failed Foreign Minister. Do you realise that we have almost nothing with which to face the French should they attack now? Everything we have is in Poland."

"Dear God in heaven," shrieked Goebbels. "They could march completely unopposed on Berlin."

"Too much of a gamble," muttered Goering. "It was all just too much of a gamble."

"Quiet, all of you." Hitler's commanding voice speared them all into silence and they set their gazes hopefully upon their Führer.

That man felt sick to his stomach. He'd gambled, bluffed and been called. He looked at Ribbentrop and said, "What now, eh – what now?"

Hitler knew what they were all feeling; he felt the same but many times over. He was also beginning to experience odd twinges of overwhelming loneliness. Sometimes he found himself wishing that he had backed off. The surrealness of it all baffled him. Like an uninterrupted dream, it went on and on. A relentless parade of situations, people and events that he seemed able to play with and control at will. It was all, all of it, more akin to a cinematic production than anything to do with real life. He felt like one of those orchestra leaders waving their baton over an eagerly obedient gang of untrained musicians. All so eerily random. Until now. Now he rather felt, for the very first time, that he wouldn't mind asking somebody else what he should do. He wasn't too sure. In fact, he had no idea at all. Ribbentrop had let him down and now he, Hitler, must act firmly and pump some iron into the thinning blood of his henchmen. He fought down the urge to tremble as it tickled his spine. He dare not at this stage, or any other come to that, show weakness or uncertainty to his henchmen nor anyone else at large. That way led to total failure and, without doubt, his own end.

"You pusillanimous drawing room warriors," he snarled at them.

Goering, the first world war fighter ace, bridled at that but threw his glare at the ashen faced Ribbentrop rather than his Führer. "D'you think I wasn't prepared for this?" Their leader smiled archly. He sure as hell wasn't prepared but he knew that he mustn't let them see how badly shaken he truly was. He had bluffed the world before, he could and would do it again. He pointed to Goering. "Get General Jodl and the other army chiefs here now, right now! I want the war room filled with your Luftwaffe seniors and a complete rundown of anticipated losses on the Polish front. The English want a war, that race of inbred island perverts. I shall give them a war to remember gentlemen. Believe me. This plays right into my hands. I shall crush them like the vermin that they are. Have faith gentlemen and believe in me. Believe in your Führer!"

The gilded Führer office of the New Reich Chancellery rang with a lustily bellowed set of Sieg Heils.

Same Day. Office of SS Oberführer Johann Rattenhuber.

Misch sat before his commanding officer, Oberführer Rattenhuber. The man's normally expressionless face was, as usual, expressionless. He stared at Misch and found himself wondering about the talented young SS man. Their own particular jewel in an otherwise rather dull and rusty looking crown. Oh yes, he could call upon killers aplenty, assassins and wannabee assassins abounded in all corners of the Reich. But killers with *his* degree of talent? Rare! So rare that neither Rattenhuber nor Himmler wanted to see the young man's talents wasted or worse still, abused. They must keep him in reserve for those times, and they were bound to arise sooner or later, when his particular talents were needed. As head of the RSD, Rattenhuber controlled all service protection and control around the Führer. Nominally, of course, Reichsführer Himmler was in charge, but in reality Rattenhuber answered to Hitler first hand. Close proximity to the Führer meant that Hitler saw him in passing and spoke with him almost every day. If he could keep young Misch under his wing, then that's what he would do. Rattenhuber had no wish, however, to cross or gainsay the Reichsführer. The man was too powerful. Also, he was Rattenhuber's main ally against the machinations of the ever plotting, scheming and poisonous Obergruppenführer Reinhard Heydrich.

So, when his good friend Wilhelm Mohnke had asked for a favour, which just so happened to have the tacit support of the Reichsführer, Rattenhuber was inclined to listen. Misch, it turned out, had been born in Alt Siolkowice in Silesia smack on the Polish border. Mohnke had an operation going on somewhere north and needed a Polish speaker who could handle himself in a tight spot if necessary. Not that Mohnke anticipated any problems; it was simply that there weren't that many Polish speakers in his command. Rattenhuber had little to do with front-line activities but he had agreed to loan out Misch for old times' sake and because the job should suit a man of Misch's talents. The assignment entailed high level, but brief, intelligence gathering.

Although some distance away from the somewhat fluid front lines of the Polish campaign it might be dangerous and required a resourceful and quick-thinking operative. It was an 'in and out' mission with the elimination of any obstacles purely down to the operative concerned. There might be a few of those obstacles popping up, but not likely anything that the redoubtable Misch couldn't handle. Fascinating! All lies, of course. God alone knew what the Reichsführer and Mohnke might have cooked up. Mohnke was cast iron solid, but Himmler was inclined to some pretty leery flights of fancy at times. The main thing, however, that had piqued Rattenhuber's interest, was Mohnke's unqualified insistence that this job was of the most vital importance to the Reich. The job might not seem like much on the surface but it required a steady hand and strong nerves. Mohnke, of course, knew Rochus Misch quite well from earlier days and had been instrumental in persuading Misch to join the SS. They had met up again once since then and Mohnke regarded Misch as a class act. Rochus Misch, as far as Mohnke was concerned, was the complete package.

Rochus nodded acceptance. Not that he was given a choice. But Rattenhuber, although generally ruthless and uncaring, always attempted to make it appear to his prodigy that he had some leeway. After a fashion he did. Once set on a course, Rochus Misch was left to his own considerable devices as to how best to accomplish the desires of his superiors. This particular assignment, though, seemed a little outside his normal purview. Not that such a thing bothered him at all. He loved the challenge of new experiences, unrehearsed and ad hoc made life all the more exciting.

SS Hauptsturmführer Wilhelm Mohnke sat across from his friend, or rather, friendly acquaintance, for Rochus Misch did not own to having friends. He was friendly enough to most, never stepping outside the persona of an open-faced charmer happily at one with the world. Nobody really knew what switched him on, or off for that matter. On the surface he was easy to get along with and never rocked anybody's boat. Almost a yes-man in his eagerness to avoid argument and confrontation. So agreeable, always. And yet, there was that innate coldness, calculating and unfathomable. An odd character but one couldn't help liking him, thought Mohnke. Now why was that? True, over the years they had broken bread and shared a beer. But always there was that chasm between them, between the rest of humanity it seemed, as far as Misch was concerned. Why did one like so much a man that clearly didn't give a rat's arse whether you lived or died? Folk were strange; like this damn missive he'd received from Reichsführer SS Heinrich Himmler. Himmler had enclosed a transcript of an outgoing message from the Abwehr main office of a certain Oberst Hans Oster to a contact in Warsaw. The message had been expertly encrypted but a female colleague of the sending cryptographer, who was also on the SS payroll and who shared an office next to his in Friedrickstrasse, became suspicious about the furtiveness of the operator involved and so, she quietly and efficiently investigated. Knowing only the origin of the encrypted message and nothing of its coded contents, she passed the thing on as soon as she was able. Complete decoding in such a short space of time was impossible. However, what they did know was that an Abwehr agent was on the move and that he was carrying something, something small and of great importance. Himmler wanted possession of whatever it was that the Abwehr agent was carrying. Not just wanted – demanded! At the very least, the Reichsführer wanted to know *what* it was that those Abwehr swine were up to. Or heads would roll!

Hans Oster was deputy head of the Abwehr, the Reich's official military intelligence service. Himmler had been trying to gain control of it for years, but the Abwehr chief, Admiral Canaris, had thus far outwitted him. Himmler wanted the Abwehr disbanded and its members inducted into the SS. As an aside, he would dearly love to see Canaris shot. He neither liked nor trusted the worthy Admiral and the feeling of out and out loathing was icily reciprocated, although, it must be said, with considerably more savoir-faire by the urbane admiral. Canaris, fearing outright conflict which he must inevitably lose went to great lengths to maintain cordial relations with Himmler, Heydrich and the SS in general.

He had operatives embedded within the Navy, Army, Air Force and just about anywhere else that one cared to mention. It was an organisation that Himmler was desperate to get his hands on. What Canaris and his Abwehr did not have, however, were the enormous resources of the SS. Hitler, as usual, did nothing to alleviate the internecine bickering even as it clogged up the vital intelligence highway. As always, he preferred his subordinates to be at one another's throats. And, of course, as Canaris and his deputy, Oster, well knew, such a situation must lead, sooner or later, to a full-blown disaster.

Himmler doubted the loyalty of Canaris and believed him to be in league with foreign powers but, despite using all his and Heydrich's massive resources, he could prove nothing. Canaris was an expert in backroom dealing and, for the moment at least, was easily outfoxing his black clad hunter. Not a particularly moralistic man, Wilhelm Canaris was, nevertheless a decent one. He loathed what was happening in Germany and if there was one man on the planet that both he and Hans Oster despised, it was Adolf Hitler. They did what they could to hinder the Führer and some of his more messy and unpleasant plans without *appearing* to be obstructive. They were after all in uniform and bound to serve. For Admiral Canaris and Oberst Oster, though, that service meant the preservation of Germany and her people; not, as Oster put it, that disgusting mountebank, Hitler, and his gang of hedonistic perverts. Over the past few years, Abwehr agents had gathered reliable and documented evidence concerning the activities of Hitler, his associates and aims, if, as Canaris pointed out, aims was the correct word. To have aims required the process of logical thought, and neither Canaris nor Oster had seen much evidence of any such thing. If the governments of the world were to be made aware of the ineptitude of this goose-stepping, Sieg Heiling and erroneously called, totalitarian state, Germany would become a laughing stock overnight. But foreign governments were running scared, they didn't want to know. Turning the good old blind eye was the safest bet for them they reckoned. Herr Hitler would get his just deserts sooner or later, from somewhere or other. And in any case, the admiral was only too well aware of SS and Gestapo scrutiny. Every call, every move, even so much as a raised eyebrow and there they were sniffing around like starving hyenas. Naturally enough the Abwehr did the same, but the SS had by far the bigger muscles and, of course, when it came to glamour for recruitment purposes, nobody could top the Hugo Boss SS uniforms, jaunty caps and shiny SS flashes and badges. Not to mention the fringe benefits.

For Canaris and Oster it was all very simple. One could philosophise and chatter 'til God's bunions ran red but the upshot of it all was, if Hitler reigned supreme for much longer, if he attained even more power in the world than he possessed right now, then, both men were in no doubt, there would be utter chaos with no proper rule at all. As Canaris, educated and always thoughtful, pointed out to his friend and colleague, Oster. "Divide and rule, my dear Hans, only works for small minded despots, kings and ninnies who have no real thought or care for the future of their people. Such men live only for the moment and for themselves. We must do all we can to impede him, Hans. No risk too great, no sacrifice refused. Hitler *must* be stopped. Or at least," this last came with a sigh of what sounded a little too much like resignation, "slowed down."

"Which is why we are now doing that which *must* be done, admiral." Oster raised a placating hand as an expression of pain and sadness crossed the Abwehr head's features. "I know what this is costing you, sir. It is tearing at my innards, as well. But we must continue with the action that we have set in motion. Unspeakably heart wrenching as it is, sir, nothing else will work. Every effort we make is simply swatted aside by the Gestapo or the SS. They are already deeply suspicious of us. If Hitler decides to listen more closely to them he'll have us all, our families included, ripped to shreds."

"I am fully aware of that, Hans," Canaris replied heavily. "Our families suffering is the one thing that gives me pause. But what must be done, must be done, eh?"

Oster nodded. At least one assassination attempt had failed and quite possibly more from other, unknown quarters. It wasn't that Hitler was difficult to get to, he wasn't, not for men like Oster and Canaris. The likelihood, though, of a successful face to face assassination was remote, and the outlook in the aftermath of any such attempt for anybody even remotely connected with Canaris, Oster and the Abwehr would be very bleak indeed. The Abwehr must at all costs survive, as it contained the only worthwhile elements of resistance to Hitler and Nazism within the armed forces. Or so Oster and his boss believed, anyway.

"He's on his way then?" Asked Canaris.

He should be there and waiting by now."

"No problems, so far?" Canaris clucked at his own trite question. Clearly, if there had been any problems Oster would have informed him.

"None," replied Oster, politely shaking his head. "Unfortunately it has been necessary to transmit, as the Poles insisted, details of handover location only at the last minute. All heavily encrypted," he added reassuringly as his boss looked up sharply.

"I hope they appreciate what we are giving them," Canaris looked grim. "I also hope, with all my heart that we have not made a mistake and that the cost in German lives will not be disproportionate to any gain by us. I should have great difficulty reconciling my conscience with our actions were that to be so, I fear." He turned briefly away from Oster.

Oster looked sympathetically at his chief. "Try not to worry overmuch, admiral. We have done what we had to. The war is as good as done. The Poles have a few days left in them. So it's not as though we are giving away vital campaign plans. They will be able to forward the information, thus enabling the British and the French to act on the intelligence they garner and prevent Hitler from doing any further damage. They merely have to move forward threateningly and Hitler will take fright and pull back. The stuff with Poland is pretty well over and done with, we can't change that. But he certainly won't be interested in a fight with the British and French if they are fully mobilized and on our border. He's not ready and from what I could ascertain when we saw him yesterday, he's shaking in his boots. Putting on a front, but scared witless."

"It's a shame that the British simply refuse to believe what we say, Hans. Why must they be so constantly distrustful? This giving them so much of our cypher materials and encryption array could go horribly wrong."

"Sir," Oster's face became a grim mask. "If our actions stop, harm or help to eliminate *that* man, then nothing about it can be wrong. I tell you, admiral, truthfully, that I would rather see one million German soldiers march to their deaths than see him, Herr Hitler, live so much as another day. He destroys German honour, culture and decency. By God, Admiral, I *will* see him dead!"

Canaris's silver hair shone with a brief quicksilver flash as he turned his head under the light. He gave Oster a sad but determined smile. "We can only hope that all this ends quickly and not with the doom-laden scenario of a million dead. With luck and God's justice, we shall soon see the end of that creature, Hans. The general staff will *have* to act once they realise that an unwinnable war is about to begin because of Hitler's moronic intransigence. Germany will be lost if they don't."

All that Oberst Oster, Admiral Canaris and the Abwehr could do had been done. Soon, unless fate conspired against them, the final key, Bomba, or Kryptologiczna, would be in British hands, thus putting the final touches to the years of encryption work that the Poles had already put in. No more need for more investigation or guesswork by them. They would soon have it all: Enigma.

"What d'you know about the Abwehr, Misch"? Mohnke lit a cigarette and watched the smoke spiral lazily toward the single lamp above his camp desk. Mohnke didn't much go in for frippery and much preferred minimalist surroundings. He felt more at home in a Tank than an office but here he was. The cramped adjoining office contained three coding clerks and a teleprinter. Through the small and rather misted-up office window opposite his desk, the SS clerks could be observed beavering away at a very busy office routine.

Rochus sat, his lazy half-smile turning downward slightly at the question. "I can't say that I know too much, Herr Hauptsturmführer," he answered, wondering why his superior officer wanted to know. It was fairly well inculcated into the SS ranks that the Abwehr were the beasties of German intelligence; half-witted, unpleasant and not to be trusted. It went without saying, of course, that the precise opposite was true.

Mohnke waved a hand and pushed his cigarette case across to Misch. "No need for sirs and salutes when we are alone Misch. We've known one another for too long to bother with such formalities."

Rochus dropped his gaze as he reached for the cigarette case and withdrew a short, thick Bremaria. Ignoring the etiquette of rank Mohnke leaned across and lit it for him, watching Misch closely as he inhaled the first long drag. Was that a change that he had just spotted in Misch's expression – his eyes? It was, it most certainly was. Why? Not keen on the offer of familiarity, perhaps? That must be it. Fair enough. He would confine future chats to discussions and instructions.

As Mohnke explained what he could of Misch's projected assignment the young SS man's expression remained calm and pleasant, as always. But inside his mind, contrary thoughts whirled. Sarcastic and uncomplimentary thoughts. He remembered taking a young lady, her name escaped him, to see the spy movie 'Alarm at Midnight.' They had sat engrossed by the players, the plot and the events as they unfolded. The hero, played by the ultra-handsome Gustav Fröhlich, was a master spy, heroic and determined. Quick with his always ready but well concealed pistol, and even quicker with his lightening fists, he had seemed the very epitome of dashing, fearless and always on the ball German manhood. He had cunningly prepared his missions with painstaking detail with the help of his spy boss, a suitably taciturn and grizzled individual played by Walter Franck, at a glamourous HQ in Berlin. Maps with dots, timetables with coded marks and squiggles, all so very professional and believable. Not a bit like this monotoned and, in all honesty, not terribly informative spiel being spouted so earnestly by the friendly Hauptsturmführer in front of him. He was to be ready to leave at a moment's notice, estimated to be within the hour, yet the only briefing that he'd received was a quick pep talk from Wilhelm Mohnke about how important all this was, and so on. Disappointing, really, but such was life. Glamour it would seem was confined to theatre dressing rooms and celluloid.

An Abwehr agent, name unknown, would be travelling to Usedom, an island just off the German/Polish border nestling in the Baltic. The only information that Mohnke had been able to pass on to Misch, was that the Abwehr agent was likely already in transit, possibly even at his destination. From the current information available they now had less than twenty-four hours to intercept that agent and retrieve the object in transit before a handover could take place. The answer to Misch's natural question, "And that object is?" was met with an apologetic, "Well, there's the thing, Misch. We don't actually know. Sorry!" The Abwehr knew, of course, but the SS, unfortunately, did not.

Rochus Misch's calm smile didn't falter one bit as he stared his superior officer straight in the eye. He leaned forward ever so slightly and, enunciating his words very carefully said, "So, sir, I am to follow a man, or woman, of whom I have no knowledge or description."

"If necessary, Misch, yes."

"No name, no rank, not even intelligence as to from where he or she might be departing, nor even how he might be travelling?"

Mohnke almost cringed as he realised the whole operation looked more like a hastily arranged works-outing set up by drunks than the professional intelligence operation that it was supposed to be. All so rushed. But what could he do? An order from Himmler was like a command from God. And Himmler, in no uncertain terms, had commanded his trusted subordinate, Hauptsturmführer Wilhelm Mohnke, to perform a minor miracle. To wit, to apprehend or kill an espionage agent and retrieve whatever it was that this unknown individual was carrying and bring it back. The amateurish paucity of information was stunning.

He found it difficult to meet Misch's eye as he endeavoured to reassure his questioning agent.

"Not as yet, Misch, no. But don't you worry yourself over details. Leave it to us. We'll get the information that you need, mark my words." Mohnke wished he had swallowed those words before allowing them to leave his mouth. How trite and hollow it must have sounded. He drew hard on his still burning cigarette. He might just as well have said, "Don't you worry your pretty little head," or some such. Damn this kind of work. He should be at the front. That's where his talents lay, leading fighting soldiers and shedding blood; not fartarsing around with this clandestine spy stuff. Nevertheless, he continued with his attempt to impart some kind of confidence in the outcome to the mildly questioning Misch.

"The SS has someone in place in the office concerned. And I mean, *directly* in place. They are working even as we speak, to discover the identity of this enemy agent and, Misch, they are risking life and limb by doing so. I am assured that they will obtain all, or at least some, of the information that we need to proceed."

Misch's expression didn't change even slightly. Risking life and limb? In an office in Germany, a German official, surrounded by Germans, was in mortal danger because he sought the identity of a fellow German in a similar line of work in order to help succour the security of the Third Reich. Who, then, were the enemy? Oh well, thought Misch, if this lot had raging diarrhoea they'd probably have to set up an organization to fund and find enough toilet paper to go round and they'd undoubtedly make a mess even of that! He almost smiled at his unintended pun.

"It would help enormously, sir," Misch gave a small almost apologetic shrug of those broad shoulders, "if we had some inkling of *exactly* where this supposed meeting might be taking place. It would surely help, sir, in bringing this mission to a successful conclusion." That maddeningly calm smile had the cheek to widen. Misch was, Mohnke realised, taking the piss right royally. And, reckoned Mohnke, as he was the man expected to accomplish this lunatic foray into God-knows-what-or-where, he had every right to do so.

Mohnke had no knowledge of espionage tactics or methods but now he leaned forward with a determined air. Just then, however, a uniformed clerk knocked and entered waving a sheet of teletyped paper. Both men could hear the teleprinter chattering away in the background.

"This came in a few minutes ago, Herr Hauptsturmführer." It looks Important!"

"Decoded?"

"Indeed, sir, yes."

The clerk passed a decoded and translated copy of the original message to Mohnke along with the original.

"Ah-ha!" Mohnke waved a dismissing hand at the clerk. "Straight back when there's more and quick as you can make it – right?"

"Sir!" The clerk clicked his heels smartly and departed quietly closing the door behind him.

Mohnke's narrow face creased into a smile. "Well, now, Rochus Misch. We have a start. Pen and paper," he ordered and watched as Misch complied by simply taking the required items from the top of Mohnke's desk. Misch waited, looking at Mohnke expectantly.

"As I said earlier, Usedom. The meeting is arranged, according to latest intelligence, for 09.30hrs tomorrow morning. Now, my friend, the *exact* location will be Ahlbeck Pier. You will need to be in the restaurant at the beach end of the pier close enough to it to make your intercept. And...."

The door flew open with an unceremonious crash as the clerk came marching back in. "There's more sir." With the aura of a man producing schnapps for an alcoholic, he carefully placed upon the desk three more sheets of teletyped information. "All decoded, Herr Hauptsturmführer and, if I may say, sir, quicker than anyone might have reasonably expected." Delighted with his work and that of his code breaking speed-typing colleagues, he waited expectantly for the praise which he thought must surely be forthcoming.

Mohnke, known as a tough character but generally fair, looked up at his underling with narrow eyes. The clerk, an SS senior private, shuddered, suddenly realising that he had allowed himself to be over excited and over familiar. Shit! Why hadn't he kept his mouth shut?

"If what you have supplied here is without error, Oberschütze Steiff, you shall be promoted. If there is an error, even the smallest, you will be transferred to guard duty at Dachau. Clear?"

It certainly was. Steiff nodded and wondered, not for the first time, why he had volunteered for that wretched signals and cypher course. It would be the death of him. Bloody officers. Bastards, the lot of 'em. Turning smartly he left the two men to whatever it was they were up to and went to make damn sure that neither of his colleagues could have made any kind of mistake. If they had and he ended up posted as a guard to Dachau concentration camp, he would make damn sure that it was them that needed guarding.

Mohnke glanced over the papers in front of him and smiled.

"Here," he waved Misch over to him. Leaning back as Misch stood over him with one hand on the back of his chair Mohnke stabbed a heavy forefinger at the first sheet.

"That's him, Misch. No name but a good enough description. Height and build. And here, my friend," he waved one of the teletyped sheets in front of Misch, "is his facial description. Oh, Misch, just look at this. He's unibrowed, dark haired, swarthy complexion and says here, got a massive overbite. Buck toothed. Stocky, five eight, one hundred and sixty pounds. Heavens, Misch, you won't be able to miss him."

"Carrying anything?" Misch enquired softly. Both men studied the recently arrived information for a few moments. There was no mention made of a briefcase, hold-all or any other carrying device. "Nothing," Mohnke replied. "Means he's carrying paper or something so portable that it fits in his pocket, or," Mohnke waved a cautionary finger, "Stitched into the lining of his jacket. This looks like being very up close and personal, Misch, wouldn't you say?"

"Certainly looks as though it might be."

"Just the way you like it, Rochus, eh?" Mohnke treated his subordinate to a wide grin as he slapped him lightly on the back.

"Couldn't be better," growled Misch. "I'd best think about making a move, sir. Anything else of interest there?" He nodded at the spread-out sheets of paper. The information they contained was sparse but should prove adequate. They now had the precise meeting point and location. The Abwehr agent would be carrying the item of interest and be handing it over to a Polish contact at Usedom. What that item was nobody, outside the Abwehr and their partners in Poland, knew. Whatever it might be it was neither large nor heavy. Easily concealed, then. Documents, Mohnke guessed. Whatever it might be, Misch would get it and bring it back.

They discussed the mission for some further few minutes before Misch departed, as ready as he could be with an assignment arranged in such haste. He had time for a quick sloosh-down, check his weapon and his proposed route and then he was off. This was a new one, following and retrieving. He couldn't help but be curious about what it was that his quarry carried. He smiled inwardly. He would find out soon enough. He gave some thought to the agent and his Polish contact. Were they seasoned killers – experts at urban concealment? More than likely. So best be even more careful and watchful than normal.

Another learning curve, thought Rochus, to himself. He and Mohnke had briefly discussed the mission and, provided he retrieved the item in question, he had a free hand with the Abwehr agent and the Pole. Rochus Misch had permission to do what he wished with and to them. Might all be very interesting.

t was as he was leaving Mohnke's small office in the newly acquired Goleniow area, now firmly in German hands, that Rochus began to feel a distinct tingling of unease. The battered SD issue DKW F8 stood eighty metres down the road which ran alongside the small river Ina. He had opted for the car rather than train or bus because anonymity was more easily retained with such travel. Trains and buses invariably seemed to attract people bent upon opening conversations with complete strangers and sharing parts of their boring lives with them. No thanks! Not for Rochus Misch.

He would have to temporarily leave the car of course once he reached the pedestrian crossing into Ahlbeck. Short enough, just a few minutes' walk but it was a route to be careful of because of its openness.

Misch suddenly felt the hairs on the back of his neck stand on end. He shivered. Something was very badly wrong. It was that description of the Abwehr agent. All of a sudden alarm bells were ringing in his head. He stopped just feet away from his car as realisation dawned. He suddenly knew who that description applied to – of all the bloody... As he turned to go back, the blow that hammered into his lower back took every breath of wind out of him. He staggered forward a couple of paces, bewildered. What had happened? He felt himself falling and half turned just as a second hammer blow beat into his chest just above the heart. Rochus Misch fell heavily to the pavement as the few passers-by stared in astonishment and fear. None reacted immediately nor came to his aid.

At a shade under three hundred metres such a shot was nothing more than bread and butter money to any halfway decent sniper. But the shooter had failed with his first shot, and he knew it. Which was why it had been necessary to take a second. Rank, amateurish crap. The shooter cursed. No time now, though, to ponder his sudden inability to hit an easy target. He had to go. Get back and report. Had the second shot been sufficient? Well, Rochus Misch would not be going anywhere soon and so, thought the shooter, a job reasonably well done. Two rounds from a tuned K98k should be enough to kill an elephant let alone a thin-skinned SS lout. The sniper smiled, packed his gear and left hot foot for his master awaiting in Stettin.

Monday. September 4th. Abwehr HQ 76/78 Tirpitzufer. Berlin.

Oster knocked ash from the end of his cigarette and smiled at the admiral. "It all went rather well, I thought."

"Went well?" Canaris chortled. "That oaf Himmler will be positively incandescent with fury. I can see him now waving his arms around and shrieking imprecations. Threatening dire retribution against all those responsible, their families, pets and property."

"The handover went perfectly." Oster was grinning. "Usedom? Did they truly believe all that?"

"They most certainly did," replied Canaris, indicating to Oster that he should help himself to more schnapps if he wished. "And they lost their top man. One of them anyway."

"All the better for us." Oster poured himself a generous measure of his favoured corn schnapps. Canaris tried not to raise an eyebrow at the size of the measures that his valued subordinate enjoyed throwing back. No sipping the stuff with Hans Oster.

"We have the SS rattled at long last."

"Rattled?" Oster interrupted. "They're flapping around like headless chickens. The airwaves are positively crackling with their coded obscenities. I tell you, sir, we've got them on the run. For the time being at least."

"Do not underestimate them, Hans. They will come after us once they've recovered from this setback. That swine Himmler, not to mention his bloodthirsty pack, have long memories and massive resources. Be careful Hans, ultra-careful in all your dealings and trust nobody."

Oster shrugged and sighed. That last from the admiral struck home. Nobody could be trusted implicitly. "Hewel did well, sir."

Canaris nodded agreement. "One of our better men. Shame to lose him but needs must. We have an opportunity to place him directly at Ribbentrop's shoulder. Having one of our own that deeply embedded is a priceless asset to the Abwehr and our future work."

The admiral was referring to young Walther Hewel. A rising diplomat and Abwehr sympathiser. A Nazi party member since nineteen-thirty-three but now a man thoroughly disillusioned with everything concerning Nazism. Outwardly the charming and urbane Hewel didn't appear to have changed his political beliefs or motifs in any way at all. Such a course would be far too difficult and treacherous to navigate safely, so he did what he could for his friends in the Abwehr.

Oster agreed with his bosses' assessment of the tall, outwardly deferential Hewel. He had become a pearl beyond price in internecine battles between the rival German intelligence agencies. Ribbentrop had been impressed with Hewel's diplomatic skills and requested his secondment not realising that he was an Abwehr collaborator. For Canaris and Oster it was an excellent outcome. They could now be assured of accurate reports about what was going on in the Foreign Office and, hopefully, of discussions between Hitler and Ribbentrop.

"Do you suppose," mused Canaris, "that the SS has any idea of what actually went on? Be a rum do if they ever found out."

"Not so much as an inkling," Oster said with almost a sneer of confidence. Himmler spends most of his time at that joke of a research centre of his at Wewelsburg."

"Ah yes," Canaris smiled. "He does love his voodoo and Ju-Ju dances, that one." Both men laughed. They had a mutual contempt for the Reichsführer and his esoteric practices. They might have laughed less had they known precisely what went on in Himmler's turreted domain.

"Do you suppose that the British will respond to our little gift?" Asked Oster.

"Well, the Poles have the details. Getting it all abroad might prove problematic but we do know for certain that the British have agents in Poland. They still have encryption work to do, a lot of it. What we've given them are limited specs of Abwehr Enigma only but they've got people who can crack the rest. Not child's play. The four-rotor model will likely prove tough to crack. They'll have to sort the Wehrmacht, Kriegsmarine and Reichchancellery cyphers separately. But Hans, we've given them a fine start on what would have been an impossible task."

"Quite right, sir, we have."

"So," the admiral began to rise from his chair signifying the end of their meeting. "No problem with our field agent?"

"None," Oster shook his head. "Safely returned to his normal place and just a little put out that he didn't make the kill he expected."

"Pah!" Canaris waved a dismissing hand. "He immobilised their operative, remained unseen and unsuspected, and the operation was a success. That's all that matters. The fewer lives taken the better."

"Quite so, sir," agreed Oster.

Same Day. SS HQ Prinz-Albrecht-Strasse. Berlin.

The office of the Reichsführer SS positively deafened its occupants with a veil of menacing silence. Himmler sat staring at the object of his ire as it stood manfully before him, ready for whatever might be thrown his way. The light, as always and as intended, reflected menacingly from his metal framed pince-nez. His small fingers caressed the length of a long silver-plated Montblanc fountain pen with gradually increasing pressure. Reichsführer SS Heinrich Himmler was not in the best of moods but was, however, determined to make the best of things. After all – what was it but just another raging cock-up by his much-vaunted security services? And of course, it all reflected upon him as its commander-in-chief. He realised now that he should have taken more care, perhaps put Heydrich in charge of the operation. But he had been unable to resist the pull of slamming it home to the wretched Abwehr and their even more wretched and upper-crust commander, Wilhelm Canaris. It had all looked too good to be true, and that was precisely how it had turned out, too good to be true. He'd ordered a steak and been served a sausage. God damn it he had been so sure that the man standing before him, the loyal, ruthless and determined Hauptsturmführer Mohnke, could and indeed should have succeeded. He had not! Failure so dismal as to be hysterically funny to his enemies and a general kick into the cruelly exposed Teutonic nuts of the SS had been the result of that ill-conceived escapade.

Himmler looked up at Mohnke and then down at the papers before him on the desk. "You almost lost one of our best men," he nodded and held up a restraining hand as Mohnke made to reply. "No more words from you, Hauptsturmführer, not until I say. That man will now in all likelihood be forever a cripple – thanks to you." The tone was terrifyingly menacing and Mohnke had the appalling vision of his family being dragged screaming behind the gates of one of the more awful of the concentration camps springing up all over Germany like spots on a pubescent teenager. Himmler had the satisfaction of noticing a distinct tremble from the tough SS officer. It almost made all this worthwhile. He must trot down to Wewelsburg soon and recharge his batteries.

"Our operative lay in the street with not one but two high velocity bullets in him. How he survived for so long, Mohnke, is nothing short of a miracle. When I say, so long, I refer of course to the fact that it was some ten minutes before anyone went to his aid. Ten minutes, Hauptsturmführer, after the injured man was shot down and bleeding like a stuck pig, RIGHT OUTSIDE YOUR FRONT DOOR!"

Mohnke, tough and ruthless as he was rolled his eyes in despair. It was all too awful. What a complete and utter mess. They hadn't known that Misch had been gunned down until someone came in off the street and asked to use the phone 'cos there was an injured man outside. Too busy with his own work it had never even occurred to Mohnke or his section men that Misch could be in any danger so close to home. Wrong, and badly Wrong! Misch, though, had somehow survived and was receiving the best care possible.

Now, of course, there was damage limitation. The Abwehr had struck a heavy blow and the SS still had no idea what was contained in that intelligence handover – if anything. Had it all been an Abwehr hoax – a trick to embarrass the SD? The truly awful thing, however, the thing that was doubtless making him and indeed the entire SD a laughing stock throughout the corridors of Abwehr HQ, was the description which he had so innocently passed on to Misch and which Misch had so gullibly accepted.

"Rather more to the point," Himmler's eyes were boring into the discomfited Mohnke's bloodshot orbs with horrible intensity, "is this description. Can I refer to it as that – a *description*? You sent Misch off on a mission to chase down, kill, maim or just terrorise this man," he tapped a sheet of A4. "A unibrowed individual with a distinctly heavy overhang of protruding but very even teeth, Five feet eight inches tall, blue eyes, very hairy hands, high forehead and swept back hair and wearing a casual brown suit. The man in question, according to your intelligence, would be found at Usedom. Correct?"

Mohnke nodded sadly.

"You know now, of course, who you have described here don't you, Mohnke? Please say that you do."

"Mohnke nodded again and wished with all his heart that he could drop dead right then and there.

"Yes, Mohnke. The man that you have described here is most certainly at Usedom. He happens to be there on an official visit for the Führer, and that casual brown suit you mention is in fact his official Party uniform. And here's the thing, Mohnke, something which you so belatedly seem to have realised, he just so happens to be Rudolf Hess, deputy Führer of the Third Reich and Reichsleiter of the Nazi Party. Was that who you wanted Misch to knock about, Hauptsturmführer Mohnke, our beloved deputy Führer? Well was it?"

"I fear that there is nothing I can say to excuse the woeful performance of my duties, Herr Reichsführer." Mohnke was a firm and disciplined soldier but he was beginning to feel his blood rise at the vicious carping from his superior. He was a soldier not a spy and had never pretended to be anything different. "I accept, sir, whatever punishment the Reichsführer deems appropriate."

"Oh, you accept, do you," Himmler's tone was acid. "And what, Hauptsturmführer Mohnke, would you consider an adequate reward for this latest piece of music hall buffoonery?" He watched as Mohnke's face reddened beneath his onslaught. Himmler waved a dismissive hand. It was done. Mohnke had done his best; a good soldier in the wrong job.

Mohnke waited with bated breath for Himmler's judgement to come crashing down on his head. His main concern now was his father. The old man was doddery and extremely vulnerable.

"Running around in tanks and killing people is more your forte, Hauptsturmführer. So, back to the Leibstandarte, take command of the 1st battalion and kill for Germany."

Mohnke's mouth hung open in disbelief. Reprieve – from Himmler? It was beyond belief. Himmler, though, was no fool. Mohnke would always be useful, but not in the intelligence field.

"Wrong place, wrong time, Mohnke. The way it is. Now get out!"

A stunned Hauptsturmführer saluted, shouted a clipped Heil Hitler and got himself away from the snake's den as fast as he could do so without actually running.

And now, Himmler sat back and arched his forefingers thoughtfully under his nose, time to have a little chat with Obergruppenführer Reinhard Heydrich. Certain things needed doing, setting up and no more mistakes. It was time to strike terror into people. If he couldn't yet put the fear of God into the intellectual head of the Abwehr chief, he knew whereabouts he could. It was time to begin working on the truly great picture of a future Europe. To create and then bring to fruition a magnificent idea with which he had been tinkering for quite some time. The more he thought about it the more deliciously appealing it became. He was being too soft, too caring of others. It was time he displayed his dark side to the world. It never did occur to him that most people already regarded him as very dark indeed.

The knock on his door was brief and light. Becker, his aide, popped a neatly trimmed blond head around the heavy edge as he announced the arrival of Gruppenführer Heydrich. The tall figure of his protégé came striding in as though he owned the place. There was not much doubt in the Reichsführer's suspicious mind that Heydrich's abilities might soon be used against him in a bid for more power and influence. Given the chance, the Gruppenführer would oust him without a blink of conscience. That's what made the man so outrageously useful, his ability to sniff out weakness and eradicate it. Himmler knew that he had a tiger by the tail in his dealings with the man they called 'Iron Heart' Heydrich. But thus far the gains had far outweighed the risks. Heydrich learnt and adapted very quickly, but so did his boss. As long as they both had a similar number of enemies against whom it was, at times, expedient to combine in order to crush, the status quo would remain unaltered. However, once the pendulum swung in favour of one or the other, those razor-sharp knives would be unleashed in an orgy of flesh and reputation slicing horror. In the meantime, though, an uneasy peace reigned.

"Heil Hitler." Heydrich's rather squeaky voice brought the usual demi smile to the Reichsführer's lips. That voice. So at odds with the general appearance of the man. As always, it amused him and, as always, he gave just the barest, most subtle hint of that amusement. If it annoyed the Gruppenführer there was no way of telling. Heydrich smiled icily in return as Himmler returned a clearly enunciated "Heil Hitler' to you Herr Gruppenführer. Please sit. How are we today?"

Heydrich sat before Himmler at his desk. "We, Herr Reichsführer, are very well, thank you. You wished to see me?"

"Indeed, Her Gruppenführer I do. I most certainly do." The thin little smile again, almost a visible determination to annoy the fearsome Gruppenführer sitting before him. Any reaction would be a victory, however small. But – nothing! Heydrich sat waiting, returning the Reichsführer's fixed smile with an even colder one of his own.

Himmler gave in first. A quick, irritated flick of his left wrist, something of a giveaway he had, a weakness that Heydrich had certainly spotted, brought their little contest to an abrupt end.

"I have something for you to do, Reinhard."

Heydrich gave him a doubtful look but said. "How interesting, Herr Reichsführer. Local or abroad?"

"Oh," Himmler smiled cunningly and for the first time, Heydrich felt a quiver of uncertainty. "Abroad, my dear Gruppenführer. Very much abroad and very much up your particular alley, if I may say so."

Heydrich looked at his boss dispassionately. "I can't wait to hear about it, Herr Reichsführer."

"I want, My dear chap, for you to organise a, no, I'm getting ahead of myself; first let me fill you in on my idea. In Poland, as you know, there are various enemies of the state. The constantly annoying Polish intelligentsia and, of course, the ever-present *Jews*. These people that are not only a nuisance, they are superfluous to the Reich and to our needs. Frankly, and I know that you agree, their existence is an affront to all decent Germans like ourselves."

"Yes indeed, Herr Reichsführer," Heydrich nodded in agreement and wondered where the hell his fantasy dwelling commander was going with all this.

"I want them gone, Heydrich."

"Gone?" Heydrich enquired, determined not to appear flummoxed, but unsure as to the Reichsführer's true meaning.

"Yes, my friend. Gone, eradicated, removed from this earth. Or, for want of better words Herr Gruppenführer – Utterly Destroyed!"

"I see," Heydrich drawled in his urbane manner. "And how do you intend to accomplish this?"

"I?" Himmler scoffed theatrically. "Not I, my dear fellow. *You!* You are the very man to accomplish this mammoth task and in so doing, you will please not only me but our beloved Führer, Adolf Hitler. He finds the continued existence of this, this scum, to be an affront to himself and the German people. You will go to Poland, my dear

Gruppenführer with my full authority to raise a brigade, or as many as you deem fit, dedicated to the extermination of the aforementioned human garbage." He paused as Heydrich's head jerked back slightly at his last comment. "You disagree with my assessment that they are human garbage?"

Heydrich smiled beatifically. "Not at all. But I do disagree with your assessment that they are in any way human, Herr Reichsführer."

For once Heinrich Himmler chortled with genuine amusement.

"Quite right, Reinhard. Quite right. That's my gentle nature coming out again." This time it was Heydrich who grinned with amusement. The Reichsführer had cracked a funny and that was rare enough to warrant a grin of disbelief at any time.

"A dedicated group, you say, Herr Reichsführer?" Himmler nodded. "In that case," mused Heydrich. "How does Einsatzgruppen sound?"

"First rate. I knew that you would dream up something with strength and purpose. Einsatzgruppen. Yes, an excellent designation." Himmler scribbled the word down.

"We are speaking, I believe, of approximately one hundred thousand Polish intelligentsia." Heydrich was already computing supply costs. The amount of ammunition required would be astronomic. Bullets were the only sure method of extermination. The Americans had tried poisoning the ground and a variety of other methods in their massive efforts to get rid of the indigenous population. The only reliable method, though, had proven to be bullet or blade. Messy, slow and horribly expensive but always reliable.

Himmler nodded. "See to them first. If there *is* to be any future resistance it will come from them; the fomenting of it, anyway. Get rid of them and any ideas that they may have."

"More than one million Jews," Heydrich pursed his lips.

"That, is a huge order, I know," conceded Himmler. "But the execution of it should undoubtedly, shall we say, prove immensely satisfying."

"Indeed," Heydrich nodded agreement, "What we need, though," he said thoughtfully, "is a more professional system of extermination. Something that we don't have at the moment but I shall work on it Herr Reichsführer."

"Do so, Heydrich. Success here will lead to promotion; of that you may rest assured."

"I should begin immediately." Reinhard was feeling quite excited about his new task. It was huge and the possibilities for advancement were stunning in their scope. He would put together entire battalions all under the umbrella of the Einsatzgruppen commanded and created by him, Reinhard Heydrich. Four to five thousand to begin with, he mused. Killers all and his to use as he saw fit. Real power and fame beckoned and he was quite certain of the best way to use it. Himmler and Hitler wanted the Jews exterminated, along with various other groups of undesirables. He, Heydrich, would give them what they wanted.

September 29. Recovery Ward 7. Hospital Camp at Bayrischzell. Bavaria.

Recovery had been slow and painful. The wounds he received would have been ruinous to most other men. Rochus Misch, though, was not most other men. Lung pierced, spleen damaged, one kidney gone and a ruptured liver. He should have been dead but was not. His splendid constitution quite simply refused to give in, and so Rochus, still in pain and unable to sit, or even move unaided, stared up at the instigator of his current woes, Wilhelm Mohnke.

"At least you've come out of it in one piece," said Mohnke. "Well," he added, "more or less anyway."

Misch remained silent for a while. Silent and staring. His eyes glued to the rank insignia on Mohnke's collar patches.

"I see you've been promoted, sir," he muttered. There was no animosity in his tone nor in his expression, and yet Mohnke felt the accusation like a knife to the heart. His hand went defensively to the brand new and shiny Sturmbannführer flashes on his lapels. In view of the latest small catastrophe, he had been 'bumped' up by Himmler in an abortive effort to show the Abwehr that the SS were not in the least bothered by the recent events in Poland and were on top of all matters that concerned them. The Abwehr, of course, were not in the least impressed.

Mohnke gave a half-hearted smile. "I'm off to the front. Taken command of the 3rd battalion."

"Nice one," Misch managed a smile. "War's done and you get your own battalion. Just what you always wanted, sir."

"Misch," Mohnke looked around and lowered his voice. "I'm sorry, OK? My fault and I own to it. Out of my depth and all that. If I could go back and change things, I would."

"No, sir," Misch managed to place a comforting hand on Mohnke's wrist. "Not your fault and if we could go back in time things would work out exactly the same 'cos that's the way things are."

Mohnke's face remained immobile but tears threatened behind his eyes. He knew Rochus Misch as well as any man or woman on this earth, and he knew beyond doubt that Misch's forgiveness was genuine. Misch smiled, it was as though the ineptness of Mohnke and the SS, not to mention Himmler himself, were merely a fact of life to be accepted and simply filed away.

Mohnke sighed. He envied Misch his fatalism.

"Look here now, Misch," Mohnke nodded and patted Misch's hand in an affectionate return gesture. "The doctors here say that you will recover, mostly, anyway. A few ongoing niggles and such, but you will get better and be fully active again. So, your promotion...."

"No!" That came out with astonishing vehemence and heads on the ward turned toward them. Misch frowned an apology. "No promotion. Sir, not for me. Not ever."

"Listen to me, Rochus," demanded Mohnke. "I said that you'll make a full recovery but your, shall we say, SS travelling days are over. Over, Rochus, understand that! So now we must think of what you can do that will still serve the Reich and also keep you active in a manner that suits your temperament – that won't drive you to depression through boredom."

"And?" Misch writhed slightly beneath his protective coating of sheets and blankets. "When you're done here," Mohnke was almost whispering, "You are to report to Rattenhuber in Berlin. He has a place for you but your duties will be of a secret nature and entail reporting directly to him."

"Those duties being?" Enquired Misch.

"He'll tell you when you see him. But I can promise you you'll find them interesting and something of a doddle compared with what you've been used to." He didn't mention to Misch that he would be getting a cushy billet for fear that the redoubtable Rochus might object. What Misch didn't know, and Wilhelm Mohnke and Rattenhuber both did, was that the war was far from over. It had barely begun. Rattenhuber was convinced that Misch could still be extremely useful, whereas Mohnke wanted to keep his injured friend away from any future front-line warfare if at all possible. It transpired that there was a position open that Rochus Misch could fill more than adequately if willing. The full details, though, were rather difficult to impart over a hospital bed in a busy Ward.

"Come on, sir. After all this time we have another secret between us?"

Mohnke hesitated. Misch was right, though. He deserved to be told *something*.

"You are Leibstandarte, Misch. Rattenhuber wants you on his team as one of the Führer's personal bodyguards. Now, my friend. This war is far from over. The Führer intends to destroy communism for good and that war when it comes will be huge. Bigger and more destructive than anything you can imagine. Not to mention those creepy British and their garlic riddled friends across the border. They will need seeing to sooner or later, believe me. So, my cushy number as you infer it to be may not be quite so cushy after all. Lively, though, Misch, eh? Certainly very lively. You, however, will be well away from all the evils of this cruel and unjust world, protecting the Führer and engaging in what you love best." Misch smiled enquiringly. "Travel, Misch. You should get in a lot of travel whilst guarding our beloved leader."

"Thank you." Misch knew that Mohnke had put the feelers out for him and requested that Rattenhuber take him on. It was his reward and he accepted it, considering himself lucky to receive anything at all. What he didn't know was that Himmler had at first wanted him shot and swept out of the way because of any future embarrassment that might be caused should Misch open his mouth a little too much. Rattenhuber had dissuaded him by singing Misch's praises to the Führer who in turn had demanded that this paragon of SS loyalty be transferred to Rattenhuber and the Führer HQ. And so, once recovered and getting about passably well, SS Scharführer Rochus Misch reported to SS Standartenführer Johann Rattenhuber in Berlin for his new assignment.

CHAPTER 23

1943: The Berghof, Obersalzberg.

Frenzied, sweaty and decidedly unpleasant to view for all but the most enthusiastic voyeur, the frantically shrieking and leg thrashing couple seemed closer to an agonizing death rather than the very apex of physical pleasure. He, Hermann Fegelein, wounded hero from the eastern front where he had, according to him, battled manfully against the mighty hordes of bestial communism and emerged alive, triumphant and crowned in glory. To hear Hermann tell it, his courage was legendary and his actions beyond saintly. Along the way he managed to considerably enrich his monetary larder with a fair-sized amount of looted goods. Gold, jewellery, hard cash and even sacks of coffee had been gathered up and dispatched homeward, thus greatly increasing the size of Hermann Fegelein's not terribly secret coffers.

In the course of his more arduous duties on the eastern front Hermann had been awarded the Iron Cross 2nd class after receiving a wound in his right buttock from a Soviet sniper. A 'crap' shot joked his commander as Hermann was wheeled off to a hospital ward. Nevertheless, a wound was a wound and Hermann was further rewarded with a series of promotions culminating in his present rarefied rank of SS General. Brigadeführer Fegelein it now was. A far cry from the mouthy little stable boy of a few years ago. Hermann had slaughtered first Jews, and then Russian partisans by the thousands during his tenure on the death littered eastern front. But late in 1941 Reichsführer Himmler had flown into a supreme hissy fit, complaining bitterly that the number of Jews currently being slaughtered was far too low. He didn't want ten, twenty or thirty thousand dead. Himmler wanted them dead in their millions. Part of the problem was the method used to kill the unwanted Jews. The constant close-up slaughter on a daily basis was taking its toll on even the most hardened of his grey clad killers. And the cost in ammunition was horrifying.

To instil a little Nazi fervour into his sometimes queasy, or simply worn-down Einsatzgruppe selectees, Standartenführer Fegelein, as he then was, had set a staggeringly efficient example of leading the way by personally disembowelling captured Russian and Polish Jews with a bayonet. All deliberately done in front of his wide eyed and staring Einsatzgruppe teams to bolster their enthusiasm for the job at hand. He, Hermann Fegelein, would set the example of what was to be. And he did it very thoroughly. Old men, young men, women, children. They were all the same to him – Jews! He particularly enjoyed gutting small babies in front of their shrieking mothers. The precise effect that these demonstrations had upon his men was impossible to tell. What was clear from then on, however, was the enormous effort and enthusiasm displayed by all ranks under his command. Each man was determined to follow orders to the letter and went out of his way to look as though he enjoyed every brutal second of it. A wise decision if for no other reason than the glaring fact that their bayonet wielding leader, despite his movie actor features, cute blue eyes and blond hair, was not a man to be crossed. Not by privates and corporals he wasn't.

Then had come the sniper's bullet, an end to active service, promotion to Brigadeführer and, hopefully, a cushy billet for the remainder of the war. That pleased Hermann no end. He hadn't gone Jew killing out of preference nor because he much gave a damn about Jews one way or another. Putting it simply, Einsatzgruppe had been for him the only way to rapid career advancement. How else could somebody like him, lots of mouth but precious little talent, rise so high in such a short space of time? Oh, yes, Hermann knew himself well enough. No illusions there. So, to hell with the eastern front, or any damn battlefront for that matter. If he could skive it out, use his wits and stay clear of harm's way, that would do him very nicely. Let other mugs do the fighting and the dying. Hermann had seen and done more than enough, thank you very much my dear old Führer.

He had not, though, ceased his perpetual seeking and grasping for more. It was his nature and even though it should have been obvious, even to him, that he was pushing things too far he carried right on doing what he did. He took foolish risks and made enemies unnecessarily seemingly without any real thought for the possible consequences. He quite simply felt himself to be entitled and, therefore, what he wanted *must* be. He loathed what he referred to as the 'Concentration Camp Snobs', the doctors and lawyers that ran the camps and considered themselves to be a cut above the rest of the SS. He didn't like them and they sure as hell despised him. Flashy Fegelein, as he had become known, was a born intriguer, a naturally loud braggart, and a liar to the extent that even Albert Speer found him to be a despicable character. Now, though, he had true blue battle scars to show off and no one was going to stop him from rising even further, not if he could help it. Caution was for old men waffling from their rocking chairs.

Some might have said that making a bee-line for the sexually rampant but repressed Eva Braun was a damn fool thing to do. But Hermann knew what he was about. He could sniff Eva and he could certainly sniff old Uncle Wolf. Fegelein knew instinctively what was going on there and, Hitler being what he was, knew damn well that Fegelein knew. The Führer was also well aware of what the libertine SS officer was up to, but he let it go. Needs must and his Eva most certainly had a variety of needs.

H e lay back, his well-formed but rather small body shining with perspiration. Chest heaving, heavy eyed and sated he twisted slightly with discomfort resulting from a somewhat too enthusiastic partner who looked to all intents and purposes as if she were ready to go again. My God, thought Hermann with a virtual reality grin, the randy mare is ready for another round. "Not yet, sweety," he muttered, caressing her well-muscled and beautifully shiny back. Smooth skinned, heavy breasted and wide hipped, Eva was the very essence of a superbly healthy German peasant girl. To have said as much to her face, though, would have sent her into a screaming rage that made even Adolf Hitler's hysterical shrieking seem tame. Without doubt, thought Hermann, she is the greatest lay I have ever had. Randy, insatiable, accommodating and incredibly inventive, those words didn't even begin to do justice to the Führer's paramour. Nevertheless, she was no 'Die Dame' magazine fashion model. Eva hated her peasant roots but there was no hiding the reality of one's antecedents in a Germany that valued the racial purity of its citizens above all else.

Eva turned her pleasant, broad featured face toward him and smiled. Quite plain, really, he mused. Plain she might be but dear God in his harem heaven, she was sexy as any woman had a right to be.

She reached across him and took a cigarette from his gold case on the bedside table. Obligingly she stuck it in his mouth and lit it for him and then, after his first puff, took it from him and drew heavily upon it herself. Adolf wasn't aware that she occasionally indulged her craving for nicotine, but then the wrinkled old git wasn't aware of a lot of things about her. After three more draws on the illicit white papered stick of death she plonked the offending item back into Hermann's eager mouth. Observing him as he drew heavily, inhaled and then blew out a long thin stream of smoke, she suddenly threw one full fleshed thigh across his belly and straddled him like an Amazon mounting a war horse. She lifted her breasts and moaned in a deep sensual manner which she knew men found irresistible. Sweat dripped from the opening pores of her body as more moans escaped her, and that broad face for all its plump cheeked peasant wideness was as coquettish as hell.

Hermann grinned at her. His burgeoning erection was still quite painful after their last intensive bout but what the hell, there was no way that he could resist her.

"Tell me," he enquired and waited.

"Tell you what my manly hero?" she smiled and raised an eyebrow.

"Has our beloved Führer ever seen this side of you? Not prying. Just curious, you understand."

"You can't be serious." Eva abruptly became mood-breakingly serious as an expression of acute distaste crossed her face. "He only gets off on corpses and nut-jobs."

"Yeh, I thought as much. Very weird bloke, our Adolf."

"I tried once, you know. I tried to get him interested. What a damn waste of time that turned out to be. I mean, really! Embarrassing or what? And God, Hermi, he stinks. I know it's not his fault entirely, but the man has the body odour of a sewer. And as for his breath – awful!"

"But you stay, though, my sweet, don't you?"

"As if I could get away. You know what he would do. Anyway – why should I go? Look at the life I have, all the treats, the staff, the houses; people at my beck and call. Even those stuck-up generals call me ma'am. All except for you, of course. You're my very own *special* general; aren't you, Hermi?"

He smiled and caressed the nape of her neck.

"Anyway, he lets me have my own way. I can have pretty well anything my little heart desires." She affected a girlish giggle and adopted a phoney coquettish pose. Herman gave her the toothy grin which women so adored and men utterly despised. "As long as I don't argue, that is. I've got my own little domestic empire here, Schatzi, so what do I care what he does with the rest of the world?"

"As long as you get your goodies, yeh?"

"In a nutshell, my blond warrior." She drew a finger along the jagged scar on his right buttock. "We both know what we want poppet and we know how to get it. We are two sides of the same coin. Just the same, the two of us."

"Survivors, you mean?"

"Oh – at the very least that, Schatzi ."

"So right, Eva," he said, "so very right. We've made it all this way from nothing and nowhere and that's how it's going to stay. Until the party ends, that is."

Eva's tussled head jerked back in surprise at that last remark from her lover. "Ends – what do you mean, Hermi – until the party ends?"

"Well," Fegelein drew on his cigarette. "You know the old saying, sweets. All good things *must* come to an end."

"Oh, you!" Thoughts of further sex flew from her mind as she prodded Hermann hard in his chest and then, drawing one leg up under her chin, began nervously rubbing her toes. "What can you mean, mister dramatic, *all* coming to an end?"

He sighed fondly. In so many ways Eva was as naïve as a virgin choir boy. Automatically using an inbuilt and highly effective cunning, she had dropped smoothly into the role that had been worked out for her by uncle Wolf and his crony, Joey Goebbels, effortlessly convincing all, or at least most, that she was nothing more than a harmless, not to mention brainless, clotheshorse. A necessary Führer accessory; to be seen and rarely, certainly not in public, heard. Whilst that description was in many ways accurate, it did not quite hit the mark. Eva was a ferocious self-seeker and utterly, in her soft beguiling way, devoted to her own personal improvement and well-being. Oh, she would wave a feminine hand in a superbly convincing display of distress over the misfortune of others, but in reality, Eva didn't give much thought to the problems of humanity. She knew about the killings of countless Jews all over Europe and could not have cared less: not her problem. She was the centre of her own universe and important unto herself before all others. Which was why she instinctively understood the actions of those around her. Eva, without being a member of the Nazi party, nevertheless slotted in perfectly.

The fact that she didn't know uncle Wolf, as she liked to call him, as well as she thought sometimes annoyed Hermann. Eva needed to wise up a little to the actualities around her. She honestly believed all that Führer spouted guff about secret wonder weapons and how the war was going well, etc. She swallowed it all hook line and sinker. He couldn't blame her, so did millions of others – cretins the lot of them if they honestly believed that Germany was going to get out of this mess without being crushed like a loathsome insect by an unforgiving world. Odd, really, about Eva. Part of her couldn't stand close proximity to the Führer, but another part sincerely admired the screw-loose leader of the Reich, like he was the second coming; a sort of Jesus in a Panzer perspective. She sincerely believed that Hitler could and would win this war and that whilst he was in charge all would be well. A foolishly simplistic and unworldly view for a woman so engrossed with her own well-being. But what the hell! He didn't adore her for her intelligence and he was sure that he would be able to convince her of the hopelessness of their situation before too much longer. Stalingrad had been bad, but the Führer's next offensive promised a whole lot worse.

"Ach, forget I said anything, sweets," He waved a hand dismissively, not wanting to wreck the mood nor the prospect of another round of hectic, sexual rough and tumble.

"Nope," she rolled onto her back. "I want to know what you meant, Hermann. So – come on, tell me. You know something and I know you and that look in your eyes when you get all serious and meaningful."

"I know nothing!" He protested with dramatic comedy intonation. "Nothing at all."

"Yes you do," she prodded him hard in his ticklish third rib. "You do-you do-you-do! Confess, Schatzi or no more nookie for you." She couldn't help but giggle, "Not for another hour, anyway. Now, Hermi, come on. Tell me....please!"

He looked at her and then with uncharacteristic gentleness took her hand and kissed the palm. Did it matter if he told her what he knew? Wasn't exactly that deeply hidden a secret.

"Oh, well. I don't know all the ins and outs, Eva, sweetheart."

"Yes!" She nodded eagerly. Cajoling secrets was something that she adored doing. It made her feel powerful and superior.

"There's a big offensive about to get under way out in the east. The Führer wants to hand the Russians a big beating. There's this salient called Kursk. Been there since after Stalingrad…."

"Oh!" Eva's hand flew to her mouth at the mention of that ill-fated city. The graveyard of the once formidable German sixth army.

"Not out there again."

"Of course out there, sweetie, where the hell else for Christ's sake? Anyway, you know what a salient is, yes?"

"Something that protrudes out from a straight line. Yes of course, Schatzi, I know what a salient is." She frowned as she aimed a playful slap at his blond head.

"OK, long story short. As far as I can gather, we're throwing everything we've got at the Russians in order to straighten that line and then, according to the Führer and his pet magician, Field Marshal Eric, whose a clever boy then, von Manstein, all will be well and we can go right ahead and win the war, as the Russians, will be too battered, exhausted and used up to resist the might of the almighty Wehrmacht – I don't think!" He threw up both hands in exasperation.

"Ooh," Eva squealed prettily. "A big offensive means we win, yes?"

"NO!"

"I don't understand," her voice now slightly tremulous at Hermann's suddenly harsh tone. "Addi would never make an offensive if he didn't think it would be successful. I know he wouldn't."

Fegelein sighed very heavily and refrained from reciting the myriad failed offensives previously ordered by their glorious Führer. Offensives? What did she know, the poor girl?"

"Eva, poppet, all I can say is stay away from Berlin. You're well out of harm's way here. Do not on any account leave. Understand?"

"Don't tell me what to do, Hermi, I don't like it. I am the Führer's," she hesitated, "the Führer's……."

"You are the Führer's piece of pretend totty, Eva. And when this latest venture with all the remaining military resources left available to us on the eastern front fails, those Russian bastards are going to come for us, sweets, and they won't be very bloody polite about who they kill, maim, rape or slaughter. Understand?"

"Stop it, Hermi, you're scaring me." Eva was wide-eyed. She had never heard her ever confident lover talk like this. It was, well, it was just so defeatist! So un-German and wishy-washy. What on earth was the matter with him, her hero? She allowed tears to fill her eyes and drop prettily down her swelling bosom. She had asked the question but certainly didn't like the answer and what it had implied. She needed reassurance and cuddles and a lot of rampant sex. Hermann had implied that defeat was a possibility, earlier hinting that there was a spy within the Führer's inner circle. How else could the Soviets always seem to know what was coming? Adolf refused to acknowledge any such thing and put it down to chance. Hermann, though, was quite sure that a spy was concealed deep within. But wasn't that typical of war – spies everywhere? Surely nothing too much to worry about.

Some twenty minutes later, with the room rank with the smell of sweaty bodies, sex and stale tobacco, the two rolled apart and gazed at one another fondly.

"Hermi, I've been thinking," said Eva dreamily.

"Oh-oh," Herman smirked tiredly. It paid to be wary when Eva thought deeply about anything. "Go on then, sweets. Spill those haricots."

"You quite like Gretl, don't you?" She gazed at him thoughtfully.

"Your sister? I'spose so. Not in the way that I like you though." He squeezed her affectionately.

"Oh, I know, I know."

"So?"

"Well, she's dreamy about you, Hermi. I mean – big time! She thinks I don't know but she is crazy about you."

Hermann shrugged. It was nothing new to him, a woman finding him dreamy. He had become used to female displays of affection. Those that didn't display any such adoration of his person he easily ignored. "OK," he muttered, tentatively. "And so?"

"You should marry her."

That got him, right enough. "What!" He shot upright into a sitting position. "Marry your sister? I thought you loved me."

"I do, Schatzi, I do. But just think. With all that's going on and this Himmler thing that's been worrying you...."

She hit a nerve with that one. Himmler had never much liked the dislikeable but outwardly competent Hermann Fegelein and the grapevine whispered that the Reichsführer SS was having thoughts on promoting him and sending him back to the jolly old eastern front. Well, not if Hermann Fegelein had anything to do with it. It was merely rumour, of course, but a wise man should always be ready with protective measures.

"Go on," he whispered, already beginning to see where his lover was going with her burgeoning plan

"Marry her, Schatzi, she'll go along with it 'cos she adores you, and you'll be in the family so to speak. Close to the Führer, close to everything that's going on, and most importantly, close to me. Good, eh?"

"Sweetheart," Fegelein was thinking now of Himmler's reaction. Fuck the son-of-a-bitch! "You're a genius. It'll work and think of the fun. All that illicit messing around. You, me and Gretl; the things we could get up to, sweets."

"Yes," Eva looked ready to go yet again for another round of their hectically energetic sex romps. "That had crossed my mind." She nibbled his earlobe

"Gretl has a nice figure you know."

"Yes, Hermi, I do know. So?" She smiled, knowing damn well what was coming next.

"I was thinking, poppet that, perhaps, just perhaps, a threesome might go down pretty nicely. What d'you think." He smiled lasciviously.

"A ménage à trois? You disgusting little SS devil you," she laughed. Gretl wouldn't mind at all and neither would she.

That was it. All set up. Hermann would marry Gretl and be closer to Eva and no suspicion would be aroused. Excellent!

CHAPTER 24

July 1943: Führer HQ, Rastenburg.

Operation Citadel, the great offensive that had so worried Brigadeführer Hermann Fegelein turned out to be a worse disaster than even he had envisaged. He had observed the latest in an increasingly long line of German military tragedies as it unfolded moment by moment. Not first-hand admittedly, but more than close enough, thank you very much. The heavily concreted Führer HQ at Rastenburg, more than one thousand kilometres away to the west, was as close as he wanted to be to a decidedly violent and rapidly approaching front line. He was now Himmler's liaison with the Führer and had semi-permanent quarters in the complex which he shared with Hitler's personal physician, the loathsome Theodore Morell. He came daily into contact with the Wehrmacht's top field commanders and planners and was not impressed with a single one of them. Always whining excuses in their snotty accents to a thoroughly pissed off Führer. And where one might ask, thought Fegelein, was the almighty Führer's supposedly omniscient brain when you needed something inventive or imaginative? Stand fast – Die bravely – No retreat! Blah-blah-Blah! Same load of old horse shit. But, as Hermann well knew, such is life.

The Russians had known every single move that the Wehrmacht and the SS had made well in advance and acted accordingly by utterly smashing the German armoured forces and slaughtering their infantry. The losses in men and material were catastrophic. Not even Albert Speer, the great architect himself, could make good the now gaping deficit in all arms. Yet still, no orders or questions concerning the possibility of a spy within the Wolfsschanze complex had been issued. Ludicrous!

Hitler had called off the failing and ruinously costly offensive when the news came that American and British forces had invaded Italy. Field Marshal von Manstein, the southern sector commander of operation Citadel, had rocked up in a bullet riddled Storch which broke a wheel on landing, and begged the Führer to allow him to continue. Victory was close, he promised. Just one more push. But Hitler, the man who always condemned retreat and quitting as out and out cowardice, told the appalled Field Marshal that he, Manstein, didn't understand the bigger picture. What was left of German Panzer forces must now be sent to Italy to bolster up Mussolini.

Manstein, known as the epitome of German officer class good manners had finally lost it with his Führer, an individual whom he detested to the very depths of his aristocratic being. The Führer of the Third Reich, in Manstein's opinion, displayed all the mental capabilities of a highly strung baboon.

"To hell with the Italians," he hissed. "What use are they? The war, the future of the Reich, will be decided here, Führer, in the east. Italy is irrelevant. Surely even YOU can see that! Lose here and you might just as well go to Stalin and offer to be his boot-boy. The initiative will be permanently lost to us. There will be no going back. This war will be done – lost! Do you understand what I am saying?"

Amazingly, Hitler didn't lose his temper nor even so much as try to shout von Manstein down. The one commander in the entire Wehrmacht that Adolf Hitler respected was standing before him, Eric von Manstein. And even Hitler didn't have the heart to yell at the defeated Field Marshal.

He tiredly waved his arms at the ashen faced and distraught commander of the southern front at Kursk. Poor fool thought that this battle still meant something: Tosh! Had it ever? It was all delaying tactics, desperate attempts to stave off the inevitable; to stay alive and hope that something might turn up later and save them all, especially himself. His head sank upon his chest. Being a demi-God had been hellish good fun in the early days when there had been lots of money, millions of willing young men ready to fight and die for their infallible Führer and a myriad of adoring worshippers hanging on to his every plagiarised word. Demi Gods, however, were supposed to have answers and he had none. All he could do was apportion blame and keep it as far away from himself as possible. It was becoming increasingly difficult to retain his savoir-faire as he received the never-ending reports of defeat from all quarters of his crumbling Nazi empire, not just daily but on an almost hourly basis. One disaster to the next. What to do? As Goebbels might say: 'Blag it out, Adolf. What else can you do?'

"Go away, Manstein," he said in a not unfriendly manner. "You are tired. I hereby relieve you of duty. Hand over to Field Marshal Model and then go on leave for a while. You need rest."

"Führer, I will not......"

That was enough. Now Hitler roared from the depths of his aching belly. "Get out of my sight you God damned wretched failure. GET OUT!" Manstein spun on his heel and left the Führer's presence. Walking through the now open HQ doorway he turned to General Jodl, his face contorted with hatred and contempt. "The man's a bloody moron, Jodl." With that Field Marshal Eric von Manstein, the last great military hope of the Third Reich marched off into history. He was done. Eric Manstein would not soldier for Hitler again.

Standing beside the huge map table, Jodl turned to his companion Field Marshal Wilhelm Keitel. "That went well, then."

"Clearly" responded Keitel, sniffing over his neatly trimmed little moustache. "What now, I wonder."

"Gentlemen." Brigadeführer Fegelein saluted smartly. "Is the Führer available?" A couple of busy looking aides made their way back and forth and an occasional officer appeared from one of the many HQ complex corridors that littered the place like a funfair horror castle. The dull hum of electricity and ringing phones added their monotonous tones to the muted chatter echoing throughout the HQ.

Keitel and Jodl looked up from the war map. Neither of them much liked the loud self-serving little SS general.

"What is it Herr Fegelein?" Asked Keitel waspishly as Jodl pointedly looked back at his map.

Fegelein smiled a little lopsidedly. "If you please, Herr Field Marshal, I am addressed as Brigadeführer or Herr General. If you please, of course."

"I do not please, Fegelein. I designate as *I* please, and I am *not* pleased to refer to you as Herr General. Clear?"

"Oh, I think that you should, Herr Field Marshal," said a new voice. "Politeness and form cost nothing. Come now. Let the Wehrmacht and the SS be friends, as they should be, eh?"

SS Reichsführer Himmler strode into the large map room. His hazel eyes glinting as ever from behind his steel pince-nez. Keitel hesitated. He had the rank but not the backbone to stand up to Reichsführer Himmler, the Reich's infamous all powerful and much feared chief policeman. Himmler's activities within and without the Reich were well known to Wilhelm Keitel. The assassination of Reinhard Heydrich last year had cleared a deadly rival out of the way thus enabling Himmler to gather ever more power and authority into his greedy hands. Great Gods, he was more avaricious even than Albert Speer when it came to the sneaky misappropriation of offices and power. These days he was known as a man who, with a stroke of his pen, could sign away the lives of any and all those foolish enough to stand against him. If not them, then those that they most cared about.

"Ah, Herr Reichsführer. What a delight to see you." Another interloping voice boomed out as the squat, brown uniformed figure of Reichsleiter Martin Bormann entered and added an even less pleasant aspect to the already gloomy atmosphere of the map room.

Fegelein grinned widely. He enjoyed seeing toffee nosed fools like Keitel being shot down by his powerful SS master. Keitel, whilst avoiding Himmler's glacial eyes, glared savagely at Fegelein.

"Likewise, I'm sure," responded the unsmiling Himmler.

"And how may we aid the Reichsführer today?" Bormann's tone was ingratiating although he was one of the few men with no reason to fear the SS chief. Hitler relied upon his private secretary completely and not even Heinrich Himmler could make a dent in his armour. Bormann, by the same token, did not make powerful men his enemies unless there was good reason. For the time being at least, he preferred to remain on friendly terms with the powerful SS Reichsführer. Generals, thought Bormann, as he continued with his oily smile, come and go; as do politicians. Himmler, though, was like the proverbial flea on a dog's back; always there, always watching and always ready for blood.

"I have some excellent news for the Fuhrer," said Himmler with a wave of his eagle topped silver baton.

"It will need to be," said Keitel, indicating the war map with a gnarled forefinger.

"Ah-hah!" Himmler strode over as though he were a Valkyrie coming to the rescue. "Problems, are there? Perhaps I can help." He leaned forward over the map table and scanned the myriad lines, marker penned contours and wood plinthed miniature flags designating various units. "Hmm." He nodded as though knowing what he was looking at. Jodl, who had been holding one such flag in his left hand, suddenly slammed it down onto the map table. "Oh, noticed something have you, Herr Reichsführer?" Jodl was generally a calm individual happiest when he was moving bodies and machines around on a map such as the one before him. "Perhaps we may now have the benefit of your......" Keitel's gently restraining hand prevented him from completing a sentence that was assuredly going to be insulting to the well-meaning Reichsführer.

"And what pray tell, Herr Generaloberst," Himmler's small even teeth were showing as he fixed his gaze upon the Wehrmacht's chief of operations, "do I seem to have missed, if anything?" He gave a small condescending smile and looked back at the map. "All seems in order, Herr General. Wouldn't you say?"

Fegelein could barely contain a wince of horror at the Reichsführer's dreadful display of military ignorance. SS or no, he found himself looking away.

"You are aware are you not, Herr Reichsführer of the recent battle some one thousand kilometres away at Kursk?"

"Recent? You mean it's over? How did we do?"

Jodl stared at him, shocked and even Keitel, so unusually for him, threw up his arms in despair. Fegelein felt a fit of the giggles coming on, not helped by Bormann's owl-like gaze.

"Do? You ask, how did we do?" Jodl's bald head turned down, its high domed crown pointing toward Himmler like a threatening missile. "Well, as you so cleverly surmised, Reichsführer, it most certainly *is* over and frankly, not to put too fine a point on it, we didn't do terribly well. Damn near catastrophic, truth be told. We lost over one thousand tanks, amongst them our best and newest Panther tanks. In men, well, at least two hundred thousand gone, probably more. And we lost some seven to eight hundred aircraft during the course of the battle which, as you now realise, is over."

"We lost, then?" Squawked Himmler, rather theatrically looking around as though this latest disaster had come about because his advice had not been sought.

"Hardly a glowing success, so yes, put like that, we lost."

"We most certainly did not." Hitler stormed into the room pointing an accusing finger at his operations chief. "I have lulled them, those bestial Slavic dogs, into a sense of false security. This will work to our favour, you'll see. I have new plans, and, mark my words," he waved an admonishing finger at them all, "new weapons with which to deal with those scum. Oh, yes, my friends. They shall soon see what it means to challenge the might of the German Wehrmacht." He looked across at Himmler. "Ah, Himmler." He frowned slightly in momentary confusion. "What are you doing here? Did I send for you?"

Throwing a stiffly correct but completely ignored Hitler salute, Himmler replied, "Not directly my Führer, no. But I do have good news. Wonderful news from the," he glanced furtively toward Jodl and Keitel, "*other* front, my Führer."

"The other front?" What was the damn man talking about? There were so many.

Himmler looked meaningfully toward the entrance of Hitler's private office; the inner sanctum, so to speak. And then, as the Führer made no move nor displayed acknowledgement that he had the remotest idea of what the Reichsführer was getting at, said, "I'm sure that Brigadeführer Fegelein, as my SS liaison officer, has been keeping you up to date with events, my Führer."

Fegelein nodded furiously in affirmation. In reality, he had done no such thing. He'd been far too busy seeking further sexual conquests, chasing after Gretl Braun and generally feathering his own nest. Then, of course, there had been this ghastly waste of time, men and money, the battle of Kursk. It had taken days to fight, conclude and then extricate all those shattered divisions before the Russians could launch their offensive. Everyone, including Hitler, had been too shaken to care much about what else was going on in the rest of the world. And then had come the invasion of Sicily by the British and Americans. Fegelein had guessed right. Nobody at the Wolfsschanze in Rastenburg gave a monkey's toss anymore about Jews, Camps or Red Cross parcels from Switzerland. It was all going to pot and he had enjoyed a brief few moments with one of Hitler's secretaries before renewing his literary and telephonic pursuit of Gretl Braun. Himmler's orders had been to keep the Führer informed about the success of the extermination camps directly under Himmler's control. The Reichsführer had adopted the now deceased Reinhard Heydrich's excellent plan for a Final Solution to the Jewish problem. Gas not bullets was the key and mighty gas chambers of death had been constructed throughout the conquered territories and the Reich itself. The thought, the planning, quite literally everything that made the Final Solution in any way practicable was all down to the cold genius of Reinhard Heydrich. His remorseless thoroughness and dedication to detail had enabled huge advancement in the Reich's dedicated efficiency with regard to curtailing unwanted human life. Himmler, however, made sure that he took the credit. His camps provided the means, his Totenkopf SS did the killing and so, to his mind, it was only right and fair that he be awarded the kudos. After all, this was his life's work. Hard and exhausting work it was, too.

Hitler glanced at the smiling Fegelein. Obsequious little turd, in Hitler's opinion, but Eva and Gretl seemed to like and trust him. For the life of him, he couldn't remember whether Fegelein had spoken to him about Himmler's business or not. What had once been a cornerstone of Nazi ideology had of late become the sole province of the SS leader and upholder of State morals, Heinrich Himmler.

The Führer sighed and looked away from Fegelein and straight at his SS chief. That man rocked back on his heels just oozing self-satisfaction and smugness. Had the fellow no concept at all of what had happened in the east? What was happening in the south and what was at any time about to happen in the west? Clearly not. Oh well. Hitler turned slightly to one side and gestured toward his office. Might as well join Himmler in his fantasy world for an hour or two. With all said and done, the Reichsführer's stories of human destruction, mutilation and disposal were always entertaining.

As the small party consisting of Hitler, Bormann, Himmler and Fegelein moved away toward the Führer's private office, Himmler turned briefly to Fegelein and said almost in a whisper, "Not you, Fegelein. Remain here and play with some maps." Fegelein's embarrassment at being treated in such a cavalier manner was eased somewhat when Hitler surprisingly said to Bormann, "Check with Misch on the switchboard, Bormann, that there's nothing new come in." It was astoundingly clear, that whatever it was that Himmler wanted to say to the Führer, the great leader wanted to hear it in private. That even Martin Bormann was excluded came as a small shock to Jodl and Keitel. Clearly Hitler had some foreknowledge of what his top policeman had to say and the news he wished to deliver.

"Of course my Führer." A smart click of shiny heels and Bormann departed on his errand. He knew his master too well to show even the slightest degree of discontent or intransigence. Hitler picked up on that sort of thing very quickly indeed and the Hitler axe could fall swiftly and messily on an unwary head. Anyway, Bormann knew well enough that he could barge into any Führer meeting with barely even the flimsiest of excuses. The Führer had never yet thrown him out once he had wormed his way in.

Fegelein mooched sulkily over to a wall map and made a pretence of studying it with great care.

With Hitler and Himmler gone Jodl waved a hand over the table map. "Nothing," he said despondently to his colleague. Keitel traced a knowing finger along an imaginary line, a long line it seemed to Fegelein as he observed them from the corner of his eye. "The Führer's genius will see us through, Jodl. It is the one constant that we may rely upon."

"Oh, Keitel, really!" The operations chief turned to the Field Marshal. "Look, man. There's nothing there." He pointed forcefully to the imaginary line Keitel had drawn across the map. "We have nothing with which to plug those gaps. All that is left for us is a massive retreat. To attempt to hold on will be calamitous. No amount of genius is going to help us, Keitel my friend. We need tanks by the hundreds, guns and men by the tens of thousands. Where, where in God's name are we to get them? From that supercilious ponce Albert Speer?"

"Tut!" Keitel gave his subordinate a swift slap on the arm and looked with alarm at the SS General that was Hermann Fegelein. To speak so in front of such creatures was dangerous indeed.

They needn't have worried. Hermann Fegelein was well aware of the true state of things. The much-lauded new tank, the Panther, had proven to be an absolute failure because the wretched things, despite being state of the art, just kept breaking down. Components broke after a hundred or so miles. There was a huge difference between limited trials and actual battle testing. Even so, no one could figure out why so many of them kept grinding to a premature halt. Hermann Fegelein knew why, 'cos it was bloody obvious to anybody with half a brain. All those lovely tanks had been built using slave labour; ergo, it stood to reason – surely, that unwilling slave workers would sabotage production whenever they could without over much danger to themselves? Small but vital parts were being deliberately weakened before insertion into their active machine part. Simplicity itself. After a hundred or so kilometres the wretched tanks broke down and just lay around like useless lumps of metal. But the skilled workers that Germany needed were all off at the front fighting and dying for the Führer, so slaves were all they had. Bit of a cleft stick and no way out other than adopting lengthy checking procedures at the production factories. Unfortunately, all that was being done was a lot of head-in-sand posturing. It didn't much matter now anyway. The final really big battle had already been fought and lost. Hermann shook his head, not caring who saw his negative motion. If he had seen it then why hadn't others? Then he smiled. Of course. The answer came in one word. Greed!

The small sitting room adjoining the Führer's office was sparsely but comfortably furnished and Himmler found himself hoping that Hitler might suggest they adjourn to that room for the anticipated briefing. Once in there and seated, Himmler knew very well that the Führer would order tea and cake, as he always did when he sat within the somewhat bourgeoise and cosy confines of his private little sitting room. No such luck today, however. The Führer seemed rather distracted. A fact which the SS chief put down to worry over the recent turn of events. Well, he, Heinrich Himmler, would soon bring smiles of joy to his revered leader's face when he imparted his wonderful news.

Hitler gestured to a high-backed chair with thinly cushioned arms and Himmler eased his skinny, black clad frame carefully into it. Hitler, though, remained standing. For the first time, Himmler noticed how pale his boss had become. Pale, wrinkled and worn. Heavens, he thought with no change of facial expression, the man has aged twenty years in just a few months. Why hadn't Fegelein told him? The Führer was ill and needed rest or, perish the thought, retirement!

The Führer's pale, blue-eyed gaze rested upon his feared police chief making that man tremble ever so slightly. Why was it, wondered Himmler, that Hitler could still put the fear of hell itself into him even after all this time? He broke fearful wind as quietly as he could and hoped that the Führer hadn't noticed.

"Well, Himmler. Good news you said? So, let's hear it. Elucidate, inform and for God's sake don't be too long about it. I have things to do."

"Of course, my Führer." Himmler cleared his throat and began. "The Final Solution, my Führer, is in full swing!"

"The what?"

"The Final Solution, my Führer. That which you commanded be done is now being done and, if I may say, it is turning out to be more successful than we could have imagined." With a ludicrously delicate gesture of his right hand and folded forefinger before his mouth, he cleared his throat again. "Thanks to my idea of using transportable gas and creating gas rooms large enough to...."

"Yes, yes. Spare me the details." Hitler now remembered his shrieked demands to Himmler three years ago in Berlin. But hadn't the now deceased Heydrich been involved in some fashion? He shifted a slightly trembling hand irritably. What did it matter who did what as long as it was done? But even he wasn't prepared for the clipped two-word statement of numbers that came next. He stepped from behind his desk and was unable to prevent his eyes from widening with astonishment. Smilingly, Himmler awaited a verbal reaction to the statement which had so astonished his Führer.

"HOW MANY?"

"We should pass the two million mark," he shrugged and moved his head from side to side like a man gauging the odds on a prize fight, "before the end of September."

To accompany his fishy eyed stare the Führer now added the pouting *ooh* of a guppy fish. Never had he dreamt that such figures were attainable. He almost flopped into the nearest available wall hugging chair as his heart began beating out an unsteady rhythm of utter disbelief. Yes, he had commanded the utter obliteration of the Jews from the face of the earth, but honestly? He'd never been convinced that it would happen. Two million and rising! Surprise? Astonishment? Those two words failed utterly to describe his feelings at that moment. He crossed his legs and in the same motion uncrossed them again, whilst at the same time attempting to disguise the fact that he suddenly found it difficult to breathe normally. Desperately the Führer of the Third Reich fought to regain his equilibrium. What had once been a dream was now becoming reality. Extermination! How the hell had Himmler brought it all about so quickly?

"You should," Hitler was somehow managing to appear nonchalant and in control, even though his pulse rate was now extremely erratic. "You should save a few for labour purposes, you know. Might be useful to us before we dispose of them in total."

Himmler smiled with delight at his Führer's reaction and obviously heartfelt, almost tearful pleasure. "Please, my Führer. Have no qualms on that score. Herr Speer, our supremely competent Armaments minister, has already been allocated some one hundred and twenty thousand Jews for his work projects. He assures me that when their usefulness is over he will see to their dispatch."

Hitler sat, looking inquiringly.

"Herr Speer has stated that most of them will be worked to death and those that refuse to pass away after making themselves useful to the Reich will simply be allowed to starve in the purpose-built underground caverns in which they are being kept. The sites will be filled in, like, well much the same as landfill, my Führer. Herr Speer is not a man to waste medicines or other luxuries on enemies of the State."

Hitler nodded. So Speer was as avaricious as the rest of them. Pity! He had hoped for better from his suave minister of Armaments. Nevertheless, Himmler's news was cheering indeed and God knew how much he needed a fillip after the never-ending stream of bad news. It hadn't escaped him, though, that his only lasting victory seemed to be over an unarmed and largely unresisting foe. The adjective *pathetic* was making a savage attempt to pierce his conscious mind but he thrust it firmly back into the putrescence of its origin.

A light but rapid tapping came at his office door and without being invited the stocky figure of Martin Bormann thrust its way in.

Hitler looked at his secretary with irritation. "Yes Bormann, what is it?"

"Your pardon, my Führer, but this just came in. The Russians have attacked and taken Bolkhov. Generaloberst Weiss has requested permission to withdraw. Jodl and Keitel agree that it might be...."

"Tsk" Hitler waved his hands. "What have I said about retreat? Why do I persistently need to repeat myself, Bormann? Retreat leads to defeat. Weiss – that is 2nd army, yes?" Bormann nodded. "You tell Keitel that he may tell Weiss, order Weiss, to stand firm. Clear? Not one step back until I have had a chance to look over and judge things for myself."

"Might I enquire as to when that might be, my Führer," asked Bormann. Even he was looking a little tentative at this latest piece of bad news.

"When might *what* be, man?"

"Your, erm, intervention in this matter my Führer. It does seem to be rather urgent."

"Oh for heaven's sake." He turned to Himmler with spread hands. "You see what I have to contend with here, Himmler. Inadequacy and mediocrity. I'm surrounded by it; surrounded by it twenty-four hours of every damned day. I must do everything myself. Very well Bormann. How far past Bolkhov have the Russians advanced?"

"Reports say more than 100 kilometres, my Führer."

"What?" That brought Hitler up sharply. "How can that be? 2nd army should have at least held them for……"

"There no longer is a second army to speak of," Jodl's voice although soft, thundered into and around the Führer's office like a drunken echo. He entered and stood by the open door as he gazed around. Himmler rose, not at all sure what was going on only knowing that whatever it was, it was pretty bad.

All eyes now upon him, Jodl continued. "Weiss's request for permission to withdraw was more by way of a politeness. He had already withdrawn to a line further back where he attempted to stop the Russian seventh and ninth tank armies along with the fifth guards' army. What is left of the 2nd army is now almost completely encircled and the flanks of army groups north and centre are directly threatened with annihilation if we don't act fast."

"Why was I not told earlier?" Demanded Hitler as he strode out to the map room.

"You were," muttered Jodl under his breath. "You just weren't listening."

Himmler, taken aback to hear such an ill-concealed blasphemy from the ever critical but loyal Jodl, followed with a deep frown and joined his Führer as he pored over fresh maps of the rapidly changing and deteriorating situation. About to suggest as to what might be the best thing to do tactically, he glanced around and decided better of it. This most definitely was not the time for small talk and braggadocio. What it was, was time to get the hell out of there!

Stepping back smartly from the large oblong table. "I take leave my Führer in order to continue with my duties to the Reich." He flung up his right arm in the obligatory Hitler salute and was mortified to see that he was being ignored. He, Himmler, was not used to being ignored regardless of the situation. A low murmur of subdued voices wafted around the now uniform littered map table as staff and line officers awaited Hitler's next words. Hitler was not so much ignoring his police chief; he had simply forgotten that he was there. Mortified and reddening with stiff armed embarrassment the Reichsführer lowered the outstretched arm, bowed ever so slightly from the waist, spun smartly to his left and marched out. With a swift glance at the packed and busy surroundings of the map table, Fegelein followed his chief out of the command complex to where Himmler was boarding his personal locomotive waiting just 200 metres away on the narrow gauge Rastenburg railway line. A great black, steam chugging monstrosity with pike hung swastika flags across its front buffers and main frame.

Himmler turned to his liaison officer as he climbed the steps to his main carriage compartment. "Keep an eye on things here, Fegelein. Now mark my words; I want reports and updates every day. Understand?"

"Should I continue to report directly to Obergruppenführer Wolff, sir?"

Himmler came down from the single step that he had climbed. "No, Fegelein." A cunning look crossed the Reichsführer's quasi mongoloid features. "You have special clearance so you will report all matters directly to me, no matter how trivial they may seem. Clear?"

Fegelein nodded discreetly, aware that even now they were probably being observed. "And if you are not available for some reason, Herr Reichsführer?"

"Then you wait, man. I won't have our SS business being blasted all over the Reich through open communication lines or loose lipped couriers. Got that?" Again Fegelein nodded.

"Oh," Himmler turned once more as he reached the top step to his carriage car, "Find that damned spy, Fegelein. It'll mean a hefty promotion if you do." With that, the Reichsführer disappeared into his window blacked pullman and off on his way to Berlin. Fegelein threw up a brisk farewell Hitler salute, bellowed Sieg Heil over the whistling and chugging of the powering up locomotive, spun on his heel and went immediately to his own quarters.

Things were not working out quite as he had anticipated. All the chasing of Eva Braun, her sister, and the material delights of being close to the centre of power, now threatened to be counter-productive. To do deals he needed to be in town; any bloody town, not stuck out in this godforsaken concrete wilderness, drinking ersatz coffee whilst fighting off mosquitos, malaria and diarrhoea. He hadn't seen anything of Eva or Gretl for months now. Those girls were busy partying away in the luxurious alpine setting of the Eagles Nest on the Obersalzberg. Lucky bitches! He had leeway, plenty of it; he had spare time and a reasonable amount of influence and clout but he could not figure a way of using those assets to advance his search for loot. Even his rank and SS status could not get him beyond the electrified fences and murderously efficient guards. Only a Führer pass could do that. More than once the worsening state of military affairs had set off alarm bell warnings in his head. He really did need to add to his illegally acquired stash of portable goodies before the good times ceased to roll, which, judging by the lines on the war room maps, could be any time soon. Hermann was a firm believer in the physical worth of bullion and cash. He wasn't one for faffing around with promissory notes and worthless international bonds. Cash in the hand; that was Hermann Fegelein's philosophy. If he had been an educated man he might have done well to have read the accounts of Napoleon's retreat from Moscow where, through force of circumstance, that emperor's pecunious marshals had been obliged to abandon their hard-won loot by the mud roads and hedgerows of Russia, Ukraine and Poland. But by Hermann's reasoning if you couldn't feel it, look at it or hear it jangle, then, it didn't exist.

Hermann Fegelein harboured a strong, ever growing and totally forbidden feeling, that defeat was inevitable. Back back and further back they were being pushed by the vengeful Russians. Well, by the vengeful pretty well everybody. Those sodding English had stirred up the pot, as they always did, and got the Americans at it. The Americans, of course, two-faced as ever, were delirious with joy at the prospect of wrecking that supercilious bunch of tea drinking farts and copping hold of what remained of their empire. Good business, as far as they were concerned. Unfortunately, though, not so good for the Third Reich and its current deviantocracy. Hermann, now convinced that Hitler's dream of a one-thousand-year Reich was going to end in a flood of Nazi tears, had been seeking an escape route for himself and Eva *if* he could get her to accompany him. Difficult, as Eva was still quite convinced that the Führer would pull a big hairy rabbit out of his black bag of tricks and save the day. Hermann was more realistic about the Reich's chances. They stood, in his view, at nil, zero, sweet sod all!

As he entered his accommodation complex he bumped into a frantic looking Dr. Theodor Morell.

"Such a rush Herr Doctor," quipped Fegelein as he made way for the plump, unwholesome looking individual squeezing past him with the remains of a pastry in one hand and a doctor's bag in the other.

"It's the Führer," squawked Morell. "He's calling for me. Great distress, I fear. I must get on, Herr Brigadeführer."

"Stomach again, is it?" enquired Fegelein giving a real go at appearing to be solicitous.

"Yes, I fear so. All the stress, you see. It's enough to kill a normal man, Herr Brigadeführer."

"Ah," Fegelein gave a small shiny cheeked smile. "Not our Führer, though, eh? A bit of stress won't do him in any time soon, I'll bet you."

Morell had squeezed past and was oblivious to the SS general's sarcasm. "Quite right, quite right." He waved a podgy, pastry filled hand and continued on his way. "See you later, Herr Brigadeführer."

"Hopefully not," muttered Fegelein under his breath as he mooched off to his quarters and a well-earned slug of Brandy.

Lying on the couch in his sitting room, the Führer moaned with discomfort. These pains were becoming worse. Was he dying? The thought made him shudder. His sight was bad, his limbs trembled, his stomach ached and he hadn't had a proper bowel movement in weeks. Constipation was such a bitch! Those people out there, the generals and the soldiers et al, always complaining about something. Weak spirited ninnies with precious little backbone. The truth was, he felt unbidden tears threaten but fought them back, only he knew the true meaning of daily suffering. The work he had to do and the things with which he must put up were almost beyond him. Did none of them appreciate the sacrifices he made for them, the German people? Of course not. Selfish swine, the lot of them.

He writhed again as a deeply unpleasant rumbling in his belly forced acid and bile up into his throat and savagely promoted an unwelcome increase in his almost ever-present heartburn. What the devil was wrong with him? His guts felt as though they were holding enough gas to fill one of von Zeppelin's old airships.

"Give me one of your injections, Morell, and something to buck me up. I cannot afford to be tired or listless at this time. Hurry man, hurry!"

Three syringes lay on the small occasional table beneath Morell's dirt encrusted fingernails. Heinz Linge had entered but Hitler waved him away. He preferred to keep his medical doses and scripts as private as possible. Word of his astonishingly huge intake of various potent chemicals had got around, though. There was just no helping it. With the best will in the world, people talked, and some talked with a joyful viciousness.

Morell tapped the brim-full syringe of a compound containing various vitamins and chemical additives, of which strychnine was the main ingredient. It was a conglomeration of his own devising and would have been thoroughly condemned by any halfway competent medic. Theodor Morell was a dab hand at creating all manner of overnight cures: quack cures, as some called them. He had used them sparingly on the Führer at first, as he well knew the results of over indulging with these particularly toxic compounds. In the short term his remedies had worked quite well. Hitler, however, with no knowledge at all regarding the ingredients of the potentially lethal cocktails he was daily ingesting, had insisted that the doses continue and Morell, wishing to please and just too downright terrified to refuse, not only injected but increased the doses to pacify his fearsomely grumpy Führer. The result on a placebo dependent psyche such as Hitler's was inevitable. Markedly deteriorating health and total addiction. Other of Morell's genius cures contained well above any recommended safety doses for the variety of addictive drugs that he used with such reckless abandon: Pervitin, morphine and more than forty other drugs were now the familiar daily course of injections poured into the Führer's system by Morell's grubby hands and sharp needles.

Sometimes, but not too often, Morell felt a tad guilty. Quack though he was, even he knew that his prescriptions bordered upon criminal over indulgence and downright negligence of his patient's health. But what could he do? Adolf Hitler was the leader, the lord of all he surveyed; the destroyer of all and anything that he wished. He most certainly would be the destroyer of chubby little old Theodor Morell should that man refuse or disobey the will of his Führer and deny him his creature comforts.

The fact was, Morell had never encountered anyone with quite such a propensity for self-pity and nostrum swallowing as the arm waving, constantly yakking Führer of the Third Reich. The man wanted a cure for even the slightest ache or pain, many of which were not real but products of a fearful hypochondriac's imagination. And so, Theodor Morell created potent pick-me-ups for imaginary disorders. Pick-me-ups which made Hitler feel as though he were ten feet tall and could conquer the world; for a while, anyway. His private little laboratory back in Berlin had, since his association with Hitler began, come more to resemble an American Ice Cream parlour than a laboratory. Bubbling and frothing little pots and vials of varying colours and with what seemed to be attractively sippable frothy layers atop each one. Morell had himself come perilously close to death inhaling some of the more deadly of his pharmaceutical experiments. What had become clear to the doctor, however, was that strong poisons if used sparingly and with expertise could be healing aids and wonderful revitalizers; but only if taken sparingly. And that was where his problem with the

Führer lay. That man did nothing sparingly: it was all or nothing all the time. Morell had tried to gently ween the Führer away from his vegetarian diet and on to some meat products, even a little dairy. Hitler, though, would have none of it. No meat and no cheesy, eggy things either. Green leaves, berries and lots of cakes. A dreadful diet. The Führer insisted that all those green lettuce leaves and cabbage stalks were good healthy eating and nothing could dissuade him. The fact was, though, Hitler's digestive system was unable to digest all those leaves which, once swallowed, didn't pass through but simply flattened against his stomach lining and lay there in glistening repulsiveness until they rotted completely away, at which time they would join in some form or another the general exodus toward his aching bowels. All that putrefying vegetation inside him, Morell knew, was the reason for Hitler's vile breath and chronic constipation; not to mention his meteorism. It was a problem that plagued many vegetarians but with Hitler it had become extreme through stress and over medication for his ongoing variety of must heal ailments. It could all be cured if only the man would rest a little and listen. But how the hell did you tell the leader of the Third Reich that he stank like a camel and had breath like a corpse? Morell decided early on that discretion was by far the better part of valour and, after being shouted down once or twice, kept his mouth shut unless he was quite certain that it was something that the Führer wanted to hear. He was the man with the cure-all syringe and he was doing pretty damn well out of it. No point in rocking this keelless boat.

"**C**ome on, Morell. I do not have all day."

"Of course, Führer, of course." Another quick, professional tap on the body of the liquid-filled syringe and then a sharp intake of breath as he realised that the vein he needed was being deliberately obtuse. Well, of course not deliberately, he leaned his fat head back a little and cursed himself, that was just silly. But he had slapped that damn vein into subcutaneous submission just seconds earlier. Yet there it was – gone! Sighing heavily he replaced the syringe, bent over the recumbent Führer, raised his flaccid arm a little and gave it a slap.

"Ah, slappy, slappy." He said jovially. Well, wasn't every day a man got to smack the Führer of the Third Reich like a naughty schoolboy.

"Shut up and get on with it," the Führer snarled. Normally he was pretty gentle with bottom of the list underlings, only bullying folk such as generals, politicians and the like. But Morell sat in the middle of that hierarchical ladder and so was inclined to receive the best and the worst of the Führer's moods.

"Yes, my Führer, of course." Slap-slap-slap! Nothing. "A touch obstinate today, Führer,"

Hitler's ire was rising by the second. He wanted relief and he wanted it now. That was the only reason for the disgusting little doctor's presence here. His upper lip began a slow journey over his sucrose rotting teeth; a warning snarl was on its way.

Thwack!

"Ouch!" Hitler almost jerked his arm away but Morell, although an out of condition, lardy type of individual was far the stronger.

"There, sir. Got the little devil up at last. All's well. Eh?" Truth was, the expression on Hitler's face was alarming, to say the least. Morell shook slightly as sweat began trickling down his face, his back and a variety of different places that weren't at all pleasant to think on.

That Führer stare was unsettling as Morell plunged the needle into a vein that was disappearing more rapidly than an avenue of retreat for one of Hitler's beleaguered armies. Hitler clearly required treatment for what might be a vein disease or an increase in his current circulation problem. A sclerotherapy procedure, more injections, might help but Morell hesitated to suggest even more additions to an already monumental amount of medication and vitamins prescribed and taken by the Führer.

With surprising deftness he plunged in the second needle and like a vaudeville juggler thrust in the third. The last being an effort to ease the Führer's constipation.

"There, sir. All done. You should try and get some rest now, my Führer, you really should," Morell tried to sound like a genuinely caring medical practitioner but his oily smile was less than convincing. He straightened up and awaited the Führer's dismissal.

"How long before it works?"

"Ah – which one, my Führer?"

Hitler looked pointedly at his rather swollen gut."

"You should experience relief within the hour, my Führer. It might be," he paused and searched for the right words, "a little ferocious initially due to the, erm, previous lack of facilitation with regard to the required movement, so to speak." Again that olive-oil smile. A joke sat on the tip of his tongue but he knew better than to give it verbal form. The Führer abhorred the thought of being considered anything less than a very grave and worthy individual; infallible, even. He was extremely serious about his projected persona, as indeed were all dictators.

Hitler nodded at his physician. "Very well. I'll call if I need you further, Morell. Now leave. I have things to do."

A slight bow from the waist and Morell departed. At least non-military types like himself weren't expected to go around bellowing out all those ridiculous exclamations of Sieg Heil. However, knowing how much Hitler loved his little acknowledgements, he did manage to throw up a scruffy looking salute before he exited through the, for him, too narrow doorway.

With Morell gone Hitler heaved himself into a sitting position grunting with effort as he did so. Morell, thought the Führer gloomily was right, he needed more exercise but there was so little time. Did Stalin have this problem – Churchill? Probably, not, he thought. If the most recent photographic evidence was anything to go by, Churchill was a fat little pig of a man and Stalin a moustachioed chain-smoking rat featured oaf. Odious creeps, the pair of them. War-mongering sons of bitches! He would have them; he would have them all! Yes, he'd have them strung up in public; see how they liked those potatoes.

The Pervitin was working now. Coursing through his system like a comic book superhero and giving him the kind of pseudo energy that made him, for a while at least, able to carry on with the disaster that was fast becoming his Third Reich. There was still no sign of any easing in the bloating of his belly nor any signals from the nether regions that his bowels were ready to ease that condition any time soon. Nevertheless, he was rapidly feeling ready to take on the world – again. He didn't much care for Morell as a man but he was one hell of a knowledgeable medico. Far in advance of those conventional buffoons that attended Himmler and Goering. Letters and qualifications meant nothing; it was a man's innate ability to do a job that counted. Just like Adolf himself.

But even as drugs livened up his sluggish system and gave thought to his otherwise moribund mind, a stark fact about his condition kept nagging away at the Reich's leader. He was becoming forgetful. His normally good memory was a shadow of its former fact-retaining self. He was doing a good job of hiding it, and as yet it was in no way hindering his ability to continue with his work, his destiny. But it was there, the encroaching weakness, and he was acutely aware of his diminishing retentive powers.

The officers gathered around the map table looked up as Hitler returned. Jodl answered calmly when asked about the newest developments. It was becoming a habit of the Führer's to enquire deeply into events when he had been absent from the decision-making core for even a few minutes.

"The situation around Bolkhov has stabilised, my Führer. Von Seidlitz was able to counterattack quite heroically from the south with remnants of 7th Panzer and Holst's battle group. Temporary, I should say, but for the time being at least we are holding them."

"Yes – holding them! Yes! Just as I said we should and now have proven that we can. Yes!"

"Unfortunately, my Führer," stated Keitel pointing at the map with self-important grim foreboding, "The British have taken Syracuse and Catania."

"What?" Hitler stared furiously at the area to which his Field Marshal was pointing and then up at the tall Wehrmacht chief.

"Well, not there, precisely my Führer," spluttered Keitel with embarrassment.

"Oh, really, Keitel – not there? Are you sure? Then why, man, are you pointing to an area some eight thousand kilometres away from that which you speak?" Hitler waved his arms dramatically. "Dear God in heaven is this the best we can do? You Keitel, have just intimated that the goddamned English have somehow landed in Russia and if," he stared down again at the map, "I have my directions right, Herr Field Marshal, they are at present having tea somewhere in the region of Smolensk!"

"Ah, yes. Your pardon, my Führer. Foolish of me. I forgot myself for a moment."

"Clearly," agreed Hitler looking around the room for affirmation. A few barely concealed smirks and polite coughs but nobody looked directly at the discomfited Field Marshal: there but for the grace of God, and all that kind of stuff. Generals like Guderian or Rundstedt would have responded to Hitler's baiting with icy fury, but Keitel admired his Führer beyond all reason and would never raise a doubt or question concerning his abilities and God given genius. Keitel was devoted to his Führer. As for the less put-upon Jodl. That man was simply a practical example of his brethren in the officer corps. He had given his oath, formally acknowledged Hitler as his liege lord and happily accepted the bangles and offices that came with his sworn obedience to the Third Reich's supremo. No questions, just obedience but a firm enough foot stamp if the Führer overstepped the socially acceptable mark. That was Alfred Jodl. The consummate professional.

"As I hope most of you know," the Führer said slowly and sarcastically, "Syracuse is in Italy...."

"Well, sir," chimed in the upper crust major Freytag von Loringhoven, "not precisely *in*, but, rather, part of. It's not de facto *in* Italy. You see?" He smiled a handsome smile and Hitler erupted like a lava spitting volcano.

"Don't you dare contradict me – don't you DARE!"

"Oh, well, I say, sir. I'm most dreadfully sorry. I didn't mean, I mean there was no intent to be disrespectful, sir. None at all. I crave the Führer's indulgence." The aristocratic head lowered and von Loringhoven avoided the Führer's eyes. It was a scary moment but it didn't hurt to dent that pompous little world destroyer's ego a little now and then.

Hitler waved off the major's excuses with a contemptuous "Pah!" Then turned his attention back to the flag dotted map. "IX Panzer and the attendant grenadier divisions on their way to Italy?" Keitel and Jodl nodded in unison.

"Along with XXl Panzer corps as you ordered, my Führer," stated Jodl.

"Bit bloody late if you ask me," muttered von Loringhoven under his breath.

For a short while longer the officers around the map table listened to a variety of suggestions from one another as to the best way to contain the coming Russian offensive. Then Hitler, bowels at last showing signs of moving with true Third Reich thoroughness, excused himself until the next briefing scheduled two hours hence.

CHAPTER 25

July 21 1944: Obersalzberg

Nothing could quite rival the beauty of Obersalzberg in summer, not in Eva's view. Nor in the view of her happily chattering sister, Gretl. They were sitting together on the low wall surrounding the Berghof, the Führer's alpine retreat and gazing down at Berchtesgaden some twelve hundred feet below them. It was a head spinning aspect to those fearful of heights. Indeed, Adolf had warned Eva more than once about her overly athletic fooling around on that wall's narrow ledge. The alpine chalet was comfortable but not overly luxurious, big but not massive. The terrace, though, was delightfully spacious with more than enough room for cavorting dogs when the Führer was in residence, and for energetic, cartwheeling and back-flipping maidens such as Eva. She loved to show off her prowess, which, whilst being extremely limited in the professional sense, was streets ahead athletically of anything that the somewhat pot-bellied and office-bound individuals of Hitler's entourage could hope to accomplish. Last summer, Martin Bormann had been observed openly drooling over her leg spreading handstand, and that whilst his wife had been sitting right next to him. Eva had pretended not to notice and then promptly performed an enticingly revealing cartwheel performance a mere few feet from the gawping Reichsleiter. Naturally, when Hitler had dragged his attention away from Ribbentrop, his foreign minister, and turned his fatherly gaze upon her, she had skipped and giggled and become all innocent and girlie. Leaving the ape-chested, big-bellied Bormann trying desperately to look elsewhere. Particularly anywhere else but at that blasted Alsatian bitch of Hitler's, Blondie. The damn thing had stalked up and sat right at his feet, tongue hanging out and panting like a sea breeze. Bormann had crossed his legs and pretended to pay court to his very long-suffering wife.

Today, however, and for a good few days previously, the Berghof was empty of any of the Führer's self-seeking coterie. Only the very pretty SS guards haunted the terrace and rooms of the echoing Berghof. Eva had noticed a short while ago, that one fellow, not an SS man but a little Wehrmacht gefreiter kept on hand to service the large bronze elevator, liked to yodel. Especially in the cool sweetness of early evening.

The harmless looking gefreiter was regarded as something of a mascot by the much larger SS boys and he would occasionally yodel like a true mountain boy as he stood tip-toeing on the north face of the Berghof's surrounding wall. The echo was a spectacularly glorious sound of in-tune humanity totally at odds with the nondescript appearance of its creator. Just one, high, perfectly delivered falsetto note from the little gefreiter would echo from the mountain walls around them for what seemed like an age. His lightning-fast changes of pitch as he sped up his routine were just downright impossible to imitate even for a professional singer. Gefreiter Henke was a miracle of sound. At times he could turn his bass to falsetto warbling into something resembling Jazz, and then he could drop it all to a slow mournful tone that would bring tears to the eyes of a Tibetan monk. Of course, another reason that gefreiter Henke was tolerated with such hand-clapping bonhomie was the fact that he, and he alone knew the intricate workings of the massive bronze lift which enabled entry and release to and from the Berghof. There had been only the one breakdown so far, but Eva would never forget being stuck at the top of the world with no way down but a sheer rock face. Henke had been flown in three years ago and had not departed since; not even on leave. He loved his job, his yodelling and his safety. The Berghof was a much better place to be than the eastern front.

"Where's little Henke?" Enquired Eva of her sister. "Let's have a sing-song and a party."

Gretl was all for it but a glance around the terrace showed that gefreiter Henke was nowhere near.

"What's that blond boy's name," Eva waggled a finger impatiently at a tall young SS guard, who, in the absence of any superior rank of note was meandering about the terrace looking tall and important.

"Oh, I don't know," Gretl ran her index finger around her sensuous lips and pouted at her sister. "Stonkybonnvonfuhrer, or something like that," she giggled and Eva frowned. "Well," Gretl mock frowned back. "Why do they insist upon using such silly titles? All so grandioso and stuff. Too soppy if you ask me. Whatever's wrong with gefreiter, or feldwebel and good old-fashioned ranks like that? Oh no. It's got to be stumbunführer this and bingbonführer that. Truly silly, Evi, honestly."

"Not so silly when it's Brigadeführer Fegelein, though, is it?" Eva shot back with a huge, knowing smile. "It's all quite alright being the wife of an SS Brigadeführer with all the goodies that entails. Oh yes, little sister. I've seen the way you perk up when men stand rigid for SS Big-wig Hermann Fegelein".

"EVA!" Gretl threw back her head in mock outrage and then giggled lasciviously. "Yeah, you're right. It really is one hell of an aphrodisiac."

"As if you need one when Hermann's around."

Gretl's soft red lips spread across her face in a wide and very sensual smile. "Right again, Evi." Then a small frown shadowed her pretty face. "But I hardly ever see him, sis. He's always off with the Führer at that Head Quarters in Poland or wherever. Can't you have a word with him and get Hermann on duty closer to home – to me?"

"Gretl, you know that I never interfere with what Adi says or does, not even a little. He's very strict about that."

"Oh," Gretl scoffed angrily. "He's strict about everything as long as it's not him being denied. I don't think he knows what real sacrifice is, honestly I don't."

"Shush that kind of talk, Gretl, right now." Eva glanced around. Hitler's official girlfriend she may well be but a few wrong words could so easily change all that. Eva liked and enjoyed her privileged position and didn't want anyone, least of all her spoilt and lippy sister, jeopardising it in any way. Adolf was fine with her putting in her two pennies worth just so long as it was about routine and unimportant domestic matters. Were she so much as to even touch upon something like military postings and such, there would be no telling what his reaction might be: she could make a well-informed guess, though.

Eva had taken what was for her an enormous risk putting her sister forward as a suitable marriage partner for her beloved Hermann. But really, she had done it more in the hope that she would get Hermann closer to her, not her sister. It wasn't working out too well at the moment because her high-ranking SS beau, and now Gretl's husband, was kept insanely busy running to-and-fro between Himmler and the Führer, thus making his visits a longed-for rarity. She, Hermann and Gretl, were playing such a deliciously dangerous game. Old bossy boots tolerated her little peccadillos, much preferring them to the alternative of having to engage in such trysts himself. But it was unlikely that her all-seeing sugar daddy would approve of such decadent licentiousness as a threesome: it was all rather too French.

Eva caught the eye of the wandering SS guard and beckoned him over. She had never taken the trouble to learn what the various uniform insignia and collar flashes denoted. The ranks of the various guards around her were a complete mystery to her and Gretl. They were all one to them. She pointed a finger and smiled questioningly. The soldier responded with a smart click of the heels, the puffing out of a muscular chest and a staccato introduction.

"Scharführer Gunther Weiss, Fraulein. How may I be of service?"

In more ways than one, mused Eva looking squarely at the width of the Hugo Boss enclosed shoulders. This boy was a veritable powerhouse beneath all that SS finery.

"The Wehrmacht man, Henke, I believe. Have you seen him, Scharführer?" She let the consonants slide from her tongue like an invitation. SS types loved all that. Silly boys. So easy to handle but basically not very bright, not even by her standards.

"The Wehrmacht gefreiter? He that repairs the elevator?"

Eva and Gretl nodded together. Scharführer Weiss pursed his lips and looked heavenward for a moment as if seeking inspiration. Hands slapped firmly behind his back he spun abruptly and called out to a colleague. "Menzner, Come here."

"Yes, Herr Scharführer?"

"That Wehrmacht type, Henke. Have you seen him?"

"Yes, sir. He left first thing this morning with Oberschutze Kleist. Both off duty, sir, of course. He had expressed an interest in visiting Dachau. Said he'd never been to a camp and was curious to see what they were like."

Weiss paused for a moment before saying, "Who gave clearance for this?"

"I believe, Herr Scharführer, that Oberschutze Kleist has a relative on the command staff at the camp. It was likely he that gave authorisation. He is due back at the Berghof before 18:30 hrs, sir."

Weiss didn't like what he had just heard. He didn't like it one bit. The popular little gefreiter had gone on a sightseeing trip to Dachau. Aided and abetted by the doubtless well-meaning Oberschutze Kleist. What on earth had induced Henke to want to visit one of those places, Dachau in particular, and what the hell had motivated Kleist into accommodating him? A desire to show off his officer ranking relative, probably. Damn fool!

"Well," Eva interrupted. "When he gets back send him up here, will you? We want to hear a little good old fashioned alpine singing."

It was a two-hour and twenty-minute drive from Dachau to Obersalzberg and they were easily on time to get back to the Berghof before the 18:30 hrs time limit, by which time Kleist would have to report for duty as set by the guard roster in the separate SS barrack hall at the lower reaches of the main building.

As far as Paul Henke was concerned the time of day no longer mattered, not one bit. The wind had been dragged from his sails with a savagery that he had not imagined existed, reducing his normally ebullient personality to that of a condemned man being handed a sentence of death by evisceration. He had been curious for some time about the places he had heard referred to as so-called concentration camps. His only living relative, an aunt in Leipzig, had also been curious and had written asking him if he had any knowledge of such places. His aunt had said that rumours were going around that bad, dreadful things went on in the camps. But, of course, she didn't believe a word of such calumnies: Germans didn't do such things. Although, she conceded, it was war, after all, so prisoners and law breakers should expect to be punished if they did wrong. That was only right and proper. Such men, violent men, needed to be kept under control and learn their lesson. But, his aunt had continued, they were saying that women too were incarcerated in these places. Could that be right? Surely not! And also, she had heard, that horrible and disgusting things were done to them — to the men as well. Not true, of course, but could he ask, perhaps, one of his important SS friends?

Paul asked, and being popular had been invited on a guided tour by his current companion, Oberschutze Hans Kleist. Kleist had a cousin at Dachau who was an Obersturmführer, a rank equivalent in the Wehrmacht of Oberleutnant, which for Henke ranked him with the Gods. Kleist's cousin had been most obliging and Gefreiter Henke received an almost full tour of the facility known as Dachau. The Obersturmführer had assumed, as Henke worked in close proximity to many of the high and mighty of the Reich, that he was au fait with the Reich's radical internment system: Kleist had assumed as much, also. Wrong! Henke got the shock of his life. He hadn't recovered from it and wasn't likely to any time soon.

"An eye-opener, eh?" Kleist's expert hands on the wheel of the two door Kubelwagen were an instant transmitter of confidence to any passenger that might be fearful of the narrow roads and increasingly higher altitudes along which they sped with sometimes terrifyingly devil-may-care abandon. Rubber burning on tight bends, under-steer around long non-barriered curves, and just a generally very robust and juvenile method of attempting to put the fear of God into the little Wehrmacht gefreiter sitting hunched in the passenger seat. All just good clean fun between the lads, nothing more than that.

However, Kleist's display of automotive bravado and skill was completely wasted because Paul Henke didn't give a monkey's toss. He barely even noticed the death-defying manoeuvres being so adroitly accomplished by the SS warrior beside him.

"I said, Kleist repeated. "Quite an eye-opener, wasn't it?"

Henke turned his drawn features to Kleist's wheel enclosing hands and then to his smooth, unlined face. His companion clearly thought that he had done Henke a big favour. The man had asked and he had received. He also quite clearly laboured under the misconception that Paul Henke was happy with what he'd seen and in all likelihood was very grateful, just as he should be. Kleist had pulled on taut family strings to get that tour.

Gefreiter Henke had never witnessed the battlefront. Always being able to find the right job, a timely excuse, or a more important place to be. He was that kind of man. Non-threatening, self-serving, just trying to get through life peaceably type of fellow. His particular set of skills, a God given ability to fix small and large mechanical and electrical motors and coils etc, made him valuable to people that kept small and intricate machines at their disposal. And so, Gefreiter Paul Henke was kept at the disposal of his betters and would continue to be so disposed of for the foreseeable future. But that future, as far as

Henke was concerned, had just come to a shuddering halt. The stifling, heart stopping nightmare he had so recently witnessed, and all in the name of fun and recreation, refused to leave him. The images of human beings in terrible agony, the sounds of their screams still rang in his ears. With such great pleasure had the obliging Obersturmführer cousin of Kleist shown them the state-of-the-art gas chambers. With just a little tut-tutting he had acquiesced to Kleist's request for permission to witness the extermination procedure. Henke had been in a state of barely mobile shock; he hadn't previously been aware that such a thing, such a system existed. The shuffling lines of naked men and women, mostly Jews, being herded toward the chambers put him in mind of pigs being driven toward the slaughter house. So tamely they went, although fouling themselves all the while. With some pride the Obersturmführer had pointed out that the men and women were separated into different lines and entered different chambers. "Must maintain some sense of decency," he'd said, smilingly. "We are not monsters, after all."

Dreadful though it was, that wasn't the worst of it. Kleist's cousin was called away to some emergency or other, and so an SS Schutze, nothing more than a Private soldier really, was called over and ordered to complete the tour on behalf of the Obersturmführer until he could return.

As they passed the clearly labelled Medical Experimentation block Kleist drew to a halt. Dead bodies lay in all death's undignified vileness outside the main entrance to the facility, presumably awaiting collection. It wasn't simply that the bodies were naked and discarded like so much trash, it was the number and the appalling state of them. Some male, some female, all bore marks of the most frightful torture. Henke was by now utterly speechless but his friend Kleist enquired for them. "What on earth goes on here, then?"

"Well, amongst other things," explained their guard, "the doctors experiment here, to see how much pain an individual can take before passing out."

"With?" began Kleist.

"With scalpels and things, but without anaesthetic" replied the guard, grinning widely. "The doctors perform surgeries like appendectomies, cancer removal, or just plain cut things out for the hell of it to see whether or not the patient can survive. All in a good cause, mind. It helps them gauge how much our lads at the front can endure. Well thought out, eh?"

"Without anaesthetic!" Henke managed to gasp out.

"That's right," came the reply. "Can't just go wasting the stuff on sub-humans now, can we?" At that precise moment three shots rang out. Even Kleist almost flew out of his skin.

"Don't worry," laughed the guard. "It's just some of the lads having target practice. He pointed downwind and Henke turned to see three Death's Head guards calmly aiming and firing at a milling group of inmates some eighty metres away outside a cluster of wooden huts behind an electrified fence: a compound within a compound.

"Jews, again?" Enquired Kleist attempting to appear nonchalant.

"Nope. They'll be Poles," came the answer. "We get 'em all in here, you know. Jews, Poles, Russian, Pansies and all sorts. We get 'em, and we deal with 'em properly."

Henke wanted to speak but he couldn't trust himself to open his mouth for fear of the gathering vomit that might spurt out over all and sundry. Not that it would matter here, though. The place was nothing more than a stinking cesspit of human disgrace anyway.

The guard pointed again to the small compound with the electric fence surrounding it. "We keep the women in there," he said, and then suddenly frowned. "Can't say I agree with what goes on with some of the higher-ups what go visiting in there." He frowned again, this time more deeply. "Not that it's any of my business, you understand. No, none of my bloody business at all."

"Don't worry," Kleist said reassuringly. "Mum's the word, matey. We're just here on a day out, not to go spilling tales. Alright?"

The guard nodded, clearly relieved.

Henke, surprised and relieved to find a man who was capable of displaying any measure of humanity in this island of filth, said, "Do the women have no protection at all, then?"

"The women?" The guard looked at him as though he were the village idiot. "It's the officers I bother about, mate. I don't know how they can do it. Lowering themselves to go and fiddle with those sub-human bitches. Jews and Slavs – awful! Polluting their pure blood like that. It baffles me, it really does."

More shots rang out as the Pole shooting guards continued with their practice. Henke knew that he had to get away but knew also, that he must wait for Kleist. They continued slowly on their tour and after each unwilling step Henke felt himself walking deeper into a black hole from which he would never return.

The Berghof loomed in front of them. "Well, my little Wehrmacht chum. Enjoy the trip? Arbeit macht frei, eh? Not for those buggers it won't. Phew. I should say not."

Henke nodded and forced words through tightly compressed lips. "A fabulous day, Hans, can't thank you enough."

"My pleasure, matey. It does folk good to see how we of the SS have things under control. A firm grip we keep, Paul, and make no mistake."

"Saw that," answered Henke. "Saw that very clearly."

"We're showing the world what order and discipline mean, that's a fact. They'll thank us in the end," he laughed loudly. "When we've kicked the shit out of them and shown them who's boss."

Henke didn't bother to argue or disagree. What would be the point other than to guarantee himself one of Kleist's lovingly executed kickings?

The wide fronted garage doors sat in front of them like a signal ending the day's festivities. The jackshaft of the treble width doors rattled as Kleist engaged the remote.

"You go on up, Paul. I've stuff to see to down here before I report for guard duty. Off you trot." He gave a careless wave of dismissal and with considerable relief Henke alighted from the car and made his way to the elevator. Kleist watched him disappear into the ornately designed bronze machine and tutted. The little sod actually looked depressed.

Henke hadn't had a lot of time to put his thoughts in order on the 124-metre ride up to the Berghof proper but it didn't matter. He put any thought of writing to his aunt about the day's experience right out of his head. If any such missive were to be read by someone else it would spell her doom, and the authorities had a nasty habit of reading people's mail: Hell – it would probably be read before it even left the Berghof. Above all right now he wanted a shower. Dear God, the stink that was on him. He reeked of death, excrement and putrefaction. Or so he felt, anyway. Was this the Germany that his friends, those poor innocent fools, had fought and died for? How many Hans Kleists et al were there? That answer didn't require a great deal of thought and was there winging its way around his dismayed mind before the control panel bell rang signifying the completion of his upward journey. Not just hundreds, but many, many thousands. The doors slid open with a smooth whisper, reminding him that today he had not carried out his usual twice daily maintenance check. Fuck it and fuck the lot of 'em! He breathed in deeply but found that he couldn't stop himself from shaking. He was suddenly angry. Angrier than he had ever been in his life.

Light flooded into the spacious elevator interior and faces turned toward the pale faced gefreiter standing uncertainly between the shiny open doors.

"Ah-ha!" A male voice called out. It was one of the guards. "He's here Fraulein Braun."

"Who?" enquired a high feminine voice.

"The yodeller," laughed the guard. "At your excellency's pleasure Ma'am."

"Oooh, wonderful," came another female trill. This time from Gretl Braun. "Tell him to yodel, Eva, please! We need some gaiety; some real music. Not that hideous Wagner crap that your fella keeps playing on the gramophone." Quite a lot of alcohol had been doing the rounds. Even the guards were looking rosy cheeked and shiny eyed.

"Oh, what's his damn name again?" asked Eva.

"It's Henke, I think," replied her sister. "Yes, I'm quite sure, Gefreiter Henke. He's," she waved a dramatic hand whilst holding aloft a glass of champagne in the other, "he's the elevator man, you see. An indispensable chappie for all our clever-clog technical stuff." With that, she fell back giggling into the heavily cushioned wicker garden chair with a thud. As her well-shaped legs flew up attractively into the evening air, one shoe went flying off into nowhere never to be seen again. "Oh, bugger," she moaned plaintively. "I don't 'spose anyone could get that for me?" The likelihood of her request being obliged was every bit as remote as she supposed, for apart from the nattily attired guards, they were the only ones out on the terrace.

"Henke," called out Eva. "Oh that's much too formal," she blew a fussy, wine fuelled raspberry. "What's his first name, Gretl?"

"Oh, how the bloody hell should I know," muttered the very tipsy Gretl leaning forward out of her chair which creaked complainingly as she did so.

"Hey, gefreiter Pumpkin Boy. Give us a song. One of your lovely yodelling songs for the Führer's lovely-lovely, and for little old me *and*, mustn't forget, our glorious, beautifully mannered protectors, the always there when you need them, SS." Her voice dropped seductively on the final two consonants and she stroked her throat with a suggestive hand.

Henke mooched away from the elevator, glanced at a couple of the guards and then trod slowly toward the two sisters. Nobody noticed his more rigid than normal actions nor the enormously enlarged pupils glowering stygian black from his widening eyes.

As he approached with just the trace of a despairingly insane smile tugging at his lips, his mind saw not the cutely curved and over indulged women seated gaily before him, but the naked and abused women shuffling to their deaths just a few hours before at the camp. How would the fortitude of these two female pillars of Nazism compare with the poor terrified creatures that he'd witnessed being herded to their brutal end by pitiless sons-of-bitches using cattle prods and rifle butts? No dignity allowed them; just filth, befoulment and degradation. And yet, there they sat, gay, happy and bleatingly annoying with their high-pitched insistence upon having a good time.

He stood before them. Small, insignificant and whey-faced. His left hand constantly moving just ever so slightly forward and back, as though there was a point that he desperately needed to make but couldn't quite recall it.

"A yodel, little Henke," sang Eva. "One of those beautifully high long ones. We love them best, don't we Gretl."

"Eh? Oh ja," Gretl treated him to what she considered a seductive smile. "Nice and high. That's how we like it my sis and me."

Henke ignored Gretl Braun and just stood staring at Eva. "They squeal, you know. Just like pigs before they die. They squeal really loudly." He looked down at his regulation boots. "You know – I think that I even trod in their shit. Just like dogs' mess. It was everywhere." He gave a shuddering sigh.

"What on earth are you on about," Eva didn't much care what he was on about, she just wanted her song but even in her tipsy state she could see that the little soldier was badly upset about something. Gretl hadn't noticed but she was becoming annoyed at Henke's reluctance to do his yodelling party-piece. Eva leaned back and yawned. "Come on now," she hesitated and then looked up brightly, "Paul, isn't it?" She nodded with sudden certainty. "Yes, that's it. Well, come along, Paul. Don't be a party pooper." She threw her arms wide. "Give us our song."

Henke looked around then up at the sky. "Jesus bloody Christ!" He shook his head and tears appeared like great pools in his eyes. He turned and walked to the surrounding wall and with a surprisingly nimble hop, landed delicately on the 10-centimetre-wide ledge. The women looked on, waiting expectantly for his high, perfect yodel to burst forth and echo throughout the mighty Obersalzberg and its surrounding peaks and crags. He stood for a while staring at them with a disconcertingly penetrating gaze and then said, quite softly and with no trace of rancour, "The awful thing is, you all know and not one of you gives a damn. Goodbye!" With that, he turned to face the cool emptiness surrounding the Berghof, stuck one foot out in front of him like a bather testing the water, and then slowly, very slowly, tilted forward to then vanish into the 124-metre space between him and the rocky ground below where he landed with a life ending splat.

Gretl sat staring at the spot where he had been for a moment before turning to her sister. "I......I don't believe that I've just seen that. Eva?" Taken by a sudden fit of trembling she called again. "Eva!" Eva, though, was in precisely the same state of disbelief as her shocked sister.

The sound of running boots approaching had them both looking at the fast-moving SS guard who, from the other side of the long terrace had seen everything. From below an alarm was sounding and the sound of men running and doors slamming reverberated around the upper and lower areas of the Berghof. The motors of the elevator could be heard whining and then the sliding doors opening and closing as men moved hastily in all directions. Within minutes the terrace was full of armed SS men all disconcertingly cocking fully loaded sub-machine guns and glaring around deeply into the encroaching gloom of the evening as if expecting to see giant blood seeking bats.

Sturmbannführer Walther Hassel came running over to them.

"Did you see, Sturmbannführer?" squeaked Eva. "Did you see what he did? Unbelievable! I don't believe what he just did. He saw it," she pointed at the guard by the wall who was now standing rigidly to attention in the presence of his commanding officer. "Why did he do that?"

"Fraulein Braun." The SS officer lightly clicked his heels without even glancing to see where Henke had thrown himself and his life from the Berghof wall. "You must come inside – now!"

"But I...."

Incredibly and with never before displayed roughness the Sturmbannführer seized Eva by the elbow, hauled her to her feet and then gestured to Gretl. "You too, Frau Fegelein. Forgive me, ladies. But needs must and your safety and protection are of paramount importance."

"Protection?" Gretl said, thoroughly confused. "But he's gone didn't you see or hear anything?"

"Take your hand off of me, Sturmbannführer or I shall report your appalling behaviour." Eva's eyes were wide with anger. Commanding officer of the Berghof security or not, how dare this SS lout lay hands upon her. Just wait until she told Adolf about his effrontery. The commander shrugged. "Apologies but with the greatest respect, what must be done must be done." He spun around and barked orders to two newly arrived NCOs.

"All doors and windows barred and shuttered. Protective steel blinds to be lowered and kept lowered until I command otherwise. Go!"

By now Gretl had become far too tipsy and confused to function sensibly. "What protection mister SS man? He's gone. Jumped, for whatever reason. I dare say you'll find out in due course after you've interrogated," she began giggling uncontrollably, "after you've interrogated the corpse. If," she threw back what remained of her champagne, "if you can piece together what's left of him, that is." Her head went back and she shrieked with drunken laughter. "I mean, locking all the windows and doors – what's he going to do eh? You don't think that he might be just a little out of it by now?"

"Gretl," Eva spoke sharply. "That's enough. The poor man's dead. Show a little...."

Sturmbannführer Hassel had had more than enough. "There has been an attempt on the Führer's life," he cut in. "As yet we have no certain knowledge of how things stand."

Both women were shocked into immediate silence. "Now," Hassel stood to one side and gestured toward the living quarters of the

Berghof. "Inside please. We must guard against all eventualities."

Neither woman so much as moved but stood rigid, staring at Hassel as though he had descended from heaven in a rickshaw.

"It was a bomb, apparently," he conceded in the hope of getting them moving. "Designed to wipe out the Führer and all those closest to him at the Wolfsschanze."

Eva's trembling hand went out to the Sturmbannführer and Gretl too moved uncomfortably closer. He carefully gathered them up in encircling arms and guided them gently but firmly into the house. There he ordered an ageing footman to bring coffee for the ladies whilst he went to the phone and demanded an immediate line to Reserve Army HQ in Berlin. After a few minutes of conversation, he suddenly shot to attention and lapsed into respectful silence as he listened to someone at the other end whose voice he had recognised and who was clearly of a much superior rank. SS men stood by all the windows and doors. Now, Eva could see what was alarming them. The prospect of a coup, if the Führer were dead or incapacitated, was all too horribly real. She felt suddenly very afraid. And then her stomach lurched and everything that she had eaten that evening threatened to come flying up from her gut. Acidic bile swamped her tongue and she swallowed uncomfortably. All thought of poor old Henke was now completely gone from her mind, and Gretl's, too. What of Hermann? Had he been close to the Führer when the bomb went off? Dear God what a bitch of an evening! Her entire position, so carefully crafted and maintained might be threatened. And her lover, the outrageously gorgeous little SS general, her very own Hermann, might be lying a bomb broken ruin in that hell-hole at Rastenburg. Alright, so she shared him with Gretl but she nevertheless regarded him as hers by right. Tears of self-pity appeared at the corners of her eyes. At her side Gretl gulped noisily as she reluctantly arrived at a similar conclusion: Brigadeführer Hermann Fegelein, her Hermann, might well be a victim of that dreadful bomb. Gretl's face mirrored Eva's as they reached for and clasped one another's hot, trembling hands.

There came a loud clack as the SS commander hung up the receiver and marched over to them.

"Berlin is under curfew. Traitors attempted to seize power illegally, the filthy swine. They shall suffer Fraulein; of that you may rest assured. By the bones of Bismarck, they shall suffer!"

"Oh, for heaven's sake. I don't care about all that, I don't. How is…?"

"The Fuhrer," shouted the Sturmbannführer triumphantly, "is alive." He stared around the room almost misty-eyed with joy. "I have just spoken with Herr Goebbels and he assures me and commands that I pass on to Fraulein Braun his best wishes and assurances that the Führer has survived the perfidious attempt on his life and is in full control. The ringleaders of the traitorous gang are being rounded up as we speak." He smiled down at Eva with a fatherly, not to mention condescending, nod of satisfaction.

"Were there any casualties?" asked the rapidly sobering Gretl.

"I am given to understand, Frau Fegelein that there were indeed casualties and that it was a miracle that anyone at all survived. The Führer hails divine providence. Indeed he does."

"And my husband, Brigadeführer Fegelein?"

"Ah. No news as yet, Ma'am but I am sure that all is well. The general is a tough fellow."

"But no news," Eva almost whimpered. She quickly realised her error. She should have made an immediate and enthusiastic display of jumping up and down with delight at the first mention of Adolf's lucky escape but for the life of her she couldn't. Where was Hermann? She saw the expression of confusion cross the SS commander's features. Quickly she composed herself.

"Thanks be to God and his angels for our deliverance," she intoned with deeply dredged up sincerity. "The Führer is saved." She put both arms around a sobbing Gretl. "Hermann will be fine, Gretl. "The Führer would never allow anything to happen to him. You know that, don't you; hmm?"

The Wolfsschanze: Rastenburg. 13.00hrs Earlier That Same Day.

"**W**hat happened – what happened?" His ears hurt like the devil and there was pain in his left arm and one of his legs. "What the bloody hell?" Something was sticking out from his right thigh. It looked like a finger. Great heaven, was it his? No, thank God, no it wasn't but it had most certainly until very recently belonged to someone. He slapped ineffectually at the unwanted fleshy protrusion but only succeeded in bending it slightly to the left. His head swam as he tried desperately to regain some kind of equilibrium. He was lying on the debris strewn concrete floor of the main conference room of the Wolfsschanze. Yes – yes! It was coming back to him now. The explosion. Massive! Dimly at first but then more swiftly realisation made its clawing way into his senses. A Bomb! Assassination? Good grief! He heaved himself up as best that he could into a sitting position and then returning dizziness had him slump heavily back again.

"Be still, Fegelein." It was Morell suddenly looming into view like some malodorous angel of quack medicine and bending concernedly over him. He jabbed something into Hermann's good leg and then deftly removed the protruding finger. "Not yours, I think, but let's be certain." He abruptly seized Fegelein's hands in his own and turned them with an examiner's thoroughness. Hermann shrieked with agony as his previously unnoticed broken left arm made stern protest under such rough handling. "Ah, sorry, dear fellow." Morell ran rough hands over the offended arm. "A break. Just above the elbow. We'll have you carted off to the surgical ward as soon as possible and have you fixed up in no time." He waved at a pair of waiters now conscripted as stretcher bearers. With a reassuring pat on the ankle Morell disappeared from view as he waded through debris and bodies in search of others that might require his skills. The removed finger lay where he had left it. A grimly silent testament to the temporary nature of any attachment in time of war.

The injection of whatever Morell had thrust into his system was working admirably. The pain gradually sank into the background and Hermann was able to look around. The conference room was a wreck. Moans and whimpering pleas for help emitted from the many uniformed bodies lying, or rather, writhing about intermingled with a wide variety of curses and demands of 'where was God when he was needed? And Why Me?' Those and similar comments rang out through the thick haze of almost impenetrable dust and grit that clung heavily all around. Suddenly he froze. The Führer – had they killed the Führer? If that were so then for him personally it was a real disaster. For years now he, Hermann Fegelein, had worked tirelessly to gain access to those nearer the seat of power, to become physically closer to the arbiter of their destiny and giver of all things rich and good. Now it seemed that he might have got his silly self just a little *too* close. It crept unwanted into his mind and he had to know; who the hell was responsible for it? This attempt at a mass killing? for that was precisely what it was, a mass killing. Why had he, an important SS commander, known nothing? Had there been no intelligence? His heart skipped a beat. The Reichsführer. He'd lay money that the cunning devil knew something, perhaps everything about what had gone on. He shook his head and mildly berated himself. You, Hermann, he thought, need to buck up, rest and find a good strong drink. Stop your stupid imaginings man. But were they imaginings? The injection was pulling his mind into stupor and his eyes were closing when he was cruelly brought back to bright and unwanted reality by an apparition of pure comedy.

Standing above him, wild-eyed with trousers in tatters, one trouser leg completely gone revealing an unattractive, pasty white leg, his hair burnt and standing on end stood the Führer of the Third Reich, Adolf Hitler. Dark smudges all over his face had him looking more like an auditioning actor for a Minstrel show than the Reich's commander-in-chief. Hermann just lay there gawping. If only Stalin could see this, he thought, as his mind threatened to wander beneath the onslaught of what he saw before him.

"Destiny," shrieked Hitler, his arms waving dramatically. "Ah, Fegelein? Have you survived?" The Führer squinted down at the recumbent SS officer who attempted a weak smile of affirmation.

"Good, good. As you see, Fegelein, destiny guides me. I have been saved for the Reich that I may continue my good work. And those most worthy have been selected by providence to remain by my side. You see, Fegelein – you see? It was divine providence: a miracle." Both arms raised in a powerful, for him, fist thrusting gesture of Hitlerian defiance. "We shall overcome all obstacles." He waved at everybody he could see. "You have witnessed a miracle and I your Führer have survived the outlandish, the disgraceful plot of our enemies. Have faith! It has been written!" He suddenly became glassy eyed, turned, staggered like an old drunk leaving a bar and would have fallen had not the battered, bruised but ever loyal Keitel caught him just in time.

Roughly and with no show of gratitude he shoved his adoring Field Marshal away from him and then pointed a trembling finger at Fegelein.

"I hereby promote you Fegelein for your exceptional loyalty. You stood with your Führer in time of mortal danger.

Hermann listened in a daze. This was a comedy show, surely? There was nothing real here at all. Well, surreal, possibly, but even that adjective barely described the utter lunacy of what was going on at the moment. Vaguely he heard the Führer loudly promote him to Gruppenführer and Lt. General of the Waffen SS. Now that really *was* a promotion.

CHAPTER 26

July 1944

Himmler paced around in a small never decreasing circle and worried about the constant pain in his stomach. General Walter Schellenberg, his favourite but not particularly effective spymaster, sat in a corner and watched through narrowed eyes. The plot on Hitler's life had failed dismally and even at that moment the perpetrators were being rounded up. The main culprits were either dead or in custody undergoing the kind of interrogation that had even the toughest of them singing like tickled canaries. Men who had thought that they were safe were being dragged out of their houses, barracks and cars at all times of the day and night. The list of those involved was truly staggering. It must be somewhat depressing, Schellenberg mused, for their cake chomping fantasist of a Führer to realise that so many of his own wanted him dead, obliterated – gone! He concealed a flesh wobbling shudder. The savagely vengeful Führer had relieved that avalanche of depression somewhat by ordering his interrogating henchmen to be as brutal as was humanly possible. It was an order that his Gestapo fiends and SS nasties carried out with unbridled enthusiasm.

Sitting just as quietly and directly opposite from Schellenberg was Friedrik Lehmann, today in his full Gruppenführer finery. However, he had determined that after this meeting there would be no more donning of the SS uniform for him. It had become far too much of an attention-grabbing advertisement for horror. This war was irretrievably lost, along with most of the mercantile and financial gains it had initially brought to the Party. That left individuals such as himself, planners and speculators, very much in profit and Bank happy, provided they had planned their escape routes accordingly. As he and the leaders amongst his influential little group had always known, there would at some point be the butcher's bill to pay, and that bill was shortly to be presented to those that were owing. Black uniforms with Death's Head badges and SS insignia would soon, he knew, be on the 'what not to wear' list. Divorce was very definitely on the cards. It had been a good, productive marriage of great convenience and he had provided for himself a more than satisfactory separation settlement. First, though, the uniform along with its emblems had to go. What was once a feared totem of a mighty Reich had now become nothing more than a wretched display of posing losers trying desperately to hang on to what had once been. Too few of the vainglorious fools had any real sense of what was coming. When a State resorted to hanging its own citizens on lamp posts in its own streets one knew well enough that the end was near.

He briefly studied Schellenberg. A handsome man who looked uber smart in his very finely tailored light green Major General of police uniform. He also held the rank of SS Brigadeführer but considered the cut and colour of the police general's uniform to be greatly superior. Schellenberg, Lehmann knew, wanted above all else to always look good. The normally chain-smoking police general glanced back at Lehmann and smiled coldly. Schellenberg knew what Lehmann thought of him and could not have cared less; he was a chain smoker, though, and just a little over two hours in the fanatically non-smoking Reichsführer's company was an agony of nicotine denied hell. He brushed imaginary cigarette ash from the top of his jodhpur style pants.

"Sir," his voice for one so seemingly effete was surprisingly deep and authoritative. "I reiterate," glancing again across at Lehmann and hoping for some support he leaned forward in his chair. "With all the confusion you should now, NOW sir, take control of the Reich. The SS will obey you to the hilt, to the last man, Herr Reichsführer. Now is the time to put into action the ideas which you so plainly outlined just four days ago. The Führer may not be dead but he is most certainly incommunicado at least for the time being." Schellenberg didn't care whether Hitler was alive or dead. He only knew that if they were to save anything at all of what remained of the Third Reich, then, they must act now, 'cos otherwise they were all headed to hell in a slop bucket. He suddenly stood erect and slapped out a crisp Nazi salute. Walter Schellenberg was one of the few men able to bring off that particular piece of Nazi theatre with any kind of panache. He did, in fact, look pretty damn good doing it.

"Heil the Führer. Heil Himmler."

Lehmann gave his neatly manicured fingernails a quick inspection and smiled. Not bad. Not bad at all. Heil Himmler? Had a nice familiar ring to it. With just the lightest touch of sarcasm he said,

"A somewhat more careful approach might be more appropriate, Walter. It's now pretty clear that Hitler, the Führer, is not dead. Always a somewhat unlikely scenario if you ask me. Furthermore, and I say this with the greatest respect, we have no proof that the SS in its entirety will support our esteemed Reichsführer. I speak of the Waffen SS, of course. They are every bit as likely to support some deranged general or other."

Himmler paused his pacing and looked from one to the other of his subordinates. News from Rastenburg was still sketchy. Certainly there had been an attempt on the Führer's life but then, that was no surprise as he, Himmler, had known about it anyway. Well, he had been able to hazard what turned out to be a pretty accurate guess, at least. The bomber/assassin Stauffenberg had left a trail of clues that a lobotomised grave digger could have followed. Really, all so inept. The Reichsführer now held all the important cards; all his to do with as he wished. It required only the will to succeed. The reputation of the feared SS chief would in many cases be sufficient to ensure obedience.

Canaris and Oster of the Abwehr were done. He had all the information concerning their traitorous dealings with the enemy over the years and would arrest them both very soon and happily extract further information from their vile, lying lips before he had those lips sliced off. He would teach that pair what it meant to mock Heinrich Himmler.

Lehmann glanced at his watch. He had been one of the original *Friends of the Reichsführer group* way back in 1935. It had been immensely profitable all round. Himmler had risen to power and prominence and the group had made vast fortunes on the back of the many concentration camps. Time now though, to decamp. Himmler, as Lehmann had discovered some years previously, was the ultimate vacillator. It would be the death of him, Lehmann reckoned. The Reichsführer seemed unable to function without the sanction and approval of his master Adolf Hitler. Even when that man had been reported dead, Himmler had been unable to take any real action but constantly demurred. Favouring first one course of action and then drifting toward another. Hopeless! Hitler, as it transpired, although somewhat damaged, was still very much alive. He was, however, in no position to defend himself before a powerful and determined attack. A coup now, fronted by the Reich's chief of the SS and all state police, plus the reserve army in Berlin, was bound to succeed. But Himmler merely vacillated, made important sounding noises, hummed and dithered until the opportunity for successful action was gone. Hitler's always loyal propaganda minister, Goebbels, had seized the initiative and now was commanding in Berlin. Defences were being shored up. True-blue Nazi majors were being immediately promoted to generals, corporals to captains and so on. This wolf was not going to whine nor roll over and show its submissive belly. The beast was surviving. Goebbels was in touch with the Führer and the likelihood of any coup led by Heinrich Himmler succeeding had become remote. Too remote by far for Friedrik Lehmann to want to bother with.

Lehmann coughed lightly and prepared to make his excuses. It was all completely academic. He would bet his life that Himmler would never dare mount any kind of coup. It went totally against his leader obeying psyche. Even if they had brought him Hitler's head on a plate, Lehmann knew that the Reichsführer would still have vacillated interminably. Nevertheless, Schellenberg was a clever and manipulative devil, so, let him have his say and attempt to live out his fruitless dream. He, Lehmann was off to healthier climes.

"If you will excuse me, Herr Reichsführer," said Lehmann softly as he rose to his neatly booted feet. Himmler's steel grey eyes glittered behind his pince-nez but he nodded permission for Lehmann to continue. "My appointment with Armaments minister Speer necessitates my leaving. With your permission, of course."

"Yes. By all means, Lehmann. Be sure to pass on my best regards to Herr Speer, won't you."

"Naturally, Reichsführer." Lehmann had no intention of doing any such thing. The two men despised one another. If there was one man in the world that Himmler wanted to kill but could not, that man was Albert Speer. Speer always wanted, needed, more Jews for his projects and constantly worked to circumvent Himmler's total control over all Jews in Reich controlled territories. Occasionally they had cooperated, come together in mutual support but too often they were at loggerheads. Bribes and favours abounded, retribution and firing squads answered back. Nevertheless, for the past couple of months the two men had made firm efforts at rapprochement to facilitate their own aims. They loathed one another but were making an effort to get on, Führerprinzip notwithstanding.

A lazy but gracefully executed Hitler salute and Lehmann made his exit. Schellenberg was pleased to see him go. Lehmann was a man holding high SS rank but, as far as Schellenberg could see, merely played at what he considered to be a contemptible little game. Rumoured to be filthy rich but never making an outward display of those riches. Something of an untrustworthy enigma. Yes, Schellenberg was glad to see him go.

"Will you act now, Herr Reichsführer?" Schellenberg's tone was becoming insistent and to Himmler, more than a little annoying. People seemed to think that because of a few little military reverses on the battlefronts, they could become over-familiar with their betters. Well – not in this office!

"And do what?" The Reichsführer demanded icily. "Wave my magic SS wand and defeat the Russians and their allies in a flash? Is that what you expect, my dear Schellenberg?"

"Well…." The police general gestured with both hands open. "Surely, sir, a word from you and things could be, well, put in motion so to speak."

"No," Himmler scratched the side of his nose thoughtfully. "I don't think so." He withdrew a sheet of paper from beneath the blotting pad on his desk. "Know what this is?"

Schellenberg bit back the savagery of a reply that flew to his lips. How the bloody hell could he possibly know what it was that the Reichsführer was waving in front of him?

"No sir. No idea at all."

"Then, I shall elucidate," said Himmler in his best schoolmaster's tone. "I have been in touch with a man called Bernadotte."

Schellenberg shook his head. He had no idea who this Bernadotte might be. So he asked the question.

"And who might that be, sir."

"What he is, Schellenberg, my dear fellow, and you should know seeing as how you are the principal spymaster of the SS. My eyes and ears, so called," he nodded accusingly at his subordinate and that man slouched his superbly accoutred shoulders under the obvious put-down.

"Any ideas?" The Reichsführer asked, clearly not expecting a positive response.

Schellenberg shrugged hopelessly. "None sir."

"Well," Himmler sighed. "He just so happens to be vice president of the Swedish Red Cross. He and I have spoken on other occasions, just a few you understand, and I have decided to put out peace feelers."

"What!" Taken totally unawares Schellenberg reeled backward. Had he heard right – the always convinced of final victory SS Reichsführer, Hitler's mainstay and most loyal support was sneaking around looking for peace?

"Tentatively at the moment, it is true. But thanks to my dear General Wolff, I have been put in touch with a man who can, hopefully, facilitate such matters. Surprised?"

"Oh. Well, you know." Christ on a broomstick, he needed a cigarette now. He waved a seemingly indifferent hand. "Just a little, Herr Reichsführer. You have always seemed so devoted to and confident of victory therefore I, amongst so many others, never dreamt that you harboured any doubts about the outcome of the war."

"Ah, that," Himmler smiled his icy smile. "I don't have any doubts my dear fellow. None at all. We are star crossed; I fear. Or, rather, this Reich as it presently stands is utterly buggered! It is now a question of saving what we can from the wreckage of Hitler's, shall we say, misguidance."

Schellenberg felt a distinct shortage of breath at the Reichsführer's damning admission of his true opinion of the Führer and his leadership. He also felt a stirring of unease deep in his belly. Why was Himmler confiding so dangerous a secret to him? Of course, the answer came almost as quickly as the question had formed. Himmler somehow knew of his dealings with the British. Dealings in which he sought to cover his own rather grubby wartime tracks as defeat loomed ever closer. The paranoic Reichsführer had watchers and spies everywhere, but the abrupt and unexpected realisation that his master had known all along of the clandestine workings of the AMT-V1 office, *his* office, came as a skin tightening shock. As Himmler's spymaster and head of AMT-V1, control of all foreign and much domestic intelligence was Schellenberg's and he had considered himself to be almost bulletproof. Now, it would seem, that even he had been closely watched. He managed what he hoped was an urbane smile of soldierly confidence and companionable agreement, for he knew by now that Himmler was playing one of his much-loved cat-and-mouse games. One toe pointed so much as a fraction in the wrong direction and it would be chop-chop-chop for him. Walter Schellenberg was a born survivor. He could switch from fawning waiter to cold-eyed mass killer in less than the bat of an eyelid. He decided upon the 'I am your man and shall be always by your side' approach. It generally worked with freaks and fantasists such as Himmler. Even so, the police general thought ruefully, Himmler had switched fantasies with remarkable ease and aplomb. Had he underestimated the man? No, not underestimated, misjudged. They had all misjudged this chinless, black clad instigator of sadism and death standing so innocuously, like an overdressed wages clerk, beside his desk. Time to play his trump card: verbal grovelling, and if that didn't work the revelation of some ultra-secret affairs of other high ranking SS members.

Taking in a deep breath Schellenberg spoke slowly and with heart-warming sincerity. "I can assure you Herr Reichsführer that I and my department have always admired your thoughts and actions and will guarantee to..."

Himmler cut across him with a hiss so loud that it resembled iced water being thrown over molten rock. "Lend your full support and undivided loyalty? I'm sure you will!" He stared at Schellenberg for a full minute. That man lowered his eyes, coughed delicately so as to display his complete subservience and awaited his master's next utterance. Himmler had him all ends-up. He could not, dared not go against the man who knew but pointedly ignored the fact that his first wife had been half Jewish and so, ipso facto the son from that marriage was deemed a Jew. A most frightful embarrassment to his SS adherent father who now deeply regretted his early infatuation with Käthe Kortekamp. Such a pretty girl, although a little older. Sweet natured, obliging and an absolute gem in every way other than the fact that she never gathered up the courage to tell him of her Jewish birth and background. She had naively hoped that he would never find out. Although only a seamstress, she had supported him financially and it had never occurred to him that she was a Jew. When he found out he erupted in a storm of rage and disbelief and ended their short marriage whilst at the same time disavowing their infant son. It was too late, though, to hide it from the likes of Himmler and Heydrich. Perilously close to breaching the recently enshrined Nuremburg Laws, Walter had feared for his career, perhaps even his life. Himmler, though, valued his services even then and had allowed Otto, the son of that ill-fated union, to remain in relative comfort and safety. Little Otto became what was referred to in the Third Reich, as a privileged Jew; rather like a protected wildlife species. For the mother, Käthe, however, there was no such clemency. She was shipped off to Ravensbruck concentration camp where she died some five months later. Schellenberg barely knew his son and never once visited him but he did his best to keep him alive. A fact of which Himmler was well aware. One wrong move would most certainly see the agonizing death of the boy. Walter often dwelt upon the exigencies of life; his life anyway. Not to protect the child would have those above him sneering with distaste and contempt. What kind of man, Jew or Gentile, would not protect his own child regardless of the cost? Even amongst the callous evil of Nazi hierarchy family meant something. One's offspring may be nature's misfortune but nevertheless, they *were* one's own flesh. And a damn nuisance too, as far as Walter Schellenberg was concerned.

"Loyalty binds me, Herr Reichsführer," said Schellenberg smartly clicking his heels and puffing out his chest. The phrase had suddenly come to him out of the blue. He couldn't for the life of him remember from where it originated. Probably some second rate play he'd seen somewhere. It sounded good though, so he stood there waiting for a response.

"Yes, of course it does. But here's the thing, Schellenberg." Himmler rocked slightly back and forth on his booted feet. The elevated insteps, giving him an added five centimetres in height, were beginning to irritate the soles of his feet. Gods, he clicked his tongue in self-pity. The things he had to suffer to keep up morale boosting appearances.

"I may need, my dear Schellenberg, to make use of your no doubt profound loyalty in the very near future. It will be tested, General, mark my words. That, along with your extreme talent in the field of covert operations."

"The Reichsführer need only command," Schellenberg murmured, wondering what the hell Himmler was droning on about. The man constantly cloaked the outstandingly obvious inside a cloak of mystery and suspense.

"I wish only to serve, Herr Reichsführer." Oh, for heaven's sake! He almost stamped his foot in annoyance. Even to a man known for his ability to transcend all normal levels of grovelling, that sounded just *too* whingeingly awful.

"And so you shall, Walter. So you shall." There it was. The use of the first name. Himmler was being nice to him. Like a tiger licking one's face just before it bites your head clean off.

"I want you, Walter, using all the facilities of your very excellent AMT-V1 office," he paused a second, "Such fine, fine people you have there, Walter." A cold, ugly smile crossed the Reichsführer's pasty little face. "Utterly trustworthy types – to a man."

Schellenberg gulped and felt his bowels turning to water. So there it was. Himmler had his own men within the very heart of Schellenberg's little espionage empire. The son-of-a-bitch! He, Schellenberg, had trained, vetted and promoted each of those men personally.

"Are you still listening, Walter?" Himmler smiled again but a little more warmly this time. "You seemed to have drifted off for a moment."

"Oh, no, certainly I am listening, Herr Reichsführer. And yes, sir. They are all such good men. A credit to the Third Reich, sir, if I may say so?"

"Oh, yes, indeed you may." Himmler's eyes belied the gentle expression on his face. Schellenberg attempted briefly to exert some form of masculinity and return a stare to those vine snake eyes but failed miserably.

"Now, to business and then you must get away to your duties."
Schellenberg nodded as his chief continued. "What I want,
Schellenberg is, as I mentioned previously, for you to use the full
resources of your office to arrange, monitor and ensure security for
further meetings with Bernadotte. You will transcribe all future
meetings and, of course, arrange transport. Further still, and this
may come as a surprise to you, I want you to negotiate with this
Swedish Count, that's the Bernadotte fellow, to arrange the release
of, shall we say, three thousand Jews."

Schellenberg, for no particular reason that came to mind, suddenly
thought of his son, Otto, ensconced somewhere in Berlin and living
hopefully a secure little life, despite the savage bombing day and night.
He found himself tapping his pockets uselessly in a knowingly fruitless
effort at discovering a notepad and pen.

"Righto. Three thousand I believe you said, Herr Reichsführer? If
I could just write that down."

Himmler pursed his lips and looked at the ceiling. "It's not a damn
recipe, Schellenberg and SS generals are not expected to trot around
like hotel waiters with order pads. The details you need are already on
your desk awaiting your total and undivided attention."

"Which, of course, sir, they shall receive." It was the shock and
confusion caused by this latest revelation from the Reichsführer that
had Walter, normally so cool, calm and calculating, now going all of a
fluster. Here was the man, standing directly in front of him, the man
whose one real goal in life, as he had so drearily repeated ad infinitum
over the years, was the unquestioned and unquestionable eradication
of the entire Jewish race by whatever means possible; and now here
was that very same man advocating some kind of deal which would see
the release of many hundreds of them. The Himmler that the Third
Reich knew and loved, trusted and admired, would sooner be hung
naked on a Synagogue door than agree to such a thing. Monstrous!
Unbelievable and, to say the least, as far as Walter Schellenberg was
concerned, more than a little strange. How the devil had this come

about? What on earth had Himmler been up to these past few months, or was it years?

"It is likely," Himmler continued, "that either Bernadotte or one of his aides might try to up the ante. I want you to make it quite clear to all concerned, Schellenberg, they'll get what they pay for. Understood? Three thousand Jews for Bernadotte to do what the devil he likes with in return for advantageous and non-protracted peace negotiations when the time comes. At a later stage, if all goes well, we can discuss the release of a further three thousand, along with, say, six hundred prisoners of war and some three hundred females. Dependent entirely, of course, upon the criteria that I stipulated being met in full. No tricks, right?"

Schellenberg nodded somewhat less than enthusiastically.

"I am fairly certain," Himmler went on, "that I shall be ensconced by our future friends, the Americans, as the overall Reich police chief and, possibly," he smirked condescendingly, "As Reichpresident. That I am highly regarded by our allied friends is patently obvious."

"It is?" Schellenberg couldn't help but display some doubt about that last statement from the Reichsführer

"Of course, my dear fellow. They need me. Who else will be able to keep law and order in an appropriate manner? I possess the knowledge, the manpower and the clout."

"And the, er, camps, sir?"

"Oh, yes. Well, we'll have to scale those back a little."

"A *little?*" He didn't know whether to laugh or cry.

"Why, yes. We borrowed the ideas from them after all. They should be flattered, don't you think?"

Schellenberg felt his legs becoming rubbery. Bubbling somewhere down in his belly was a shriek of laughter that threatened to burst forth at any moment.

"Anyway, you know what's expected of you, Schellenberg. Get these negotiations going. You will have a pool of ten thousand Jews to negotiate with. That should do you for a while. If you need more just ask. Keep away from Speer and above all, Schellenberg, do *not* breathe a word of what we have discussed outside of this office. Hitler must never know. It would cloud matters beyond redemption and end the lives of more than you can possibly imagine."

Wrong! Schellenberg could easily imagine the loss of life and the awfulness of its ending all too well. He moved toward the door.

"It shall be as you say, Herr Reichsführer." His right arm made to throw out the usual Hitler salute but under the circumstances, it seemed rather a pointless thing to do so he left it. Just as he reached the door, Himmler asked. "Tell me, Schellenberg."

"Yes, Herr Reichsführer?"

"When I meet Eisenhower, should I bow or offer my hand?"

Frozen-faced, as if seeing his superior for the first time, Schellenberg said, "I rather think that a straightforward cap salute should do the trick, sir."

"Yes," murmured Himmler. "You're probably right. Oh – and one other thing before you leave." There was that icy 'coming to get you look' again.

"Yes, sir?"

"Arrest General Hans Oster immediately. Understand? Alive and well and ready for interrogation. The swine is guilty of treason." A flick of the wrist dismissed Schellenberg to his duties and he departed. Poor Hans Oster. There would soon be a lot of chickens coming home to roost. He wondered how much longer the Abwehr chief, Admiral Canaris could stay out of it all. The Reichsführer SS was clearing the decks and desks of all those that might cause him problems. Just keep doing as you're told, Walter, dear boy, he told himself. He made a mental note to check up on Hermann Fegelein. It was odd that Himmler never mentioned his top liaison officer. Information was power and Walter felt a growing need for more information. And Fegelein had lots of it.

CHAPTER 27

August 1944: Gestapo Headquarters, Berlin.

The former Decorative Art Museum had lost much of its former charm. In fact, it had lost it all. There were no longer exquisitely manufactured tables and chairs on show to an admiring public. No expertly turned ceramics and glassware, no beautifully woven textiles. The only expertly turned metalware now in the place consisted of padlocks and metal framed interrogation tables and chairs at the lower levels. Here, at ground level, the furniture was sturdy and functional but with no pretensions to art or sublimity of form. As for pictures. The old museum hadn't been known for bothering much with the 'fine arts', as they were known but some of the walls were adorned with prints of Frederick the Great and Adolf Hitler. The same pattern repeated itself on the two vast floors above where the Third Reich's police and intelligence services beavered away day and night attempting to make sense of the encroaching horror that was fast approaching Berlin from what seemed to be all corners of the earth.

General Walter Schellenberg made his way down the wide and damp concrete stairs to the long corridored and many roomed basement area below. Down here, in a maze of soundproofed and steel doored rooms one could, if one listened intently, hear the screams of the damned. The stench of disinfectant and carbolic was pretty well overwhelming. The frightful mess that people in extremis could make was truly quite appalling and the reek of human waste clung to the walls, floors, everywhere; there was just no disguising what manner of place this was beneath the regal exterior of what had once been part of the old government quarter on the venerable Prinz-Albrecht-Strasse. It was human devised hell; a place where human beings had the chance to show off to one another just how far, since the days of the Roman Colosseum, humanity had advanced in areas of inducing pain and terror. From the good old standby of raw bone crunching beatings to electric needles and nerve extraction, the Third Reich could congratulate itself. In this, if nothing else, it quite possibly was a world leader.

Schellenberg had stepped out in his SS Brigadeführer uniform today. It made sense as he needed access to certain areas of the Gestapo HQ and his nice, crisp SS general's uniform, if not as snazzy as his police effort, looked the part. Heavily badged and scary; Just the ticket.

Poor old Hans Oster had been arrested two days ago, just as Himmler had ordered, and was at present subject of the rather probing and unpleasant ministrations of a wonderfully gifted Gestapo operative, or torturer to use plainer language. Walter despised the American manner of using euphemisms for unpleasant events or actions. A spade was a spade and that was the end of it.

General Oster had been taken as he entered his Abwehr office and brought without ceremony immediately to Gestapo HQ. His interrogation had begun the moment he entered the downstairs room, 310. Stripped of his general's red stripe uniform, questioning of the unfortunate Oster had begun well before Schellenberg was able to arrive. Walter was no softy but he was harbouring some small hope that he might be able to save his friendly acquaintance at least *some* unnecessary pain. A few soft-spoken words, vague promises, just enough to gain his trust and get some relevant information. That Hans

Oster would eventually talk he had no doubt; everybody did in the end, but talk about what? That was the question. Oster might have tripped up but that didn't negate the fact that he was a clever old sod and had stuck his fingers in many pies.

With his highly polished boots rhythmically slapping the concrete floor with each measured stride, Schellenberg arrived at room 310. He made an abrupt gesture and the single accompanying guard leaned forward and pushed open the heavy steel door.

The room was of medium size and well-lit by two 100-watt bulbs which hung with eye stabbing brightness from the heavily white-washed ceiling.

A slim man of slightly above average height sat across from the badly beaten and trembling Hans Oster. The general's wrists were securely clamped by iron embossed leather straps to a steel framed chair with a commode-like seat. The chair itself was drilled into the floor but not so the long metal table beside which it sat. The table shone with a metallic menace and contained various curves, indentations, wickedly curved hooks and stays which, along with the thick, sweat hardened leather straps placed at intervals around the scratched and shiny work surface, could be used to restrain a victim in any variety of horribly unpleasant and previously unimagined positions. Sitting at a smaller and far less offensive looking table by the far wall, was a short blond female stenographer. Her little state-of-the-art steno machine sat before her and her chubby red-nailed fingers were poised above the keys like a bird of prey ready to claw out the entrails of its latest victim. No mini-brained shorthand scribbling harpy here. The high rank of their current object of attention demanded that every word, grunt, groan and shriek be taken down with the greatest accuracy.

Oster's feet were bare and he was stripped down to his red striped trousers which were by now badly stained. Clearly, the trousers had recently been thrown back on and Oster's body had received a great deal of previous pain and indignity from the clerkish looking man sitting cross legged in front of him. Oster's chest, back and belly were a mass of dark bruises and facially he had been beaten almost beyond recognition. His nether regions, Schellenberg knew, would already be a mass of yellow and black bruising.

Had they started with the electrodes yet, Schellenberg wondered? It didn't much look like it. That little box with its innocuous looking wires and pads sat as yet unused on a medical trolly to one side of the interrogator, a man by the name of Obersturmführer Gustav Nagel. The studious looking SS officer had followed protocol and, after a medical examination to ensure that the almost sixty-year-old general could withstand severe interrogation, had begun with the softening up process of a non-lethal but very thorough beating just to get things going. For that, he would have used a now absent junior NCO rather than crack his own precious knuckles on a hard target like someone's skull. They had men aplenty trained and ready to do such work.

Nagel uncrossed his legs and stood before his ranking superior.

"Herr Brigadeführer. We have been expecting you, sir."

"Preliminaries done with, then?"

"Yes, sir, indeed they are." He gestured toward the stenographer. "Everything that the prisoner has said we have on record. Some quite interesting stuff, sir. I'll make sure to send you a transcript of the detainee's responses later today."

"Good." Schellenberg nodded. "Now, you can get out."

Nagel looked up, startled out of his calm demeanour by Schellenberg's abrupt tone of command.

Schellenberg turned slightly toward the door and gestured heavily. "The both of you – out. Now!"

"With respect Herr Brigadeführer," protested Nagel, "you do not have the authority to command here."

"What?" Schellenberg leaned forward threateningly. "What did you just say Obersturmführer?"

Nagel quailed beneath the ferocious glare of his SS superior and glanced involuntarily at his stenographer.

"I am here," snapped Schellenberg using his best snarl to great effect, "at the express orders of the Reichsführer SS Heinrich Himmler. Do you understand? The Reichsführer himself no less, and he demands my absolute attention to every detail and awaits my report, Obersturmführer. I am to interrogate the prisoner personally in any way that I see fit and I see fit to see you GONE!"

"I.... I" the smooth manner had completely left the interrogator by now. This was way out of order and beyond anything that he had encountered before but to gainsay a Brigadeführer with Himmler's carte blanch could be a very bad move indeed. He rose and gestured to the stenographer to do the same.

"Of course, sir, Herr Brigadeführer. But I must, sir, of necessity put this down in my report."

"As you wish. Now leave."

Almost on tip-toe Nagel and the stenographer scuttled past. The normally omnipotent Obersturmführer's ego was more than a little put out by all this. He and the little blonde had a thing going and she was apt to reward him handsomely with her favours whenever he allowed her to be in attendance during the more frightful and scream inducing interrogations. Her excitement at the conclusion of one of her ever-so-handsome SS beau's exquisite sessions in these cold, terrifying rooms was almost beyond description. Sexually enthusiastic didn't even come close. Rampant and loaded with expletive shrieking perversion might have been nearer the point. She was certainly noisy, hip grindlingly insatiable and, when it came right down to it, unbelievably accommodating to a man of Nagel's very strange tastes. It was an excellent arrangement and now this bastard Schellenberg had come in and ruined it all for him. He'd made Nagel look and feel inferior, small in every way. Well, one never knew. Perhaps, just perhaps, the handsome and oh-so-suave SS and Police general might himself end up in here one day, strapped to a chair before a grinning Obersturmführer Gustav Nagel gleefully displaying his electrodes and needles along with his buxom little blonde.

Walter toed the heavy door shut as they left and then turned to the broken figure in the chair. He was known as a glib, rather facetious man prone to a flippant turn of phrase but none such sprang to his lips right now. He had known Hans Oster in his glory days as the man rose through the officer ranks all the way up to major general and second in command of the now doomed Abwehr. There was precious little that was glorious about Major General Hans Oster now, nor ever would be again.

Walter sat casually on the seat that Nagel had just vacated and looked long and hard at Oster. He tried to appear complacent but what was the point? Oster was beyond giving two twists of a baboon's tail of caring about impressions whether feigned or real. Barely able to breathe through his ripped and bleeding nose, one eye completely and grotesquely shut with the other so badly damaged that there was just the barest slit for Oster to peer through. Teeth? Pretty well all gone; two of them were firmly embedded deep within the uncontrollably shaking general's upper lip. His left ear no longer bore any resemblance to an auditorial organ at all; it was reduced to a messy, congealed lump of what now looked like the discarded remnants of processed meat. The remains of it were stuck revoltingly to the side of his swollen cheek. Poor old devil, thought Schellenberg, sadly. What a bloody awful comedown. Might as well get on, though. Quicker this was all done the quicker he could get out of this hell-hole.

"What on earth induced you to be so stupid, Hans?" he enquired gently. "Dear God man, look where it has led you."

Oster's breath came in rasping heaves. They had been rougher than they should have been but, then, there had been the pouting little blonde to impress. Sons of bitches, thought Walter. Nevertheless, the gentle approach might work pretty well now. An older man once subjected to this kind of ego breaking treatment was liable to crack and burst into tears at the first approach of anything that might appear to be a concern for his well-being. With a first-rate impression of a man deeply concerned for another's welfare, Schellenberg leaned forward and smiled sadly.

"My poor chap. Truly, if there were something that I could do to bring all this to an end, I would do it. Please believe me Hans." He touched the shaking and broken general lightly on a bruised shoulder whilst at the same time trying hard to force a tear from the corner of either eye. "I am going to do all within my power, Hans, to halt this criminality. But, Hans, my dear fellow, you have to give me *something*. Himmler's got himself all hot and bothered and there's no telling what awful things he might do: you know, family, children, that kind of thing." Hiding his distaste for the smell emanating from the ageing former Abwehr deputy head, Walter placed his own handsome and well coiffured head close to Oster's good ear. In a conspiratorial whisper he murmured, "We have arrested and dealt with all those connected with the bomb plot at Rastenburg. What we want Hans, is for you to tell us what role, precisely, Canaris played in all this. Not just now but over the years. Tell us, me, Hans and this treatment stops. I'll have you whistled away to a safe camp where you can rest and heal. No more pain or humiliation. Come on now – what do you say?"

"Fuck you, you bland, useless oaf." Oster spat blood and sputum forcing Schellenberg to reel back as nasty bits splattered his lovely uniform and pristine features. Just as his face was beginning to turn into a snarl of anger, Oster burst into tears.

"I'll tell you," he whimpered. "I'll tell you but you won't like it. Even a selfish swine like you will want to throw up."

Schellenberg stared for a moment and then gathering himself together, he said. "Go on, then Hans but be warned. Anything like that again," he indicated the small spatters of blood on his black uniform, all trace of mister nice guy now completely gone, "and I shall personally place those electrodes," he jerked his head toward the medical trolley holding the threatening gadgets, "in the vilest reaches of your body imaginable. Clear?"

"I'll tell you, Walter Schellenberg. There's no one else and no other way – and it must be told."

"For God's sake go on, then." Schellenberg was impatient to know what it was that despite his awful and agonizing situation, had the once imperturbable Hans Oster in such a tear-dropping flap of guilt.

As the minutes rolled by, and Oster's once cultured but now hoarse and ragged tones droned on, Schellenberg's expression, changed from one of deliberately studied boredom to one of smirking disbelief. Then, after listening for a few minutes more, a tic appeared beneath his left eye. Slow at first but gathering pace, as Oster continued with his confession. Colour drained from the tautening skin around Schellenberg's face until his pallor pretty well matched that of his prisoner. The betraying tic worked like a maggot on a flame and Schellenberg actually slapped his own eye in an attempt to still its horror betraying origins. Oster became silent and all that could be heard was the harsh, uneven breathing of both men. Schellenberg it was who broke the silence. There was no disbelief on his face now, and certainly no sign of a smirk. He stared at Hans Oster as if seeing him for the first time. Slowly, almost like an old man rising from a wheelchair, he rose and took three heel scuffling steps away from the prisoner and then turned with a clawed hand and a semi wave of realization at Oster.

"You," a pursed lipped whistle of air escaped from Schellenberg as he attempted to frame his words. "You are telling me, trying to tell me, that...." He rammed clenched fists into the sides of his legs and threw his head back, shaking it to and fro in a paroxysm of, what? He didn't know. Disbelief, despair, anger? He marched straight at the head hanging Oster, leaned forward and grabbed him by the throat. "You did that – it was YOU? You son of a bitch. You vile piece of filth Oster. How the fuck could you?" Probably for the first and only time in his life major general of police and Brigadeführer of the SS, Walter Schellenberg, was so profoundly shocked at the actions of another human being that he was finding extreme difficulty in forming his words. Indeed, at that moment any cogent thought or action was impossible. There was just a dull feeling growing inside of him, about the insane inevitability of it all. There had never been any chance at all of victory; not from the very beginning. Even with Hitler's hopelessly inept leadership they might have stood some kind of chance of an at least limited success. That the entire thing was a monumental but nevertheless avoidable disaster on a never-before-seen scale of death and destruction, was down to the broken, snivelling secret bagging son-of-a-bitch trembling in a metal chair before him.

"You vile, treacherous insect!" In a move so unlike him, Schellenberg's right hand came down in an almighty open-handed slap across Oster's face.

"It had to be done. It was for the best." Oster protested through heaving, blood spatting sobs. "We thought it was for the best. Truly."

"Seriously? Did you? Well, my snivelling old friend. How wrong you were eh? How bloody wrong you were!"

"Oh – dear God, Schellenberg. The man's inhuman. Who could have known that the swine would continue regardless of the loss of life?"

"German lives, Oster. German lives! Millions of them. Our pilots, soldiers and sailors dead, slaughtered like cattle, and now our civilians are perishing in their tens of thousands. And don't get me started on Stalingrad, you son-of-a-bitch, and Kursk. Shit on a shovel, Oster. You knew all the time that our armies would be annihilated and yet you said nothing! The enemy knew it all, every damn move we made. Jesus wept; I can scarcely believe it. I really can't! Every time Hitler took a crap they knew about it. Those battles over the skies of Britain, all Rommel's oh-so-clever tactics in North Africa, every eastern offensive and every damn ship and troop movement. They had it all laid out in front of them from the very beginning and you said *nothing*." He waved his hands in disgust. "Pah! Of course you said nothing because you, you wrinkled fucking wretch of a man, you were too scared to come forward. Dear God in heaven how they must have laughed." Schellenberg paused, collecting himself and trying to formulate his next move in this insane scenario. Ah, yes. He'd almost forgotten, such had been his astonishment and disbelief. Mustn't forget the next big question.

Now," he rammed the knuckle of his index finger into the ugly remains of Oster's ruined ear. "You said, we. Who else? Not lower order drones. I want to know who eased the way for you. Had to be somebody right at the top, eh? Tell me now, Hans, and it had better be the truth or I'll see your wife, sons and those ugly old aunts of yours stripped and given up for medical experiments at Auschwitz."

Oster looked despairingly at his tormentor. "What's the point, Schellenberg? You'll hang with the rest of them. You know that, don't you."

"Last time, Oster. Tell me. It was Canaris, wasn't it? Good old Wilhelm up to his damn tricks, even then."

Oster nodded. "Yes, but it was my idea, you see. I, we, were certain that with a torrent of small early defeats Hitler would be brought down by the general staff, or some other Wehrmacht outfit working behind the scenes. There were several, you know. Yes," Oster sighed and coughed up a small globule of blood. "Yes, of course you know. Won't be much that you haven't found out by now."

"Don't be so sure *Herr* Oster. There are those able to hold out a lot longer than weaklings such as yourself." That comment, as much an attempt to regain a measure of his former equilibrium than offend Oster, failed. Oster's confession, driven part by fear of more excruciating pain and part by an overwhelming sense of guilt, had left him feeling hollow and at a complete loss. The tragedy of the entire thing was almost too much to bear. Oster's deals with British Intelligence early on in the war, his handing over of the plans and details of the state and armed forces code generating cypher machine known as Enigma, had ensured that the Third Reich had no chance at all of winning the war once the allies had centred their strength and aims. Like a chess player whose opponent has been given every single one of his moves in advance, the Reich was able to continue playing for a while but only at the cost, quite literally, of all its pieces on the board. Admiral Canaris had put the resources of the Abwehr behind Oster's plan and it had worked in so far as giving the allies up to minute high level information. Where it had gone wrong, though, was the sad failure to kill, or remove Adolf Hitler. Both Canaris and Oster had overestimated the leading generals' will and ability to bring Hitler down in the wake of those defeats. Fortitude had been severely lacking amongst the High Command of the Wehrmacht as each man jostled parsimoniously for position and favour. The saddest thing, as far as Schellenberg could see was that, notwithstanding all the accurate intelligence warnings sent their way, the Allies were initially unable to resist German military talent and tenacity. The splendid Wehrmacht had defied the odds time and time again despite the spies and their treasonous efforts.

Schellenberg swallowed hard. Only when the defeats mounted in scope and intensity had people felt that something needed to be done. Courage could only take an army so far. As entire divisions were thrown against a happily awaiting enemy, betrayal won out. So brilliantly was the Allied intelligence subterfuge carried out that, regardless of numerous warnings, the Nazi leader refused even now to believe that his prized cypher machine was at fault and, more to the point, really didn't seem to care. It was as though, with total victory being denied him, the Führer transferred his throbbing lust for destruction to something much closer to home. A more obedient target for his strange and ungovernably growing perversion; Germany itself and everything dear to the Reich, Adolf Hitler seemed to want to see annihilated! At the start it had been the Jews Hitler had screamed must be eradicated. Now, it would appear that it was the Germans and Germany itself that he wanted to see wiped from the face of the earth.

General Gehlen, the chief intelligence officer of the eastern front had warned Hitler time and time again of Soviet assault movements, weapons and numbers. His work was painstaking and brilliantly accurate but Hitler called him a dolt and refused to heed his warnings and excellent advice. The defeats continued and losses mounted with the army chiefs raising barely a word of protest. Men like Guderian and von Manstein were quickly moved on to lesser commands. The officer corps that Oster and Canaris had counted on to use its strength and high moral values with which to bring Hitler down was now so weakened and humiliated by their Nazi chiefs and mistresses that as an opposition they were less useful than a masturbating eunuch.

Oster and Canaris had, however, succeeded after a fashion. Hitler would be destroyed along with his minions. Unfortunately, so would a large part of Germany and her population.

Damned amateurs! Schellenberg gazed with loathing at the man he had once admired as being an urbane, well-educated military thinker.

He lit a cigarette and took a massively long drag before inhaling to the very depths of his lungs. Oh, well, he thought. It's done so what the hell? Best report to Himmler and ascertain what the chinless one wanted to do. But there was another thing. With all that had gone on and with Oster spilling names like a clumsy waiter, one or two of those named individuals rang a bell in Schellenberg's head. Those names led back to the SS and, therefore, to both Heydrich and Himmler: but which of them, or was it both? Obviously their names didn't crop up in any way at all, but some of the individuals coming out of this bit of woodwork could only, as Schellenberg well knew, have done what they were purported to have done under the protection of Himmler or Heydrich. Whatever, he couldn't possibly pass on such accusatory supposition to the Reichsführer. This was all just too much insider knowledge for any man to be comfortable with. Who the hell had done what and why? He had no idea. And he didn't like where his imagination and suspicions were taking him. Alarm bells were ringing in his ears and his head ached. Another cigarette and this time his abused airways protested with a harsh rattle as he dragged down tar and nicotine into the depths of his lungs. He held the glowing end of the cigarette in front of Oster's barely focusing good eye.

"You are done, Hans. Silly, silly man. You thought you were being so very smart, didn't you? But I can tell you now you fool, that you never had the vaguest idea of what was going on. Not one iota! And you still don't see it. You'll go down in German history not just as the greatest traitor ever, but as a complete nonsense of a man — a moron! As I remember, you believe in God. Start praying. You've made your confession and now I suggest you keep that flapping mouth of yours shut. I shall ensure that there are no further interrogations, so no reason for you to go ratting off again. Remember your children, yes?" With that, he roughly swiped the remains of his cigarette across Oster's woeful face and departed the room. He must frame his report extremely carefully. If Himmler ever gained an inkling of what he, Schellenberg, now suspected, then Brigadeführer Schellenberg would be joining Oster and co on the chicken wire gallows that awaited them. Heavens! He might even precede them. No thanks. Discretion and distance; that was the key now. Close this interrogation and get Oster silenced as soon as possible.

Himmler leaned back with an icy smile of satisfaction. Got him at last! That pig Canaris was in his web and would suffer agonies before he died. He had ordered Schellenberg to arrest the Admiral and have him incarcerated along with Oster at Flossenburg concentration camp. There would be a trial of sorts, and then he, Himmler, would ensure that both were hung naked from meat hooks. They could watch one another die in disgrace as the wire gouged into their necks forcing their eyes to bulge from their sockets as each of them kicked and struggled for air, jerking, writhing and ridiculous in their naked shame filled death. Then, he would forward film of the event to the eagerly awaiting Führer. Hitler loved such things provided that, of course, they were filmed and sound recorded with taste and professionalism. The Führer hated tat of any kind. It wasn't Himmler's idea of a way to spend an evening, watching such things. He merely did what had to be done. Fear must be instilled but he did not feel the need to personally watch. He preferred not to dwell on the subject of voyeurism, as it might lead him to uncomfortable conclusions about others and, with all said and done, who was he to judge?

Things had worked out splendidly and the Abwehr was at last in his hands. It had taken a little longer than anticipated but what did that matter? Now, he had it all.

He understood only too well why Oster had been unable to speak about his crime and error sooner. He would have been personally blamed for every single one of Germany's defeats and woes: Pariah wouldn't have been the word for it. Such an outcome would have suited Himmler wonderfully well. But, of course, Himmler tapped a finger on the desk, when it came right down to it, Oster *was* to blame. Dear God! When he thought of Stalingrad and Kursk. The conceited fool deserved his shameful death. He really should have spoken out – he *really* should have.

Now, though, it was all working out so very well. The Reichsführer was a man who collected things. Not toy cars or knick-knacks and stuff like that. He liked to collect offices, agencies and departments, no matter how small or insignificant seeming. Heinrich liked to accrue far more than he needed. No man in the Third Reich, or anywhere else in the world for that matter, had as many offices, functions and responsibilities as Reichsführer SS Heinrich Himmler. He was quietly obsessive about his collection and his collecting. The Abwehr, an organization that he had been working and scheming to get his hands on for more than five years was his at last. He now controlled every single Police force, SS group and Crime agency in the Reich and the conquered territories, what remained of them, anyway. Every local police and security department was his, along with all attendant paraphernalia. He controlled every phone tap, every prison sentence and every drop of panic induced sweat in the homes and offices of the Third Reich. He clapped his hands together. All this should be very useful when the war ended and the Allies sought him out for his assistance in controlling a conquered Germany. Yes – he was utterly convinced that he would be of supreme value to Eisenhower and co. How could it not be?

CHAPTER 28

December 1944: Berlin

V on Loringhoven glanced over at Fegelein and shrugged as that man sauntered by. He didn't bother to salute despite Fegelein's higher rank. Had the SS officer insisted von Loringhoven was quite sure that he would be capable of summoning an appropriate response. Fegelein was, after all, his social inferior and breeding did still count amongst those who considered such things important. And without doubt, the gauche braggart that was Gruppenführer Hermann Fegelein, very definitely envied those with impeccable breeding. He would never admit to it, of course. But von Loringhoven and his ilk could smell the envy and borderline subservience of such men. It was what made creatures like Fegelein so offensively rude and bullying in an effort to make up for their self-perceived inferiority.

They had been back in the capital for five days and what a wreck the place was. The Chancellery dripped with the aura of defeat. And, as is so common in times of dire human despair and distress, from the depths of the human barrel rose a black scum of irresistibly spreading putrescence. Out in the streets and suburbs of the once great and proud city, previously unemployable riff-raff, the very dregs of the city's last manpower reserve roamed, creating further obscene vileness in an already terrified and dying city. Dressed in badly fitting, outdated and second-hand SS uniforms, they patrolled all areas of Berlin summarily beating, shooting and generally mistreating anybody they considered to be harbouring defeatist tendencies. More than a few lamp posts held the swinging bodies of confused, often elderly men who had fallen foul of the latest ghastly addition to the stunned and oppressed Berliners. This untrained army of battlefront skivers and violence addicted society rejects now had licence to carry out their dreams of slaughtering others and all within the law. Like the Witchfinders of ye olde merry England, there was no one to stop them slaking their unquenchable thirst for depravity.

Berliners now endured, along with day and night bombing raids and constant shelling, their very own home-grown horror. The Order Police. Not even the Kripo or Gestapo would employ these men and some few women. They patrolled the streets carrying their ever ready to use sub-machine guns and, strangely with ammunition now at a premium, were constantly popping off their weapons in displays of Latin American style bravado. There wasn't one of them that could run more than one hundred metres without dropping in a gasping heap and only a few that could go more than a few hours without alcohol and just as many that needed regular attention for a variety of sexually transmitted diseases. As the Russians drew ever closer to Berlin, so the Order Police held even greater sway over a confused and demoralized populace. Hitler demanded that every traitor, malcontent and defeatist be executed immediately. Without, of course, specifying in any way how such defeatism and treachery might be identified.

Although innocent of any crime or wrongdoing, starving, food-seeking civilians caught out on the streets were liable to the most extreme of penalties. Such as the small boy of around eleven years of age who at that moment was being held by a thick wristed Neanderthal having supreme fun as he drew terrified shrieks of pain and fear from the child.

"Papa, Papa," the little boy begged his wide-eyed struggling father for help. "Make him stop. Please, papa, he's hurting me. Papa, please!"

The boy's father howled in an agony of despair as he watched the rope being tied around his little son's scrawny neck. They hadn't had a hot meal or bathed for weeks now. The mother waited at their bomb ruined home hoping upon hope that the ill-fated males of her family might soon return with food of some description – any description just so long as it was edible, so that she might feed herself and their three-year-old daughter. Perhaps a little to spare for their starving neighbour and possibly even hoard a little. It would be so good to have something to put by for later. Her husband and son had been out scavenging for more than three hours now and were well overdue. Scavenging, of course, was illegal. A defeatist pastime punishable by death. The Führer would not tolerate displays of defeatism such as beggars and scavengers, so the Party took draconian steps to discourage all and any analogous activity. Husband and son wouldn't be returning. Not now, not ever. They had been condemned as defeatist scum, enemies of the Reich, thieves and malcontents. Or so the spotty faced young officer in charge of this particular group of Order Police had determined. His six brutal men, all dressed in an approximation of uniforms and in various stages of gross physical unfitness, needed some fun and action. It was scary being out on the streets with all these wretched bombs and things falling out of the sky. He was indeed scared, aggravated and tired of desperately trying to hide his fear and uncertainty from the paunchy thugs that he commanded. He found, however, that a good way of relieving his natural anxiety was to inflict hell upon others and thus stand back and enjoy their pain and discomfiture. It didn't allay his fear but it sure as hell took the edge off it for a while.

The child's face was drenched in tears and snot as he made final almost animal appeals to his father before the noose was tightened around his neck, choking off any further audible communication with his parent and their tormentors. He groaned with the kind of belly deep mortal fear that makes normal men shudder as he saw his father jerk with terror when a noose was placed, loosely at first, about his own neck.

"We have done nothing," he managed to gasp through his pain and fear. "Why must you do this to us.... why?"

Spotty face smirked. "Why not?"

His men roared with amusement at the wit of their leader. Such fun. The doomed man had nothing of value on him, more's the pity, but his death and that of his brat should be fun to watch; there was that, at least.

"Please," sobbed the father. "Spare my boy. What in God's name has he done to deserve this? Please, don't hurt him. Oh...."

A gesture from the acting Oberscharführer and the child's madly struggling little body left the ground as the uniformed thug holding the rope which was looped over the protruding strut of the lamp post pulled it taut and began heaving until the boy hung, jerking and kicking. As he swung before them all, eyes bulging out of their sockets, urine flooding down his skinny, underdeveloped little legs, they laughed and applauded. The laughter died a little when blood began spouting from the child's eyes and it seemed that his puny spine must surely break during a series of titanically violent death spasms. The small, undernourished frame, though, refused to die and lingered on. It had barely begun life's journey and had no intention of departing easily but depart it did, eventually.

The father, now beyond anything human bit through his tongue and cared not one bit when the rope that encircled his neck was drawn taut and three of the brutes surrounding him drew him up to join his son in unfair, undignified and unforgivably inflicted death.

Gruppenführer Fegelein listened as shells popped off all around. His apartment was something of a shambles after his absence. It had been neat enough on his return what with his little red-headed friend running in and out and occasionally cleaning it, but within just a few days he had managed to make it look scruffy and unkempt.

He peered out of a cracked window. At least they were all, miraculously, still in place. Most window frames in and around Berlin these days were just boarded up holes in a wall.

From just a few miles away in an easterly direction the Wehrmacht was battling heroically against overwhelming odds. It was costing the Soviets six men for every German soldier killed, seven tanks for every German tank knocked out and it was best not to mention aircraft. But Russia had the goods, the supplies and reserves: Germany didn't. German losses couldn't be made good, whereas the Soviets had men and tanks aplenty. Too many, really. Reserves and replacements were constantly bumping into each other, getting lost and causing all manner of confusion, snarl-ups and various degrees of panic all along the battlefront and behind. Of the three million men advancing on the German capital it was quite usual to find that some quarter of a million of them seemed to have gone missing as they lumbered around the German countryside searching for jump-off points, supply depots or quite simply, someone to tell them what to do and where to go. It was all very well comrades Stalin and Marshall Zhukov shrieking that they must take Berlin and smash the vile Germans but with maps and higher intelligence at a premium, not too many were fully or even partly aware of the direction in which they should be travelling. It was a logistical and nerve shredding nightmare! Nevertheless, somehow the vast and ridiculously ungainly Soviet colossus was moving closer each day, each hour, really, to Berlin.

Hermann had managed a brief visit to the Berghof where, after several exhausting sessions of carnal slobbering, he was quite sure that he had impregnated his adoring wife, Gretl Braun, sister of the woman that *he* adored, Eva. Eva had happily taken her share of what remained of Hermann's sexual energies during the course of his frenetic two-day alpine visit. Overjoyed that his wounds had not been too serious nor in any way disabling, both young women had made their concern and happiness over his limp free survival very clear. Almost overwhelmingly so.

Poor Hermann was exhausted. Even his seemingly unending day and night killing sprees as an Einsatzgruppen commander hadn't left him feeling so completely done in.

He enjoyed his time with the girls at Hitler's mountain retreat immensely. First rate food, excellent wine, glorious views and fresh unpolluted air. Who could ask for more? Time, though, was at a premium and Hermann, although enjoying his invalid break, knew that there was work to be done. It made sense for the girls, particularly Eva, to go where they would be safe. Certainly they must stay south but other than that he had no iron-clad idea. Well away from Berlin, that much was obvious but Eva was making sounds that he didn't much like. Gretl was fine. She would go wherever he told her to go and that meant, temporarily at least, a nice little chalet in the Jachenau valley. She would be as safe as it was possible to be down there and she could wait quietly until he sent someone for her. That was enough; job and duty done. Eva though, had mentioned trotting off to Berlin for a few days to see Adolf. Silly idea and far too dangerous but she was a woman used to getting her own way. Whereas Gretl seemed to have at least some kind of grasp on the seriousness of the general situation, Eva dropped ever more readily into a dream world where everything would turn out OK in the end. Not terribly likely but there was no convincing her. She had become far too accustomed to the rarefied, airy-fairy existence of the always accommodated and obeyed first lady, more-or-less, of the Third Reich. Nasty old reality was no longer allowed entry into her world. A bombed, crumbling ruin, to her, simply meant something that was going to look so much nicer when it was rebuilt or repaired. Life was simple and pretty for Eva and she wanted it to remain so. The always clear and slender atmosphere high up at alpine Berchtesgaden aided and abetted fully in Eva's 'everything's fine' fantasy. The awful ruin that was now Berlin might open her eyes but Hermann didn't want her anywhere near the place. It seemed, though, that there was no way he could stop her. Not even Hitler could prevent her from rocking up if she so chose. He loved her but for the life of him, he couldn't figure out why. Especially as, for a man as violently selfish as he, such an emotion was bound, sooner or later, to bring disaster.

Working in the Chancellery was becoming daily more difficult. The Führer was constantly being advised, nagged might be a better word, to make a bee-line for the Alpine redoubt as soon as possible because it was now pretty obvious to even the most pig-headed die-hards, that the Russians were going to be battering at the gates of the city quite soon. Ninth Army commander, General Busse had forecast a matter of weeks before Berlin would suffer complete encirclement. Beyond belief! It was almost upon them, the unthinkable, the unbelievable – the end!

My plans, thought Fegelein angrily, might all go up in smoke. They certainly would if the Russians accomplished a complete encirclement. He needed to get out before that happened but his high rank and responsibilities to the Führer and Himmler, plus his inability to forecast or control the movements of his lover, made it almost impossible to do a simple runner. There was another thing; Himmler's constant demands for updates and his continuous probing with peace feelers toward a not particularly interested enemy had placed Hermann Fegelein in an awkward position. There would be hell to pay should such dealings ever leak out, as they may well do at some stage. Fegelein had himself gathered and kept three damning copies of Himmler's correspondence with Count Bernadotte along with various offers of groups of Jews for sale, exchange and so on. These he kept for future insurance but he was well aware that if *he* had such damning evidence of the high and mighty Reichsführer's betrayal, then so indeed might others.

Himmler's clumsiness in dealings with the allies was a puzzle to him. For a man so paranoid about his personal security that all visitors and staff were searched top to toe on a regular basis, his slackness and naivety were stunning. Even his subordinate's homes were carefully watched with their comings and goings carefully monitored. Normally the safety-first SS overlord missed nothing and risked nothing. Yet here he was going out on a very tenuous limb indeed. The Reichsführer was becoming desperate and wanted to safeguard his future and now realized that haste was of the essence. Yes – that had to be it. Himmler might make a show of sounding off enthusiastically about how much faith he had in the Führer and the soon to be unveiled super weapons but only a man who realised that the jig was pretty well up took risks like this. Unfortunately, those risks also involved Hermann Fegelein, and Hermann wasn't at all sure that the Allies would be quite as forgiving as the Reichsführer seemed to think. How many millions? Hermann and his little Einsatzgruppe had slaughtered more than twenty thousand way back in 1940. He would never forget how proud he had been to reach that figure, only to have Himmler personally berate him for not killing more. The death count was far too low, Himmler had admonished with some irritation and wagging of forefinger. Increase the amount or suffer the consequences of demotion. Typical! That man had thrown up all over the place at the sight of blood and had almost died of horror when he visited Auschwitz. A case of 'Don't do as I do – Do as I say,' and no mistake. Like his master, Adolf Hitler, Himmler had never killed, never fired meaningful shots at an enemy and never suffered the horror of hand-to-hand combat to the death. They merely pretended that they knew all about suffering in order to get others to suffer for them.

Bloody Hell, thought Hermann. I'm leaving it a bit late to get all philosophical. The ground beneath him suddenly shook and trembled making his dusty, bottle and paper strewn dining table shake noisily. Dust and flecks of paint drifted down from the ceiling as he took a look out of the small bay window of his living room.

Tanks! Brand new Tiger Mk II models, three of them along with about two hundred slouching panzer grenadiers. They'd be off to the eastern front which, as rotten luck would have it, was now less than twelve miles away. He sighed and lit a cigarette. They'd probably run out of fuel before they got there or very soon afterwards. Albert Speer might have done miracles with producing lots of tanks, planes and trucks but he'd done sweet bugger all about getting fuel to run the bloody things. What a waste of time it all was.

He smirked as one of the men trailing behind what remained of the Reich's panzer glory, fell out of line and attempted to hide behind a massive pile of rubble. His attempt was almost immediately unsuccessful. A Wehrmacht sergeant strode up to the kneeling soldier who comically tried to bury himself within the solid pile of rubble before him in a vain hope that the sergeant wouldn't see him. Hermann could have laughed himself silly at the sight had it not been so horribly tragic. Upon men such as these Hitler now depended for his survival. It was only now that he noticed that the men outside his window were not proper soldiers at all, least of all panzer grenadiers. They were old men and some little boys, children of around twelve to fifteen years of age.

"Oh, for fucks sake." Hermann rose from his chair and for a moment, just a moment, his better side almost came to the fore. He was an SS General and a Gruppenführer of the SS. He could go out there and stop this. He could send those little boys home, the old men, too. Jesus, he looked again, they were *really* old. Idiot! he thought, as he realised that he was being a sentimental fool. SS generals did not concern themselves with the plight of old men and children. They must look out for themselves. Not my bloody fault, all this, he thought angrily as a shot cracked viciously from outside. The tanks and attendant infantry, Volkssturm and Hitler Youth combined, it turned out, hadn't so much as paused whilst the little drama of death unfolded quickly before Fegelein's window begrimed view.

The sergeant trotted off to catch up with his men leaving the raggedly uniformed old man lying beside the pile of rubble. All out in the open. No attempt at concealment or burial; not so much a few bricks to cover the poor old sod. Hermann stared for a second at the slightly twisted corpse and tutted disapprovingly. Not a day under seventy that one. Just how long did anyone think that men such as that could fight? It wasn't as though they were brimming over with energy.

He toyed with the idea of not going back to the Chancellery. It was a dangerous place to be and Hitler seemed adamant about not fleeing the city. What a pratt! The man prated on and on about being ready and willing to die, adamant in his oft repeated proclamations that death was easy and would be a welcome release from all his trials and tribulations. Well, death was on its merry and totally unconcealed way.

Had the Führer finally reached the stage where he no longer cared about the continuance of his precious and, in his view, supremely important, life? Or did he honestly believe that if he repeated the old 'we shall be victorious' slogans often enough that sufficient followers would be dumb enough to believe in him yet *again* and redouble their efforts, march out and heroically save the Reich from destruction? Super weapons, new armies and situation saving miracles? Piffle! The Führer, Fegelein realised, would move heaven and earth to ensure even a few hours more of life – his life. That the man was devoted to death and destruction was blindingly obvious to anybody with even half a functioning neuron. But just as obviously, the ranting, 'let's do Armageddon' persona of Adolf Hitler, was decidedly reluctant to visit that doom laden scenario directly upon himself.

The phone rang. It was Rochus Misch from the Chancellery. He was wanted there at once. Now, thought Fegelein, there was an odd and interesting fellow. Always around when something needed doing; always got a Führer pass, a Rattenhuber pass and, at times a Reichsführer SS Himmler, pass. All those passes and yet he, SS Gruppenführer Hermann Fegelein had never been aware of why they were issued. Misch had travelled the length and breadth of the Reich with those passes, and a good few of the territories as well. Always first class or personal pilot etc. Incredible! Who and what was he really? Hermann could never quite put a finger on the always calm and self-controlled Rochus Misch.

As his battered little Kubelwagen stuttered into life, Fegelein adjusted the rake of his smart SS emblemed cap. With his rank he could have had round-the-clock services of a motor pool driver, but with some of the trips that he took and the visits that he made, an extra set of a nosey, enquiring eyes simply would not do. Everyone reported on or about everyone else these days. Besides, most of the available motor pool drivers were worse than useless.

A loud grinding sound erupted from beneath his right foot as he depressed the clutch and eased forward the gear lever. Hermann grimaced as the lever shuddered and shook protestingly in his gloved hand and noisily refused to enter its prescribed working slot in the gearbox. He immediately flicked his ankle swiftly up and down over the clutch pedal and expertly double-clutched whilst at the same time forcefully thrusting the gear lever forward. He was rewarded with the sound of something heavy slamming into something solid but yielding. He had managed to shift it into first gear. The clutch was worn all to hell and likely to stay that way as nobody bothered much with routine servicing anymore; if it moved, it was fine. Oil, spark plugs and lubricants of all types were almost impossible to get. Of course, the clutch might be aided by an adjustment but who could be bothered to crawl under the thing to check? All the skilled mechanics had been sent to the front ages ago, leaving the sick, lame and lazy who could just barely manage to drive their charges a dozen or so miles before complaining of some unbearable pain or illness. Erich Kempka, the Führer's driver, once just a chauffeur but now a Gruppenführer like himself, had plenty of vehicles down in the motor pool. Kempka ran all the transport, fuel allocation and such like for all those concerned with High Command and government bigwigs. He had plenty of cars but precious little fuel. One had to be ever so nice to good old Erich if one wanted a can of fuel, diesel, petrol or ersatz oil. He could still get it, though, if you could match his price. Luckily, although not liking Gruppenführer Fegelein in any way, Kempka had been the recipient of a couple of very lucrative favours from Himmler's SS liaison chief, favours that necessitated adequate and willing reciprocation, so they perforce got on well enough. Sometimes they even went so far, after a drink or two and many feigned expressions of mutual trust and goodwill, as to exchange gossipy information concerning the great and the good, or not so good in most cases.

Getting the little dust cart of a military vehicle up into third gear had been an experience in patience that Hermann was unaccustomed to exerting. The bloody thing coughed continually, bucked and spat and more than once threatened to expire. It was only a little more than three kilometres to the Chancellery and he could have walked it easily enough. The trouble was that during the course of any such walk through bombed and shell ravaged Berlin, the attendant masses of dust would be inclined to cling in no small measure to his pristine and showy SS uniform. It was quite likely that he would rock up at the Chancellery looking like an overworked plasterer's labourer and there was no way that he would willingly allow that to happen. Not willingly. But this mechanical wreck of a car was clearly about to expire.

As he slowed to a halt he observed some fifty metres ahead and to the right of him a group of Order Police harassing, and probably about to shoot, hang or kick to death a boy of about sixteen. No attendant adult appeared to be responsible for the youth and Fegelein realised that it was just the Order Police having their fun. Anger rose from within. A heavy rage which demanded to burst forth. There was too much of this random, indiscriminate killing. Far, far too much! It offended Hermann's sensibilities, which was to say, his sense of order and oblation. Yes, certainly, he had been an Einsatzgruppe commander and had killed, and killed and then killed some more. But they, he and his men, had done it *properly!* Not this willy-nilly, randomly generated opiate for brain dead ne'r do wells and skivers. No discipline, no order. He slowly got out of the car, his hand caressing the exposed butt of the 9mm Luger holstered at his hip. He, as representative of the *real* SS, would teach those imitation heroes a lesson that they would never forget.

He kicked shut the door of the Kubelwagen, barely noticing it swing crazily off its hinges as he did so, and made to cross the road. At just that moment a Mercedes roared up and came to a halt beside him. What the hell!

A smooth, handsome countenance peered out at him from the rear passenger seat as the window was wound down. The occupant took in the expired Kubelwagen, the holster gripping right hand of Fegelein and the Gruppenführer's curiously enraged expression.

"You don't want to leave anything in there, dear boy," came the cultured tones of an aristocrat. A slender, cigarette holding hand waved gracefully toward the Kubelwagen. "Might be hell to pay. Secrets and all that, eh?" A chuckle and then the hand beckoned. "Need a lift? Hop in, there's plenty of room."

Just for a second Hermann hesitated, head back and staring at the Order Police as they continued going about their frightful business. Then he turned to the Mercedes and its occupant. Major Freytag von Loringhoven. A mere bloody major yet here he was trolling around in a supercharged Mercedes with a driver who looked fit enough to go fifteen rounds with Max Schmeling. Son-of-a-bitch, how did he manage it? But of course, the holier than thou, always super sweet-smelling blue-bloods remained well and truly on top of the human heap. Even the Gestapo's sterilizing ill will had barely managed to put a tick into that centuries bred sneering upper lip of the Junkers. They simply had to lift an eyebrow to inspire a loyalty and devotion that even Adolf Hitler in his shrieking heyday couldn't hope to equal. Without ever mentioning it, the Führer had quietly ceased his hunting down and killing off of the old aristocracy. They could be extremely useful and, by the same token, an absolute pest. An unkillable parasite that would last as long as humanity itself. Adolf used them when and as best he could, and quietly had them removed from the scene at every treason riddled opportunity they gave him.

Loringhoven was right, of course. His attaché case was in the back of the Kubelwagen and contained some important time and travel schedules plus his travelling SS general's official stamp along with his SS Gruppenführer's pass to all areas. He strode back to the Kubelwagen, retrieved his black leather attaché, then returned in casual, matter-of-fact style to the Mercedes where, with a flourish, he presented it to the socially vastly superior von Loringhoven. Socially superior maybe, but as regards military rank, vastly inferior. Fegelein was about to make some kind of sarcastic comment but von Loringhoven spoke first.

Taking the attaché from Fegelein's outstretched hand he said, "I say, Herr Fegelein. Look over there."

Fegelein almost exploded beneath that ego prodding barb. The aristocratic git dared talk down to *him?*" Look at what, dear boy?"

Von Loringhoven, if he noticed the aggressive tone and manner of the SS general, completely ignored it.

"Those fellows over there. Aren't they some of your old mob? The Order Police, or something like that?" He chuckled loudly and Fegelein distinctly heard the sickly sound of phlegm slapping at the back of the major's nasal passages, "Good heavens. It looks as if they are saluting us. Well, you at least."

Hermann turned and saw the patrol group leader and his four underlings standing rigidly to attention in the rubble with their right arms thrown out in a parody of an SS Hitler salute. They were shrieking Heil Hitler as loudly as their raucous voices could manage. Their reaction was hardly surprising. Real SS Gruppenführers and SS Generals such as he were rarely seen in public these days. For bottom of the barrel types like the handful of Order Police honouring him from across the way, Hermann Fegelein was more glamourous than a Hollywood movie star. He walked around to the front of the car glaring at the sad Sieg Heiling excuses for soldiers. Just then an unbroken droning of powerful engines filled the air and he glanced up.

"Get back here Fegelein," called von Loringhoven. "Not waiting old son. Look up there!"

A darkening of the Berlin sky showed only too clearly what von Loringhoven was yelling about. Air raid. The aircraft were high and spread over a huge distance. How many? Hermann had no idea. He didn't even know if this was an area on their list. It was purely residential with no nearby factories but he knew the Allies liked to bomb civilians and shatter their morale. From time immemorial there was something that drove people to the pleasure of slaughter, to the macabre joys of maiming those that couldn't fight back. As Fegelein knew only too well, though, it was a fun game that soon palled and it had its own heavy price.

Remaining as dignified as he could he made his way the few steps back to the car. As he climbed in the back and settled down beside his hated ally-in-escape the hairs on his neck stood on end as he heard a tell-tale whistling from above.

"Oh Shit. We're going to be right in the middle of it." Off to their right, the little group of frozenly saluting Order Police abruptly disappeared from the earth. A medium sized bomb landed smack, bang in the middle of them ending the sixteen-year-old's misery in an instant and casting to the four winds the various constituent parts, bits and pieces of his violently unkind tormentors.

"Get to the Chancellery garage quick as you can, Hans," shouted von Loringhoven.

"Right away, sir." Notwithstanding the various potholes and craters, the Mercedes roared off at speed. Hans knew his job and the route expertly. The Chancellery garage was underground and well shielded from bomb attacks. Getting there, however, might be difficult during the course of a raid. No choice but to go for it hell for leather, though. All around massive explosions erupted, fire and steel flew through the air and Fegelein cursed loudly as even through the suspension springs and thick rubber tyres of the Mercedes the ground could be felt shaking and bucking crazily. On more than one occasion nearby explosions caused the rear of the heavy vehicle to lift and lurch with both rear wheels leaving the ground simultaneously and crashing back down with a sickening crunch. Back breaking doesn't describe this trip, thought von Loringhoven hoping upon hope that his companion was more uncomfortable than he.

"You know what?" he shouted over the noise. Fegelein gave him a glance of dislike but nevertheless attempted a grin. "No – what?"

"I rather think that the Führer will be going underground pretty soon now, what with all this coming down on us on an almost twice daily basis. Not to mention the British at night."

Both men fell heavily against one another as Hans was forced to break and swerve when a bomb landed and detonated some twenty yards in front of them. It was a close thing and as they hurtled down into the Chancellery garage all three men heaved huge sighs of relief.

The Führer had indeed decided that underground was the best place to be under the current circumstances. Already huge quantities of papers were being bundled into boxes and dragged down the long previously concealed staircase to the Führerbunker many feet below. The air conditioning had been installed but didn't appear to be functioning properly and neither did the rather complicated and gravity challenged sewerage and water system. Hitler didn't care. The bombs had been bad enough but, as von Loringhoven pointed out, the constant day and night shelling from the now frighteningly close Soviet armies, was doing the poor old dear's head in. "Says he can't work with all the noise, poor chap." So down into the concrete Bunker of finality they all trundled.

CHAPTER 29

April 5 1945: The Berghof.

Bags packed, seven in total and Eva was all ready to go. Gretl was loud with tearful dissent over her sister's pending departure and begged that she stay until Hermann's people came and took them to that nice little house in Jachenau. As sisters they should remain together. It would be safer because who on earth could tell where things were going or where they might all end up? Gretl, never having flown on Eva's high flights of fantasy, was more down to earth than her sister. Her little general, Hermann, had hinted for ages that the war was lost, could not possibly be won. On his last visit Hermann had stated categorically that it was all over bar the final death agonies. He explained in reasonably non-technical terms exactly why and what they should do. Gretl had agreed with her husband. She wanted Eva to remain close by despite the fact she had become a little jealous of her closeness to Hermann. Wherever Eva was, that's where Hermann would also be, or at least attempt to be.

She had always known that their shared SS general favoured Eva over her and, although at the outset she had smilingly tolerated the arrangement, she had grown to resent it. Gretl knew that he'd only married her to improve his position with Hitler and to be closer to Eva but she tolerated that because she loved him so much that she would do anything to keep him. Hitler knew well enough what Hermann was all about but he turned a blind eye.

The real trouble was Eva.

She was totally caught up in the Führer's fairy tale miracles and the certainty of his final and inevitable victory. His, the Führer's, destiny was assured and inviolate. Nothing could impede his God-planned mission. And Eva swallowed every word of it. In a way Gretl understood why her sister refused to relinquish her hold on what had been, until recently, a wildly lived and happily real fantasy. She didn't want it to stop and she stubbornly persisted in believing that, if she wished and believed hard enough, all her fantasies would continue uninterrupted as shining and gloriously obedient reality.

Another reason that had Gretl longing for a peaceful area of safety was the fact that she was most certainly pregnant. Not showing yet but she had missed twice and knew very well that something was growing inside her. She must and would protect and nurture Hermann's child with her life. Berlin, from what she had been told was a nightmare of destruction.

"But, Eva," Gretl laid a restraining but loving hand on her sister's arm. "They say that the water and power sources in Berlin are cut off and that there is bombing, day and night. It's so unsafe, sis. Not to mention the trip. Think of all those nasty allied planes. You've heard them flying around up there. They shoot up anything that they see. Honestly, Eva, they are barbarians and thugs. Stay here with me and come with me to Jachenau. You'll love the house and it's so safe and quiet, Eva. Please say you will."

"Oh, you are being silly," Eva scoffed smilingly at her younger sister. "You do so exaggerate, Gretl. It's not as bad as you say. Nothing like it. And anyway, I happen to know that Adi's arranged spacious living quarters for himself and some others downstairs underneath the Chancellery. They say that it has all sorts of bomb proof shields and stuff like that, so there's nothing at all to concern yourself with. Now do stop worrying so, and help me with these cases." In truth, Eva was more excited about another bout of heavy sex and slobbering with Hermann than anything else. She would flounce in and demand that her beloved Führer accept her arrival as a sign of ultimate love, fealty, sacrifice and all that other wordy stuff, and he would award her all manner of verbal accolades lauding her womanly courage, etc. She would insist upon staying for a few days just to be close to him, as she should be. He, of course, as she knew so well, would determinedly protest against hazarding her safety and regretfully but firmly refuse her noble gesture. Excellent! She would then quietly depart to Hermann's cosy flat and get uproariously drunk and engage in endless bouts of rampant sex with her beau. This time without the panting and ever eager presence of younger sister, Gretl. Her Hermann was an SS Gruppenführer and an SS General to boot. He could arrange everything for them. What a delightful surprise he would get when he saw her arrive in all her glory. She could barely wait.

April 7. 1945: The Bunker

Fegelein needed to make a call but not down here. Schellenberg had managed to relay a cryptic message to him informing him that Himmler was making increasingly overt moves to distance himself from Hitler and the Reich. Unbelievable! The architect of hellish death for millions was attempting to jump ship in the honest belief that the allies would approve and understand him and his motives; a piece of monumentally stupid reasoning. The SS Reichsführer was doomed. As yet, Hermann had no idea how far whatever action Himmler was taking had moved along. But as the liaison officer between the SS Chief and the Führer of the Reich, it was his job to keep Hitler informed. Well – sod that!

Shooting the messenger was all too accurate a description for those relaying bad news down here in this joke of a 'last stand'.

He was feeling nervous and that was not a sensation which Hermann could tolerate for very long without a stiffener, anything strongly alcoholic would do. Such plans as he had made now appeared to have been wildly optimistic. Time was pretty well up for all of them. The Russians were inexorably closing off every gap that might lead to a bullet and wound free exit from Berlin. Only a few routes still lay open beyond Berlin's rapidly shrinking military perimeter but they wouldn't remain so for very much longer. Soon all avenues of escape would be closed to any but the hardiest and most determined of escapees. One could still, at a pinch, fly out, but that would mean ordering the reluctant remains of any available Luftwaffe squadron to brave the allied dominated skies above the city. They were less than keen to face such impossible odds and Goering, the Luftwaffe chief, had precious little control over what was left of his once formidable air force. There was, of course, Hans Bauer's Fieseler Storch. It could be requisitioned but the only man with authority to give such permission, apart from the Führer himself, was that barrel-bellied rat, Bormann. So, no hope there. But he must think of something. It wasn't desertion that he was contemplating, not really. For all practical purposes the war was over and he'd done more than his bit. There was nothing left to do other than save oneself and outwit the brain-dead cretins who considered that they should all die out there in some inferno gutted and shell riddled street. No thanks! He had no intention of obeying the current trend of dying so that another might live. That other of course being the great repudiator of death himself, Adolf Hitler. A man who seemed determined to live beyond the one thousand years that his glorious Third Reich had singularly failed to attain.

His reverie was cut short in jaw-dropping fashion. The normally steady equilibrium of Hermann Fegelein was struck with a metaphorical hammer so hard that his knees buckled and onrushing dizziness swung his world all topsy-turvy.

A buzz of surprise mixed with hums of astonishment came from the entrance of the Vorbunker. She waltzed in like Marlene Dietrich at an award ceremony. All smiles and hand waving to an adoring public. A silk handkerchief flicked delicately beneath her nose as the smell of the

Bunker made itself known to its newest visitor. Eva Braun. Herman gawped, as did they all, and yet he could say nothing. Not a damn thing. The Führer's woman, his paramour, was here in the flesh. She actually did a twirl and the tiniest hip flip. In heaven's name! His fists clenched and he took half a step forward but was forestalled by the bulky figure of Reichsleiter Martin Bormann placing his thick necked form directly in front of her. What do – what to do? Hermann felt like bursting into tears. Had she not listened to a word that he'd said at the Berghof?

Behind the glamourous apparition of the immaculately made-up and beautifully coiffured and dressed Eva, stood three uniformed flunkies in various stages of box and bag steadying discomfort. She had brought an entire wardrobe of clothes and accessories down into the Bunker. Fegelein slapped a hand to his head and turned away. Unable to speak nor even so much as form a single coherent thought he lurched back against the condensation running wall and let his back slide down almost a full two feet.

"My dear Fraulein Braun," Bormann was all gushing Maître d' complete with unctuous smile as, with two sausage thick fingers, he took Eva's hand and raised it to his thin lips. "If you would wait just a moment or two, fraulein, I shall inform the Führer that you are here. Is he expecting you?" he asked, knowing full well that Eva Braun was most certainly not expected. Eva was no threat to Martin Bormann and as such he was inclined to tolerate her presence be it in Berlin or the Berghof. She had rebuffed his much earlier sexual overtures but as he, Martin Bormann, had been instrumental in encouraging the Hitler/Braun relationship there had been no repercussions. Eva had always had sense enough not to overly tease or tempt the males within the Nazi hierarchy and kept her fun and games confined to the lower ranks who were a lot more fun, an awful lot better looking and generally less demanding. Until Hermann, of course. He had queered her pitch more than just a little. She could see him out of the corner of her eye and was loving every moment of his astonishment and discomfiture.

Men needn't always have their own way. She was a woman with a mind of her own, so she told herself, anyway. She couldn't help but play up to her captive Bunker audience although the smell was worse than anything she had been expecting. Heavens above didn't they use soap and water down here? She could smell, what was it? yes, foot odour mixed with sweat and unwashed nylons. It reminded her of one of Adolf's long since departed vegetarian cooks, Frau Hinke from Leipzig, or somewhere. There were other smells, all rather ghastly, and she wondered what it must be like down in the further reaches of the Bunker. She had expected something rather more glamorous than this. After the Berghof, the glorious Reich Chancellery and all the luxury hotels and houses, this was unbelievably tatty. What on earth had Adolf been thinking? What this place needed, she decided, was a woman's touch, no doubt about that. Not hers, though, oh dear me no. Her attendants and accompanying baggage were for show only, to add realism to her brilliantly thought up charade lest anyone have the nerve to doubt her motive. But in all honesty, not even for her lovely little SS general could she envisage living down here in this gigantic hole in the ground with all the great unwashed and their rancid odours. No-no-no!

"I'm not expected, as it happens," she answered brightly. "I am here," her tone dropped to one more in keeping with the solemness of the situation, "to share with you all the trials and tribulations that have beset the Reich. We *shall* overcome. This both I and the Führer know." In her best stage actress manner she dramatically threw her head back and waited for the applause and exclamations of joy and wonder.

Nothing much happened and after a few mercifully brief seconds of Eva standing there posing with her rather heavy nose pointed melodramatically toward the ceiling, a blank-faced Bormann said, "I'll inform the Führer immediately, Fraulein Braun." Was the woman stark staring mad? He shrugged his heavy shoulders and made his way to Hitler's rooms some small distance down the main corridor. Braun had been an excellent choice as the Führer's silent partner. Odd in a way that the females in Hitler's life all resembled, after a fashion, his father. Eli Raubal, Hortense Gruber and now, Eva Braun. All three had heavy heads and broad faces resembling Hitler's long dead father, Alois, over whose death he had shed copious tears at the graveside. Nothing at all like the daintier features of his mother, Klara, over whom he had shed not so much a single tear even though he nursed her through her dying days. All that aside, Hitler didn't like dainty unless it was in males. Very odd but not worth going into at this stage of affairs. Bormann enjoyed his little secrets garnered through time, patience and ruthless skulduggery. Time to get the old boy out of his rooms and see how he reacted to this latest turn of events with the now determined to be noticed, Eva.

Fegelein stared at his foolishly behaving lover hoping to gain her attention and bring this particular piece of lunacy to an end. She looked straight at him and smiled brightly, as though she were having the time of her life. The truth, however, was that the journey had unsettled her hugely. The state of Berlin had shocked her and slightly addled her senses. Its ruin was beyond belief. So awful had been the sights that met her eyes as they drove deeper into the city, that she had pulled down the blinds in the rear of the big Mercedes to block out such unwelcome horrors. And now she was here, she couldn't wait to get away again. This place quite simply was not safe! Nothing at all was as she had thought it would be. Hermann had told her that things were bad but not for one instant had she anticipated such a monumental catastrophe.

Linge assisted his shuffling Führer toward the Vorbunker. Both the Führer and his high-ranking valet were pretty much immune by now to the smells and humidity of the Bunker. Not, though, to the reek of tobacco smoke. Hitler paused his slow, step hesitant progress and turned to Linge. "I won't tolerate it, Linge. You hear me? Find out who they are, the smokers, and have them punished."

"Of course, my Führer." Linge nodded sympathetically. "I shall arrange their transfer to the front as soon as we discover the culprits."

"The Front," sniggered Hitler with a rare display of humour. "You won't have far to send them, then, Linge, eh?"

"Indeed not, my Führer," agreed the valet.

"What can she want, I wonder?" muttered the Führer. "Not a place for ladies down here. Not good at all." Secretaries and clerks were fine but not ladies and certainly not Eva Braun. He had just received the news that she had arrived and was eager to see him

Eva smiled with sparkly eyes and moist lips. It was a look that she had been practising for almost a year now and she was sure that she had it off perfectly. This was her moment. In all the years that she and Adolf had been together this was going to be her first moment in the eye of the general public. It did of course suit her to disregard the fact that the two of them had never been truly together in the strict sense of a loving relationship. And this journey into a damp overpopulated tomb could hardly be described as a flash-bulb popping introduction to the great and the good. Nevertheless, it was all she had and this was her moment in the spotlight. Perhaps, she gave a round lipped pout at an imaginary camera, history would record her wonderful offer of sacrifice for the greater good. That would indeed be a super thing, to go down in history as the Führer's loyal and courageous partner. For a moment or two she was able to bask in the glory of her imagination. Gleefully she soaked up the wide-eyed stares of those around her. It was all rather spoilt by a series of thunderous and floor shaking explosions from above as the Russians, completely unaware of her performance, renewed their merciless shelling of the capital.

An even greater comedown was the wretched state of the once awe-inspiring figure that appeared before her. Somehow, God alone knew how, she stifled a nervous laugh. She hadn't seen her pretend beloved for quite some time now what with all the constant problems of this silly war. The smile on her round face froze and the pout turned into an oooh! How could this have happened? True, Adolf had never been the most handsome of men, nor smooth or elegant. Power, though, had rendered him *ultra*-sexy: power and money were inclined to have that effect. The women of the Reich had trembled with sexual anticipation at the merest thought of his attention. But this, this *thing* standing before her was more of a ruin than the city he was so determinedly wrecking. Awful!

"Fraulein Braun. How good it is to see you. What are you doing here in this dangerous place, my dear?"

Ruin or not there was nothing much wrong with his voice. It still retained that odd quality, a strangely attractive but guttural baritone. It was mildly hypnotic when he spoke in conversational key, which was probably why most folk dozed off during his after-dinner discourses. Nevertheless, it could become devastatingly effective when raised in anger or to make a point. They said that the strange timbre of his voice was because he had been gassed during the first world war. She had never asked. Adolf could be funny about such things, well, he could be funny about many things.

Right now, though, he had miffed her right royally. Why could he not have said, 'Eva, my love. How wonderful it is to see you', instead of just standing and looking at her as though she were a cheap perfume seller on a Reeperbahn market stall? The cheek of it! Well, she wasn't about to allow herself to be put down again. Now was the time to make her mark and be recognised for who and what she was; The Führer's woman, his paramour, inamorata, mistress; whatever. It didn't matter. Fame and recognition mattered and it was time that she had her share of it. Bull by the horns time, Eva, she decided fiercely. Sweaty little hands clenched tight she regained her smile, looked directly at the saggy old bag of trembling bones that she was about to claim as her one great love, and said proudly, firmly, "Adolf, my Führer," here we go, she thought, "I am here before you, my love, with all that I am."

His watery, pale blue eyes stared seemingly unseeing and certainly not comprehending. "Yes," he answered. "I can see that. And how good it is to see you. Come. We shall talk in my study."

On no, thought Eva. It has to be here. Everybody must see, or rather witness what happens next. There must be no mistake, no misunderstanding. Her place in history depended upon a sympathetic audience, on her acting skills and what she said within the next few minutes.

"My Führer, Adolf Hitler," she squawked. "Where others might desert you in your time of need," oh, yes. She had heard the rumours. "I, the woman who has remained quietly in the background until now, I profess my undying devotion to you, my Führer, my Adolf. Here I am and here I shall remain forever by your side throughout whatever may transpire."

"Ah, well, that is very thoughtful of you, my dear." Adolf nodded in a somewhat abstracted fashion as he turned his decidedly bewildered countenance to Bormann. "You hear that, Bormann? She wants to stay here – with me. What d'you make of that, eh?" His expression twisted slightly and was clearly confused.

Bormann slapped his podgy hands together in feigned delight. There were, though, more important things to consider at the moment than the foibles of the Führer's bit of totty. That said, the chances were that the poor old sod couldn't remember whether he had invited her down here or not.

"A wonderful idea, my Führer." He turned his ice-like smile toward Eva, his hard, mole-like features keeping deeply hidden the mood of devilment welcomingly running over him, just as it had so often before. Such moods were invariably detrimental to others. He did unpleasant things to people for no other reason than the joy it gave him to witness and be the cause of intense pain and despair. If he had a raison d'etre, it was to stir things up and observe the suffering of those fools stupid enough to drift too close to his sticky and destructive web.

Martin Bormann had risen to dizzy heights within the Third Reich because of his infallible ability to read people; men and women both. And he had sussed Eva's little game very quickly. A little playtime, then? This should be fun.

Bormann's thick working-class accent rang out with its harsh Prussian drawl. "I imagine that Fraulein Braun will be a most welcome addition to the Bunker, my Führer. Her courage, fortitude and national socialist ethos will serve as a beacon to *all* German womanhood, and for men also!" He added condescendingly.

Bormann, you bastard, thought Eva angrily. I thought you liked me you chubby lump of lard. But she quickly moved to the attack, or so she thought.

She raised a self-deprecating hand and fluttered her fingers beneath her chin in a time honoured, I'm only a girlie, display and said directly to the Führer, "You must on no account, my Führer allow thoughts of my safety to interfere with your decision." Meaning, of course, the precise opposite. After all, what kind of male would deliberately countenance a woman being placed in danger? Unheard of and unthinkable. Wasn't it? Feeling less confident now she nevertheless continued. "I am determined to brave all risks, even to my life. Yes, my life is the price that I am prepared to pay to stand by you, Adolf, my Führer and candle of hope for a better future for our German Reich."

Hitler made to interject and Bormann's self-satisfied smirk made clear his enjoyment at Eva's self-inflicted path to hell.

"Suffering, even death itself," now she was laying it on thick. She hadn't expected to have to go this far but that wretch Bormann had forced her hand. She found herself wishing that she had listened to Hermann and Gretl and kept well away. "It is all part of what we must endure. I do not fear death, my Führer," oh, dear God but she most certainly did, "so please, I beg of you, allow me to suffer *whatever* must be suffered no matter how hellish it may be." That would surely be enough. He couldn't possibly let her remain now. Not with the threat of such imminent horrors directly confronting her innocent self. There was no way that Adolf Hitler, the protector of all Reich maidens, would allow her to suffer pain and death, no way at all.

With beaming face Martin Bormann applauded as he looked around at the assembled clerks, corporals, generals and everyday Bunker dogsbodies observing this ludicrous scene.

"Wonderful! My Führer, I congratulate you. You have found your true Gerhilde. A magnificent display of courage worthy of the Valkyries themselves. Sieg Heil!" His right arm flew up in a perfect Nazi salute to be followed, as he knew it would be, by a chorus of the same from all those anywhere near the immediate vicinity. The place echoed to three loudly bellowed Sieg Heils. There, thought Bormann. That should do it.

The ear-splitting salutation stopped Adolf dead in his tracks. Any thoughts of refusing Eva's blatantly insincere request now flew from his addled mind. The merest mention of wide winged, musclebound Valkyrie's set his timorous pulse racing dangerously. Yes, the rousing, soul invigorating tones of the Nibelungen roared in his ears, the chorus, the soaring strings, the blaring horns of Wagner, and the still echoing Sieg Heils in the Bunker; Oh God – Yes!

"Very well. It shall be so," rasped the Führer. "Stay, my Gerhilde, as an example of German courage and faith in the future. Remain here with me your Führer and you shall reap the reward for your steadfastness, I promise you!" Any promised reward was going to be completely illusory but it certainly sounded good coming from the man who was still absolute leader of the Third Reich; even if they were standing on pretty well all that remained of it. He waved an admiring finger pointedly toward Eva, who had gone a deathly shade of pale. "You have restored my faith in humanity, Eva Braun. If only my soldiers were as constant and loyal as you, my dear."

Her breath came in small gasps as she realised at last the full import of what she had done to herself. This wasn't the Adolf of old; this was a very different man. She half turned as though making to leave, for that indeed was what her body was so urgently commanding her to do – get the hell out! But people were closing in around her, smiling their congratulations, acclamations and in some instances lop-sided grins that said, you ninny!

Her blue pure silk dress was clammy against her thighs and even the long dead eyes of her furry shoulder covering stole seemed to be searching for an exit. No way out. She turned back to the Führer and, completely ignoring Bormann, said, as graciously as she could, "Together at last, as we should be, my Führer." Even now she wasn't completely aware of the utter lunacy of the situation. She had wanted theatre and she had got it – in full measure. Her tears of horror and despair were quite naturally enough taken as tokens of joy and her slightly lopsided and glassy eyed smile was rewarded by the sight of the Führer's lips drawing back over his gold bridged teeth.

"There we are, then," he acknowledged. He waved a hand toward her. "Come, my dear. We must allocate quarters for you."

Allocate quarters? It didn't, of course, sound quite in keeping with lovers being drawn closer together but Eva thanked heaven for small mercies. Even now, some eight years after the event, or non-event as it turned out, she could photographically remember her one and only attempt at physical intimacy with him. It had been in Munich at a time when everything was so happy, gay and vibrantly alive. She had tried because of the sweet cloying smell of unexpected success and the heady, surreal atmosphere surrounding them all. At the back of her mind had been the thought that perhaps she should make the effort, and that thought was accompanied by a nagging worry that it might be expected of her. It hadn't been, and the horror of the frightful embarrassment which followed still lingered with her. It had been a dreadful mistake and Adolf had become violent. The end of their relationship had loomed terrifyingly close and it had taken all her female wiles, begging skills and promises to be good in the future to make him forgive her presumption and forwardness. Privately she had fumed and later broken every vase, cup and weaker sticks of furniture that she could find. That a smelly old thing like him should regard *her* as disgusting was beyond the pale. However, she did so love the life of luxury that Adolf afforded her that it was worth a little grovelling to ensure its continuance. Anyway, she quickly realised how lucky she was not to have to endure the sexual posturing of the less than hygiene attentive Adolf Hitler. She learnt how to flatter his ego and please him in a thousand other, far less arduous and unpleasant ways.

As Linge once again took his Führer's arm supportively by the elbow he smiled at Eva sympathetically. He quite liked Eva Braun even though he couldn't stand the sight of her mouthy little SS General, Hermann Fegelein. He gently steered Hitler back in the direction from which they had appeared. Eva, wearing a pair of not quite yet fashionable platform shoes with sequin sides, tottered along awkwardly behind them. Balance was a problem with this kind of shoe when moving at so slow a pace on an unhealthily slippery floor. Her SS porters struggled along as best they might.

"Bormann," Hitler's voice was just a tad quavery now, he was feeling tired and there would soon be another military briefing to endure.

"Yes, my Führer," Bormann answered in his usual unctuous fashion as he too cast a less than sympathetic smile toward Eva.

"Shift Goebbels into his family room and allocate those quarters to Fraulein Braun. He should spend more time with his children anyway whilst they are down here. Why did he bring them, by the way – did he say?"

"His wife's idea, I believe, my Führer. Frau Goebbels always likes to have her family close by."

"Damn stupid idea if you ask me, eh Linge?" His ever-loyal valet nodded agreeably as he eased his Führer over two small steps leading past the conference area of the Bunker.

"Anyway, Bormann. See to it. See to it at once. Give Herr Goebbels my regards and have him shift his gear immediately. And some tea and cake for Fraulein Braun. I need to rest now." He turned to Eva. "I shall see you for supper, my dear. Right now I fear that I have overmuch to do. Just call on Bormann here for anything you need. You will probably want to chat with the secretaries, eh? Woman stuff and all that kind of thing. Fine girls, all of them. You'll get on famously, my dear. Arrange that Bormann, will you?"

More unctuous smiling and nodding from Borman. Joseph Goebbels, the self-important club footed one, was going to be absolutely furious with this turn of events. Being compelled to share his unloving and vindictive wife's quarters along with their noisy ever boisterous and laughing children would infuriate the hell out of him. And as for his wife, Magda? If there was one person whom she loathed and found more contemptible than her philandering husband it was Eva Braun. Sometimes, thought Bormann with a certain amount of glee, it's almost worth being stuck down here.

The truth of the matter, in Bormann's opinion, was that there was no reason for Joseph or Magda Goebbels to remain in the Bunker, let alone have their children down here. The Führer had more or less told the Propaganda Minister to go as there was not one damn thing that he could accomplish, not anymore. Hitler was bored with Goebbels constantly carping rhetoric which much of the time mirrored his own. Although at one time valuing his abilities he had never much liked the man. As for Magda? She was nothing more than a fanatically adoring bore. Bormann gave a grin which revealed tiny but even teeth behind very thin lips. Poor old Magda. All she wanted in life was to be tied to the Führer's ankles and be dragged around by him everywhere, quite literally everywhere, that he went. The grin turned to pursed lips. How could a woman be so depraved as to fancy a man in such a disgusting manner? And to lust after the Führer – silly woman. Both she and her husband gave total devotion to the Führer as their reasons for remaining in the Bunker. Had he been a little too naïve, thought Bormann, in agreeing to come down here? He could only exert control over those directly within his physical sphere. To get things back on an even keel he needed to be above ground and controlling a communications network that functioned fully nationwide not this rag tag of torn cables, public phones and Rochus Misch's flickering but local switchboard. Unfortunately, to be above ground and exerting control meant getting the Führer to agree to popping his head up and making a bee-line for the south before it was too late. Fat chance! Bormann sighed heavily. Without the Führer he was nothing. All the fear that he engendered and the respect that was his on demand, emanated from his master and because he was his master's most trusted servant. He signed papers for the Führer, used the Führer stamp in his name, had his absolute trust and confidence. But without that shambling wreck he, Martin Bormann was nothing! He had indeed appealed to the Führer to go south where there were armies that were still loyal and intact but he, for whatever reason, steadfastly refused and when Hitler made his mind up about something, anything at all, he never altered it. Never.

So, all he could do was make the best of things and continue as though nothing was wrong. Deep down in his ever common-sense psyche, he knew that the war was lost; he simply didn't want to admit that he might lose what he had. Nevertheless, everything had its season and this particular season was now, clearly, drawing to a frosty close. Perhaps it might be time to take closer heed of von Loringhoven's doings and, of course, Fegelein. He tapped the bridge of his broad, bully's nose. And then, of course, there was the ever-enigmatic devil himself, that keeper of secrets, Rochus Misch. Might be time, reckoned the Reichsleiter, to check on some of those exit plans that he knew various others had been planning.

CHAPTER 30

April 1945: Berlin, The Bunker

Joseph Goebbels and his wife, Magda glared at one another. The enforced closeness and the constant racket from their children were not going down too well with either of them.

"Bombs, shells, noisy children and now you," complained Joseph miserably. "This is just too damn awful."

"Isn't it, though," retorted Magda. "Perhaps you should put out a bulletin to all those cossetted Berliners. Remind them all of how lucky they are, hmm?" she purred, almost daring him to start a row.

"Happy then, are we, having our face put out by the superior being that is Eva Braun?" Joseph sneered irritatingly. "I just bet that you are. Well, my dear ever loyal Magda, remember in the days to come that it was you who insisted upon remaining with the Führer. It was your bounden duty, or so you said. And now, here you are."

"Here *we* are", snapped Magda. "God alone knows how far beneath the surface."

"Not what you had in mind?" He teased. "Well, old girl, you didn't have to drag yourself all the wretched way down here. If you'd taken my advice you would have waved bye-bye from the Chancellery steps and then gone on your way *with* the children." His heavy, misshapen foot increased its floor slapping rhythm. "Heaven only knows what you were trying to prove. You probably gave Eva Braun the idea and Christ knows she was quick enough off the mark. And the children! What on earth possessed you, you foolish...." He stopped abruptly as he remembered only too well what a monumental fury his wife could unleash if pushed to her unnaturally close limit. She was a good deal bigger than he and prone to outbursts of physical violence. Once, a few years ago, after she'd learnt about yet another of his affairs with an outrageously pretty Czechoslovakian actress, she had violently attacked him in the hallway of their large Berlin mansion. A loosened tooth, which he refused forever to mention, and finger marks from a hefty slap had been his reminders of that particular encounter. Not that he had allowed Magda to get away with her furious abuse of his person. Once he had managed to calm her down by threatening to shoot her, Joseph warned her that if she ever attacked him like that again he would send her favourite servant, Heide Floss, to the dental experimentation unit at Wewelsburg castle where Himmler's manic and gleefully sadistic experimenting dentists, trainees most of them, would introduce her to a variety of prolonged and agonizingly awful dental procedures.

Knowing that he would make good on any such threat, Magda reined in her natural high temper and confined her dislike and contempt for her husband to the almost equal violence of her words which, she found, Joseph could more than match with viciously unkind rhetoric. Not a match made in heaven but a match for each other they certainly were. And so, as time went by, Joseph continued with his various affairs and Magda less than surreptitiously pursued her own.

Relapsing into a mutually sulky silence they sat waiting for their energetic little brood to come down from their much-enjoyed daily activity of tormenting of the upper Bunker SS guards. The children's antics such as shrieked out name calling directed at various adults, horribly unfunny practical jokes and the like, were downright annoying to many of the Bunker residents. Others, however, smiled and nodded indulgently at the Goebbels children as they laughed and cavorted in the manner that children the world over do as they take advantage of over-indulgent adults. They adapted with amazing resilience to Bunker life. There were, though, some few amongst the Bunker inhabitants that found the Goebbels brood an extreme annoyance which they would dearly like to see eliminated. Nosey, noisy brats constantly turning up and demanding attention, food or something to do. At least two of the SS guards in the Bunker were former Einsatzgruppen members and as far as they were concerned the best place for noisy children was on the sharp end of a bayonet. But, unfortunately for them, they were now governed by a new protocol of restraint, so when the ghastly creatures that were children approached them, they evinced smiles of tolerance and care which barely got beyond the first and tiniest twitch of the lower lip and never got close to the eyes.

Joseph knew intimately of his wife's devotion and completely incomprehensible love for the Führer. The Führer was also well aware of Magda's absurd, obscenity lusting devotion and whilst not outwardly discouraging it, kept it well beyond arm's length. Flattery and devotion were all very well; a dictator's bread and butter, in fact. But fleshly contact and all such vileness thereby entailed, Never! Why were women drawn to Hitler to such an unhealthy extent, he wondered – had always wondered? And yet, Adolf, for all his outward display of respect for women, couldn't tolerate being too close to them, either physically or emotionally. What did Magda really and truly want from their fading Führer, he asked himself? Hell – what did it matter – what did any of it matter anymore? But the children. What was to become of them? That he, Joseph Goebbels, must end his life if their admittedly slapdash and ludicrously amateurish effort at European domination failed, he had always known. Those were the stakes. But he was well aware that Magda would never take her own life. Like Hitler, she lacked the courage to ultimately end it all. Hitler's attitude and his childlike refusal to acknowledge the harsh reality of their gamble, for that's precisely what it had been, came as a shock to Joseph Goebbels. He had always suspected that there was something of the tart about Adolf, but he had never figured him as being a whinging coward. Surely he couldn't have been so wrong about the man to whom he had devoted his intelligence, his very life? Such a thing now seemed distinctly possible and it put him, and some few others, in a quandary. Joseph knew that he couldn't allow himself to be taken alive and he had already made provisions. But the Führer, what about him? In some ways Goebbels blamed himself. He had always supported Adolf's ridiculous lies and fairy tales about new weapons and huge new armies that would ensure final victory for the Reich, but only while there was the remotest hope of relief, even if it were to be only temporary. But to hash out such platitudes now was not merely feeble and worthless; on a personal level it was utterly demeaning. Only the weak and feeble minded needed to be bolstered by such dreams and now, he realised, that description was and always had been the correct classification for the Führer of the Third Reich; a dreamer too weak to even countenance the existence of any kind of reality. Well, it was all ending in blood and horror but at least he'd enjoyed more than his fair share of fun. He sighed so forcibly that dribble flew from his lower lip.

Magda looked closely at her husband. She didn't like him, never had very much, not really. She had got herself close to Joseph, and then married him, because such a move enabled her to get close to the Führer, Adolf Hitler. Joseph was Hitler's confidant, a close and trusted colleague. That meant that she, Magda, could be close as well. That had been her plan and it had worked almost to perfection. The only fly in the ointment being that her glorious Führer, whilst at all times being charming and accommodating to her foibles and wishes, kept her very much at a safe distance. All smiles and charming words but no touchy-touchy. Not ever.

She had been entranced, infatuated with Adolf Hitler from the first moment she set eyes on him. Oh yes, she had heard all the strange and weird stories that went around about the Führer, but they hadn't concerned her then, or now. Magda cared not one iota what the rest of a mean-spirited, unworthy world thought; if there was one human being that loved Adolf Hitler without judgement or reservation, that person was Magda Goebbels.

And now, here she was with ultra-bright and always something to say husband, Joseph, the great Propaganda Minister, Goebbels. Not a muscle nor a working sinew was to be seen anywhere on that scrawny little body, but he possessed a mouth like a Hercules with mechanical gums. She said nothing, just sat glowering. She glowered because she knew that he hated it. Her piercing bright blue eyes, whilst never meeting his, glowered and glared at him like an incubus on heat. The club foot in its heavy ankle raised shoe tapped more earnestly, and the rapid rhythm of his floor beating deformity became gradually louder until it began to quite severely affect Magda's already jangled nerves.

"Will you stop that infernal noise, Joseph?"

"Of course," he said, not unkindly. He was starting to feel just a bit agitated. Even in the present circumstances, possibly because of them, he felt a sudden urge for sexual release. Those urges which had landed him in fairly deep water more than once over the years. Murderous husbands and insanely irate lovers screaming melodramatically for his blood. Charges of rape, molestation and sexual harassment, all had been levelled at him at one time or another. Not that he cared. He had managed all too easily to lie or simply threaten his way out of trouble. Joseph knew how to survive the anger of the masses and their morals, and laugh whilst doing it.

Running his right index finger over an eyebrow he leaned forward slightly over the edge of his chair. A suggestive grin and a typical Goebbels flick of the wrist as he made to rise and go toward her. Well, why not? She was female, she was here and she was his wife, after all, so why the hell not?

"NO! And keep your damn hands to yourself, Jo Goebbels or you'll regret it."

But, as she thought later, whilst his slimy, greedy little body slithered all over hers; what else was there to do?

CHAPTER 31

April 27 1945: Berlin, The Bunker

No point in even pretending to pretend now. It had been like co-habiting with the living dead down in the Bunker, and for a man with Hermann Fegelein's strong desire for survival, it was no place to be. Fegelein had had enough. He had passed on a few remaining but not overly important intelligence bits and pieces to his master, Himmler, just a couple of days ago. He had been forced to do this through a coded message sent via Mohnke's beleaguered and crumbling HQ, which was falling rapidly back from the Brandenburg Gate. That fiery, white hot metal shrieking horror of a battle front was now less than 800 metres distant from the Bunker, so there was no time to lose. Mohnke himself had said that the position was utterly hopeless and that his command would cease to exist after the next Soviet attack.

So, no goodbyes, no tearful farewells. To hell with the lot of 'em; he'd just upped and scarpered away like the petty nobody that he had once been. He'd had more sense than to appear furtive in his movements. No one questioned the openly departing SS Gruppenführer as he sallied forth in yet another motor pool acquisition courtesy of good old Erich Kempka. Kempka had guessed what Fegelein was up to but had better sense than to ask questions. Nobody in their right mind wanted to remain here in this hellhole. He, too, would be taking his leave as soon as was possible. Hopefully, he and a few of his armed motor pool drivers might be able to break through to the west if they were stealthy and smart enough.

Not much in the way of fuel and Hermann realised that he should have departed a good week earlier, at least. He had banked on at least one of the highways or minor roads on Berlin's southern axis remaining open. Schellenberg's Intelligence reports had been pretty thorough and stated that the British and Americans would not be advancing any further; they had taken the Ruhr and crossed the Rhine. The victorious Western Allies therefore agreed that Berlin should be a prize for the eager Russians. Under normal circumstances that should have given him sufficient time to get to the still functioning Tegel airfield. With the Tempelhof runways under constant attack and by now pretty well unusable, only the small private field at Tegel remained available to those fleeing who could still find a serviceable plane and bribe someone to fly them out. Such attempts were certainly dangerous, what with the Allies' total command of the air, but it was the only way to put any worthwhile mileage between themselves and the advancing Russians. Unfortunately, however, those Russians, God damn them all to hell, had moved with incredible speed, crushed any resistance and closed off that last avenue of escape. Berlin was now encircled by a ring of vengeful steel. Any possible way out would involve crawling through tunnels, sewers and the like, slapping on all sorts of silly disguises and inevitably paying out huge sums in bribes. His supposed partner in escape, Luftwaffe Oberst Horst Dickel would have long since departed or died. No news from him and no way of obtaining any. So, no nice little hideaway in a Bavarian valley for him. There wasn't enough fuel in the car to get him even ten miles beyond the city limits and that, of course, was assuming he could make it that far. Walk it? Not bloody likely. To attempt that would mean leaving his ill-gotten gains here in Berlin. What a damn, bloody mess!

It was just as well that Eva had refused to come. She still could not face the fact that the end had at last arrived. And, of course, with the Russians not knowing who she was, if caught she would undoubtedly be raped, repeatedly. That was their way and anyway, hadn't he and his Einsatzgruppe buddies done the same? Oh, yes. It was sad, but poor Eva was going to find that there was a high price to pay for being a willing participant in the Third Reich's Nibelungen fantasy.

He got out of the car and felt an unaccustomed twist of depression forcing his mood down into a darker pit. He had thought that it would be relatively easy and instead it was turning out to be downright impossible. He kicked the car door shut. Inside the apartment, as he well knew, the little redhead awaited him; his replacement for Eva. Didn't come close, truth be told but better than nothing. She had for a while now made herself useful by doing the occasional spring clean, eagerly initiating frantic sex and, very importantly, not talking too much. She just let him get on with his own style of empty yak and rarely interrupted. Her place had been bombed to a ruin and so she pretty well lived in. He didn't mind. It was company when he was here and the sex wasn't too bad. She would be all pretend smiles and lust, over eager to please 'cos SS General Hermann Fegelein was her ticket to safety. Hah! He grimaced. Fat lot she knew. He didn't blame her, though. If anything on two legs, or four, come to that, would offer to save Herman Fegelein, then, he, Hermann, would be ever so obligingly grateful in ways that would shock even his very open-minded redhead. But that wasn't going to happen. He'd mucked up in a big way and for the life of him, he couldn't see a way out. He hoped that Liza had cleaned the place whilst he'd been in the Bunker. Clean sheets and a nice smell would be nice; yes, that would be ever so nice. Vaguely, as he entered his abode, he wondered if Liza and Eva might have liked one another had they met. Not likely. Eva would have had Liza working as her servant within a day; perhaps even minutes.

Even as he entered his apartment moves were afoot some few kilometres away to bring him back to the increasingly straw grasping

Führer. Sick, health failing to the very bottom of his allotted bucket depth, Hitler was calling for Hermann Fegelein. "Where is Fegelein?" was the current bleat. And with good reason.

Unbeknownst to Fegelein and because of the content of his last transmitted report upon conditions and command in the Bunker, Himmler had contacted the allies directly and his transmissions had been sent, insanely, in the clear. No coding, no enigmatic phrases; just a plea for peace negotiations to be opened with *him*. No mention of Hitler, Goebbels or any Reich ministers – just *him*.

In other words, Heinrich Himmler had made his move to take over what remained of the Third Reich and poor old Hermann Fegelein didn't know a damn thing about it. That such a man as Himmler, the great Concentration Camp creator and instigator of appalling death for millions, could even consider treachery had driven Adolf to the very edge of what little remained of his sanity. Neither, as far as men like Loringhoven and Bormann were concerned, did it say an awful lot for the mental capacity of the chin receded Reichsführer. It was the end of Heinrich Himmler and the tragedy, as far as Hermann Fegelein would be concerned, was that he was going to discover all this far too late.

He was blind drunk within the first hour of his arrival at the apartment. Liza, lying naked on the bed beside him was also sozzled. He awoke to take a leak, drank some more, put a record on the neatly edged Metz gramophone, dragged poor naked Liza from the bed and hurled her around in a dancing frenzy only to come to a staggering halt when, barely conscious, she threw up all over him. Somehow he dragged her to the bathroom but lost track of things after that. Some eight hours later he awoke again. Barely compos mentis, he was vaguely aware of an alarm bell sounding from somewhere deep within the narrowing recess of his mind. He should be up and about doing things, something, anything but what the hell was it? Another bottle followed by another bout of mindless and instantly forgettable sex. Couldn't have been that bad, though, his alcohol-invaded neurons dreamily reckoned, because Liza was moaning, almost bellowing, far more loudly than usual. Dimly he wondered why she was moaning. Was she in pain? No, surely not. She was always noisy during sex. He knew that she did a lot of moaning and groaning because she thought it pleased and aroused him; it didn't. It got on his nerves and wrecked his concentration.

Someone was slapping his face. What the hell? It was Liza. Slap-Slap-Slap! She was lying beside him, and rolling back and forth to give momentum to her slapping. Her hand raised and her smooth white shoulder stretched back as she prepared to deliver yet another stinging slap.

"What the hell d'you think you're doing?" he croaked. The words were barely comprehensible and a stream of bubbling drool followed immediately after them.

"Door," she mumbled.

"What?"

"Door! There's someone hammering on the door. Can't you hear it?"

"Couldn't care less," he mumbled and lapsed immediately back into a welcome stupor.

Liza squeaked with alarm as the door gave way beneath increasingly violent hammering from large SS-issue boots.

It all might not have been so bad had Hermann been ready, calm and in command of his senses. People back in the Bunker were initially merely curious as to why he was absent and men were sent to check. There had been two previous visits and polite knocks on his door all of which had been ignored. Hardly surprising bearing in mind the state of Hermann and his lady friend but the callers weren't to know that. What might have been a mere light interrogation was going to be very different now that suspicions were aroused and Himmler's treachery known to all. Gruppenführer Fegelein was, after all, Himmler's liaison officer in the Bunker; his one, his only conduit to the Führer, or rather, his apish watcher, Martin Bormann. Normally, Hermann would have used his wits and eased his way out of this now delicate and highly dangerous situation. But he was pissed out of his mind and feeling foolishly aggressive at having his slumber interrupted. Being married to Eva's sister and now so close to the focal point of Nazi power had given him delusions of grandeur. Always conceited, he had begun to think of himself as untouchable. As he was soon to find out, though, neither he, Himmler, Goering nor anyone else in the Third Reich was untouchable as long as Martin Bormann ruled the Führer's fantasy fuelled roost.

No less than six SS men tramped into his bedroom ignoring the squealing protests of the drunk, carelessly naked, Liza.

"Hermi," she shook him as hard as she could. "Tell these men to get out. It's not right." At last, covering herself with a part of the sheet she glared up at the tall man who was obviously in charge. Even drunk she could see the rakish slant of his cap and the casual stance of a man used to being in control.

"You need to get out before he wakes up," shrieked Liza. But a winding tendril of fear thrust its way through her lower belly. These men wouldn't dare storm in like this unless they had a good reason and an awful lot of authority. The tall officer, SS Obersturmbannführer Peter Högl, wagged an expensively gloved finger at her. "Just be quiet, madam, and all will be fine."

"But...."

"Did you not hear what I said?" Hissed the SS officer. "Be quiet!"

He marched noisily over to where Hermann was lying and snoring happily away; every second that passed drew him deeper into a darkening pit of drunken slumber.

"Sieg Heil, Herr Gruppenführer," he roared. He didn't like Fegelein. But, still, the man had rank, although with luck that might soon change. Even so, for the time being he must tread with at least a modicum of care, just in case.

"Imbibed a little too much have we, Herr Gruppenführer, sir?" He laid a gentle hand on the recumbent Fegelein's shoulder and shook it briskly for a couple of seconds.

"Time to rise, sir. You're wanted by the Führer."

"Führer who?" Hermann came just ever-so-slightly out of his stupor. He could register the word Führer but it didn't mean much to him, not at the moment. Fear didn't so much as tickle his emotional surface. All he felt was a small irritation at the oaf disturbing him.

The Obersturmbannführer's fists clenched at his sides. He would dearly love to slap some sense into the drunken little slob on the bed. This man, this SS General Fegelein, had got away with far too much in past. Big mouthed, conceited and untrustworthy. Horrible little man. Whatever might be heading Fegelein's way, Högl hoped sincerely that it would be painful and unpleasant.

Brave men were fighting to their last breath just three or four hundred metres away, and here was this disgrace of a senior SS officer drunk out of his mind. Even the short trip to Fegelein's apartment was now fraught with danger and necessitated skirting around desperately fighting Wehrmacht and Volkssturm units as the Russians drew ever closer.

"Search the place," ordered Högl. Those had been Bormann's orders before he left the Bunker. "Then," he glanced contemptuously down at Fegelein. "Get this gentleman dressed." Hermann's black, beribboned Gruppenführer's uniform lay in an untidy, carelessly thrown heap on the bedroom floor. Angrily Högl picked it up, jacket, trousers, shirt and tie, and dumped it all unceremoniously atop the still recumbent Fegelein. That man merely hiccupped, swallowed and snored in response.

The sound of drawers being opened, slammed shut and in all cases clumsily emptied bounced off the walls of the apartment. Some distance away, a massive artillery bombardment turned the wide laned Wilhelmstrasse into a giant's golf course as new craters, some more than twenty feet deep, appeared as if out of nowhere. But the earth-shaking racket gave no pause to the searching SS men. The Russians seemed incapable of aiming their shells and so threw their exploding ordnance arbitrarily into the city. There was precious little order or method to the Soviet bombardments, which meant that attempting to dodge the incoming shells, whilst a natural reaction, was pretty much a waste of time. After so many months of indiscriminate aerial bombardment, and now constant shelling, this was just another day at the office.

The apartment didn't take long to search and nothing incriminating or even remotely dodgy had been revealed. It was time to leave. Högl didn't want to get trapped by the advancing Russians on the way back.

"Get him dressed," he ordered his men and then, gesturing toward Liza, "leave her here. She's of no interest." He looked more closely at the red-headed Liza. Actually, under any other circumstance, he would have been very interested indeed. Now, unfortunately, was not the time for dalliance nor even lustful thoughts. Liza was looking rather downcast at her exclusion from the neatness trashing search and the fact that she was considered to be of no importance whatsoever. She knew that the officer in charge was looking at her, so she dropped the sheet a little further over both breasts in an effort to gain further attention. She knew that she was attractive, desirable, and it now would seem, quite possibly available. The Obersturmbannführer, however, had turned away, his attention taken by something else.

A small black attaché lay close to where Hermann's clothes had been carelessly thrown. Not expecting anything out of the ordinary, Högl bent and lifted the shiny little case for a brief inspection. On the bed Hermann was now awake and swearing blue murder at his enforced enclothment. He would doubtless have found conversing normally next to impossible, but every nuance, consonant and vowel of his drunken cursing was vividly enunciated in glaringly articulate detail.

Just as they managed to get him fully dressed and in at least some semblance of neat SS-style order, Obersturmbannführer Peter Högl let out a loud gasp and then whistled like an Adlon hotel porter signalling for a customer's car. As his men turned to see what had so provoked their commander's breathy sounds, Högl waved two pages of flimsy A4 paper toward Fegelein.

"Trouble has found you, Herr Gruppenführer," He glanced again at the papers in his hand. "Oh dear, sir. I'd say that this is trouble in a big way." To his staring and inquisitive men he said, "Get him into the car and back to the Bunker." He gave Liza a lovely little half salute, Nazi-style, and watched as the still loudly protesting Hermann Fegelein was dragged rather than escorted, out of the apartment into the unforgiving hell that was Berlin.

Poor, foolish Hermann. The documents that he had copied and kept to be used as blackmail should he ever need to protect himself against the dupe seeking of his superiors were the papers that Högl had waved so condemningly before him as they hauled him from the apartment. He felt a brief moment of loss, as from the corner of his eye his excellent peripheral vision revealed Liza's pretty breasts waving a forlorn and desperate to be noticed bye-bye. He had important things to do, but, one never knew, perhaps later; if, of course, the place was still standing.

CHAPTER 32

April 28 1945: Berlin, The Bunker

Eva had pleaded with Adolf for almost an hour but to no avail. She hadn't dared put too much of a case because she knew from the outset that it would be hopeless. She felt, though, that she owed it to Hermi to do the best that she could for him.

Whilst not initially being too concerned over Hermann's absence, the Führer had become decidedly agitated when, immediately after the discovery of Himmler's treachery, Gruppenführer Fegelein was still nowhere to be found. His prolonged absence aroused deep, and correctly formed, suspicion. However, despite Bormann's glee and obvious desire to see the blonde little Gruppenführer destroyed, Adolf had resisted the calls for his destruction. Fegelein was, after all, married to Eva's sister, and the very last thing he needed was a hissy-fitting paramour shedding floods of tears in front of the already unsteady Bunker minions. But when Obersturmbannführer Högl rocked up and produced documented evidence that Fegelein had not only known about Himmler's vile treachery and concealed it but that he might also have colluded in it, Adolf became positively incandescent with eye-bulging rage. Yet again, engulfed with fury and self-pity, the once mighty Führer of the Third Reich knocked ferociously on the door of apoplexy and seemed within seconds of a lip writhing death. He didn't die, though.

After still another prolonged period of wailing on about how unfair life was and how he wasn't appreciated by those around him, he shrieked for Fegelein's head. Death! Only his brother-in-law's relationship with Eva saved Hermann Fegelein from a truly frightful and agonizing end. He would be shot. To Hermann's pleas that he at least be allowed to see the Führer and put his case before him, Hitler spat with fury and ignored them. Obersturmbannführer Peter Högl would do the honours. The Obersturmbannführer was only too happy to do so.

Two hours later, still drunk, still swearing and utterly unrepentant, former Gruppenführer and SS General Hermann Fegelein turned to face the men who had first dragged him from his apartment and now had dragged him, still swearing right royally, into the Chancellery garden. Only Peter Högl was aiming a weapon at him. The rest of his squad just stood with weapons held loosely, observing the proceedings. Proper form, etiquette and so on, should be adhered to, even here beneath the ever-widening umbrella of bombs, shells and foul-mouthed panic. Having lower orders from the ranks shooting high ranking SS officers, even former SS officers, simply was not on, not in his view. And right now it was his view that counted. Anyway, he wanted this pleasure all for himself.

Hermann sneered at his former junior in rank. It was all over but the truth was he'd known that months ago. With all said and done Hermann was no coward and was well aware that compared with many others, men at Stalingrad, Kursk, Poles and Jews, etc, he had had a damn good run. Bluffed it, loved it, and now it was done. Anyway, he was too drunk to be afraid of a sodding thing. Even now, though, as he puffed out his chest for the final time, he couldn't help but notice the strangely satisfied expression in Högl's eyes. He briefly and quite pointlessly wondered why the man disliked him so much. Well, what the hell did it matter now? He gave his very best cheeky-chappie grin and threw up his right arm as if to give a final Hitler salute. Instead, though, and with great gusto which brought small grins to the observing SS squad, he closed his fist and in the age-old gesture of defiance and contempt stuck up his middle finger and roared out, just as the first shots left Högl's MP40, "Fuck Hitler and Fuck his bloody Reich!" He was dead before he hit the ground. Less than one week later the daughter whom he would never see, was born. For reasons of her own, Gretl named the child Eva Barbara, after husband Hermann's one and only true love.

Von Loringhoven watched Peter Högl stomp through the Bunker and march up to Bormann's door where he stopped, waited thoughtfully for a second, then just threw open the door and without further ado clomped straight in. Now that was odd, thought von Loringhoven. Not many would dare enter the Reichsleiter's den in such a peremptory manner, not even with the current state of affairs.

Fegelein's execution had caused considerable disquiet in the nether reaches of the Bunker. Unpopular he may have been but his closeness to the Hitler family, the inner circle, so to speak, and his abrupt and brutal demise, had done nothing to bolster any remaining confidence amongst Hitler's still hard-working subterranean staff. If Fegelein, then who next? Two of the secretaries were in tears with one of them hair tearingly hysterical. Christina Schroeder was her name and many were the happy trysts that she and the now dead Hermann Fegelein had enjoyed in various corners of the Reich Chancellery and latterly the Bunker. Disbelief abounded amongst those females that had rather fancied the dashing young SS Gruppenführer; he had seemed so indestructible and they had all believed him utterly loyal to the Führer despite his big mouth and massive ego.

But now, he was gone, thus showing that the Führer could and would terminate the existence of any one of them without so much as a blink.

Even von Loringhoven was feeling unsettled by the suddenness of the latest dismissal from life that had been Hermann Fegelein. Rank was no longer any kind of protection and Himmler's pathetic peace wheedling posturing would be funny were it not so devastatingly indicative of the Nazi hierarchy. The architects and arbiters of the hell that had been unleashed upon the world were, almost as one, attempting to save their skins and crawl away. Like pus searching for scabs in which to hide they slithered hither and thither. Once so loving of the limelight, now so tremblingly avoiding any kind of light at all. Loringhoven sneered a sneer so long that it made even his aristocratically handsome face seem ugly. Would he miss the occasionally shared cigarette breaks with Fegelein? Not in the least. He had tolerated him because he had to; good riddance, as far as von Loringhoven was concerned. But who was next?

"Excuse me, Bernd," the very large figure of Hitler's surgeon, Obersturmbannführer Ludwig Stumpfegger, eased past the only slightly less tall but slenderer figure that was Bernd Freytag von Loringhoven. The two got on well. Stumpfegger's SS rank was little more than an honorary title which enabled him to carry out his Führer duties without hindrance.

Loringhoven made way for the six-foot five-inch SS surgeon. Stumpfegger was also an accomplished medical practitioner and as such Hitler found him invaluable as a skilled jack-of-all-trades. The Führer had been at something of a loss after the departure of the gross and foul-smelling Theodor Morell. Stumpfegger, however, didn't much enjoy his work for the Führer. The Reich's commander in chief constantly demanded aids and cures that the SS surgeon simply could not, or would not supply. Stimulants in pill form, such as the quackish Morell had supplied, Stumpfegger refused point blank to prescribe. The leader of a nation should not be on fantasy inducing psychotropic drugs, not in his opinion. It was only because of his intimate knowledge of treatment for various ailments afflicting Hitler that he remained in the position which he now held. Another doctor, Ernst Schenck, was kept on hand in order to supply Hitler with his favourite addictions.

Apart from some clerks mingling at the far end of the Vorbunker corridor they were alone. Von Loringhoven laid a light and furtively probing hand upon Stumpfegger's wrist.

"Any news, Ludwig?" he gave a short flick of his head toward where Hitler's rooms were situated.

Feeling and looking like a second-rate actor in an American crime movie, Stumpfegger glanced around, then, lowering his head from its great height said very softly, "No, not really. There is talk of," he hesitated, "well, you know, Bernd, there is talk of someone doing the right thing and just relieving us all of a great problem."

"He won't do it himself? Unbelievable!" Loringhoven sighed and joined the surgeon in his furtive eye flicking glances up and down the corridor. "This is insane; just damn well stupidly insane. It must stop."

"Even Goebbels has come around to our way of thinking," said Stumpfegger. "I heard him making some veiled comments to Walter Hewel and General Jodl. That wife of his, though. She'll happily inform on, or kill anyone she even remotely suspects of working against the Führer."

"I know," hissed Loringhoven. "But see here, Ludwig. Talk won't get us anywhere, it's action that is needed. And you my friend, are in the best position of us all. Can't you just give the wretch something and put him out of our misery!"

"Me?" Stumpfegger jerked back in horror. "Look, Bernd," he stopped talking as General Mohnke came thundering along the corridor on his way to the daily Hitler briefing. He nodded briefly at the two tall officers as he passed and then turned back to them. They could see the exhaustion clearly on his face. Black rings circled sunken, bloodshot eyes and his skin was a ghastly pallor. Adding to the aura of hell on earth that he'd brought with him to the Bunker, there was something that looked as though it might be flesh and bone sticking revoltingly from the sleeve of his filthy battle begrimed tunic. Dear God, thought Loringhoven, he looks almost as bad as Hitler.

"Seen Misch?" demanded Mohnke brusquely.

"You mean Scharführer Misch?" Stumpfegger replied rather stupidly, as there was only one Misch in the Bunker and everyone was aware of him.

"Yes. Him. Seen him?"

"I imagine he'll be down at his phones now that the switchboard seems to have given up the ghost."

"Ah." Mohnke shrugged his shoulders. "I see." Just as he was about to continue on his journey he paused and said, "You might want to think about making yourselves scarce in a few hours. There's going to be some rather nasty visitors dropping in and wanting to do a nice little booted jig on anything German."

"Why, general," Loringhoven smiled conspiratorially. "That might be construed as defeatist talk. Men have been shot for less, sir."

"Really, major?" Mohnke smiled back at him. "And just who the fuck d'you think does all the shooting around here, eh?" He stalked off. "Remember what I said. Seventy-two hours maximum."

As the SS commander of the Bunker's outer defences disappeared into the far reaches of the Bunker, Stumpfegger frowned and said, "Sounds bad, eh, Bernd?"

"Oh", Loringhoven waved a languid hand. "When hasn't it?" Then he shook his head and threw off all vestige of devil-may-care pretence and admitted. "Yes, Ludwig, and coming from Mohnke, I'd say it's pretty damn final." He looked almost appealingly at the massive SS surgeon. "For heaven's sake, can't you of all people come up with something? Whilst the Führer still breathes we are stuck down here just waiting to die. You're one of the few with the access and the tools!"

Stumpfegger blinked, licked his lips and said, "It's not as easy as you seem to think, Bernd. It's difficult, you see, to end a man when you've just finished repairing his anal fistula."

"His what?"

"Precisely." With that Stumpfegger sloped off.

That left precious few others who might be able to, or even consider eliminating Hitler. There was, of course, himself. But how? Only a select few were permitted to carry firearms and he wasn't one of them. So, that left him with his bare hands. Now that he thought about it, if he could just get the man alone for a few minutes how difficult could it be? The Führer was a physical wreck. Nothing much more than one hundred and thirty pounds of brittle and ailing human wreckage: it could be done. However, he would need an appointment, even down here, which would mean going through Bormann. That man would never allow him, nor anyone else, sole access to the Führer. Even now, the Reichsleiter guarded his privileges more ferociously than a latter-day Cerberus. Could he handle them both? No, not before Bormann shrieked loud enough to be heard and help arrived. Loringhoven had yet another problem which nagged constantly at his mind whenever his thoughts drifted to removing the Reich's wilting leader. His oath: they had all taken that binding oath to the Führer and despite everything that had been done by him and in his name, he, Bernd Freytag von Loringhoven, felt bound by it, just as so many of them still did. Damn it to hell! Why were they all so stupid – how could an oath be more important than the survival of a nation? He had to put it to the back of his mind and obey his conscience; simple as that! He went after Stumpfegger determined to force his point before it was too late.

CHAPTER 33

April 29 1945: Berlin, The Bunker

Walter Hewel, diplomat extraordinaire and the now despised Foreign Minister von Ribbentrop's liaison officer to the Führer, sat opposite his leader gazing at him sadly. He remembered the early days when the Führer had radiated power, confidence and, yes, even charm; all he radiated now was a repulsive smell.

In Hewel's view, the Führer had been misled and ill-advised by a coterie of self-seeking and perverted hedonists. The poor man had sacrificed his health, body and to some extent his mind for the sake of his people and the Reich. He was a hero cast in the true iron fast Germanic mould, but he had been grievously misled. That's how Walter saw his ailing Führer. He had been wrong and even now was not fully aware of the horrors that his master had unleashed upon the world. Hitler and his henchmen and women had proven to have hearts of steel possessing a ruthlessness that was totally alien to a more humanely inclined soul. The shadowy assistance he had lent the Abwehr some years ago he had quickly terminated when he realised that he was being used by men cleverer than himself for purposes that he did not fully comprehend. Sensibly, even though he knew that they still wanted his services, he sided with Ribbentrop against Canaris and his Abwehr purely out of a natural desire for self-preservation.

Hewel, however, although he had been put together with a far gentler and more passive mixture than most of the Nazi leadership was, nevertheless, imbued with a single mindedness of purpose which in its own way could be quite terrifying. He was ever so slightly chubby, smooth-faced and had the appearance of a very nice chap, which he was. The Party hierarchy thought of him as far too humanitarian in his views. It was rumoured that he had once complained to Himmler about the wilful slaughtering of foreign peoples, in particular the Jews. Himmler had scoffed him out of his office and snickered unkindly when Walter had gone to Hitler with his off-the-wall theories of kindness and compassion being tools far better suited to the retention of conquered territories than the recklessly in-vogue methods of constant terror and brutality. But Walter, of course, had missed the point completely. In a deviocracy, such as the Third Reich, brutality was *the* tool to have and use to show off one's power. It was a known fact amongst the Nazi intelligencia, that utter brutality was the key to a better life and so, many thousands of them became well practised in the use of it. It was all part of an unspoken and unofficial dogma but nevertheless real for all that. To display flagrant or even restrained disrespect to this well founded and deep belief would mean ostracization, at the very least! The Third Reich was no place for heretics. The Führer had given Hewel a metaphorical pat on the head and smiled him on his way. Walter Hewel was tolerated by the Nazi royalty for one salient reason and that was his absolute and unimpeachable, or so it was thought, loyalty to the Nazi party. Whilst others screamed and cursed, ran for their lives and betrayed everything that they had sworn to protect and hold dear, Walter stood firm, like a rock. The soft looking man with the cute little paunch had transpired to be tougher and a lot more worthwhile than the majority of Himmler's black-clad SS killers and Gestapo interrogators.

As far as he was concerned, once a man chose a course, bed or wife, then that was it; he died either with it, or for it!

Walter, however, was no idiot. His peculiar methods over the years and his apparent determination to stand by what he believed in, even in the face of sharp criticism, had gained him a good deal of respect from those within the Party who were not quite so enamoured by the Führer or at ease with his doings worldwide.

Hitler was gazing dolefully back at him. The normally ever-present Bormann had been dismissed from the Führer's presence. Hewel was the one man on earth that Adolf Hitler was quite sure would not harm him. Even Bormann was happy enough to leave him alone with his still occasionally mercurial meal ticket, safe in the knowledge that Walter was not a man for conspiracies, plots or assassinations.

Hitler attempted a smile but it was quite hopeless. The right side of his face refused to move and all he managed was a child-scaring grimace.

"What is it, Hewel? I don't see much of you these days. So much to do what with making sure that we win this war." He leaned forward from his chair. "Which we shall, my young friend. Make no mistake……"

"Sir! Führer – my Führer. Stop it. Please!"

"What did you say?" Hitler was nonplussed at being spoken to in such a way.

"My Führer." Hewel stood and looked down at the beaten old lump before him. He searched for words but Hitler waved an impatient hand.

"Sit down, Hewel and get control of yourself."

Walter sat; hands slapped over both knees. He knew what he had to say and hated having to say it. But even if it meant his life he would, nevertheless, speak the truth to his Führer, in full. This had to end.

"Now," Hitler spoke with amazing calm and for him, remarkable gentleness, as if he knew what was coming. "What is it you want, young man, eh?"

"Well, sir." Hewel managed through tight lips. "Firstly, my Führer, I wish to ask for one of the capsules that Herr Stumpfegger has provided. The reason being," and here he looked directly at his Führer and locked eyes with the man who had been for so long his absolute master, "because I believe that the war is lost and I have no desire to continue living under Soviet conquerors, sir. "Or," he shrugged, "if I am to be honest, any other conqueror. I will make an end of it my Führer, here in the Bunker."

The expected outburst didn't arrive. Hitler just sat staring at him with watery eyes. Then, abruptly and without a word, reached into his tunic pocket and withdrew a small metal pill box. It was no larger than a child's thumbnail and the Führer handed it to him wordlessly.

Hewel took the proffered pill holder and opened it. Inside there nestled a small round capsule.

"Cyanide," whispered Hitler, conspiratorially. "Keep the lid shut until you need to use it else it can lose potency over time. You know, Hewel," his eyes wandered slightly as his mind travelled back, "I had the most awful disagreement with Speer about the war. Did you know that?"

"No, my Führer. I didn't."

"It was a week ago, I think. He refused to admit that the war could still be won; just wouldn't go along with my thinking, you see. I've rubbed him out of the government, you know. I finished my testament, oh yes, and made sure that he has no future part to play in the future Reich. None! I will admit, that things are not too good here in Berlin. But men like Speer must never be allowed to control the actions of the future Reich."

Future Reich – what future Reich? Walter had precious little idea of what the Führer was talking about. Testaments, arguments with a minister? It was all one to him. He had a vague recollection of one of the secretaries getting in a tizz when that oaf Fegelein was shot and Goebbels yelling something to her about a testament. Was that what Hitler was going on about?

There was no more time for any of this self-indulgence.

"I am sure that the armaments minister feels bereft, my Führer. I believe that Herr Speer always did his best for you and the Party."

"Not damn well near enough," growled Hitler, "not by a long shot, he didn't. Betrayed me, he did, in the end, just like the rest. He betrayed me. Why? I made him, made him what he is. I gave him everything he ever needed and see how he repaid me. Damn-damn-swine!" His brown speckled hands began moving erratically back and forth, up and down and his head was jerking agitatedly from side to side. All these were clear warning signs that he was about to go off again on one of his interminable self-pitying monologues. Walter knew that if he didn't stop him there would be copious tears, recriminations in the vilest language imaginable, all followed by lip spraying vomit from the sick old man before him. Poor fellow, he thought. My poor, poor Führer: to be brought to such a pass as this!

Hewel knew how much Hitler had depended upon Albert Speer and just how much he revered and envied that man's style, superior education and mental talents. If Adolf Hitler ever truly liked and admired any human being, that being was the urbane Albert Speer. Walter had got on quite well with Speer, although the armaments minister was inclined to poke fun at the easy-going diplomat because of the antics of his ludicrous boss, Joachim von Ribbentrop. But Walter had always known what the charming Albert was about. He had conned Adolf Hitler because Hitler adored him. Speer was clever, right enough. Probably the cleverest man in the party. They got on because they shared a similar level of educational attainment. Unlike the majority of those around them, they were both highly educated men, men whose imagination went beyond the need or desire for unnecessary violence. They spoke the same language, but they certainly didn't harbour the same thoughts. Walter quite liked being around Speer because of his very dry and wittily sarcastic sense of humour, but he knew him to be a lying, cold-hearted manipulator. But that was life in politics, so no point in bemoaning or judging.

Valuable time was being wasted. Walter rose and before the Führer could get any further with his diatribe, said firmly, "My Führer. You must listen to me." Dribble was already running down Hitler's chin but he looked up sharply. Walter dropped into a friendly crouch so that he might be eye to eye with the Führer. He almost lay a tentative hand upon his leader's constantly trembling knee but thought better of it.

"The time has come, my Führer. You must not be taken alive. The disgrace and humiliation of such an event would be beyond bearing for all Germans."

"Then why don't they make sure that it doesn't happen?" Wailed the Führer. "Why am I betrayed by those that have best cause to remain true? Why-Why?" Tears appeared and began to flow down grizzled cheeks. It was an ugly sight to see; the Führer of the Third Reich sobbing and whimpering like the self-pitying old man that he was.

"Sir," Hewel protested. "This won't do. Remember who you are."

"Oh!" Hitler's whine turned to a roar of outrage. His fist clenched and he threw a feeble punch at Hewel's head. It landed but with less force than a floating tissue. "Get out!" The roar had become a squeak. The lion a mouse. Hewel reared back. He had to get through to the man. The future of all Germans and any subsequent self-respect that they might hold for themselves depended upon him convincing the Führer to act now, within the hour. Germany must have something glorious to look back on. The fight to the finish was all that remained, but beyond that there must be pride in the achievements of the Reich's fallen heroes; Siegfried and Gotterdammerung were all very well but some semblance of truth around the myth needed to be preserved. Better that all Germany be destroyed than their once brilliant and courageous leader be taken in disgrace and revealed as a whining heap of self-pity. Such a thing must never, *never* be allowed to happen.

The door flew open as Martin Bormann thundered in. "Just what the devil's going on here?" he demanded angrily. "I heard shouting."

Hitler sat, writhing in his chair and Hewel was at last beginning to lose patience with it all. The Führer was clearly beyond any kind of rationality. It was Bormann, and Bormann alone, who was keeping this wretched charade from coming to a close. But for what possible reason?

With a trembling, liver spotted hand the Führer pointed accusingly at Hewel who had risen to his full five-feet-eleven inches, which was more than enough to have him towering above the portly Reichsleiter.

"He wants me dead," growled the Führer. This man whom I have trusted for years has stated to my face, Bormann, TO MY FACE – that I should die here and now. What d'you think of such an outrageous piece of chicanery, eh?"

"Unbelievable villainy, my Führer." Bormann looked suitably outraged, his acting skills, honed over the last five years of sneaky subservience to the Führer, were by now almost matchless.

A loud rapping came on the only partly closed 'Führer quarters' gas proof door. Bormann turned savagely toward whoever it might be and snarled, "Not now. We are in conference. Get away at once!"

"I most certainly will not and don't you ever take that tone with me again Herr Reichsleiter Bormann." Joseph Goebbels pressed his puny shoulder against the creaking steel door and heaved it further open. The Propaganda Minister took things in at a glance. He clumped in club footedly and stood directly above Hitler.

"My Führer," he gave Adolf his best smarmy smile which dropped abruptly as he transferred his gaze to Bormann.

"Now look here, Herr Goebbels......." Bormann opened his mouth preparing to verbally slap down the Propaganda Minister but that man effortlessly waved his utterance aside.

"Forgive me my Führer if I interrupt the ramblings of your secretary...."

Bormann's face reddened at this maddening display of disrespect. Hitler looked from one to the other. There had been a time not so long ago when such juvenile bitching would have been grist to his ever-turning mill, but now he just felt confused. What the devil did they all want? He was beginning to feel decidedly out of sorts, even more so than usual. He needed a pick-me-up. And some cake; he wanted some cake. That always made him feel better.

"I have a request from the secretaries. They would like to leave, if you would allow them to do so, of course. I said that I would put it to you as there is nothing more that they can do for us down here. Might be best to let them go."

"They'll probably be picked up in minutes once they're out there if they try it on their own. They could end up being shot, raped, or both. Can't they see that?" Bormann said in his know-it-all fashion.

"You think that they'll have a better chance tramping through what remains of Berlin with a squad of armed to the teeth soldiers, then? Nobody'll notice that little lot, that's for sure, eh, Herr Reichsleiter Bormann?"

Bormann's fat fists clenched as he struggled to retain his composure. "I am merely saying, that they are our responsibility and we should do everything possible to protect them. Not just send the poor girls out with no plan or means of survival."

"A plan had been formulated," replied Goebbels and it has a reasonable chance of success if they follow it to the letter."

"Well, in this situation," snarled Bormann, "I should say that there's fat chance of anything going to plan, *Herr* Minister."

Hitler raised a limpish looking arm as he attempted to interpose but he was ignored. He coughed and wriggled a little and his head drooped as Goebbels, his dislike of the Reichsleiter now showing far more obviously than before, raised his voice in reply, "Well, Reichsleiter Bormann, as we are discussing plans, designs and shall we say, shenanigans, how are your attempts at message sending to Herr Himmler, eh?"

Bormann's jaw dropped and even Hewel gasped. Himmler was supposed to be under arrest but such was his power and the numerical strength of his bodyguard, that nobody at this stage of the war, could spare the men to arrest him, nor felt much inclined to do so. One full division of Totenkopf SS he had kept for his personal use and no one much cared to take them on.

The fact was that he, Bormann, had been trying to get in touch with Schellenberg to ascertain Himmler's precise whereabouts in order to arrange command handover of the Totenkopf troops to SS General Karl Wolf, who would then, hopefully, use it to march on Berlin and rescue them all; well, rescue him, anyway and the Führer. But the way that Goebbels had put it, he had been trying to contact the Reich's greatest traitor and now Hitler's most hated and despised enemy for clandestine reasons of his own. Utter rubbish!

"Contact was necessary to safeguard the Führer," protested Bormann with chest heaving vehemence. As you very well know, Herr Goebbels."

Dear God, thought Goebbels, any minute now he's going to start beating his thorax like an ape. He amended his thought. Like the ape that he is. "Seriously?" Goebbels smirked.

"Yes, damn it! Seriously," yelled Bormann. "An entire division of SS Totenkopf that should be here protecting us…I mean, the Führer, is just sitting idly by, waiting hand and foot upon that man, Himmler. The unmitigated swine has been keeping them back for his personal use. Criminal, I tell you – criminal!"

"A division?" What should have been a roar was more of an irritated bleat but clearly the Führer had been jolted back to reality. "Why did I not know?" He rose and raised both arms. "Traitors the whole goddamned lot of you. Miserable, rotten to the core vile ingrates. Is this what I deserve after all my sacrifice? Ungrateful buggers. Get out! Get out!" He took three tottering steps to the right and then two more to the rear and collapsed into the cheap and shoddy looking sofa.

He just sat. Head shaking from side to side repeating himself over and over. "Charlatans. Charlatans all. All of them. Where's Linge? I want some cake."

"Perhaps I should fetch Fraulein Braun," suggested Hewel, simply for something to ease the rising tension.

Both Goebbels and Bormann turned to look at the always charming Walter Hewel. It was a difficult situation because the three men at that moment sharing Hitler's living quarters were all high-ranking officials.

"Fraulein Braun?" Goebbels's tone was less than enthusiastic. Hewel and Bormann glanced sharply at the Führer but he made no response. Someone had to ease the rising tension and say something nice, or at least volunteer to accept the odium just waiting to spill all over them from the furious, cake demanding Führer.

"I said, where's Linge," moaned Hitler. As if on cue, Heinz Linge appeared. A tray was clasped in his white gloved hands and atop it were cup, saucer, delicately sliced pieces of lemon, sugar lumps and, thank heaven, the all-important cake. It was cream cake with apple filling and a large sprinkling of heavily sugared almonds over the top. An outrageous extravagance which was glaringly out of place with its surroundings.

"Here, Linge, here." Hitler waved him over impatiently. Pour tea and cut me a slice." He gestured commandingly at the cake. Linge smiled and obeyed instantly. No matter what and no matter where, Heinz Linge always knew what his Führer wanted. Hewel shook his head in a slightly bewildered fashion. The man Linge was a marvel. Goebbels nodded at the Führer's valet. It was well done and the awful tension was receding by the minute as Hitler's happy meter rose in accordance with the pleasuring of his very sweet tooth. Things were abruptly spoiled by the dramatic appearance of General Wilhelm Mohnke barging into the now extremely cramped quarters of the supreme commander. He threw up an immaculately executed Hitler salute and bellowed the obligatory "Sieg Heil my Führer." Hitler, about to reach for his beloved cake, paused and looked up at his SS protector.

"What is it Mohnke? More bad news?"

"As you failed to appear for your usual military briefing my Führer, I felt it necessary to report to you as soon as was possible and in person."

Hitler nibbled delicately upon his thick, cream packed tasty and made a small, almost girlish sound of appreciation. His yellowish tongue flicked out and around his lips as he reached for and popped a sugar lump into his mouth and then promptly sipped at his tea. A small gurgling sound emanated from his lips as he slurped through the fleshy lemon slice swimming atop his thin, porcelain cup.

Mohnke allowed his saluting arm to drop casually to his side. He looked around at the others before continuing. "Perhaps, sir, we should reconvene in the conference room. Jodl and Krebs are there and we hope to hear from Weidling before too long, that's assuming, of course, well," he shrugged, "it's not certain that he can get through."

As if deliberately trying to postpone the inevitable deluge of bad news that he knew must be coming, Hitler took another mouthful of his delicious cake and mulched it slowly around his mouth. Crumbs of creamy apple touched sponge trickled down his grey already stained tunic and nestled over his dark trousered lap like snow on a blackboard.

Mohnke's cheeks hollowed as he breathed in and out very deeply. Ignoring any kind of protocol he bent over the Führer and spoke urgently into his ear.

There was a gasp and then Hitler said, "All of them – so soon? Surely we have reserves? We must. I know we must. Enough to hold them for a little while longer. That is all that I ask, Mohnke. There are things, vital things that I as Führer must do. I still have so much left to do. It is beyond your understanding Mohnke, but I must have more time. More time!" The cup fell to the floor and Linge moved to pick it up. Mohnke turned to the others and said, "Twenty hours at the very most. They are quite literally here. The only reason that they have not hammered down the door of the Bunker is because at this precise moment they are devoting all their attention to the Reichstag. That's where they think the Führer is holding out and that entire area has become an inferno. Our forces are fighting to the death but we are quite literally now within their battle boundary. You must all go now, settle your affairs and such, or suffer the consequences. There is nothing left in the way of an organized defence."

Goebbels, Hewel and Bormann stared at one another. What now?

They had all known that this moment was coming and yet they were totally unprepared. An evil smell pervaded the small room. Nerves were becoming very frayed.

Goebbels said, "My Führer, I believe that it is time to end this."

Hewel nodded. "I was saying as much before Reichsleiter Bormann entered."

"Oh, I know what you were up to right enough," snarled Bormann. "Don't you worry yourself about that, Herr Diplomat. The Führer's safety is paramount. It is *all* that concerns me, nothing else."

The smell was growing worse, almost suffocatingly awful, and it was now accompanied by hellish sounds from someone's noisily overwrought belly.

"Enough of this bickering," snapped Goebbels. "We must ascertain what the Führer feels about all this."

Mohnke wrinkled his nose. He had the distinct feeling that the Führer had already let them all know exactly how he felt.

"Whatever you command, my Führer," continued the Propaganda Minister, "I, your loyal servant, shall obey." He threw his head back and adopted the same set-jawed and determined expression that he had liked to use whilst extolling the Führer's virtues during his Nazi rally speeches in former times.

All three men turned toward their sofa ensconced Führer and waited for his decision. A pregnant pause ensued which was followed by a strangled cough, a wheezing gasp and a slapping of hands against thighs as the Führer jerked convulsively as though enduring a silent coughing fit. His right hand flapped, clenched, opened and then fell claw-like onto its owner's lap.

Mohnke, who had been obscuring the view of the others by standing directly in front of Hitler whilst he spoke, suddenly turned and bent forward. Were they seeing things right? Did the heroic general actually reach out and touch the Führer? He had indeed. Straightening up he turned back slowly to face the three men. Linge, standing behind the sofa was white-faced with angst. He still held the fallen cup and now stood, as though undecided as to where he should put it.

Mohnke ran a tired hand across his forehead. What a supreme bloody waste it all was.

"The Führer," he intoned, feeling like a second-rate actor performing at a village hall, "is dead!"

A moment's stunned silence was followed by a unison movement forward as they all crowded around to view the now bug-eyed and very dead Führer of the Third Reich. Their surge forward was followed almost immediately by an olfactory rendered necessity to retreat at least a few feet from the stiffening corpse. The final awfulness of death, against which he had so determinedly but hopelessly fought, now claimed the once mighty master of the Third Reich. Hewel was shocked and horribly upset by what he saw. The scene was beyond disgusting. That Hitler had been dying whilst they had been arguing was bad enough, and although his end must have been quick, the manner of it defied all effort at dignified description. For the German Führer, Adolf Hitler, such a death was unacceptable and must never be publicised or known elsewhere.

"Oh, dear God!" Goebbels lurched back as an enormous expulsion of gas emanated loudly from the dead Führer. He knew that this sort of thing happened to the recently departed but had never personally witnessed it. Awful – too awful!

What to do? None of them really knew. Now that he was gone, it seemed impossible that he was in fact, really *gone*.

Mohnke decided to take charge of these civilian weaklings and set the ball rolling. "Heart attack I'd say. Anyway, I shall go and fetch Doctor Stumpfegger and then I'm going to halt that madness up there." He pointed brusquely upwards.

"No – no! Wait a moment." Said Hewel in a more determined manner than was usual for him. "You can't."

"What d'you mean – I can't?" Mohnke's tone was close to being threatening.

"Get Stumpfegger, by all means," replied Hewel. "But this," he pointed at the dead man on the sofa, "say nothing of this to anyone and certainly don't go making any ceasefires on your own account. We have things to consider down here. Not least...." He raised two defensively calming hands towards Mohnke and the about to yell, Bormann, "Not least," he repeated, "what has just this minute happened."

"He's right," Goebbels cut in as, in a show of support he went and stood directly beside the diplomat. "Look around. We need a story. Something to give the people. What the nation does not need is a vision nor even the slightest knowledge of THIS!" He waved his hands around the room. "Dear God in heaven," his eyes filled. "Is this what the Third Reich, the Führer, we ourselves, is *this* how we end? Look at him for crying out loud. Thousands, tens of thousands of Germans have died for him, and even more are still dying for him. FOR HIM, not us or the state but HIM." He waved a despairing hand at the swelling body on the sofa. God, it was becoming more disgusting by the minute, "Is that the image you want the soldiers still fighting to preserve the life of the Führer to see? Do you think that they, any one of them should be so brutalised as to have any such knowledge thrust upon them? He was their hero, their God, their goddamned everything. Now look at him. The almighty Führer, our most glorious and revered leader slain – BY A BLOODY CREAM CAKE! And he died, may I point out," here Goebbels's face became a mask of genuine emotion, "squelched in a mountain of his own excrement. Nobody must ever know how he died; Not ever!"

"A fair point," agreed the nodding Mohnke. "So," he pointed at Goebbels and Hewel, "think up a story. It had better be quick 'cos we don't have much time." He marched off to locate Stumpfegger whilst the others faffed around throwing out scatty ideas for all kinds of make-believe accounts of what had happened. Bormann was close to panic. That brutal face and powerful, thick-set body efficiently hid the heart and soul of an absolute coward. Without his boss and mentor he possessed little power. He needed to contact Hitler's designated successor, Admiral Dönitz, in Schleswig Holstein. Hitler had placed the navy chief in command of that entire area but as yet Dönitz would know nothing of Hitler's demise. It was time for some telegraphic bluffing. All he had to do was conceal the Führer's death from the avian featured admiral, issue some kind of phoney directive that ordered his placement at the new seat of government and all would be well. Admiral Karl Dönitz was a man who believed in total devotion to duty and the rule of law. The problems of getting himself up to Schleswig Holstein he would consider later. In the meantime, going along with Goebbels's demand for complete secrecy regarding Hitler's death suited him very well, for the moment. Time to join in the discussion.

Hewel it was whose mind worked clearest and fastest, and Goebbels added colourful and moderately believable touches of his own. He made quick and salient points as to how they should organize things. He also, even though he knew his own end was fast approaching, added some valuable insight as to how to best stage manage the whole affair in the hours to come. It would be necessary to bring others into the scheme. And then the hard bit, giving intelligent people the lie to relate later but never telling them the actual truth. Mohnke and Stumpfegger would, of course, be aware of what was being done. A plan of sorts was formulated with remarkable speed in that room and its sole object was the perpetuation and spread of the myth of a magnificently brave Führer fighting heroically to the last. The interior comms were still working and Goebbels blasted out commands and threats to each and every department chief still in the Bunker.

Mohnke arrived with Stumpfegger a short while later. "Heart attack," confirmed the SS surgeon. "Brought about, probably, by asphyxia; choking. Not much doubt that the cake was the culprit. He'd been showing signs of worsening arterial sclerosis for some time now, and frankly, his addiction to cream cakes and pastries didn't help matters. The Führer owned a diseased heart and it quite simply stopped. He was what, fifty-six years old? He had the body of an eighty-year-old and I dread to think of the condition of his internal organs. Without a post-mortem I can't tell you more."

"I don't think we need be bothering ourselves with that kind of detail,"said Goebbels.

"We really should get him moved," suggested Mohnke.

"Yes, yes," Hewel agreed, making sure that he spoke softly to the SS general. "Now," he deftly took centre stage. "We need Misch. It will be his job to sort out Eva Braun and find us that registrar. Wagner is his name. The Führer had him here to witness his testament. He's probably still upstairs by the section guardhouse. Now, Linge," he gestured to the always immaculate valet, Obersturmführer Heinz Linge, who, very shortly after the original shock of his master's death, had quickly overcome any reservations he might have had about what was being planned and had even made a couple of very useful suggestions. "Would you inform Misch of what is needed and as quickly as you can, please."

"Tell him that the command comes from me," interjected Mohnke. "He'll be far less likely to argue or question. Tell him everything"

"It shall be as you say, Herr General." Linge smoothly made his way out of the room without even the semblance of a salute.

Stolz, the SS Guard Commander had already been ordered by Mohnke to keep everybody within the strictest confines of their workplaces and to allow nobody in or out of the Bunker until commanded by Goebbels or Mohnke to do so. The sudden surge of muzzle pointing discipline came as a shock to the inhabitants of the Bunker who immediately began questions as to why – what was the point?

Rochus Misch swung into action without question and with no waste of time. He did, though, throw Heinz Linge a massively speculative look, to which the Obersturmführer responded with an elegant shrug from his neatly proportioned shoulders.

He had been given the most loathsome job. Apparently the order came from Mohnke, but it had Joseph Goebbels written all over it.

He was ordered to find Wagner, a registrar, and then to sort out the women and that meant only one thing.

Locating Walter Wagner was both quick and easy. He was indeed at the section guard house of the SS awaiting escort back to the front after witnessing Hitler's will and red jacketed testament. The testament, copied out three times, had been entrusted to three stalwarts, two of them soldiers and the other a press attaché, with orders to deliver them to the relevant worthies named inside the front cover. The three men had promised, all stern-faced, to deliver the historically vital documents, as ordered, and promptly, with courageous demeanour, departed on their appointed duties. Once outside, however, the three officers deciding that the printed ravings of a dead madman held no particular value to history, simply threw the testaments into the gutter and made their individual attempts to escape the ruin of Berlin.

Wagner, the registrar, now sat in the Bunker conference room. A marriage certificate was being typed up by Hitler's most efficient secretary, Gertrude Junge. All Wagner, as a legally appointed Registrar, had to do was sign the document and then he would be sent on his merry way.

Incredibly, over Hitler's bloated and stinking corpse, a workable plan had been formulated and was already being obediently followed. It was intellectually scruffy, barely believable, but Goebbels and Hewel were convinced that it would work. After all, what else was there? A very small group would know the real truth, a larger group of those formally close to Hitler would be fed a bare-faced and totally ludicrous lie but in the absence of anything else would believe that *they* knew the truth. As for the rest? Well, as Goebbels pointed out, whoever bothered to ask the little man what he thought or saw? Privates and corporals, cleaners and clerks etc. Such folk meant nothing! When it was all over, the only questions to be asked would be asked of the upper-class personnel, the elite, so to speak. Those who had been close to the centre; the Bormanns, Hewels and Mohnkes of this subterranean world. Then on down to any kind of officer, Minister, personal secretary, military confidants and suchlike; the aforementioned would be quickly briefed by Hewel and Goebbels of the fairy tale version of what had happened and then sworn to secrecy. They would all, of course, sooner or later, reveal what they knew, or thought that they knew. As long as they went along with the rough outline of the great lie all should be well. Such stories invariably contradicted one another anyway. As for the mass, those little people who even now gathered around outside the Führer's private quarters expectantly awaiting some kind of news, who on earth would ever seek them out for information? Historians and investigators would only be interested in what the leading personalities, the movers and the shakers had to say. The plan was that they be confronted with accomplished liars who would convincingly feed to them all the absurd tripe that they wanted to hear. It should make plausible copy, and by the time anyone got around to checking their stories against those of the hoi polloi it would be too late. The myth of the Third Reich, the fantasy death of its Siegfried like Führer, would be perpetuated for all time, hopefully. More to the point: their part in the great struggle would be lionized, respected, and revered by those that came after them.

"It's too damn risky and doesn't have the slightest touch of realism," protested Bormann.

"We're going ahead with it," replied Goebbels. "It will work. Besides which, there's no other choice."

"Just think of the confusion," put in Hewel. "There will be a million questions, all asked by foreign interrogators, journalists and the like. In such a circumstance as this," he waved his hands around, "they will in all likelihood believe anything we tell them. What choice will they have?"

"Howling hell!" Bormann gagged and looked around desperately. More than anything he wanted to get out of this place, its vile stench and its attendant aura of utter doom and gloom. He hadn't been able to contact Dönitz directly but a message had got through to his HQ. He needed now to get out. Hewel and Goebbels, though, were quite right in their estimation of the situation. That reeking *thing* on the sofa was smelling worse by the minute.

The trouble was the believability of their story.

"Look," said Bormann. "We all know how sick and feeble the old boy was."

God in heaven! Thought Hewel. That was a far cry from the unctuous utterings that usually sprang from the Reichsleiter's mouth when mentioning his Führer.

"Constantly trembling hands, physically feeble, almost blind and, truth be told, unable to walk unaided. Let us be real here. The man couldn't even *hold* a pistol let alone stick one to his head and fire the bloody thing. Nobody will ever believe it."

"Yes they will," snarled Goebbels. "They'll believe anything that I choose to tell them and I tell them, and you, Herr Bormann, that the Führer, Adolf Hitler shot himself rather than be taken by the enemy. He bravely ended his life, fighting in defence of his beloved capital, Berlin. He also bit on a cyanide capsule to ensure that the Russians could not inflict the indignity of capture upon him. As to your statement that he did not possess the strength to shoot himself. Here, problem solved." Goebbels withdrew a small Walther PP.32 from his inner jacket pocket and fired a round straight into Hitler's lolling head. The reaction was a lifelike jerk, a comic flick of his right arm followed by further slumping down the sofa.

Bormann almost jumped out of his skin whilst Hewel took a step back in initial alarm.

"The Führer," hissed Goebbels. "Has just shot himself." He checked his watch. "Time is 15:30 hours. All agreed?"

A series of watch checks followed by affirmative nods.

"Good. Now, let's get on with the rest of it, shall we?"

From outside the Führer's Bunker apartment came the sound of loud rejoicing. Bormann, with so much to do, eased his way out. The door had not been completely shut and the sound of the shot had been quite widely heard at this level.

Clerks, junior ranks and general dogsbodies together with red-lipped typists were shouting and laughing gleefully. Cigarettes were being lit and schnapps was being downed by the cupful. How the news had got out, gunshot notwithstanding, was a mystery. The workspaces for staff were a small way away from the entrance door to the Führer apartment and even though not fully closed, the thick steel door and massive concrete walls would have muffled the sound of a pistol shot beyond any certainty as to its precise origin. Had Mohnke said something, or Misch, perhaps? That didn't seem too likely. More probably the SS guard commander, Stolz or one of his men had leaked it. Bastard! They weren't yet ready for full disclosure.

"What the devil d'you all think you're doing, eh?" Roared Bormann in a voice which just a few hours ago would have put the fear of God into anyone of them. Loose sheets of A4-sized paper began flying through the air. It was an odd, but passable version of bunting and they began to sing happily.

"The old bastards dead," a facially scarred little Wehrmacht private sneered. Their cheers and loud acclamations of delight mixed with some of the vilest anti-Führer insults that he had ever heard shocked Bormann to the core. He'd had no idea that his former master was *this* unpopular. Poor Martin Bormann had earnestly believed that, despite everything, the little people down here loved their Führer, their Uncle Wolf. He'd also harboured the secret fantasy that they might even have a glowing respect for himself, the all-seeing Reichsleiter. Clearly, such was not the case.

Two of the girls were dancing on a wide desk to the hoots and bellows of both male and female occupants of the corridor. It had taken mere minutes to transform these outwardly humble and obedient drones into wild, table turning horrors.

"Enough!" Roared Bormann breathing a huge sigh of relief as Stolz turned up at his side with two SS guards.

"Back to work before I have you all shot." He turned his small beady eyes on the guard commander. "See that they continue with their duties, Sturmführer, I'll be back shortly."

The SS commander barely even glanced at Bormann as he nodded. Duties? Other than sticking up their middle fingers and blowing raspberries, it was difficult to see what else this lot might be capable of. The trap door had been opened and a lot of pent-up emotional nasties were about to be released.

As Bormann scuttled off Stolz gestured to one of his men.

"Shoot anyone that tries to leave. Clear?" The man nodded but not with any degree of enthusiasm. Wouldn't be long now before the whole thing collapsed, thought Stolz. He was finding it more and more difficult to resist the urge to turn about and walk to the Bunker exit and then just keep right on walking; it was something that he would have to do sooner or later anyway. The SS loyal unto death stuff was all wearing a bit thin these days. As he looked more closely at his two men, he realised that he wasn't the only one with those thoughts. Beckoning the remaining guard to follow him, Stolz retraced his steps back toward the Goebbels apartment where further important duties awaited him, or so he had been told.

CHAPTER 34

April 30 1945: The Bunker, Berlin.

"I can't! Honestly, Misch, get away from me." Rochus glared down at Eva Braun, his six-foot-plus frame dwarfing her as she shrank back from him. The woman was treading a far finer line than she could possibly imagine. She needed to obey him now, there was no time for arguments or tantrums. If she persisted with this silly bout of near hysteria then all Hewel's mewling wouldn't be able to save her. He would have to do what he must do.

"You say he's dead but where's the proof? And now you're saying that I should agree to be his bloody wife – a dead man's wife. Are you all insane? It's madness. I don't understand any of this." Eva broke into wretched sobs of self-pity, disbelief, horror, all rolled into one ugly, snot-dripping howl.

"You don't have to agree to anything," replied Misch. "Most of it's done. But if you want to have any chance at survival you'll do as you're told. Now, you must come with me."

Misch took Eva by the arm and propelled her down toward her own quarters which lay adjacent to the Führer's. His forceful strength and cast-iron demeanour showed a very different and far more terrifying Rochus Misch. This was not the Rochus that she knew. Nobody ever had manhandled her in such a manner as he was doing now. The world, her world, had gone completely insane and hysteria bubbled beneath her once cheery surface. She had experienced a total lack of comprehension about what was happening to her and all around her. Realisation, though, was now forcing its way into her brain. Despite the terror and confusion, her natural and very powerful instinct for survival was at last kicking in. As Misch dragged her, all loose-lipped and watery-eyed toward what was going to be some kind of crazy necro-style wedding, she fought to regain her composure. She was no fool, despite what others might think, and had seen enough to know that her previously so effective 'helpless little damsel' routine was over and done. She only had to feel the rough handed way that Misch tugged and dragged her around to know that much. Beyond doubt now, her survival was going to be down to nobody else but herself. That realization, factual as it was, made her shudder. But she would do whatever it took to make it out. The one thing that Eva had absolutely no intention of doing was dying: not down here, not up there, nor anywhere else if she could avoid it.

Nothing, though, could have prepared her for the horror that awaited in the Führer apartment. On the way, she was subjected to leers and jeers. And unbelievably smoke, of all things, was blown into her face. A far cry from her triumphant entry of such a short while ago. Everything that Hermann had warned her of was coming hideously true. Oh, how she wished that she had listened to him. Misch, a man who had always been so courteous and obliging was now very clearly ensuring that she was seen by as many people en route to the Führer apartment as was possible. There was no more mister nice guy. Steel-eyed Rochus Misch was all deadly seriousness and Eva was not merely scared stiff of what was going on around her, she was now terrified of a man that she had previously considered a friend. They, Bormann, Goebbels and that nice Herr Hewel were demanding that she sign a marriage certificate that was even now, as she tottered along, her wrist clasped firmly in Misch's powerful hand, being typed up by a secretary. It was some kind of plan they had concocted for posterity and therefore most likely to be just a load of meaningless tat designed to preserve their towering egos. It had been made very plain to her that, if she didn't sign, then, she must remain and die, with the very realistic threat of multiple rape thrown into the mix. If her identity were to be discovered then she would undoubtedly be paraded, tortured and humiliated before being executed. If, on the other hand, she were sensible and *did* sign, then she would be shown a way out. A difficult and dangerous journey, yes, but at least with a chance of survival. And, as Misch had so unkindly pointed out; against all advice, she had arrived down here and brought the now attendant problem upon herself. If she wished to survive, then, out into the ruin that was Berlin she must go, and yes, she must go alone. It wasn't much of a chance nor anything much of a choice. Those wretched men, no longer under the spell of their Führer, clearly didn't give a damn about her. Any lingering shreds of fantasy rescue and deliverance were replaced by ice-cold realism in her psyche. It was all over and she was right royally scuppered!

Her supposed beloved was by now well beyond even the most expert embalmer's ministrations and Eva, naturally enough, was violently sick the moment she set eyes upon, and got a whiff of the new, so to speak, Adolf.

She didn't even read the document that was thrust in front of her but automatically began to sign with her real name, Braun.

"No!" Goebbels grabbed her wrist with surprising strength. "With *his* name, you fool." He jerked his head toward the dead Hitler and there was much clucking and knowing masculine nodding at such typically female thoughtlessness. Eva bit her lip and held back any response that she might have made. Even now, terrified and uncertain as she was, she was utterly sick to death of the sneering patronization of the males around her. Self-serving mother's boys every single one of them. As always, out for nothing but themselves. True enough, so was she, but she was a woman and therefore, in her opinion, thoroughly entitled.

She held back the tears that threatened to engulf her and cast another glance at her dead Führer. For an instant she felt her heart shudder as she remembered the way it had once been. How Godlike he had seemed; him and all those men around him. Now, though, she saw the reality of it all. Just another bunch of egos on the make: that's all they had ever been. The funny looking little man who was the registrar, Walther Wagner, was hustled out and back from whence he came. The poor fellow was dead within an hour of his registering and witnessing the strange 'marriage' of Hitler and Braun. He was a staunch Nazi and so the powers that be, or what remained of them, had decided not to end his life themselves. The Russians obligingly did the job for them with a barrage of artillery shells. As the once respected public official made his way back to his unit, one such shell sent the thoroughly dismembered Wagner to his own particular Valhalla.

B ag packed, just a small brown valise, and, distressingly, dressed down to servants clothes, Eva Braun departed with Misch, who was now as completely devoted to shrouding her presence as he had previously been to advertising it. The distance from the Führer's apartment to the concrete staircase leading up and out to the old Reich Chancellery was short enough, a few metres only. The staff had only moments ago been shifted toward the Vorbunker in preparation for a breakout. Now scared witless they mingled and twittered and hovered the merest smidgen above total panic. To remain down here meant death but, then, any attempt to face what lay outside probably meant death, as well.

The few that did pass Misch and Eva as they made their way out were far too preoccupied with their own problems to pay any attention to a scruffy cleaner and the tall SS man. En route they passed the Goebbels' quarters and clearly something was going on in there but whatever it was it was none of their concern.

At the foot of the stairs two SS guards blocked their exit to the upper level but even they were not particularly attentive toward their duty and without even a glance at Eva, they nodded Misch through. As the two of them reached the mid Bunker level they heard the guards coming up after them. Not in chase but just two more soldiers deciding that enough was enough.

The old Chancellery was an utter ruin and the once beautiful grounds now resembled a first world war no-man's land. It was cold, hideously noisy and the atmosphere was thick with dust and cordite. Eva's knee-length coat was a pre-war cheapy from some downmarket store, the style of which had been long out of fashion even then; and the dress that Misch had insisted that she wear she wouldn't normally have been seen dead in. Light blue and of what had once been a bright patterned floral design, the faded shapes of the photo printed flowers now resembled dull grey and badly formed pastries on a dress that was two sizes too large for the current wearer. The scarf was a typical peasant style full head covering, grey in colour, and was deliberate in its available face and head concealment. Her shoes and stockings, though, would be a giveaway for anyone showing real interest in the identity of the wearer. Bespoke shoes and expensive nylons; costly and these days almost completely unattainable items for the average woman.

Eva hadn't enquired as to where the clothes and scarf came from. They were hers now and that was that. She idly supposed that one of the secretaries or female clerks would be the willing recipient of her clothes left in the Bunker. A slight twinge of possession loss gripped her but she quickly shook it off. They were welcome. Rape in silk or old cotton; it was all the same.

Unbeknownst to her, the truth was that the clothes she now wore still retained the fleshly warmth and human stains of their former owner. And the fact that she, Eva Braun was still alive, was down to the intervention of none other than Walther Hewel. The others had all been for eliminating her. Goebbels in particular had been most keen to see her ended. The story to go out would be that the Führer had rewarded his faithful companion, Eva Braun, with the gift of marriage and she, so very bravely, had resolutely determined to share his fate: death by suicide. Thus had the Führer and his faithful partner in life perished: For Germany!

Hewel had argued, quite forcibly, that Eva should be given the opportunity to escape. Nobody at large would ever recognize her. She had, after all, been kept firmly in the background. No national newspaper pictures and no cinema newsreels had ever revealed her existence; she was just known, in general, to have been around. Eva Braun was de facto, the Führer's wife. How would they settle their consciences in the years to come, when the myth that they were jointly perpetuating became the accepted fact, with the knowledge that they had murdered the heroine of the story? Reluctantly the others agreed and Hewel's idea for replacing Eva with a female cleaner was put immediately into operation.

Rosa Lagrosse had remained in the Bunker because there was nowhere else to go. Her small room in Seltze Strasse was now just a bombed ruin. She had migrated to Germany in the late thirties to find work as a housekeeper in Berlin where she met and fell in love with a young Wehrmacht corporal who had since been ripped apart by red hot shrapnel at a place called Kursk, somewhere in Russia. Her poor corporal had spent his final moments in a living hell and cursing Adolf Hitler.

Because of the huge losses on all battlefronts, willing menial workers were at something of a premium in early-nineteen-forties Germany. So the authorities had looked kindly upon Rosa's application to remain and allowed her continuing employment. Much good it did her in the end, but there wasn't much else for her.

Deep in the Bunker, Rosa lived in a tiny cubby-hole with her buckets and brooms and tried to stay out of the way. They didn't look much alike, she and Eva Braun, but as Misch, who had been brought in to lend his expertise to the situation, had pointed out, who would ever notice? She would burn with the corpse of the Führer and that would be that. None there fancied arguing at this stage. They just wanted it all done with. So Misch, in his usual accomplished way, carried out the deed. Rosa Lagrosse died of a broken neck. Misch had been merciful and the poor woman suffered no pain. Death had been instantaneous.

Eva Braun's replacement in death, Rosa Lagrosse, was sat, side by side with the Führer in ugly, rigor bloated death.

Eva had been given a route that, she was informed, whilst it might be messy was still, by and large, navigable. She had also been given a cyanide capsule in the event that she was caught.

Up and out into the Old Chancellery grounds with Misch now gently pushing her in a westerly direction. She shuddered and became stone still as a series of shells fell not more than fifty metres away. A squad of Volkssturm came ambling by doubtless on their way to oblivion somewhere.

"One kilometre to Bertzhof tunnel," said Misch, "and from there you continue west for twelve kilometres. Once at the other end you must head south. Got that?"

Eva nodded. Bright-eyed with fright and knowing that she was going to have to work her muscular legs like fury if she was to have more than a rabbit's chance in hell of success.

"Dirty yourself up a little," suggested Misch. "You're not likely to be recognized but it doesn't do to take chances."

He turned to go back to the Bunker. "Rochus," Eva said, tearfully. "Please, I......."

"Just go and whatever you do, don't let them take you alive. Now GO!"

Alone, terrified, but no quitter if and when it came to preserving her own life, Eva did as she was bid and headed toward the Bertzhof tunnel. As she walked she occasionally paused to stoop and gather some dust and muck from the ground. Any woman walking around out here would look like a bombed-out victim and she must appear the same. She also fingered the loaded Walther PPK. If necessary she could and would use it. Hermann had ensured that she knew how to use a firearm and she had no qualms. She would most certainly use it before resorting to the cyanide capsule. To hell with that! The PPK had been Adolf's. Well, at least the old sod had left her something worthwhile in the end.

A spattering of gunfire close by made her pause. She glanced around. How far was it she had come, two hundred metres? Were those soldiers that she could see in the dust laden gloom? She was about to move forward when she saw the shape of their metal headgear. Caution gripped her and she sank down on her haunches and stared hard at the approaching figures. They too were moving with extreme caution. Bent double they sidled nervously closer to where she squatted. They were no more than twenty metres distant and she could see the weapons clasped in their hands. Rifles and submachine guns and there were about twelve of them possibly more and they were....oh, dear God! They were Russians and headed in a direct line for the Bunker. Desperately she sank even further into the gloom of the surrounding hell and eased herself deep into the rubble of a fallen wall which lay close by. There she lay, the former first lady of the Third Reich. Eva Braun lay and waited, and waited.

CHAPTER 35

A Little Later: Berlin, The Bunker

Rochus returned to the Bunker amidst a storm of ricocheting bullets two of which tore through his uniform but left not so much as a scratch on his body. He went quickly down to the lower Bunker and on toward the main exit at the Vorbunker. Once there he found his senses almost overwhelmed by the meaningless jabbering and hysterical hand flapping normally associated with the kinds of unfortunates that both they and Hitler had been so keen to dispose of through euthanasia a few years ago. Everybody wanted to get out and none of them wanted to die; the uncertainty of what lay just metres from the front door had most of them in a buttock twitching panic.

The news had gone out that the Führer was dead by his own hand; he'd died, it was said, like an absolute hero with his loyal and beloved wife dying by his side. The overall commander of Berlin, General Weidling, had communicated that he intended to throw in the towel just as soon as he could get in touch with the Soviet high command. In reality, just as soon as he could find someone above the rank of corporal to whom he could legitimately surrender. They were all on their own, he had said. Nothing left to do other than try and make it out of Berlin. He wished them good luck and that was the last they heard from him. Meanwhile, savage fighting continued above the Bunker.

Every street, alley and house was a battleground. The best chance seemed to stay with General Mohnke who, with the twenty remaining SS soldiers under his command, almost all that remained of the inner ring defences, had formed a small perimeter. If anyone could get out it must surely be him. But Rochus knew that the chances of any of them escaping the Russians in large armed groups were slim to none. Solitary escapees might get beyond the steel ring around them but anyone in a uniform stood little chance. Particularly the once prized SS uniforms; they needed to be got rid of in favour of whatever else might be at hand. Anything would do as long as it wasn't the hated and horribly obvious Hugo Boss designed Waffen and Totenkopf SS lounge suits that had once been all the rage. Rochus shook his head. None of them had thought this part of it out very well. Time had placed a firm stranglehold upon ideas and creativity.

He had, though, one last task to perform before he could in good conscience depart and see to his own safety.

Bormann was arguing with Stumpfegger about the best route to Schleswig-Holstein. Misch almost burst out laughing. The Reichsleiter, if that he still was, had changed from his brown party uniform into the grey/green of an SS Sturmbannführer. Did he really think that that would help? What a damn fool. Stumpfegger had at least managed to find a Wehrmacht uniform into which he was able to squeeze his giant frame.

Generals Krebs and Burgdorf roamed around, becoming less sober by the minute, wondering why no one was bothering to salute them anymore or even call them, sir. They pointed self-importantly at their hand-held maps but had as little idea of what was best to do as the rest of them.

Krebs, highly educated and a Russian speaker turned to his colleague, Burgdorf and said, "I could always have a go at contacting the Russian High Command, you know, Wilhelm. Might be worth a try."

"Why not?" Responded Bergdorf. His eyes were watery with a surfeit of schnapps. "You'll need that Misch fella, though. He's the one with the electronic know-how and all that." Krebs, himself no stranger these days to the numbing joys of strong alcohol became suddenly distracted by something that he could see in an alcove further down the corridor.

"What's that?" He moved toward the alcove and Bergdorf, with just the hint of a stagger, followed him.

A dog, what had once been a large, fluffy Alsatian, lay huddled and dead within the alcove. Some of the animal had been eaten away by rats that had already nibbled at a thigh, both ears and a section of nostril.

"What on earth?" muttered Bergdorf.

"That'll be the Führer's bitch, Blondi," said Krebs. He bent slightly and sniffed. "Cyanide poisoning."

"What – commit suicide, did she?" said Burgdorf with an attempt at humour.

"Very funny, Wilhelm. Not exactly, though. Stumpfegger and some Wehrmacht Feldwebel were trying out the efficacy of those cyanide capsules that doctor Morell knocked up before he left for pastures new."

"Seems they work well enough."

"Seems so. Got yours?" Krebs idly toed the head of the dead animal.

Burgdorf shook his head. "A stiff drink and a bullet, I think, Hans. And you?"

"The same, I s'pose."

Erich Kempka, Hitler's former driver and chief of the motor pool, stood with the harder than Krupp steel, Otto Gunsche. They were conversing quietly in a corner where even the panic-stricken clerks and typists gave them a wide berth. Misch waved them over. "We have things to do," he spoke purposefully and calmly.

"I've sorted as much gasoline as should be necessary," muttered Kempka.

"Then let's to it," rasped Gunsche in his usual monotoned way.

Down the stairs and on to the Führer apartment they went with

Misch leading the way. As they entered the Führer sitting room Linge appeared from the bedroom. "Got her away, OK?" he enquired

Misch shrugged. "Best that could be expected. She might make it. Who knows. Where's Hewel?"

"I don't know. He muttered something about having things to see to and then just shot off," answered the still immaculate former valet.

Gunsche nodded his great ugly head. "He'll have to top himself. No other way for the likes of him."

Linge pointed to a blanket folded neatly on the floor. "I could only find the one." They needed blankets so that the bodies might be covered as they carried them up through the Vorbunker and into the Chancellery garden for burning. The last thing they wanted was for the screaming mass of desperately waiting to exit former Reich employees catching a glimpse of the very dead and head lolling Führer and his supposed lady.

Gunsche sat the corpses close together on the sofa and then leaned back to survey his handywork. There was just the one thing left to do before the final burning. A proposed modelling for a selective few of the dead couple, cuddling like dying love birds on the sofa, in order to give their stories a more dramatic credence when later related.

Goebbels appeared at the doorway. Gunsche waved a hand at the figures on the sofa. He had Rosa's head leaning coyly on Hitler's left shoulder, with her rigor solid fingers clasped together like extremely fat earthworms. Hitler by now was looking like a man who had been on a full carbohydrate diet for weeks and was now about to explode. Misch eased forward and lowered Rosa's head covering her face with her hair. The hair was similar colouring to Eva's but the body was somewhat fuller. Oh, well. Who the devil was going to notice? Just about everybody, that's who.

"Ludicrous," snapped Goebbels. Just get them up top and burn the bloody things. Don't allow anyone to look too closely."

Linge had a strange smirk on his face and clearly, he was seeing the funny side of things. The proposed modelling didn't have a hope in hell of convincing anybody that this woman was Eva Braun. And the dead Hitler most certainly did *not* present a picture that was likely to engender adoration amongst the living nor future generations. The entire thing was macabre and honestly, even to Otto Gunsche, not a man known for his sense of humour, almost too hysterically funny.

Linge pointed theatrically at Rosa's dead feet and ankles. Poor dead Rosa was not, of course, wearing fashionable shoes nor fashionable nylon stockings. The obvious giveaway that this woman most patently was *not* Eva Braun, the glamorous clothes horse of Berchtesgaden, were the darned, odd coloured socks draped around her thick and somewhat hairy ankles. Darned inexpertly, with the addition of trailing cotton from beneath the foot in her very worn left shoe. The first lady of the Third Reich down at heel and wearing darned socks? Hardly likely!

"Well," Linge shrugged and gave Gunsche a small grin. "The idea was good."

Without ceremony and with somewhat brutal and uncaring haste, Misch dragged both bodies from the sofa and causally let them collapse together on the floor.

"Only the one blanket?" He asked Linge.

"Sorry, yes. It's a big one but there just aren't any left around."

"And we don't have time to go looking," added Goebbels. "Wrap them up together and carry them up. Do it now whilst we still can."

Misch, strong as he was, needed the assistance of Gunsche to get both bodies all the way up to the Chancellery garden. The stairs were steep and the struggle through the heaving mass of people crammed into the forward end of the Vorbunker was as hideous as it was comic. Rosa's thick, besocked feet dangled from beneath the single blanket in which both she and the Führer were wrapped and, horror upon horror, the Führer's head popped out from beneath its woolly hideaway on two devastatingly embarrassing occasions.

Somehow they managed and the final deed was done.

Dumped together with a Portuguese cleaner in a shallow pit just outside his final command centre, Adolf Hitler's remains were burnt and his one-thousand-year Reich came to a stuttering and inglorious end – almost. The Reich might have come to an end but though the author might be dead the tragedy played on.

There remained now the final agony as, like a hideously wounded monster from some Jurassic hell, the dying Reich writhed in abject defeat and humiliation bellowing and shrieking its unbearable anguish for its enemies to hear and gloat over. The torment that it had inflicted upon others was now being shovelled up well above the letter box level of expected reprisal.

Rochus Misch went back down to the Bunker for the final time. Freytag von Loringhoven, ever the suave man about town had already departed. Dressed in an ordinary grey suit, wearing a trilby hat and carrying a small brown leather suitcase and an umbrella he had looked for all the world like a middle-class tourist from the Rhine on his way to a sightseeing tour. Freytag was gone, heaven knows where but he was at least, off and away.

Krebs and Burgdorf, still making frantic calls for a cease fire to some Russian operator a hundred metres away, vied with each other in unsteady, alcohol fuelled attempts to pour more schnapps into obstinately sliding glasses on their shared table. They gave up and simply shared the bottle, drinking noisily from its mouth. The conversation then became belchingly serious as they discussed their approaching demise. Burgdorf drunkenly and very earnestly suggested that they die like duellists; far more soldierly than putting a bullet through one's own head. But as the hours wore on and alcohol took an ever-stronger hold they realised, the both of them, that they had best look to their own devices. A pistol barrel in the mouth was more certain than a gunfight between two drunken old men. They then began to ostentatiously check and cock their little service pistols in preparation for their proposed action.

Magda Goebbels sighed with relief after the effort of slaughtering her six children. It was done for the best of reasons and she felt no guilt. A world without the Führer was not a world that she wanted her children to ever witness let alone grow up in. Life without the Führer would be nothing, not worth living. To hell with God and all that cartoon clap-trap, the Führer, the wonderful Adolf Hitler was her God, *their* God. Without him there was nothing and so they all must die. And so they all *had* died by her unerring hand, or hands in Helga's case. The entire little brood had been doctored with a heavy sedative and then Magda had crushed a cyanide capsule between their soft little lips. Helmut, the only boy, had stirred and called for his papa but had been dead within seconds. Helga, though, the eldest and therefore, Magda supposed, the least susceptible to the sedative, had awoken fully. Bright, clear blue eyes wide with panic and bewilderment, thirteen-year-old Helga had struggled and pleaded with her mother not to hurt her. Why, mother, she wept, what had she done wrong? It took every ounce of strength from Magda's powerful hands to throttle the life out of her desperately attempting to survive firstborn. The little devil had wriggled and struggled like a fury, damn her! Magda was exhausted. But it was at last done. All dead and now it was her turn. Now she must join them in death and be once again with her beloved Führer. That was, of course, if such an afterlife existed.

There was, though, a problem. As she raised the small PPK to her head, her finger gently squeezing the trigger, she found that she couldn't make that final pull on the mechanism that would end her life. She was afraid. She looked at her dead children and then down at the pistol. A grimly determined expression crossed her face as she once again raised the weapon to her head, then with a muttered curse transferred it so that the barrel was in her mouth: the index finger tightened hard on the trigger and her eyes closed as she exerted all her willpower in an effort to accomplish this one final act for her Führer – But no! Nothing. She couldn't do it. Oh Lord! She sank back against the iron frame of the bunk beds that held her dead children.

A sound at the door had her looking up. She was dry-eyed but definitely furious with herself. Joseph entered slowly, staring first at the beds and then at the woman that had slaughtered his children. They had discussed what should be done but in reality, he had never thought that she would do it, kill her own children.

They stood a while, wordlessly staring at one another. Then, slowly, Joseph withdrew his weapon, eased back the hammer and fired. The bullet entered Magda's blond head and she fell dead to the floor where he calmly left her. It must now be, of course, his turn. Upstairs or down? What did it matter? Misch would see to the disposal. That was one man who could always be relied upon. A final kiss for each of his dead children, a blank glance at the woman who bore them, and Joseph Goebbels departed this world with a bullet neatly planted through his brain via his once so persuasive mouth.

Rochus surveyed the scene of familial slaughter with an unfeeling eye. His mind ran with the volumes of information that he had acquired over the last few years. Lots and lots of it. He knew a great deal about the people that had run this mess from its inception to its messy end. But like a good soldier he had kept his head down, carried out his duties calmly and efficiently, done as he was told and survived; up to this point, at least. He knew as no one else knew, precisely what had happened down here right from the very beginning. The great spy that Himmler had been so keen to apprehend was in fact no spy at all, and the little spy that no one had suspected had remained just that because Rochus, rather than make waves and get involved, had elected to remain quiet. Any spy at this stage was, after all, merely a surplus to anybody's requirements. He had allowed Mr Naughty, as he liked to call him whenever his mind dwelt upon the subject, to remain unmolested. As for the other? Getting involved with that sort at any stage might have meant his own head and Rochus was very much in agreement with the three wise monkeys, 'Neither see, speak nor hear evil.' A man lived longer that way.

He cast his eyes once again over the dead bodies of the Goebbels family. He had indeed promised that he would burn the corpses when all was done but to hell with it. They were dead, so was the Third Reich. It was time to go.

Rochus moved swiftly up the stairs and out into the night. His friend Mohnke was with a small group someway up ahead and Rochus decided to follow at a distance rather than join the group.

En route, he saw Bormann lumbering around obviously lost and close to complete panic. Rochus moved stealthily in the shadows, making sure to avoid the rotund and heavily perspiring man of whom even Himmler had once been afraid.

Swiftly and expertly he put distance between himself and the Bunker and then stopped dead. Slowly he raised his hands and bit slightly on his lower lip. Oh, well. It hadn't been such a bad war.

CHAPTER 36

May 23 1945: Lüneburg, North Germany.

Albert Speer howled. Tears fell in a torrent from a usually dry and calm featured face. The normally so difficult to read Albert was now revealing his feelings and then some. Outside the small temporary cell in which he was being held, a guard looked briefly through the spy hole of the cell door. He saw Speer positively snivelling, almost wailing with what was surely unbearable grief. Eyes cast upward in the direction of a generally supposed heaven, Albert Speer resembled a badly drawn caricature of saintly martyrdom. The only things missing from this picture of abject tragedy were some flesh piercing arrows sticking out from bloodily penetrated limbs. He sobbed, snivelled, snorted loudly and then managed to calm himself.

Hitler, his erstwhile friend and mentor was dead. That however wasn't the reason for his almost hysterical outburst of weeping and breast beating. He had heard some hours previously that his former partner in a variety of nefarious misdeeds, Heinrich Himmler, was unfortunately *not* dead. He had been captured. That news had sent him into a total panic. Himmler would be questioned and Himmler would talk and Heinrich bloody Himmler knew a damn sight too much about Albert Speer. Transport Speer, under a variety of pseudonyms, had not merely been responsible for transporting troops and war munitions to the various factories and battle fronts. The Speer transport organization had delivered countless thousands of Jews to the camps, Auschwitz in particular, and with Himmler's written authority and connivance, to his own munitions and defence works where they were forced to work in appalling conditions. Some of Speer's workplaces were located deep underground where there weren't even the most basic of sanitation facilities and no medical care. They died in their hundreds, frozen, starved and worked to death. And all under *his* auspices.

Albert had been clever, right enough. Precious little in the way of written commands and receipts, dockets etc, could be laid at his door. But Himmler? He knew everything and Albert had no doubt at all that the chinless wonder would blab out everything. All his caution and cleverness would be in vain. The allied judicial authorities, or their investigators anyway, were already part way eating out of his hand. With luck, he might get away with his part in the horrors that played out in Nazi Germany. The Americans and British were so insanely gullible. Not so the Russians, however. It was going to be a close-run thing but he reckoned that his chances were good. He was charming and urbane and more to the point, absolutely plausible. He was totally unlike the bullying, sadistic killers that the experienced but slightly naïve investigators were accustomed to dealing with. He, Albert Speer, came across as a well-meaning gentleman. Misled by others in a cruel system of which he had very little knowledge. Or so he very persuasively said. With his talent for dissembling he had a better than even chance of avoiding the gallows. But not if Himmler ran off at the mouth. Should the former SS chief give him up, and Albert was certain that he would if only to save himself, then, it was all over. Albert Speer: just another war criminal.

And then, oh thank God, the news had come. The shiny helmeted American corporal who had come around with the canister of steaming cocoa that evening had the most wonderful tidings to impart as he ladled the sweet chocolate brown liquid into Albert's proffered tin mug. Heinrich Himmler was dead! Died, apparently, by his own evil hand, so said the corporal. He'd concealed a cyanide capsule in one of his teeth and after some unseemly writhing and jerking departed life whilst in British hands. Was the corporal sure? Albert had asked tremblingly. Dead as mutton, answered the corporal happily. It took some five minutes for the news to sink in and then Albert Speer gave vent to his true feelings. He howled with joy, screamed with relief and like a footballer who has just scored a goal, ran around his six-by-nine cell in a frenzy of self-congratulation. He was saved. With luck and skill he would escape the noose. Sure he would be imprisoned but at least he wouldn't have to face up to the awfulness of his own death.

He dried his tear encrusted eyes, blew his snot swamped nose and composed his features into their normal smug, holier-than-thou and butter would never melt in *this* mouth attitude and forced himself to concentrate on his lies and explanations. He tutted. Never again must he allow himself to become so emotional unless, of course, he was facing his official accusers.

August,1981: Munich

An old man now and, with all said and done, satisfied with the way that his life had turned out because it might have been one hell of a lot worse, Albert Speer strolled along the Stachus Passagen in Munich's city centre. Released from incarceration in Spandau prison in nineteen sixty-six after serving a paltry twenty years he had since made a small fortune with his tell-all books and global TV appearances. Everyone, it seemed, wanted a little piece of the 'good German', Albert Speer. Admittedly, though, of late, things had shown distinct signs of becoming awkward. Little slip-ups that he had made all those years ago were beginning to surface beneath the lazar-like searching and scrutiny of skilled scoop hunters; reporters and biographers alike were beginning to twitch their inquisitive noses in his direction once again. It was looking a tad dangerous and he was being hard pressed to keep down one or two deeply disturbing and incriminating truths. His closer than the norm relationship with Himmler and their mutually beneficial business dealings were being, if not widely discussed, at least pointedly questioned in some literary areas. Why couldn't those wretched people just let it all go? It was over and done with. Time to forget and move on. It didn't occur to him or his ego that one way of prodding historical ferrets to forget all about him might be to stop grandstanding, disappear and thus become rather more easily forgettable. But that wasn't Albert. He enjoyed the limelight and as the last few years had shown, he could and would talk about himself and the Third Reich interminably to anyone who cared to listen. He had his 'the good German', routine down pat by now and thoroughly enjoyed every performance he gave; unless, of course, he was asked an awkward question; needle-like they seemed more inclined to slip in these days. But there was precious little point in worrying. He was on top of things and had the right people keeping him there. All would be well.

Since nineteen seventy-eight he had been heavily involved in an affair with Frieda Schenk, a very attractive woman some forty years his junior. Something had clicked inside Albert when they met and he was now enjoying a full-throttle Indian summer romance. Frieda, a well-educated German national living in London, had come to him some time ago ostensibly to research facts for her book. It had quickly become obvious, however, that her main interest, wrinkles or no, was Albert himself. They began an affair and whenever he was in London, or travelling abroad, she joined him. It wasn't looks, money or power that attracted Frieda; it was Albert's knowledge of living, of what he had seen, done and been a part of. Frieda couldn't get enough of the urbane former Nazi minister. The only other man that might have got a look in had he been alive, would have been Adolf Hitler.

Speer was due in London in a few days for yet another TV programme about the war and his part in the final days as a 'good German' trying to save Berlin from the horrors of Hitler's Nero

Decree; the final orders for the destruction of anything that might help sustain life. Frieda would be meeting him at the airport and Albert decided that he should take her a small gift; a trinket of some kind. Nothing too expensive, fat chance of that. Albert liked to keep hold of his money. A small bauble, though, should do nicely.

Passing by an older style fancy goods shop his eye fell upon some not cheap but not outrageously expensive bracelets and coloured necklaces. Not things that he would consider purchasing for his lovely Frieda but quite possibly for his wife on her next birthday.

As he moved nearer to the well-stocked window for a closer look his attention was caught by the broad beam and sagging waistline of what appeared to be the owner. She had her back to the window and was shuffling some stock from one drawer to another.

As if knowing that she was being stared at she turned and their eyes met.

For just a few seconds but it seemed like hours they stood there, staring at each other. Speer's heart almost stopped as the portly old woman in the shop, her eyes wide with recognition and fear, slowly raised a plump, well-manicured finger to her lips in a shushing gesture. In an almost childlike manner, Albert responded to the woman's gesture by copying it exactly. The woman turned back to her work and Albert feeling as though the earth were moving beneath his feet, slowly walked away.

Unbelievable. After all this time. Here and hidden in plain sight. Other than himself she had outdone the whole lot of them.

Three days later, shortly after giving yet another splendid TV performance before a live audience, Albert was found dead in his London hotel room. He was seventy-six years of age and it was said that his heart gave out. Of those who had known him well, only his long-suffering wife, six children and four or five tradesmen turned up. He was not, it seems, greatly missed.

Epilogue

March 9, 1980: Hamburg

The two old men stared down kindly at a third old man, who lay sick and dying but in a comfortable bed of his own. Friedrik Lehman leaned forward not enjoying the feeling of his once slim but now weighty belly pushing up against his diaphragm. It inhibited his breathing but, then, he was an old man and lucky to have survived so long. He was also in better condition than the dying man who lay before him. Something of a hero he was. His companion, too, deserved recognition for the part played in the final act of one of history's greatest tragedies.

Lehman was the last survivor of the all-powerful cabal of businessmen and industrialists that had run and dominated Germany for such an unexpectedly short time. That was before the unpleasantly eccentric elected leader of the Reich went quite startlingly off the rails. Although there had been warning signs aplenty, the group had considered that the brutality loving Adolf Hitler knew what was good for him and would continue to toe the cabal's quite flexible line. Lehman, cautious as always had placed his own man as close to the Führer as was possible. It was that man who lay dying before them. Oddly, he was the youngest of the three but the cancer eating away at his belly was no respecter of age.

The business enterprises of the old cabal had all prospered, despite the efforts at destruction of a mad Führer and all, with the exception of Lehman's, were now run on a global scale by highly enthusiastic offspring. American and Swiss banking protection and collaboration had protected them as Lehman had known that they would. The pre-war set-up had worked admirably. Money spoke beyond race, religion and politics.

The second man in the sick room was no business bigshot. He too, though, had played a part in the finale in spite of his previous loyalties.

It could, of course, have been so different. But they had, it was true, fundamentally misjudged Adolf Hitler. They had, in fact, completely overestimated him. Like his pathetically inept paintings, Hitler's view of war and the world had lacked perspective. A little war – a big war, he had been unable to balance in his mind the different perspectives required by the mind's eye to see accurately any kind of picture from a distance. Little war = good: nice fat profits. Big war = bad: low profits. His inability for contextual thinking showed in his drawings and what passed for paintings. A one-trick pony barely described the man's incompetence and lack of foresight. They should have seen it but they hadn't. Shame on them all.

Hitler had barely bothered to rule Germany; in fact, he hadn't ruled it at all. His butterfly mind refused to buckle down to the boring and mundane tasks of actually running the country and he flitted disastrously from one pie in the sky idea to the next. His Gauleiters had seen to all the mundane stuff of ruling the nation and people. Hitler had been too happy enjoying his wars, even to the extent of losing them. To him, playing warlord had been far more rewarding than playing politics.

Nevertheless, the cabal had prospered, made money and grown even richer than before.

A small gasp from the bed drew Lehman further forward to share the sick man's final seconds on earth.

Bald now and sunken faced but he had clearly once been a handsome man. The eyes, still bright and beautifully blue gazed up at Lehman and his companion without a hint of fear or reproach.

"Nobody ever guessed," whispered the dying man. "Not even close."

Lehman and his companion nodded and gave sad little smiles.

Another gasp of pain and then the dying man smiled and whispered something. Lehman leaned even further forward.

"What was that, old friend?" He lent his ear to the dying man's mouth. Again the whisper came, this time just a little louder and followed by a strangled giggle and then a sharp exhalation of dying breath: it was over.

At nine-thirty on that Friday morning Heinz Linge closed his eyes for the last time and died.

Lehman smiled and looked across at the other man.

"What did he say?" came the question.

"He said," Lehman gave a small twisted grin. "You know that he always had a sense of humour, Wilhelm."

"Yes, yes, I know. So what did he say?"

"Well, what he said was," Lehman spoke slowly. Then snapped his hands out at the wrists. "The Butler did it." He looked admiringly at the stiffening corpse. "At death's door and he cracks a joke."

Wilhelm Mohnke looking poker-faced suddenly broke into a toothy grin and lightly tapped his colleague's right arm.

"But it was no joke, though, Friedrik, was it?"

Heinz Linge although displaying a not entirely phoney devotion to Hitler, had been placed in his position as valet/butler to the Führer by carefully orchestrated moves and removals of various inner circle staff members. He had made his reports and been accurate in so doing. All of Hitler's closely attendant menials, drivers, pilots, servants and the like, were noticeable for their cute good looks. Linge, knowing full well that Hitler was personally and physically attracted to him, made very sure that he was never too far away. By nineteen-forty-three he had come to realise that his perpetual drug taking had rendered Hitler incapable of exercising full and proper control of his own faculties, let alone exercising any kind of proper control over the vast armies that he commanded. He watched as Hitler disintegrated before his eyes beneath the torrent of quack medicines that Theodor Morell constantly administered to him.

Under orders from Lehman, by nineteen-forty-four Linge himself was adding cyanide to the Führer's meals in an effort not only to rid the Reich of a massive problem but to help end the man's mental and physical suffering. Hitler's constitution, however, displayed a remarkable ability to absorb such small doses and merely led him onward on the certain feeling that he was invincible and could not be wrong about anything. Like the old mad Russian monk Rasputin, Hitler refused to die and seemed impervious to anything but direct assault.

Linge had had no idea that Mohnke was connected to Lehman in any way until the day of Hitler's death. A plan, of sorts, was cobbled together that would suit the purposes of both men. Reasons were academic; results were what counted now.

When they had all been down in the Führer apartment on that final day, and Hitler had called for his cream cake and tea, Heinz Linge had taken the bull by the horns and quite simply concealed not one, but two cyanide capsules deep within the surfeit amount of cream that Hitler always insisted upon. The Führer ate cakes like a pig at a bucket and so, Linge secreted the capsules deep within the cake and waited all of a tremble. Mohnke was standing directly in front of the Führer and blocking the view of that man to the others. Hitler, as usual, stuffed the cake straight into his mouth but suddenly stopped dead, choked a little and attempted to sit bolt upright. His teeth had snapped shut and his tongue had discovered the foreign objects within his cake. At that moment, Mohnke had turned and seen the Führer turning a startling shade of red, with huge clots of cream and spittle spluttering forcibly from within his mouth as he attempted to spit it out. A glance at Linge showed that the man was close to panic. Mohnke's powerful right hand, so used to dealing death to the Reich's enemies, reached out and expertly took Hitler by the jaw forcing the feebly struggling man to swallow the full-strength capsules. And there was an end of it, really; after all that it had taken a mere few seconds. No glamorous death no glorious political bequests to a suffering people. Hitler died as he had lived: badly. And as Heinz Linge stated at the end of his own life: The Butler really did do it.